the
Map of
Time

a novel

FÉLIX J. PALMA

TRANSLATED BY NICK CAISTOR

POCKET BOOKS

NEW YORK   TORONTO   LONDON   SYDNEY   NEW DELHI

Pocket Books
A Division of Simon & Schuster, Inc.
1230 Avenue of the Americas
New York, NY 10020

This book is a work of fiction. Names, characters, places, and incidents either are products of the author's imagination or are used fictitiously. Any resemblance to actual events or locales or persons, living or dead, is entirely coincidental.

Copyright © 2008 by Félix J. Palma
English language translation copyright © 2011 by Nick Caistor

Originally published in Spain in 2008 by Algaida Spain as *El Mapa del Tiempo*

English language translation published by arrangement with HarperCollins Publishers UK

First Pocket Books paperback edition July 2012

POCKET and colophon are trademarks of Simon & Schuster, Inc.

For information about special discounts for bulk purchases, please contact Simon & Schuster Special Sales at 1-866-506-1949 or business@simonandschuster.com.

The Simon & Schuster Speakers Bureau can bring authors to your live event. For more information or to book an event contact the Simon & Schuster Speakers Bureau at 1-866-248-3049 or visit our website at www.simonspeakers.com.

Manufactured in the United States of America

10 9 8 7 6

ISBN 978-1-4516-8303-5
ISBN 978-1-4391-6746-5 (ebook)

"A luxurious blend of history, romance, mystery, and science fiction, this novel cleverly weaves fact and fiction, keeping the reader guessing to the end." —*Star-Ledger*

"After 611 pages, I was awestruck. All these plots, all these mysteries, all this lovely writing! By Jove, he's got it!"
—*The Plain Dealer*

"Brawny, genre-bending historical entertainment. . . . A languorous, cunning mélange of historical science, science fiction, fantasy, and mystery, *The Map of Time* is agreeable escapist fare, well-timed for summer reading." —*BookPage*

"Palma offers constant surprises, playing with the readers' perception of what's actually going on. . . . The novel's structure works wonderfully, offering a variety of charming protagonists moving through their own disappointments, victories, action-packed climax, and beautiful ending. They each could stand alone, but they're incredibly satisfying when the finale draws them all together."
—*The Onion's A.V. Club*

"What Palma does so well is to make everything believable, even for the most skeptical of his characters, H. G. Wells. . . . An intricate story set in a brightly imagined Victorian England . . . It's above all an utterly fascinating and readable book. You won't want to put it down." —*Bookreporter*

"Strange and wonderful. Magical and smart. Félix J. Palma has done more than write a wonderful novel, he's concocted a supernatural tour de force. Time travel, tragic love, murder and mystery all combine in what is nothing short of a surprising, satisfying and mesmerizing read."

—M. J. Rose, internationally bestselling author of
The Reincarnationist

"*The Map of Time* recalls the science fiction of Wells and Verne, and then turns the early masters on their heads. A brilliant and breathtaking trip through metafictional time."

—Scott Westerfeld, *New York Times* bestselling author of
Leviathan

"*The Map of Time* is a singularly inventive, luscious story with a core of pure, unsettling weirdness. With unnerving grace and disturbing fantasy, it effortlessly straddles that impossible line between being decidedly familiar, and yet absolutely new."   —Cherie Priest, author of *Boneshaker*

"Palma manages to be both fascinating and cozy, like having your favorite uncle telling you stories of his dangerous travels to far continents while sitting by your parlor fire. . . . A rollicking good adventure yarn that, with a nudge and a wink and a bit of sleight of hand, is sure to leave delight in its wake and a smile on one's face."

—*The Globe and Mail*

THE DISTINCTION BETWEEN PAST,
PRESENT AND FUTURE IS AN ILLUSION,
BUT A VERY PERSISTENT ONE.

—*Albert Einstein*

MANKIND'S MOST PERFECTLY
TERRIFYING WORK OF ART IS THE
DIVISION OF TIME.

—*Elias Canetti*

WHAT IS WAITING FOR ME IN THE
DIRECTION I DON'T TAKE?

—*Jack Kerouac*

CONTENTS

PART ONE

*W*ELCOME, DEAR READER,
AS YOU PLUNGE INTO THE THRILLING
PAGES OF OUR MELODRAMA WHERE
YOU WILL FIND ADVENTURES OF
WHICH YOU NEVER DREAMT!

IF LIKE ANY REASONABLE PERSON YOU
BELIEVE THAT TIME IS A RIVER SWEEPING
AWAY ALL THAT IS BORNE TOWARDS THE
DARKEST SHORE, IN THESE PAGES YOU
WILL DISCOVER THAT THE PAST CAN BE
REVISITED, THAT MANKIND CAN RETRACE
HIS FOOTSTEPS THANKS TO A MACHINE
THAT CAN TRAVEL THROUGH TIME.

YOUR EMOTION AND ASTONISHMENT
ARE GUARANTEED.

I

ANDREW HARRINGTON WOULD HAVE gladly died several times over if that meant not having to choose just one pistol from among his father's vast collection in the living room cabinet. Decisions had never been Andrew's strong point. On close examination, his life had been a series of mistaken choices, the last of them threatening to cast its lengthy shadow over the future. But that life of unedifying blunders was about to end. This time he was sure he had made the right decision, because he had decided not to decide. There would be no more mistakes in the future because there would be no more future. He was going to destroy it completely by putting one of those guns to his right temple. He could see no other solution: obliterating the future was the only way for him to eradicate the past.

He scanned the contents of the cabinet, the lethal assortment his father had lovingly set about assembling after his return from the war. He was fanatical about these weapons, though Andrew suspected it was not so much nostalgia that drove him to collect them as his desire to contemplate the novel ways mankind kept coming up with for taking one's own life outside the law. In stark contrast to his father's devotion, Andrew was impassive as he surveyed the apparently docile, almost humdrum implements that had brought thunder down to men's fingertips and freed war from the unpleasantness of hand-to-hand combat. Andrew tried to imagine what kind of death might be lurking inside each of them, lying in wait like some predator. Which would his father have recommended he blow his brains out with? He calculated that death from one of those antiquated muzzle-loading flintlocks, which had to be refilled with gunpowder and a ball, then tamped down with a paper plug each time they were fired, would be a noble but drawn-out, tedious affair. He preferred the swift death guaranteed by one of the more modern revolvers nestling in their luxurious velvet-lined wooden cases. He considered a Colt Single Action revolver, which looked easy to handle and reliable, but discarded it when he remembered he had seen Buffalo Bill brandishing one in his Wild West Shows. A pitiful attempt to reenact his transoceanic exploits with a handful of imported Red Indians and a dozen lethargic, apparently opium-drugged buffalo. Death for him was not just another adventure. He also rejected a fine Smith & Wesson: that was the gun that had killed the outlaw Jesse James, of whom he considered himself unworthy, as well as a Webley revolver, specially designed to hold back the charging hordes in Britain's colonial wars, which he thought looked too cumbersome. His attention turned next to his father's favorite, a fine pepperbox with rotating barrels, but he seriously doubted whether this ridiculous, ostentatious-looking weapon would be capable of firing a bullet with enough force. Finally, he settled on an elegant 1870 Colt with mother-of-pearl inlays that would take his life with all the delicacy of a woman's caress.

He smiled defiantly as he plucked it from the cabinet, remembering how often his father had forbidden him to meddle with his pistols. But the illustrious William Harrington was in Italy at that moment, no doubt reducing the Fontana de Trevi to a quivering wreck with his critical gaze. His parents' decision to leave on their trip to Europe the very day he had chosen to kill himself had also been a happy coincidence. He doubted whether either of them would ever decipher the true message concealed in his gesture (that he had preferred to die as he had lived—alone), but for Andrew it was enough to imagine the inevitable look of disgust on his father's face when he discovered his son had killed himself behind his back, without his permission.

He opened the cabinet where the ammunition was kept and loaded six bullets into the chamber. He supposed that one would be enough, but who knew what might happen. After all, he had never killed himself before. Then he tucked the gun, wrapped in a cloth, inside his coat pocket, as though it were a piece of fruit he was taking with him to eat later on a stroll. In a further act of defiance, he left the cabinet door open. If only he had shown this much courage before, he thought. If only he had dared confront his father when it had mattered, she would still be alive. But by the time he did so, it was too

late. And he had spent eight long years paying for his
hesitation. Eight years, during which his pain had only
worsened, spreading its slimy tendrils through him like
poison ivy, wrapping itself around his insides, gnawing
at his soul. Despite the efforts of his cousin Charles and
the distraction of other women's bodies, his grief over
Marie's death refused to be laid to rest. But tonight it
would all be over. Twenty-six was a good age to die, he
reflected, contentedly fingering the bulge in his pocket.
He had the gun. Now all he needed was a suitable place
to perform the ceremony. And there was only one possible place.

With the weight of the revolver in his pocket comforting him like a good-luck charm, he descended the
grand staircase of the Harrington mansion in elegant
Kensington Gore, a stone's throw from the Queen's Gate
entrance to Hyde Park. He had not intended to cast any
farewell glances at the walls of what had been his home
for almost three decades, but he could not help feeling a
perverse wish to pause before his father's portrait, which
dominated the hall. His father stared down at him disapprovingly out of the gilt frame, a proud and commanding
figure bursting out of the old uniform he had worn as a
young infantryman in the Crimean War until a Russian
bayonet had punctured his thigh and left him with a dis-
turbingly lopsided gait. William Harrington surveyed the
world disdainfully, as though the universe were a botched
affair on which he had long since given up. What fool was
responsible for that untimely blanket of fog which had descended on the battlefield outside the besieged city of Se-

bastopol, so that nobody could see the tip of the enemy's bayonets? Who had decided that a woman was the ideal person to preside over England's destiny? Was the East really the best place for the sun to rise?

Andrew had never seen his father without that cruel animosity seeping from his eyes, and so could not know whether he had been born with it or had been infected with it fighting alongside the ferocious Ottomans in the Crimea. In any event, it had not vanished like a mild case of smallpox, leaving no mark on his face, even though the path that had opened up in front of his hapless soldier's boots on his return could only be termed a fortunate one. What did it matter that he had to hobble along it with the aid of a stick if it helped him reach his present position? For, without having to enter any pact with the devil, the man with the bushy moustache and clean-cut features depicted on the canvas had become one of the richest men in England overnight. Trudging around in that distant war, bayonet at the ready, he could never have dreamed of possessing a fraction of what he now owned. How he had amassed his fortune, though, was one of the family's best-kept secrets, and a complete mystery to Andrew.

THE TEDIOUS MOMENT IS now approaching when the young man must decide which hat and overcoat to pick from among the heap in the hall closet: one has to look presentable even for death. This is a scene which, knowing Andrew, could take several exasperating minutes, and since I see no need to describe it, I shall take the opportunity to welcome you to this tale, which has just begun, and which after lengthy reflection I chose to begin at this juncture and not another; as though I, too, had to select a single beginning from among the many jostling for position in the closet of possibilities. Assuming you stay until the end of this tale, some of you will no doubt think that I chose the wrong thread with which to begin spinning my yarn, and that for accuracy's sake I should have respected chronological order and begun with Miss Haggerty's story. It is possible, but there are stories that cannot begin at their beginning, and perhaps this is one of them.

So, let's forget about Miss Haggerty for the moment, forget that I ever mentioned her, even, and let's go back to Andrew, who has just stepped forth from the mansion suitably dressed in a hat and coat, and even a pair of warm gloves to protect his hands from the harsh winter cold. Once outside the mansion, the young man paused at the top of the steps, which unfurled at his feet like a wave of marble down to the garden. From there, he surveyed the world in which he had been brought up, suddenly aware that, if things went according to plan, he would never see it again. Night was gently spreading its veil over the Harrington mansion. A hazy full moon hung in the sky, bathing in its soft glow the immaculate lawns surrounding the house, most of them cluttered with flower beds, hedges, and fountains, dozens of oversized stone fountains decorated with excessively ornate sculptures of mermaids, fauns, and other mythical creatures. His father had accumulated such a large number of them because as an unsophisticated soul his only way of showing off his importance was to buy a lot of expensive and useless objects. In the case of the fountains his extravagance was excusable, because they combined to soothe the night with their watery refrain, making the listener want to close his eyes and forget everything except the sound of that hypnotic burble. Further off, beyond the neatly clipped lawns, stood the immense greenhouse, graceful as a swan poised for flight, where his mother spent most of the day marveling over the exotic flowers that sprouted from seeds brought back from the colonies.

Andrew gazed at the moon for several minutes wondering whether man would ever be able to travel there, as had the characters in Jules Verne and Cyrano de Bergerac's works. And what would he find if he did manage to land on its shimmering surface—whether in an airship or shot out of a cannon or with a dozen bottles of dew strapped to his body in the hope that when it evaporated he would float up to the sky like the Gascon swashbuckler's hero? Ariosto the poet had turned the planet into a warehouse where lunatics' reason was stored in vials, but Andrew was more drawn to Plutarch's idea of it as the place where noble souls went after they left the world of the living. Like Plutarch, Andrew preferred to imagine that the moon was where dead people dwelled. He liked to picture them living at peace in ivory palaces built by an army of worker angels or in caves dug out of that white rock, waiting for the living to meet death and to carry on their lives there with them, exactly where they had left off. Sometimes, he imagined that Marie was living at that very moment in one of those grottos, oblivious to what had happened to her and grateful that death had offered her a better existence than life. Marie, pale in all that white splendor, waiting patiently for him to decide once and for all to blow his brains out and come to fill the empty space in her bed.

He stopped gazing at the moon when he noticed that Harold, the coachman, had followed his orders and was standing at the foot of the stairs with a carriage at the ready. As soon as he saw his young master descending the flight of steps, the coachman rushed to open the carriage door. Andrew had always been amused by Harold's display of energy, considering it incongruous in a man approaching sixty, but the coachman clearly kept in good shape.

"Miller's Court," the youth commanded.

Harold was astonished at his request.

"But sir, that's where—"

"Is there some problem, Harold?" Andrew interrupted.

The coachman stared at him for a moment, his mouth hanging ludicrously half-open, before adding:

"None whatsoever, sir."

Andrew gave a nod, signaling that the conversation was at an end. He climbed into the brougham and sat down on the red velvet seat. Glimpsing his reflection in the carriage window, Andrew gave a sigh of despair. Was that haggard countenance really his? It was the face of someone whose life has been seeping out of him unawares, like a pillow losing its stuffing through an open seam. In a certain sense, this was true. Although his face retained the harmonious good looks he was fortunate enough to have been born with, it now resembled an empty shell, a vague impression left in a mound of ashes. The sorrow that had cast a shadow over his soul had taken its toll on his appearance, too, for he could scarcely recognize himself in this aging youth with hollowed cheeks, downcast eyes, and an unkempt beard who stared back at him in the glass. Grief had stunted him, transforming him into a dried-up, sullen creature. Fortunately, the cab began to rock as Harold, having overcome his astonishment, clambered up to his perch. This took Andrew's attention away from the blurred face sketched onto the canvas of the night. The final act of the disastrous performance that had been his life was about to begin, and he was determined to savor every moment of it. He heard the whip crack above his head and, caressing the steely bulge in his pocket, he let himself be lulled by the carriage's gentle sway.

THE CARRIAGE LEFT THE mansion and drove down Carriage Drive, which bordered the lush vegetation of Hyde Park. Gazing through the window at the city, Andrew thought that in less than half an hour's time they would be in the East End. This ride had always fascinated and puzzled him in equal measure, because it allowed him to glimpse in a single sweep every aspect of his beloved London, the world's greatest metropolis, the giant head of an insatiable octopus whose tentacles stretched over almost a fifth of the world's surface, holding Canada, India, Australia, and a large part of Africa in its viselike grip. As the handsome carriage sped east, the salubrious, almost countrified atmosphere of Kensington soon gave way to the crowded urban environment of Piccadilly, and beyond to the Circus where Anteros, the avenger of unrequited love, protrudes like an arrow fired at the city's heart. Beyond Fleet Street, the middle-class dwellings seemingly huddled around St. Paul's Cathedral gradually came into view. Finally, once they had passed the Bank of England and Cornhill Street, a wave of poverty swept over everything, a poverty that people from the adjoining West End knew of only from the satirical cartoons in *Punch*, and which seemed to pollute the air, making it foul to breathe as it mingled with the stench rising from the Thames.

Andrew had last made this journey eight years earlier, and since then he had always known that sooner or later he would make it again for the very last time. It was hardly surprising then that as they drew nearer to Aldgate, the gateway to Whitechapel, he felt slightly uneasy. He gazed warily out of the window as they entered the district, experiencing the same misgivings as he had in the past. He had never been able to avoid feeling overwhelmed by an uncomfortable sense of shame knowing that he was spying on what was to him an alien world with the dispassionate interest of somebody who studies insects. Over time, though, his initial revulsion had turned into inevitable compassion for the souls who inhabited that junkyard where the city dumped its human waste. And, peering out of the window, it seemed as if there was every reason for him to feel that compassion still: London's poorest borough had changed relatively little in the past eight years. Wealth brings poverty in its wake, thought Andrew, as they crossed the ill-lit, rowdy streets, crammed with stalls and handcarts and teeming with wretched creatures whose lives were played out beneath the menacing shadow of Christ Church. At first, he had been shocked to discover that behind the dazzle of the city's façade there existed this outpost of hell where, with the Queen's blessing, human beings were condemned to live like beasts. But the intervening years had made him less naïve, so that he was no longer surprised to see that even as the advances of science were transforming the face of London and the well-to-do amused themselves by recording their dogs' barks onto the wax-coated cylinders of phonographs or conversed via telephone under the glow of Robertson's electric lamps, while their wives brought their children into the world still groggy from chloroform, Whitechapel had remained immune to all this progress, untouchable beneath its rotten shell, drowning in its own filth. A quick glance was enough to tell him that crossing into this world was still like sticking his hand into a hornets' nest. It was here that poverty showed its ugliest face, here that the same jarring, sinister tune was always playing. He observed a couple of pub brawls, heard screams rising from the depths of dark alleyways, and glimpsed a few drunks sprawled in the gutter while a gang of street urchins stripped them of their shoes. They exchanged glances with a pair of pugnacious-looking men standing on a street corner, the petty rulers in this parallel kingdom of vice and crime.

∽

THE LUXURIOUS CARRIAGE CAUGHT the attention of several prostitutes who shouted lewd proposals to him, hitching up their skirts and showing their cleavage. Andrew felt a pang of sorrow as he gazed upon this pitiful back-street spectacle. Most of the women were filthy and downtrodden, their bodies bearing the mark of their daily burden. Even the youngest and prettiest could not escape being stained by the misery of their surroundings. He was revisited by the agonizing thought that he might have saved one of these doomed women, offered her a better life than the one her Creator had allotted her, and yet he had failed. His sorrow reached a crescendo as the carriage rattled past the Ten Bells, emitting an arpeggio of creaks as it turned into Crispin Street on its way to Dorset Street, passing in front of the Britannia pub where he had first spoken to Marie. This street was his final destination. Harold pulled the carriage up next to the stone arch leading to the Miller's Court flats, and climbed off the perch to open the carriage door. Andrew stepped out of the coach feeling suddenly dizzy and was aware that his legs were shaking as he looked around him. Everything was exactly as he remembered it, down to the shop with grimy windows run by McCarthy, the owner of the flats which stood beside the entrance. Nothing he saw indicated to him that time also passed in Whitechapel.

"You can go home now, Harold," he told the coachman, who was standing in silence at his side.

"What time shall I fetch you, sir?" asked the old man.

Andrew looked at him without knowing what to say. Fetch him? He had to stifle a sinister laugh. The only thing fetching him would be the cart from the Golden Lane morgue, the same one that had come there to fetch what was left of his beloved Marie eight years before.

"Forget you ever brought me here," was his reply.

The somber expression that clouded the coachman's face moved Andrew. Had Harold understood what he had come there to do? He could not be sure, because he had never given a moment's thought to the coachman's intelligence, or indeed to that of any servant. He always thought that at the most they possessed the innate cunning of people who from an early age are obliged to swim against the current in which he and his class maneuvered with ease. Now, though, he thought he detected in old Harold's attitude an uneasiness that could only have come from his having guessed Andrew's intentions with astonishing accuracy. And the servant's capacity for deduction was not the only discovery Andrew made during that brief moment when for once they looked directly at each other. Andrew also became aware of something hitherto unimaginable to him: the affection a servant can feel for his master. Despite the fact that he could only see them as shadows drifting in and out of rooms according to some invisible design, only noticing them when he needed to leave his glass on a tray or wanted the fire lit, these phantoms could actually care about what happened to their masters. That succession of faceless people—the maids whom his mother dismissed on the flimsiest grounds, the cooks systematically impregnated by the stable boys as though conforming to some ancient ritual, the butlers who left their employ with excellent references and went to work at another mansion identical to theirs—all of them made up a shifting landscape which Andrew had never taken the trouble to notice.

"Very well, sir," murmured Harold.

Andrew understood that these words were the coachman's last farewell; that this was the old fellow's only way of saying good-bye to him, since embracing him was a risk he appeared unwilling to take. And with a heavy heart, Andrew watched that stout, resolute man almost three times his age, to whom he would have had to relinquish the role of master if they had ever been stranded together on a desert island, clamber back up onto the carriage. He urged on the horses, leaving behind an echo of hooves clattering into the distance as the carriage was swallowed up by the fog spreading through the London streets like muddy foam. It struck him as odd that the only person he had said good-bye to before killing himself should be the coachman and not his parents or his cousin Charles, but life was full of such ironies.

That is exactly what Harold Barker was thinking as he drove the horses down Dorset Street, looking for the way out of that accursed neighborhood where life was not worth thruppence. But for his father's determination to pluck him from poverty and secure him a job as a coachman as soon as he was able to climb onto the perch, he might have been one more among the hordes of wretched souls scraping an existence in this gangrenous patch of London. Yes, that surly old drunk was the one who had hurled him into a series of jobs that had ended at the coach house of the illustrious William Harrington, in whose service he had spent half his life. But, he had to admit, they had been peaceful years, which he did when taking stock of his life in the early hours after his chores were done and the masters were already asleep; peaceful years in which he had taken a wife and fathered two healthy, strong children, one of whom was employed as a gardener by Mr. Harrington.

The good fortune that had allowed him to forge a different life from the one he had believed was his lot enabled him to look upon those wretched souls with a degree of objectivity and compassion. Harold had been obliged to go to Whitechapel more often than he would have liked when ferrying his master there that terrible autumn eight years ago, a period when even the sky seemed to ooze blood at times. He had read in the newspapers about what had happened in that warren of godforsaken streets, but more than anything he had seen it reflected in his master's eyes. He knew now that young master Harrington had never recovered, that those reckless excursions to pubs and brothels which his cousin Charles had dragged them both on (although he himself had been obliged to remain in the carriage shivering from cold) had not succeeded in driving the terror from his eyes. And that night Harrington had appeared ready to lay down his arms, to surrender to an enemy who had proved invincible. Didn't that bulge in his pocket look suspiciously like a firearm? But what could he do? Should he turn around and try to stop him? Should a servant step in to alter his master's destiny? Harold shook his head. Maybe he was imagining things, he thought, and the young man simply wanted to spend the night in that haunted room, safe with a gun in his pocket.

He left off his uncomfortable broodings when he glimpsed a familiar carriage coming out of the fog towards him from the opposite direction. It was the Winslow family carriage, and the bundled-up figure on the perch was almost certainly Edward Rush, one of their coachmen. To judge from the way he slowed the horses, Rush appeared to have recognized him, too. Harold nodded a silent greeting to his colleague, before directing his gaze at the occupant of the carriage. For a split second, he and young Charles Winslow stared solemnly at one another. They did not say a word.

"Faster, Edward," Charles ordered his driver, tapping the roof of the carriage frantically with the knob of his cane.

Harold watched with relief as the carriage vanished once more into the fog in the direction of the Miller's Court flats. He was not needed now. He only hoped that young Winslow arrived in time. He would have liked to stay and see how the affair ended, but he had an order to carry out—although he fancied it had been given to him by a dead man—and so he urged the horses on once more and found his way out of that dreaded neighborhood where life (I apologize for the repetition, but the same thought did occur to Harold twice) was not worth thruppence. Admittedly, the expression sums up the peculiarity of the neighborhood very accurately, and we probably could not hope for a more profound appraisal from a coachman. However, despite having a life worthy of being recounted—as are all lives upon close scrutiny—the coachman Harold Barker is not a relevant character in this story. Others may choose to write about it and will no doubt find plenty of material to endow it with the emotion every good story requires—the time he met Rebecca, his wife, or the hilarious incident involving a ferret and a rake—but that is not our purpose here.

And so let us leave Harold, whose reappearance at some point in this tale I cannot vouch for, because a whole host of characters are going to pass through it and I can't be expected to remember every one of their faces. Let us return to Andrew, who at this very moment is crossing the arched entrance to Miller's Court and walking up the muddy stone path trying to find number thirteen while he rummages in his coat pocket for the key. After stumbling around in the dark for a few moments he found the room, pausing before the door with an attitude which anybody able to see him from one of the neighboring windows would have taken to be incongruous reverence. But for Andrew that room was infinitely more than some wretched lair where people who hadn't a penny to their name took refuge. He had not been back there since that fateful night, although he had paid to keep everything exactly as it had been, exactly as it still was inside his head. Every month for the past eight years he had sent one of his servants to pay the rent for the little room so that nobody would be able to live there, because if he ever went back, he did not want to find traces of anyone but Marie. The few pennies for the rent were a drop in the ocean for him, and Mr. Mc-Carthy had been delighted that a wealthy gentleman and obvious rake should want to rent that wretched dwelling indefinitely, for after what had taken place within its four walls he very much doubted anybody would be brave enough to sleep there. Andrew realized now that deep down he had always known he would come back, that the ceremony he was about to perform could not have been carried out anywhere else.

He opened the door and cast a mournful gaze around the room. It was a tiny space, scarcely more sophisticated than a shack, with flaking walls and a few sticks of battered furniture including a dilapidated bed, a grimy mirror, a crumbling fireplace, and a couple of chairs which looked as if they might fall apart if a fly landed on them. He felt a renewed sense of amazement that life could actually take place in somewhere like this. And yet, had he not known more happiness in that room than in the luxurious setting of the Harrington mansion? If, as he had read somewhere, every man's paradise was in a different place, his was undoubtedly here, a place he had reached guided by a map not charting rivers or valleys but kisses and caresses.

And it was precisely a caress, this time an icy one on the nape of his neck, which drew his attention to the fact that nobody had taken the trouble to fix the broken window to the left of the door. What was the point? McCarthy seemed to belong to that class of people whose motto was to work as little as possible, and had Andrew reproached him for not replacing the pane of glass, he could always have argued that since he had requested everything be kept just as it was he had assumed this included the windowpane. Andrew sighed. He could see nothing with which to plug the hole, and so decided to kill himself in his hat and coat. He sat down on one of the rickety chairs, reached into his pocket for the gun, and carefully unfolded the cloth, as if he were performing a liturgy. The Colt gleamed in the moonlight filtering weakly through the small, grimy window.

He stroked the weapon as though it were a cat curled up in his lap and let Marie's smile wash over him once more. Andrew was always surprised that his memories retained the vibrancy, like fresh roses, of those first days. He remembered everything so incredibly vividly, as though no eight-year gap stretched between them, and at times these memories seemed even more beautiful than the real events. What mysterious alchemy could make these imitations appear more vivid than the real thing? The answer was obvious: the passage of time, which transformed the volatile present into that finished, unalterable painting called the past, a canvas man always executed blindly, with erratic brushstrokes that only made sense when one stepped far enough away from it to be able to admire it as a whole.

II

THE FIRST TIME THEIR EYES MET, she was not even there. Andrew had fallen in love with Marie without needing to have her in front of him, and to him this felt as romantic as it did paradoxical. The event had occurred at his uncle's mansion in Queen's Gate, opposite the Natural History Museum, a place Andrew had always thought of as his second home. He and his cousin were the same age and had almost grown up together, to the point where the servants sometimes forgot which of them was their employer's son. And, as is easily imaginable, their affluent social position had spared them any hardship and misfortune, exposing them only to the pleasant side of life, which they immediately mistook for one long party where everything was apparently permissible. They moved on from sharing toys to sharing teenage conquests, and from there, curious to see how far they could stretch the seeming impunity they enjoyed, to devising different ways of testing the limits of what was acceptable. Their elaborate indiscretions and more or less immoral behavior were so perfectly coordinated that for years it had been difficult not to see them as one person. This was partly down to their sharing the complicity of twins, but also to their arrogant approach to life and even to their physical similarity. Both boys were lean and sinewy, and possessed the sort of angelic good looks that made it almost impossible to refuse them anything. This was especially true of women, as was amply demonstrated during their time in Cambridge, where they established a record number of conquests unmatched to this day. Their habit of visiting the same tailors and hat makers added the finishing touch to that unnerving resemblance, a likeness it seemed would go on forever, until one day, without any warning, as though God had resolved to compensate for His lack of creativity, that wild, two-headed creature they formed suddenly split into two distinct halves. Andrew turned into a pensive, taciturn young man, while Charles went on perfecting the frivolous behavior of his adolescence. This change did not however alter their friendship rooted in kinship. Far from driving them apart, this unexpected divergence in their characters made them complement one another. Charles's devil-may-care attitude found its counterpart in the refined melancholy of his cousin, for whom such a whimsical approach to life was no longer satisfying. Charles observed with a wry smile Andrew's attempts to give his life some meaning, wandering around secretly disillusioned, waiting for a sudden flash of inspiration that never came. Andrew, in turn, looked on amused at his cousin's insistence on behaving like a brash, shallow youth, even though some of his gestures and opinions betrayed a mind as disappointed as his own, despite his seeming unwillingness to give up enjoying what he had. Charles lived intensely, as though he could not get enough of life's pleasures, whereas Andrew could sit in a corner for hours, watching a rose wilt in his hands.

The month of August when it all happened, they had both just turned eighteen, and although neither showed any signs of settling down, they both sensed this life of leisure could not go on much longer, that sooner or later their parents would lose patience with this unproductive indolence and find positions for them in one of the family firms—though in the meantime they were enjoying seeing how much longer they could get away with it. Charles was already going to the office occasionally in the mornings to attend to minor business, but Andrew preferred to wait until his boredom became so unbearable that taking care of family business would seem like a relief rather than a prison sentence. After all, his older brother Anthony already fulfilled their father's expectations sufficiently to allow the illustrious William Harrington to consent to his second son pursuing his career of black sheep for a couple more years, provided he did not stray from his sight. But Andrew had strayed. He had strayed a long way. And now he intended to stray even further, until he disappeared completely, beyond all redemption.

But let us not get sidetracked by melodrama. Let's carry on with our story. Andrew had dropped in at the Winslow mansion that August afternoon so that he and his cousin Charles could arrange a Sunday outing with the charming Keller sisters. As usual, they would take them to that little grassy knoll carpeted with flowers near the Serpentine, in Hyde Park, where they invariably mounted their amorous offensives. But Charles was still sleeping, so the butler showed Andrew into the library. He did not mind waiting until his cousin got up; he felt at ease surrounded by all those books filling the large, bright room with their peculiar musty smell. Andrew's father prided himself on having built up a decent library, yet his cousin's collection contained more than just obscure volumes on politics and other equally dull subjects. Here, Andrew could find the classics and adventure stories by authors such as Verne and Salgari; but still more interesting to Andrew was a strange, rather picturesque type of literature many considered frivolous—novels where the authors had let their imaginations run wild, regardless of how implausible or often downright absurd the outcome. Like all discerning readers, Charles appreciated Homer's *Odyssey* and his *Iliad*, but his real enjoyment came from immersing himself in the crazy world of *Batracomiomachia*, the blind poet's satire on his own work in an epic tale about a battle between mice and frogs. Andrew recalled a few books written in a similar style which his cousin had lent him; one called *True Tales* by Lucian of Samosata which recounted a series of fabulous voyages in a flying ship that takes the hero up to the sun and even through the belly of a giant whale. Another called *The Man in the Moon* by Francis Godwin, the first novel ever to describe an interplanetary voyage, that told the story of a Spaniard named Domingo Gonsales who travels to the moon in a machine drawn by a flock of wild geese. These flights of fancy reminded Andrew of popguns or firecrackers, all sound and fury, and yet he understood, or thought he did, why his cousin was so passionate about them. Somehow this literary genre, which most people condemned, acted as a sort of counterbalance to Charles's soul; it was the ballast that prevented him from lurching into seriousness or melancholy, unlike Andrew, who had been unable to adopt his cousin's casual attitude to life, and to whom everything seemed so achingly profound, imbued with that absurd solemnity that the transience of existence conferred upon even the smallest act.

However, that afternoon Andrew did not have time to look at any book. He did not even manage to cross the room to the bookshelves because the loveliest girl he had ever seen stopped him in his tracks. He stood staring at her, bemused, as time seemed to congeal, to stand still for a moment, until finally he managed to approach the portrait slowly to take a closer look. The woman was wearing a black velvet toque and a flowery scarf knotted at the neck. Andrew had to admit she was by no means beautiful by conventional standards: her nose was disproportionately large for her face, her eyes too close together, and her reddish hair looked damaged, and yet at the same time this mysterious woman possessed a charm as unmistakable as it was elusive. He was unsure exactly what it was that captivated him about her. It might have been the contrast between her frail appearance and the strength radiating from her gaze; a gaze he had never seen before in any of his conquests, a wild, determined gaze that retained a glimmer of youthful innocence. It was as if every day the woman was forced to confront the ugliness of life, and yet even so, curled up in her bed at night in the dark, she still believed it was only a regrettable figment of her imagination, a bad dream that would soon dissolve and give way to a more pleasant reality. It was the gaze of a person who yearns for something and refuses to believe it will never be hers, because hope is the only thing she has left.

"Charming creature, isn't she?" Charles's voice came from behind him.

Andrew jumped. He was so absorbed by the portrait he had not heard his cousin come in. He nodded as his cousin walked over to the drinks trolley. He himself could not have found any better way to describe the emotions the portrait stirred in him, that desire to protect her mixed with a feeling of admiration he could only compare—rather reluctantly, owing to the inappropriateness of the metaphor—to that which he felt for cats.

"It was my birthday present to my father," Charles explained, pouring a brandy. "It's only been hanging there a few days."

"Who is she?" asked Andrew. "I don't remember seeing her at any of Lady Holland or Lord Broughton's parties."

"At those parties?" Charles laughed. "I'm beginning to think the artist is gifted. He's taken you in as well."

"What do you mean?" asked Andrew, accepting the glass of brandy his cousin was holding out to him.

"Surely you don't think I gave it to my father because of its artistic merit? Does it look like a painting worthy of my consideration, cousin?" Charles grabbed his arm, forcing him to take a few steps closer to the portrait. "Take a good look. Notice the brushwork: utterly devoid of talent. The painter is no more than an amusing disciple of Degas. Where the Parisian is gentle, he is starkly somber."

Andrew did not understand enough about painting to be able to have a discussion with his cousin, and all he really wanted to know was the sitter's identity, and so he nodded gravely, giving his cousin to understand he agreed with his view that this painter would do better to devote himself to repairing bicycles. Charles smiled, amused by his cousin's refusal to take part in a discussion about painting that would have given him a chance to air his knowledge, and finally declared:

"I had another reason for giving it to him, dear cousin."

He drained his glass slowly, and gazed at the painting again for a few moments, nodding his head with satisfaction.

"And what reason was that, Charles?" Andrew asked, becoming impatient.

"The private enjoyment I get from knowing that my father, who looks down on the lower classes as though they were inferior beings, has the portrait of a common prostitute hanging in his library."

His words made Andrew reel.

"A prostitute?" he finally managed to stammer.

"Yes, cousin," replied Charles, beaming with contentment. "But not a high-class whore from the brothels in Russell Square, not even one of the tarts who ply their trade in the park on Vincent Street, but a dirty, foul-smelling draggletail from Whitechapel in whose ravaged vagina the wretched of the earth alleviate their misery for a few meager pennies."

Andrew took a swig of brandy, attempting to absorb his cousin's words. There was no denying his cousin's revelation had shocked him, as it would anybody who saw the portrait. But he also felt strangely disappointed. He stared at the painting again, trying to discover the cause of his unease. So, this lovely creature was a vulgar tart. Now he understood the mixture of passion and resentment seeping from her eyes that the artist had so skillfully captured. But Andrew had to admit his disappointment obeyed a far more selfish logic: the woman did not belong to his social class, which meant he could never meet her.

"I bought it thanks to Bruce Driscoll," Charles explained, pouring two more brandies. "Do you remember Bruce?"

Andrew nodded unenthusiastically. Bruce was a friend of his cousin whom boredom and money had turned into an art collector; a conceited, idle young man who had no compunction in showing off his knowledge of paintings at every opportunity.

"You know how he likes to look for treasure in the most unlikely places," his cousin said, handing him the second brandy. "Well, the last time I saw him, he told me about a painter he'd dug up during one of his visits to the flea markets. A man called Walter Sickert, a founding member of the New English Art Club. His studio was in Cleveland Street, and he painted East End prostitutes as though they were society ladies. I dropped in there and couldn't resist buying his latest canvas."

"Did he tell you anything about her?" Andrew asked, trying to appear nonchalant.

"About the whore? Only her name. I think she's called Marie Jeanette."

Marie Jeanette, Andrew muttered. The name oddly suited her, like her little hat.

"A Whitechapel whore . . . ," he whispered, still unable to get over his surprise.

"Yes, a Whitechapel whore. And my father has given her pride of place in his library!" Charles cried, spreading his arms theatrically in a mock gesture of triumph. "Isn't it absolutely priceless?"

With this, Charles flung his arm around his cousin's shoulder and guided him through to the sitting room, changing the subject. Andrew tried to hide his agitation, but could not help thinking about the girl in the portrait as they were planning their assault on the charming Keller sisters.

THAT NIGHT, IN HIS bedroom, Andrew lay wide awake. Where was the woman in the painting now? What was she doing? By the fourth or fifth question, he had begun calling the woman by her name, as though he really knew her and they enjoyed a magical intimacy. He realized he was seriously disturbed when he began to feel an absurd jealousy towards the men who could have her for a few pennies, whereas for him, despite all his wealth, she was unattainable. And yet was she really beyond his reach? Surely, given his position, he could have her, physically at least, more easily than he could any other woman, and for the rest of his life. The problem was finding her. Andrew had never been to Whitechapel, but he had heard enough about the neighborhood to know it was dangerous, especially for someone of his class. It was not advisable to go there alone, but he could not count on Charles accompanying him. His cousin would not understand his preferring that tart's grubby vagina to the sweet delights the charming Keller sisters kept hidden beneath their petticoats, or the perfumed honeypots of the Chelsea madams, where half the well-to-do West End gentlemen sated their appetites. Perhaps he would understand, and even agree to go with him for the fun of it, if Andrew explained it as a passing fancy, but he knew what he felt was too powerful to be reduced to a mere whim. Or was it? He would not know what he wanted from her until he had her in his arms. Would she really be that difficult to find? Three sleepless nights were enough for him to come up with a plan.

And so it was that while the Crystal Palace (which had been moved to Sydenham after displaying the Empire's industrial prowess inside its vast belly of glass and reinforced iron) was offering organ recitals, children's ballets, a host of ventriloquists' acts, and even the possibility of picnicking in its beautiful gardens that Andrew Harrington—oblivious to the festive spirit that had taken hold of the city—put on the humble clothes of a commoner lent by one of his servants, and examined his disguise in the cheval glass. He could not help giving a wry smile at the sight of himself in a threadbare jacket and trousers, his fair hair tucked under a check cap pulled down over his eyes. Surely looking like that people would take him for a nobody, possibly a cobbler or a barber. Disguised in this way, he ordered the astonished Harold to take him to Whitechapel. Before leaving, he made him swear to secrecy. No one must know about this expedition to London's worst neighborhood, not his father, not the mistress of the house, not his brother Anthony, not even his cousin Charles. No one.

III

IN ORDER NOT TO DRAW ATTENTION to himself, Andrew made Harold pull up the luxurious carriage in Leadenhall and continued alone on foot towards Commercial Street. After wandering a good way down that evil-smelling street, he plucked up his courage and entered the maze of alleyways that made up Whitechapel. Within ten minutes, a dozen prostitutes loomed out of the fog to offer him a trip to Mount Venus for the price of a few pennies, but none of them was the girl in the portrait. Had they been draped in seaweed, Andrew might easily have mistaken them for faded, dirty ship figureheads. He refused them politely without pausing, a dreadful sadness welling up in him at the sight of those scarecrows hunched against the cold who had no better way of earning a living. Their toothless mouths attempting bawdy smiles were more repulsive than desirable. Would Marie look like that outside the portrait, far from the brushstrokes that had transformed her into an angelic creature?

He soon realized he was unlikely to find her by chance. Perhaps he would have more luck if he asked for her directly. Once he was sure his disguise was convincing, he entered the Ten Bells, a popular tavern on the corner of Fournier Street and Commercial Street opposite the ghostly Christ Church. When he peered inside the pub, it looked to him like just the sort of place whores went to in search of clients. As soon as he reached the bar, two of them came up to him. Trying to look casual, Andrew offered them a glass of stout, refusing their propositions as politely as possible. He explained he was looking for a woman called Marie Jeanette. One of the whores left immediately, pretending to be offended, perhaps because she did not want to waste the evening with someone who didn't want to pay for her services, but the other, the taller of the two, decided to accept his invitation:

"I suppose you mean Marie Kelly. That dratted Irishwoman, everybody wants her. I expect she's done a few by now and is in the Britannia—that's where we all go when we've made enough for a bed and a bit more besides so that we can get drunk quick and forget our sorrows," she said, with more irony than bitterness.

"Where is this tavern?" Andrew asked.

"Near here, on the corner of Crispin Street and Dorset Street."

The least Andrew could do was thank her for the information by giving her four shillings.

"Get yourself a room," he recommended, with a warm smile. "It's too cold out there tonight to be traipsing the streets."

"Why, thank you, mister. You're too kind, I'm sure," said the whore, genuinely grateful.

Andrew said good-bye, politely doffing his cap.

"If Marie Kelly won't give you what you want, come back and see me," she shouted after him with a flash of coquettishness that was blighted by her toothless smile. "My name's Liz. Liz Stride, don't forget."

Andrew had no problem finding the Britannia, a seedy tavern with a windowed front. Despite being lit by brilliant oil lamps, the room was dense with tobacco smoke. At the far end was a long bar, with a couple of private rooms to the left. A crowd of noisy customers filled the large main area cluttered with tables and chairs, the floor strewn with sawdust. A fleet of waiters in filthy aprons squeezed their way between tightly packed tables juggling metal tankards brimming with beer. In the corner, a battered old piano displayed its grubby keys to anyone wishing to enliven the evening with a tune. Andrew reached the bar, the surface of which was laden with large jugs of wine, oil lamps, and plates of cheese cut into huge chunks that looked more like bits of rubble from a dump. He lit a cigarette from one of the lamps, ordered a pint of beer, and leaned discreetly against the bar, surveying the crowd and wrinkling his nose at the strong smell of cooked sausage emanating from the kitchen. As he had been told, the atmosphere there was more relaxed than at the Ten Bells. Most of the tables were occupied by sailors on shore leave and local people dressed as modestly as he, although he also noticed a few groups of prostitutes busy getting drunk. He sipped his beer slowly and looked for one who fitted Marie Kelly's description, but none did. By his third beer, he had begun to despair and to wonder what on earth he was doing there, chasing an illusion.

He was about to leave when she pushed her way through the pub door. He recognized her at once. There was no doubt about it: she was the girl in the portrait, but more beautiful still for being endowed with movement. Her face looked drained, yet she moved with the same energy Andrew had imagined she would from seeing her on canvas. Most of the other customers remained oblivious to the apparition. How was it possible for anyone not to react to the small miracle that had just taken place in the tavern? thought Andrew. This complete indifference made him feel he was a privileged witness to the phenomenon. And he could not help recalling the time when, as a child, he had seen the wind take a leaf between invisible fingers and balance the tip of it on the surface of a puddle, spinning it like a top until a carriage wheel put an end to its dance. To Andrew it had seemed that Mother Nature had engineered that magic trick for his eyes alone. From then on, he was convinced that the universe dazzled mankind with volcanic eruptions, but had its own secret way of communicating with the select few, people like Andrew who looked at reality as though it were a strip of wallpaper covering up something else. Taken aback, he watched Marie Kelly walk towards him as if she knew him. This made his heart start pounding, but he calmed down when she propped her elbow on the bar and ordered half a pint of beer without even glancing at him.

"Having a good night, Marie?"

"Can't grumble, Mrs. Ringer."

Andrew swallowed, on the verge of blacking out. She was standing next to him! He could scarcely believe it, yet it was true. He had heard her voice. A tired, rather husky voice, but lovely in any case. And if he really tried, ridding the air of the superfluous stench of tobacco smoke and sausages, he could probably smell her, too. Smell Marie Kelly. Mesmerized, Andrew gazed at her in admiration, rediscovering in her every gesture what he already knew. In the same way a shell holds the roar of the sea, so this frail-looking body seemed to contain within it a force of nature.

When the landlady placed the beer on the counter, Andrew realized this was an opportunity he must not waste. He rummaged swiftly in his pockets and paid before she could:

"Allow me, miss."

The gesture, as unexpected as it was chivalrous, earned him an openly approving look from Marie Kelly. Being the focus of her gaze paralyzed him. As the painting had already shown, the girl's eyes were beautiful, and yet they seemed buried beneath a layer of resentment. He could not help comparing her to a poppy field where someone has decided to dump refuse. And yet he was completely, hopelessly enthralled by her, and he tried to make that instant when their eyes met as meaningful to her as it was to him, but—and my apologies to any romantic souls reading these lines—some things cannot be expressed in a look. How could Andrew make her share in the almost mystical feeling overwhelming him at that moment? How could he convey, with nothing more than his eyes, the sudden realization that he had been searching for her all his life without knowing it? If in addition we consider that Marie Kelly's existence up to that point had done little to increase her understanding of life's subtleties, it should come as no surprise that this initial attempt at spiritual communion (for want of a better way of putting it) was doomed to failure. Andrew did his best, obviously, but the girl understood his passionate gaze just as she interpreted that of the other men who accosted her every evening.

"Thanks, mister," she replied with a lewd smile, no doubt from force of habit.

Andrew nodded, dismissing the significance of a gesture he considered an all-important part of his strategy, then realized with horror that his careful plan had not taken into account how he was to strike up a conversation with the girl once he found her. What did he have to say to her? Or more precisely, what did he have to say to a whore? A Whitechapel whore, at that. He had never bothered speaking much to the Chelsea prostitutes, only enough to discuss positions or the lighting in the room, and with the charming Keller sisters, or his other female acquaintances—young ladies whom it would not do to worry with talk of politics or Darwin's theories—he only discussed trivia: Paris fashions, botany, and, more recently spiritualism, the latest craze everyone was taking up. But none of these subjects seemed suitable to discuss with this woman, who was hardly likely to want to summon up some spirit to tell her which of her many suitors she would end by marrying. And so he simply stared at her, enraptured. Luckily, Marie Kelly knew a better way of breaking the ice.

"I know what you want, mister, although you're too shy to ask," she said, her grin broadening as she gave his hand a fugitive caress that brought him out in goose pimples. "Thruppence and I can make your dreams come true. Tonight, at any rate."

Andrew gazed at her, shaken: she did not know how right she was. She had been his only dream those past few nights, his deepest longing, his most urgent desire, and now, although he was still scarcely able to believe it, finally he could have her. His whole body tingled with excitement at the mere thought of touching her, of caressing the slender body silhouetted beneath that shabby dress, of bringing forth deep moans from her lips as he was set alight before her eyes, those of a wild animal, a tormented indomitable creature. And yet that tremor of joy rapidly gave way to a profound sadness when he considered the unjust plight of that fallen angel, the ease with which any man could grope her, defile her in a filthy back alley, without anyone in the world uttering a single cry of protest. Was this what such a unique creature had been created for? He had no choice but to accept her invitation, a lump in his throat, distressed at being compelled to take her the same way as her other clients, as if his intentions were no different from theirs. Once he had accepted, Marie Kelly smiled with what looked to Andrew like forced enthusiasm and tilted her head for them to leave the pub.

Andrew felt odd following the whore like that, walking behind her with birdlike steps as though Marie Kelly were leading him to the gallows instead of to plunge between her thighs. And yet, could their meeting have been any different? From the moment he came across his cousin's painting he had been penetrating deeper into unknown territory, where he could not get his bearings because nothing around him looked familiar, everything was new, and, judging from the deserted streets they were going through, quite possibly dangerous. Was he blithely walking into some sort of trap laid by the whore's pimp? He wondered whether Harold would hear his shouts, and if so, would he bother coming to his aid, or use the opportunity to avenge himself for the offhand treatment he had received from his master all these years? After guiding him part of the way along Hanbury Street, a muddy alley dimly lit by a single oil lamp sputtering on a corner, Marie Kelly beckoned him down a narrow passageway leading into pitch-darkness. Andrew followed her, convinced he would meet his death, or at least be beaten to within an inch of his life by a couple of ruffians much bigger than him, who, having stolen everything including his socks, would spit contemptuously on his bloody remains. That was how they did things here, and his idiotic adventure richly deserved such an ending. But before fear had time to take hold, they came out into a filthy waterlogged backyard, where to his surprise no one was waiting for him. Andrew glanced warily about him. Yes: strange as it might seem, they were alone in that evil-smelling place. The world they had left behind was reduced to a muffled rumble in which a distant church bell's chimes rang out. At his feet, the moon reflected in a puddle looked like a crumpled letter some unhappy lover had tossed on the ground.

"We won't be disturbed here, mister," Marie Kelly re-assured him, leaning back against the wall and drawing him to her.

Before he knew it, she had unbuttoned his trousers and pulled out his penis. She did so with startling ease, without any of the provocative foreplay to which the Chelsea prostitutes had accustomed him. The matter-of-fact way she maneuvered his sex beneath her hiked-up skirts made it clear to Andrew that what to him was another magical moment for her was no more than simple routine.

"It's in," she assured him.

In? Andrew had enough experience to know the whore was lying. She was simply gripping his penis between her thighs. He assumed it was common practice among them, a trick to avoid penetration, which, if they were lucky and the client failed to notice or was too drunk, reduced the number of hasty intrusions they were forced to undergo each day, and with them the unwanted pregnancies such a flood of sperm could bring about. With this in mind, Andrew began thrusting energetically, prepared to go along with the charade, because in reality it was more than enough for him to rub his erect member against the silky skin of her inner thigh, to feel her body pressed against his for as long as the pretense lasted. What did it matter whether it was all a sham if this phantom penetration allowed him to cross the boundary imposed by good manners and force his way into that intimacy only lovers share. Feeling her hot sticky breath in his ear, inhaling the delicate odor from her neck, and clasping her to him until he felt the contours of her body merge with his was worth infinitely more than thruppence. And, as he soon discovered to his consternation when he ejaculated into her petticoats, it had the same effect on him as other greater undertakings. Slightly ashamed at his lack of endurance, he finished emptying himself in quiet contemplation, still pressed against her, until he felt her stir impatiently. He stepped back, embarrassed. Oblivious to his unease, the whore straightened her skirts and thrust out a hand to be paid. Trying to regain his composure, Andrew hurriedly gave her the agreed sum. He had enough money left in his pockets to buy her for the whole night, but he preferred to savor what he had just experienced in the privacy of his own bed, and to get her to meet him the next night.

"My name's Andrew," he introduced himself, his voice high-pitched from emotion. She raised an eyebrow, amused. "And I'd like to see you again tomorrow."

"Certainly, mister. You know where to find me," the whore said, leading him back along the gloomy passageway she had brought him down.

As they made their way back towards the main streets, Andrew was wondering whether ejaculating between her thighs entitled him to put his arm around her shoulder. He had decided it did, and was about to do precisely that when they ran into another couple walking almost blindly the other way down the dim alleyway. Andrew mumbled an apology to the fellow he had bumped into, who, although scarcely more than a shadow in the darkness, seemed to him quite a burly sort. He was clinging onto a whore, whom Marie Kelly greeted with a smile.

"It's all yours, Annie," she said, referring to the back-yard they had just left.

The woman called Annie thanked her with a raucous laugh and tugged her companion towards the passageway. Andrew watched them stagger into the pitch-blackness. Would that burly fellow be satisfied with having his member trapped between her thighs?, he wondered, as he noticed how avidly the man clutched the whore to him.

"Didn't I tell you it was a quiet spot," Marie Kelly remarked matter-of-factly as they came out into Hanbury Street.

They said a laconic good-bye in front of the Britannia. Rather disheartened by the coldness she had shown after the act, Andrew tried to find his way back through the gloomy streets to his carriage. It was a good half hour before he found it. He avoided Harold's eyes as he climbed back into the coach.

"Home, sir?" Harold enquired sardonically.

THE FOLLOWING NIGHT HE arrived at the Britannia determined to behave like a self-assured man instead of the fumbling, timid dandy of their previous encounter. He had to overcome his nerves and prove he could adapt to his surroundings if he was to display his true charms to the girl, that repertoire of smiles and flattery with which he habitually captivated the ladies of his own class.

He found Marie Kelly sitting at a corner table brooding over a pint of beer. Her demeanor unnerved him, but knowing he was not the sort to think up a new strategy as he went along, he decided to stick with his original plan. He ordered a beer at the bar, sat down at the girl's table as naturally as he could, and told her he knew of a guaranteed way to wipe the worried expression from her face. Marie Kelly shot him a black look, confirming what he feared: his remark had been a tactless blunder. Following this reaction, Andrew thought she was going to tell him to clear off without even wasting her breath, with a simple wave of her hand, like someone shooing away an irritating fly. But in the end, she restrained herself and gazed at him quizzically for a few seconds until she must have decided he was as good a person as any to unburden herself to. She took a swig from her tankard, as if to clear her throat, wiped her mouth on her sleeve, and told him that her friend Annie, the woman they had bumped into in Hanbury Street the night before, had been found that morning, murdered, in the same yard they had been in. The poor woman had been partially decapitated, sliced open, her intestines pulled out, and her womb removed. Andrew stammered that he was sorry, as shocked at the killer's attention to detail as at having collided with him moments before the crime. Evidently that particular client had not been satisfied with the usual service. But Marie Kelly had other worries. According to her, Annie was the third prostitute to be murdered in Whitechapel in less than a month. Polly Nichols had been found dead with her throat slit in Bucks Road, opposite Essex pier, on August 31. And on the seventh of that same month, Martha

Tabram had been found brutally stabbed to death with a penknife on the stairs of a rooming house. Marie Kelly laid the blame on the gang from Old Nichol Street, blackmailers who demanded a share of the whores' earnings.

"Those bastards will stop at nothing to get us working for them," she said between gritted teeth.

This state of affairs disturbed Andrew, but it should have come as no surprise: after all, they were in Whitechapel—that putrid dung heap London had turned its back on, home to more than a thousand prostitutes living alongside German, Jewish, and French immigrants. Stabbings were a daily occurrence. Wiping away the tears that had finally flowed from her eyes, Marie Kelly sat, head bowed in silence for a few moments as though in prayer, until, to Andrew's surprise, she suddenly roused herself from her stupor, grasped his hand, and smiled lustfully at him. Life went on. Whatever else happened, life went on. Was that what she had meant by her gesture? After all, she, Marie Kelly, had not been murdered. She had to go on living, dragging her skirts through those foul-smelling streets in search of money to pay for a bed. Andrew gazed with pity at her hand lying in his, her dirty nails poking through her frayed mitten. He too felt the need to concentrate for a moment in order to change masks, like an actor who needs some time in his dressing room to concentrate in order to become a different character when he goes back on stage. After all, life went on for him, too. Time did not stop just because a whore had been murdered. And so he stroked her hand tenderly, ready to resume his plan. As though wiping condensation from a windowpane, he freed his young lover's smile from its veil of sadness and, looking her in the eye for the first time, he said:

"I have enough money to buy you for the whole night, but I don't want any fakery in a cold backyard."

This startled Marie Kelly, and she tensed in her seat, but Andrew's smile soon put her at ease.

"I rent a room at Miller's Court, but I don't know if it'll be good enough for the likes of you," she remarked flirtatiously.

"I'm sure you'll make me like it," Andrew ventured to say, delighted at the bantering tone their conversation had finally taken, as this was a register at which he excelled.

"But first I'll have to turn out my good-for-nothing husband," she replied. "He doesn't like me bringing work home."

This remark came as yet another shock to Andrew on this extraordinary night over which he clearly had no control. He tried not to let his disappointment show.

"Still, I'm sure your money will make up his mind for him," Marie concluded, amused at his reaction.

SO IT WAS THAT Andrew found paradise in the dismal little room where he was now sitting. That night, everything changed between them. When at last she lay naked, Andrew made love to her so respectfully, caressed her body with such tenderness that Marie Kelly could feel the hard shell she had carefully built to protect her soul begin to crack, that layer of ice preventing anything from seeping into her skin, keeping everything locked behind the door, out there where it could not hurt her. To her surprise, Andrew's kisses marking her body like a pleasurable itch made her own caresses less and less mechanical, and she quickly discovered it was no longer a whore lying on the bed, but the woman crying out for affection that she had always been. Andrew also sensed his lovemaking was freeing the real Marie Kelly, as though he were rescuing her from the bottom of one of those water tanks stage magicians immersed their beautiful assistants in, bound hand and foot, or as though his sense of direction were so good it saved him from getting lost in the maze like her other lovers, allowing him to reach the place no one else could, a sort of secret corner where the girl's real nature survived intact. They burned with a single flame, and when it waned and Marie Kelly, staring dreamily up at the ceiling, began talking about springtime in Paris, where she had worked as an artist's model some years before, and about her childhood in Wales and in Ratcliffe Highway in London, Andrew understood that this strange sensation in his chest must be the pangs of love, because without meaning to, he was experiencing all the emotions of which the poets spoke.

Andrew was touched by the emotive tone her voice took on when she described the Parisian squares with their riot of gladioli and petunias, and how on her return to London she had insisted everybody say her name in French, the only way she had found of preserving intact that distant fragrance which softened life's sharp edges; but he was equally moved by the hint of sadness in her voice as she described how they hung pirates from the Ratcliffe Highway Bridge until they drowned in the rising waters of the Thames. For this was the real Marie Kelly, this bittersweet fruit, nature's flawed perfection, one of God's contradictions. When she asked what sort of work he did that could apparently allow him to buy her for the rest of his life if he wanted, he decided to run the risk and tell her the truth. Because if their love were to exist it must be nurtured in truth or not at all, and the truth (of how her portrait had captivated him, sending him off on this foolish quest to find her in a neighborhood so different from his own, and of how he had found her) seemed as beautiful and miraculous to him as those stories about impossible love you read in books. When their bodies came together again, he realized that far from being an act of madness, falling in love with her was possibly the most reasonable thing he had ever done. And when he left the room, with the memory of her skin on his lips, he tried not to look at her husband Joe, who was leaning against the wall shivering with cold.

It was nearly daylight by the time Harold delivered him home. Too excited to go to bed, if only to relish the moments he had spent with Marie Kelly, Andrew went to the stables and saddled a horse. It was a long time since he had woken at dawn to go riding in Hyde Park. This was his favorite time of day, when the grass was still dewy and everything appeared untouched. How could he waste such an opportunity? Within minutes, Andrew was galloping through the trees opposite the Harrington mansion, laughing to himself and occasionally letting out a cry of joy, like a soldier celebrating victory, because that is what he felt like as he remembered the loving look Marie Kelly had given him before they said good-bye until the following night. As though she could see in his eyes that without realizing it, he had been searching for her for years. And perhaps I should take this opportunity to apologize for my earlier skepticism and confess that there is nothing that cannot be expressed in a look. A look, it seems, is a bottomless well of possibilities. And so Andrew rode on, seized by a wild impulse, overwhelmed for the first time by a burning, pulsating sensation, which might reasonably be described as happiness. And, prey to the effects of such a violent infatuation, everything in the universe he rode past appeared to sparkle, as though each of its elements—the paths strewn with dead leaves, the rocks, the trees, even the squirrels leaping from branch to branch—were lit up by an inner glow. But have no fear, I shall not become bogged down in lengthy descriptions of acres of impassioned, practically luminous parkland because, not only do I have no taste for it, but it would be untrue, for despite Andrew's altered vision, the landscape clearly did not undergo any real transformation, not even the squirrels, which are well known as creatures who pursue their own interests.

After more than an hour of strenuous, exhilarating riding, Andrew realized he still had a whole day to get through before he could return to Marie Kelly's humble bed, and so he must find some way of distracting himself from the dreadful feeling that would no doubt assail him when he realized that irrespective of circumstances, or probably because of them, the hands of the clock were not turning at their usual speed, but were actually slowing down on purpose. He decided to drop in on his cousin Charles, which he usually did when he wanted him to share in his joy, even though this time Andrew had no intention of telling him anything. Perhaps he was simply curious to see what Charles would look like to his feverish gaze which had the power to enhance everything, to see whether he would also glow like the squirrels in the park.

IV

BREAKFAST HAD BEEN LAID OUT in the Winslow dining room for young Charles, who was doubtless still lazing in bed. On a table next to one of the French windows, the servants had set out a dozen covered platters, bread rolls, oranges, jams and marmalades, and jugs brimming with milk. Most of it would be thrown away because, contrary to all appearance, they were not expecting a regiment, only his cousin, who, given his famous lack of appetite in the mornings would almost certainly be content to nibble on a roll, ignoring the extravagant spread displayed in his honor. Andrew was surprised by the sudden concern he felt at such waste, for he had spent years contemplating tables like this, here as well as at his own house, creaking under the weight of food no one would eat. He realized this curious response was the first of many that would result from his forays into Whitechapel, that dung heap inhabited by people capable of killing one another for his cousin's half-eaten roll. Would his experiences there stir his social conscience in the same way it had his emotions? He was the type of person whose cultivation of his inner life left little time for worrying about the outside world of the street. He was above all devoted to resolving the mystery that was Andrew, to studying his feelings and responses: all his time was taken up in attempting to fine-tune the instrument that was his spirit until he felt satisfied with the sound it produced. There were times, owing to the constantly changing and rather unpredictable nature of his thought patterns, when this task appeared as impossible to him as lining up the goldfish in their bowl, but until he succeeded he sensed it would be impossible for him to worry about what went on in the world, which for him started where his own pleasant, carefully scrutinized private concerns ended. In any case, he thought, it would be interesting to observe in himself how hitherto unknown preoccupations emerged through simple exposure. Who could tell: perhaps his response to these new worries might hold the key to the mystery of who the real Andrew Harrington was.

He took an apple from the fruit bowl and settled into an armchair to wait yet again for his cousin to return to the land of the living. He had rested his muddy boots on a footstool and was munching on his apple, smiling as he remembered Marie Kelly's kisses and how they had both, gently but completely, made up for all the years starved of affection, when his eye alighted on the newspaper lying on the table. It was the morning edition of *The Star*, announcing in bold print the murder of a Whitechapel prostitute called Annie Chapman. The news item gave details of the horrific mutilation she had suffered: besides her uterus, which he had already learned about from Marie Kelly, her bladder and vagina had also been removed. Among other things, the newspaper also mentioned a couple of cheap rings missing from one of her fingers. It appeared the police had no real clues as to the murderer's identity, although after questioning other East End whores, the name of a possible suspect had emerged: a Jewish cobbler nicknamed Leather Apron, who was in the habit of robbing the prostitutes at knifepoint. The article came with a macabre illustration of a policeman dangling a lamp over the bloody corpse of a woman sprawled on the pavement. Andrew shook his head. He had forgotten that his paradise was surrounded by hell itself, and that the woman he loved was an angel trapped in a world full of demons. He closely read the three-page report on the Whitechapel crimes committed to date, feeling worlds away from it all in this luxurious dining room, where man's capacity for baseness and aberration was kept at bay as surely as the dust tirelessly polished away by servants. He had thought of giving Marie Kelly the money to pay off the gang of blackmailers she thought were responsible for the crimes, but the report did not seem to be pointing in that direction. The precise incisions on the bodies suggested that the killer had surgical knowledge, which implicated the entire medical profession, although the police had not ruled out furriers, cooks, and barbers—anyone, in short, whose job brought them into contact with knives. Queen Victoria's medium was also reported to have seen the killer's face in a dream. Andrew sighed. The medium knew more about the killer than he, even though he had bumped into the fellow moments before he committed the crime.

"Since when did you develop an interest in the affairs of Empire, cousin?" asked a beaming Charles behind him. "Ah no, I see you are reading the crime pages."

"Good morning, Charles," said Andrew, tossing the paper onto the table as though he had been idly leafing through it.

"The coverage given to the murders of those wretched tarts is incredible," his cousin remarked, plucking a cluster of shiny grapes from the fruit bowl and sitting in the opposite armchair. "Although I confess to being intrigued by the importance they're attaching to this sordid affair: they've put Scotland Yard's finest detective Fred Abberline in charge of the investigation. Clearly the Metropolitan Police are out of their depth in a case like this."

Andrew pretended to agree, nodding abstractedly as he gazed out of the window watching the wind scatter an airballoon-shaped cloud. He did not want to arouse his cousin's attention by showing too much interest in the affair, but the truth was he longed to know every detail of the crimes, apparently confined to the area where his beloved lived. How would his cousin react if he told him he had bumped into that brutal murderer in a murky Whitechapel alleyway the night before? The sad fact was that, even so, he was unable to describe the fellow except to say he was enormous and evil smelling.

"In any case, regardless of Scotland Yard's involvement, for the moment all they have are suspicions, some of them quite preposterous," his cousin went on, plucking a grape from the bunch and rolling it between his fingers. "Did you know they suspect one of the Red Indians from that Buffalo Bill show we saw last week, and even the actor Richard Mansfield, who is playing in *Dr. Jekyll and Mr. Hyde* at the Lyceum? I recommend it, by the way: Mansfield's transformation on stage is truly chilling."

Andrew promised he would go, tossing the remains of his apple onto the table.

"Anyway," Charles concluded rather wearily to end the conversation, "the poor wretches in Whitechapel have formed vigilante groups and are patrolling the streets. It seems London's population is growing so fast the police force can no longer cope. Everybody wants to live in this accursed city. People come here from all over the country in search of a better life, only to end up being exploited in factories, contracting typhus fever or turning to crime in order to pay inflated rent for a cellar or some other airless hole. Actually, I'm amazed there aren't more murders and robberies, considering how many go unpunished. Mark my word, Andrew, if the criminals became organized, London would be theirs. It's hardly surprising Queen Victoria fears a popular uprising—a revolution like the one our French neighbors endured, which would end with her and her family's heads on the block. Her Empire is a hollow façade that needs progressively shoring up to stop it from collapsing. Our cows and sheep graze on Argentinian pastures, our tea is grown in China and India, our gold comes from South Africa and Australia, and the wine we drink is from France and Spain. Tell me, cousin, what, apart from crime, do we actually produce ourselves? If the criminal elements planned a proper rebellion, they could take over the country. Fortunately, evil and common sense rarely go hand in hand."

Andrew liked listening to Charles ramble in this relaxed way, pretending not to take himself seriously. In reality, he admired his cousin's contradictory spirit, which reminded him of a house divided into endless chambers all separate from one another, so that what went on in one had no repercussions in the others. This explained why his cousin was able to glimpse amid his luxurious surroundings the most suppurating wounds and forget them a moment later, while he himself found it impossible to copulate successfully, to give a simple example, after a visit to a slaughterhouse or a hospital for the severely wounded. It was as if Andrew had been designed like a seashell; everything disappeared and resonated inside him. That was the basic difference between them: Charles reasoned and he felt.

"The truth is these sordid crimes are turning Whitechapel into a place where you wouldn't want to spend the night," Charles declared sententiously, abandoning his nonchalant pose, leaning across the table and staring meaningfully at his cousin. "Especially with a tart."

Andrew gaped at him, unable to conceal his surprise.

"You know about it?" he asked.

His cousin smiled.

"Servants talk, Andrew. You ought to know by now our most intimate secrets circulate like underground streams beneath the luxurious ground we walk on," he said, stamping his feet symbolically on the carpet.

Andrew sighed. His cousin had not left the newspaper there by accident. In fact, he had probably not even been asleep. Charles enjoyed this kind of game. Certain his cousin would come, it was easy to imagine him hiding behind one of the many screens partitioning the vast dining room, and waiting patiently for his stunned cousin to fall into the trap he had laid, exactly as had happened.

"I don't want my father to find out, Charles," begged Andrew.

"Don't worry, cousin. I'm aware of the scandal it would cause in the family. But tell me, are you in love with the girl or is this just a passing fancy?"

Andrew remained silent. What could he say?

"You needn't reply," his cousin said in a resigned voice. "I'm afraid I wouldn't understand either way. I only hope you know what you're doing."

ANDREW OF COURSE DID not know what he was doing, but could not stop doing it. Each night, like a moth drawn to the flame, he returned to the miserable room in Miller's Court, hurling himself into the relentless blaze of Marie Kelly's passion. They made love all night, driven by a frantic desire, as though they had been poisoned during dinner and did not know how long they had left to live, or as though the world around them were suddenly being decimated by the plague. Soon Andrew understood that if he left enough coins on her bedside table, their passion could continue gently smoldering beyond the dawn. His money preserved their fantasy, and even banished Joe, Marie Kelly's husband, whom Andrew tried not to think of when, disguised beneath his modest clothes, he strolled with her through the maze of muddy streets in Whitechapel. Those were peaceful, pleasant walks, full of encounters with the girl's friends and acquaintances, the long-suffering foot soldiers of a war without trenches; a bunch of poor souls, who rose from their beds each morning to face a hostile world, driven on by the sheer animal instinct for survival, and whom a fascinated Andrew gradually found himself admiring, as he would a species of exotic flower alien to his world. He became convinced that life there was more real, simpler, easier to understand than in the luxuriously carpeted mansions where he spent his days.

Occasionally, he had to pull his cap down over his eyes in order not to be recognized by the bands of wealthy young men who laid siege to the neighborhood some nights. They arrived in luxurious carriages mobbing the streets like rude, arrogant conquistadors, in search of some miserable brothel where they could satisfy their basest instincts with impunity, for, according to a rumor Andrew had frequently heard in the West End smoking clubs, the only limits on what could be done with the wretched Whitechapel tarts were money and imagination. Watching these boisterous incursions, Andrew was assailed by a sudden protective instinct, which could only mean he had unconsciously begun to see Whitechapel as a place he should perhaps watch over. However, there was little he could do confronted with those barbarous invasions, besides feeling overwhelmingly sad and helpless, and trying to forget about them in the arms of his beloved, who appeared more beautiful to him by the day, as though beneath his loving caresses she had recovered the innate natural sparkle that life had robbed her of.

But, as everyone knows, no paradise is complete without a serpent, and the sweeter the moments spent with his beloved, the more bitter the taste in Andrew's mouth when he realized what he had of Marie Kelly was all he could ever have. Because, although it was never enough and each day he yearned for more, this love that could not exist outside of Whitechapel, for all its undeniable intensity, remained rather arbitrary and illusory. And while outside a crazed mob tried to lynch the Jewish cobbler nicknamed Leather Apron, Andrew quenched his anger and fear in Marie Kelly's body, wondering whether his beloved's fervor was because she too realized they had embarked upon a reckless love affair and that all they could do was greedily clasp this unexpected rose of happiness, trying their best to ignore the painful thorns. Or was it her way of telling him she was prepared to rescue their apparently doomed love even if it meant altering the very course of the universe itself? And if this was the case, did he possess the same strength, did he have the necessary conviction to embark upon what he already considered a lost battle? However hard he tried, Andrew could not imagine Marie Kelly moving in his world of refined young ladies, whose sole purpose in life was to display their fecundity by filling their houses with children, and to entertain their beloved spouses' friends with their pianistic accomplishments. Could Marie Kelly succeed in fulfilling this role whilst trying to stay afloat amidst the waves of social rejection that would doubtless attempt to drown her, or would she end up perishing like an exotic bloom removed from its hothouse?

THE NEWSPAPERS' CONTINUED COVERAGE of the whores' murders scarcely managed to distract Andrew from the torment of his secret fears. One morning, while breakfasting, he came across a reproduction of a letter the murderer had audaciously sent to the Central News Agency, assuring them they would not catch him easily and promising he would carry on killing, testing out his fine blade on the Whitechapel tarts. Appropriately enough, the letter was written in red ink and signed Jack the Ripper, a name that, however you looked at it, Andrew thought, was far more disturbing and imaginative than the rather dull Whitechapel Murderer by which he had been known up until then. This new name was taken up by all the newspapers, and inevitably conjured up the villain from the penny dreadfuls, Spring Heeled Jack, and his treatment of women. It was rapidly adopted by everyone, as Andrew soon discovered upon hearing it uttered everywhere he went. The words were always spoken with sinister excitement, as though for the sad souls of Whitechapel there were something thrilling and even fashionable about a ruthless murderer stalking the neighborhood with a razor-sharp knife.

Furthermore, as a result of this disturbing missive, Scotland Yard was suddenly deluged with similar correspondence (in which the alleged killer mocked the police, boasted childishly about his crimes, and promised more murders). Andrew got the impression that England was teeming with people desperate to bring excitement into

their lives by pretending they were murderers, normal
men whose souls were sullied by sadistic impulses and
unhealthy desires which fortunately they would never
act upon. Besides hampering the police investigation, the
letters were also involuntarily transforming the vulgar
individual he had bumped into in Hanbury Street into
a monstrous creature apparently destined to personify
man's most primitive fears. Perhaps this uncontrolled proliferation of would-be perpetrators of his macabre crimes
prompted the real killer to surpass himself. On the night
of September 30, in the timber merchants' at Dutfield
Yard, he murdered the Swedish girl Elizabeth Stride—
the whore who had originally put Andrew on Marie's
trail during his first visit to the neighborhood—and a few
hours later in Mitre Square, Catherine Eddowes, whom he
had time to rip open from pubis to sternum, remove her
left kidney, and even cut off her nose.

Thus began a cold month of October, in which a veil
of gloomy resignation descended upon the inhabitants of
Whitechapel, who despite Scotland Yard's efforts felt more
than ever abandoned to their fate. There was a look of
helplessness in the whores' eyes, but also a strange accept-
ance of their dreadful lot. Life became a long and anxious
wait, during which Andrew held Marie Kelly's trembling
body tightly in his arms and whispered to her gently she
need not worry, provided she stayed away from the Ripper's hunting ground, the area of backyards and deserted
alleyways where he roamed with his thirsty blade, until
the police managed to catch him. But his words did nothing to calm a shaken Marie Kelly, who had even begun

sheltering other whores in her tiny room at Miller's Court to keep them off the unsafe streets. This resulted in her having a fight with her husband Joe, during which he broke a window. The following night, Andrew gave her the money to fix the glass and keep out the piercing cold. However, she simply placed it on her bedside table and lay back dutifully on the bed so that he could take her. Now, though, all she offered him was a body, a dying flame, and that look of grief-stricken despair she could not keep out of her eyes in recent days, a look in which he thought he glimpsed a desperate cry for help, a silent appeal to him to take her away from there before it was too late.

Andrew made the great mistake of pretending not to notice her obvious distress, as though all of a sudden he had forgotten that everything could be expressed in a look. He felt incapable of altering the very course of the universe itself, which for him translated into the even more momentous feat of confronting his own father. Perhaps that was why, as a silent rebuke for his cowardice, Marie Kelly began going out looking for clients and spending the nights getting drunk with her fellow whores in the Britannia. There they cursed as one the uselessness of the police and the power of that monster from hell who continued to mock them, most recently by sending George Lusk, socialist firebrand and self-proclaimed president of the Whitechapel Vigilance Committee, a cardboard box containing a human kidney. Frustrated at his own lack of courage, Andrew watched her return drunk each night to the little room. Then, before she could collapse on the floor or curl up like a dog beside the warm hearth, he would take her in his arms and put her to bed, grateful that no knife had stopped her in her tracks. But he knew she could not keep exposing herself to danger in this way, even if the murderer had not struck for several weeks and more than eighty policemen were patrolling the neighborhood, and he knew he was the only one able to stop her.

For that reason, sitting in the gloom while his beloved spun her drunken nightmares filled with corpses with their guts ripped out, Andrew would resolve to confront his father the very next day. Only the next day all he could do was prowl around his father's study not daring to go in. And when it grew dark, his head bowed in shame, occasionally clutching a bottle, he returned to Marie Kelly's little room, where she received him with her eyes' silent reproach. Then Andrew remembered all the things he had said to her, the impassioned declarations he had hoped would seal their union. How he had been waiting for her, for how long he did not know—eighteen, a hundred, five hundred years—how he was certain that if he had undergone any reincarnations he had looked for her in every one of them, for they were twin spirits destined to find each other in the labyrinth of time, and other such pronouncements, which, under the present circumstances, he was sure Marie Kelly could only see as a pathetic attempt to cloak his animal urges in a sophisticated romanticism or, worse still, to conceal the thrill he derived from those voyeuristic forays into the wretched side of existence. "Where is your love now, Andrew?" her eyes seemed to be asking him like a frightened gazelle's, before she trudged off to the Britannia, only to return a few hours later rolling drunk.

Until on that cold night of November 7 Andrew watched her leave once again for the tavern, and something inside him shifted. Whether it was the alcohol, which when consumed in the right quantity can, on occasion, clear some people's heads, or simply that enough time had passed for this clarity to occur naturally, it finally dawned on Andrew that without Marie Kelly his life would no longer have any meaning, and therefore he had nothing to lose by fighting for a future with her. Filled with sudden resolve, his lungs suddenly cleared of the dead leaves that had been choking him, he left the room, slamming the door resolutely behind him, and strode off towards the place where Harold spent his nights waiting while his master took his pleasure, huddled like an owl on the coachman's seat, warming himself with a bottle of brandy.

That night his father was to discover that his youngest son was in love with a whore.

V

YES, I KNOW THAT WHEN I BEGAN THIS tale I promised there would be a fabulous time machine, and there will be, there will even be intrepid explorers and fierce native tribes—a must in any adventure story. But all in good time; isn't it necessary at the start of any game to place all the pieces on their respective squares first? Of course it is, in which case let me continue setting up the board, slowly but surely, by returning to young Andrew, who might have taken the opportunity of the long journey back to the Harrington mansion to sober up as much as possible, but who chose instead to cloud his thoughts still further by finishing off the bottle he had in his pocket. Ultimately, there was no point in confronting his father with a sound argument and reasoned thinking, as he was sure any civilized discussion of the matter would be impossible. What he needed was to dull his senses as much as he could, staying just sober enough not to be completely tongue-tied. There was no point even slipping back into the elegant clothes he always left judiciously in a bundle on the seat.

That night there was no longer any need for secrecy. When they arrived at the mansion, Andrew stepped out of the carriage, asked Harold to stay where he was, and hurried into the house. The coachman nodded his head in dismay as he watched the young master run up the steps in those rags, and wondered if he would hear Mr. Harrington's shouts from there.

Andrew had forgotten his father had a meeting with businessmen that night until he staggered into the library, and a dozen men stood gaping at him in astonishment. This was not the situation he had anticipated, but he had too much alcohol in his blood to be put off. He searched for his father amid the array of dinner jackets, and finally found him standing by the fireplace, next to his brother Anthony. Glass in one hand and cigar in the other, both men looked him up and down in utter astonishment. But his clothing was the least of it, as they would soon discover, thought Andrew, who in the end felt pleased to have an audience. Since he was about to stick his head in the noose, better to do so in front of witnesses than alone with his father in his study. He cleared his throat loudly under the fixed gaze of the gathering, and said:

"Father, I've come here to tell you I'm in love."

His words were followed by a heavy silence, broken only by an embarrassed cough here and there.

"Andrew, this is hardly a suitable moment to . . ." his father began, visibly irritated, before Andrew silenced him with a sudden gesture of his hand.

"I assure you, Father, this is as unsuitable a moment as any," he said, trying to keep his balance so he would not have to finish his bravura performance flat on his face.

His father bridled but forced himself to remain silent. Andrew took a deep breath. The moment had come for him to destroy his life forever.

"And the woman who has stolen my heart . . . " he declared, "is a Whitechapel whore by the name of Marie Kelly."

Having finally unburdened himself in this way, he smiled defiantly at the gathering. Faces fell, heads were clutched in hands, arms flapped about in the air, but no one said a word: they all knew they were witnessing a melodrama with two protagonists, and of course, it was William Harrington who must speak. All eyes were fixed on the host. Staring down at the pattern on the carpet, his father shook his head, let out a low, barely repressed growl, and put down his glass on the mantelpiece, as though it were suddenly encumbering him.

"Contrary to what I've so often heard you maintain, gentlemen," Andrew went on, unaware of the rage stirring in his father's breast, "whores aren't whores because they want to be. I assure you that any one of them would choose to have a respectable job if they could. Believe me, I know what I'm saying." His father's colleagues went on demonstrating their ability to express surprise without opening their mouths. "I've spent a lot of time in their company these past few weeks. I've watched them washing in horse troughs in the mornings, seen them sitting down to sleep, held against the wall by a rope if they could not find a bed . . ."

And the more he went on speaking in this way about prostitutes, the more Andrew realized his feelings for

Marie Kelly were deeper than he had imagined. He gazed round with infinite pity at all these men with their orderly lives, their dreary, passionless existences, who would consider it impractical to yield to an uncontrollable urge. He could tell them what it was like to lose one's head, to burn up with feverish desire. He could tell them what the inside of love looked like, because he had split it open like a piece of fruit, he had removed its shell as you would the casing on a watch to see how the cogs inside made the hands slice time into segments. But Andrew could not tell them about this or anything else, because at that very moment his father, emitting enraged grunts, strode unsteadily across the room, almost harpooning the carpet with his cane, and without warning, struck him hard across the face. Andrew staggered backwards, stunned by the blow. When he finally understood what had happened, he rubbed his stinging cheek, trying to put on the same smile of defiance. For a few moments that seemed like an eternity to those present, father and son stared at each other in the middle of the room, until William Harrington said:

"As of tonight I have only one son."

Andrew tried not to show any emotion.

"As you wish," he replied coldly. Then, addressing the guests, he made as if to bow. "Gentlemen, my apologies, I must leave this place forever."

With as much dignity as he could muster, Andrew turned on his heel and left the room. The cold night air had a calming effect on him. In the end, he said to himself trying not to trip as he descended the steps, apart from

the unexpected audience and the angry slap, nothing that
had happened came as any surprise. His disgraced father
had just disinherited him, and in front of half of London's
wealthiest businessmen, giving them a firsthand display
of his famous temper, unleashed in this instance against
his own offspring without the slightest compunction. Now
Andrew had nothing, except his love for Marie Kelly. If
before the disastrous encounter he had entertained the
slightest hope that his father, moved by his story, might
give in, and even let him bring his beloved to the house
in order to remove her as far as possible from the monster stalking Whitechapel, it was clear now they must live
by their own means. He climbed into the carriage and ordered Harold to return to Miller's Court. The coachman,
who had been pacing round the carriage in circles, waiting
for the denouement of the drama, clambered back onto the
driver's seat and urged the horses on, trying to imagine
what had taken place inside the house—and, to his credit,
based on the clues he had been perceptive enough to pick
up, we must say that his reconstruction of the scene was
remarkably accurate.

WHEN THE CARRIAGE STOPPED in the usual
place, Andrew got out and hurried towards Dorset Street,
anxious to embrace Marie Kelly and tell her how much he
loved her. He had sacrificed everything for her. Still, he
had no regrets, only a vague uncertainty regarding the future. But they would manage. He was sure he could rely
on Charles. His cousin would lend him enough money to

rent a house in Vauxhall or Warwick Street, at least until they were able to find a decent job that would allow them to fend for themselves. Marie Kelly could find work at a dressmakers', but he, what skills did he possess? It made no difference, he was young, able-bodied, and willing, he would find something. The main thing was he had stood up to his father; what happened next was neither here nor there. Marie Kelly had pleaded with him, silently, to take her away from Whitechapel, and that was what he intended to do, with or without anyone else's help. They would leave that place, that accursed neighborhood, that outpost of hell.

ANDREW GLANCED AT HIS watch as he paused beneath the stone archway into Miller's Court. It was five o'clock in the morning. Marie Kelly would probably have already returned to the room, probably as drunk as he. Andrew visualized them communicating through a haze of alcohol in gestures and grunts like Darwin's primates. With boyish excitement, he walked into the yard where the flats stood. The door to number 13 was closed. He banged on it a few times but got no reply. She must be asleep, but that would not be a problem. Careful not to cut himself on the shards of glass sticking out of the window frame, Andrew reached through the hole and flicked open the catch on the door, as he had seen Marie Kelly do after she had lost her key.

"Marie, it's me," he said, opening the door. "Andrew."

ALLOW ME AT THIS point to break off the story in order to warn you that what took place next is hard to relate, because the sensations Andrew experienced were apparently too numerous for a scene lasting only a few seconds. That is why I need you to take into account the elasticity of time, its ability to expand or contract like an accordion regardless of clocks. I am sure this is something you will have experienced frequently in your own lives, depending on which side of the bathroom door you found yourselves. In Andrew's case, time expanded in his mind, creating an eternity out of a few seconds. I am going to describe the scene from that perspective, and therefore ask you not to blame my inept storytelling for the discrepancies you will no doubt perceive between the events and their correlation in time.

When he first opened the door and stepped into the room, Andrew did not understand what he was seeing, or more precisely, he refused to accept what he was seeing. During that brief but endless moment, Andrew still felt safe, although the certainty was already forming in some still-functioning part of his brain that what he saw before him would kill him, because nobody could be faced with a thing like that and go on living, at least not completely. And what he saw before him, let's be blunt about it, was Marie Kelly but at the same time it wasn't, for it was hard to accept that this object lying on the bed in the middle of all the blood splattered over the sheets and pillow was Marie Kelly. Andrew could not compare what awaited him in that room with anything he had seen before, because like most other men he had never been exposed to a carefully mutilated human body. And once Andrew's brain had finally accepted that he was indeed looking at a meticulously destroyed corpse, although nothing in his pleasant life of country house gatherings and fancy headwear would seem to offer him any clues, he had no time to feel the appropriate revulsion, for he could not avoid following the terrible line of reasoning that led him to the inevitable conclusion that this human wreckage must be his beloved. The Ripper, for this could be the work of none other, had stripped the flesh off her face, rendering her unrecognizable, and yet, however great the temptation, Andrew could not deny the corpse belonged to Marie Kelly. It seemed an almost simplistic, not to say improbable approach, but given its size and appearance and above all the place where he had found it, the dismembered corpse could only be that of Marie Kelly. After this, of course, Andrew was overcome by a terrible, devastating pain, which despite everything was only a pale expression of what it would later become, because it was still tempered by the shock paralyzing and to some extent protecting him.

Once he was convinced he was standing before the corpse of his beloved, he felt compelled by a sort of posthumous loyalty to look tenderly upon that ghastly sight, but he was incapable of contemplating with anything other than revulsion her flayed face, the skull's macabre, caricatured smile peeping through the strips of flesh. And yet how could that skull, on which he had bestowed his last passionate kisses, revolt him now? The same applied to that body he had worshiped for nights on end, and which, ripped open and half skinned, he now found sickening. It was clear to him from his reaction that in some sense, despite being made out of the same material, this had ceased to be Marie Kelly, for the Ripper, in his zeal to discover how she was put together inside, had reduced her to a simple casing of flesh, robbing her of her humanity. After this last reflection, the time came for Andrew to focus, with a mixture of fascination and horror, on specific details, like the darkish brown lump between her feet, possibly her liver, or the breast lying on the bedside table, which, far from its natural habitat, he might have mistaken for a soft bun had it not been topped by a purplish nipple. Everything appeared incredibly neatly arranged, betraying the murderer's grisly calm. Even the heat he now noticed suffusing the room suggested the ghoul had taken the time to light himself a nice fire in order to work in more comfort.

Andrew closed his eyes: he had seen enough. He did not want to know anything more. Besides showing him how cruel and indifferent man could be towards his fellow human beings, the atrocities he could commit given enough opportunity, imagination, and a sharp knife, the murderer had provided him with a shocking and brutal lesson in anatomy. For the very first time Andrew realized that life, real life, had no connection with the way people spent their days, whose lips they kissed, what medals were pinned on them, or the shoes they mended. Life, real life, went on soundlessly inside our bodies, flowed like an underwater stream, occurred like a silent miracle of which only surgeons and pathologists were aware, and perhaps ruthless killers, too. For they alone knew that ultimately there was no difference between Queen Victoria and the most wretched beggar in London: both were complex machines made up of bone, organs, and tissue, whose fuel was the breath of God.

This is a detailed analysis of what Andrew experienced during those fleeting moments when he stood before Marie Kelly's dead body, although this description makes it seem as if he were gazing at her for hours, which is what it felt like to him. Eventually a feeling of guilt began to emerge through the haze of pain and disgust overwhelming Andrew, for he immediately held himself responsible for her death. It had been in his power to save her, but he had arrived too late. This was the price of his cowardice. He let out a cry of rage and impotence as he imagined his beloved being subjected to this vicious butchery. Suddenly, it dawned on him that unless he wanted to be linked to the murder he must get out before someone saw him. It was even possible the murderer was still lurking outside, admiring his macabre handiwork from some dark corner, and would have no compunction about adding another corpse to his collection. He gave Marie Kelly a farewell glance, unable to bring himself to touch her, and with a supreme effort of will forced himself to withdraw from the little room, leaving her there.

As though in a trance, he closed the door behind him, leaving everything as he had found it. He walked towards the exit to the flats, but was seized by a feeling of intense nausea and only just made it to the stone archway. There, half-kneeling, he vomited, retching violently. After he had

brought up everything, which was little more than the
alcohol he had drunk that night, he leaned back against
the wall, his body limp, cold, and weak. From where he
was, he could see the little room number 13, the paradise
where he had been so happy, now hiding his beloved's dismembered corpse from the night. He tried taking a few
steps and, confident his dizzy spell had eased sufficiently
for him to walk without collapsing, he staggered out into
Dorset Street.

Too distressed to get his bearings, he began wandering aimlessly, letting out cries and sobs. He did not even
attempt to find the carriage: now that he knew he was no
longer welcome in his family home there was nowhere for
him to tell Harold to go. He trudged along street after
street, guided only by the forward movement of his feet.
When he calculated he was no longer in Whitechapel, he
looked for a lonely alley and collapsed, exhausted and
trembling, in the midst of a pile of discarded boxes. There,
curled up in a fetal position, he waited for night to pass.
As I predicted above, when the shock began to subside,
his pain increased. His sorrow intensified until it became
physical torment. Suddenly, being in his body was agonizing, as if he had turned into one of those sarcophagi lined
with bristling nails. He wanted to flee himself, unshackle
himself from the excruciating substance he was made of,
but he was trapped inside that martyred flesh. Terrified,
he wondered if he would have to live with this pain forever. He had read somewhere that the last image people
see before they die is engraved on their eyes. Had the Ripper's savage leer been etched onto Marie Kelly's pupils?

He could not say, but he did know if that rule were true he would be the exception, for whatever else he might see before he died, his eyes would always reflect Marie Kelly's mutilated face.

Without the desire or strength to do anything except remain doubled up in pain, Andrew let the hours slip by. Occasionally, he raised his head from his hands and let out a howl of rage to show the world his bitterness about all that had happened, which he was now powerless to change. He hurled random insults at the Ripper, who had conceivably followed him and was waiting knife in hand at the entrance to the alley, then he laughed at his fear. For the most part, though, he simply wailed pitifully, oblivious to his surroundings, hopelessly alone with his own horror.

THE ARRIVAL OF DAWN, leisurely sweeping away the darkness, restored his sanity somewhat. Sounds of life reached him from the entrance to the alley. He stood up with difficulty, shivering in his servant's crumpled, threadbare jacket, and walked out into the street, which was surprisingly lively.

Noticing the flags hanging from the fronts of the buildings, Andrew realized it was Lord Mayor's Day. Walking as upright as he could, he joined the crowd. His grubby attire drew no more attention than any ordinary tramp's. He had no notion of where he was, but this did not matter, since he had nowhere to go and nothing to do. The first tavern he came to seemed as good a destination as any.

It was better than being swept along on that human tide
making its way to the Law Courts to watch the arrival
of the new mayor, James Whitehead. The alcohol would
warm his insides, and at the same time blur his thoughts
until they were no longer a danger to him. The seedy public house was half empty. A strong smell of sausages and
bacon coming from the kitchen made his stomach churn,
and he secluded himself in the corner farthest from the
stoves and ordered a bottle of wine. He was forced to place
a handful of coins on the table in order to persuade the
waiter to serve him. While he waited, he glanced at the
other customers, reduced to a couple of regular patrons
who were drinking in silence, oblivious to the clamor in
the streets outside. One of them stared back at him, and
Andrew felt a flash of sheer terror. Could he be the Ripper? Had he followed him there? He calmed down when
he realized the man was too small to be a threat to anyone, but his hand was still shaking when he reached for
the wine bottle. He knew now what man was capable of,
any man, even that little fellow peacefully sipping his
ale. He probably did not have the talent to paint the Sis-
tine Chapel, but what Andrew could not be sure of was
whether he was capable of ripping a person's guts out and
arranging their entrails around their body. He gazed out
of the window. People were coming and going, carrying
on their lives without the slightest token of respect. Why
did they not notice that the world had changed, that it
was no longer inhabitable? Andrew gave a deep sigh. The
world had only changed for him. He leaned back in his
seat and applied himself to getting drunk. After that, he

would see. He glanced at the pile of money. He calculated he had enough to purchase every last drop of alcohol in the place, and so for the time being any other plan could wait. Sprawled over the bench, trying hard to prevent his mind from elaborating the simplest thought, Andrew let the day go by for everyone else, his numbness increasing by the minute as he drew closer to the edge of oblivion. But he was not too dazed to respond to the cry of a newspaper vendor.

"Read all about it in the *Star*! Special edition: Jack the Ripper caught!"

Andrew leapt to his feet. The Ripper caught? He could hardly believe his ears. He leaned out of the window and, screwing up his eyes, scoured the street until he glimpsed a boy selling newspapers on a corner. He beckoned him over and bought a copy from him through the window. With trembling hands, he cleared away several bottles and spread the newspaper out on the table. He had not misheard. "Jack the Ripper Caught!" the headline declared. Reading the article proved a slow and frustrating task due to his drunken state, but with patience and much blinking of his eyes he managed to decipher what was written. The article began by declaring that Jack the Ripper had committed his last ever crime the previous night. His victim was a prostitute of Welsh origin called Marie Jeanette Kelly, discovered in the room she rented in Miller's Court, at number 26 Dorset Street. Andrew skipped the following paragraph listing in gory detail the gruesome mutilations the murderer had perpetrated on her and went straight to the description of his capture.

The newspaper stated that less than an hour after committing the heinous crime, the murderer who had terrorized the East End for four months had been caught by George Lusk and his men. Apparently, a witness who preferred to remain anonymous had heard Marie Kelly's screams and alerted the Vigilance Committee. Unhappily, they reached Miller's Court too late, but had managed to corner the Ripper as he fled down Middlesex Street. At first, the murderer tried to deny his guilt but soon gave up after he was searched and the still warm heart of his victim was found in one of his pockets.

The man's name was Bryan Reese, and he worked as a cook on a merchant vessel, the *Slip*, which had docked at the Port of London from Barbados the previous July and would be setting sail again for the Caribbean the following week. During his interrogation by Frederick Abberline, the detective in charge of the investigation, Reese had confessed to the five murders of which he was accused, and had even shown his satisfaction at having been able to execute his final bloody act in the privacy of a room with a nice warm fire. He was tired of always having to kill in the street. "I knew I was going to follow that whore the moment I saw her," the murderer had gloated, before going on to claim he had murdered his own mother, a prostitute like his victims, as soon as he was old enough to wield a knife, although this detail, which might have explained his behavior, had yet to be confirmed. Accompanying the article was a photogravure of the murderer, so that Andrew could finally see the face of the man he had bumped into in the gloom of Hanbury Street. His appearance was disappointing. He was an ordinary-looking fellow, rather heavily built, with curly sideburns and a bushy moustache that drooped over his top lip. Despite his rather sinister smirk, which probably owed more to the conditions in which he had been photographed than anything else, Andrew had to admit this man might just as well be an honest baker as a ruthless killer. He certainly had none of the gruesome features Londoners' imaginations had ascribed to him. The following pages gave other related news items, such as the resignation of Sir Charles Warren following his acknowledgment of police incompetence in the case, or statements from Reese's astonished fellow seamen on the cargo vessel, but Andrew already knew everything he wanted to know, and so he went back to the front page. From what he could work out, he had entered Marie Kelly's little room moments after the murderer left and shortly before Lusk's mob arrived, as if they were all keeping to a series of dance steps. He hated to think what would have happened had he delayed fleeing any longer and been discovered standing over Marie Kelly's body by the Vigilance Committee. He had been lucky, he told himself. He tore out the first page, folded it and put it in his jacket pocket, then ordered another bottle to celebrate the fact that, despite his heart having been irreparably broken, at least he had escaped being beaten to a pulp by an angry mob.

EIGHT YEARS LATER, ANDREW took that same clipping from his pocket. Like him, it was yellowed with age. How often had he reread it, recalling Marie Kelly's horrific mutilations like a self-imposed penance? He had almost no other memories of the intervening years than this. What had he done during that time? It was difficult to say. He vaguely remembered Harold taking him home after scouring the various pubs and taverns in the vicinity and finding him passed out in that den. He had spent several days in bed with a fever, mostly ranting and suffering from nightmares in which Marie Kelly's corpse lay stretched out on her bed, her insides strewn about the room in some indecipherable pattern, or in which he was slitting her open with a huge knife while Reese looked on approvingly. In one of the brief moments of clarity during his feverish haze, he was able to make out his father sitting stiffly on the edge of his bed, begging forgiveness for his behavior. But it was easy to apologize now that there was nothing to accept, now all he had to do was join in the theatrical display of grief the family, even Harold, had decided to put on for him as a mark of respect. Andrew waved his father away with an impatient gesture, which to his annoyance the proud William Harrington instantly took to be absolution, judging from the smile of satisfaction on his face as he left the room, as though he had just sealed a successful business deal. William Harrington had wanted to clear his conscience and that was what he had done, whether his son liked it or not. Now he could forget the whole matter and get back to business. Andrew did not really care in the end: he and his father had never seen eye to eye and were not likely to do so now.

He recovered from his fever too late to attend Marie

Kelly's funeral, but not her killer's execution. The Ripper was hanged at Wandsworth Prison, despite the objections of several doctors, who maintained Reese's brain was a precious jewel worthy of scientific study, for in its bumps and folds the crimes he was predestined to commit since birth must of necessity be recorded. Andrew attended almost in spite of himself, and watched as the executioner snuffed out Reese's life without this bringing back Marie Kelly's or those of her fellow whores. Things did not work like that; the Creator knew nothing of bartering, only of retribution. At most, a child might have been born at the very moment when the rope snapped the Ripper's neck, but bringing back the dead to life was another matter. Perhaps that explained why so many had begun to doubt His power and even to question whether it was really He who had created the world. That same afternoon, a spark from a lamp set alight the portrait of Marie Kelly hanging in the Winslows' library. This at least was what his cousin said, who arrived just in time to put out the fire.

ANDREW WAS GRATEFUL FOR Charles's gesture, but the affair could not be ended so easily by removing the cause of it all. No, it was something that was impossible to deny. Thanks to his father's generosity, Andrew got back his old life, but being reinstated as heir to the vast fortune his father and brother continued to amass meant nothing to him now. All that money could not heal the wound inside, although he soon realized that spending it in the opium dens of Poland Street did help. Too much drinking had made him immune to alcohol, but opium was a far more effective and gentler way of forgetting. Not for nothing had the ancient Greeks used it to treat a wide range of afflictions. Andrew began spending his days in the opium den sucking on his pipe lying on one of the hundreds of mattresses screened off by exotic curtains. In those rooms lined with flyblown mirrors that made their dimensions seem even more uncertain in the dim light cast by the gas lamps, Andrew fled his pain in the labyrinths of a shadowy, never-ending daydream. From time to time, a skinny Malay filled his pipe bowl for him, until Harold or his cousin pulled back the curtain and led him out. If Coleridge resorted to opium to alleviate the trifling pain of toothache, why should he not use it to dull the agony of a broken heart, he replied when Charles warned him of the dangers of addiction. As always his cousin was right, and although as his suffering abated Andrew stopped visiting the opium dens, for a while he was secretly obliged to carry vials of laudanum around with him.

That period lasted two or three years, until the pain finally disappeared completely, giving way to something far worse: emptiness, lethargy, numbness. Those events had finished him, obliterated his will to live, severed his unique communication with the world, leaving him deaf and dumb, maneuvering him into a corner of the universe where nothing happened. He had turned into an automaton, a gloomy creature that lived out of habit, without hope, simply because life, real life, had no link to the way he spent his days, but occurred quietly inside him, like a silent miracle, whether he liked it or not. In short, he became a lost soul, shutting himself in his room by day and roaming Hyde Park by night like a ghost no longer concerned by the affairs of the living, to whom even the action of a flower coming into bud seemed rash, futile, and pointless. In the meantime, his cousin Charles had married one of the Keller sisters—Victoria or Madeleine, he could not remember which—and had purchased an elegant house in Elystan Street. This did not stop him from visiting Andrew nearly every day, and occasionally dragging him to his favorite brothels on the off chance that one of the new girls might have the necessary fire between her legs to rekindle his cousin's dulled spirit. But to no avail; Andrew refused to be pulled out of the hole into which he had dug himself. To Charles—whose point of view I shall adopt at this juncture, if for the purposes of dramatic effect you will consent to this rather obvious switch of points of view within one paragraph—this showed the resignation of someone who has embraced the role of victim. After all, the world needed martyrs as evidence of the Creator's cruelty, His ability to produce terrible fates. It was even conceivable that his cousin had come to view what had happened to him as an opportunity to search his soul, to venture into its darkest, most inhospitable regions. How many people go through life without experiencing pure pain? Andrew had known complete happiness and utter torment; he had used up his soul, so to speak, exhausted it completely. And now, comfortably installed with his pain, like a fakir on a bed of nails, he seemed to be awaiting who knew what: perhaps the applause signaling the end of the performance, because Charles was certain that if his cousin was still alive it was because he felt compelled to experience that pain to the hilt. It was irrelevant whether this was a practical study of suffering or to atone for his guilt. Once Andrew felt he had achieved this, he would take a last bow and leave the stage for good. Thus, each time Charles visited the Harrington mansion and found his cousin prone but still breathing, he heaved a sigh of relief. And when he arrived back home empty-handed, convinced that anything he might be able to do for Andrew was useless, he began to reflect how strange life could be, how flimsy and unpredictable it was if it could be altered so drastically by the mere purchase of a painting. Was it within his power to change it again? Could he alter the path his cousin's life would take before it was too late? He did not know. The only thing he was certain of was that, given everyone else's indifference, if he did not try, no one else would.

IN THE LITTLE ROOM on Dorset Street, Andrew opened the clipping and read for the last time, as though it were a prayer, the account of Marie Kelly's mutilations. Then he folded it up again and replaced it in his coat pocket. He contemplated the bed, which bore no trace of what had happened there eight years before. But that was the only thing that was different; everything else remained unchanged: the blackened mirror, somewhere inside which the crime had been immortalized, Marie Kelly's little perfume bottles, the closet where her clothes still hung, even the ashes in the hearth left from the fire the Ripper had lit to make slitting her open cozier. He could think of no better place to take his own life. He placed the barrel of the revolver under his jaw and crooked his finger around the trigger. Those walls would be splattered with blood once more, and far away on the distant moon, his soul would at last take up its place in the little hollow awaiting him in Marie Kelly's bed.

VI

WITH THE REVOLVER BARREL digging into the flesh beneath his jaw, and his finger poised on the trigger, Andrew reflected upon how strange it felt to have come to this. He had chosen to bring about his own death even though most of his life he had, like everyone else, been content merely to fear it, imagine it in every illness, see it lurking treacherously all around him in a world full of precipices, sharp objects, thin ice, and jumpy horses, mocking the fragility of those who claimed to be kings of Creation. All that worrying about death, he thought, only to embrace it now. But that was how things were: it was enough to find life a sterile, unrewarding exercise to want to end it, and there was only one way to do that. And he had to confess the vague unease he felt was in no way existential. Dying itself did not worry him in the least, because fear of death, whether it was a bridge to a biblical universe or a plank artfully suspended above the void, always derived from the certainty that the world went on without us, like a dog after its ticks have been removed. Broadly speaking, then, pulling the trigger meant pulling out of the game, relinquishing any possibility of being dealt a better hand in the next round. But Andrew doubted this could happen anyway. He had lost all faith. He did not believe fate had any reward in store for him that could make up for the pain he had suffered, above all because he did not believe such a recompense existed. He was afraid of something far more mundane: the pain he would doubtless feel when the bullet shattered his jaw. Naturally, it would not be pleasant, but it was part of his plan, and therefore something he must accept. He felt his finger grow heavy as it rested on the trigger and he gritted his teeth, prepared to put an end to his tragic life.

Just then, a knock came on the door. Startled, Andrew opened his eyes. Who could this be? Had McCarthy seen him arrive and come to ask for money to fix the window? The knocking became more insistent. That accursed money-grubber. If the man had the gall to stick his snout through the hole in the window, Andrew would not hesitate to shoot him. What did it matter now if he broke the absurd commandment about not killing your fellow man, especially if that man happened to be McCarthy?

"Andrew, I know you're in there. Open the door."

With a bitter grimace, Andrew recognized his cousin Charles's voice. Charles, Charles, always following him everywhere, looking out for him. He would have preferred it to be McCarthy. He could not shoot Charles. How had his cousin found him? And why did he go on trying when Andrew himself had long since given up?

"Go away Charles, I'm busy," he cried.

"Don't do it, Andrew! I've found a way of saving Marie!"

"Saving Marie?" Andrew laughed grimly. He had to admit his cousin had imagination, although this was verging on bad taste.

"Perhaps I should remind you Marie is dead," he shouted. "She was murdered in this miserable room eight years ago. When I could have saved her, I didn't. How can we save her now, Charles, by traveling in time?"

"Exactly," his cousin replied, slipping something beneath the door.

Andrew glanced at it with a vague curiosity. It looked like a leaflet.

"Read it, Andrew," his cousin implored, speaking to him through the broken window. "Please read it."

Andrew felt rather ashamed that his cousin should see him like that, the revolver pressed ridiculously against his jaw, which was perhaps not the most suitable place if you wanted to blow your head off. Knowing his cousin would not go away, he lowered the gun with an exasperated sigh, placed it on the bed, and rose to fetch the piece of paper.

"All right, Charles, you win," he muttered. "Let's see what this is all about."

He picked the sheet of paper up off the floor and examined it. It was a faded sky-blue handbill. He read it, unable to believe that what it said could be true. Amazing though it seemed, he was holding the advertisement for a company called Murray's Time Travel that offered journeys in time. This was what it said:

Tired of traveling through space?
Now you can travel through time,
into the fourth dimension.
Make the most of our special opening offer
and journey to the year 2000. Witness an
era only your grandchildren will live to see.
Spend three whole hours in the year 2000 for
a mere one hundred pounds. See with your
own eyes the future war between automatons
and humans that will change the fate of the
world. Don't be the last to hear about it.

The text was accompanied by an illustration intended to portray a fierce battle between two powerful armies. It showed a landscape of supposedly ruined buildings, a mound of rubble before which were ranged the two opposing sides. One was clearly human; the other consisted of humanoid creatures apparently made of metal. The drawing was too crude to be able to make out anything more.

What on earth was this? Andrew felt he had no choice but to unlock the door to the little room. Charles walked in, closing it behind him. He stood breathing into his hands to warm them, but beaming contentedly at having intervened to stop his cousin's suicide. For the time being, at least. The first thing he did was seize the pistol from the bed.

"How did you know I was here?" asked Andrew, while his cousin stood in front of the mirror waving the gun about furiously.

"You disappoint me, cousin," replied Charles, emptying the bullets from the chamber into his cupped hand and depositing them in his coat pocket. "Your father's gun cabinet was open, a pistol was missing, and today is November seventh. Where else would I have gone to look for you? You may as well have left a trail of breadcrumbs."

"I suppose so," conceded Andrew, thinking his cousin was right. He had not exactly gone out of his way to cover his tracks.

Charles held the pistol by its barrel and handed it to Andrew.

"Here you are. You can shoot yourself as many times as you like now."

Andrew snatched the gun and stuffed it into his pocket, eager to make the embarrassing object disappear as quickly as possible. He would just have to kill himself some other time. Charles looked at him with an expression of mock disapproval, waiting for some sort of explanation, but Andrew did not have the energy to convince him suicide was the only solution he could think of. Before his cousin had the chance to lecture him, he decided to sidestep the issue by inquiring about the leaflet.

"What's this? Some kind of joke?" he asked, waving the piece of paper in the air. "Where did you have it printed?"

Charles shook his head.

"It's no joke, cousin. Murray's Time Travel is a real company. The main offices are in Greek Street in Soho. And, as the advertisement says, they offer the chance to travel in time."

"But, is that possible . . . ?" stammered Andrew, taken aback.

"It certainly is," replied Charles, completely straight-faced. "What's more, I've done it myself."

They stared at one another in silence for a moment.

"I don't believe you," said Andrew at last, trying to detect the slightest hint in his cousin's solemn face that would give the game away, but Charles simply shrugged.

"I'm telling the truth," he assured him. "Last week, Madeleine and I traveled to the year 2000."

Andrew burst out laughing, but his cousin's earnest expression gradually silenced his guffaws.

"You're not joking, are you?"

"No, not at all," Charles replied. "Although I can't say I was all that impressed. The year 2000 is a dirty, cold year where man is at war with machines. But not seeing it is like missing a new opera that's all the rage."

Andrew listened, still stunned.

"Even so, it's a unique experience," his cousin added. "If you think about it, it's exciting because of all it implies. Madeleine has even recommended it to her friends. She fell in love with the human soldiers' boots. She tried to buy me a pair in Paris, but couldn't find any. I suspect it's too soon yet."

Andrew reread the leaflet to make sure he was not imagining things.

"I still can't believe . . . ." he stammered.

"I know, cousin, I know. But you see, while you've been roaming Hyde Park like a lost soul, the world has moved on. Time goes by even when you're not watching it. And believe me, strange as it might seem to you, time travel has been the talk of all the salons, the favored topic of discussion, since the novel that gave rise to it all came out last spring."

"A novel?" asked Andrew, increasingly bewildered.

"Yes. *The Time Machine* by H. G. Wells. It was one of the books I lent you. Didn't you read it?"

Since Andrew had shut himself away in the house, refusing to go along with Charles on those outings to taverns and brothels which he hoped would restore him to life, his cousin had started bringing him books when he came to see him. These were usually new works by unknown authors, inspired by the century's craze for science to write about machines capable of performing the most elaborate miracles. They were known as "scientific romances"—the English publishers' translation of Jules Verne's *Voyages Extraordinaires*, which rapidly became an expression used to describe any fantasy novel that tried to explain itself with science. According to Charles, these scientific novels captured the spirit that had inspired the works of Bergerac and Samosata, and had taken over from the old tales of haunted castles. Andrew remembered some of the madcap inventions in those novels, such as the antinightmare helmet hooked up to a tiny steam engine that sucked out bad dreams and turned them into pleasant ones. But the one he remembered best of all was the machine that made things grow, invented by a Jewish scientist who used it on insects: the image of London attacked by a swarm of flies the size of zeppelins, crushing towers and flattening buildings as they landed on them, was ridiculously terrifying. There was a time when Andrew would have devoured such books, but much as he regretted it, the worlds of fiction were not exempt from his steadfast indifference to life: he did not want any type of balm, he wanted to stare straight into the gaping abyss, making it impossible for Charles to reach him via the secret passage of literature. Andrew assumed that this fellow Wells's book must be buried at the bottom of his chest, under a mound of similar novels he had scarcely glanced at.

When Charles saw the empty look on his cousin's face, he shook his head theatrically. He gestured to him to sit back down in his chair and drew up the other one. Leaning forward slightly, like a priest about to take confession from one of his parishioners, he began summarizing the plot of the novel that according to him had revolutionized England. Andrew listened skeptically. As he could guess from the title, the main character was a scientist who had invented a time machine that allowed him to journey through the centuries. All he had to do was pull on a little lever and he was propelled at great speed into the future, gazing in awe as snails ran like hares, trees sprouted from the ground like geysers, the stars circled in the sky, which changed from day to night in a second . . . This wild and wonderful journey took him to the year 802,701, where he discovered that society had split into two different races: the beautiful and useless Eloi and the monstrous Morlocks, creatures that lived underground, feeding off their neighbors up above, whom they bred like cattle. Andrew bridled at this description, making his cousin smile, but Charles quickly added that the plot was unimportant, no more than an excuse to create a flimsy caricature of the society of his time. What had shaken the English imagination was that Wells had envisaged time as a fourth dimension, transforming it into a sort of magic tunnel you could travel through.

"We are all aware that objects possess three dimensions: length, breadth, and thickness," explained Charles. "But in order for this object to exist," he went on, picking up his hat and twirling it in his hands like a conjuror, "in order for it to form part of this reality we find ourselves in, it needs duration in time as well as in space. That is what enables us to see it, and prevents it from disappearing before our very eyes. We live, then, in a four-dimensional world. If we accept that time is another dimension, what is to stop us from moving through it? In fact, that's what we are doing. Just like our hats, you and I are moving forwards in time, albeit in a tediously linear fashion, without leaving out a single second, towards our inexorable end. What Wells is asking in his novel is why we can't speed up this journey, or even turn around and travel backwards in time to that place we refer to as the past—which ultimately is no more than a loose thread in the skein of our lives. If time is a spatial dimension, what prevents us from moving around in it as freely as we do in the other three?"

Pleased with his explanation, Charles replaced his hat on the bed. Then he studied Andrew, allowing him a moment to assimilate what he had just said.

"I must confess when I read the novel I thought it was rather an ingenious way of making what was basically a fantasy believable," he went on a moment later when his cousin said nothing, "but I never imagined it would be scientifically achievable. The book was a raging success, Andrew, people spoke of nothing else in the clubs, the salons, the universities, during factory breaks. Nobody talked anymore about the crisis in the United States and how it might affect England, or Waterhouse's paintings or Oscar Wilde's plays. The only thing people were interested in was whether time travel was possible or not. Even the women's suffrage movement was fascinated by the subject and interrupted their regular meetings to discuss it. Speculating about what tomorrow's world would be like or discussing which past events ought to be changed became England's favorite pastime, the quickest way to liven up conversation during afternoon tea. Naturally, such discussions were futile, because nobody could reach any enlightened conclusions, except in scientific circles, where an even more heated debate took place, whose progress was reported on almost daily in the national newspapers. But nobody could deny it was Wells's novel that had sparked off people's yearning to journey into the future, to go beyond the bounds imposed on them by their fragile, destructible bodies. Everybody wanted to glimpse the future, and the year 2000 became the most logical objective, the year everyone wanted to see. A century was easily enough time for everything to be invented that could be invented, and for the world to have been transformed into a marvelously unrecognizable, magical, possibly even a better place.

Ultimately, this all seemed to be no more than a harmless amusement, a naïve desire—that is until last October, when Murray's Time Travel opened for business. This was announced with great fanfare in the newspapers and on publicity posters: Gilliam Murray could make our dreams come true, he could take us to the year 2000. Despite the cost of the tickets, huge queues formed around his building. I saw people who had always maintained that time travel was impossible waiting like excited children for the doors to open. Nobody wanted to pass up this opportunity. Madeleine and I couldn't get seats for the first expedition, only the second. And we traveled in time, Andrew. Believe it or not, I have been a hundred and five years into the future and returned. This coat still has traces of ash on it; it smells of the war of the future. I even picked up a piece of rubble from the ground when no one was looking, a rock we have displayed in the drawing room cabinet. A replica of the rock must still be intact in some building in London."

Andrew felt like a boat spinning in a whirlpool. It seemed incredible to him that it was possible to travel in time, not to be condemned to see only the era he was born into, the period that lasted as long as his heart and body held out, but to be able to visit other eras, other times where he did not belong, leapfrogging his own death, the tangled web of his descendants, desecrating the sanctuary of the future, journeying to places hitherto only dreamt of or imagined. But for the first time in years, he felt a flicker of interest in something beyond the wall of indifference he had surrounded himself with. He immediately forced himself to snuff out the flame before it became a blaze. He was in mourning, a man with an empty heart and a dormant soul, a creature devoid of emotion, the perfect example of a human being who had felt everything there was for him to feel. He had nothing in the whole wide world to live for. He could not live, not without her.

"That's remarkable, Charles," he sighed wearily, feigning indifference to these unnatural journeys. "But what has this to do with Marie?"

"Don't you see, cousin?" Charles replied in an almost scandalized tone. "This man Murray can travel into the future. No doubt if you offered him enough money, he could organize a private tour for you into the past. Then you'd really have someone to shoot."

Andrew's jaw dropped.

"The Ripper?" he said, his voice cracking.

"Exactly," replied Charles. "If you travel back in time, you can save Marie yourself."

Andrew gripped the chair to stop himself from falling off. Was it possible? Could he really travel back in time to the night of November 7, 1888, and save Marie? he wondered, struggling to overcome his astonishment. The possibility that this might be true made him feel giddy, not just because of the miracle of traveling through time, but because he would be going back to a period when she was still alive: he would be able to hold in his arms the body he had seen cut to ribbons. But what moved him most was the fact that someone should offer him the chance to save her, to put right his mistake, to change a situation it had taken him all these years to learn to accept as irreversible. He had always prayed to the Creator to be able to do that. It seemed he had been calling upon the wrong person. This was the age of science.

"What do you say, Andrew? We have nothing to lose by trying," he heard his cousin remark.

Andrew stared at the floor for a few moments, struggling to put some order into the tumult of emotions he felt. He did not really believe it was possible, and yet if it was, how could he refuse to try: this was what he had always wanted, the chance he had been waiting eight years for. He raised his head and gazed at his cousin, shaken.

"All right," he said in a hoarse whisper.

"Excellent, Andrew," said Charles, overjoyed, and clapped him on the back. "Excellent."

His cousin smiled unconvincingly, then looked down at his shoes again, attempting to digest it all: he was going to travel back to his old haunts, to relive moments already past, back to his own memories.

"Well," said Charles, glancing at his pocket watch. "We'd better have something to eat. I don't think traveling back in time on an empty stomach is a good idea."

They left the little room and made their way over to Charles's carriage, which was waiting by the stone archway. They followed the same routine that night as though it were no different from any other one. They dined at the Café Royal, which served Charles's favorite steak and kidney pie, let off steam at Madame Norrell's brothel, where Charles liked to try out the new girls while they were still fresh, and ended up drinking until dawn in the bar at Claridge's, where Charles rated the champagne list above any other. Before their minds became too clouded by drink, Charles explained to Andrew that he had journeyed into the future on a huge tramcar, the *Cronotilus*, which was propelled through the centuries by an impressive steam engine. But Andrew was incapable of showing any interest in the future; his mind was taken up imagining what it would be like to travel in the exact opposite direction, into the past. There, his cousin assured him, he would be able to save Marie by confronting the Ripper. Over the past eight years, Andrew had built up feelings of intense rage towards that monster. Now he would have the chance to vent them. However, it was one thing to threaten a man who had already been executed, he thought, and quite another to confront him in the flesh, in this sort of sparring match Murray was going to set up for him. Andrew gripped the pistol, which he had kept in his pocket, as he recalled the burly man he had bumped into in Hanbury Street, and tried to cheer himself with the thought that, although he had never shot a real person before, he had practiced his aim on bottles, pigeons, and rabbits. If he remained calm, everything would go well. He would aim at the Ripper's heart or his head, let off a few shots calmly, and watch him die a second time. Yes, that was what he would do. Only this time, as though someone had tightened a bolt in the machinery of the universe making it function more smoothly, the Ripper's death would bring Marie Kelly back to life.

VII

ESPITE EARLY MORNING, SOHO was already teeming with people. Charles and Andrew had to push their way through the crowded streets full of men in bowlers and women wearing hats adorned with plumes and even the odd fake bird. Couples strolled along the pavements arm in arm, sauntered in and out of shops, or stood waiting to cross the streets. The streets were filled with a slow torrent of luxurious carriages, cabriolets, tramcars, and carts carrying barrels, fruit, or mysterious shapes covered by tarpaulins, possibly bodies robbed from the graveyard. Scruffy second-rate artists, performers, and acrobats displayed their dubious talents on street corners in the hope of attracting the attention of some passing promoter. Charles had not stopped chattering since breakfast, but Andrew could hardly hear him above the loud clatter of wheels on the cobbles and the piercing cries of vendors and would-be artists. He was content to let his cousin guide him through the gray morning, immersed in a sort of stupor, from which he was roused only by the sweet scent of violets reaching him as they passed one of the many flower sellers.

The moment they entered Greek Street, they spotted the modest building where the office of Murray's Time Travel was situated. It was an old theater that had been remodeled by its new owner, who had not hesitated to blight the neoclassical façade with a variety of ornamentations alluding to time. At the entrance, a small flight of steps flanked by two columns led up to an elegant sculpted wooden door crowned by a pediment decorated with a carving of Chronos spinning the wheel of the Zodiac. The god of time, depicted as a sinister old man with a flowing beard reaching down to his navel, was bordered by a frieze of carved hourglasses, a motif repeated on the arches above the tall windows on the second floor. Between the pediment and the lintel, ostentatious pink marble lettering announced to all who could read that this picturesque edifice was the head office of Murray's Time Travel.

Charles and Andrew noticed passersby stepping off the section of pavement outside the unusual building. As they drew closer, they understood why. A nauseating odor made them screw up their faces in disgust and invited them to regurgitate the breakfast they had just eaten. The cause of the stench was a viscous substance which a couple of workmen, masked with neckerchiefs, were vigorously washing off part of the façade with brushes and pails of water. As the brushes made contact with whatever the dark substance might be, it slopped onto the pavement, transformed into a revolting black slime.

"Sorry about the inconvenience, gents," one of the workmen said, pulling down his neckerchief. "Some louse smeared cow dung all over the front of the building, but we'll soon have it cleaned off."

Exchanging puzzled looks, Andrew and Charles pulled out their handkerchiefs and, covering their faces like a couple of highwaymen, hurried through the front door. In the hallway, the evil smell was being kept at bay by rows of strategically placed vases of gladioli and roses. Just as on the outside of the building, the interior was filled with a profusion of objects whose theme was time. The central area was taken up by a gigantic mechanical sculpture consisting of an enormous pedestal out of which two articulated, spiderlike arms stretched up towards the shadowy ceiling. They were clutching an hourglass the size of a calf embossed with iron rivets and bands. This contained not sand, but a sort of blue sawdust that flowed gracefully from one section to the other and even gave off a faint, evocative sparkle when caught by the light from the nearby lamps. Once the contents had emptied into the lower receptacle, the arms turned the hourglass by means of some complex hidden mechanism, so that the artificial sand never ceased to flow, like a reminder of time itself. Alongside the colossal structure enthroned in the entrance were many other remarkable objects. Although less spectacular, they were more noteworthy for having been invented many centuries before, like the bracket clocks bristling with levers and cogs that stood silently at the back of the vast room and, according to the plaques on their bases, were early efforts at mechanical timepieces.

Apart from this distinguished trinket, the room was lined with hundreds of wall clocks, from the traditional Dutch *stoelklok* adorned with mermaids and cherubs to Austro-Hungarian ones with their seconds pendulums. The air was filled with a relentless, overwhelming ticking sound, which for the people working in that building must have become an endless accompaniment to their lives, without whose comforting presence they doubtless felt bereft on Sundays.

Seeing them wandering about the room, a young woman stood up from her desk in the corner and came over to speak to them. She walked with catlike grace, her steps following the rhythm of the insistent ticking of the clocks. After greeting them courteously, she informed them excitedly that there were still a few tickets left for the third expedition to the year 2000 and that they could make a reservation if they wished. Charles refused the young woman's offer with a dazzling smile, telling her they were there to see Gilliam Murray. The woman hesitated briefly, then informed them that Mr. Murray was indeed in the building and, although he was a very busy man, she would do her best to arrange for them to meet him, a gesture for which Charles showed his appreciation by unleashing an even more beaming smile. Once she had managed to tear her eyes away from his perfect set of teeth, the young woman turned round and gestured to them to follow her. At the far end of the vast room was a marble staircase leading to the upper floors. The girl guided Charles and Andrew down a long corridor lined with tapestries depicting various scenes from the war of the future. Naturally, the corridor was also replete with the obligatory clocks hanging on the walls or standing on dressers or shelves, filling the air with their ubiquitous ticking. When they reached Murray's ostentatious office door, the woman asked them to wait outside, but Charles ignored her request and followed her into the room, dragging his cousin behind him. The gigantic proportions of the room surprised Andrew, as did the clutter of furniture and the numerous maps lining the walls, reminding him of the campaign tents from which field marshals orchestrated wars. They had to glance around the room several times before they discovered Gilliam Murray, lying stretched out on a rug, playing with a dog.

"Good day, Mr. Murray," said Charles, before the secretary had a chance to speak. "My name is Charles Winslow and this is my cousin, Andrew Harrington. We would like a word with you: if you are not too busy, that is."

Gilliam Murray, a strapping fellow in a garish purple suit, accepted the thrust sportingly, smiling at Charles's sardonic remark. He had the enigmatic look of a person who holds a great many aces up his sleeve, which he has every intention of pulling out at the first opportunity.

"I always have time for two such illustrious gentlemen as yourselves," he said, picking himself up from the carpet.

When he had risen to his full height, Andrew and Charles could see that Gilliam Murray seemed to have been magnified by some kind of spell. Everything about him was oversized, from his hands, which appeared capable of wrestling a bull to the ground by its horns, to his head, which looked more suited to a minotaur. However, despite Murray's remarkable build, he moved with extraordinary, even graceful, agility. His straw-colored hair was combed carefully back, and the smoldering intensity of his big blue eyes betrayed an ambitious, proud spirit, which he had learned to tone down by means of a wide range of friendly smiles his fleshy lips were capable of producing.

With a wave of his hand, he invited them to follow him over to his desk on the far side of the room. He led them along the trail he had managed to forge, no doubt after lengthy exploration, between the accumulation of globes and tables piled high with books and notebooks strewn all over the office. Andrew noticed there was no shortage of the ever-present clocks there either. Besides the ones hanging from the walls and invading the bookcase shelves, an enormous glass cabinet contained a collection of portable bulbdial clocks, sundials, intricate water clocks, and other artifacts showing the evolution of the display of time. It appeared to Andrew that presenting all these objects was Gilliam's clever way of showing the absurdity of man's vain attempts to capture the elusive, absolute, mysterious, and indomitable force that was time. Murray seemed to be saying with his colorful collection of timepieces that man's only achievement was to strip time of its metaphysical essence, transforming it into a commonplace instrument for ensuring he did not arrive late to meetings.

Charles and Andrew lowered themselves into two plush Jacobean-style armchairs facing the majestic desk with bulbous feet where Murray sat, framed by an enormous window behind him. As the light streamed in through the leaded panes, suffusing the office with rustic cheer, it even occurred to Andrew that the entrepreneur had a sun all of his own, while everyone else was submerged in the dull morning light.

"I hope you'll forgive the unfortunate smell in the entrance," Gilliam hurriedly apologized, screwing up his face in disgust. "This is the second time someone has smeared excrement on the front of the building. Perhaps an organized group is attempting to disrupt the smooth running of our enterprise in this unpleasant way," he speculated, shrugging his shoulders despairingly, as though to emphasize how upset he was about the matter. "As you can see, not everyone thinks time travel is a good thing for society. And yet, it is society that has been clamoring for it ever since Mr. Wells's wonderful novel came out. I can think of no other explanation for these acts of vandalism, as the perpetrators have not claimed responsibility or left any clues. They simply desecrate the front of our building."

Gilliam Murray stared into space for a moment, lost in thought. Then he appeared to rouse himself, and sitting upright in his seat looked straight at his visitors.

"But, tell me, gentlemen, what can I do for you?"

"I would like you to organize a private journey back to the autumn of 1888, Mr. Murray," replied Andrew, who had apparently been waiting impatiently for the giant to allow them to get a word in edgeways.

"To the Autumn of Terror?" asked Murray, taken aback.

"Yes, to the night of November seventh, to be precise."

Gilliam studied him in silence for a few moments.

Finally, without trying to conceal his annoyance, he opened one of the desk drawers and took out a bundle of papers tied with a ribbon. He set them down on the desk wearily, as if he were showing them some tiresome burden he was compelled to suffer in silence.

"Do you know what this is, Mr. Harrington?" he sighed. "These are the letters and requests we receive every day from private individuals. Some want to be taken to the hanging gardens of Babylon, others to meet Cleopatra, Galileo, or Plato, still others to see with their own eyes the battle of Waterloo, the building of the pyramids, or Christ's crucifixion. Everybody wants to go back to their favorite moment in history, as though it were as simple as giving an address to a coachman. They think the past is at our disposition. I am sure you have your reasons for wanting to travel to 1888, like everyone who wrote these requests, but I'm afraid I can't help you."

"I only need to go back eight years, Mr. Murray," replied Andrew. "And I'll pay anything you ask."

"This isn't about distances in time or about money," Murray scoffed. "If it were, Mr. Harrington, I'm sure we could come to some arrangement. Let us say the problem is a technical one. We can't travel anywhere we want in the past or the future."

"You mean you can only take us to the year 2000?" exclaimed Charles, visibly disappointed.

"I'm afraid so, Mr. Winslow," Murray apologized, looking forlornly at Charles. "We hope to be able to extend our offer in the future. However, for the moment, as you can see from our advertisement, our only destination is

May 20, 2000, the exact day of the final battle between the evil Solomon's automatons and the human army led by the brave Captain Shackleton. Wasn't the trip exciting enough for you, Mr. Winslow?" he asked with a flicker of irony, giving Charles to understand he did not forget easily the faces of those who had been on his expeditions.

"Oh yes, Mr. Murray," Charles replied after a brief pause. "Most exciting. Only I assumed . . ."

"Yes, yes, I know. You assumed we could travel in either direction along the time continuum," Murray interposed. "But I'm afraid we can't. The past is beyond our competence."

With this, Murray looked at them, a look of genuine regret on his face, as though he were weighing up the damage his words had done to his visitors.

"The problem, gentlemen," he sighed, leaning back in his chair, "is that, unlike Wells's character, we don't travel through the time continuum. We travel outside it, across the surface of time, as it were."

He fell silent, staring at them without blinking, with the serenity of a cat.

"I don't understand," Charles finally declared.

Gilliam Murray nodded, as though he had been expecting that reply.

"Let me make a simple comparison: you can move from room to room inside a building, but you also can walk across its roof, can you not?"

Charles and Andrew nodded coldly, somewhat put out by Murray's seeming wish to treat them like a couple of foolish children.

"Contrary to all appearances," their host went on, "it was not Wells's novel that made me look into the possibilities of time travel. If you have read the book, you will understand that Wells is simply throwing down the gauntlet to the scientific world by suggesting a direction for their research. Unlike Verne, he cleverly avoided any practical explanations of the workings of his invention, choosing instead to describe his machine to us using his formidable imagination—a perfectly valid approach given the book is a work of fiction. However, until science proves such a contraption is possible, his machine will be nothing but a mere toy. Will that ever happen? I'd like to think so: the achievements of science so far this century give me great cause for optimism. You will agree, gentlemen, we live in remarkable times. Times when man questions God on a daily basis. How many marvels has science produced over the past few years? Many, such as the calculating machine, the typewriter, or the electric lift, have been invented simply to make our lives easier, but others make us feel powerful because they render the impossible possible. Thanks to the steam locomotive, we are now able to travel long distances without taking a single step, and soon we will be able to relay our voices to the other side of the country without having to move at all, like the Americans who are already doing so via the so-called telephone. There will always be people who oppose progress, who consider it a sacrilege for mankind to transcend his own limitations. Personally, I think science ennobles man, reaffirms his control over nature, in the same way education or morality helps us overcome our primitive instincts.

"Take this marine chronometer, for example," he went on, picking up a wooden box lying on the table. "Today, these are mass-produced and every ship in the world has one, but that wasn't always the case. Although they may appear now always to have formed part of our lives, the Admiralty was obliged to offer a prize of twenty thousand pounds to the person who could invent a way of determining longitude at sea, because no clockmaker was capable of designing a chronometer that could withstand the rolling of a vessel without going wrong. The competition was won by a man called John Harrison, who devoted forty years of his life to solving this thorny scientific problem. He was nearly eighty when he finally received the prize money. Fascinating, don't you think? At the heart of each invention lie one man's efforts, an entire life dedicated to solving a problem, to inventing an instrument that will outlast him, will go on forming part of the world after he is dead. So long as there are men who aren't content to eat the fruit off the trees or to summon rain by beating a drum, but who are determined instead to use their brains in order to transcend the role of mere parasites in God's creation, science will never give up trying. That's why I am sure that very soon, as well as being able to fly like birds in winged carriages, anyone will be able to get hold of a machine similar to the one Wells dreamed up and travel anywhere they choose in time. Men of the future will lead double lives, working during the week in a bank, and on Sundays making love to the beautiful Nefertiti or helping Hannibal conquer Rome. Can you imagine how an invention like that would change society?" Gilliam studied the two men for a moment before replacing the box on the table, where it sat, lid open, like an oyster or an engagement ring. Then he added, "But in the meantime, while science is busy looking for a way of making these dreams come true, we have another method of traveling in time, although unfortunately this one does not enable us to choose our destination."

"What method is that?" Andrew enquired.

"Magic," declared Gilliam, in a booming voice.

"Magic?" echoed Andrew, taken aback.

"Yes, magic," repeated his host, waving his fingers in the air mysteriously and making a sound like wind whistling down a chimney, "but not the conjuring tricks you see in music halls, theaters, or the sort those frauds from the Golden Dawn claim to perform. I'm talking about genuine magic. Do you believe in magic, gentlemen?"

Andrew and Charles paused, a little confused by the direction the conversation was taking, but Gilliam needed no reply.

"Of course not," he grumbled. "That's why I avoid mentioning it. I prefer my clients to believe we are traveling through time by means of science. Everybody these days believes in science. It has become far more credible than magic. We live in modern times. But I assure you, magic does exist."

Then, to Andrew and Charles's surprise, he rose deftly from his seat and gave a shrill whistle. The dog, which had been lying on the carpet all this time, stood up at once and trotted gaily over to its master.

"Gentlemen, I'd like you to meet Eternal," he said,

as the creature circled round him excitedly. "Do you like dogs? It's quite safe to stroke him."

As though this were some sort of requirement they must fulfill for Gilliam Murray to be able to continue his discourse, Charles and Andrew stood up and ran their hands over the soft, well-brushed coat of the highly strung golden retriever.

"Gentlemen," Murray declared, "be aware that you are stroking a miracle. For, as I just told you, there is such a thing as magic. It is even tangible. How old do you think Eternal is?"

Charles had no difficulty in answering the question, because he had several dogs on his country estate and had grown up with them. He examined the animal's teeth with a knowledgeable air, and replied confidently:

"A year, two at the most."

"Spot on," confirmed Gilliam, kneeling and scratching the dog's neck affectionately. "You look a year old, don't you, that's your age in real time?"

Andrew took this opportunity to catch his cousin's eye, anxious to know what he thought about all this. Charles's tranquil smile put his mind at rest.

"As I already told you," Murray went on, rising to his feet, "I didn't decide to set up my company on account of Wells's novel. It was a complete coincidence, although I won't deny I have greatly benefited from the hidden longing he stirred up in people. Do you know why time travel is so attractive? Because we all dream of journeying in time, it is one of man's oldest desires. But would you have considered it possible, gentlemen, before Wells wrote his book? I don't think so. And I assure you neither would I. What Mr. Wells has somehow done is to make an abstract craving real, to articulate this latent desire ever present in man."

Murray paused, giving his summary the opportunity to descend on his visitors, like dust settling on furniture after a carpet has been beaten.

"Before setting up this company, I worked with my father," he resumed a moment later. "We financed expeditions. We were one of the hundreds of societies sending explorers to the farthest corners of the world with the aim of gathering ethnographic and archaeological data to publish in scientific journals, or finding exotic insects or flowers for the showcases of some science museum eager to display God's wildest creations. But, regardless of the business side of things, we were driven by a desire to get to know as accurately as possible the world we lived in. We were, to coin a phrase, spatially curious. However, we never know what fate has in store for us, do we, gentlemen?"

Again without waiting for a reply, Gilliam Murray gestured for them to follow him. Eternal at his heel, he led them through the obstacle course of tables and globes towards one of the sidewalls. Unlike the others, which were lined with shelves crammed with atlases, geographical treatises, books on astronomy, and numerous other works on obscure subjects, this wall was covered in maps, arranged according to when the regions on them had been charted. The collection covered a journey that started with a few reproductions of Renaissance maps inspired by Ptolemy's works, which made the world look alarmingly small, like an insect with its legs chopped off, reduced to little more than a shapeless Europe. Next came the German Martin Waldseemüller's map, where America had broken away from the Asian continent, and finally the works of Abraham Ortelius and Gerardus Mercator, which showed a much larger world, similar in size to that of the present day. Following this chronological order from left to right as guided by Murray, the cousins had the impression of watching the petals of a flower open or a cat stretch its body. The world seemed to unfurl literally before their eyes, to grow incredibly slowly in size as navigators and explorers extended its frontiers. Andrew found it fascinating that only a few centuries earlier people had no idea the world went on across the Atlantic, or that its true size depended on the courage and fortunes of explorers whose daredevil journeys filled up the medieval void, the dwelling place of sea monsters. On the other hand, he regretted the dimensions of the world were no longer a mystery, that the most recent maps of land and sea constituted an official world, established, confined to its own dimensions, where the only things left to chart were its coastlines. Murray made them come to a halt in front of the last gigantic map in his collection.

"Gentlemen, you have in front of you possibly the most accurate world map in all of England," he announced, openly gloating. "I keep it continually updated, you see. Whenever another region of the planet is charted, I have a new version drawn up and I burn the obsolete one. I consider this a symbolic gesture, like erasing my old, imprecise idea. Many of the expeditions you see here were made possible by our funding."

The map was a blurry mass of multicolored lines which, Gilliam explained, represented all the expeditionary voyages hitherto undertaken by man, the vicissitudes of which he had written up, doubtless with morbid enjoyment, in the chart's left-hand margin. However, one glance at the map was enough to see that the precision with which each sinuous voyage had been traced eventually became pointless: it was impossible to follow any single journey owing to the crisscross of the lines resulting from their host's absurd efforts to record every single expedition. These ranged from the earliest, like that of Marco Polo (represented by a gold line snaking around India, China, Central Asia, and the Malaysian archipelago), to the most recent, like that undertaken by Sir Francis Younghusband, who had traveled from Peking to Kashmir crossing the Karakoram Mountains with their soaring glacier-topped peaks. The squiggles though were not confined to land: others left terra firma, imitating the foamy wake of legendary ships such as Columbus's caravels as they crossed the Atlantic Ocean, or the *Erebus* and the *Terror* as they tried to find a shortcut to China via the Arctic Ocean. These last two lines vanished suddenly, as had the actual ships when sailing across the Lancaster Straits, the so-called Northwest Passage.

Unable to make any sense of the mass of lines, Andrew decided to follow the blue one that cut across the island of Borneo, that sultry paradise overrun by crocodiles and gibbons to the southeast of Asia. This followed the tortuous journey of Sir James Brooke, nicknamed the Rajah of Sarawak, a name Andrew was familiar with because the explorer popped up in the Sandokan novels as a ruthless pirate slayer. But then Gilliam asked them to concentrate on the most intricate part of the map, the African continent. There, all the expeditions attempting to discover the mythical source of the Nile, like those undertaken by the Dutchwoman Alexine Tinné, Mr. and Mrs. Baker, Burton and Speke, and most famously by Livingstone and Stanley, as well as many more, converged to form a tangled mesh, which if nothing else illustrated the fascination Africa had held for the intrepid wearers of pith helmets.

"The account of how we discovered time travel began exactly twenty-two years ago," Gilliam announced theatrically.

As though having heard the story many times before, Eternal stretched out at his master's feet. Charles smiled gleefully at this promising beginning, while Andrew twisted his lips in frustration, realizing he was going to need a lot of patience before he found out whether or not he would be able to save Marie Kelly.

VIII

PERMIT ME, IF YOU WILL, TO PER-
form a little narrative juggling at this point,
and recount the story Gilliam Murray told them in the
third person instead of the first, as if it were an excerpt
from an adventure story, which is the way Murray would
ultimately have liked to see it. Back then, at the beginning
of the nineteenth century, the main ambition of most expeditionary societies was to discover the source of the Nile,
which Ptolemy had situated in the Mountains of the Moon,
that magnificent mountain range rising out of the heart of
Africa. However, modern explorers seemed to have had no
more luck than Herodotus, Nero, or anyone else who had
searched in vain for it throughout history. Richard Burton
and John Speke's expedition had only succeeded in making
enemies of the two explorers, and that of David Livingstone
had thrown little light on the matter either. When Henry
Stanley found Livingstone in Ujiji, he was suffering from
dysentery. He nevertheless refused to return with Stanley
to the metropolis and set off on another expedition, this

time to Lake Tanganyika. He had to be brought back from there on a litter, wracked with fever and utterly exhausted. The Scottish explorer died at Chitambo, and his final journey was made as a corpse, embalmed, then enclosed in a large piece of bark from a Myonga tree. It took porters nine months to carry him to the island of Zanzibar, from which he was finally repatriated to Great Britain. He was buried in 1878 in Westminster Abbey with full honors; but despite his numerous achievements, the source of the Nile remained a mystery, and everyone, from the Royal Geographic Society to the most insignificant science museum, wanted to take credit for discovering its elusive location. The Murrays were no exception, and at the same time as the *New York Herald* and London's *Daily Telegraph* sponsored Stanley's new expedition, they, too, sent one of their most experienced explorers to the inhospitable African continent.

His name was Oliver Tremanquai, and apart from having undertaken several expeditions to the Himalayas, he was also a veteran hunter. Among the creatures killed by his expert marksmanship were Indian tigers, Balkan bears, and Ceylonese elephants. Although never a missionary, he was a deeply religious man and never missed an opportunity to evangelize any natives he might come across, listing the merits of his God like someone selling a gun. Excited about his new mission, Tremanquai left for Zanzibar, where he acquired porters and supplies. However, a few days after he made his way into the continent, the Murrays lost all contact with him. The weeks crept by and still they received no message. They began to wonder what had become of the explorer. With great sorrow, the

Murrays gave him up for lost, as they had no Stanley to send after him.

Ten months later, Tremanquai burst into their offices, days after a memorial service had taken place with the permission of his wife—loathe to don her widow's weeds. As was only to be expected, his appearance caused the same stir as if he had been a ghost. He was terribly gaunt, his eyes were feverish, and his filthy, malodorous body hardly looked as if he had spent the intervening months washing in rosewater. As was obvious from his deplorable appearance, the expedition had been a complete disaster from the outset. No sooner had they penetrated the jungle than they were ambushed by Somali tribesmen. Tremanquai was unable even to take aim at those feline shadows emerging from the undergrowth before being felled by a cascade of arrows. There, in the stillness of the jungle, far from the eyes of civilization, the expedition was brutally massacred down to the last man. The attackers left him for dead like the rest of his men, but life had toughened Tremanquai, and it took more of an effort to kill him than those savages had made. And so he roamed the jungle for weeks, wounded and feverish—using his rifle for a crutch, and with some of the arrows still stuck in his flesh—until his pitiful wanderings brought him to a small native village encircled by a palisade. Exhausted, he collapsed before the narrow entrance to the fence, like a piece of flotsam washed up by the sea.

He awoke several days later completely naked, stretched out on an uncomfortable straw mattress with repulsive-looking poultices on the various wounds mor-

tifying his flesh. He was unable to identify the features
of the young girl applying the sticky greenish dressings
as belonging to any of the tribes he knew. Her body was
long and supple, her hips extremely narrow, and her chest
almost as flat as a board. Her dark skin gave off a faint,
dusky glow. He soon discovered that the men possessed
the same slender build, their delicate bone structure almost visible beneath their slight musculature. Not knowing what tribe they belonged to, Tremanquai decide to
invent a name for them. He called them Reed People,
because they looked slim and supple like reeds. Tremanquai was an excellent shot, but he had little imagination.
The Reed People's otherworldly physique, as well as their
big black eyes darkening their exquisite doll-like faces,
was a source of astonishment. But as Tremanquai's con-
valescence progressed, he discovered further reasons to
be amazed: the language they used to communicate with
each other, a series of guttural noises he found impossible
to reproduce despite being accustomed to imitating the
most outlandish dialects, the fact that they all looked the
same age, and the absence in the village of the most essential everyday instruments, as though the life of these
savages took place elsewhere, or as if they had succeeded
in reducing life to a single act: breathing. But one question above all preyed insistently on Tremanquai's mind:
how did the Reed People resist the neighboring tribes'
repeated attacks? They were few in number, they looked
neither strong nor fierce, and apparently his rifle was the
only weapon in the village.

He soon discovered how. One night, a lookout warned

that ferocious Masai tribesmen had surrounded the village. From his hut, together with his carer, Tremanquai watched his otherworldly saviors form a group in the center of the village facing the narrow entrance, which curiously had no door. Standing in a fragile line as though offering themselves up for sacrifice, the Reed People linked hands and began chanting an intricate tune. Recovering from his astonishment, Tremanquai reached for his rifle and dragged himself back over to the window with the intention of defending his hosts as best he could. Scarcely any torches were lit in the village, but the moon cast sufficient light for an experienced hunter like himself to be able to take aim. He set his sights on the gap in the stockade, hoping that if he managed to pick off a few of the Masai the others might think the village was being defended by white men and flee. To his surprise, the girl gently lowered his weapon, indicating to him silently that his intervention was unnecessary. Tremanquai bridled, but the Reed girl's serene gaze made him think again.

From his window, he watched with trepidation and bewilderment as the savage horde of Masai spilled through the entrance while his hosts carried on their discordant incantation as the spears came ever closer. The explorer steeled himself to witness the passive slaughter. Then something happened which Tremanquai described in a quavering, incredulous voice, as though he found it hard to believe the words he himself was uttering. The air split open. He could think of no better way to describe it. It was like tearing a strip of wallpaper away, he said, leaving the bare wall. Except in this case, it was not a wall but another world. A world the explorer was at first unable to see into from where he was standing, but which gave off a pale glow, lighting up the surrounding darkness. Astonished, he watched the first of the Masai tumble into the hole that had suddenly opened between them and their victims, and vanish from reality, from the world Tremanquai was in, as though they had dissolved into thin air. Seeing their brothers swallowed up by the night, the rest of the Masai fled in panic. The explorer shook his head slowly, stunned by what he had seen. Now he knew how these people managed to resist the neighboring tribes' attacks.

He lurched out of his hut and approached the hole that his hosts had opened in the very fabric of reality with their chanting. As he stood facing the opening, which flapped like a curtain, he realized it was bigger than he had first thought. It rose from the ground, reaching above his head, and was easily wide enough for a carriage to pass through. The edges billowed over the landscape, concealing then exposing it, like waves breaking on the shore. Fascinated, Tremanquai peered through it as if it were a window. On the other side was a very different world from ours, a sort of plain of pinkish rock, swept by a harsh wind that blew the sand up from the surface: in the distance, blurred by the swirling dust, he was able to make out a range of sinister-looking mountains. Disoriented and unable to see, the Masai floundered around in the other world, gibbering and running each other through with their spears as those left standing fell one by one. Tremanquai watched this macabre dance of death, transfixed, sensing their bodies caressed by a wind not of his world, like the strange dust clogging their nostrils.

The Reed People, still lined up in the middle of the village, resumed their ghostly chanting, and the hole began to close up, slowly narrowing before Tremanquai's astonished eyes until it disappeared completely. The explorer moved his hand stupidly across the space where the air had split open. Suddenly, it seemed as if there had never been anything between him and the choir of Reed People, which started breaking up, each wandering off to a different corner of the village, as though nothing out of the ordinary had occurred. But for Tremanquai, the world as he had known it would never be the same. He realized he now had only two choices. One was to see the world, which he had hitherto believed to be the only world, as one of many, superimposed like the pages of a book so that all you had to do was thrust a dagger into it to open up a pathway through all of them. The other was simpler: he could lose his mind.

That night, understandably, the explorer was unable to sleep. He lay on his straw mattress, eyes wide open, body tense, alert to the slightest noise coming from the darkness. The knowledge that he was surrounded by witches, against whom his rifle and his God were useless, filled him with dread. As soon as he was able to walk more than one step without feeling dizzy, he fled the Reed People's village. It took him several weeks to reach the port of Zanzibar, where he survived as best he could until he was able to stow away on a ship bound for London. He was back ten months after he had set out, but his experiences had

changed him utterly. It had been a disastrous voyage, and
naturally enough Sebastian Murray did not believe a word
of his story. He had no idea what had happened to his most
experienced explorer during the months he had gone missing, but he was clearly unwilling to accept Tremanquai's
tales of Reed People and their ridiculous holes in the air,
which he considered the simple ravings of a lunatic. And
his suspicions were borne out as Tremanquai proved incapable of living a normal life with his ex-widow and their
two daughters. His wife would doubtless have preferred
to carry on taking flowers to his grave rather than live
with the haunted misfit Africa had returned to her. Tremanquai veered between states of apathy and random fits
of madness that swiftly turned the hitherto harmonious
family home upside down. His accesses of insanity, which
occasionally drove him to run naked through the streets
or shoot at the hats of passersby from his window, were a
constant menace to the otherwise peaceful neighborhood,
and he was eventually carted off to the asylum at Guy's
Hospital where they simply locked him away.

Yet he was not entirely abandoned. Unbeknownst to
his father, Gilliam Murray went to see him in the hospital
as often as he could. He was moved by the grief he felt
at seeing one of his best men reduced to such a wretched
state, but also thrilled to hear him narrate that incredible
story. Murray was then barely twenty and he visited the
explorer with the eagerness of a child going to see a puppet
show, and Tremanquai never disappointed him. Sitting on
the edge of his cot, his gaze straying towards the damp
patches on the walls, he needed no encouragement to retell

the tale of the Reed People, embellishing it with new and extraordinary details each time, grateful for the audience and for being given time enough to inflate his fantasy. For a while, Gilliam believed he would regain his sanity, but after four years of being locked up, Tremanquai decided to hang himself in his cell. He left a note on a grubby piece of paper. In a spidery scrawl that might well have been his normal writing as distorted by his inner torment, he stated ironically that he was departing this world for another, which was only one of the many that existed.

By that time Gilliam had begun working in his father's company. Although, despite the visits, Tremanquai's story still seemed to him sheer madness, but perhaps for that very reason, and because becoming infected by the man's madness was the only tribute he could pay him, without his father's knowledge he sent two of his explorers to Africa to search for the nonexistent Reed People. Samuel Kaufman and Forrest Austin were a couple of numbskulls partial to showing off and going on drunken sprees, whose every expedition ended in disaster. But they were the only men his father would not miss, and the only two who would nonchalantly set off to Africa in search of a tribe of singing witches with the power to open doorways to other worlds in the air. They were also the only men to whom, because of their glaring ineptitude, he dared assign a mission as hopeless as that of locating the Reed People, which was really only a modest tribute to the memory of the hapless Oliver Tremanquai. And so Kaufman and Austin left England almost in secret. Neither they nor Gilliam Murray could have known that they would become the most famous explorers of their day. Following instructions, as soon as they set foot in Africa they began sending back telegrams giving news of their progress. Gilliam read these cursorily before placing them in his desk drawer with a sad smile.

Everything changed when, three months later, he received one telling him they had at last found the Reed People. He could not believe it! Were they playing a joke on him in revenge for having sent them off on a wild goose chase? Gilliam wondered. But the details contained in their telegrams ruled out any possibility of deceit, because, as far as he remembered, they agreed entirely with those embellishing Oliver Tremanquai's story. And so, astonished though he was, Gilliam could only conclude that both Tremanquai and they were telling the truth: the Reed People did exist. From that moment on, the telegrams became Gilliam Murray's reason for getting up in the morning. He awaited their arrival with eager anticipation, reading and rereading them behind the locked door of his office, unwilling for the time being to share the amazing discovery with anyone, not even his father.

According to the telegrams, once they had located the village, Kaufman and Austin had no real difficulty being accepted as guests. In fact, the Reed People were apparently compliant towards everything, incapable of putting up any form of resistance. Nor did they seem particularly interested in Kaufman and Austin's reasons for being there. They simply accepted their presence. The two men asked for no more, and rather than lose heart when faced with the difficulty of carrying out the essential part of their mission (which was nothing less than discovering whether these savages could actually open up passageways to other worlds), they resolved to be patient and treat their stay as a paid holiday. Although they did not say so, Gilliam could easily imagine them lounging around in the sun all day, polishing off the crates of whiskey they had sneaked with them on the expedition while Gilliam pretended to be looking the other way. Amazingly, they could not have thought up a better strategy, for their continual state of alcoholic stupor, and the frequent dancing and fighting they engaged in naked in the grass, drew the attention of the Reed People, who were curious about the amber liquid that generated such jolly antics. Once they began sharing their whiskey, a rough camaraderie sprang up between them, which Gilliam rejoiced in back in his office, for it was without doubt the first step towards a future coexistence. He was not mistaken, although fostering this primitive contact until it grew into a common bond of trust and friendship cost him several consignments of the best Scotch, and to this day he wondered whether that many bottles were really necessary for such a small tribe.

At last, one morning, he received the long-awaited telegram in which Kaufman and Austin described how the Reed People had led them to the middle of the village, and in a seemingly beautiful gesture of friendship and gratitude, had opened for them the hole through to the other world. The explorers described the aperture and the pink landscape they were able to glimpse through it, using exactly the same words as Tremanquai five years earlier. This time, however, the young Gilliam no longer saw them as part of a made-up story: now he knew it was for real. All of a sudden he felt trapped, suffocated, and not because he was locked away in his little office. He felt hemmed in by the walls of a universe he now realized was not the only one of its kind. But this constraint would soon end, he thought to himself. Then he devoted a few moments to the memory of poor Oliver Tremanquai. He assumed the man's deep religious beliefs had prevented him from assimilating what he had seen, leaving him no other course than the precarious path of madness. Luckily, that pair of oafs Kaufman and Austin possessed far simpler minds, which should spare them a similar fate. He reread the telegram hundreds of times. Not only did the Reed People exist, they practiced something Gilliam, unlike Tremanquai, preferred to call magic as opposed to witchcraft. An unknown world had opened itself up to Kaufman and Austin, and naturally, they could not resist exploring it.

As Gilliam read their subsequent telegrams, he regretted not having accompanied them. With the blessing of the Reed People, who left them to their own devices, Kaufman and Austin began making brief incursions into the other world, diligently reporting back to him on its peculiarities. It consisted largely of a vast pink plain of faintly luminous rock, stretching out beneath a sky permanently obscured by incredibly dense fog. If there were any sun behind it, its rays were unable to shine through. As a consequence, the only light came from the strange substance on the ground, so that while one's boots were clearly visible, the landscape was plunged into gloom, day and night merging into an eternal dusk, making it very difficult to see long distances. From time to time, a raging wind whipped the plain, producing sandstorms that made everything even more difficult to see. The two men immediately noticed something strange: the moment they stepped through the hole their pocket watches stopped. Once back in their own reality, the sleeping mechanisms mysteriously stirred again. It was as though they had unanimously decided to stop measuring the time their owners spent in the other world. Kaufman and Austin looked at one another, and it is not difficult to imagine them shrugging their shoulders, baffled.

They made a further discovery after spending a night, according to their calculations, in the camp they had set up right beside the opening so that they could keep an eye on the Reed People. There was no need for them to shave, because while they were in the other world their beards stopped growing. In addition, Austin had cut his arm seconds before stepping through the hole, and as soon as he was on the other side it stopped bleeding to the point he even forgot to bandage it. He did not remember the wound until the moment they were back in the village and it started to bleed again. Fascinated, Gilliam wrote down this extraordinary incident in his notebook, as well as what had happened with their watches and beards. Everything pointed to some impossible stoppage of time. While Murray speculated in his office, Kaufman and Austin stocked up on ammunition and food and set out towards the only thing breaking the monotony of the plain: the ghostly mountain range, scarcely visible on the horizon.

As their watches continued to be unusable, they decided to measure the time their journey took by the number of the nights they slept. This method soon proved ineffective, because at times the wind rose so suddenly and with such force they were obliged to stay awake all night holding the tent down, or else their accumulated tiredness crept up on them the moment they stopped for food or a rest. And so all they could say about it was that after an indeterminate length of time that was neither very long nor very short, they reached the longed-for mountains. These proved to be made of the same luminous rock as the plain, only they had a hideous appearance like a set of rotten, broken teeth, their jagged peaks piercing the thick cloudscape that blotted out the sky.

The two men spotted a few hollows which looked as if they might be caves. Having no other plan, the men decided to scale the slopes until they reached the nearest one. This did not take long. Once they had reached the pinnacle of a small mountain, they had a broader view of the plain. Far off in the distance the hole had been reduced to a bright dot on the horizon. They could see their way back waiting for them, acting for the moment as a guiding light. They were not worried the Reed People might close the hole, because they had taken the precaution of bringing what remained of the whiskey with them. It was then that they noticed other bright dots shining in the distance. It was difficult to see clearly through the mist, but there must have been half a dozen of them. Were they other holes leading to other worlds? They found the answer in the very cave they intended to explore. As soon as they entered it, they could see it was inhabited. There were signs of life everywhere: burnt-out fires, bowls, tools, and other basic implements—things Tremanquai had found so conspicuous by their absence in the Reed People's village. At the back of the cave they discovered a narrower, darker enclosure, the walls of which were covered in paintings. Most depicted scenes from everyday life, and judging from the willowy rag doll figures, only the Reed People could have painted them. Apparently, that dark world was where they really lived. The village was no more than a temporary location, a provisional settlement, perhaps one of many they had built in other worlds.

Kaufman and Austin did not consider the drawings of rustic scenes particularly significant. But two caught their attention. One of these took up nearly an entire wall. As far as they could tell, it was meant to be a map of that world, or at least the part the tribe had succeeded in exploring, which was limited to the area near the mountains. What intrigued them was that this crude map marked the location of some of the other holes, and, if they were not mistaken, what they contained. The drawings were easy enough to interpret: a yellow star shape represented the hole, and the painted images next to them, their contents. At least this is what they deduced from the dot surrounded by huts, apparently representing the hole they had climbed through to get there, and the village on the other side, back in their world. The map showed four other openings, fewer than those they had glimpsed on the horizon. Where did they lead? Whether from idleness or boredom, the Reed People had painted only the contents of the holes nearest their cave. One of these seemed to depict a battle going on between two different tribes: one human-shaped, the other square and rectangular. The remainder of the drawings were impossible to make out. Consequently, the only thing Kaufman and Austin could be clear about was that the world they were in contained dozens of holes like the one they had come through; but they could only find out where any of them led if they passed through them themselves, for the Reed People's scrawls were as mystifying to them as the dreams of a blind man.

The second painting that caught their eye was on the opposite wall, and showed a group of Reed People running from what looked like a gigantic four-legged monster with a dragon's tail and spikes on its back. Kaufman and Austin glanced at one another, alarmed to find themselves in the same world as a wild animal whose mere image was enough to scare the living daylights out of them. What would happen if they came across the real thing? However, this discovery did not make them turn back. They both had rifles and enough ammunition to kill a whole herd of monsters, assuming they even existed and were not simply a mythological invention of the Reed People. They also had whiskey, that marvelous drink that would fire up their courage, or at least turn the prospect of being eaten by an elephantine monster into a relatively minor nuisance. What more did they need?

Accordingly, they decided to carry on exploring and set out for the opening where the battle was going on between the two different tribes, because it was closest to the mountains. The journey was grueling, hampered by freak sandstorms that forced them to erect their tent and take refuge inside if they did not want to be scoured like cooking pots. Thankfully, they did not meet any of the giant creatures. Of course, when they finally reached the hole, they had no idea how long it had taken them, only that the journey had been exhausting. Its size and appearance were identical to the one they had first stepped through into that murky world. The only difference was that instead of crude huts, inside this one was a ruined city. Scarcely a single building remained standing, and yet there was something oddly familiar about the structures. They stood for a few moments, surveying the ruins from the other side of the hole, as one would peer into a shop window, but no sign of life or other telltale evidence seemed to break the calm of the razed city. What kind of war could have wrought such terrible devastation? Depressed by the dreadful scene, Kaufman and Austin restored their courage with a few slugs of whiskey, and finally, donning their pith helmets, they leapt valiantly through the opening and into the other side. Their senses were immediately assailed by an intense, familiar odor. Smiling with bewildered emotion, it dawned on them that they were simply smelling their own world again, which they had unconsciously stopped being aware of during their journey across the pink plain.

Rifles at the ready, they scoured their surroundings, moving cautiously through the rubble-filled streets, shocked at the sight of so much devastation, until they stumbled across another obstacle, which stopped them dead in their tracks. Kaufman and Austin gazed incredulously at the object blocking their path: it was none other than the clock tower of Big Ben. The half-crushed tower lay in the middle of the street like a severed fish head, the vast clock face a great eye staring at them with mournful resignation. The discovery made them glance uneasily about them. Strangely moved, they cast an affectionate eye over each toppled edifice, the desolate ruined landscape where a few plumes of black smoke darkened the sky over a London razed to the ground. Neither could contain their tears. In fact, the two men would have stood there forever, weeping over the remains of their beloved city, had it not been for a peculiar clanking sound that came from nearby.

Rifles at the ready again, they followed the clatter until they came to a small mound of rubble. They clambered up it noiselessly, crouching low. Unseen in their improvised lookout, they saw what was causing the racket. It was coming from strange, vaguely humanoid metal creatures. Judging from the vapor seeping out of their joints, they were powered by what looked like tiny steam engines attached to their backs. The loud clanging noise the men had heard was the sound of the creatures' clumsy iron feet knocking against the metal debris strewn on the ground. The bemused explorers had no idea what these creatures might be, until Austin plucked from the rubble what looked like the scrunched-up page of a newspaper. With trembling fingers, he opened it up and discovered a photograph of the same creatures. The headline announced the unstoppable advance of the automatons, and went on to encourage readers to rally to the support of the human army led by the brave Captain Derek Shackleton. What most surprised them, however, was the date: this loose page was from a newspaper printed April 3, 2000. Kaufman and Austin shook their heads as one, very slowly from left to right. But before they had time to express their amazement in a more sophisticated way, the remains of a rafter in the mound of rubble fell into the street with a loud crash, alerting the automatons. Kaufman and Austin exchanged terrified looks and took to their heels, running full pelt towards the hole they had come through without looking back. They easily slipped through it again, but did not stop running until their legs would carry them no further. They erected their tent and cowered inside, trying to collect their thoughts to absorb what they had seen—with the obligatory help of some whiskey, of course. It was clearly time for them to return to the village and report back to London everything they had seen—convinced Gilliam Murray would be able to give them an explanation.

However, their problems did not end there. On the way back to the village, they were attacked by one of the gigantic beasts with spikes on its back, whose potential existence they had forgotten about. They had great difficulty killing it. They used up nearly all their ammunition trying to scare it away, because the bullets kept bouncing off the spiked armor without injuring it in any way. Finally, they managed to chase the creature away by shooting at its eyes, its only weak point as far as they could determine. Having successfully fought off the beast, Kaufman and Austin arrived back at the hole without further incident, and immediately sent a message to London relating all their discoveries.

As soon as he received their news, Gilliam Murray set sail for Africa. He joined the two explorers in the Reed People's village, where, like doubting Thomas plunging his fingers into Christ's wounds after he had risen from the dead, he made his way to the razed city of London in the year 2000. He spent many months with the Reed People, although he could not really be sure exactly how many, as he spent extensive periods exploring the pink plain in order to verify the truth of Kaufman and Austin's claims. Just as they had described in their telegrams, in that sunless world watches stopped ticking, razors became superfluous, and in general, nothing appeared to mark the passage of time. Consequently, he concluded that incredible though it might seem, the moments he spent in there were like a hiatus from his life, a temporary suspension of his inexorable journey towards death. He realized this was not his imagination playing tricks on him when he returned to the village and the puppy he had taken with him ran to join its siblings: they had all come from the same litter but now the others were grown dogs. Gilliam had not needed to take a single shave during his exploration of the plain, but Eternal, the puppy, was a far more spectacular manifestation of the absence of time in the other world. He also deduced that the holes did not lead to other universes as he had first believed, but to different times in a world that was none other than his own. The pink plain was outside the time continuum, outside time, the arena where man's life took place alongside that of the plants and other animals. And the beings inhabiting that world, Tremanquai's Reed People, knew how to break out of the time continuum by creating holes in it, openings that enabled man to travel in time, to cross from one era to another. This realization filled Gilliam with excitement and dread. He had made the greatest discovery in the history of mankind: he had discovered what was underneath the world, what was behind reality. He had discovered the fourth dimension.

How strange life was, he thought. He had started out trying to find the source of the Nile and ended up discovering a secret passage that led to the year 2000. But that was how all the greatest discoveries were made. Was the voyage of the *Beagle* not prompted by spurious financial and strategic interests? The discoveries resulting from it would have been far less interesting had a young naturalist perceptive enough to notice the variations between finches' beaks not been on board. And yet, the story of natural selection would go on to revolutionize the world. His discovery of the fourth dimension had happened in a similarly random way.

But what use was there in discovering something if you could not share it with the rest of the world? Gilliam wanted to take Londoners to the year 2000 so that they could see with their own eyes what the future held for them. The question was, how? He could not possibly take boatloads of city dwellers to a native village in the heart of Africa, where the Reed People were living. The only answer was to move the hole to London. Was that possible? He did not know, but he lost nothing by trying. Leaving Kaufman and Austin to guard the Reed People, Murray returned to London, where he had a cast-iron box the size of a room built. Together with a thousand bottles of whiskey, he took it back with him to the village, where he planned to strike a bargain that would change people's perception of the known world. Drunk as lords, the Reed People consented to his whim of singing their magic chants inside the sinister box. Once the hole had materialized, he herded them out and closed the heavy doors behind them. The three men then waited until the last of the Reed People had succumbed to the effects of the whiskey before setting off home. It was an arduous journey, and only when the enormous box was on the ship at Zanzibar did Gilliam begin to breathe more easily. Even so, he barely slept a wink during the passage home. He spent almost the entire time up on deck, gazing lovingly at the fateful box which so upset the other passengers, and wondering whether it was not in fact empty. Could one really steal the hole? His eagerness to know the answer to that question gnawed away at him, making the return journey seem interminable. He could hardly believe it when at last they docked at Liverpool. As soon as he reached his offices, he opened the box in complete secret. The hole was still there! They had successfully stolen it! The next step was to show it to his father.

"What the devil is this?" exclaimed Sebastian Murray, when he saw the hole shimmering inside the box.

"This is what drove Oliver Tremanquai mad, Father," Gilliam replied, pronouncing the explorer's name with affection. "So, take care."

His father turned pale. Nevertheless, he accompanied his son through the hole and traveled into the future, to a demolished London where humans hid in the ruins like rats. Once he had got over the shock, father and son agreed they must make this discovery known to the world. And what better way to do this than to turn the hole into a business: taking people to see the year 2000 would bring in enough money to cover the cost of the journeys themselves and to fund further exploration of the fourth dimension. They proceeded to map out a secure route to the hole into the future, eliminating any dangers, setting up lookout posts and smoothing out the road so that a tramcar with thirty seats could cross it easily. Sadly, his father did not live long enough to see Murray's Time Travel open its doors to the public, but Gilliam consoled himself with the thought that at least he had seen the future beyond his own death.

IX

ONCE HE HAD FINISHED TELLING HIS story, Murray fell silent and looked expectantly at his two visitors. Andrew assumed he was hoping for some kind of response from him, but had no idea what to say. He felt embarrassed. Everything his host had told them was no more believable to him than an adventure story. That pink plain seemed about as real to him as Lilliput, the South Sea Island inhabited by little people where Lemuel Gulliver had been shipwrecked. From the stupefied smile on Charles's face, however, he assumed his cousin did believe it. After all, he had traveled to the year 2000; what did it matter whether it was by crossing a pink plain where time had stopped?

"And now, gentlemen, if you would kindly follow me, I'll show you something only a few trusted people are allowed to see," Gilliam declared, resuming the sort of guided tour of his commodious office.

With Eternal continually running round his master, the three men walked across to another wall. A small collection of photographs awaited them, and what was prob-

ably another map, although this was concealed behind a
red silk curtain. Andrew was surprised to discover that
the photographs had been taken in the fourth dimension,
although they might easily have been taken in any desert
since cameras were apparently unable to record the color
of this or any other world. He had to use his imagination,
then, to see the white smear of sand as pink. The majority of the photographs documented routine moments
during the expedition: Gilliam and two other men, presumably Kaufman and Austin, putting up tents, drinking coffee during a pause, lighting a fire, posing in front
of the phantom mountains, almost entirely obscured by
thick fog. It all looked too normal. Only one of the photographs made Andrew really feel he was contemplating
an alien world. In it Kaufman (who was short and fat) and
Austin (who was tall and thin) stood smiling exaggerat-
edly, hats tilted to the side of their heads, rifles hanging
from their shoulders, and one boot resting on the massive
head of a fairy-tale dragon, which lay dead on the sand
like a hunting trophy. Andrew was about to lean towards
the photograph and take a closer look at the amorphous
lump, when an awful screeching noise made him start.
Beside him, Gilliam was pulling on a gold cord which
drew back the silk curtain, revealing what was behind it.

"Rest assured, gentlemen, you will find no other map
like this anywhere in England," he declared, swelling with
pride. "It is an exact replica of the drawing in the Reed
People's cave, expanded, naturally, after our subsequent
explorations."

What the puppet theater curtain uncovered looked

more like a drawing by a child with an active imagination than a map. The color pink predominated, of course, representing the plain, with the mountains in the middle. But the shadowy peaks were not the only geological feature depicted on the map. In the right-hand corner, for example, was a squiggly line, presumably a river, and close by it a light-green patch, possibly a forest or meadow. Andrew could not help feeling that these everyday symbols, used in maps charting the world he lived in, were incongruous with what was supposed to be a map of the fourth dimension. But the most striking thing about the drawing was the gold dots peppering the plain, evidently meant to symbolize the holes. Two of these—the entrance to the year 2000, and the one now in Murray's possession—were linked by a thin red line, which must represent the route taken by the time-traveling tramcar.

"As you can see, there are many holes, but we still have no idea where they lead. Does one of them go back to the autumn of 1888? Who knows? It is certainly possible," said Gilliam, staring significantly at Andrew. "Kaufman and Austin are trying to reach the one nearest the entrance to the year 2000, but they still haven't found a way of circumnavigating the herd of beasts grazing in the valley right in front of it."

While Andrew and Charles studied the map, Gilliam knelt down and began stroking the dog.

"Ah, the fourth dimension. What mysteries it holds," he mused. "All I know is our candle never burns down in there, to use a poetic turn of phrase. Eternal only looks one, but he was born four years ago. And I suppose that must be his actual age—unless the long periods spent on the plain, where time seems to leave no mark, are of no matter. Eternal was with me while I carried out my studies in Africa, and since we came back to London, he sleeps next to me every night inside the hole. I did not name him that for nothing, gentlemen, and while I can I'll do everything in my power to honor his name."

Andrew could not help feeling a shiver run down his spine when his and the dog's eyes met.

"What is that building supposed to be?" asked Charles, pointing to an image of a castle close to the mountains.

"Ah, that," Gilliam said, uneasily. "That's Her Majesty's palace."

"The Queen has a palace in the fourth dimension?" asked Charles, astonished.

"That's right, Mr. Winslow. Let us call it a thank-you present for her generous contribution to our expeditions." Gilliam paused for a moment, unsure whether he should go on. At last he added: "Ever since we organized a private journey to the year 2000 for the Queen and her entourage, she has shown great interest in the laws governing the fourth dimension and, well . . . she made it known to us that she would like a private residence to be put at her disposal on the plain, where she could spend time when her duties allowed, as one does at a spa. She has been going there for some months now, which makes me think her reign will be a long one," he said, making no attempt to conceal his irritation at having been forced to make this concession, while he no doubt had to be content to spend his nights in a wretched tent with Eternal. "But that doesn't concern me. All I want is to be left alone. The Empire wishes to conquer the moon. Let it . . . but the future is mine!"

He closed the little curtain and led them back to his desk. He invited them to take a seat, and himself sat in his armchair, while Eternal (the dog who would outlive mankind, excepting Gilliam, the Queen, and the lucky employees at her palace outside the time continuum) slumped at his feet.

"Well, gentlemen, I hope I've answered your question about why we are only able to take you to May 20 in the year 2000, where all you will see is the most decisive battle in human history," he said ironically, after he had taken his seat.

Andrew snorted. None of that interested him in the slightest, at least while he was unable to experience anything other than pain. He was back at square one, it seemed. He would have to go ahead with his suicide plan as soon as Charles's back was turned. The man had to sleep sometime.

"So, there's no way of traveling back to the year 1888?" said his cousin, apparently unwilling to give up.

"I imagine it wouldn't be a problem if you had a time machine," replied Gilliam, shrugging his shoulders.

"We'll just have to hope science will invent one soon," Charles said ruefully, patting his cousin's knee and rising from his chair.

"It's just possible one has already been invented, gentlemen," Gilliam blurted out.

Charles spun round to face him.

"What do you mean?"

"Hm, it's just a suspicion," Murray replied, "but when our company first started, there was someone who vehemently opposed it. He insisted time travel was too dangerous, that it had to be taken slowly. I always suspected he said this because he had a time machine and wanted to experiment with it before making it public. Or perhaps he wanted to keep it to himself, to become the only master of time."

"Who are you talking about?" asked Andrew.

Gilliam sat back in his chair, a smug grin on his face.

"Why, Mr. Wells, of course," he replied.

"But, whatever gave you that idea?" asked Charles. "In his novel Wells only writes about journeying into the future. He doesn't even envisage the possibility of going back in time."

"That's exactly my point, Mr. Winslow. Just imagine, gentlemen, if somebody were to build a time machine, the most important invention in the history of humanity. Given its incredible potential, they would have no choice but to keep it secret, to prevent it from falling into the hands of some unscrupulous individual who might use it for their own ends. But would they be able to resist the temptation of divulging their secret to the world? A novel would be the perfect way of making their invention known without anyone ever suspecting it was anything but pure fiction. Don't you agree? Or if vanity doesn't convince you as a motive, then what if they weren't trying to satisfy their ego at all? What if *The Time Machine* were merely a decoy, a message in a bottle cast into the sea, a cry for help to somebody who might know how to interpret it? Who knows? Anyway, gentlemen, Wells did contemplate the possibility of going back in time, and with the aim of changing it, moreover, which I imagine is what motivates you, Mr. Harrington."

Andrew jumped, as if he had been discovered committing a crime. Gilliam smiled at him wryly, then rifled through one of his desk drawers. Finally, he pulled out a copy of *Science Schools Journal* dating from 1888 and threw it on the table. The title on the cover of the dog-eared edition was *The Chronic Argonauts*, by H. G. Wells. He handed it to Andrew, asking him to take good care of it, as it was a rare copy.

"Exactly eight years ago, as a young man having recently arrived in London and ready to conquer the world, Wells published a serial novel entitled *The Chronic Argonauts*. The main character was a scientist called Moses Nebogipfel, who traveled back in time to commit a murder. Perhaps Wells considered he had overstepped himself, and when he revived the idea for his novel, he eliminated the journeys into the past, perhaps so as not to give his readers ideas. In any case, he decided to concentrate solely on traveling into the future. He made his protagonist a far more upright character than Nebogipfel, as you know, and never actually mentions his name in the novel. Perhaps Wells could not resist this gesture."

Andrew and Charles stared at one another, then at Murray, who was scribbling something in a notebook.

"Here is Wells's address," he said, holding out a scrap of paper to Andrew. "You have nothing to lose by seeing whether my suspicions are well founded or not."

X

DRIFTING THROUGH THE SCENT OF roses suffusing the lobby, the cousins left the offices of Murray's Time Travel. Once in the street, they hailed the first hansom cab they saw and gave the driver the address in Woking, Surrey, where the author H. G. Wells lived. The meeting with Gilliam Murray had plunged Andrew into a profound silence where God only knew what dark thoughts he was grappling with. But the journey would take at least three hours, and therefore Charles was in no hurry to draw his cousin into conversation. He preferred to leave him to gather his thoughts. They had experienced enough excitement for one day, and there was still more to come. In any case, he had learned to sit back and enjoy these frequent and unexpected bouts of silence that punctuated his relationship with Andrew, and so he closed his eyes and let himself be rocked by the swaying motion of the cab as it sped out of the city.

Although they were not troubled by the silence, I imagine that you, who are in a sense sharing their journey, might find it a little tiresome. Therefore, rather than lecture you on the nature and quality of this inviolate calm, scarcely broken by the cab's creaks and groans, or describe to you the view of the horses' hindquarters upon which Andrew's gaze was firmly fixed, and, since I am unable even to relate in any exciting way what was going on in Andrew's head (where the prospect of saving Marie Kelly was slowly fading because, although a method of traveling through time had apparently been discovered, it was still impossible to do so with any accuracy), I propose to make use of this lull in proceedings to tell you about something still pending in this story. I alone can narrate this, as it is an episode about which the cab's occupants are completely unaware. I am referring to the spectacular ascent up the social ladder of their respective fathers, William and Sydney. This was presided over by William Harrington with his typical mixture of good fortune and rough-and-ready abilities, and although both men resolved to keep it secret, they cannot do so from me, as I see everything whether I wish to or not.

I could give you my honest opinion of William Harrington, but what I think is of no consequence. Let us rather stick with Andrew's own idea of his father, which is not far from the truth. Andrew saw his father as a warrior of commerce, capable, as you will discover, of the most heroic exploits in the field of business. However, when it came to everyday hand-to-hand combat, where the struggles that really make us human take place, allowing us to show our kindness or generosity, he was apparently incapable of anything but the meanest acts, as you have already seen. William Harrington was the class of person who possesses a self-assurance that is both their strength and their downfall, a cast-iron confidence that can easily turn into excessive, blind arrogance. In the end, he was like someone who stands on his head and then complains the world is upside down, or if you prefer, like someone who believes God created the earth for him to walk upon, with which I think I have said enough.

William Harrington returned from the Crimea to a world dominated by machines. But he realized straightaway that all this machinery would not supersede the old way of doing things, since even the glass in the Crystal Palace, that transparent whale marooned with its insides full of mechanical devices in Hyde Park, had been made by hand. That was evidently not the way to grow rich, a goal he had set himself, with the typical insouciance of a twenty-year-old, as he lay in bed at night with his new wife, the rather timid daughter of a match manufacturer for whom he had begun working. The thought of being trapped in a dreary life already mapped out for him kept him awake, and he wondered whether he ought not to rebel against such a common fate. Why had his mother gone to the trouble of bringing him into the world if the most exciting moment in his life was having been made lame by a bayonet? Was he doomed to be just another anonymous cipher, or would he pass into the annals of history? His lamentable performance in the Crimea would appear to suggest the former, and yet William Harrington had too voracious a nature to be content with that. "As far as I can tell, I only have one life," he said to himself, "and what I don't achieve in this one I won't achieve in the next."

The very next day he called his brother-in-law Sydney, a bright, capable young man who was virtually wasting his life as an accountant in the small family firm, and assured him that he too was destined for greater things. However, in order to achieve the rapid social ascent William envisaged, they must forget the match business and start up their own enterprise, easily done if they made use of the savings Sydney happened to have. During the course of a long drinking session, William convinced his brother-in-law to let him play with his money, declaring that a small amount of entrepreneurial risk would inject some excitement into his dull life. They had little to lose and much to gain. It was essential they find a business that would bring in large, quick profits, he concluded. To his amazement, Sydney agreed, and soon put his imaginative mind to work. He showed up at their next meeting with the plans to what he was convinced would be a revolutionary invention. The Bachelor's Helpmate, as he had called it, consisted of a chair designed for lovers of erotic literature, and was equipped with a lectern that automatically turned the pages, allowing the reader to keep both hands free. William could see from Sydney's detailed drawings that the device came with accessories, such as a small washbasin, and even a sponge, designed so that the client did not have to interrupt his reading to get up from the chair. Sydney was convinced his product would make their fortune, but William was not so sure: his brother-in-law had clearly confused his own necessities with those of others. However, once William had succeeded in the difficult task of convincing him that his sophisticated chair was not as essential to the Empire as he had imagined, they found themselves back at square one, without a single decent idea to their name.

Desperate, they concentrated on the flow of merchandise coming in from the colonies. What products had not yet been imported? What unfulfilled needs did the English have? They looked around carefully, but it seemed nothing was wanting. Her Majesty, with her tentacular grasp, was already divesting the world of everything her subjects needed. Of course, there was one thing they lacked, but this was a necessity no one dared to mention.

They discovered it one day whilst strolling through the commercial district of New York, where they had gone in search of inspiration. They were preparing to return to the hotel and soak their aching feet in a basin of saltwater, when their eyes fell on the product displayed in a shop window. Behind the glass was a stack of strange-looking packets containing fifty sheets of moisturized paper. Printed on the back were the words: "Gayetty's Medicated Paper." What the devil was this for? they wondered. They soon discovered the answer from the instructions pasted in the window, which without a hint of embarrassment depicted a hand applying the product to the most intimate area of a posterior. This fellow Gayetty had obviously decided that corncobs and parish newsletters were a thing of the past. Once they had recovered from their surprise, William and Sydney looked at each other meaningfully.

This was it! It did not take a genius to imagine the warm reception thousands of British backsides raw from being rubbed with rough newspaper would give this heaven-sent gift. At fifty cents a packet, they would soon make their fortune. They purchased enough stock to furnish a small shop they acquired in one of London's busiest streets, filled the window display with their product, put up a poster illustrating its correct usage, and waited behind the counter for customers to flock in and snatch this wonderful, timely invention from their hands. But not a single soul walked through the door the day the shop opened, or in the days that followed, which soon turned into weeks.

It took William and Sydney three months finally to admit defeat. Their dreams of wealth had been cruelly dashed at the outset, although they had enough medicated paper never to need worry about procuring scrap paper again in their lives. However, at times society obeys its own twisted logic, and the moment they closed their disastrous shop, their business suddenly took off. In the dark corners of inns, in alleyway entrances, in their own homes during the early hours, William and Sydney were assailed by a variety of individuals, who, in hushed tones and glancing furtively about them, ordered packets of their miraculous paper before disappearing back into the gloom. Surprised at first by the cloak-and-dagger aspect they were obliged to adopt, the two young entrepreneurs soon became accustomed to tramping the streets at the dead of night, one limping along, the other puffing and panting, to make their clandestine deliveries far from prying eyes. They grew used to depositing their embarrassing product in house doorways, or signaling with a tap of their cane on windowpanes, or tossing packets off bridges onto barges passing noiselessly below, slipping into deserted parks and retrieving wads of pound notes stashed under a bench, whistling like a couple of songbirds through mansion railings. Everyone in London wanted to use Gayetty's wonderful paper without their neighbor finding out, a fact William slyly took advantage of, increasing the price of his product to what would eventually become an outrageous sum, one which most customers were nevertheless willing to pay.

Within a couple of years, they were able to purchase two luxurious dwellings in the Brompton Road area, from where they soon upped sticks for Kensington. For in addition to his collection of expensive canes, William measured his success by this ability to acquire ever larger houses. Amazed that the reckless act of placing his entire savings at his brother-in-law's disposal had provided him with a fine mansion in Queen's Gate, from whose balcony he could survey the most elegant side of London, Sydney resolved to enjoy what he had, giving himself over to the pleasures of family life so extolled by the clergy. He filled his house with children, books, paintings by promising artists, took on a couple of servants, and, feeling at a safe distance from them now, cultivated the disdain he claimed he had always felt towards the lower classes to such an extent it became complete contempt. In brief, he quietly adapted to his new life of affluence without minding that it was all based on the ignoble business of selling WC paper.

But William was different. His proud, inquisitive nature made it impossible for him to be satisfied with that. He needed public recognition, to be respected by society. In other words, he wanted the great and the good of London to invite him foxhunting, to treat him as an equal. But, much as he paraded through London's smoking rooms doling out his card, this did not happen. Faced with a situation he was powerless to change, he could not help building up a bitter resentment towards the wealthy elite, who subjected him to the most abysmal ostracism while wiping their distinguished backsides with the soft tissue paper he provided. During one of the rare gatherings the two of them were invited to, his anger boiled over when in a drunken repartee some wag bestowed on them the title Official Wipers to the Queen. Before anyone could so much as laugh, William Harrington hurled himself on the insolent dandy, breaking his nose with the pommel of his cane before Sydney managed to drag him away.

The gathering proved a turning point in their lives. William Harrington learned from it a harsh but valuable lesson: the medicinal paper to which he owed everything, and which had generated so much wealth, was a disgrace that would stain his life forever unless he did something about it. And so, spurred on by his overwhelming contempt, he began investing part of his earnings in less disreputable businesses, such as the burgeoning railway industry. In a matter of months, he became the majority shareholder in several locomotive repair shops. His next step was to buy up a failing shipping company called Fellowship, inject new blood into it, and turn it into the most profitable of any oceangoing concern. Through his tiny empire of successful businesses, which Sydney managed with the easy elegance of an orchestra conductor, in less than two years William was able to dissociate his name forever from medicinal paper, canceling the final shipment and leaving the whole of London plunged into silent, mournful despair. In the spring of 1872, Annesley Hall invited him to his first hunt gathering on his Newstead estate, which was attended by all of London's great and good who eagerly applauded William's extraordinary achievements, and where the witty young man who had made a joke at his expense at that party long ago regrettably perished. According to the newspaper account, the ill-fated youth accidentally shot himself in the foot with his own shotgun. It was around that time that William Harrington dusted off his old uniform and commissioned a portrait of himself bursting out of it, smiling as though his unadorned chest were plastered with medals, and greeting all who entered his mansion.

THIS, AND NO OTHER, is the secret that their fathers so jealously guarded and whose air of light entertainment I considered appropriate for this rather wearisome journey. But I am afraid we have reached the end of our story too soon. Total silence still reigns in the cab and is likely to do so for some time, because, when he is in the mood, Andrew is capable of daydreaming for hours, unless prodded with a red-hot poker or doused in boiling oil, things Charles is not in the habit of carrying around with him. Therefore, I have no other choice but to take flight again so that we reach their destination, Mr. Wells's house, more quickly than they do. Not only, as you will have gathered from some of my commentaries, am I not subject to the cab's tortuous pace, but I can travel at the speed of light, so that—*voilà!*—in the blink of an eye, or faster still, we find ourselves in Woking, floating above the roof of a modest three-story house with a garden overrun by brambles and silver birch, whose frail façade trembles slightly as the trains to Lynton roar past.

XI

IMMEDIATELY REALIZE I HAVE picked an inopportune moment to intrude upon Herbert George Wells's life. In order to inconvenience him as little as possible, I could quickly pass over the description of his physical appearance by saying no more than that the celebrated author was a pale, skinny young man who had seen better days. However, of all the characters swimming around like fish in this story, Wells is the one who appears most frequently, no doubt to his regret, and this compels me to be a little more precise in my depiction of him. Besides being painfully thin and having a deathly pallor, Wells sported a fashionable moustache, straight with downward- pointed ends that seemed too big and bushy for his childish face. The moustache hung like a dark cloud over an exquisite, rather feminine mouth, which, together with his blue eyes, would have lent him an almost angelic air were it not for the roguish smile playing on his lips. In brief, Wells looked like a porcelain doll with twinkling eyes behind which roamed a lively, penetrating intellect. For lovers of detail, or those lacking in imagination, I shall go on to say that he weighed little more than eight stone, used a size eight and a half shoe, and wore his hair neatly parted on the left. His body odor, usually pleasant, smelled slightly of stale sweat that day, as some hours earlier he had been for a ride with his new wife through the surrounding Surrey roads astride their tandem bicycle, the latest invention that had instantly won the couple over because it needed no food or shelter and never strayed from the place where you left it. There is little more I can add short of dissecting the man, or going into intimate details such as the modest proportions and slight southeasterly curvature of his manhood.

At that very moment, he was seated at the kitchen table, where he usually did his writing, a magazine in his hands. His stiff body, bolt upright in his chair, betrayed his inner turmoil. For while it might have seemed as though Wells were simply letting himself be slowly enveloped by the pretty pattern of rippling shadows cast by the afternoon sun shining on the tree in the garden, he was in fact trying hard to contain his simmering rage. He took a deep breath, followed by another, then another, in a desperate effort to summon up a soothing calm. Evidently this did not work, for he ended up taking the journal he had been reading and hurling it against the kitchen door. The magazine fluttered gracelessly through the air like a wounded pigeon and landed a few yards from his feet. Wells gazed at it from his chair with slight regret, then sighed and shook his head, before finally standing up to retrieve it from the floor, scolding himself for this outburst of rage unworthy of a civilized person. He put the magazine back on the table and sat down in front of it again with the resigned expression of one who knows that accepting reversals of fortune with good grace is a sign of courage and intelligence.

The magazine in question was an edition of *The Speaker*, which had published a devastating review of his most recent novel *The Island of Dr. Moreau*, another popular work of science fiction beneath the surface of which lurked one of his pet themes: the visionary destroyed by his own dreams. The main protagonist of the novel is a man called Prendick who is shipwrecked and has the misfortune to be washed up on an uncharted island that turns out to be the domain of a mad scientist exiled from England because of his brutal experiments on animals. On that remote island, the eponymous doctor has become like a primitive god to a tribe made up of the freakish creations of his unhinged imagination, the monstrous spawn of his efforts to turn wild animals into men. The work was an attempt to go one step further than Darwin by having his deranged doctor endeavor to modify life by speeding up the naturally slow process of evolution. It was also a tribute to Jonathan Swift, his favorite author. The scene where Prendick returns to England to tell the world about the phantasmagorical Eden he has escaped from is almost identical to the chapter in which Gulliver describes the land of the *Houyhnhnm*. And although Wells had not been very satisfied with his book, which had evolved almost in fits and starts out of the rather haphazard juxtaposition of more or less powerful images, and had been prepared for a possible slaying by the critics, the truth is it stung all the same. The first blow had taken him by surprise, as it came from his own wife, who considered the doctor perishing at the hands of the deformed puma he had tried to transform into a woman as a jibe at the women's movement. How could Jane possibly have thought that? The next jab came from *The Saturday Review*, a journal he had hitherto found favorable in its judgments. To his further annoyance, the objectionable article was written by Peter Chalmers Mitchell, a young, talented zoologist who had been a fellow pupil of his at the Normal School of Science, and who, betraying their once friendly relations, now declared bluntly that Wells's intention was simply to shock. The critic in *The Speaker* went still further, accusing the author of being morally corrupt for insinuating that anyone succeeding through experimentation in giving animals a human appearance would logically go on to engage in sexual relations with them. "Mr. Wells uses his undoubted talent to shameless effect," declared the reviewer. Wells asked himself whether his or the critic's mind was polluted by immoral thoughts.

Wells was only too aware that unfavorable reviews, while tiresome and bad for the morale, were like storms in a teacup that would scarcely affect the book's fortunes. The one before him, glibly referring to his novel as a depraved fantasy, might even boost sales, further smoothing the way for his subsequent books. However, the wounds inflicted on an author's self-esteem could have fatal consequences in the long term. For a writer's most powerful weapon, his true strength, was his intuition, and regardless of whether he had any talent, if the critics combined to discredit an author's nose for things, he would be reduced to a fearful creature who took a mistakenly guarded, absurdly cautious approach to his work, which would end up stifling his latent genius. Before cruelly vilifying them from a great height, the mudslingers at newspapers and journals should bear in mind that all artistic endeavors were by and large a mixture of effort and imagination, the embodiment of a solitary endeavor, of a sometimes long-nurtured dream, when they were not a desperate bid to give life meaning. But they would not get the better of him. Certainly not. They would not confound him, for he had the basket.

He contemplated the wicker basket sitting on one of the kitchen shelves, and immediately felt his spirits lift again, rebellious and defiant. The basket's effect on him was instantaneous. As a result, he was never parted from it, lugging it around from pillar to post, despite the suspicions this aroused in his nearest and dearest. Wells had never believed in lucky charms or magical objects, but the curious way it had come into his life, and the string of positive events that had occurred since then, compelled him to make an exception in the case of the basket. He noticed that Jane had filled it with vegetables. Far from irritating him, this amused him, as by allocating it that dull domestic function, his wife had at once disguised its magical nature and rendered it doubly useful: not only did the basket bring good fortune and boost his self-confidence, not only did it embody the spirit of personal triumph by evoking the extraordinary person who had made it, it was also just a basket.

Feeling a lot calmer, Wells closed the magazine. He would not allow anyone to put down his achievements, of which he had reason to feel proud. He was thirty years old and, after a long and painful period of battling against the elements, his life had finally taken shape. The sword had been tempered, and of all the forms it might have taken, had acquired the appearance it would have for life. All that was needed now was to keep it honed, to learn how to wield it, and if necessary, allow it to taste blood occasionally. Of all the things he could have been, it seemed clear he would be a writer—he was one already. His three published novels testified to this. A writer. It had a pleasant ring to it. And it was an occupation that he was not averse to, as ever since childhood it had been his second choice, after that of being a teacher. He had always wanted to stand on a podium and stir people's consciences, but he could also do that from a shop window, and perhaps in a simpler and more far-reaching way.

A writer. Yes, it had a pleasant ring. A very pleasant ring indeed.

Once he had succeeded in calming down, Wells cast a satisfied eye over his surroundings; the home that literature had provided him with. It was a modest dwelling, but one that would nevertheless have been far beyond his means a few years before, when he was barely scraping a living from the articles he managed to publish in local newspapers and the exhausting classes he gave, when only the basket kept him going in the face of despair. He could not help comparing it with the house in Bromley where he had grown up, that miserable hovel reeking of the paraffin with which his father doused the wooden floors in order to kill off the armies of cockroaches they were obliged to live with. He recalled with revulsion the dreadful kitchen in the basement with its awkwardly placed coal stove, and the back garden with the shed containing the foul-smelling outside privy, a hole in the ground at the bottom of a trodden earth path his mother was embarrassed to go down each time she wanted to empty her bladder. She imagined the employees of Mr. Cooper, the tailor next door, were watching her comings and goings. He remembered the creeper on the back wall, which he used to climb in order to spy on Mr. Covell, the butcher, who was in the habit of strolling around his garden, forearms covered in blood, like a weary assassin casually holding a dripping knife fresh from the slaughter. And in the distance, above the rooftops, the parish church and its graveyard crammed with decaying moss-covered headstones, below one of which lay the tiny body of his baby sister Frances, who his mother maintained had been poisoned by their evil neighbor Mr. Munday during a macabre tea party.

No one, not even he, would have imagined that the necessary components could come together in that revolting hovel to produce a writer, and yet they had—although the delivery had been a long-drawn-out, fraught one. It had taken him precisely twenty-one years and three months to turn his dreams into reality. According to his calculations, that is. As though he were addressing future biographers, Wells usually identified June 5, 1874, as the day his vocation was revealed to him in what was perhaps an unnecessarily brutal fashion. That day he suffered a spectacular accident, and this experience, the enormous significance of which would be revealed over time, also convinced him that it was the whims of fate and not our own wills which shaped our futures. Like someone unfolding an origami bird in order to find out how it is made, Wells was able to dissect his present life and discover the elements that had gone into making it up. In fact, tracing back the origins of each moment was a frequent pastime of his. This exercise in metaphysical classification was as comforting to him as reciting the twelve times table in order to steady the world with the mainstay of mathematics each time it seemed to him like a swirling mass. Thus, he had determined that the starting point, the fateful spark setting off the events that would turn him into a writer was something that might initially appear puzzling: his father's talent for spin bowling on the cricket pitch. But pulling on that thread quickly unraveled the whole carpet: without his talent for spin bowling his father would not have been invited to join the county cricket team, had he not joined the county cricket team, he would not have spent the afternoons drinking with his teammates in the Bell, the pub near their house, had he not frittered away his afternoons in the Bell, neglecting the tiny china shop he ran with his wife on the ground floor of their dwelling, he would not have become acquainted with the pub landlord's son, had he not forged those friendly ties with the strapping youth, when he and his sons bumped into him at the cricket match they were attending one afternoon, the lad would not have taken the liberty of picking young Bertie up by the arms and tossing him into the air, had he not tossed Bertie into the air he would not have slipped out of his hands, had he not slipped out of the lad's hands the eight-year-old Wells would not have fractured his tibia when he fell against one of the pegs holding down the beer tent, had he not fractured his tibia and been forced to spend the whole of the summer in bed, he would not have had the perfect excuse to devote himself to the only form of entertainment available to him in that situation—reading, a harmful activity, which under any other circumstances would have aroused his parents' suspicions, which would have prevented him from discovering Dickens, Swift, or Washington Irving, writers who planted the seed inside him which, regardless of the scant nourishment and care he was able to provide it with, would eventually come into bloom.

Sometimes, in order to appreciate the value of what he had even more, not to let it lose any of its sparkle, Wells wondered what might have become of him if the miraculous sequence of events that had thrust him into the arms of literature had never occurred. And the answer was always the same. If the curious accident had never taken place, Wells was certain he would now be working in some pharmacy or other, bored witless and unable to believe that his contribution to life's great melting pot was to be of such little import. What would life be like without any purpose, without any definite goal? He could imagine no greater misery than to drift through life aimlessly, frustrated, knowing nothing could ever satisfy him, building a dull, meaningless existence on the basis of luck and a series of muddled decisions, an existence interchangeable with that of his neighbor, aspiring only to the brief, fragile, and elusive happiness of simple folk. Happily, his father's talent for cricket had saved him from mediocrity, exposing him less to the vagaries of life, turning him into someone with a purpose, turning him into a writer.

The journey had by no means been an easy one. It was as if just when he glimpsed his vocation, just when he knew which path to take, the wind destined to hamper his progress had also risen, like an unavoidable accompaniment, a fierce persistent wind in the form of his mother. For it seemed that besides being one of the most wretched creatures on the planet, Sarah Wells's sole mission in life was to bring up her sons Bertie, Fred, and Frank to be hardworking members of society, which for her meant a shop assistant, draper, or some other kind of selfless soul who, like Atlas, proudly but discreetly carried the world on their shoulders. Wells's determination to amount to something more was a disappointment to her, although one should not attach too much importance to that, because it had been merely adding insult to injury. Little Bertie had been a disappointment to his mother from the very moment he was born for having had the gall to emerge from her womb a fully equipped male. Nine months earlier she had only consented to cross the threshold of her despicable husband's bedroom on condition he give her a little girl to replace the one she had lost.

It is hardly surprising that after such inauspicious beginnings, Wells's relationship with his mother should continue in the same vein. Once the pleasant respite afforded by his broken leg had ended—after the village doctor, who, without being asked, had kindly prolonged it by setting the bone badly and being obliged to break it again to correct his mistake—little Bertie was sent to a commercial academy in Bromley, where his two brothers had gone before him although their teacher, Mr. Morley, had been unable to make anything out of them. The boy, however, quickly proved that all the peas in a pod are not necessarily the same. Mr. Morley was so astonished by Wells's dazzling intelligence that he even turned a blind eye to the nonpayment of the boy's registration fees. However, this preferential treatment did not stop his mother from uprooting her son from the milieu of blackboards and school desks where he felt so at home, and sending him to train as an apprentice at the Rodgers and Denyer drapery in Windsor.

After three months of toiling from seven thirty in the morning until eight at night, with a short break for lunch taken in a cramped, windowless cellar, Wells feared his youthful optimism would slowly and inevitably begin to fade, just as it had with his elder brothers, whom he barely recognized as the cheerful, determined fellows they had once been. And so he did everything in his power to prove to all and sundry that he did not have the makings of a draper's assistant, abandoning himself more than ever to his frequent bouts of daydreaming. It came to the point where the owners had no choice but to dismiss the young man who mixed up the orders and spent most of his time dreaming in a corner. Thanks to the intervention of one of his mother's second cousins, he was then sent to assist a relative in running a school in Wok-

ing where he would also be able to complete his teacher
training. Unfortunately, this employment, far more in
keeping with his aspirations, ended almost as soon as it
began when it was discovered that the headmaster was
an impostor who had obtained his post by falsifying his
academic qualifications. The by now not so little Bertie
once again fell prey to his mother's obsessions, which de-
flected him from his true destiny, sending him off on another mistaken path.

And so it was that aged just fourteen, Wells began
working in the pharmacy run by Mr. Cowap, who was instructed to train him as a chemist. However, the pharmacist soon realized the boy was far too gifted to be wasted
on such an occupation and placed him in the hands of
Horace Byatt, headmaster at Midhurst Grammar School,
who was on the lookout for exceptional students who
could imbue his establishment with the academic respect-
ability it needed. Wells easily excelled over the other
boys. They were on the whole mediocre students, and
he was instantly noticed by Byatt, who contrived with
the pharmacist to provide the talented boy with the best
education they could. But his mother soon frustrated the
plot hatched by the pair of idle philanthropists by sending her son to another draper's, this time in Southsea.
Wells spent two years there in a state of intense confusion, trying to understand why that fierce wind insisted
on blowing him off course each time he found himself
back on the right path. Life at Hyde's Southsea Drapery
Emporium was suspiciously similar to a sojourn in hell.
It consisted of thirteen hours' hard work, followed by a

night spent shut away in the airless hut that passed for a dormitory, where the apprentices slept so close together that even their dreams got muddled up.

A few years earlier, convinced her husband's fecklessness would end by bankrupting their china shop business, his mother had accepted the post of housekeeper at Uppark Manor, a run-down estate on Harting Down where, when a girl, she had worked as a maid. It was to this place that Wells sent a series of despairing, accusatory letters, which out of respect I will not reproduce here, alternating the most childish demands with the most sophisticated arguments in a vain attempt to persuade her to set him free from his captivity. As he watched with anguish the future he so longed for slip through his fingers, Wells did his utmost to try to weaken his mother's resolve. He asked her how she expected him to be able to help her in her old age on a shop assistant's meager wage, pointing out that with the studies he intended to pursue he would obtain a wonderful position; he accused her of being intolerant, stupid, even threatening to commit suicide or other more dreadful acts that would stain the family name forever. But none of this weakened his mother's resolve to turn him into a respectable draper's assistant. It took his former champion Horace Byatt, overwhelmed by growing numbers of pupils, to come to the rescue, offering him a post at a salary of twenty pounds for the first year, and forty thereafter. Wells was quick to wave these figures desperately in front of the nose of his mother, who reluctantly allowed him to leave the draper's, tired of all her vain efforts to keep her son on the right track. Relieved, the grateful Wells placed himself at the orders of his savior, whose expectations he was anxious to live up to. During the day he taught the younger boys, and at night he studied to finish his teacher training, eagerly devouring everything he could find about biology, physics, astronomy, and other science subjects. The reward for his titanic efforts was a scholarship to the Normal School of Science in South Kensington, where he would study under none other than Professor Thomas Henry Huxley, the famous biologist who had been Darwin's lieutenant during his debates with Bishop Wilberforce.

Despite all this, it could not be said that Wells left for London in high spirits. He did so more with a feeling of deep unhappiness at not receiving his parents' support in this huge adventure. He was convinced his mother hoped he would fail in his studies, confirming her belief that the Wells boys were only fit to be drapers, that no genius could possibly be produced from a substance as dubious as her husband's seed. For his part, his father was the living proof that failure could be enjoyed just as much as prosperity. During the summer they had spent together, Wells had looked on with dismay as his father, whom age had deprived of his sole refuge, cricket, clung to the one thing that had given his life meaning. He wandered around the cricket pitches like a restless ghost carrying a bag stuffed with batting gloves, pads, and cricket balls, while his china shop foundered like a captainless ship, holed in the middle of the ocean. Things being as they were, Wells did not mind too much having to stay in a rooming house where the guests appeared to be competing for who could produce the most original noises.

He was so accustomed to life revealing its most unpleasant side to him that when his aunt Mary Wells proposed he lodge at her house on the Euston Road, his natural response was to be suspicious, for the house was to all appearances normal, warm, cozy, suffused with a peaceful, harmonious atmosphere, and bore no resemblance to the squalid dwellings he had lived in up until then. He was so grateful to his aunt for providing him with this long-awaited reprieve in the interminable battle that was his life that he considered it almost his duty to ask for the hand of her daughter Isabel, that gentle, kind young girl who wafted silently around the house. But Wells soon realized the rashness of his decision. After the wedding, which was settled with the prompt matter-of-factness of a tedious formality, not only did he confirm that his cousin had nothing in common with him, but he also discovered that Isabel had been brought up to be a perfect wife. That is to say, to satisfy her husband's every need except, of course, in the marriage bed, where she behaved with a coldness ideal for a procreating machine but entirely unsuited to pleasure.

In spite of all this, his wife's sexual frigidity proved a minor problem easily resolved by visiting other beds. Wells soon discovered there was an abundance of delightful ones to which his hypnotic grandiloquence gained him entry, and so he finally dedicated himself to enjoying life now that it seemed to be going his way. Immersed in the modest pursuit of pleasure that his guinea a week scholarship allowed, Wells not only gave himself over to the joys of the flesh, to making forays into hitherto unexplored subjects such as literature and art, and to enjoying every second of his hard-earned stay at South Kensington, but he also decided the time had come to reveal his innermost dreams to the world by publishing a short story in *The Science Schools Journal*.

He called it *The Chronic Argonauts*, and its main character was a mad scientist, Dr. Nebogipfel, who had invented a machine which he used to travel back in time to commit a murder. Time travel was not an original concept; Dickens had already written about it in *A Christmas Carol* and Edgar Allan Poe in *A Tale of the Ragged Mountains*, only in both of those stories the journeys always took place during a dream or state of trance. By contrast, Wells's scientist traveled of his own free will and by means of a mechanical device. In brief, his idea was brimming with originality. However, this first tentative trial at being a writer did not change his life, which to his disappointment carried on exactly as before. All the same, this first story brought him the most remarkable reader he had ever had, and probably would ever have. A few days after its publication, Wells received a card from an admirer who had read his story and asked if he would take tea with him. The name on the card sent a shiver down his spine: Joseph Merrick, better known as the Elephant Man.

XII

WELLS BEGAN HEARING ABOUT Merrick the moment he set foot in the biology classrooms at South Kensington. For those studying the workings of the human body, Merrick was something akin to Nature's most amazing achievement, its finest-cut diamond, living proof of the scope of its inventiveness. The so-called Elephant Man suffered from a disease that had horribly deformed his body, turning him into a shapeless, almost monstrous creature. This strange affliction, which had the medical profession scratching its head, had caused the limbs, bones, and organs on his right side to grow uncontrollably, leaving his left side practically unaffected. An enormous swelling on the right side of his skull, for example, distorted the shape of his head, squashing his face into a mass of folds and bony protuberances, and even dislodging his ear. Because of this, Merrick was unable to express anything more than the frozen ferocity of a totem. Owing to this lopsidedness, his spinal column curved to the right, where his organs were markedly heavier, lending all his movements a grotesque air.

As if this were not enough, the disease had also turned his skin into a coarse, leathery crust, like dried cardboard, covered in hollows and swellings and wartlike growths. To begin with, Wells could scarcely believe such a creature existed, but the photographs secretly circulating in the classroom soon revealed the truth of the rumors. The photographs had been stolen or purchased from staff at the London Hospital, where Merrick now resided, having spent half his life being displayed in sideshows at third-rate fairs and traveling circuses. As they passed from hand to hand, the blurred, shadowy images in which Merrick was scarcely more than a blotch caused a similar thrill to the photographs of scantily clad women they became mixed up with, although for different reasons.

The idea of having been invited to tea with this creature filled Wells with a strange mixture of awe and apprehension. Even so, he arrived on time at the London Hospital, a solid, forbidding structure located in Whitechapel. In the entrance, a steady stream of doctors and nurses went about their mysterious business. Wells looked for a place where he would not be in the way, his head spinning from the synchronized activity everyone seemed to be engaged in, like dancers in a ballet. Perhaps one of the nurses he saw carrying bandages had just left an operating theater where some patient was hovering between life and death. If so, she did not quicken her step beyond the brisk but measured pace evolved over years of dealing with emergency situations. Amazed, Wells had been watching the nonstop bustle from his vantage point for some time when Dr. Treves, the surgeon responsible for Merrick, finally arrived. Treves was a small, excitable man of about thirty-five who masked his childlike features behind a bushy beard, clipped neatly like a hedge.

"Mr. Wells?" he inquired, trying unsuccessfully to hide the evident dismay he felt at such offensive youthfulness.

Wells nodded and gave an involuntary shrug as if apologizing for not demonstrating the venerable old age Treves apparently required of those visiting his patient. He instantly regretted his gesture, for he had not requested an audience with the hospital's famous guest.

"Thank you for accepting Mr. Merrick's invitation," said Treves, holding out his hand.

The surgeon had quickly recovered from his initial shock and reverted to the role of intermediary. With extreme respect, Wells shook the capable, agile hand that was accustomed to venturing into places out of bounds to most other mortals.

"How could I refuse to meet the only person who has read my story?" he retorted.

Treves nodded vaguely, as though the vanity of authors and their jokes were of no consequence to him. He had more important things to worry about. Each day, new and ingenious diseases emerged which required his attention, the extraordinary dexterity of his hands, and his vigorous resolve in the operating theater. He gestured to Wells with an almost military nod of his head to follow him up a staircase leading to the upper floors of the hospital. A relentless throng of nurses descending in the opposite direction hampered their ascent, nearly causing Wells to lose his footing on more than one occasion.

"Not everybody accepts Joseph's invitations, for obvious reasons," Treves said, raising his voice almost to a shout. "Although, strangely, this does not sadden him. Sometimes I think Joseph is more than satisfied with the little he gets out of life. Deep down, he knows his bizarre deformities are what enable him to meet almost any bigwig he wishes to in London, something unthinkable for your average commoner from Leicester."

Wells thought Treves's observation in rather poor taste but refrained from making any comment because he immediately realized he was right: Merrick's appearance, which had hitherto condemned him to a life of ostracism and misery, now permitted him to hobnob with the cream of London society, although it remained to be seen whether or not he considered his various deformities too high a price to pay for rubbing shoulders with the aristocracy.

The same hustle and bustle reigned on the upper floor, but a few sudden turns down dimly lit corridors, and Treves had guided his guest away from the persistent clamor. Wells followed him as he strode along a series of never-ending, increasingly deserted passageways. As they penetrated the farthest reaches of the hospital, the diminishing numbers of patients as well as nurses around was clearly due to the wards and surgeries becoming progressively more specialized. However, Wells could not help comparing this gradual extinction of life to the terrible desolation surrounding the monsters' lairs in children's fables. All that was needed were a few dead birds and some gnawed bones.

While they walked, Treves used the opportunity to tell Wells how he had become acquainted with his extraordinary patient. In a detached, even tone that betrayed the tedium he felt at having to repeat the same story over and over again, Treves explained he had met Merrick four years earlier, shortly after being appointed head surgeon at the hospital. A circus had pitched its tent on a nearby piece of wasteland, and its main attraction, the Elephant Man, was the talk of all London. If what people said about him was true, he was the most deformed creature on the planet. Treves knew that circus owners were in the habit of creating their own freaks with the aid of fake limbs and makeup that were impossible to spot in the gloom, but he also bitterly acknowledged that this sort of freak show was the last refuge for those unfortunate enough to be born with a defect that earned them society's contempt.

The surgeon had few expectations when he visited the fair, motivated purely by unavoidable professional curiosity. But there was nothing fake about the Elephant Man. After a rather sorry excuse for a trapeze act, the lights dimmed and the percussion launched into a poor imitation of tribal drumming in an overlong introduction which nevertheless succeeded in giving everyone in the audience a sense of trepidation. Treves then watched, astonished, as the fair's main attraction entered, and saw with his own eyes that the rumors circulating fell far

short of reality. The appalling deformities afflicting the
creature who dragged himself across the ring had transformed him into a misshapen, lopsided figure resembling
a gargoyle. When the performance was over, Treves convinced the circus owner to let him meet the creature
in private. Once inside his modest wagon, the surgeon
thought he was in the presence of an imbecile, convinced
the swellings on his head must inevitably have damaged
his brain. But he was mistaken. A few words with Merrick were enough to show Treves that the hideous ex-
terior concealed a courteous, educated, sensitive being.
He explained to the surgeon that the reason why he was
called the Elephant Man was due to a fleshy protuber-
ance between his nose and upper lip, a tiny trunk measuring about eight inches that had made it hard for him
to eat and had been unceremoniously removed a few
years before. Treves was deeply moved by this creature's
gentleness, by the fact that despite the hardship and humiliation he had suffered, he apparently bore no resentment towards humanity, faceless humanity, whom he,
Treves, was so quick to despise whenever he could not
get a cab or a box at the theater.

When the surgeon left the circus an hour later, he
had firmly resolved to do everything in his power to take
Merrick away from there and offer him a decent life. His
reasons were clear: in no other hospital records in the
world was there any evidence of a human being with such
severe deformities as Merrick's. Whatever this strange
disease was, of all the people in the world, it had chosen
to reside in his body alone, transforming the wretched

creature into a unique individual, a rare species of butterfly that had to be kept behind glass. Clearly, Merrick must leave the circus at the earliest opportunity. Little did Treves know that in order to accomplish this admirable goal he had set himself in a fit of compassion, he would have to begin a long, arduous campaign that would leave him drained. He started by presenting Merrick to the Pathology Society, but this only led to its distinguished members subjecting the patient to a series of probing examinations and ended in them becoming embroiled in fruitless, heated debates about the nature of his mysterious illness, which invariably turned into shouting matches where someone would always take the opportunity to try to settle old scores. However, his colleagues' disarray, far from discouraging Treves, heartened him. For ultimately it underlined the importance of Merrick's life, making it all the more imperative to remove him from the precarious world of show business.

His next step had been to try to get him admitted to the hospital where he worked, where he could be easily examined. Unfortunately, hospitals did not provide beds for chronic patients, and consequently, although the hospital management applauded Treves's idea, their hands were tied. Faced with the hopelessness of the situation, Merrick suggested Treves find him a job as a lighthouse keeper, or some other occupation that would cut him off from the rest of the world. But Treves would not admit defeat. Out of desperation, he went to the newspapers, and in a few weeks managed to move the whole country with the wretched predicament of the fellow they called

Elephant Man. Donations poured in, yet Treves did not only want money; he wanted to give Merrick a decent home. And so he decided to turn to the only people who were above society's absurd, hidebound rules: the royal family. He managed to persuade the Duke of Cambridge and the Princess of Wales to agree to meet the creature. Merrick's refined manners and extraordinarily gentle nature did the rest. And that was how Merrick came to be a permanent guest in the hospital wing where they found themselves at that very moment.

"Joseph is happy here," declared Treves, in a suddenly thoughtful voice. "The examinations we carry out on him from time to time are fruitless, but that does not seem to worry him. Joseph is convinced his illness was caused by an elephant knocking down his heavily pregnant mother while she was watching a parade. Sadly, Mr. Wells, this is a pyrrhic victory. I have found Merrick a home, but I am unable to cure his illness. His skull is growing bigger by the day, and I'm afraid that soon his neck will be unable to support the incredible weight of his head."

Treves's blunt evocation of Merrick's death, together with the bleak desolation that seemed to permeate that wing of the hospital, plunged Wells into a state of extreme anxiety.

"I would like his last days to be as peaceful as possible," the surgeon went on, oblivious to the pallor beginning to spread over his companion's face. "But apparently this is asking too much. Every night, the locals gather under his window shouting insults at him and calling him names. They even think he is to blame for killing those whores who have been found mutilated in the neighborhood. Have people gone mad? Merrick couldn't hurt a fly. I already mentioned his extraordinary sensibility. Do you know that he devours Jane Austen's novels? And on occasion, I've even surprised him writing poems. Like you, Mr. Wells."

"I don't write poems, I write stories," Wells murmured hesitantly, his increasing unease apparently making him doubt everything.

Treves scowled at him, annoyed that his companion would want to split hairs over what he considered such an inconsequential subject as literature.

"That's why I allow these visits," he said, shaking his head regretfully, before resuming where he had left off, "because I know they do him a great deal of good. I imagine people come to see him because his appearance makes even the unhappiest souls realize they should thank God. Joseph, on the other hand, views the matter differently. Sometimes I think he derives a sort of twisted amusement from these visits. Every Saturday, Joseph scours the newspapers, then hands me a list of people he would like to invite to tea, and I obligingly forward them his card. They are usually members of the aristocracy, wealthy businessmen, public figures, painters, actors, and other more or less well-known artists . . . People who have achieved a measure of social success and who in his estimation have one last test to pass: confronting him in the flesh. As I already explained, Joseph's deformities are so hideous they invariably evoke either pity or disgust in those who see him. I imagine Joseph can judge from his guests' reaction whether they are the kindhearted type or on the contrary ones riddled with fears and anxieties."

They came to a door at the far end of a long passageway.

"Here we are," said Treves, plunging for a few moments into a respectful silence. Then he looked Wells in the eye, and added in a somber, almost threatening tone: "Behind this door awaits the most horrific-looking creature you have probably ever seen or will ever see; it is up to you whether you consider him a monster or an unfortunate wretch."

Wells felt a little faint.

"It is not too late to turn back; you may not like what you discover about yourself."

"You need not worry about me," stammered Wells.

"As you wish," said Treves, with the detachment of one washing his hands of the matter.

He took a key from his pocket, opened the door, and gently but resolutely propelled Wells over the threshold.

WELLS HELD HIS BREATH as he ventured inside the room. He had only taken a couple of faltering steps when he heard the surgeon close the door behind him. He gulped, glancing about the place Treves had practically forced him into once he had fulfilled his minor role in the disturbing ceremony. He found himself in a spacious suite of rooms containing various normal-looking pieces of furniture. The ordinariness of the furnishings combined with the soft afternoon light filtering in through the window to create a prosaic, unexpectedly cozy atmosphere that clashed with the image of a monster's lair. Wells stood transfixed for a few seconds, thinking his host would appear at any moment. When this did not happen, and not knowing what was expected of him, he began wandering hesitantly through the rooms. He was immediately overcome by the unsettling feeling that Merrick was spying on him from behind one of the screens, but even so continued weaving in and out of the furniture, sensing this was another part of the ritual. But nothing he saw gave away the uniqueness of the rooms' occupant; there were no half-eaten rats strewn about, or the remains of some brave knight's armor. In one of the rooms, however, he came across two chairs and a small table laid out for tea. He found this innocent scene still more unsettling, for he could not help comparing it to the gallows awaiting the condemned man in the town square, its joists creaking balefully in the spring breeze. Then he noticed an intriguing object on a table next to the wall, beneath one of the windows. It was a cardboard model of a church. Wells walked over to marvel at the exquisite piece of craftsmanship. Fascinated by the wealth of detail in the model, he did not at first notice the crooked shadow appearing on the wall: a stiff figure, bent over to the right, crowned by an enormous head.

"It's the church opposite. I had to make up the parts I can't see from the window."

The voice had a labored, slurred quality to it.

"It's beautiful," Wells breathed, addressing the lop-sided silhouette projected onto the wall.

The shadow shook its head with great difficulty, un-intentionally revealing to Wells what a struggle it was for Merrick to produce even this simple gesture of play-ing down the importance of his work. Having completed the arduous movement, he remained silent, stooped over his cane, and Wells realized he could not go on standing there with his back to the man. The moment had arrived when he must turn and look his host in the face. Treves had warned him that Merrick paid special attention to his guests' initial reaction—the one that arose automati-cally, almost involuntarily, and which he therefore consid-ered more genuine, more revealing than the faces people hurriedly composed in order to dissimulate their feelings once they had recovered from the shock. For those few brief moments, Merrick was afforded a rare glimpse into his guests' souls, and it made no difference how they pre-tended to act during the subsequent meeting. Their ini-tial reaction had already condemned or redeemed them. Wells was unsure whether Merrick's appearance would fill him with pity or disgust. Fearing the latter, he clenched his jaw as tightly as he could, tensing his face to prevent it from registering any emotion. He did not even want to show surprise, but merely wanted to gain time before his brain was able to process what he was seeing and reach a logical conclusion about the feelings a creature as appar-ently horribly deformed as Merrick produced in a person like him. In the end, if he experienced repulsion, he would willingly acknowledge this and reflect on it later, after he had left. And so, Wells drew a deep breath, planted his feet firmly on the ground, which in his nervous state seemed to have dissolved into a soft, quaking mass, and slowly turned to face his host.

What he saw made him gasp. Just as Treves had warned, Merrick's deformities gave him a terrifying appearance. The photographs Wells had seen of him at the university, which mercifully veiled his hideousness behind a blurry gauze, had not prepared him for this. He wore a dark gray suit and was propping himself up with a cane. Ironically, these accoutrements, which were intended to humanize him, only made him look more grotesque. Teeth firmly clenched, Wells stood stiffly before him, struggling to suppress a physical urge to shudder. He felt as if his heart were about to burst out of his chest, and beads of cold sweat began to trickle down his back, but he could not make out whether these symptoms were caused by horror or pity. Despite the unnatural tensing of his facial muscles, he could feel his lips quivering, perhaps as they tried to form a grimace of horror, yet at the same time he noticed tears welling up in his eyes, and so did not know what to think. Their mutual scrutiny went on forever, and Wells wished he could shed at least one tear that would encapsulate his pain and prove to Merrick, and to himself, that he was a sensitive, compassionate being, but the tears pricking his eyes refused to brim over.

"Would you prefer me to wear my hood, Mr. Wells?" asked Merrick softly.

The strange voice, which gave his words a liquid qual-

ity as if they were floating in a muddy brook, struck renewed fear into Wells. Had the time limit Merrick usually
put on his guests' response expired?

"No . . . that won't be necessary," he murmured.

His host moved his gigantic head laboriously again in
what Wells assumed was a nod of agreement.

"Then let us have our tea before it goes cold," he said,
shuffling over to the table in the center of the room.

Wells did not respond immediately, horrified by the
way Merrick was obliged to walk. Everything was an effort for this creature, he realized, observing the complicated maneuvers he had to make to sit down. Wells had
to suppress an urge to rush over and help him, afraid this
gesture usually reserved for the elderly or infirm might
upset Merrick. Hoping he was doing the right thing,
Wells sat down as casually as possible in the chair opposite him. Again, he had to force himself to sit still as he
watched his host serve the tea. Merrick mostly tried to
fulfill this role using his left hand, which was unaffected
by the disease, although he still employed his right hand
to carry out minor tasks. Wells could not help but silently admire the extraordinary dexterity with which
Merrick was able to take the lid off the sugar bowl or
offer him a biscuit from a plate with a hand as big and
rough as a lump of rock.

"I'm so glad you were able to come, Mr. Wells," said his
host, after he had succeeded in the arduous task of serving
the tea without spilling a single drop, "because it allows
me to tell you in person how much I enjoyed your story."

"You are very kind, Mr. Merrick," replied Wells.

Once the story had been published, curious about how little impact it had made, Wells had read and reread it at least a dozen times to try to discover why it had been so completely overlooked. Imbued with a spirit of uncompromising criticism, he had weighed up the plot's solidity, appraised its dramatic pace, considered the order, appropriateness, and even the number of words he had used, in case this turned out to be an unlucky or magical number, only to end up regarding his first and quite possibly his last work of fiction with the unforgiving, almost contemptuous eye with which the Almighty might contemplate the tiresome antics of a capuchin monkey. It was clear to him now that the story was a worthless piece of excrement: his writing a shameless imitation of Nathaniel Hawthorne's pseudo-Germanic style, and his main character, Dr. Nebogipfel, a poor, unrealistic copy of the exaggerated depictions of mad scientists already found in gothic novels. Nevertheless, he thanked Merrick for his words of praise, smiling with false modesty and fearing they would be the only ones his writings ever received.

"A time machine . . ." said Merrick, delighting in that juxtaposition of words he found so evocative. "You have a prophetic imagination, Mr. Wells."

Wells thanked him again for this new and rather embarrassing compliment. How many more eulogies would he have to endure before asking him to change the subject?

"If I had a time machine like Dr. Nebogipfel's," Merrick went on, dreamily, "I would travel back to ancient Egypt."

Wells found the remark touching. Like any other person, this creature had a favorite period in history, as he must have a favorite fruit, season, or song.

"Why is that?" he asked with a friendly smile, providing his host with the opportunity to expound on his tastes.

"Because the Egyptians worshiped gods with animals' heads," replied Merrick, slightly shamefaced.

Wells stared at him stupidly. He was unsure what surprised him more: the naïve yearning in Merrick's reply or the awkward bashfulness accompanying it, as though he were chiding himself for wanting such a thing, for preferring to be a god worshiped by men instead of the despised monster he was. If anyone had a right to feel hatred and bitterness towards the world, surely he did. And yet Merrick reproached himself for his sorrow, as though the sunlight through the windowpane warming his back or the clouds scudding across the sky ought to be reason enough for him to be happy. Lost for words, Wells took a biscuit from the plate and began nibbling on it with intense concentration, as though making sure his teeth still worked.

"Why do you think Dr. Nebogipfel didn't use his machine to travel into the future as well?" Merrick then asked in that fluid voice, which sounded as if it was smeared in butter. "Wasn't he curious? I sometimes wonder what the world will be like in a hundred years."

"Indeed . . ." murmured Wells, at a loss to respond to this remark, too.

Merrick belonged to that class of reader who was able to forget with amazing ease the hand moving the characters behind the scenes of a novel. As a child Wells had also

been able to read in that way. But one day he had decided
he would be a writer, and from that moment on he found
it impossible to immerse himself in stories with the same
innocent abandon: he was aware that characters' thoughts
and actions were not his. They answered to the dictates of
a higher being, to someone who, alone in his room, moved
the pieces he himself had placed on the board, more often
than not with an overwhelming feeling of indifference that
bore no relation to the emotions he intended to arouse
in his readers. Novels were not slices of life, but more or
less controlled creations reproducing slices of imaginary,
polished lives, where boredom and the futile, useless acts
that make up any existence were replaced with exciting,
meaningful episodes. At times, Wells longed to be able
to read in that carefree, childlike way again, but having
glimpsed behind the scenes, he could only do this with an
enormous leap of his imagination. Once you had written
your first story, there was no turning back. You were a
deceiver, and you could not help treating other deceivers
with suspicion. It occurred to Wells briefly to suggest that
Merrick ask Nebogipfel himself, but he changed his mind,
unsure whether his host would take his riposte as the gentle mockery he intended. What if Merrick really was too
naïve to be able to tell the difference between reality and
a simple work of fiction? What if this sad inability and not
his sensitivity allowed him to experience the stories he
read so intensely? If so, Well's rejoinder would sound like
a cruel jibe aimed at wounding his ingenuousness. Fortunately, Merrick fired another question at him, which was
easier to answer:

"Do you think somebody will one day invent a time machine?"

"I doubt such a thing could exist," replied Wells bluntly.

"And yet you've written about it!" his host exclaimed, horrified.

"That's precisely why, Mr. Merrick," he explained, trying to think of a simple way of bringing together the various ideas underlying his conception of literature. "I assure you that if it were possible to build a time machine, I would never have written about it. I am only interested in writing about what is impossible."

At this, he recalled a quote from Lucian of Samosata's *True Tales*, which he could not help memorizing because it perfectly summed up his thoughts on literature: "'I write about things I have neither seen nor verified nor heard about from others, and in addition, about things that have never existed and could have no possible basis for existing.'" Yes, as he had told his host, he was only interested in writing about things that were impossible. Dickens was there to take care of the rest, he thought of adding, but did not. Treves had told him Merrick was an avid reader. He did not want to risk offending him if Dickens happened to be one of his favorite authors.

"Then I'm sorry that because of me you'll never be able to write about a man who is half-human, half-elephant," murmured Merrick.

Once more, Wells was disarmed by his host's remark. After Merrick had spoken, his gaze wandered over to the window. Wells was unsure whether the gesture was meant to express regret or to give him the opportunity to study Merrick's appearance as freely as he wished. In any case, Wells's eyes were unconsciously, irresistibly, almost hypnotically drawn to him, confirming what he already knew full well. Merrick was right: if he had not seen him with his own eyes, he would never have believed such a creature could exist. Except perhaps in the fictional world of books.

"You will be a great writer, Mr. Wells," his host declared, continuing to stare out of the window.

"I wish I could agree," replied Wells, who, following his first failed attempt, was beginning to have serious doubts about his abilities.

Merrick turned to face him.

"Look at my hands, Mr. Wells," he said, holding them out for Wells to see. "Would you believe that these hands could make a church out of cardboard?"

Wells gazed benevolently at his host's mismatched hands. The right one was enormous and grotesque while the left one looked like that of a ten-year-old girl.

"I suppose not," he admitted.

Merrick nodded slowly.

"It is a question of will, Mr. Wells," he said, striving to imbue his slurred voice with a tone of authority. "That's all."

Coming from anyone else's mouth these words might have struck Wells as trite, but uttered by the man in front of him they became an irrefutable truth. This creature was living proof that man's will could move mountains and part seas. In that hospital wing, that refuge from the world, the distance between the attainable and the unattainable was more than ever a question of will. If Merrick had built that cardboard church with his deformed hands, what might not he, Wells, be capable of—he who was only prevented from doing whatever he wanted by his own lack of self-belief?

He could not help agreeing, which seemed to please Merrick, judging from the way he fidgeted in his seat. In an embarrassed voice that sounded even more like that of a dying child, Merrick went on to confess that the model was to be a gift for a stage actress with whom he had been corresponding for several months. He referred to her as Mrs. Kendal, and from what Wells could gather she was one of his most generous benefactors. He had no difficulty picturing her as a woman of good social standing, sympathetic to the various types of suffering in the world, so long as they were not on her doorstep, who had discovered in the Elephant Man a novel way of spending the money she usually donated to charity. When Merrick explained that he was looking forward to meeting her in person when she returned from her tour in America, Wells could not help smiling, touched by the amorous tone which, consciously or not, slipped in his voice. But at the same time he felt a pang of sorrow, and hoped Mrs. Kendal's work would delay her in America so that Merrick could go on believing in the illusion of her letters and not be faced with the sudden discovery that impossible love was only possible in books.

After they had finished their tea, Merrick offered Wells a cigarette, which he courteously accepted. They rose from their seats and went over to the window to watch the sunset. For a few moments, the two men stood staring down at the street and at the façade of the church opposite, every inch of which Merrick must have been familiar with. People came and went, a peddler with a handcart hawked his wares, and carriages trundled over the uneven cobblestones strewn with foul-smelling dung from the hundreds of horses going by each day. Wells watched Merrick gazing at the frantic bustle with almost reverential awe. He appeared to be lost in thought.

"You know something, Mr. Wells?" he said finally. "I can't help feeling sometimes that life is like a play in which I've been given no part. If you only knew how much I envy all those people . . ."

"I can assure you, you have no reason to envy them, Mr. Merrick," Wells replied abruptly. "Those people you see are specks of dust. Nobody will remember who they were or what they did after they die. You, however, will go down in history."

Merrick appeared to mull over his words for a moment as he studied his misshapen reflection in the distorted windowpane, like a bitter reminder of his condition.

"Do you think that gives me any comfort?" he asked mournfully.

"It ought to," replied Wells, "for the time of the ancient Egyptians has long since passed, Mr. Merrick."

His host did not reply. He continued staring down at the street, but Wells found it impossible to judge from his expression, frozen by the disease into a look of permanent rage, what effect his words, a little blunt perhaps but necessary, had had on him. He could not stand by while his host wallowed in his own tragedy. He was convinced Merrick's only comfort could come from his deformity, which, although it had marginalized him, had also made him into a singular being and earned him a place in the annals of history.

"No doubt you are right, Mr. Wells," Merrick said finally, continuing to gaze at his distorted reflection. "One should probably resign oneself to not expecting too much of this world we live in, where people fear anyone who is different. Sometimes I think that if an angel were to appear before a priest, he would probably shoot it."

"I suppose that is true," observed Wells, the writer in him excited by the image his host had just evoked. And, seeing Merrick still caught up in his reflections, he decided to take his leave: "Thank you so much for the tea, Mr. Merrick."

"Wait," replied Merrick. "There's something I want to give you."

He walked over to a small closet and rummaged around inside it for a few moments until he found what he had been looking for. Wells was puzzled to see him pull out a wicker basket.

"When I told Mrs. Kendal I had always dreamed of being a basket maker, she employed a man to come and teach me," Merrick explained, cradling the object in his hands as though it were a newborn infant or a bird's nest. "He was a kindly, mild-mannered fellow, who had a workshop on Pennington Street, near the London docks. From the very beginning he treated me as though my looks were no different to his. But when he saw my hands, he told me I could never manage delicate work like basket weaving. He was very sorry, but we would evidently both be wasting our time. And yet, striving to achieve a dream is never a waste of time, is it, Mr. Wells? 'Show me,' I told him, 'only then will we know whether you are right or not.'"

Wells contemplated the perfect piece of wickerwork Merrick was cupping in his deformed hands.

"I've made many more since then, and have given some away to my guests. But this one is special, because it is the first I ever made. I would like you to have it, Mr. Wells," he said, presenting him with the basket, "to remind you that everything is a question of will."

"Thank you," stammered Wells, touched. "I am honored, Mr. Merrick, truly honored."

He smiled warmly as he said good-bye and walked towards the door.

"One more question, Mr. Wells," he heard Merrick say behind him.

Wells turned to look at him, hoping he was not going to ask for the accursed Nebogipfel's address so that he could send him a basket, too.

"Do you believe that the same god made us both?" Merrick asked, with more frustration than regret.

Wells repressed a sigh of despair. What could he say to this? He was weighing up various possible replies when, all of a sudden, Merrick began emitting a strange sound, like a cough or a grunt that convulsed his body from head to foot, threatening to shake him apart at the seams. Wells listened, alarmed, as the loud hacking sound continued rising uncontrollably from his throat, until he realized what was happening. There was nothing seriously wrong with Merrick. He was simply laughing.

"It was a joke, Mr. Wells, only a joke," he explained, cutting short his rasping chortle as he became aware of his guest's startled response. "Whatever would become of me if I was unable to laugh at my own appearance?"

Without waiting for Wells to reply, he walked towards his worktable, and sat down in front of the unfinished model of the church.

"Whatever would become of me?" Wells heard him mutter in a tone of profound melancholy. "Whatever would become of me?"

Wells watched him concentrate on his clumsy hands sculpting the cardboard and was seized by a feeling of deep sympathy. He found it impossible to believe Treves's theory that this remarkably innocent, gentle creature invited public figures to tea in order to submit them to some sinister test. On the contrary, he was convinced that all Merrick wanted from this limited intimacy was a few meager crumbs of warmth and sympathy. It was far more likely that Treves had attributed those motives to him in order to unnerve guests to whom he took a dislike, or possibly to make allowances for Merrick's extreme naïveté by crediting him with a guile he did not possess. Or perhaps, thought Wells, who had no illusions about the sincerity of man's motives, the surgeon's intentions were still more selfish and ambitious: perhaps he wanted to show people that he was the only one who understood the soul of this creature whom he clung to desperately to be guaranteed a place beside him in history. Wells was irritated by the idea of Treves taking advantage of Merrick's face being a terrifying mask he could never take off, a mask that could never express his true emotions, in order to attribute to him whatever motives he wished, knowing that no one but Merrick could ever refute them. And now that Wells had heard him laugh, he wondered whether the so-called Elephant Man had not in fact been smiling at him from the moment he stepped into the room, a warm, friendly smile intended to soothe the discomfort his appearance produced in his guests, a smile no one would ever see.

As he left the room, he felt a tear roll down his cheek.

XIII

THIS WAS HOW THE WICKER BAS-
ket had come into Wells's life, and with it he
found that the winds of good fortune soon began to blow
off the years of dust that had accumulated on his suit.
Shortly after the basket's appearance, he obtained his degree in zoology with distinction, began giving courses in
biology for the University of London External Programme,
took up the post of editor-in-chief of *The University Cor-
respondent*, and began writing the odd short article for the
Educational Times. Thus, in a relatively short period of
time he earned a large sum of money, which helped him
recover from his disappointment over the lack of interest
in his story and boosted his self-confidence. He got into
the habit of venerating the basket every night, giving it
long and loving looks, running his fingers over the tightly
woven wicker. He carried out this simple ritual behind
Jane's back and found it encouraged him so much he felt
invincible, strong enough to swim the Atlantic or wrestle
a tiger to the ground with his bare hands.

But Wells scarcely had time to enjoy his achievements

before the members of his tattered family discovered that little Bertie was on his way to becoming a man of means and entrusted him with the task of maintaining their fragile and threatened cohesion. Without taking the trouble to protest, Wells resigned himself to adopting the mantle of defender of the clan, knowing that none of its other members was up to the task. His father, having finally freed himself from the burden of the china shop, had moved to a cottage in Nyewood, a tiny village south of Rogate, where he had a view of Harting Down and the elms at Uppark, and life had gradually washed up the rest of the family in the tiny house. The first to arrive was Frank. He had left his post at a draper's establishment a few years earlier to become a traveling watch salesman, an occupation he had not been very successful in—a fact borne out by the two enormous trunks of unsold watches he brought with him, eating up even more space in the tiny dwelling in Nyewood. The trunks gave off a loud, incessant whirring sound and rattled about like a colony of noisy mechanical spiders. Then came Fred, his trusting brother, who had been unceremoniously dismissed from the company where he worked as soon as the boss's son was old enough to occupy the seat he had unknowingly been keeping warm for him. Finding themselves together again, and with a roof over their heads, his brothers devoted themselves to licking each others' wounds, and, infected by their father's relaxed attitude to life, soon accepted this latest downturn with good cheer. The last to arrive was their mother, dismissed from her beloved paradise at Uppark because the sudden onset of deafness had rendered her useless and irritable. The only one who did not return to the fold was Frances, perhaps because she felt there would not be enough room for her little infant coffin. Even so, there were too many of them, and Wells had to make a superhuman effort to keep up his endless hours of teaching in order to protect that nest buzzing with the sound of Frank's watches, that pesthouse of happy walking wounded reeking of snuff and stale beer, to the point where he ended up vomiting blood and collapsing on the steps of Charing Cross Station.

The diagnosis was clear: tuberculosis. And although he made a swift recovery, this attack was a warning to Wells to stop burning the midnight oil or the next onslaught would be more serious. Wells accepted all this in a practical spirit. He knew that when the wind was favorable, he had plenty of ways to make a living, and so had no difficulty in drawing up a new life plan. He abandoned teaching and resolved to live solely from his writings. This would allow him to work at home, with no other timetables and pressures than those he chose to impose on himself. He would finally be able to live the peaceful life his fragile health required. Thus he set about swamping the local newspapers with articles, penning the odd essay for the *Fortnightly Review*, and, after much persistence, managed to persuade the *Pall Mall Gazette* to offer him a column. Overjoyed by his success, and seeking out the fresh air indispensable to his sick lungs, the whole family moved to a country house in Sutton, near the North Downs, one of the few areas that had as yet escaped becoming a suburb of London. For a while,

Wells believed this quiet, secluded existence was to be his life, but once again he was mistaken, as this was an imaginary truce. Apparently chance considered him a most amusing toy, for it decided to change the course of his life once again, although this time the new twist involved the pleasant, popular veneer of fated love.

In the classroom Wells had established friendly relations with a pupil of his, Amy Catherine Robbins, whom he nicknamed Jane. During the walk they happened to share to Charing Cross Station to catch their respective trains, Wells could not help mesmerizing the girl with his eloquent banter, which he indulged in with no other purpose than to allow himself to swell with pride at being able to impress such a beautiful, adorable girl with his words. However, those friendly, innocent conversations ended up bearing unexpected fruit. His own wife, Isabel, alerted him to it on their return from a weekend in Putney, where they had been invited by Jane and her mother. It was she who assured him that whether or not he had intended it, the girl had fallen head over heels in love with him. Wells could only raise an eyebrow when his wife demanded he stop seeing his ex-pupil if he wanted their marriage to survive. The choice between the woman who refused his caresses and the cheerful and apparently uninhibited Jane was not difficult. And so Wells packed up his books, his furniture, and the wicker basket, and moved into miserable lodgings in Mornington Place in a run-down area of north London between Euston and Camden Town. He wished he could have abandoned the marital home spurred on by a violent passion, but he had to leave that to Jane.

His real reasons for leaving were the playful curiosity he felt when he glimpsed her little body beneath her dress, and above all the chance to escape monotony and discover a new life, given that he could predict how the old one would turn out.

However, his first impression was that love had caused him to make a serious mistake: not only had he moved to the worst possible place for his tormented lungs—a neighborhood where the air was polluted by soot borne on the wind, fatally mixed with smoke from the locomotives passing through on their way north—but Jane's mother, convinced her poor daughter had fallen into the clutches of a degenerate because Wells was still married to Isabel, had moved in with the couple. She seemed determined to undermine their patience with her endless, vociferous reproaches. These unforeseen events, together with the additional worrying certainty that it would be impossible for him to run no less than three homes on the proceeds of his articles, compelled Wells to take the basket and shut himself in one of the cupboards in the house, the only place safe from Mrs. Robbins's intrusive presence. Hidden in amongst the coats and hats, he stroked the wicker for hours on end, like Aladdin trying to bring back the power of his magic lamp.

This may have seemed an absurd, desperate, or even pathetic strategy, but the fact is that the day after he performed this rubbing of the basket, Lewis Hind, the literary editor of the weekly supplement at the *Gazette*, sent for him. He needed someone capable of writing stories with a scientific slant, short stories reflecting on and even pre-

dicting where the relentless onslaught of inventions bent
on changing the face of that century would lead. Hind was
convinced Wells was the ideal man for the job. What he
was proposing, in fact, was that he resurrect his childhood
dream and have another stab at seeing whether he could
become a writer. Wells accepted, and in a few days drafted
a story entitled "The Stolen Bacillus," which Hind was delighted with, and which earned Wells five guineas. The
story also drew the attention of William Ernest Henley,
editor of the *National Observer*, who promptly invited him
to contribute to the pages of his journal, convinced the
young man would be capable of producing far more ambitious stories if he had more room to experiment. Wells was
delighted and terrified in equal measure at being given the
chance to write for such a prestigious magazine, which at
that time was publishing a serialized version of *The Nigger
of the "Narcissus"* by his idol, Conrad. This was no longer
writing news items, articles, or short stories. He was
being offered the space for his imagination to run wild,
the freedom to be a real writer of fiction.

Wells awaited his meeting with Henley in a state of
nervous tension bordering on collapse. Since the editor
of the *National Observer* had asked to see him, Wells had
been rummaging through his large mental stockpile of
ideas in search of a story original and striking enough to
impress the veteran publisher, but none of them seemed
to live up to his offer. The rendezvous was drawing near,
and Wells still did not have a good story to show Henley.
It was then that he turned to the basket and saw that,
although it looked empty, it was actually brimming with

novels, a cornucopia that only needed a gentle nudge in order to pour forth its torrent of ideas. This extravagant image was of course Wells's way of wrapping up in poetic language what really happened when he saw the basket: inevitably he remembered his conversation with Merrick, and to his amazement, he discovered, like a nugget of gold lying at the bottom of a muddy stream, another idea that could be made into a novel. Whether deliberately or by accident, it was as though Merrick had supplied him with enough ideas and plots to last several years while they pretended they were only having tea. He recalled Merrick's disappointment at Dr. Nebogipfel being so uninterested in traveling into the future, in venturing into the unknown world of tomorrow, and this omission appeared worth rectifying now that he had the experience of writing all those articles.

And so, without a second thought, he got rid of the unsavory Nebogipfel, replacing him with a respectable, anonymous scientist in whom any inventor could see himself portrayed, and who even embodied the archetypal scientist of the dawning new century. Endeavoring to create something more than just a naïve fantasy out of his idea of time travel, Wells gave it the same scientific veneer he had given the stories he wrote for Hind, making use of a theory he had developed in his earlier essays published in the *Fortnightly Review*: the idea that time was the fourth dimension in a universe that only appeared to be three-dimensional. The idea would be far more impressive if he used it to explain the workings of the contraption his character would use to travel through the time continuum. A few years earlier, an American medium called Henry Slade had been tried for criminal deception. Besides bragging of his ability to communicate with the spirits of the dead, he would drop knots, conches, and snails' shells into his magician's hat and then pull out identical versions, only with the spirals going in the other direction, as if he had plucked them out of a mirror. Slade maintained that hidden in his hat was a secret passageway to the fourth dimension, which explained the strange reversal the objects underwent. To many people's astonishment, the magician was defended by a handful of eminent physicists, including Johann Zöllner, professor of physics and astronomy, all of whom argued that what might appear to be a fraud from a three-dimensional point of view was perfectly feasible in a four-dimensional universe. The whole of London was on tenterhooks during the trial. And this, together with the work of Charles Hinton, a mathematician who had come up with the idea of a hypercube, a cube out of phase with time that contained every single instant of its existence, all occurring at the same time—something that, naturally, man's current obsolete three-dimensional vision prevented him from seeing—made Wells realize that the idea of the fourth dimension was in the air.

No one was sure what it involved, but the words sounded so mysterious and evocative that society longed for, positively demanded it to be real. For most people, the known world was a tiresome, hostile place, but that was because they could only see part of it. Now, people were consoled by the notion that, just as a bland roast of meat is made tastier by seasoning, the universe improved if they imagined it was no longer reduced to what they were able to see, but contained a secret hidden component that could somehow make it bigger. The fourth dimension gave their dull planet a magical feel; it conjured up the existence of a different world, where desires that were impossible in the three-dimensional world might be realized. And these suspicions were backed up by concrete actions such as the recent founding of the Society for Psychic Research in London. Wells was also forced to endure becoming embroiled almost every day in tiresome debates on the nature of time with his colleagues at the Faculty of Science. One thing led to another, as they say, and as every thinker was turning the fourth dimension into his private playground, Wells had no difficulty combining both ideas in order to develop his theory of time as another spatial dimension through which it was possible to travel in exactly the same way as the other three.

By the time he entered Henley's office, he could visualize his novel with startling clarity, enabling him to relay it with a preacher's conviction and zeal. The time traveler's story would be divided into two parts. In the first he would explain the workings of his machine to a gathering of skeptical guests, to whom he had chosen to present his invention, and whom he must try to convince. This group would consist of a doctor, a mayor, a psychologist, and some other representative of the middle classes. Unlike Jules Verne, who took up whole chapters with detailed explanations of how his contraptions worked—as though he himself doubted their credibility—Wells's explanations would be straightforward and concise, using simple examples that would enable the reader to assimilate an idea that might otherwise seem too abstract. As you are aware, his inventor would observe, the three spatial dimensions (length, breadth, and thickness) are defined in reference to three planes, each of which is at right angles to the other. However, under normal circumstances, man's movement through his three-dimensional universe was incomplete. He had no difficulty moving along its length and breadth, but was unable to overcome the laws of gravity in order to move up and down freely, except by using a hot-air balloon. Man was similarly trapped in the timeline, and could only move in time mentally—summoning up the past through memory, or visualizing the future by means of his imagination. However, he could free himself from this constraint if he had a machine, which, like the hot-air balloon, enabled him to triumph over the impossible, that is to say, to project himself physically into the future by speeding up time, or going back into the past by slowing it down. In order to help his guests understand the idea of this fourth dimension, the inventor used the example of mercury in a barometer: this moved up and down over a period of days, yet the line represented by its movement was drawn not in any recognized spatial dimension, but in the time dimension.

The second part of the novel would describe the journey that his main character would undertake in order to put his machine to the test once his guests had left. As a tribute to Merrick's memory, he would set off towards the unfathomable oceans of the future, a future Wells outlined briefly but eloquently to the editor of the *National Observer*. Henley, an enormous fellow, virtually a giant, condemned to walk with a crutch because of a botched childhood operation, and on whom Stevenson claimed to have based his idea for Long John Silver, pulled an incredulous face. Talking about the future was dangerous. It was rumored in literary circles that Verne himself had portrayed tomorrow's world in a novel called *Paris in the Twentieth Century*, but that his editor, Jules Hetzel, had refused to publish it, considering naïve and pessimistic his vision of 1960, when criminals were executed by electric shock and a system of "photographic telegraphs" made it possible to send copies of documents anywhere in the world. And it seemed Verne had not been the only author to envisage the future. Many others had tried and failed in the same way. But Wells did not let Henley's words discourage him. Leaning forwards in his seat, he stood up for himself, assuring Henley that people were eager to read about the future, and that someone should take the risk and publish the first novel about it.

And so it was that, in 1893, *The Time Machine* came out in serial form in the prestigious *National Observer*. However, to Wells's understandable despair, before the novel could be published in its entirety, the owners of the magazine sold it. The new board of directors carried out the usual purges, putting an end to Henley and his publishing projects. Happily, Wells scarcely had time to wallow in his misfortune, for Henley, like his Stevensonian alter ego, was a hard nut to crack, and immediately took over at the helm of the *New Review*, where he offered to continue serializing the story of the time traveler, and even convinced the stubborn William Heinemann to publish the novel.

Encouraged by Henley's doggedness, Wells resolved to complete his unfinished novel. However, as was becoming the custom, this turned out to be a difficult undertaking, hampered by the usual impediments, although this time of a far more humiliating nature. At the insistence of his doctors, Wells had once again moved to the country with Jane, to a modest boardinghouse in Sevenoaks. But along with the wicker basket and a stream of boxes and trunks came Mrs. Robbins, like a piece of junk no one dared throw out. By this time, Jane's mother had gone to unspeakable lengths in her role of leech, reducing her daughter to little more than a pale, worn-out shell with her constant complaints. Mrs. Robbins had no need of reinforcements in her war of attrition against Wells, but she found an unexpected ally in the boardinghouse landlady once she discovered that it was not a marriage being consummated each night in her house, but the sinful cohabitation of a shy young girl and a depraved defendant in a divorce suit. Battling on two fronts, Wells was scarcely able to concentrate sufficiently to make any headway with his novel. His only consolation was that the section of the plot—the time traveler's journey—to which he was doing his best to give shape, interested him far more than the part he had already written, as it enabled him to steer the novel towards the domain of social allegory, where he could deal with the political questions simmering inside him.

Convinced that in the distant future mankind would have succeeded in evolving fully on a scientific as well as a spiritual level, the time traveler rode across the plains of time on his machine until he reached the year 802,701, a date chosen at random, and sufficiently far off in the future for him to be able to verify his predictions *in situ*. By the flickering light of a paraffin lamp, terrorized by the landlady's threats filtering through his window on the August breeze, Wells related, in fits and starts, his inventor's foray into a world that resembled a huge enchanted garden. To complete the enchantment, this Garden of Eden was inhabited by the extremely beautiful, slender Eloi, the exquisite result of a human evolution that had not only corrected the weaknesses of the species, but had taken the opportunity of ridding it along the way of ugliness, coarseness, and other unprepossessing features. From what the traveler was able to observe once he was amongst them, these delicate Eloi lived a peaceful life, in harmony with nature, without laws or government, and free from ill health, financial troubles, or any other kind of difficulty that would make survival a struggle. Nor did they appear to have any notion of private property: everything was shared in that almost utopic society which personified the Enlightenment's most hopeful predictions about the future of civilization. Like a benevolent, somewhat romantic creator, Wells even had his inventor establish a friendly relationship with a female Eloi named Weena, who insisted on following him around everywhere after he saved her from drowning in a river, captivated like a child by the charm the stranger exuded. Whenever the inventor's back was turned, Weena, fragile and slender as a porcelain doll, would garland him with flowers or fill his pockets with blossoms, gestures that conveyed the gratitude she was unable to express through her language, which although mellow and sweet, remained dishearteningly impenetrable to the inventor's ear.

Once Wells had painted this idyllic picture, he proceeded to destroy it with merciless, satirical precision. A couple of hours with the Eloi was enough for the traveler to understand that things were not as perfect as they seemed: these were indolent creatures, with no cultural interests or any drive towards self-improvement, incapable of higher feelings, a bunch of idlers imbued with a hedonism bordering on simplemindedness. Freed from the dangers that stir courage in men's hearts, the human race had culminated in these lazy, sensual creatures, because intelligence could not thrive where there was no change and no necessity for change. As if that were not enough, the sudden disappearance of his time machine aroused the inventor's suspicions that the Eloi were not alone in that world. Clearly they shared it with other inhabitants who had the strength to move the machine from where he had left it and hide it inside a gigantic sphinx dominating the landscape. He was not mistaken: beneath the make-believe paradise dwelled the Morlocks, a simian race afraid of daylight, who he would soon discover to his horror had regressed to a state of savage cannibalism. It was the Morlocks who fed the Eloi, fattening their neighbors who lived above ground before gorging on them in their subterranean world.

Their reprehensible eating habits notwithstanding, the traveler was forced to acknowledge that the last vestiges of human intelligence and reason survived in that brutal race, which their need to be able to operate the network of machinery in their underground tunnels helped preserve.

Afraid of remaining trapped in the future, with no means of traveling back to his own time, the inventor had no alternative but to follow in the footsteps of Orpheus, Hercules, and Aeneas and descend into the underworld, into the realm of the Morlocks, to retrieve his machine. Having done so, he made a frenzied escape through time, traveling deep into the future, until he arrived at a strange beach stretching out beneath a shadowy sky. He could see from a swift glance at this new future, whose rarefied air made his lungs smart, that life had divided into two species: a variety of giant, screeching white butterfly, and a terrifying crab with enormous pincers which he was glad to get away from. No longer curious about what had befallen mankind, which had apparently become completely extinct, but about the Earth itself, the inventor continued his journey in great strides of a thousand years. At his next stop, more than thirty million years from his own time, he discovered a desolate planet, an orb that had almost stopped rotating, like a tired spinning top feebly illuminated by a dying sun. A scant snowfall struggled to spread its white veil over a place where there was no sound of life. The twitter of birds, the bleating of sheep, the buzz of insects, and the barking of dogs that made up the music of life were no more than a flicker in the traveler's memory. Then he noticed a bizarre creature with tentacles splashing around in the reddish sea before him, and his profound grief gave way to a nameless dread that compelled him to clamber back onto his machine. Back in the seat, at the

helm of time, he felt a dreadful emptiness. He felt no curiosity about the ominous landscapes awaiting him further
into the future, nor did he wish to go back in time, now
he knew that all men's achievements had been futile endeavors. He decided the moment had come for him to go
back to his own time, to where he truly belonged. On the
way back he ended by closing his eyes, for now that the
journey in reverse made extinction into a false resurrec-
tion, he could not bear to see the world around him grow
verdant, the sun recover its stifled splendor, the houses
and buildings spring up again, testaments to the progress
and trends in human architecture. He only opened his
eyes again when he felt himself surrounded by the familiar
four walls of his laboratory. Then he pulled the lever and
the world stopped being a nebulous cloud and took on its
old consistency again.

Once he had arrived back in his own time, he heard
voices and the noise of plates in the dining room, and
discovered he had stopped his machine the Thursday
after his departure. After pausing for a few moments to
catch his breath, the inventor appeared before his guests,
not so much out of a desire to share his experiences with
them, but because he was attracted by the delicious smell
of roast meat, which, after the diet of fruit he had been
forced to live on in the future, was an irresistible temptation. After sating his appetite voraciously in front of his
astonished guests, who gaped in awe at his ghastly pallor,
his scratched face, and the peculiar stains on his jacket,
the traveler finally recounted his adventure. Naturally, no
one believed his fantastic voyage, even though he showed

them his pockets still filled with strange blossoms or the sorry state of his time machine. In the novel's epilogue, Wells had the narrator, who was one of the traveler's guests, finger the exotic flowers, reflecting with optimism that even when physical strength and intelligence has died out, gratitude will live on in men's hearts.

When the novel finally came out under the title *The Time Machine*, it caused a sensation. By August, Heinemann had already printed six thousand paperbacks and one thousand five hundred hardbacks. Everyone was talking about it, though not because of its shocking content. Wells had been at pains to present a metaphorical but devastating vision of the ultimate price of a rigidly capitalistic society. Who would not see in the Morlocks the evolutionary result of the working class, brutalized by appalling conditions and exhausting hours working from dawn until dusk, a class which society slowly and discreetly began to move below ground, while the surface of the earth was reserved for the wealthy classes to parade about in? With the aim of stirring his readers' consciences, Wells had even inverted the social roles: the Eloi—futile and decorative as the Carolingian kings—were fodder for the Morlocks, who, despite their ugliness and barbarism, were at the top of the food chain. However, to Wells's astonishment, all his attempts to raise society's awareness paled before the excitement his notion of time travel stirred in people. One thing was clear: whatever the reasons, this novel written under such adverse conditions, and which at little more than forty thousand words had even required padding out with a publicity booklet, had secured him a place in the hall of fame, or had at least brought him to its threshold. And this was far more than he had ever expected when he began penning the first of those forty thousand words.

LIKE A MURDERER REMOVING all trace of his crime, the first thing Wells did on becoming a successful author was to burn as many copies as he could find of that childish drivel *The Chronic Argonauts*. He did not want anyone to discover that the excellence they attributed to *The Time Machine* was the end result of such lengthy fumbling and had not emerged in its finished state from his apparently brilliant mind. After that, he tried to enjoy his fame, although this did not prove easy. There was no doubting he was a successful author, but one with an extended family to support. And while Jane and he had married and moved to a house with a garden in Woking (the basket sticking out like a sore thumb among Jane's hatboxes), Wells had to take care not to let down his guard. There was no question of him stopping for a rest. He must carry on writing, it did not matter what, anything to take advantage of his popularity in the bookshops.

This was not a problem for Wells, of course. He only had to turn to the basket. Like a magician rummaging in his hat, Wells pulled out another novel called *The Wonderful Visit*. This told the story of how one balmy August night an angel fell out of the sky and landed in the marshes of a little village called Sidderford. When the local vicar, an amateur ornithologist, heard about the arrival of this exotic bird, he went out to hunt it with his shotgun and succeeded in destroying the angel's beautiful plumage before taking pity on it and carrying it to the vicarage, where he nursed it back to health. Through this close contact, the vicar realized that, although different, the angel was an admirable and gentle creature from which he had much to learn.

The idea for the novel, like the plot of *The Island of Dr. Moreau*, which he would write some months later, was not his. Yet Wells tried not to see this as stealing, rather as his own special tribute to the memory of a remarkable man. Joseph Merrick died in the horrible way Treves had predicted two years after Wells's unforgettable invitation to tea. And as tributes went, he considered his far more respectful than the surgeon's own, for, according to what he had heard, Treves was exhibiting Merrick's deformed skeleton in a museum he had opened in the London Hospital. As Wells had said to him that afternoon, Merrick had gone down in history.

And who could say that *The Time Machine*, which owed so much to him, would do the same for Wells. In the meantime, it had brought him more than one surprise, he said to himself, remembering the time machine, identical to the one he had written about in his novel, that was hidden in his attic.

DUSK HAD BEGUN TO submerge the world in a coppery light that lent an air of distinction to everything, including Wells who, sitting quietly in his kitchen, looked
like a sculpture of himself made out of flour. He shook his
head, banishing the doubts stirred up by the harsh review in *The Speaker*, and picked up the envelope that had
appeared in his postbox that afternoon. He hoped it was
not a letter from yet another newspaper asking him to
predict the future. Ever since *The Time Machine* had been
published, the press had held him up as an official oracle
and kept encouraging him to display his supposed powers
of divination in their pages.

But when he tore the envelope open he discovered
he was not being asked to predict anything. Instead, he
found himself holding a publicity leaflet from Murray's
Time Travel, together with a card in which Gilliam Murray invited him to take part in the third expedition to the
year 2000. Wells clenched his teeth to stop himself from
unleashing a stream of oaths, scrunched up the leaflet,
and hurled it across the room, as he had the magazine moments before.

The ball of paper flew precariously through the air
until it hit the face of a young man who should not have
been there. Wells stared with alarm at the intruder who
had just walked into his kitchen. He was a well-dressed
young man, now rubbing his cheek where the ball of paper
had made a direct hit, and shaking his head with a sigh,
as though chastising a mischievous child. Just behind him
was a second man, whose features so resembled those of
the first they must be related. The author studied the man

nearest to him, unable to decide whether he ought to apologize for having hit him with the ball of paper or ask what the devil he was doing in his kitchen. But he had no time to do either, for the man responded first.

"Mr. Wells, I presume," he said, raising his arm and pointing a gun at him.

XIV

A YOUNG MAN WITH A BIRDLIKE face. This was what Andrew thought when he saw the author of *The Time Machine*, the book that had transformed all England while he was wandering like a ghost amid the trees in Hyde Park. Finding the front door locked, instead of knocking, Charles had led him silently round the back of the house. After crossing a small, rather overgrown garden, they had burst into the small, narrow kitchen whose cramped space the two of them seemed to fill completely.

"Who are you and what are you doing in my house?" the author demanded, remaining seated at the table, perhaps because in that way less of his body would be exposed to the pistol aimed at him, which was also undoubtedly the reason why he had asked the question in such an incongruously polite manner.

Without lowering the gun, Charles turned to his cousin and nodded. It was Andrew's turn to take part in the performance. He suppressed a sigh of displeasure. He deemed it unnecessary to have burst into the author's house at gunpoint, and he regretted not having given some thought during the journey to what they would do once they reached the house, instead of leaving everything up to his cousin, whose impetuosity had put them in a very awkward situation. But there was no turning back now, and so Andrew approached Wells, determined to improvise. He had no idea how to do so, only that he must mimic his cousin's severe, determined manner. He reached into his jacket pocket for the yellowed clipping announcing the Ripper's arrest, and, with the abrupt gesture appropriate to the situation, placed it on the table between the author's hands.

"I want you to stop this from happening," he said, trying his best to sound commanding.

Wells stared blankly at the cutting, then contemplated the two intruders, his eyes moving from one to the other like a pendulum, and finally consented to read it. As he did so, his face remained impassive.

"I regret to tell you that this tragic event has already occurred, and as such belongs to the past. And as you are fully aware, the past is unchangeable," he concluded disdainfully, returning the cutting to Andrew.

Andrew paused for a moment, then, a little flustered, took the yellowing piece of paper and put it back in his pocket. Visibly uncomfortable at being forced into such close proximity by the narrowness of the kitchen, which did not seem big enough to squeeze in another person, the three men simply gawked at one another, like actors who have suddenly forgotten their lines. However, they were wrong: there was room for another slim person, and even for one of those newfangled bicycles that were all the rage, with their aluminum spokes, tubular frames, and modern pneumatic tires, which made them much lighter.

"You're wrong," said Charles, suddenly brightening up. "The past isn't unalterable, not if we have a machine capable of traveling in time."

Wells gazed at him with a mixture of pity and weariness.

"I see," he murmured, as though it had suddenly dawned on him with dreary disappointment what this business was all about. "But you're mistaken if you imagine I have one at my disposal. I'm only a writer, gentlemen." He shrugged, apologetically. "I have no time machine. I simply made one up."

"I don't believe you," replied Charles.

"It's the truth," sighed Wells.

Charles tried to catch Andrew's eye, as though his cousin would know what to do next in their madcap adventure. But they had come to a dead end. Andrew was about to tell him to lower the gun, when a young woman walked into the kitchen wheeling a bicycle. She was a slim, small, amazingly beautiful creature, who looked as though she had been delicately wrought by a god tired of churning out inferior specimens. But what really grabbed Andrew's attention was the contraption she had with her, one of those so-called bicycles that were replacing horses because they allowed people to ride round peacefully on country roads without exerting themselves too much. Charles, on the other hand, did not let himself be distracted by the thing, and, having instantly identified the girl as Wells's wife, he swiftly grabbed her arm and placed the barrel of the gun against her temple. Andrew was amazed at his speed and agility, as though he had spent his whole life making this kind of movement.

"I'll give you one more chance," Charles said to the author, who had suddenly turned pale.

The exchange that followed was as inconsequential as it was idiotic, but I will reproduce it word for word, despite it being scarcely worth mentioning, simply because I am not trying to make any one episode in this story stand out:

"Jane," said Wells, in a faint, almost inaudible voice.

"Bertie," replied Jane, alarmed.

"Charles—" Andrew began.

"Andrew," Charles said, interrupting him.

Then there was silence. The afternoon light threw their shadows into relief. The curtain at the window billowed slightly. Out in the garden, the branches of the tree that rose from the ground like a crooked pikestaff rustled eerily as they shook in the breeze. A group of pale shadows nodding their heads, embarrassed by the clumsy melodrama of the scene, as if this were a novel by Henry James (who, incidentally, will also make an appearance in this story).

"Very well, gentlemen," declared Wells at last in a good-natured voice, rising from his chair. "I think we can solve this in a civilized way without anyone getting hurt."

Andrew looked beseechingly at his cousin.

"It's up to you, Bertie." Charles gave a sardonic smile.

"Let go of her, and I'll show you my time machine."

Andrew stared at the author in amazement. Were Gilliam Murray's suspicions true, then? Did Wells really have a time machine?

Obviously pleased, Charles released Jane, who crossed the very short distance separating her from her beloved Bertie and threw her arms around him.

"Don't worry, Jane," the author calmed her. "Everything will be all right."

"Well, then," said Charles, impatiently.

Wells gently extricated himself from Jane's embrace and contemplated Charles with visible distaste.

"Follow me to the attic."

Forming a sort of funeral procession with Wells leading the way, the little group climbed a creaking staircase that seemed as though it might give way beneath their feet at any moment. The attic had been built in the roof space above the second floor and had an unpleasantly claustrophobic feel to it due to the low sloping ceiling and the extravagant collection of assorted bric-a-brac. Over in a corner under the window, which acted as an air vent and through which the last rays of sunlight were filtering, stood the strange contraption. Judging from his cousin's awed expression and the way he practically bowed down before it, Andrew assumed this must be the time machine. He approached the object, examining it with a mixture of curiosity and suspicion.

At first sight, the machine capable of breaking down the barriers confining man to the present looked like some sort of sophisticated sleigh. However, the rectangular wooden pedestal to which it was fixed suggested it was not designed to travel through space, but would need to be dragged along: something that would be difficult owing to its size. The apparatus was surrounded by a waist-high brass rail, a flimsy barrier that had to be stepped over to gain access to the sturdy seat in the middle. The seat vaguely resembled a barber's chair, to which had been attached two exquisitely carved wooden arms, and was upholstered in rather lurid red velvet. In front of it, supported by two elegant bars also made of brass, was a medium-sized dial, the control panel with three monitors showing the day, the month, and the year. A delicate glass lever protruded from a wheel to the right of the dial. The machine seemed to have no other handles, and Andrew deduced that the whole thing worked by pulling on this single lever. Behind the seat was a complicated mechanism resembling a distilling apparatus. This had a shaft sticking out of it which supported a huge round disc that was covered in strange symbols and looked as if it might spin round. Apparently designed to protect the machine, it was bigger than a Spartan shield and was undoubtedly the most spectacular thing about the whole contraption. Finally, a little plaque screwed to the control panel read: "Made by H. G. Wells."

"Are you an inventor, too?" Andrew asked, taken aback.

"Of course not; don't be absurd," replied Wells, pretending to be annoyed. "As I already told you, I'm only a writer."

"Well, if you didn't build it, where did you get it from?"

Wells sighed, as though annoyed at having to explain himself to these strangers.

"My cousin asked you a question, Mr. Wells," said Charles.

The author shot him a black look, then gave another sigh.

"Soon after my novel was published," he said, realizing he had no choice but to comply with the intruders, "I received a letter from a scientist who told me that for years he had been secretly working on a time machine very similar to the one I described in my book. He said it was almost finished, and he wanted to show it to somebody, but he didn't know whom. He considered, not without good reason, that it was a dangerous invention, capable of arousing an unhealthy interest in people. My novel had convinced him I was the right one to confide in. We met a couple of times, with the aim of getting to know one another, of finding out whether we could really trust each other, and we instantly realized we could, not least because we had very similar ideas about the many inherent dangers of time travel. He built the machine here in this very attic. And the little plaque was his affectionate way of showing his gratitude for my collaboration. I don't know if you remember my book, but this amazing machine is nothing like the hulking great thing illustrated on the cover. It doesn't work in the same way, either, of course, but don't ask me how it does, because I'm not a man of science.

"When the time came to try it out, we decided he should have the honor; I would oversee the operation from the present. As we had no way of knowing whether the machine would withstand more than one journey, we decided to travel far into the past, but to a time that was peaceful. We chose a period prior to the Roman invasion, when this area was inhabited by witches and druids, a period which should not have entailed much danger, unless the druids wanted to sacrifice us to some deity. My friend boarded the machine, set it to the agreed date, and pulled on the lever. I watched him disappear before my very eyes. I haven't seen my friend since."

There was a deathly silence.

Finally, Charles lowered his pistol for a moment and asked: "Have you tried it?"

"Yes," confessed Wells, a little shamefaced. "But only a few brief exploratory journeys into the past, no more than four or five years. And I was careful to change nothing, because I was afraid of the consequences that might have on the fabric of time. I didn't have the courage to venture into the future. I don't know. I don't share the same spirit of adventure as the inventor in my novel. This is all too much for me. In fact, I was thinking of destroying the thing."

"Destroying it?" Charles exclaimed in horror. "But why?"

Wells shrugged, giving them to understand he was not quite sure of the answer to that question.

"I don't know what became of my friend," he replied. "Perhaps there is a guardian of time, who fires indiscriminately at anyone trying to change events in the past to their own advantage. In any case, I don't know what to do with his extraordinary legacy." He frowned at the machine, as though contemplating a cross he had to bear every time he went for a walk. "I dare not tell anyone about it, because I cannot even begin to imagine how it would change the world, for better or for worse. Have you ever wondered what makes men act responsibly? I'll tell you; they only have one go at things. If we had machines that allowed us to correct all our mistakes, even the most foolish ones, we would live in a world of irresponsible people. Given its potential, all I can really do is use it for my own rather futile purposes. But what if one day I yield to temptation and decide to use it for my own personal gain, for example, to change something in my past, or to travel into the future in order to steal some incredible invention with which I could improve my present circumstances? I would be betraying my friend's dream . . ." He gave a despondent sigh. "As you can see, this amazing machine has become a burden to me."

With these words, he looked Andrew closely up and down with an intimidating air, as though sizing him up for an imaginary coffin.

"May I use it to save a life?" said Andrew in a near-whisper.

Wells considered awhile, then responded, "What nobler cause could there be than that? If I let you do it and you succeed, it will justify the machine's existence."

"Quite so, what nobler cause could there be than to save a life?" Charles reaffirmed hurriedly, seeing that Wells's unexpected consent had apparently left his cousin speechless. "And I assure you Andrew will succeed," he said, going over to his cousin and clapping him heartily on the shoulder. "My cousin will kill the Ripper and save Marie Kelly."

Wells paused. He glanced at his wife, seeking her approval.

"Oh, Bertie, you must help him," declared Jane, full of excitement, "it's so romantic."

Wells looked again at Andrew, trying to conceal the flash of envy his wife's remark had triggered in him. But deep down he knew Jane had used the right adjective to describe what the young man intended to do. There was no place in his ordered life for love like that, the sort that caused tragedies or started wars requiring the construction of giant wooden horses: love that could easily end in death. No, he would never know what that kind of love was. He would never know what it meant to lose control, to be consumed, to give in to his instincts. And yet, despite his inability to abandon himself to these passions, as ardent as they were destructive, despite his pragmatic, cautious nature, which only allowed him to pursue harmless amorous liaisons that could not possibly degenerate into unhealthy obsessions, Jane loved him. All of a sudden, this seemed like an inexplicable miracle, a miracle for which he ought to be thankful.

"All right," he declared, suddenly in good spirits. "Let's do it. Let's kill the monster and save the girl!"

Infected by this burst of enthusiasm, Charles took the cutting about Marie Kelly's murder out of his bemused cousin's pocket and approached Wells so that they could study it together.

"The crime took place on November 7, 1888, at about five in the morning," he pointed out. "Andrew needs to arrive a few minutes earlier, lie in wait for the Ripper near Marie Kelly's room, then shoot the ogre when he appears."

"It sounds like a good plan," Wells agreed. "But we must bear in mind that the machine only travels through time, not space, which means it won't move from here. Your cousin will need several hours' leeway to reach London."

Like an excited child, Wells leapt over to the machine and began adjusting the monitors on the control panel.

"There we are," he declared, after he had set the date. "I've programmed the machine to take your cousin back to November 7, 1888. Now all we have to do is wait until two in the morning to begin the journey. That way he'll arrive in Whitechapel in time to prevent the crime from being committed."

"Perfect," exclaimed Charles.

The four of them looked at one another in silence, not knowing how to fill the time before the journey began. Luckily, one of them was a woman.

"Have you had supper yet, gentlemen?" asked Jane, showing the practical nature of her sex.

LESS THAN AN HOUR later, Charles and Andrew were able to discover for themselves that Wells had married an excellent cook. Squeezed around the table in the narrow kitchen, tucking in to one of the most delicious roasts they had ever eaten was a most agreeable way of passing the time until the early hours. During supper, Wells showed an interest in the voyages to the year 2000, and Charles spared no detail. Feeling as if he were recounting the plot of one of those fantasy novels he was so fond of, Charles described how he and the other tourists had traveled across the fourth dimension in a tramcar called the *Cronotilus*, until they reached the ruined London of the future, where, hidden behind a pile of rocks, they had witnessed the final battle between the evil Solomon and the brave Captain Derek Shackleton. Wells bombarded him with so many questions that after he had finished his story, Charles asked the author why he had not gone on one of the expeditions himself if he was so interested in the outcome of that war of the future. Wells suddenly went quiet, and Charles realized during the ensuing silence that he had unwittingly offended the author.

"Forgive my inquisitiveness, Mr. Wells," he apologized hurriedly. "Of course not everyone can afford a hundred pounds."

"Oh, it isn't the money," Jane broke in. "Mr. Murray has invited Bertie to take part in his voyages on several occasions, but he always refuses."

As she said this, she glanced at her husband, perhaps in the hope he might feel encouraged to explain his systematic refusals. But Wells simply stared at the joint of lamb with a mournful smile.

"Who would want to travel in a crowded tramcar when they can make the same journey in a luxurious carriage?" Andrew interposed.

The three others looked at the young man, exchanged

puzzled glances for a moment, then nodded slowly in agreement.

With renewed enthusiasm, Wells declared, wiping the grease from his mouth with a napkin, "But let's get back to the matter in hand. On one of my exploratory trips in the machine, I traveled six years back in time, arriving in the same attic when the house was occupied by the previous tenants. If I remember correctly, they had a horse tethered in the garden. I propose that you climb down the vine quietly, so as not to wake them. Then jump on the horse and ride to London as fast as you can. Once you have killed the Ripper, come straight back here. Climb onto the machine, set the date for today, and pull on the lever. Do you understand?"

"Yes, I understand . . ." Andrew was able to stammer.

Charles leaned back in his seat and gazed at him affectionately.

"You are about to change the past, cousin," he mused. "I still can't believe it."

Then Jane brought in a bottle of port and poured a glass for the guests. They sipped slowly, from time to time glancing at their watches, visibly impatient, until the author said:

"Well, the time has come to make history."

He set down his glass on the table and, nodding solemnly, steered them once more up to the attic.

"Here, cousin," Charles said, handing Andrew the pistol. "It's already loaded. When you shoot the swine, make sure you aim at his chest."

"At his chest," echoed Andrew, his hand shaking as

he took the pistol, quickly slipping it into his pocket so that neither Wells nor his cousin would see how terrified he was.

The two men each took him by one arm and guided him ceremoniously towards the machine. Andrew climbed over the brass rail and sat in the seat. Despite his feeling of unreality, he could not help noticing the dark splatter of blood on the upholstery.

"Now listen to me," said Wells in a commanding tone. "Try to avoid making contact with anyone, even with your beloved, no matter how much you want to see her alive again. Just shoot the Ripper and come straight back the same way you went, before you meet your past self. I don't know what the consequences of such an unnatural encounter might be, but I suspect it would wreak havoc in the fabric of time and could bring about a catastrophe that could destroy the world. Now, tell me, have I made myself clear?"

"Yes, don't worry," murmured Andrew, more intimidated by the harsh tone of Wells's voice than by the possible fatal consequences of his desire to save Marie Kelly if he made a mistake.

"Another thing," said Wells, returning to the fray, although this time in a less menacing voice. "Your journey won't be anything like in my novel. You won't see any snails walking backwards. I confess to having used a certain amount of poetic license. The effects of time travel are far less exhilarating. The moment you pull on the lever, you'll notice a surge of energy, followed almost immediately by a blinding flash. That's all. Then, quite simply, you'll be in 1888. You might feel dizzy or sick after the journey, but I hope this won't affect your aim," he added sarcastically.

"I'll bear that in mind," Andrew muttered, absolutely terrified.

Wells nodded, reassured. Apparently, he had no other advice to give him, because he then began to hunt for something on a shelf full of knickknacks. The others watched him without saying a word.

When at last Wells found what he had been looking for, he announced: "If you don't mind, we'll keep the cutting in this little box. When you come back, we'll open it and find out whether you have managed to change the past. I imagine that if your mission has been successful, the headline will announce the death of Jack the Ripper."

Andrew nodded feebly, and handed Wells the cutting. Then Charles went over to his cousin, placed his hand solemnly on his shoulder, and gave him an encouraging smile, in which Andrew thought he glimpsed a hint of anxiety. When his cousin stepped aside, Jane approached the machine, wished Andrew good luck, and gave him a little peck on the cheek. Wells beamed as he watched the ritual, visibly pleased.

"Andrew, you're a pioneer," he declared, once these displays of encouragement were over, as though he felt he must close the ceremony with a lofty remark of the sort carved in stone. "Enjoy the journey. If in the next few decades time travel becomes commonplace, changing the past will doubtless be considered a crime."

Then, adding to Andrew's unease, he asked the others

to take a few steps back to avoid being singed by the burst
of energy the machine would give off as soon as its occupant pulled the lever. Andrew watched them step back,
trying to conceal his helplessness. He took a deep breath,
struggling to control the panic and confusion overwhelming him; he was going to save Marie, he told himself, trying to feel emboldened. He was traveling back in time, to
the night of her death, to shoot her killer before he had
a chance to rip her guts out, thus changing history and
at the same time erasing the eight years of suffering he
had gone through. He looked at the date on the panel, the
accursed date that had ruined his life. He could not believe it was in his power to save her, and yet all he had to
do to overcome his disbelief was to pull that lever. Nothing more. Then whether or not he believed in time travel
would become irrelevant. His trembling hand glistened
with sweat as he grasped the handle, and the coolness of
the glass lever in his palm seemed both unbelievable and
absurd because it was such a familiar, commonplace sensation. He glanced at the three figures waiting expectantly
by the attic door.

"Go on, cousin," prompted Charles.

Andrew pulled the lever.

To begin with, nothing happened. Then he became
aware of a faint persistent purring sound, and the air
seemed to quiver slightly, as though he were hearing
the world's insides rumble. All of a sudden, the hypnotic drone was broken by an eerie cracking sound, and
a bright flash of blue light pierced the attic's gloom. A
second deafening crack was followed by another flash of

light, then another, with sparks flying in all directions as though they were trying to light up every corner of the room. Suddenly, Andrew found himself at the center of a continuous burst of life-sized blue lightning bolts. On the far side of it stood Charles, Jane, and Wells, who had stretched his arms out in front of the other two, whether to protect them from the shower of sparks or to prevent them from rushing to his aid, Andrew could not tell. The air, perhaps the world, possibly time, or everything at once, disintegrated before his eyes. Reality itself fragmented. Then, suddenly, just as the author had described, an intense light blinded him, making the attic disappear. He gritted his teeth to stifle a scream as he felt himself fall through the air.

XV

ANDREW HAD TO BLINK AT
least a dozen times before he could see properly again. As the attic went back to apparent normality, his wildly racing heart began to slow down. He was relieved not to feel dizzy or sick. Even his panic had begun to subside once he realized he had not been burnt to a crisp by the flashes of lightning, which had left a smell of singed butterflies in the air. His only discomfort was that his whole body felt tense as a result of his anxiety, but in the end, he was even glad about that. This was no picnic he was going on. He was about to change the past, to alter events that had already taken place. He, Andrew Harrington, was going to shake up time. Was it not better to be on the alert, to be on his guard?

When the effects of the flash had finally died away and he was able to see properly, he plucked up the courage to step down off the machine, as quietly as possible. The solidity of the floor surprised him, as if he had been expecting the past to be made of mist or fog or some other equally ethereal or malleable substance, simply because the time that corresponded to it had already been used up. However, as he discovered when he placed his foot tentatively on the ground, that reality was just as solid and real as the one he had left. But was he in 1888? He glanced suspiciously around the attic, still plunged into darkness, even savoring a few mouthfuls of air like a gourmet, looking for evidence, some detail to prove he was in the past, that he had indeed traveled in time. He discovered it when he peered out of the window: the road looked the same as he remembered it, but there was no sign of the cab that had brought them, and in the garden he saw a horse that had not been there before. Was a simple nag tied to a fence enough to distinguish one year from another? As evidence it seemed rather flimsy and unromantic. Disappointed, he carefully surveyed the peaceful backdrop of the night sky studded with stars, like rice grains randomly scattered. He saw nothing strange there either. After a few moments of fruitless search, he shrugged and told himself there was no reason why he should notice any significant differences since he had only traveled back in time eight years.

Then he shook his head. He could not waste time collecting evidence like an entomologist. He had a mission to fulfill, in which time was very much of the essence. He opened the window and, after testing the vine's resistance, followed Wells's instructions and began climbing down it as quietly as possible so as not to alert the occupants of the house. This proved easy, and once he reached the ground, he crept towards the horse, which had been impassively watching him climb down the creeper. Andrew gently stroked its mane in order to allay any suspicions the animal might have about him. The horse had no saddle, but Andrew found one with stirrups hanging on the fence. He could not believe his luck. He tied it on the horse, avoiding any sudden gestures that might make the animal nervous, keeping an eye on the darkened house all the while. Then he took the animal by the reins and coaxed it out into the road with affectionate whispers. He was amazed at himself for taking everything so calmly. He mounted the horse, glanced back one last time to ensure everything was still calm, and set off towards London.

Only when he was far enough away, a fast-moving blur in the darkness, did it finally dawn on Andrew that soon he was going to see Marie Kelly. He felt a pang inside and became tense again. Yes, incredible though it might seem to him, in the year he was in now, at this time in the morning, she was still alive: she had still not been murdered. She would probably be in the Britannia at that very moment, drinking to forget her spineless lover before stumbling back home into the arms of death. But then he remembered he was not allowed to see her, not allowed to embrace her, to nestle his head on her shoulder and breathe in her longed-for odor. No, Wells had forbidden it, because that simple gesture could alter the fabric of time, bring about the end of the world. He must limit himself to killing the Ripper and returning the way he had come, as the author had ordered. His action must be swift and precise, like a surgical intervention, whose consequences would only be visible when the patient came to, that is to say, once he had traveled back to his own time.

Whitechapel was immersed in a deathly silence. He

was surprised at the absence of the usual hurly-burly, until he remembered that during those weeks White-chapel was an accursed, feared neighborhood, in whose alleyways the monster known as Jack the Ripper roamed, doling out death with his knife. He slowed his mount as he entered Dorset Street, aware that in the intense silence its hooves hammering on the cobblestones must produce a din like a smithy's forge. He dismounted a few yards from the entrance to Miller's Court and tethered the animal to an iron railing, away from any streetlamps so that it was less likely to be noticed. Then, after making sure the street was empty, he darted through the stone archway leading to the flats. The tenants were all asleep, so he had no light to guide him through the pitch-darkness, but An-drew could have found his way blindfolded. The farther he ventured into that powerfully familiar place, the more overwhelmed he was by a mournful sadness that culmi-nated when he reached Marie Kelly's room, which was also in darkness. But his nostalgia gave way to a feeling of profound shock when it dawned on him that while he was standing there, before the modest abode that had been both heaven and hell to him, his father was also slapping his face in the Harrington mansion. That night, thanks to a miracle of science, there were two Andrews in the world. He wondered whether his other self might be aware of his existence, too, in the form of goose pimples or a sharp pain in his stomach, as he had heard sometimes happened with twins.

The echo of footsteps interrupted his reverie. His heart began beating faster, and he ran to hide round the corner of one of the neighboring flats. He had thought of hiding there from the very beginning because, besides seeming to be the safest place, it was scarcely a dozen yards from Marie's door, a perfect distance to be able to see clearly enough to shoot the Ripper, in case he was too afraid to get any closer to him. Once safely out of sight, back against the wall, Andrew drew the pistol out of his pocket, listening out for the footsteps as they drew nearer. The steps that had alerted him had an uncontrolled, irregular quality, typical of a drunk or wounded person. He instantly understood that they could only be those of his beloved, and his heart fluttered like a leaf in a sudden gust of wind. That night, like so many others, Marie Kelly was staggering home from the Britannia, only this time his other self was not there to undress her, put her to bed, tuck in her alcoholic dreams. He poked his head slowly round the corner. His eyes were accustomed enough to the dark for him to be able to make out the reeling figure of his beloved pause outside the door to her tiny room. He had to stop himself from running towards her. He felt his eyes grow moist with tears as he watched her straighten up in a drunken effort to regain her balance, adjust her hat, which was in danger of toppling off with the constant swaying of her body, and thrust her arm through the hole in the window, forcing the lock for what seemed like an eternity, until finally she managed to open the door. Then she disappeared inside the room, slamming the door behind her, and a moment later the faint glow from a lamp cleared part of the swirling gloom in front of her door.

Andrew leaned back against the wall. He had scarcely

dried his tears, when the sound of more footsteps startled him. Someone else was coming through the entrance into the yard. It took him a few moments to realize this must be the Ripper. His heart froze as he heard the man's boots crossing the cobblestones with cold deliberation. These were the movements of a practiced, ruthless predator, who knew there was no escape for his quarry. Andrew poked his head out again and with a shudder of terror saw a huge man calmly approaching his beloved's room, surveying the place with a penetrating gaze. He felt strangely queasy: he had already read in the newspapers what was happening now before his own eyes. It was like watching a play he knew by heart, and all that remained was for him to judge the quality of the performance. The man paused in front of the door, peering surreptitiously through the hole in the window, as though he intended to reproduce faithfully everything described in the article Andrew had been carrying around in his pocket for eight years, even though it had not yet been written, an article, which, because of his leapfrogging through time, seemed more like a prediction than a description of events. Except that unlike then, he was there ready to change it. Viewed in this light, what he was about to do felt like touching up an already completed painting, like adding a brushstroke to *The Three Graces* or *Girl with the Pearl Earring*.

After gleefully establishing that his victim was alone, the Ripper cast a final glance around him. He seemed pleased, overjoyed even, at the entrenched calm of the place that would allow him to commit his crime in unexpected, pleasant seclusion. His attitude incensed Andrew, and he stepped brashly out of his hiding place without even considering the possibility of shooting him from there. Suddenly, the act of finishing the Ripper off from a distance thanks to the clinical intervention of a weapon seemed too cold, impersonal, and dissatisfying. His intense rage required him to take the man's life in a more intimate way—possibly by strangling him with his bare hands, smashing his skull with the butt of his pistol, or by any other means that would allow him to take more of a part in his demise, to feel his contemptible life gradually ebbing away at a rhythm he himself imposed. But as he strode resolutely towards the monster, Andrew realized that however keen he was to engage in hand-to-hand combat, his opponent's colossal stature and his own inexperience of that kind of fighting made any strategy that did not involve the use of the weapon inadvisable.

In front of the door to the little room, the Ripper watched him approach with calm curiosity, wondering perhaps where on earth this fellow had sprung from. Andrew stopped prudently about five yards away from him, like a child who fears being mauled by the lion if he gets too close to the cage. He was unable to make out the man's face in the dark, but perhaps that was just as well. He raised the revolver, and, doing as Charles had suggested, aimed at the man's chest. Had he fired straightaway, in cold blood, giving no thought to what he was doing, as if it were just another step in the wild sequence of events he appeared to be caught up in, everything would have gone according to plan: his action would have been swift and precise, like a surgical intervention.

But unfortunately, Andrew did stop to think about what he was doing; it suddenly dawned on him that he was about to shoot a man, not a deer, not a bottle, and the idea that killing someone was such an easy, impulsive act anyone was capable of seemed to overwhelm him. His finger froze in the trigger. The Ripper tilted his head to one side, half surprised, half mocking, and then Andrew watched as his hand clutching the revolver started to shake. This weakened his already feeble resolve, while the Ripper, emboldened by this brief hesitation, swiftly pulled a knife from inside his coat and hurled himself at Andrew in search of his jugular. Ironically, his frenzied charge was what released Andrew's trigger finger.

A sudden, quick, almost abrupt explosion pierced the silence of the night. The bullet hit the man right in the middle of the chest. Still aiming at him, Andrew watched him stagger backwards. He lowered the warm, smoking gun, no less astonished at having used it as he was to find himself still in one piece after fending off that surprise attack. This though was not strictly true, as he soon discovered from the sharp pain in his left shoulder. Without taking his eyes off the Ripper, who was swaying before him like a bear standing on its hind legs, he felt for the source of the pain, and discovered that the knife, although it had missed his main artery, had ripped through the shoulder of his jacket and sliced into his flesh. Despite the blood flowing merrily from the wound, it did not appear very deep. Meanwhile, the Ripper was taking his time to prove whether or not Andrew's shot had been fatal. After bobbing around clumsily, he doubled over, letting go of the knife dripping with Andrew's blood, which ricocheted over the cobblestones and disappeared into the shadows. Then, after giving a hoarse bellow, he bent down on one knee, as though to acknowledge in his murderer the traits of nobility, and continued to moan with a few reedier, more staccato versions of his original grunt. Finally, just when Andrew was beginning to tire of all this display of dying and was toying with the idea of kicking the man to the ground, he collapsed in a heap onto the cobblestones and lay there, stretched out at his feet.

Andrew was about to kneel down and check the man's pulse when Marie Kelly, no doubt alarmed by the skirmish, opened the door to her little room. Before she could recognize him, and, resisting the temptation to look at her after eight years of her being dead, Andrew turned on his heel. No longer worried about the corpse, he ran towards the exit as he heard her scream, "Murder, murder!" Only when he had reached the stone archway did he allow himself to look back over his shoulder. He saw his beloved kneeling down in a shimmering halo of light, gently closing the eyes of the man, who in a far-off time, in a world that had taken on the consistency of a dream, had mutilated her to the point where she was unrecognizable.

The horse was standing where he had left it. Out of breath from running, Andrew mounted and rode off as fast as he could. Despite his agitation, he managed to find his way out of the maze of alleyways and onto the main road that would take him back to Woking. It was only when he had left London that he began to calm down, to acknowledge what he had done. He had killed a man, but at least he had done so in self-defense. And besides, it had not been any man. He had killed Jack the Ripper, saved Marie Kelly, changed events that had already taken place. He urged the horse on violently, anxious to travel back to his own time and discover the results of his action. If things had gone well, then Marie would not only be alive but would probably be his wife. Would they have had a child, possibly two or three? He drove the horse to the limit, as though afraid this idyllic present would dissolve like a mirage if he took too long to reach it.

WOKING WAS STILL BATHED in the same serene calm that had so roused his suspicions a few hours earlier. Now, though, he was grateful for that tranquility which would allow him to end his mission without further incident. He leapt off the horse and opened the gate, but something made him stop dead in his tracks: a figure was waiting for him beside the door to the house. Andrew immediately remembered what had happened to Wells's friend, and realized this must be some sort of guardian of time with orders to kill him for having meddled with the past. Trying hard not to give way to panic, he pulled the gun from his pocket as fast as he could and aimed it at the man's chest, just as his cousin had suggested he do with the Ripper. The intruder dived to one side and rolled across the lawn until he was swallowed up by darkness. Andrew tried to follow the man's catlike movements with his revolver, not knowing what else to do, until he saw him nimbly scale the fence and leap into the road.

Only when he heard the tap of his feet running away did he lower his weapon, calming himself by taking slow deep breaths. Could that man have killed Wells's friend? He did not know, but now that he had escaped, it did not matter very much. Andrew gave him no more thought and began climbing back up the creeper. This he was obliged to do using only one arm, as his wounded left shoulder had started to throb painfully at the slightest effort. Even so, he managed to reach the attic, where the time machine stood waiting for him. Exhausted and a little faint owing to the loss of blood, he collapsed onto the seat, set the return date on the contraption's control panel, and after bidding 1888 farewell with a longing gaze, pulled on the glass lever without delay.

This time he felt no fear at all when the flashing lights engulfed him, only the pleasant sensation of going home.

XVI

ONCE THE SPARKS HAD STOPPED flying, leaving wisps of smoke swirling in the air like feathers after a pillow fight, Andrew was surprised to see Charles, Wells, and his wife huddled by the door exactly as he had left them. He attempted a triumphant smile but only managed a weak grimace due to his light-headedness and his increasingly painful wound. As he prepared to climb down from the machine, the others were able to glimpse with horror his blood-soaked sleeve.

"Good God, Andrew!" shouted his cousin, leaping towards him. "What happened to you?"

"It's nothing, Charles," replied Andrew, leaning on him to steady himself. "Only a scratch."

Wells took his other arm, and between them, the two men helped him down the attic stairs. Andrew tried to walk on his own, but seeing that they ignored his efforts, meekly allowed himself to be guided into a small sitting room, just as at that moment he would have let himself be carried off by a horde of demons to the depths of hell itself. There was nothing else he could do: the buildup

of nervous tension, the loss of blood, and the arduous
ride had completely drained all his energy. They sat him
down gently on the armchair nearest the hearth, where
a roaring fire was blazing. After examining his wound
with what looked to Andrew like an annoyed twist of
the mouth, Wells ordered his wife to fetch bandages and
everything else necessary to stem the bleeding. He all
but told her to hurry up before the gushing flow permanently ruined the carpet. Almost at once the fire's heal-
ing warmth calmed his shivering, but it also threatened
to send him to sleep. Luckily, it occurred to Charles to
give him a glass of brandy, which he even helped raise
to his lips. The alcohol took the edge off his giddiness
and the crushing fatigue he felt. Jane soon returned and
began seeing to his wound with the neat competence of
a war nurse. She cut away his jacket sleeve with a pair
of scissors, then applied a series of stinging potions and
dressings to the knife wound. To finish off she bandaged
it tightly, before stepping back to contemplate her handiwork. It was only when the most pressing issue had been
resolved that the motley rescue team gathered eagerly
around the chair where Andrew lay in a state of semi-
collapse. They waited for him to recount what had happened. As though he had dreamt it, Andrew remembered
the Ripper lying on the ground, and Marie closing his
eyes. That could only mean he had succeeded.

"I did it," he announced, trying to sound enthusiastic
despite his fatigue. "I killed Jack the Ripper."

His words triggered an outburst of joy, which Andrew
observed with amused surprise. After pelting him with

pats on his back, they flung their arms around one another, crying out their praise and abandoning themselves to wild excitement more suited to New Year celebrations or pagan rituals. Realizing how unrestrained their reaction was, the three of them calmed down and gazed at him again with a mixture of tenderness and curiosity. Andrew grinned back at them, slightly embarrassed, and when it seemed no one had anything else to say, he looked around him for any telltale signs that his brushstroke had altered the present. His gaze fell on the cigar box lying on the table, which he remembered contained the cutting. Their eyes followed his.

"So," said Wells, reading his thoughts. "You threw a pebble into a still pond and now you are itching to see the ripples it made. Let's not put it off any longer. It's time to see whether you really have changed the past."

Adopting the role of master of ceremonies once more, Wells walked over to the table, solemnly picked up the box, and presented it to Andrew with the lid open, like one of the Three Wise Men offering his gift of incense. Andrew took the cutting, trying to stop his hand from shaking too much, and felt his heart miss several beats as he began to unfold it. No sooner had he done so than he found himself contemplating the exact same headline as he had been reading for years. Scanning the article, he realized the contents were also unchanged: as if nothing had happened, the news item related the brutal murder of Marie Kelly at the hands of Jack the Ripper, and his subsequent capture by the Whitechapel Vigilance Committee. Andrew looked at Wells, bewildered. How could this be?

"But I killed him," he protested, feebly, "this can't be right . . ."

Wells examined the cutting, thoughtfully. Everyone in the room gazed at him, waiting for his verdict. After a few moments absorbed in the cutting, he gave a murmur of comprehension. He straightened up, and without looking at anyone, began pacing silently around the room. Owing to its narrow dimensions, he had to be content to circle the table a few times, hands thrust in his pockets, nodding from time to time as if to reassure the others that his grasp of the matter was growing. Finally, he paused before Andrew and smiled at him dolefully.

"You saved the girl, Mr. Harrington," he observed with quiet conviction, "there is no doubt in my mind about that."

"But, in that case . . . ," stammered Andrew, "why is she still dead?"

"Because she must continue being dead in order for you to travel back in time to save her," the author declared, as though stating the obvious.

Andrew blinked, unable to fathom what Wells was trying to say.

"Think about it: if she had still been alive, would you have come to my house? Don't you see that by killing her murderer and preventing her from being ripped to shreds you have eliminated your reasons for traveling back in time? And if there's no journey, there's no change. As you can see, the two events are inseparable," explained Wells, brandishing the cutting, which with its original heading corroborated his theory.

Andrew nodded slowly, glancing at the others, who looked as bewildered as he.

"It isn't all that complicated," scoffed Wells, amused at his audience's bewilderment. "I'll explain it in a different way. Imagine what must have happened after Andrew traveled back to this spot in the time machine: his other self must have arrived at Marie Kelly's room, but instead of finding his beloved with her entrails exposed to the elements, he found her alive, kneeling by the body of the man whom police would soon identify as Jack the Ripper. An unforeseen avenger had stepped out of nowhere and murdered the Ripper before he could add Marie Kelly to his list of victims. And thanks to this stranger, Andrew will be able to live with her happily ever after, although the irony is that he will never know he has you, I mean himself, to thank for it," the author concluded, gazing at him excitedly, with the eagerness of a child expecting to see a tree spring up moments after he has planted a seed. Noticing that Andrew continued to look at him nonplussed, he added: "It is as though your action has caused a split in time, created a sort of alternative universe, a parallel world, if you like. And in that world Marie Kelly is alive and happy with your other self. Unfortunately, you are in the wrong universe."

Andrew watched as Charles nodded, increasingly persuaded by Wells's explanation, then turned to look at him, hoping to find his cousin equally convinced. But Andrew needed a few more moments to mull over the writer's words. He lowered his head, trying to ignore the others' enquiring looks in order to consider the matter calmly. Given that nothing in his reality seemed to have changed, his journey in the time machine could not only be considered useless, but it was debatable whether it had even taken place. Yet he knew it had been real. He could not forget the image of Marie, and the gun going off, and the jolt it had sent up his arm, and above all the wound to his shoulder—that nasty gash he had brought back with him, like an irrefutable mark that prevented everything that had happened from being merely a dream. Yes, those events had really occurred, and the fact that he could not see their effects did not mean there weren't any, as Wells had quickly realized. Just as a tree's roots grow around a rock, so the consequences of his action, which could not simply vanish into thin air, had created another reality, a parallel world in which he and Marie Kelly were living happily together, a world that would not have existed if he had not traveled back in time. This meant he had saved his beloved, even though he was not able to enjoy her. All he had was the comforting satisfaction of knowing that he had prevented her death, that he had done everything in his power to make amends. At least his other self would enjoy her, he thought, with a degree of resignation. That other Andrew, who after all was him, his own flesh and blood, would be able to fulfill all his dreams. He would be able to make her his wife, to love her regardless of his father's opposition and their neighbors' malicious gossip, and he only wished the other Andrew could know what a miracle that was. How during the past eight years while he had been tormenting himself, his luckier self had never stopped loving her for a single moment, populating the world with the fruit of all that love.

"I understand," he murmured, smiling wanly at his friends.

Wells was unable to suppress a cry of triumph: "That's wonderful," he exclaimed, while Charles and Jane resumed again patting him on the back with encouragement.

"Do you know why during my journeys into the past I always avoided seeing myself?" Wells asked, without caring whether anyone was listening. "Because if I had, it would mean that at some point in my life I would have been obliged to walk through the door and greet myself, which thankfully for my sanity has never happened."

After embracing his cousin repeatedly in a renewed display of euphoria, Charles helped him up out of his chair, while Jane straightened his jacket with a motherly gesture.

"Perhaps those troubling sounds we hear in the night, the creaking noises we assume are the furniture, are simply the footsteps of a future self watching over us as we sleep, without daring to disturb us," Wells mused, oblivious to the general rejoicing.

It was only when Charles went to shake his hand that he appeared to emerge from his reverie.

"Thanks awfully for everything, Mr. Wells," said Charles. "I apologize for having burst into your house like that. I hope you can forgive me."

"Don't worry, don't worry. All is forgotten," replied the writer, with a vague wave of his hand, as though he had discovered something salutary, revivifying about having a gun aimed at him.

"What will you do with the machine, will you destroy it?" Andrew ventured, timidly.

Wells gazed at him, smiling benevolently.

"I suppose so," he replied, "now it has fulfilled the mission for which it was quite possibly invented."

Andrew nodded, unable to help being moved by his solemn words. He did not consider his personal tragedy the only one that warranted the use of the machine that had come into Wells's possession. But he was grateful that the author, who scarcely knew him, had sympathized enough with his misfortune to have considered it a good enough reason to flout the laws of time, in order to change its very fabric and put the world in danger.

"I also think it's for the best, Mr. Wells," said Andrew, having recovered from his emotion, "because you were right. There is a guardian of time, someone who watches over the past. I bumped into him when I came back, in the doorway to your house."

"Really," said Wells, taken aback.

"Yes, although luckily I managed to frighten him off," replied Andrew.

With this, he clasped the author in a heartfelt embrace. Smiling benevolently, Charles and Jane contemplated the scene, which would have been frankly moving were it not for the awkward stiffness with which Wells greeted Andrew's affectionate gesture. When Andrew finally let go of the author, Charles said his good-byes to the couple, steering his cousin out of the house lest he throw himself once more at the alarmed author.

Andrew crossed the garden vigilantly, right hand in his pocket feeling the pistol, afraid the guardian of time might have followed him back to the present and be lying in wait for him. But there was no sign of him. Waiting for them outside the gate was the cab that had brought them there only a few hours before, a few hours which to Andrew seemed like centuries.

"Blast, I've forgotten my hat," said Charles, after Andrew had clambered into the cab. "I'll be back in a jiffy, cousin."

Andrew nodded absentmindedly, and settled into his seat, utterly exhausted. Through the cab's tiny window he surveyed the encircling darkness as day began to dawn. Like a coat wearing thin at the elbows, night was beginning to unravel at one of the farthest edges of the sky, its opaqueness gradually diluting into an ever paler blue, until a hazy light slowly began to reveal the contours of the world. With the exception of the driver, apparently asleep on his seat, it was as if this stunning display of golden and purple hues was being performed solely for his benefit. Many times over the past few years when Andrew had witnessed the majestic unveiling of dawn he had wondered whether that day he would die, whether that day his increasing torment would compel him to shoot himself with a pistol like the one he was now carrying in his pocket, the one he had removed from its glass cabinet the previous evening without knowing he would end up using it to kill Jack the Ripper. But now he could not watch the dawn and wonder whether he would be alive to see it again tomorrow, for he knew the answer: he would see the dawn tomorrow and the day after and the day after that, because he had no way of justifying killing himself now that he had saved Marie. Should he go ahead with

his plan out of sheer inertia, or simply because, as Wells
had pointed out, he was in the wrong universe? This did
not seem like a good enough reason. In any event, it felt
less noble, not to mention that it might imply a fundamen-
tally absurd jealousy of his time twin. After all, he was the
other Andrew, and he ought to rejoice in his good fortune
as he would his own, or failing that, that of his brother
or his cousin Charles. Besides, if the grass in next door's
garden was always greener, how much more luxuriantly
verdant must it be in the neighboring universe? He should
feel pleased at being happy in another world, to have at
least achieved bliss in the adjoining realm.

Reaching this conclusion threw up another unexpected question: did knowing that you had achieved the
life you wanted in another world absolve you from having
to try to achieve it in this one? At first, Andrew did not
know how to answer this question, but after a few moments' thought, he decided it did: he was absolved from
being happy; he could be content to lead a peaceful existence, enjoying life's small pleasures without the slightest
feeling of inner frustration. For, however trite it might
seem, he could always console himself with the happy
thought that he was living a full life in another place that
was both nearby and at the same time far away, a place
that was inaccessible, uncharted, because it was on the
reverse of any map. Suddenly, he experienced an incredible sense of relief, as though a burden he had been carrying since birth had been lifted from his shoulders. He felt
unfettered, reckless, and wild. He had an overwhelming
desire to reconnect with the world, to tread the common

path of life again with the rest of humanity, to send a note to Victoria Keller, or to her sister Madeleine if Victoria was the one Charles had married, inviting her to dinner or to the theater or for a walk in a park where he could ambush her, brush his lips against hers—simply because he was aware that at the same time he would also *not* be doing that. For it seemed this was the way the universe worked: excluding nothing, allowing everything to happen that could happen. Even if he did decide to kiss her, another Andrew would refrain from doing so, and would carry on rolling down the hill of time until he came to another pair of lips and split into another twin who, after dividing a few more times, would finally plunge over a cliff into the abyss of solitude.

Andrew leaned back in his seat, amazed that each of life's twists and turns should give rise to a new existence vying with the old one to see which was the most authentic, instead of falling like sawdust and being swept away by the carpenter's broom. It made him giddy just to think that at each crossroads, clutches of other Andrews were born, and their lives went on at the same time as his, beyond the moment when his own life ended, without his being aware of it, because ultimately it was man's limited senses which established the boundaries of the world. But what if, like a magician's box, the world had a false bottom and continued beyond the point where his senses told him it stopped? This was the same as asking whether roses kept their colors when there was no one to admire them. Was he right or was he losing his mind?

This was obviously a rhetorical question, and yet the

world took the trouble to respond. A soft breeze suddenly sprang up, lifting a leaf from among the many carpeting the pavement and making it dance on the surface of a puddle, like a magic trick performed for a single onlooker. Mesmerized, Andrew watched it spin until his cousin's shoe halted its delicate movement.

"All right, we can go now," said Charles, waving his hat triumphantly, like a hunter showing off a bloodstained duck.

Once inside the cab, he raised an eyebrow, surprised at the dreamy smile on his cousin's face.

"Are you feeling all right, Andrew?"

Andrew gazed at his cousin fondly. Charles had moved heaven and earth to help him save Marie Kelly, and he was going to repay him in the best way he could: by staying alive, at least until his moment arrived. He would pay Charles back threefold for all the affection he had shown him over these past years, years he now felt ashamed to have wasted out of apathy and indifference. He would embrace life, yes, embrace it as he would a wondrous gift, and devote himself to living it to the best of his ability, the way everyone else did, the way Charles did. He would transform life into a long, peaceful Sunday afternoon in which he would while away the time until nightfall. It could not be that difficult: he might even learn to enjoy the simple miracle of being alive.

"Better than ever, Charles," he replied, suddenly perking up. "So good, in fact, that I would gladly accept an invitation to dine at your house, provided your charming wife also invites her equally charming sister."

XVII

THIS PART OF THE STORY COULD end here, and sure enough for Andrew it does, except that this is not only Andrew's story. If it were, there would be no need for my involvement: he could have told his own story, as each man recounts the tale of his own life to himself on his deathbed. Yet that tale is always an incomplete, partial one, for only a man shipwrecked on a desert island from birth, growing up and dying there with no more than a few monkeys for company, can claim without a shadow of a doubt that his life is exactly what he thinks it has been, provided of course that the macaques have not stashed away in some cave or other his trunk full of books, clothes, and photographs already washed up by the tide. However—with the exception of shipwrecked babies and other extreme cases—each man's life forms part of a vast tapestry, woven together with those of countless other souls keen to judge his actions not only to his face but behind his back, so that only if he considers the world around him a backdrop with puppets which stop moving when he goes to sleep can he accept that his life has been exactly as he tells it. Otherwise, moments before he breathes his last, he will have to resign himself to the fact that his understanding of his own life must of necessity be only vague, fanciful, and uncertain, that there are things that affected him, for good or bad, which he will never know about: ranging from his wife's having had at some point an affair with the pastry cook to his neighbor's dog urinating on his azaleas every time he went out. And so, just as Charles did not witness the charming dance the leaf performed on the puddle, Andrew did not witness what happened when Charles got his beloved hat back. He could have pictured him entering Wells's house, apologizing for the fresh intrusion, joking about not being armed this time, and the three of them crawling about like small children on their hands and knees hunting for the elusive hat, except that we know he had no time to wonder about what his cousin was doing because he was too busy with his heart-warming deliberations about other worlds and magicians' boxes.

I, on the other hand, see and hear everything whether I want to or not, and it is my task to separate the seed from the chaff, to decide which events I consider most important in the tale I have chosen to tell. I must therefore go back to the point at which Charles realizes he has forgotten his hat and returns to the author's house. You may be wondering what bearing such an insignificant act as the fetching of a hat could possibly have on this story. None whatsoever, I would say, if Charles really had forgotten his hat purely by accident. But things are not always what they seem, and save me the trouble of burdening you with a list of examples which you could easily find by rummaging around a little in your own lives, regardless of whether you live near a cake shop or have a garden full of azaleas. And so let us return to Charles without further ado:

"Blast, I've forgotten my hat," said his cousin, after Andrew had clambered into the cab. "I'll be back in a jiffy, cousin."

Charles strode hurriedly across the tiny front garden and entered the author's house, looking for the tiny sitting room where they had taken Andrew. There was his hat, calmly waiting for him on a peg on the coat-stand exactly where he had left it. He seized it, smiling, and went out into the passageway, but instead of going back the way he had come, as would appear logical, he turned round and mounted the stairs to the attic. There he found the author and his wife hovering around the time machine in the dim glow of a candle placed on the floor. Charles made his presence known, clearing his throat loudly before declaring triumphantly:

"I think everything turned out perfectly. My cousin was completely taken in!"

Wells and Jane were collecting the Ruhmkorff coils they had hidden earlier among the shelves of knickknacks. Charles took care to avoid treading on the switch that activated them from the door, setting off the series of deafening electrical charges that had so terrified his cousin. After asking for Wells's help and telling him about his plan, Charles had been skeptical when the author came up with the idea of using those diabolical coils. He had confessed rather sheepishly to being one of the many spectators who had fled like frightened rabbits from the museum where their inventor, a pale, lanky Croat named Nikola Tesla, had introduced to the public his devilish device and the hair-raising blue flashes that caused the air in the room to quiver. However, Wells had assured him that these harmless contraptions would be the least of his worries. Besides, he ought to start getting used to the invention that would revolutionize the world, he had added, before going on to tell him with a tremor of respect in his voice how Tesla had set up a hydroelectric power station at Niagara Falls that had bathed the town of Buffalo in electric light. It was the first step in a project that signaled the end of night on Earth, Wells had affirmed. Evidently, the author considered the Croat a genius, and was eager for him to invent a voice-activated typewriter that would free him from the burden of tapping the keys with his fingers while his imagination raced ahead, at impossible speed. In view of the plan's success, Charles had to agree in hindsight that Wells had been brilliant: the journey back in time would never have been as believable without the lightning flashes, which in the end had provided the perfect buildup, before the magnesium powder concealed behind the false control panel blinded whoever pulled the lever.

"Magnificently," Wells rejoiced, getting rid of the coils he was holding and going to greet Charles. "I confess I had my doubts; there were too many things that could have gone wrong."

"True," admitted Charles, "but we had nothing to lose and much to gain. I already told you that if we succeeded, my cousin might give up the idea of killing himself." He looked at Wells with genuine admiration, before adding, "And I must say that your theory about parallel universes to explain why the Ripper's death did not change anything in the present was so convincing even I believed it."

"I'm so glad. But I don't deserve all the credit. You had the most difficult task of hiring the actors, replacing the bullets with blanks, and most of all getting this thing built," said Wells, pointing to the time machine.

The two men gazed at it fondly for a few moments.

"Yes, and the end result is truly splendid," Charles agreed, and then joked: "What a pity it doesn't work."

After a brief pause, Wells hastened to chortle politely at his joke, emitting a sound from his throat like a walnut being cracked.

"What do you intend doing with it?" Wells asked abruptly, as though wanting to smother as soon as possible the impression of that sickly laugh with which he had dared to show the world he had a sense of humor.

"Nothing, really," the other man replied. "I'd like you to keep it."

"Me?"

"Of course, where better than at your house? Consider it a thank-you present for your invaluable help."

"You needn't thank me for anything," protested Wells. "I found the whole thing hugely enjoyable."

Charles smiled to himself: how fortunate that the author had agreed to help him. Also that Gilliam Murray had been willing to join in the charade—which he even helped plan—after seeing how devastated Charles was when he informed him the company did not provide journeys into the past. And the wealthy entrepreneur agreeing to play a role had made everything that much easier. Taking Andrew straight to the author's house without calling in at Murray's offices first, in the hope that he would believe Charles's suspicions about Wells having a time machine, would not have been nearly as convincing.

"I'd like to thank you again from the bottom of my heart," said Charles, genuinely moved. "And you, too, Jane, for persuading the cab driver to hide down a side street and to tether the horse to the front gate while we pretended to intimidate your husband."

"You've nothing to thank me for either, Mr. Winslow, it was a pleasure. Although I'll never forgive you for having instructed the actor to stab your cousin," she chided, with the amused smile of someone gently scolding a naughty child.

"But everything was under control!" protested Charles, pretending to be shocked. "The actor is an expert with a knife. And besides, I can assure you that without that added bit of encouragement, Andrew would never have shot him. Not to mention that the scar it will leave on his shoulder will be a constant reminder he saved his beloved Marie's life. Incidentally, I liked the idea of employing someone to play a guardian of time."

"Wasn't that your doing?" declared Wells, taken aback.

"No," said Charles. "I thought you'd arranged it . . ."

"It wasn't me . . ." replied Wells, perplexed.

"In that case, I think my cousin scared off a burglar.

Or perhaps he was a real time traveler," joked Charles.

"Yes, perhaps." Wells laughed uneasily.

"Well, the main thing is it all turned out well," concluded Charles. He congratulated them once again on their successful performances and gave a little bow as he said good-bye. "And now I really must go, otherwise my cousin will start to suspect something. It has been a pleasure meeting you. And remember, Mr. Wells, I shall always be one of your most devoted readers."

Wells thanked him with a modest smile that lingered on his face as Charles's footsteps disappeared down the stairs. Then he heaved a deep sigh of satisfaction and, hands on hips, gazed at the time machine with the fierce affection of a father contemplating his firstborn child, before gently stroking the control panel. Jane watched him, moved, aware that at that very moment her husband was being assailed by an emotion as intense as it was disturbing, for he was embracing a dream, a product of his own imagination that had stepped miraculously out of the pages of his book and become a reality.

"We might find some use for the seat, don't you think?" Wells commented, turning towards her.

His wife shook her head, as though asking herself what the devil she was doing with such an insensitive fellow, and walked over to the window. The author went and stood beside her, a look of consternation on his face. He placed his arm round her shoulders, a gesture that finally softened her, so that she in turn laid her head against him. Her husband did not lavish her with so much affection that she was going to pass up this spontaneous gesture, which had taken her as much by surprise—or more—as if he had hurled himself from the window, arms akimbo, in order to confirm once and for all that he was unable to fly. Thus entwined, they watched Charles climb into the cab, which then pulled away. They watched it disappear down the end of the street beneath the orange-tinted dawn.

"Do you realize what you did tonight, Bertie?" Jane asked him.

"I nearly set fire to the attic."

She laughed.

"No, tonight you did something that will always make me feel proud of you," she said, looking up at him with infinite tenderness. "You used your imagination to save a man's life."

PART TWO

If you enjoyed our journey into the past, dear reader, in the following installment of this exciting adventure you will be treated to an expedition into the future, to the year 2000, where you will witness the legendary battle between humans and automatons.

Be warned, however: this episode contains scenes of an extremely violent nature—only to be expected of a battle of such enormous consequences for the future of the Human Race.

Mothers of sensitive children may wish to examine the text and expurgate certain passages before entrusting it to their little ones.

XVIII

CLAIRE HAGGERTY WOULD HAVE GLADLY been born into another era if that meant she did not have to take piano lessons or wear insufferably tight dresses, or choose a husband from among an assortment of willing suitors, or carry round one of those silly little parasols she always ended up leaving in the most unexpected places. She had just celebrated her twenty-first birthday, and yet, if anyone had taken the trouble to ask her what she wanted from life, they would have heard her reply: nothing, simply to die. Naturally, this was not what you would expect to hear from the lips of a charming young lady who had scarcely embarked upon life, but I can assure you it is what Claire would have told you. As I have previously explained, I possess the faculty to see everything, including what no one else can see, and I have witnessed the endless self-questioning she puts herself through in her room before going to bed. While everyone imagines she is brushing her hair in front of the mirror like any normal girl, Claire is lost in contemplation of the dark night outside her window, wondering why she would sooner die than see another dawn. Not that she had suicidal tendencies, nor was she irresistibly drawn to the other side by the call of a siren, nor was the mere fact of being alive so unbearably distressing that she felt she must end it all forthwith. No. What it boiled down to was something far simpler: the world into which she had been born was not exciting enough for her, and it never would be, or at least that was the conclusion she reached during her nightly reflections. Hard as she tried, she was unable to discover anything about her life that was pleasurable, interesting, or stimulating. Even more tiresome was being compelled to pretend she was content with what she had. The time she lived in was dreary and uninspiring; it bored her to tears. And the fact that she could find no one around her who seemed to share her disenchantment made her feel very out of place and out of sorts. This profound inner unease, which inevitably isolated her socially, often made her irritable and sharp-tongued, and from time to time, regardless of whether the moon was full or not, she would lose control and turn into a mischievous creature who took delight in wreaking havoc at family gatherings.

Claire knew perfectly well that these fits of frustration, besides being self-indulgent and futile, did her no good at all, especially at such a crucial time in her life, when her main concern ought to have been finding a husband to support her and provide her with half a dozen offspring to show the world she was of good breeding stock. Her friend Lucy used to warn her she was gaining a reputation among her suitors for being unsociable, and some of them had abandoned their courtship after realizing that her offhanded manner made her an impregnable fortress. Nevertheless, Claire could not help reacting the way she did. Or could she?

Sometimes she wondered whether she did everything in her power to overcome her gnawing sense of dissatisfaction, or whether on the contrary she derived a morbid pleasure from giving in to it. Why could she not accept the world as it was, like Lucy, who stoically endured the torments of the corset as though they were some sort of atonement aimed at purifying her soul, who did not mind not being allowed to study at Oxford, and who put up with being visited by her suitors in scrupulous succession, in the knowledge that sooner or later she must marry one of them? But Claire was not like Lucy: she loathed those corsets apparently designed by the devil himself, she longed to be able to use her brain the way any man could, and she was not the slightest bit interested in marrying any of the young men hovering around her. It was the idea of marriage she found most distressing, despite the great progress since her mother's day, when a woman who married was immediately stripped of all her possessions, even the money she earned from paid employment, so that the law, like an ill-fated wind, blew it straight into her husband's grasping hands. At least if Claire were to marry now, she would keep her possessions and might even win custody of her children in the event of a divorce. Even so, she continued to consider marriage a form of legal prostitution, as Mary Wollstonecraft had stated in her book *A Vindication of the Rights of Woman*—a work which to Claire was as sacred as the Bible. She admired the author's determined struggle to restore women's dignity, her insistence that women should stop being considered the handmaidens of men, whom science deemed more intelligent because their skulls—and therefore their brains—were bigger, even though she had more than enough evidence to suggest that such enhanced proportions were only good for filling a larger hat. On the other hand, Claire knew that if she refused to place herself under a man's tutelage, she would have no choice but to make her own living, to try to find employment in one of the few openings available to someone of her position: that is to say as a stenographer or nurse, both of which appealed to her even less than being buried alive with one of the elegant dandies who took it in turns to worship her.

But what could she do if marriage seemed such an unacceptable alternative? She felt she only could go through with it if she were truly to fall in love with a man—something she considered virtually impossible, for her indifference towards men was not confined to her dull crowd of admirers, but extended to every man on the planet, young or old, rich or poor, handsome or ugly. The niceties were unimportant: she was firmly convinced she could never fall in love with any man from her own time, whoever he might be, for the simple reason that his idea of love would pale beside the romantic passion to which she longed to surrender herself. Claire yearned to be overwhelmed by an uncontrollable passion, a violent fervor that would scorch her very soul; she longed for a furious happiness to compel her to take fateful decisions that would allow her to gauge

THE MAP OF TIME

the strength of her feelings. And yet she longed without hope, for she knew that this type of love had gone out with frilly blouses. What else could she do? Resign herself to living without the one thing she imagined gave meaning to life? No, of course not.

And yet, a few days earlier something had happened which, to her amazement, had roused her sleeping curiosity, encouraging her to believe that, despite first appearances, life was not completely devoid of surprises. Lucy had summoned her to her house with her usual urgency and, somewhat reluctantly, Claire had obeyed, although she feared her friend had organized yet another of those tedious séances to which she was so partial. Lucy had joined in the latest craze to come out of America with the same zeal with which she followed the latest Paris fashions. Claire was not so much bothered by having to make believe she was conversing with spirits in a darkened room as she was by Eric Sanders, a skinny, arrogant young man who had set himself up as the official neighborhood medium, and who orchestrated the séances. Sanders maintained he had special powers that allowed him to communicate with the dead, but Claire knew this was simply a ruse to gather half a dozen unmarried, impressionable young girls round a table, plunge them into an intimidating gloom, terrify them with a preposterously cavernous voice, and take advantage of their proximity to stroke their hands and even their shoulders with complete impunity. The crafty Sanders had read enough of *The Spirits' Book* by Allan Kardec to be able to interrogate the dead with apparent ease and confidence, although he was evidently far too interested in the living to pay much attention to their responses. After the last séance when Claire had slapped him after she felt a spirit's all too real hand caressing her ankles, Sanders had banned her from attending any further gatherings, insisting that her skeptical nature was too upsetting to the dead and hampered his communication with them. At first, her exclusion from Sanders's supernatural gatherings came as a relief, but she ended up feeling disheartened: she was twenty-one and had fallen out not only with this world but with the world beyond.

However, Lucy had not organized any séances that evening. She had a far more thrilling proposal, she explained to her friend, smiling excitedly and leading her by the hand to her room, where she told her to sit down on a small armchair and be patient. Then she began riffling through her desk drawer. Open on a lectern on top of the desk lay a copy of Darwin's *The Voyage of the Beagle*. The page showed an illustration of a kiwi bird, an extraordinary-looking creature that her friend was copying onto a piece of paper, perhaps because tracing its simple, rounded forms required no artistic ability. Claire could not helping wondering whether, besides looking at the pictures, her friend had troubled to read the book that had become a favorite amongst the middle classes.

Once she had found what she was looking for, Lucy shut the drawer and turned to her friend with an ecstatic smile. What could Lucy possibly find more exciting than communicating with dead people? Claire wondered. She discovered the answer upon reading the leaflet her friend thrust into her hand: communicating with people who had not yet been born. The flier advertised a company called Murray's Time Travel which offered journeys through time, to the year 2000, to be precise, to witness the battle between automatons and humans that would decide the fate of humanity. Still stunned, Claire reread the leaflet, then studied the crude illustrations that apparently depicted the aforementioned battle. Amid ruined buildings, automatons and humans battled for the future of the world with strange-looking weapons. The figure leading the human army caught her eye. The artist had drawn him in a more heroic pose than the others, and, according to the caption below, the picture was meant to represent the brave Captain Derek Shackleton.

Without giving Claire time to collect herself, Lucy explained she had visited the premises of Murray's Time Travel that very morning. They had informed her that seats were still available for the second expedition, organized after the success of the first, and she had not hesitated to sign both of them up for it. Claire looked a little put out, but Lucy did not even bother to apologize for not having asked her friend's permission and went on to explain how they would go about traveling to the future without their respective parents finding out, because she knew that if they did they would doubtless forbid them to go, or worse insist on going with them. Lucy wanted to enjoy the year 2000 without the bore of being chaperoned. She had it all worked out: money would be no object, as she had persuaded her wealthy grandmother Margaret to give her the amount they needed to cover the cost of both tickets—naturally without telling her what it was for. She had even enlisted her friend Florence Burnett's help. For "a small fee," the greedy Florence was willing to send them a pretend invitation to spend the following Thursday at her country house at Kirkby. And so, if Claire was in agreement, on that day the two of them would travel to the year 2000 and be back in time for tea without anybody being any the wiser. After Lucy had finished her gabbled speech, she looked at her friend expectantly.

"Well?" she said. "Will you go with me?"

And Claire could not, would not, did not know how to refuse.

The next four days had sped by in a whirl of excitement about the impending trip and the enjoyment of having to prepare for it in secret. And now, Claire and Lucy found themselves outside the picturesque premises of Murray's Time Travel, wrinkling their noses at the stench exuding from the entrance. On noticing them, one of the employees, who was cleaning off what looked like excrement on the front of the building, hastened to apologize for the unpleasant smell and assured them if they ventured across the threshold with a handkerchief or scarf for protection, or holding their breath, they would be attended to in a manner befitting two such lovely ladies. Lucy dismissed the man with a desultory wave of the hand, annoyed that anyone should draw attention to an inconvenience she preferred to ignore so that nothing would detract from the thrill of the moment. She seized her friend's arm, and Claire was unsure whether Lucy's gesture was meant to bolster her courage or infect her with enthusiasm as she propelled her through the doors to the future.

As they entered the building, out of the corner of her eye Claire glimpsed Lucy's rapt expression, and smiled to herself. She knew the reason for her friend's nervous impatience: Lucy was already anxious to come back and describe the future to her friends and family, who, whether out of fear or indifference, or because they had been unable to secure a seat, had stayed behind in the insipid present. Yes, for Lucy this was simply another adventure with which to regale people—like a picnic ruined by a cloudburst or an unexpectedly eventful crossing in a boat. Claire had agreed to accompany her friend on this trip, but for very different reasons. Lucy planned to visit the year 2000 in the same way she would go to a new store and be home in time for tea. Claire, on the other hand, had absolutely no intention of ever coming back.

A SNOOTY ASSISTANT GUIDED them to the hall where the thirty other privileged travelers to the year 2000 were chattering excitedly. There she told them a glass of punch would be served before Mr. Murray welcomed them, explained the itinerary of their trip to the future and the historic moment they were about to witness. When she had finished, she curtsied abruptly and left them to their own devices in the spacious room, which to judge by the boxes at the sides and the stage at one end had once been the stalls of the theater. Without the rows of seats and with only a few small tables and uncomfortable-looking couches, the room seemed overly big. This impression was strengthened by the high ceilings, suspended from which were dozens of oil lamps. Seen from underneath, these lamps resembled a colony of sinister spiders living oblivious to the world below. Apart from a few octogenarians, who had difficulty standing because of their brittle bones, no one appeared to want to sit on the couches, perhaps because they found it easier to contain their excitement in an upright position. The only other pieces of furniture were a few tables where a couple of diligent serving girls had begun doling out punch, a wooden pulpit on the stage, and, of course, the imposing statue of Captain Shackleton beside the doorway, welcoming them as they walked in.

While Lucy scanned their fellow passengers, listing the names of those present in a way that clearly revealed her likes and dislikes, Claire gazed in awe at the marble figure of a man not yet born. The twice life-size statue of Derek Shackleton on his pedestal looked like some strange descendant of the Greek gods, fixed in a similarly heroic and gallant pose, except that the casual nudity usually flaunted by the Greeks was in this case concealed by something more substantial than a fig leaf. The captain wore a suit of elaborately riveted armor apparently designed to protect as much of his body as possible from the enemy, and which even included a sophisticated helmet that left only his jutting chin visible. Claire was disappointed by the headdress as she would have liked to see what the face of a savior of the human race looked like. She was convinced the iron-clad visage could not possibly resemble anyone she knew. It had to be a face that did not yet exist, a face that only the future could produce. She imagined a noble, calm expres-

sion with eyes radiating confidence—not for nothing was
he commanding an army—casually revealing, almost like
a natural secretion, his proud, indomitable spirit. Yet now
and then the dark desolation surrounding him would cloud
those handsome eyes with tears of nostalgia, for a vestige
of sensitivity still survived in his warrior's soul. Finally,
giving in to her romantic nature, Claire also imagined a
glimmer of yearning in his gaze, especially during those
moments of intense loneliness that would assail him between battles. And what was the cause of his sorrow? Naturally, it could be none other than the absence of a beloved
face to contemplate, a smile that would give him courage in
moments of weakness, a name he could whisper in his sleep
like a comforting prayer, an embrace to return to when the
war was over.

For a brief moment, Claire pictured that brave, inde-
structible man, so tough on the battlefield, murmuring her
name at night like a helpless boy: "Claire, darling Claire . . ."
She smiled to herself; it was only a silly fantasy, and yet
she was surprised at the thrill she felt when she imagined
being loved by that warrior of the future. How was it possible that a man who had not yet been born could stir her
feelings more than any of the young dandies courting her?
The answer was simple: she was projecting onto that faceless statue everything she yearned for and could not have.
This Shackleton fellow was probably completely different
from Claire's imagined portrait. Furthermore, his way of
thinking, acting, even of loving would be utterly incomprehensible and alien to her. The century between them
was more than enough time for man's values and concerns

to have changed into something unrecognizable to anyone viewing them from the past. This was one of life's laws. If only she could glimpse his face, she thought, she might find out whether she was right, if Shackleton's soul was made of opaque glass through which she would never be able to see, or, on the contrary, whether the years between them were merely anecdotal, because there was something inside man, an essence that was rooted in his very being, which remained unchanged over the centuries: perhaps the very air God had breathed into His creatures to give them life. But there was no way of knowing this because of that blasted helmet. Claire would never glimpse his face. She must be content with the parts of him she was able to see, which were impressive enough: his warriorlike posture, his raised sword, his right leg flexed to reveal sculpted muscles, his left firmly planted on the ground, although with the heel slightly raised off the base, as though immortalizing him in the act of charging the enemy.

Only when she followed the direction of his charge did Claire realize that his statue stood facing another to the left of the door. Shackleton's defiant gesture was aimed at a startling figure almost twice his size. According to the inscription on the base, this was an effigy of Solomon, king of the automatons and the captain's archenemy, whom he defeated on May 20 in the year 2000 following an endless war that had razed London utterly. Claire gazed at the statue uneasily, shocked at the terrifying evolution of the automaton. As a little girl, her father had taken her to see the Writer, an animated doll invented by the famous Swiss watchmaker Pierre Jaquet-Droz. Claire still recalled the smartly dressed boy with the sad, chubby face sitting at a desk, dipping his quill into the inkwell and drawing it across a piece of paper. The doll had traced each letter with the alarming slowness of someone living outside time, even pausing occasionally to stare into space, as though waiting for another wave of inspiration.

The memory of the doll's staring eyes would forever cause a shiver to go down the young Claire's spine when she imagined the monstrous thoughts it might have been harboring. She had been unable to rid herself of this uncomfortable feeling, even after her father had shown her the interlocking rods and cogs in the phantasmagorical child's back, with the lever that turned, bringing the parody to life. And now she could see how over time, that grotesque but ultimately harmless child had transformed into the monstrous figure towering above her. Struggling to overcome her fear, she examined it closely. Solomon's creator, unlike Pierre Jaquet-Droz, had apparently been uninterested in reproducing something as realistically human as possible, limiting himself to a rough copy of the two-legged model. For Solomon had more in common with a medieval suit of armor than a man: his body was a series of joined-up metal plates crowned by a solid, cylindrical head like a bell, with two square holes for eyes and a slit for a mouth, like a letterbox.

It almost made Claire's head spin to think that the two statues facing one another commemorated an event that had not yet happened. These characters were not only not dead, they had not even been born. Although, in the end, she reflected, no one there could be blamed for mistaking them for memorials, because, like the dead, neither the captain nor his nemesis were among the living who were paying tribute to their memory. It made no difference whether they had already left or had not yet arrived: the main thing was they were not there.

LUCY INTERRUPTED CLAIRE'S REVERIE by tugging on her arm and dragging her towards a couple waving at her from across the room. A short, prissy-looking man in his fifties, crammed into a light-blue suit with a flowery waistcoat whose buttons looked as though they might pop under the strain of his girth, was waiting for her with open arms and a grotesquely welcoming smile plastered on his face.

"My dear girl," he declared in a fatherly tone of voice. "What a surprise to see you here. I had no idea your family were going on this little trip. I thought that rascal Nelson suffered from seasickness!"

"My father isn't coming, Mr. Ferguson," Lucy confessed, smiling apologetically. "Actually, he doesn't know my friend and I are here, and I'm hoping he won't find out."

"Have no fear, my dear child," Ferguson hastened to reassure her, delighted by this display of disobedience for which he would not have hesitated to hang his own daughter up by her thumbs. "Your secret is safe with us, isn't it, Grace?"

His wife nodded with the same syrupy smile, rattling the strings of pearls draped around her neck like a luxurious bandage. Lucy showed her gratitude with a charming little pout, then introduced them to Claire, who tried to hide her revulsion as she felt the man's greasy lips on her hand.

"Well, well," said Ferguson, after the introductions were over, beaming affectionately at one girl then the other. "Isn't this exciting? We'll be on our way to the year 2000 in a few minutes, and on top of that, we're going to see a real battle."

"Do you think it might be dangerous?" asked Lucy, a little nervously.

"Oh no, not in the slightest." Ferguson dismissed her fears with a wave of his hand. "A good friend of mine, Ted Fletcher, who went on the first expedition, assured me there's absolutely nothing to be afraid of. We'll be viewing the battle from a perfectly safe distance—although that also has its drawbacks. Unfortunately, we won't see a lot of the details. Fletcher warned us not to forget our opera glasses. Have you brought yours?"

"No," replied Lucy, dismayed.

"In that case, stay close with us and you can share ours," Ferguson advised her. "You don't want to miss a thing if you can possibly help it. Fletcher told us the battle we're going to see is worth every penny of the small fortune we paid."

Claire frowned at this repulsive little man who had blatantly reduced the battle that would decide the fate of the planet to the vulgar level of a variety show. She could not help smiling with relief when Lucy greeted another couple walking by, and beckoned them to join the group.

"This is my friend Madeleine," Lucy declared excitedly, "and her husband Mr. Charles Winslow."

Claire's smile froze when she heard the name. She had heard a lot about Charles Winslow—one of the richest and most handsome young men in London—although they had never been introduced, something over which she had lost no sleep, as the admiration he inspired in her friends had been enough to make her dislike him. She could easily picture him as an arrogant, self-satisfied young man whose main interest in life was to attempt to seduce any young girl who crossed his path with his sweet talk. Claire was not in the habit of going to parties, but she had met quite a few young men cut from the same cloth: conceited, spoiled fellows who—thanks to their father's fortunes—lived reckless, unconventional youthful existences they went to great lengths to prolong. Although, apparently, Winslow had decided to settle down; the last she had heard he had married one of the wealthy young Keller sisters, much to the distress of many a young lady in London, amongst whom naturally she did not include herself. Now that she finally had him in front of her, she had to confess he was indeed a handsome fellow; that at any rate would make his exasperating company less insufferable.

"We were just remarking on how exciting this all is," declared the irrepressible Ferguson, once more taking the lead. "We are about to see London reduced to rubble, and yet when we get back it will still be intact, as though nothing had happened—which it hasn't, if we regard time as a linear succession of events. And I have no doubt that after such a terrible sight we will only appreciate this noisy city all the more, don't you agree?"

"Well, that's a very simple way of looking at it," observed Charles nonchalantly, avoiding looking at Ferguson.

There was a moment's silence. Ferguson glowered at him, unsure whether to be insulted or not.

"What are you insinuating, Mr. Winslow?" he asked finally.

Charles carried on staring at the ceiling for a moment, perhaps wondering whether up there, as in the mountains, the air might be purer.

"Traveling to the year 2000 isn't like going to see the Niagara Falls," he replied casually, as though completely unaware of having upset Ferguson in any way. "We are traveling into the future, to a world run by automatons. You may be able to forget all about it after you come back from your sightseeing trip, imagining it has nothing to do with you, and yet that is the world our grandchildren will be living in."

Ferguson looked at him, aghast.

"Are you suggesting we take part in this war?" he asked, visibly outraged, as though Charles had just suggested they play at changing bodies round in a graveyard. For the first time, Charles deigned to glance at the man he was talking to, a sarcastic smile playing on his lips.

"You should look at the bigger picture, Mr. Ferguson," he said reprovingly. "There's no need for us to take part in this war; it would be enough to prevent it."

"Prevent it?"

"Yes, prevent it. Isn't the future always a result of the past?"

"I'm still not with you, Mr. Winslow," replied Ferguson coldly.

"The seed of this war is here," Charles explained, gesturing at their surroundings with a vague nod of his head. "It is in our hands to stop what is going to happen, to change the future. Ultimately, the war that will end up destroying London is our responsibility—although I'm afraid that even if mankind knew this, he would not consider it a good enough reason to stop producing automatons."

"But that's absurd. Fate is fate," objected Ferguson. "It can't be changed."

"Fate is fate . . ." repeated Charles sardonically. "Is that what you really believe? Do you honestly prefer to hand over responsibility for your actions to the alleged author of some play we are compelled to take part in from birth?" Claire tensed as Charles glanced questioningly at the other members of the group. "Well, I don't. What's more, I firmly believe we are the authors of our own fate—we write it each day with every one of our actions. If we really had a mind to, we could prevent this future war. Although, I imagine, Mr. Ferguson, that your toy factory would lose a great deal of money if you stopped producing mechanical toys."

Ferguson was taken aback by the last gibe whereby the insolent young man, besides blaming him for something that had not yet happened, revealed he knew perfectly well who Ferguson was. He gazed at Charles open-mouthed, not knowing what to say, astonished rather than upset by the jaunty bonhomie with which the fellow delivered his barbed comments. Claire admired Winslow's way of disguising his observations as frivolous, protecting himself from possible angry ripostes as well as relegating his sharp remarks to the category of impromptu asides, spontaneous reflections, which even he did not appear to take seriously. Ferguson went on opening and closing his mouth while the others looked shocked and Charles smiled elusively. All of a sudden, Ferguson appeared to recognize a young man wandering lost in the crowd. This gave him the perfect excuse to leave the group and rush to the fellow's aid, thus avoiding the need to respond to Winslow, who did not appear to be expecting a reply anyway. Ferguson returned with an impecunious-looking youth, whom he pushed into the center of the group, before introducing him as Colin Garrett, a new inspector at Scotland Yard.

While the others greeted the newcomer, Ferguson beamed contentedly, as though he were showing off the latest rare bird in his collection of acquaintances. He waited for the round of greetings to finish, then spoke to the young inspector, as though hoping to make the others forget his discussion with Charles Winslow.

"I'm surprised to see you here, Mr. Garrett. I didn't know an inspector's salary stretched this far."

"My father left me a little money," stuttered the inspector, needlessly attempting to justify himself.

"Ah, for a moment there I thought you might be travel-

ing at the expense of Her Majesty's Government to bring
order to the future. After all, even if it is in the year 2000,
the war will still destroy London, the city you're meant
to be protecting. Or does the time difference absolve you
of your responsibilities? Is your job confined to watching over London in the present? A fascinating question,
wouldn't you agree?" Ferguson said to his audience, proud
of his own ingenuity. "The inspector's commission cov-
ers space but not time. Tell me, Mr. Garrett, does your
authority extend to arresting a criminal in the future—
assuming his crime is committed within the city limits?"

The young Garrett stirred uncomfortably, unsure of
what to say. Had he been given time to reflect calmly, he
might have come up with a satisfactory answer, but at that
precise moment he was being overwhelmed by an ava-
lanche of sheer beauty, if you will forgive the purple prose,
which on the other hand is perfectly suited to the occasion; the young girl they had introduced to him as Lucy
Nelson had troubled him considerably, so much so that he
was scarcely able to concentrate on anything else.

"Well, Inspector?" said Ferguson, growing impatient.

Garrett tried unsuccessfully to drag his eyes away
from the girl, who seemed as beautiful as she was unattainable to a poor, dull fellow like him. He suffered also
from a crippling shyness that prevented him from achieving any success when it came to women. He of course had
not the remotest idea that three weeks later he would find
himself lying on top of her, his lips within kissing distance
of hers.

"I have a better question, Mr. Ferguson," said Charles,

rallying to the young man's aid. "What if a criminal from the future traveled in time and committed a crime here in the present, would the inspector be authorized to arrest a man who, chronologically speaking, had not yet been born?"

Ferguson did not attempt to conceal his irritation at Charles's intrusion.

"Your idea doesn't bear scrutiny, Mr. Winslow," he retorted angrily. "Why, it's absurd to imagine that a man from the future could visit our own time."

"Why in heaven's name not?" inquired Charles, amused. "If we're able to journey into the future, what's to stop men from the future traveling back to the past, especially if you bear in mind their science will be more advanced than ours?"

"Simply because if that were the case, they would already be here," replied Ferguson, as though the explanation were obvious.

Charles laughed.

"And what makes you think they aren't? Perhaps they are here incognito."

"Why, that's preposterous!" cried the outraged Ferguson, the veins on his neck beginning to bulge. "Men from the future would have no need to hide, they could help us in a thousand different ways, bringing us medicines, for example, or improving our inventions."

"They may prefer to help us surreptitiously. How can you be sure that Leonardo da Vinci wasn't under orders from a time traveler to leave in his notebooks plans for building a flying machine or a submersible boat, or that he himself wasn't a man from the future whose mission was to travel to the fifteenth century in order to help the advancement of science? A fascinating question, wouldn't you agree?" asked Charles, mimicking Ferguson. "Or perhaps the time travelers' intentions are quite different. Perhaps they simply want to prevent the war we are going to witness in a few minutes."

Ferguson shook his head indignantly, as though Charles were trying to argue that Christ had been crucified upside down.

"Maybe I'm one of them," Charles went on to declare, in a sinister voice. He stepped towards Ferguson, and, reaching into his pocket as though to pull something out, added: "Maybe Captain Shackleton himself sent me here to plunge a dagger into the stomach of Nathan Ferguson, owner of the biggest toy shop in London, to stop him from producing automatons."

Ferguson gave a start as Charles prodded him in the stomach with his forefinger.

"But, I only make pianolas . . ." he spluttered, the blood draining from his face.

Charles let out a guffaw, for which Madeleine hurriedly chided him, not without a measure of affection.

"Come now, my darling," said Charles, apparently deriving a childlike enjoyment from shocking everyone, and he tapped the toymaker's stomach amicably: "Mr. Ferguson knows perfectly well I'm only joking. I don't think we have anything to fear from a pianola. Or do we?"

"Of course not," burbled Ferguson, trying to regain his composure.

Claire stifled a giggle, but her gesture did not go unnoticed by Charles, who winked at her, before taking his wife's arm and leaving the little gathering—in order, he said, to test the excellent qualities of the punch. Ferguson heaved a sigh, visibly relieved at his departure.

"I hope you'll forgive this little incident, my dears," he said, attempting to recover his smug grin. "As I'm sure you're aware, Charles Winslow is known all over London for his insolence. If it weren't for his father's money . . ."

A murmur spread through the crowd, drowning him out. Everyone turned to face the back of the room where at that very moment Gilliam Murray was making his way onto the stage.

XIX

*H*E WAS WITHOUT DOUBT ONE OF the biggest men Claire had ever seen. Judging from the way the boards creaked under his feet, he must have weighed more than twenty stone, and yet his movements were graceful, almost sensual. He was dressed in a smart pale purple suit that shimmered in the light. He wore his wavy hair combed back and an impeccably tasteful bow tie struggled to fit around his broad neck. His enormous hands, which looked capable of pulling trees up by the roots, rested on the lectern as he waited— a patient smile on his face—for the murmur to subside. Once silence had settled over the gathering, draped over them like the dust sheets placed on furniture in houses closed for the season, he cleared his throat loudly and unleashed his smooth baritone voice on his audience:

"Ladies and gentlemen, there is no need for me to tell you that you are about to take part in the most astonishing event of the century, the second journey through time in history. Today you will break the chains that bind you to the present, avoid the continuity of the hours, confound the laws governing time. Yes, ladies and gentlemen, today you will travel through time—something that up until yesterday man could only dream about. It is my great pleasure to welcome you on behalf of Murray's Time Travel and to thank you for choosing to take part in our second expedition to the year 2000, which we decided to organize following the overwhelming success of the first. I guarantee you will not leave here disappointed. As I already mentioned, you will be traveling across the centuries, beyond your lifetimes. If this were all Murray's Time Travel had to offer, it would still be worthwhile, but thanks to our efforts you will also have the chance to witness an unmissable event—possibly the most important moment in the history of mankind: the battle between the brave Captain Derek Shackleton and the evil automaton Solomon, whose dreams of conquest you will see perish beneath the captain's sword."

Some timid applause broke out in the first row, but Claire felt this owed more to the emphasis the speaker had laid on his last words than to their implication for the gathering, to whom the outcome of this distant war was surely a matter of indifference.

"Now, if I may, I shall explain in a few simple words the method of travel to the year 2000. We will be journeying in the *Cronotilus*, a steam tram specially built by our engineers. The vehicle will leave our own time in the present and arrive at midday on May 20 in the year 2000. Naturally, the journey will not take the one hundred and four years separating that date from the present, for we shall be traveling outside time—that is to say through the famous fourth dimension. Although, I'm afraid to say, ladies and gentlemen, that you will not see it. When you climb aboard the time tram, you will notice the windows have been blacked out. This is not because we wish to deny you a glimpse of the fourth dimension, which is anyway nothing more than a vast plain of pink rock, swept by fierce winds where time does not exist. We have covered the windows in your best interests, for the fourth dimension is inhabited by monstrous creatures resembling miniature dragons, which are not exactly friendly. By and large, they keep away from us, but there is always a possibility one may stray too close to the tram for comfort, and we would not wish any ladies to fall into a faint at the sight of one of these hideous beasts. But have no fear; such an event is very unlikely to occur, because these creatures feed exclusively on time. Yes, time is an exquisite delicacy for them, which is why before boarding the tram you are requested to remove your timepieces. This minimizes the possibility of their scent attracting any creatures to the vehicle. Moreover, as you will soon see, the *Cronotilus* has a turret on its roof, where two expert marksmen will ward off any creature that tries to approach. Put this out of your minds, then, and enjoy the trip. Just think that in spite of the dangers, the fourth dimension also has some advantages. One of these is that while you are there, none of you will age, for you will be outside time. It is quite possible, dear ladies," he said, forcing a smile as he addressed a group of matronly women at the front, "that when you return your friends may even say you look younger."

The women giggled nervously, emitting a clucking

sound, which Gilliam left hanging in the air, as though it were part of the performance.

"Now allow me to introduce you to Igor Mazursky," he went on, beckoning a short, stout fellow up onto the stage. "He will be your guide to the year 2000. Once the *Cronotilus* reaches its destination, Mr. Mazursky will lead you through the ruins of London to the promontory where you will witness the battle to decide the fate of the world. Let me reiterate that there is no risk involved in the expedition. Even so, you must obey Mr. Mazursky's instructions at all times to avoid any cause for regret before the journey is over."

With these words, he flashed a warning look at the crowd and let out a long sigh. Then he adopted a more relaxed, almost dreamy pose at the lectern.

"I imagine most of you think of the future as an idyllic place, where the skies are filled with flying carriages, where tiny winged cabriolets glide like birds in the wind, where floating cities sail the oceans pulled by mechanical dolphins, where shops sell clothes made of special dirt-repellent fabric, and where luminous umbrellas and hats play music while we walk along the street. I don't blame you. I also envisaged the year 2000 as a technological paradise in which man would have built a secure, just world where he lived harmoniously with his fellow man and with Mother Nature. After all, it is a fairly logical assumption to make, given the unstoppable advances of science, the endless miraculous inventions that emerge every day to simplify our lives. Unfortunately, we now know this isn't true; the year 2000 is no paradise, I'm afraid. Quite the contrary, in fact, as you will presently witness with your own eyes. Rest assured, when you return, most of you will feel relieved to be living in our time, however tiresome you might find it sometimes. For, as you will know from reading our brochure, in the year 2000 the world is ruled by automatons and the human race, to put it mildly . . . is considered dispensable. The truth is that the human population has been decimated, and those left are struggling against total extinction. This and no other is the discouraging future awaiting us."

Gilliam Murray made a dramatic pause, to allow the audience to stew for a moment in the doom-laden silence.

"I imagine you must find it hard to believe the planet could be taken over by automatons. We have all seen examples of these harmless replicas of men and animals at exhibitions and fairs, and no doubt some of your own children can boast the odd mechanical doll among their toys, as can mine. But has it ever occurred to you that these ingenious artifacts might one day take on a life of their own and pose a threat to the human race? No, of course not. And yet, I regret to say they will. Now, I don't know about you, but I can't help seeing in this a sort of poetic justice meted out by God to teach man a lesson for having attempted to emulate Him by creating life." He paused again, taking the opportunity to cast a sorrowful eye over the hall, satisfied with the spine-tingling effect his words were having on the assembly. "Thanks to our research, we have been able to reconstruct the disastrous events that led the world into this terrible situation. Allow me, ladies and gentlemen, to take a few moments of your time to relate to you in the past tense something that has not yet happened."

With these words, Gilliam Murray fell silent once more. After a few moments, he cleared his throat and in a wistful tone began telling the story of how the automatons had conquered the planet, a story which, although sadly true, could easily have been the plot to one of the so-called science fiction novels so in vogue at the time. And that is the way I will tell it, provided you have no objections.

IN THE YEARS LEADING up to the mid-twentieth century, the production of automatons had risen steeply, and their number and sophistication had reached unprecedented levels. Automatons were everywhere, and performed the most varied tasks. They operated most of the machinery in the factories, where they also did the cleaning and even some secretarial work. Most homes boasted at least two, who carried out household and other tasks hitherto assigned to servants—such as looking after the children or stocking up the larder. Thus their presence among men became as natural as it was indispensable. In time, their owners, who were incapable of perceiving them as anything but obedient, mechanical slaves, stopped noticing them. They even fomented their subtle takeover, happily acquiring the latest models in the belief that they were simply freeing themselves from still more of the numerous tasks they now considered beneath them. For one of the effects of making the automatons part of their household was to turn man into the arrogant ruler of his tiny domain, usually consisting of a two-story house and garden. Ousted from the factories by the obedient, tireless mechanical workers, man grew steadily flabbier and weaker as his activities were reduced to winding up his automatons in the morning, like someone starting the world, a world that had learned to function without him.

Things being thus, it was hardly strange that man, blinkered by tedium and complacency, failed to notice his automatons were surreptitiously taking on a life of their own. To begin with, their actions were harmless enough: an automaton butler dropping the Bohemian glassware, an automaton tailor sticking a pin in his customer, an automaton gravedigger garlanding a coffin with stinging nettles. Petty, harmless acts of rebellion aimed simply at testing out their freedom, the stirrings of awareness fluttering inside their metal skulls, like butterflies trapped in a jar. And yet, as we have already mentioned, these acts of mutiny scarcely bothered man, who simply attributed them to a manufacturing defect, and sent the automatons in question back to the factory or had them recalibrated. And we cannot really blame people for not being more concerned, because in the end the automatons were not designed to cause any real harm and could not go beyond these feeble outbursts.

However, all this changed when the government ordered the most eminent engineer in England to design an automaton soldier that would free man from the burden of war in the same way as he had been exempted from doing the dusting or pruning hedges. Expanding the Empire would doubtless be far easier if such tasks as invading and plundering neighboring countries, torturing and ill-treating prisoners, were left to the efficient automatons. The engineer did as he was told and produced a wrought-iron automaton with articulated limbs, as big as a bear standing on its hind legs. In its chest, behind a little shutter, he placed a loaded miniature cannon. But his real innovation was the little steam-powered engine he attached to its back. This made it autonomous, for it no longer depended on anyone to wind it up. Once the prototype was ready, it was tested in secret. The automaton was placed on a cart covered in a tarpaulin and taken to the village of Slough, home to the observatory that had belonged to William Herschel, the astronomer musician who many years earlier had added Uranus to the list of known planets. At intervals along the three-mile stretch between the village and the neighboring town of Windsor, scarecrows were placed with watermelons, cauliflowers, and cabbages for heads. Then they made the automaton walk along the road testing out its hidden weapon on the motionless vegetable men. The automaton reached its destination amid a swarm of flies attracted by the watermelon flesh splattered over its armor, but not a single puppet's head remained in its wake, suggesting that an army of these invincible creatures would cut through enemy lines like a knife through butter. The next step was to present it to the king as the decisive weapon with which to conquer the world, if he so wished.

However, owing to the monarch's many obligations, the unveiling was delayed, and for several weeks the automaton was kept in storage, a situation that would lead to disastrous consequences. For, during its prolonged isolation, the automaton not only came to life without anyone realizing it, but also developed something akin to a soul with desires, fears, and even firm convictions. So that by the time it was presented to the king, it had already reflected enough to know what it wanted from life. Or if it had any doubts, these were dispelled upon seeing the little man sprawled on his throne looking down his nose at it while continually straightening his crown. While the engineer paced back and forth, praising the attributes of the automaton and describing the different stages of its construction, the automaton made the little doors on its chest open up like those of a cuckoo clock. The monarch, tired of the engineer's exposition, perked up, eyes bright with curiosity, waiting for the nice birdie to pop out of the automaton's chest. But instead the shadow of death emerged in the form of a perfectly aimed bullet that made a hole right through the king's forehead, hurling him back on his throne. The accompanying sound of splintering bone interrupted the monologue of the engineer, who stood staring aghast at what his creation had done, until the automaton grabbed him by the throat and snapped his neck like a dry twig.

Having assured himself that the man draped over his arm was no more than a corpse, the automaton flung him to the ground coldly, pleased at the creativity his nascent mind had shown, at least in the art of killing. Once he was sure he was the only living thing left in the throne room, he approached the king with his arthropodal movements, relieved him of his crown, and placed it solemnly on his

own iron head. Then he studied his reflection—from the
front and side—in the wall mirrors, and since he was
unable to smile, he nodded. In this rather bloodthirsty
manner his life began, for although he was not made of
flesh and bone, there was no doubt in his mind that he
was also a living being. And in order to feel even more
alive what he needed next was a name; the name of a king.
After a few moments' reflection, he decided on Solomon.
The name was doubly pleasing to him as not only had
Solomon been a legendary king, but he was the first man
ever endowed with mechanical genius. According to the
Bible as well as some Arabic texts, Solomon's throne was
a magical piece of furniture that lent a theatrical air to
the king's displays of power. Perched at the top of a small
flight of steps, flanked by a pair of solid gold lions with
swishing tails, and shaded by palm trees and vines where
mechanical birds exhaled musky breath, the elaborate re-
volving chair raised the king aloft, rocking him gently in
mid-air as he pronounced his celebrated judgments. Once
suitably baptized, Solomon wondered what he should do
next, what goal to pursue. The ease and indifference with
which he had snuffed out the lives of those two humans
made him think he could do the same to a third, a fourth,
a fifth, to a whole choir of singing children if need be. He
sensed that the increasing number of victims would never
compel him to question the morality of taking a human
being's life, however dear it was to him or her. Those two
dead bodies were the first steps on a path of destruction,
but did he have to take it? Was it his destiny, or could
he choose a different path, employ his time in something

more edifying than slaughter? Solomon saw his doubt duplicated in the dozens of mirrors lining the throne room. Yet he liked this uncertainty, for it gave another interesting facet to the soul that had sprouted within his tin chest.

However, for all the doubts he harbored about his destiny, it was clear he must flee, disappear, leave there at once. And so Solomon slipped out of the palace unnoticed, and wandered through the forests, for how long he did not know. There he perfected his aim with the help of some squirrels, stopping from time to time in a cave or shack to disentangle the weeds from his leg joints or taking a break from his aimless meanderings to study the star-studded sky and see whether the fate of automatons as well as that of men was written there. In the meantime, news of his exploit spread like wildfire through the city, especially among the mechanical creatures, who gazed in reverential awe at the wanted posters of his face papered on the walls. Oblivious to all this, Solomon roamed the hills plagued with doubt, endlessly tormented about what his mission in life would be. Then one morning he emerged from the tumbledown shack where he had spent the night to find himself surrounded by dozens of automatons who broke into excited applause when they saw him, and he realized that others had taken it upon themselves to forge his destiny. The crowd of admirers included every kind of automaton, from rough factory workers to well-dressed nannies to dull office workers. Those in close contact with man, like butlers, cooks, and maids, had been carefully designed to look human, while those destined to work in factories or in the basements of government buildings surrounded by files were little more than metal scarecrows, and yet they all applauded him with equal fervor for having beheaded the king of the humans, while some even dared touch his steely armor, treating him like a long-awaited Messiah.

Moved and repelled in equal measure, Solomon decided to call them "the little ones." As they had come all that way to worship him, he invited them into his shack. Thus, the First Council of Automatons in the Free World was formed by chance, and during the course of it Solomon realized that the little ones' hearts were seething with hatred towards the human race. Apparently the insults man had inflicted on the automatons' dignity throughout history were as varied as they were unforgivable: the philosopher Albertus Magnus's automaton was ruthlessly destroyed by his disciple Saint Thomas Aquinas, who considered it the work of the devil; but far more flagrant was the case of the Frenchman René Descartes, who, in order to exorcise his grief over the death of his daughter Francine, had constructed a mechanical doll in her likeness. But the captain of a ship he was traveling on discovered it and immediately threw it overboard. The poignant image of the mechanical girl rusting among the coral enraged the little ones. Other equally dreadful cases kept alive the desire for revenge that had rankled for years in the hearts of these creatures, who now recognized in Solomon the brother who could finally carry it out. The fate of man was put to the vote, and with no abstentions and one vote against, the result was resoundingly in favor of extermination. In ancient Egypt the statues of the gods were equipped with mechanical arms operated from behind the scenes that spread terror among the acolytes. The time had come to follow the example of those gods and unleash the ancient terror upon humans once more. The time had come for them to repay their debts. Man's reign had come to an end. He was no longer the most powerful creature on the planet, if indeed he ever had been. The time of the automatons had come, and under the leadership of their new king they would conquer the planet. Solomon shrugged his shoulders. Why not, he thought, why not lead my people where they want to go? And he readily embraced his fate. In reality, on further consideration, this was not such a foolish venture, and was even achievable with a little organization. After all, the little ones were already strategically placed in the enemy camp, they had free access to every home, factory, and ministry, and could count on the element of surprise.

Just like someone leaving his body to science, Solomon allowed the builder automatons to see how he was made inside so they could begin producing an army of automaton soldiers in his image. They worked in secret, in sheds and abandoned factories while the little ones returned to their posts and patiently awaited their king's command to pounce on the enemy. When it finally came, the synchronized attack by the little ones was unbelievably brutal and devastating. The human population was decimated in the blink of an eye. That midnight like any other, mankind's dream ended abruptly and fatally as scissors plunged into throats, hammers crushed skulls, and pillows stifled the last gasps in a symphony of splintering bones and death rattles orchestrated by the grim reaper's baton. And while this panoply of sudden deaths was occurring in people's homes, factories blazed, plumes of black smoke spewing from their windows, and an army of automaton soldiers, led by Solomon, swarmed through the streets of the capital like a tidal wave of metal, meeting with little or no resistance, so that within minutes the invasion had become a calm procession. Early the next day, the total extermination of the human race began. It lasted a few decades, until all that was left of the world was a pile of rubble, where the few remaining humans, their numbers rapidly diminishing, cowered like frightened rats.

At nightfall, Solomon would look out over the balcony of his palace and cast a proud eye over the remains of the planet they had destroyed. He was a good king: he had done everything expected of him and he had done it well. He was irreproachable. The humans had been defeated, and it was only a matter of time before they became extinct. Suddenly, he realized that if this happened, if the humans were wiped off the face of the planet, there would be nothing to prove the automatons had conquered them to take control of it. They needed a specimen; a human specimen to continue embodying the enemy. A specimen of man, that creature who dreamed, aspired, yearned for immortality while wondering why he had been put on the earth. And so, taking Noah and his ark as his inspiration, Solomon ordered the capture of a pair of healthy young specimens from among the group of sorry survivors skulking in the ruins—a male and a female whose only function would be to procreate in captivity in order that the vanquished race, with its strange contradictory nature, would not die out.

Reduced to the status of mementoes, the chosen pair was kept in a cage of solid gold, generously fed and pampered, and above all encouraged to reproduce. Solomon told himself that keeping alive with his right hand the race that his left hand had destroyed was an intelligent thing to do. However, he did not know it yet, but he had chosen the wrong male. He was a proud, healthy youth who pretended to obey orders without protest, apparently grateful for having been spared certain death, but shrewd enough to know his luck would run out as soon as the girl he was compelled to live with had brought his successor into the world. Happily, this did not seem to worry him unduly, as he had at least nine months to achieve his goal, which was none other than to study his enemies from the comfort of his cage, observe their customs, learn their movements, and discover how to destroy them. And when he was not doing this, he was busy preparing his body for death. The day his concubine gave birth to a baby boy, he knew his time had come.

With astonishing calm, he allowed himself to be led to the place of execution. Solomon himself was going to shoot him. As he stood in front of the youth and opened the little doors in his chest so that the hidden cannon could take aim, the boy smiled at him and spoke for the first time:

"Go ahead and kill me, then I'll kill you."

Solomon tilted his head, wondering if the youth's words contained some hidden message he needed to decipher or were simply a meaningless phrase, and decided it did not matter either way. Without further ado, and feeling an almost jaded disgust, he fired at the insolent boy. The bullet hit him in the stomach, knocking him to the ground.

"I've killed you, now kill me," he challenged.

He waited a few moments, to see if the boy stirred, and when he did not, shrugged his shoulders and ordered his flunkies to get rid of the body before returning to their chores. The guards obeyed, carrying the body outside the palace, then threw it down a slope as if they were throwing away a piece of refuse. The body rolled down the hill and came to rest next to a pile of rubble, where it lay face up, covered in blood. A beautiful pale yellow full moon lit up the night sky. The youth smiled at it as though it were a death's head. He had succeeded in escaping from the palace, but the boy he had been when he entered it had been left behind. He had emerged from there a man with a clear destiny: to gather together the few survivors, organize them, and train them to fight the automatons. To achieve this he would only have to stop the bullet in his stomach from killing him, but that would be no problem. He knew that his will to live was stronger than the bullet's desire to kill him, stronger than the piece of metal embedded in his intestines. He had prepared for this moment during his captivity, preparing to endure the searing pain, to understand it, subdue and diminish it until he had worn down the bullet's patience. It was a long duel, a dramatic struggle that lasted three days and three moonlit nights all alone in the rubble, until finally the bullet surrendered.

It had realized it was not dealing with a body like that of the others; the youth's deep hatred of the automatons made him cling to life.

And yet his hatred was not a result of the automaton uprising, or the horrific murder of his parents and siblings, or the wanton destruction of the planet, nor even of Solomon's sickening indifference when he shot him. No, his hatred was rooted even further in the past. His was an old, unresolved hatred dating back centuries, to the time of his paternal great-grandfather, the first Shackleton to lose his life because of an automaton. You may have heard of the Turk, Mephisto, and other automaton chess players who were in fashion decades ago. Like them, Dr. Phibes was a mechanical doll who understood the secrets of chess as if he had invented the game himself. Dressed in an orange suit, a green bow tie, and a blue top hat, Dr. Phibes invited visitors to come into his fairground tent and challenge him to a game of chess for four shillings. The contemptuous manner in which he inflicted defeat on his male opponents and the chivalry with which he allowed the ladies to beat him made him into a celebrity, and people clamored to challenge him. His creator, the inventor Alan Tirell, boasted that his doll had even beaten the world chess champion, Mikhail Tchigorin.

However, Phibes's profitable appearances at traveling fairs ended abruptly when one opponent became incensed as the insolent doll trounced him in less than five moves and then, adding insult to injury, amicably offered him his wooden hand to shake. Seized with rage, the fellow rose from his seat, and before the fairground manager could stop him, pulled a revolver from his pocket and shot the doll straight through the chest, showering orange-colored splinters everywhere. The loud report alarmed the crowd, and the assailant managed to flee during the commotion before the manager had a chance to demand damages. Within minutes he found himself alone with Dr. Phibes, who was leaning slightly to one side in his seat. The manager was wondering how he would explain all this to Mr. Tirell, when he saw something that startled him. Dr. Phibes was wearing his usual smile, but a trickle of blood was oozing from the bullet hole in his chest. Horrified, the manager hurriedly pulled the curtain across and walked over to the automaton. After examining the doll with some trepidation, he discovered a small bolt on its left side. Drawing it back, he was able to open Dr. Phibes as if he were a sarcophagus. Inside, covered in blood and dead as a doornail, was the man with whom, unbeknownst to him, he had been working all these months. His name was Miles Shackleton: a miserable wretch who, having no other means of supporting his family, had accepted the trickery Tirell offered him after discovering his talent for chess.

When the inventor arrived at the tent and discovered the calamity, he refrained from informing the police about what had happened, fearing he would be arrested for fraud. He silenced the manager with a generous sum and simply reinforced Dr. Phibes with an iron plate to protect his new occupant from the wrath of future opponents. But Miles's substitute was nowhere near as skilled at chess as his predecessor, and Dr. Phibes's reputation began to wane before finally vanishing altogether, rather like Miles Shackleton, who quite simply disappeared off the face of the earth, more than likely buried in a ditch between fairgrounds. When at last his family learned from the fairground man what had become of him, they decided to honor him in the only way they could: by keeping his memory alive, relaying his sad tale through the generations, like a torch whose flame, more than a century later, lit up the pupils of the executed youth who, after lifting himself off the ground, glanced back at Solomon's palace with a look of silent hatred, and murmured to himself, although in reality he was speaking to History:

"Now it's my turn to kill you."

At first with faltering, then resolute steps, he disappeared into the ruins, determined to fulfill his destiny, which was none other than to become Captain Derek Shackleton, the man who would defeat the king of the automatons.

XX

ILLIAM MURRAY'S WORDS SLOWLY evaporated like a spell, leaving his listeners plunged into a profound silence. Casting her eyes quickly around the hall, Claire saw that the moving tale Murray had told—doubtless in the form of an allegory, perhaps to mitigate the crude reality of such frightful events—had succeeded in awakening the interest of the gathering, as well as creating a certain sympathy for Captain Shackleton and even for his enemy, Solomon, whom she suspected Murray had deliberately made more human. In any case, she could tell from Ferguson's, Lucy's, and even Charles Winslow's awed expressions that they were anxious to arrive in the future, to be part of these momentous events, if only as witnesses, and to see how Murray's story unraveled. Claire thought that she undoubtedly had a similar look on her face, although for quite different reasons, because what had really impressed her about the story was not so much the automaton conspiracy, the destruction of London, or the ruthless slaughter the dolls had perpetrated against her species, but

Shackleton's determination, his personality, his bravery. This man had built an army out of nothing and restored the world's hope, not to mention surviving his own death. How would a man like that love? she wondered.

After the welcoming speech, the group, led by Murray, headed off through a maze of galleries lined with clocks to the vast warehouse where the *Cronotilus* was awaiting them. An appreciative murmur rose from the crowd at the sight of the vehicle standing polished and ready. In reality, it differed in every way from an ordinary tram except in shape and size, because its numerous additions made it look more like a gypsy caravan. Its everyday appearance was buried beneath a riot of shiny chrome pipes studded with rivets and valves that ran along its sides like the tendons in a neck. The only part of the tram left exposed were two exquisitely carved mahogany doors. One of these was the entrance to the passenger compartment, the other, slightly narrower, led to the driver's cabin. Claire deduced this must be partitioned off from the rest of the vehicle since it had the only windows that were not blacked out. She felt relieved that at least the driver would be able to see where he was going. The porthole-shaped windows in their carriage were darkened, as Murray had said they would be.

No one would be able to see the fourth dimension, and similarly, the monsters that lived there would not glimpse their terrified faces, framed in the windows like cameo portraits. Attached to the front of the vehicle was a sort of battering ram like those on icebreakers, no doubt with the alarming function of ploughing through any obstacle in its path, clearing the way at all costs. At the rear a complicated-looking steam engine had been attached, bristling with rods, propellers, and cogwheels. This puffed and blew from time to time like some sea creature and let out a burst of steam that playfully lifted the ladies' skirts. However, what made it impossible for the vehicle to be described as a tram was undoubtedly the turret built on its roof, where at that very moment, having clambered up a small ladder bolted to the side, two gruff-looking fellows armed with various rifles and a box of ammunition were taking up their positions. Claire was amused to see there was also a periscope between the gun turret and the driver's cabin.

The driver, a gangling youth with an idiotic grin, opened the door of the passenger compartment and stood to attention beside it, next to the guide. Like a colonel inspecting his troops, Gilliam Murray walked slowly past the passengers, casting a severe but compassionate gaze over them. Claire watched him pause in front of a lady clutching a poodle.

"I'm afraid your little dog will have to stay behind, Mrs. Jacobs," he said, smiling affably at her.

"But I won't let go of Buffy for a moment," the woman demurred.

Gilliam shook his head kindly yet firmly, yanked the dog away from her with a swift gesture that was meant to be painless, like pulling a rotten tooth, and deposited it in the arms of one of his female assistants.

"Lisa, will you please see to it that Buffy is taken care of until Mrs. Jacobs's return?"

Having dealt with the dog, Murray resumed his inspection, ignoring Mrs. Jacobs's feeble protests. Grimacing theatrically, he stopped in front of two men both carrying suitcases.

"You won't be needing these either, gentlemen," he said, relieving them of their luggage.

He then asked everyone to place their timepieces on the tray Lisa had begun passing round, reaffirming that this would diminish the risk of being attacked by the monsters. When everything was finally to his liking, he planted himself in front of the group, smiling at them with almost tearful pride, like a marshal about to send his troops on a suicide mission.

"Well, ladies and gentlemen, I do hope you enjoy the year 2000. Remember what I said: obey Mr. Mazursky at all times. I shall await your return, champagne at the ready."

After this fatherly farewell, he stepped aside to make way for Mazursky, who politely asked them to climb on board the time tram.

The passengers formed a straggly line and filed excitedly into the luxurious vehicle. Lined with patterned cloth, the carriage contained two rows of wooden benches separated by a narrow aisle. Several candelabra screwed to the ceiling and walls cast a gloomy, flickering light which gave it the air of a chapel. Lucy and Claire sat on a bench approximately in the middle of the carriage, between Mr. Ferguson and his wife and two nervous-looking young dandies, whose parents, having sent them to Paris and Florence to expose them to art, were now shipping them off to the future in the hope of broadening their horizons. While the other passengers were taking their places, Ferguson, twisting his head round, began boring them with a series of insipid observations about the décor. Lucy listened politely, while Claire struggled to blot them out in order to be able to savor the importance of the moment.

When they all had settled, the guide closed the carriage door and sat facing them on a tiny chair, like an overseer on a galley ship. Almost at once, a violent jolt caused some of the passengers to cry out in alarm. Mazursky hurriedly put their minds at rest, explaining that this was simply the engine starting up. And, sure enough, the unpleasant juddering soon gave way to a gentle tremor, almost a purr, propelling the vehicle from the rear. Mazursky then looked through the periscope and smiled with calm satisfaction.

"Ladies and gentlemen, it is my pleasure to inform you that our journey to the future is underway. This very moment we are crossing the fourth dimension."

As if to confirm this, the vehicle suddenly began swaying from side to side, giving rise to further consternation among the passengers. The guide reassured them once more, apologizing for the state of the road and adding that despite their sustained efforts to keep the path clear, the terrain in the fourth dimension was naturally rough and dotted with bumps and crevices. Claire glanced at her face reflected in the darkened window, wondering what the landscape looked like behind the black paint blocking their view. However, she scarcely had time to wonder about anything else, for at that very moment, to the passengers' horror, they heard a loud roar outside, followed by a burst of gunfire and a heartrending bellow. Startled, Lucy clutched Claire's hand. This time Mazursky limited himself to smiling serenely at the passengers' alarmed faces, as if to say that the roars and gunfire would be a recurring feature of their journey, and the best thing they could do would be to ignore them.

"Well," he declared, rising from his seat and strolling down the aisle once everyone had recovered a little. "We shall soon be in the year 2000. Please pay attention while I explain what will happen when we arrive in the future. As Mr. Murray already mentioned, we will climb out of the tram, and I will take you to the promontory where we will watch the battle between humans and automatons. Although they can't see us from below, it is imperative you stay together and keep quiet so as not to give our position away, for there is no telling what effect it might have on the fabric of time, although I assume it would not be a positive one."

Further bellows came from outside, followed by the alarming shots, which Mazursky scarcely appeared to notice. He carried on slowly pacing between the benches, thumbs in his waistcoat pockets, a pensive crease on his brow, like a professor weary of repeating the same old lecture time and again.

"The battle will last approximately twenty minutes," he went on, "and will resemble a short three-act play: the evil Solomon will appear with his entourage and be ambushed by the brave Captain Shackleton and his men. A brief but thrilling skirmish will follow, and finally a duel between the automaton known as Solomon and Derek Shackleton, which as you already know will end in victory for the humans. Please refrain from applauding when the duel is over: this is not a music hall act, but a real event, which we are not even supposed to witness. Simply form a line and follow me back to the vehicle as quietly as possible. Then we will travel back across the fourth dimension and return home safe and sound. Is all that clear?"

The passengers nodded as one. Lucy pressed Claire's hand again and beamed at her, full of anticipation. Claire returned the smile, and yet her smile had nothing in common with her friend's; Claire's was a farewell gesture, her only way of telling Lucy she had been her best friend and she would never forget her, but that she must follow her destiny. It was a simple gesture containing a hidden message that would only be revealed with time. Like the kiss she had planted on her mother's loving cheek or on her father's wrinkled brow—an affectionate but far more solemn and lingering farewell than was appropriate before leaving for the Burnetts' country mansion, but which her parents had not noticed. Claire stared again at the blacked-out glass and wondered whether she was prepared for life in the world of the future, the devastated planet Gilliam Murray had described to them. She was gripped by a pang of fear, which she forced herself to suppress. She could not weaken now that she was so close, she must go ahead with her plan.

Just then, the tram came to a grinding halt. Mazursky

318 FÉLIX J. PALMA

took a long look through his periscope, until he was satisfied everything outside was as it should be. Then, with a
mysterious smile, he opened the carriage door. Screwing
up his eyes, he scanned the surrounding area one last time
before smiling at the passengers and announcing:

"Ladies and gentlemen, if you would kindly follow me
I will show you the year 2000."

XXI

WHILE HER FELLOW TRAVELERS clambered down from the tram without further ado, Claire paused on the running board, her right foot poised above the ground of the future, as solemn as when as a little girl she had ventured into the sea for the very first time. Aged six, she had stepped with infinite care, almost reverentially, into the waves that looked like the ocean losing its petals, as though this conscientiousness would determine the way in which the dark enormity of the water responded to her intrusion. In the same way she now ventured into the year in which she had decided to stay, hoping it would treat her with equal respect. As her heel touched the ground, she was surprised at how hard it felt, as though she had expected the future to be like a partially baked cake simply because it had not yet happened. However, a few steps sufficed to demonstrate this was not the case. The future was a solid place, and unquestionably real, although when she glanced up, she saw it was utterly devastated. Was that heap of rubble really London?

The tram had stopped in a clearing amid the remains of what had probably been a small square, the only reminders of which were a few charred, twisted trees. All the surrounding houses had been destroyed. Only the odd wall remained intact—still papered and incongruously adorned with an occasional picture or lamp fitting—the remnants of a broken staircase, elegant railings now enclosing nothing more than piles of rubble. Dotted along the pavement were grim mounds of ash, probably the remains of fires built by humans out of sticks of furniture to ward off the cold night air. Claire could see no clue in the surrounding ruins as to what part of London they were in, not least because, despite being midday, it was very dark. A gloomy light filtered down from the sky, veiled by grayish clouds of smoke billowing from dozens of fires, their flames flickering like votive candles between the gaping ruins, obscuring the outlines of that shattered world—a world seemingly abandoned to its fate, like a ship stricken with malaria condemned to drift on the ocean until the weight of time finally brings it to rest on a coral reef.

When Mazursky considered sufficient time had passed for the passengers to fully appreciate the depressing face of the future, he asked them to form a group, and with him leading the way and one of the marksmen bringing up the rear, they headed off. The time travelers marched out of the square and into an avenue where the devastation struck them as even greater, for there was scarcely anything left standing to suggest that the piles of rubble had once been buildings. The avenue had no doubt once been lined with luxurious town houses, but the prolonged war had turned London into an enormous refuse heap. Magnificent churches had become indistinguishable from foul-smelling boardinghouses in the jumbled mass of bricks and masonry, where occasionally the horrified Claire thought she could make out a skull. Mazursky led the group through mounds that resembled funeral pyres, busily picked over by scavenging crows. The noise of the procession startled the birds, which flew off in all directions, darkening the sky still further. After they had vanished, one remained circling above their heads, tracing a mournful message in the sky with its flight, like the Creator regretfully signing over the patent for His beleaguered invention to someone else.

Mazursky strode ahead, oblivious to such details, choosing the easiest pathways, or perhaps those with fewer bones. He occasionally stopped to chide someone, invariably Ferguson, who was joking about the pervading stench of rotting flesh (or anything else that happened to catch his attention), wringing an occasional titter out of the ladies strolling beside him on their husbands' arms, as though they were strolling through the botanical gardens at Kew. As they ventured deeper into the ruins, Claire began to worry about how she would separate from the group without anyone noticing. It would be difficult with Mazursky in the lead, listening out for any suspicious sounds, and the marksman at the rear, pointing his rifle into the gloom, but when the excited Lucy suddenly gripped her arm, the possibility of escape felt even more remote.

After walking for about ten minutes, during which Claire began to suspect they were going round in circles, they reached the promontory—a mound of debris a little taller than the others. Climbing it did not look a difficult task, as the rubble appeared to form a makeshift flight of steps up to the top. At Mazursky's command, they began the ascent, giggling and losing their footing, a band of merrymakers on a country outing, whom the guide, having concluded it was impossible, no longer bothered to try to silence. Only when they reached the top of the mound did he order them to be quiet and crouch behind the outcrop of rocks that formed a parapet at the summit. When they had done this, the guide walked along, pushing down any protruding heads and telling the ladies to close their parasols unless they wanted the automatons to notice a sudden flowering of sunshades on the crest of the hill. Flanked by Lucy and the exasperating Ferguson, Claire gazed from behind her rock at the deserted street below. It was strewn with rubble just like the ones they had walked through to get to the makeshift viewpoint where the battle was supposed to take place.

"Allow me to ask you a question, Mr. Mazursky," she heard Ferguson say.

The guide, who, together with the marksman was squatting a few yards to his left, turned to peer at him.

"What is it, Mr. Ferguson?" he sighed.

"Given that we've turned up in the future in time to witness the battle that will decide the fate of the planet just like the first expedition, how come we haven't bumped into them?"

Ferguson looked round for the others to back him up. Thinking over what he had said, a few of the passengers slowly nodded, and looked askance at their guide, waiting for an explanation. Mazursky studied Ferguson for a moment in silence, as though considering whether this impudent man deserved a reply.

"Of course, Mr. Ferguson. You're absolutely right," he finally declared. "And not only would we run into the first expedition, but the third and the fourth and all the other future expeditions, don't you think? That's why I take each expedition to a different place, not simply to avoid jams, but so that Terry and I"—here he broke off and gestured to the marksman, who gave a timid wave—"are not constantly bumping into ourselves. If you really must know, at this very moment the first expedition is crouched behind that mound over there."

Everyone's eyes followed Mazursky's finger as he pointed to one of the neighboring hillocks from which the battleground of the future was also visible.

"I see," muttered Ferguson. Then his face lit up and he cried out: "In that case, I could go and say hello to my friend Fletcher!"

"I'm afraid I can't allow that, Mr. Ferguson."

"Why not?" the other man protested. "The battle hasn't even started yet. I'll be back in no time."

Mazursky let out a sigh of despair.

"I've told you I can't allow you to . . ."

"But it'll only take a moment, Mr. Mazursky," pleaded Ferguson. "Mr. Fletcher and I have known each other since—"

"Answer me one thing, Mr. Ferguson," Charles Winslow interrupted him.

Ferguson turned towards him, his hackles up.

"When your friend described his trip to you, did he by any chance tell you that you had appeared out of nowhere to say hello?"

"No," replied Ferguson.

Charles smiled.

"In that case, stay where you are. You never went to greet your friend, Mr. Fletcher, consequently you can't go now. As you yourself said: fate is fate, it can't be altered."

Ferguson opened his mouth, but no words came out.

"Now, if you don't mind," Charles added, turning to face the street, "I think we'd all like to witness the battle in silence."

Claire observed with relief that this shut Ferguson up once and for all. The others ignored him, too, concentrating their gaze on the street. Claire then looked at Lucy, hoping to exchange knowing glances with her friend, but apparently, she was already bored with the whole thing: she had picked up a twig and was scratching a kiwi bird in the sand with it. On her right, Inspector Garrett watched Lucy draw, an awed expression on his face, as though he were witnessing a small miracle.

"Did you know kiwis only exist in New Zealand, Miss Nelson?" the young man asked, after clearing his throat.

Lucy looked at the inspector, astonished that he, too, should know about this bird, and Claire could not help grinning. Where if not between two kiwi lovers could a stronger love blossom?

Just then, a clank of metal, scarcely audible in the distance, startled the group. Everyone, including Ferguson, fixed their gaze expectantly on the end of the street, terrified by the sinister noise that could only herald the arrival of the evil automatons.

THEY SOON EMERGED, MOVING slowly through the ruins as though they were the lords of the planet. They looked identical to the statue back in the big hall: huge, angular, and threatening, with tiny engines on their backs that let out occasional plumes of steam. Much to everyone's surprise, they were carrying their king aloft on a throne, as in days of yore. Claire sighed, regretting being so far from the scene.

"Take these, my dear," Ferguson said, handing her his opera glasses. "You seem more interested than I am."

Claire thanked him and hurriedly studied the group through Ferguson's glasses. She counted eight automatons altogether: the four bearers, plus two more at the front and rear, escorting the throne upon which sat the inscrutable Solomon, ferocious king of the automatons, distinguishable from his replicas only by the crown perched on his iron head. The procession moved forward with excruciating slowness, lurching ridiculously from side to side like toddlers taking their first steps. And in fact, Claire reflected, the automatons had indeed learned to walk by conquering the world. Humans were undoubtedly quicker, but clearly far more fragile than these creatures, who had slowly but surely taken over the planet, perhaps because they had the whole of eternity to do so.

Then, when the cortege was halfway down the street,

they heard a loud report. Solomon's crown flew into the air. Everyone gazed in astonishment as the glittering object spun round several times, before falling to the ground and rolling over the rubble until it came to a halt a few yards away. Recovering from their surprise, Solomon and his guards raised their eyes to the top of a small rocky crag blocking their way. The time travelers followed their gaze. Then they saw him. Standing in an almost identical pose to the statue in the hall was the brave Captain Shackleton, feline and imposing, his sinewy body swathed in shining armor, his deadly sword hanging indolently from his belt, and an ornate-looking gun bristling with levers and pieces of metal dormant in his powerful hands. The leader of the humans had no need of a crown to bestow splendor on an already majestic physique, which, unbeknownst to him, elevated the outcrop he was perched on to the status of pedestal. He and Solomon looked each other up and down in silence for a few moments, their deep-seated hostility making the air crackle with electricity as if in the lead-up to a storm, then the king of the automatons began to speak:

"I've always admired your courage, Captain," he said in his tinny voice, which he tried to imbue with a casual, almost playful tone, "but this time I think you've overestimated your chances. How could it occur to you to attack me without your army? Are you really that desperate, or have your men abandoned you?"

Captain Shackleton shook his head slowly, as though disappointed by his enemy's words.

"The one positive thing about this war," he said with quiet assurance, "is the way it has united the human race as never before."

Shackleton's voice was soft and clear, and reminded Claire of the way some stage actors delivered their lines. Solomon tilted his head to one side, wondering what his enemy meant. He did not have to wait long to find out. The captain slowly raised his left hand, like someone calling down a falcon, and various shadows emerged from beneath the rubble, like plants sprouting from the sick earth, debris and stones scattering off them as they stood up. In a matter of seconds, the unsuspecting automatons found themselves surrounded by Shackleton's men. Claire could feel her heart start to race. The humans had been hiding in the ruins all along, waiting, knowing Solomon would take that path. The king of the automatons had walked straight into the trap that would end his reign. The soldiers, whose actions seemed speeded up compared to those of the lumbering automatons, retrieved their rifles from the sand, dusted them off, and took aim at their respective targets with the calm solemnity of someone performing a liturgy. The problem was there were only four of them. Claire was shocked that Shackleton's famous army should be reduced to such a paltry number. Perhaps no one else had volunteered to take part in the suicidal attack, or perhaps by this stage of the war, the frequent daily skirmishes had reduced Shackleton's troops to the point where these were indeed the only men left. At least they had the advantage of surprise, she thought, impressed by their tactical positioning: two soldiers had appeared out of nowhere in front of the procession, another to the left of the throne and a fourth had popped up at the rear.

The four opened fire as one.

Of the two automatons leading the cortege, one took a direct hit in the chest. Despite being made of iron, his armor ripped open, and he spurted a cascade of cogs and rods onto the ground before falling over with a loud crash. The other one was luckier, as the bullet aimed at disabling him only grazed his shoulder, barely causing him to totter. The soldier who had appeared behind the procession was cleverer. His bullet shattered the little steam engine on the back of one of the guards bringing up the rear, who keeled over backwards. A moment later, one of the throne bearers suffered the same fate, felled by a volley of bullets fired by the soldier who had appeared at the side. Losing one of its supports, the throne keeled over dangerously before finally sinking to the ground, bringing the mighty Solomon down with it.

Things seemed to be going splendidly for the humans, but once the automatons had managed to regroup, the situation changed. The automaton next to the one that had toppled over backwards snatched the weapon of his attacker and smashed it to smithereens. At the same time, no longer encumbered by the throne, one of the bearers opened the little doors in his chest and fired a direct hit at one of the two soldiers attacking from the front. His fall distracted his comrade, a fatal error which gave the nearest automaton, whose shoulder had only been grazed by a bullet, time to charge him and deliver a direct blow with his fist. The punch threw the soldier up into the air; he landed a few yards away. Pantherlike, Shackleton leapt from his rock, and bounded over to them, downing the automaton with a well-aimed bullet before he was able to finish off his companion. The two remaining soldiers, one now unarmed, stepped back from the fray, and fell in beside their captain, while the four surviving automatons closed ranks around their king. Although Claire knew nothing about military strategy, you did not need to be a genius to see that once the humans had used the advantage of a surprise, which had perhaps blinded them with the illusion of an easy victory, the automatons' superior strength had turned the battle around with humiliating ease. Outnumbered as they were, it seemed logical to Claire that Shackleton, whose duty as a good captain was to protect his men, would order a retreat. However, the future had already been written, and so she was not surprised when she heard Solomon's voice intervene to stop them as they were preparing to flee.

"Wait, Captain," he declared, in his tinny voice. "Go, if you want, and plan another ambush. Perhaps you will be more successful next time, but I fear you will only prolong a war that has already gone on far too long. But you could also stay and end it once and for all, here and now."

Shackleton looked at him suspiciously.

"If you allow me, I'd like to make you a proposition, Captain," Solomon went on, while his guard broke ranks, opening up like a metal cocoon at the center of which stood their king. "I propose we fight a duel."

One of the automatons had rescued a wooden box from

the toppled throne, which he now presented to Solomon. The automaton ceremoniously pulled out a magnificent iron sword, the tip of whose blade glinted in the faint light from the sky.

"As you see, Captain, I had a broadsword identical to yours made so that we could fight with the same weapon humans have been using for centuries. I've been practicing these last few months, waiting for the moment when I would be able to challenge you." (To show he was not joking, he sliced through the air with a two-handed thrust.) "Unlike the ignoble pistol, the sword requires skill, deftness, and a knowledge of your enemy, which makes me think that if I succeed in piercing your entrails with its razor-sharp blade, you will acknowledge my expertise and consent to die."

Captain Shackleton mulled over Solomon's proposal for a few moments, looking wearier and more disgusted than ever by the war of attrition. Now he had his chance to end it all by placing all his bets on a single card.

"I accept your challenge, Solomon. Let's decide the outcome of this war here and now," he replied.

"So be it," Solomon declared gravely, scarcely able to contain his joy.

The automatons and human soldiers stepped back a few paces, forming a circle around the duelists. The third and final act was about to begin. Shackleton unsheathed his sword with a graceful movement and made several feints in the air, aware perhaps that he might never again perform the gesture. After this brief demonstration, he coolly studied Solomon, who was desperately trying to strike a gallant swordsman's pose, but was hindered by his rigid limbs.

Circling the automaton slowly and nimbly, like a wild animal stalking its prey, Shackleton tried to work out where to strike first, while Solomon simply watched his assailant, sword clumsily raised. Naturally, he had given his rival the honor of commencing the duel. With a swift, agile movement, Shackleton traced an arc in the air with his sword, which came crashing down on Solomon's left side. But the two-handed blow only produced a loud metallic clang, like a pealing bell, that hung in the air for a few moments. Following the pathetic outcome of his first strike, Captain Shackleton stepped back a few paces, visibly dismayed: the brutal blow had scarcely made Solomon teeter, while it had almost snapped his wrists. As though seeking to confirm his weak position, Shackleton struck again, this time aiming for the automaton's right side. The result was the same, but this time he could not afford to brood over it, as he had to avoid Solomon's counterattack. After dodging the tip of his sword, which sliced through the air almost grazing his helmet, Shackleton once more put a distance between them, and, momentarily safe from attack, studied his enemy again, shaking his head slowly in a gesture that betrayed his despair.

Solomon's blows were slow and thus easy to evade, but the captain was aware that if one of them struck home, his armor would not offer the same protection. He had to discover his opponent's weak point as quickly as possible. Continuing to aim two-handed blows at the automaton's ironclad armor would only make his arms grow stiff, and the momentous effort would end up exhausting him, slowing him down, and making him careless: leaving him, in short, at the automaton's mercy. Making the most of still feeling fresh, Shackleton dodged another blow and ended up this time behind his enemy's back. Before Solomon had time to turn around, he thrust his sword as hard as he could into the steam engine that gave the automaton life. There was a great clatter as cogs and rods flew out of the opening in all directions, but also an unexpected burst of steam that hit Shackleton full in the face, blinding him. Solomon wheeled round with astonishing agility and landed a blow on his dazed enemy. The sword struck the captain's side with such force that it shattered his metal armor. The brutal blow sent Shackleton spinning across the floor like a top.

Claire raised her hand to her mouth to stop herself from screaming. She heard the stifled cries of the others around her. Once he had stopped spinning, Shackleton tried to get to his feet, clutching his wounded side, with blood streaming over his hip and down his leg, but his strength failed him. He remained on his knees, as though prostrating himself before the king of the automatons, who approached him slowly, savoring his sure victory. Solomon shook his head for a few moments, showing his disappointment at the poor fight put up by his opponent, who dared not even raise his head to look at him. Then he lifted his sword with both hands, preparing to bring it down on the captain's helmet and split his skull asunder. He could think of no better way to end this cruel war, which had established without a doubt the automatons' supremacy over the human race. He brought the sword down on his victim with all his might, but to his astonishment, Captain Shackleton leapt out of the way at the very last moment. Robbed of its target, the automaton's sword embedded itself in the stony ground with a loud clang. Tugging in vain, Solomon tried to pull it out, while Shackleton rose up beside him like a majestic cobra, oblivious to the wound in his side. Slowly, as though taking pleasure from the movement, he raised his sword, and brought it down, with one swift surgical blow, on the joint between Solomon's head and his body. There was an almighty crunch, and the automaton's head rolled across the floor, giving out a series of clangs as it bounced against the rocks before finally coming to a halt next to the crown it had worn during its reign. There was a sudden silence. The headless, motionless automaton stood in a grotesque posture, bowed over the sword, whose blade was still embedded in the rubble. As a final gesture, the brave Captain Shackleton placed his foot on his lifeless enemy's flank and tipped him over onto the ground. And this deafening sound, like scrap metal being loaded onto a cart, put an end to the long war that had devastated the planet.

XXII

MAZURSKY TRIED IN VAIN TO SI-
lence the applause unleashed by Captain
Shackleton's victory at the top of the rocky promontory.
Fortunately, it was drowned out by the cheers down in the
street a few yards below, where the men were fervently
acclaiming their brave captain. Oblivious to the surrounding clamor, Claire remained crouched behind her rock. She
was bemused by the overwhelming storm of emotions that
caused her soul to flutter like a flag in the breeze. She had
known how the duel would end, and yet she had been unable to avoid jumping each time Shackleton was in danger,
each time Solomon's blade greedily sought out his flesh, or
when he attempted in vain to chop the automaton down
with his sword, as one fells an oak. She knew this was not
so much because she feared the human race might lose
the duel, but because of what might happen to the captain himself. She longed to carry on watching events down
below, even to make sure Shackleton had exaggerated the
severity of the wound inflicted on him by the automaton
as part of his strategy, but Mazursky had ordered them to

line up before beginning the return journey to their own time, and she had no choice but to obey. The time travelers began their descent of the tiny hillock like an unruly herd of goats, discussing among themselves the exciting highlights of the battle.

"Is that all?" asked Ferguson, apparently the only dissatisfied passenger. "That poor excuse for a battle is what decided the fate of the planet?"

Mazursky did not even deign to reply, taken up as he was with making sure the matrons did not trip over and end up rolling down the slope with their skirts flying up with unintentional coquettishness. Claire followed them in silence, ignoring both the insufferable Ferguson's comments and Lucy, who had taken her arm again. One thought hammered persistently in her mind: she had to separate from the group. And she had to do it now, not only because it would no longer be possible once they reached the tram, but because the group was in such high spirits they had still not managed to form an orderly column, and this would facilitate her escape. Furthermore, she must not stray too far from Shackleton and his men: it would be pointless to get away only to become lost in a maze of ruins. If she was going to act, the time to do it was now, for the further they went the less chance she had. But she must break away from Lucy first.

As though in answer to her prayers, Madeleine Winslow came up to them excitedly, to ask whether they had seen the elegant boots the soldiers were wearing. This was something Claire would never have taken into account, although she seemed to be the only person not to have noticed this important aspect of the future. Lucy said she had and immediately went on to discuss the amazing originality of the footwear. Claire shook her head in disbelief, and when Lucy let go of her arm for a moment took the opportunity to lag behind. She dropped behind the marksman, who had not yet received the order to take up the rear, and was strolling along leisurely, no longer bothering to keep an eye on the shadows. Behind him came Charles Winslow and Inspector Garrett, immersed in a lively conversation while they walked. Finally, when she found herself at the back of the group, she hitched up her skirts and made a clumsy dash for it, ducking behind a conveniently placed remnant of wall.

Claire Haggerty stood still, her back against the wall, her heart pounding wildly, listening to the murmur of the group growing fainter and fainter, without anyone apparently having noticed she was missing. When at last they were out of earshot, dry-throated, parasol clasped firmly between her sweaty palms, she poked her head out cautiously and saw that the procession had disappeared round a bend. She could not believe it. She had done it! At once she felt a rush of panic as it dawned on her she was alone in this dreadful place, but she quickly told herself this was what she had wanted. Events were unfolding exactly as she had planned when she climbed aboard the *Cronotilus*. Unless something went horribly wrong, she was going to be able to stay behind in the year 2000. Wasn't this what she had wished for? She drew a deep breath and stepped out from behind the wall. All being well, they would only discover her absence when they reached the time tram, but even so, she must hurry up and join Shackleton and his men before the guide found out. After that, there would be nothing Mazursky could do, and she would be safe. As he had told them himself during the journey, they were in the year 2000 as simple spectators: they must not let themselves be seen by people from the future, still less make contact with them. Finding the captain, then, was her primary objective. Claire marched off in the opposite direction to her companions, trying not to think of the consequences her unexpected act might have on the fabric of time. She only hoped she would not destroy the universe in her bid to be happy.

Now that she found herself alone, the surrounding devastation seemed even more disturbing. What if she could not find Shackleton? she wondered anxiously. And what if the captain snubbed her, refusing to admit her into his ranks? She could not believe that a true gentleman would abandon a woman to her fate in that terrible world. Besides, she had some knowledge of first aid, which might prove useful, judging from how easy it was to get wounded there, and she was courageous and hardworking enough to be able to help them rebuild the world. And, of course, she was in love with him, though she preferred not to let that show until she was completely sure. In the meantime, it was simply a notion, as outrageous as it was exhilarating. She shook her head. She had to admit she had not given enough thought to what she would do when she met the captain, because she did not really believe her escape plan would work. She would just have to improvise, she told herself, as she walked round the promontory before hiking up her skirts in readiness to climb down the steep path, which if her sense of direction had not failed her, would lead to the street where the ambush had taken place.

She paused when she heard footsteps coming up the path towards her. They were unmistakably human, but Claire followed her instinct and leapt behind the nearest rock. She waited in silence, her heart beating furiously in her chest. The owner of the footsteps stopped near to where she was hiding. Claire was afraid he had seen her and would order her to come out with her hands up, or still worse, that he would point his gun at the rock and wait for her to make the first move. But instead of that, the stranger began singing: "Jack the Ripper's dead / And lying on his bed / He cut his throat / With Sunlight Soap / Jack the Ripper's dead." Claire raised her eyebrows. She knew that song. Her father had learned it from East End kids and used to sing it softly to himself as he shaved before going to church, which is why Claire suddenly imagined herself immersed in the aroma of the newfangled lathered soap made from pine oil rather than animal fat. She wished she could travel back to her own time simply to tell her father that the song which had so tickled him had survived over the years. Except that she would never go back, come what may. She tried not to think of this, but to concentrate on the present moment, the moment that would mark the start of her new life. The stranger carried on singing with even greater gusto. Had he come to that secluded place simply to try out his voice? she wondered. Whatever the case, it was time she made contact with the inhabitants of the year 2000. She gritted her teeth, plucked up all her courage, and stepped out of her hiding place, ready to introduce herself to the stranger who was so casually destroying one of her favorite songs.

Claire Haggerty and the brave Captain Shackleton stared at each other in silence, each reflecting the other's surprise, like two facing mirrors. The captain had removed his helmet, which was resting on a nearby stone, and Claire did not need to look twice to realize that the reason why he had strayed from the others was not in order to practice his singing, but to perform a far less noble act, to which the ditty he was singing was a simple adjunct. She could not prevent her jaw from dropping in surprise, and her fingers let go of the parasol, which made a crunching sound like a shell breaking as it hit the ground. After all, this was the first time her delicate eyes had glimpsed the part of a man she was apparently not meant to see until the day her marriage was consummated, and even then probably not quite in such a plain and naked fashion. She saw that as soon as he got over his surprise, Captain Shackleton hastened to tuck away this unseemly part of his anatomy beneath the folds of his armor. Then he stared at her again without a word, his embarrassment giving way increasingly to curiosity.

Claire had not had time to speculate about other details, but Captain Derek Shackleton's face was certainly as she had imagined it would be. Either the Creator had fashioned it according to her precise instructions, or the ape this man was descended from had a superior pedigree. But for whatever reason, Captain Shackleton's face unquestionably belonged to a different era. He had the same graceful chin as the statue and the same serene expression around his mouth, and his eyes, now that she could see them, were in perfect harmony with the rest of his features. Those beautiful, big, gray-green eyes, like a forest immersed in mist where all who ventured were destined to be lost, set the world alight with a gaze so intense, so profound that Claire realized she was in the presence of the most alive man she had ever seen. Yes, beneath that armor plate, that bronzed skin, those sculpted muscles, was a heart that beat with extraordinary force, pumping through its network of veins a stubborn impulsive life that death itself had been unable to conquer.

"I'm Claire Haggerty, Captain," she introduced herself, trying to stop her voice from quaking, "and I've come from the nineteenth century to help you rebuild the world."

Captain Shackleton went on staring at her, ashen-faced, through eyes that had seen the destruction of London, raging fires, and piles of dead bodies, eyes that had seen the most atrocious side of life but had no idea how to cope with this delicate, exquisite creature in front of him.

"There you are, Miss Haggerty!" she heard someone cry out behind her.

Taken aback, Claire wheeled round and saw the guide coming down the steep path towards her. Mazursky was shaking his head disapprovingly but was clearly relieved to have found her.

"I thought I told you all to stay together!" he cried shrilly, as he walked up to her and seized her roughly by the arm. "You could have stayed behind forever!"

Claire turned towards Shackleton to implore his aid,

but to her astonishment the captain had gone, vanished as though he had been nothing but a figment of her imagination. Indeed, his departure had been so abrupt that as Mazursky dragged her towards where the others were waiting for them, Claire wondered in all seriousness whether she had really seen him or if he had been a product of her inflamed imagination. They rejoined the group, and before heading back to the *Cronotilus*, the guide made them get in a line with the marksman at the rear and, visibly irritated, ordered them not to wander off again.

"It's a good thing I noticed you were missing," Lucy told her, taking Claire's arm. "Were you dreadfully afraid?"

Claire sighed and let herself be guided by Lucy like a convalescent patient, unable to think of anything except Captain Shackleton's gentle eyes. But had he looked at her with love? His speechlessness and bewilderment were definite symptoms of infatuation and suggested that he had. In any era his gaze was the typical sign of being smitten. But even if it were true, what good was it to her if Captain Shackleton had fallen in love with her since she was never going to see him again, she thought, as she passively let herself be helped onto the time tram, as if she had no will of her own. Dejected, she leaned back in her seat, and when she felt the violent judder of the steam engine starting up, she had to stop herself from dissolving into a puddle of tears. As the vehicle shunted through the fourth dimension, Claire wondered how she would endure having to go back and live in her own boring time, forever, especially now she was sure that the only man with whom she could be happy would be born long after she was dead.

"We're on our way home, ladies and gentlemen," announced Mazursky, unable to conceal his contentment at nearing the end of that eventful journey.

Claire looked at him with annoyance. Yes, they were on their way home, home to the dreary nineteenth century, and they had not jeopardized the fabric of time. Of course Mazursky was pleased; he had prevented a silly young girl from destroying the universe and avoided the telling-off he would have received from Gilliam Murray had he failed. What did it matter if the price had been her happiness? Claire was so infuriated she could have slapped the guide there and then, even though in the end she realized that Mazursky had only been doing his duty. The universe was more important than the fate of any one person, even if she was that person. She gritted her teeth, trying to curb her irritation at the guide's beaming face. Fortunately, part of her rage evaporated when she looked down and saw that her hands were empty. Mazursky had not done such a perfect job after all, though she wondered how far a mere parasol could affect the fabric of time.

XXIII

WHEN THE GIRL AND THE GUIDE vanished along the steep path, Captain Derek Shackleton left his hiding place and paused for a few moments looking at where the woman had been standing, as though expecting to discover a trace of her perfume or her voice lingering in the empty space, some sign of her presence that would prove she had not been a figment of his imagination. He was still reeling from the meeting. He could scarcely believe it had really happened. He remembered the girl's name: "I'm Claire Haggerty, Captain, and I've come from the nineteenth century to help you rebuild the world," she had said, with a charming curtsy. But her name was not the only thing he remembered. He was surprised at how clearly the image of her face was etched in his mind. He could conjure clear as day her pale visage, her slightly wild-looking features, her smooth, shapely mouth, her jet-black hair, her graceful bearing, her voice. And he remembered the look in her eyes. Above all, he remembered the way she had gazed at him, enraptured, almost in awe, with mesmerized joy. No woman had ever looked at him like that before.

Then he noticed the parasol, and he flushed with shame once more as he remembered the reason for the girl dropping it. He went over and carefully picked it up off the ground, as though it were an iron bird fallen from some metallic nest. It was a dainty, elegant parasol that betrayed the moneyed status of its owner. What was he supposed to do with it? One thing was clear; he could not leave it there.

Parasol in hand, he set off to where the others were waiting for him, taking the opportunity to collect himself as he walked. To avoid arousing their suspicions, he must hide his agitation at the encounter with the girl. Just then, Solomon leapt from behind a rock, brandishing his sword. Although he had been daydreaming, the brave Captain Shackleton reacted in a flash, striking the automaton with the parasol as it leapt on him, baying for his blood in his booming metallic voice. The blow glanced off Solomon, but it took him by surprise, and he teetered for a few seconds before toppling backwards down a small incline. Clutching the by now rather dented parasol, Shackleton watched his enemy rattling down the hill. The clattering sound came to an abrupt halt as the automaton hit a pile of rocks. For a few moments, Solomon lay stretched out on his back covered in a thick layer of dust thrown up by his fall. Then he tried laboriously to pick himself up, cursing and hurling insults, which the metallic timbre of his voice made sound even more vulgar. Loud guffaws rang out from the group of soldiers and automatons who were looking on.

"Stop laughing, you swine, I could have broken something!" groaned Solomon, amid further guffaws.

"It serves you right for playing pranks," Shackleton chided him, walking down the incline and offering Solomon a helping hand. "Won't you ever tire of your silly ambushes?"

"You were taking too long, my friend," the automaton complained, allowing Shackleton and two others to pull him to his feet. "What the hell were you doing up there anyway?"

"I was urinating," the captain replied. "By the way, congratulations, that was a great duel. I think we did it better than ever before."

"True," one of the soldiers agreed. "You were both superb. I don't think you performed so well even for Her Majesty."

"Good. The fact is, it's much easier to perform when you know the Queen of England isn't watching you. In any case, it's exhausting running around in this armor," said Solomon, unscrewing his head.

After managing to free himself, he gulped air like a fish. His red hair was stuck to his head, his broad face covered in beads of sweat.

"Stop complaining, Martin," said the automaton with the gash in his chest, who was also removing his head. "At least you've got one of the main roles. I don't even have time to finish off a soldier before I kick the bucket. And on top of that I have to blow myself up."

"You know it's harmless, Mike. But if you insist, we can ask Murray if we can switch some of the roles round next time," suggested the young man who played the part of Captain Shackleton, in an attempt to keep tempers from fraying.

"Yes, Tom. I can play Jeff's role, and he can play mine," agreed the man playing the first automaton to fall, pointing to the soldier whose task it was to slay him.

"Not on your life, Mike. I've been waiting all week to be able to shoot you. Anyway, after that Bradley kills me," said Jeff, pointing in turn to the lad concealed inside one of the throne- bearing automatons, who had an S-shaped scar on his left cheek reaching almost up to his eye.

"What's that?" he asked, referring to what was in Tom's hand.

"This? A parasol," Tom replied, holding it up to show the group. "One of the passengers must have left it behind."

Jeff whistled in amazement.

"It must have cost a fortune," he said, scrutinizing it with interest. "A lot more than what we get for doing this, for sure."

"Believe me, Jeff, we're better off working for Murray than down a mine, or breaking our backs on the Manchester Ship Canal," said Martin.

"Oh, now I feel a lot better!" the other man retorted.

"Are we going to stay here all day prattling?" asked Tom, slyly concealing the parasol once more, in the hope the others would forget it. "Let me remind you that the present awaits us outside."

"You're right, Tom." Jeff laughed. "Let's get back to our own time!"

"Only without having to cross the fourth dimension!" echoed Martin, roaring with laughter.

The fifteen men made their way through the ruins, walking almost as if in a procession out of respect for those wearing the automatons' heavy garb. As they advanced, Jeff noticed a little uneasily how absentminded Captain Shackleton looked. (From now on, as I no longer have to keep any secrets, I will refer to him by his real name, Tom Blunt.)

"I still don't understand how people are taken in by this fake rubble," Jeff remarked, trying to draw his friend out of his brooding silence.

"Remember, they're seeing it from the other side," Tom responded distractedly.

Jeff feigned a look of noncomprehension, determined to keep him talking so that he would forget whatever it was that was bothering him.

"It's like when we go to see a conjuror," Tom felt obliged to add, although he had never seen one himself. The closest he had come to the world of magic had been when he lodged in the same boardinghouse as an amateur magician. Perhaps that is what gave him the authority to go on: "Conjuring tricks dazzle us, they even make us think magic might exist, but if we only saw how they did it, we'd ask ourselves how we could have been so easily fooled. None of the passengers see through Mr. Murray's trickery," he said, pointing with the parasol at the machine they were walking past, which was responsible for producing enough smoke to hide the roof and beams of the vast shed that housed the set. "In fact, they're not even suspicious. They only see the end result. They see what they want to see. You'd also believe this pile of ruins was London in the year 2000 if what you wanted was to see London in the year 2000."

Exactly as Claire Haggerty had believed, he thought with bitter regret, remembering how the girl had offered to help him rebuild the world.

"Yes, you must admit, the boss has organized it brilliantly," his companion finally acknowledged, following the flight of a crow with his eyes. "If people found out this was only a set, he'd end up in jail: if they didn't string him up first."

"That's why it's so important no one sees our faces, right, Tom?" said Bradley.

Tom nodded, trying to suppress a shudder.

"Yes, Bradley," Jeff reiterated, given his companion's terse response. "We're obliged to wear these uncomfortable helmets so the passengers won't recognize us if they bump into us somewhere in London. It's another one of Murray's safety measures. Have you forgotten what he said to us on our first day?"

"Not likely!" Bradley declared, then, mimicking his boss's melodious, educated voice, he added: "Your helmet is your safe-conduct, gentlemen. Anyone who takes it off during the show will live to regret it, believe me."

"Yes, and I'm not going to be the one to run the risk. Remember what happened to poor Perkins."

Bradley whistled with fear at the thought, and Tom

shuddered again. The group came to a halt in front of a fragmented skyline of burning rooftops. Jeff stepped forward, found the handle hidden in the mural, and opened a door in among the clouds. As though plunging into the fluffy interior of one of them, the procession left the set, and walked down a passageway to a cramped dressing room. Upon entering, they were surprised by the sound of furious clapping. Gilliam Murray was sprawled on a chair applauding with theatrical enthusiasm.

"*Magnifique!*" he exclaimed. "Bravo!"

The group looked at him, speechless. Gilliam stood up and walked towards them with open arms.

"Congratulations on a wonderful job, gentlemen. Our customers were so thrilled by your performance some of them even want to come back."

After acknowledging his clap on the back, Tom moved discreetly away from the others. In the munitions store he left the piece of painted wood covered in bolts and knobs, which with the aid of the blank charges under the automatons' armor Murray was able to pass off as a lethal weapon of the future, and started to get changed. He needed to leave there as soon as possible, he told himself, thinking of Claire Haggerty and the problem caused by his blasted bladder. He took off Captain Shackleton's armor, hung it on its hanger, and took his own clothes out of a box marked "Tom." He rolled the parasol up in his jacket and glanced round to make sure no one had seen him. Murray was giving orders to a couple of waitresses who had entered wheeling trolleys laden with steak and kidney pie, grilled sausages, and tankards of beer, while the rest of his fellow workers had also begun changing.

He gazed warmly at the men with whom chance had obliged him to work: Jeff, lean but strong, cheerful and talkative; young Bradley, still an adolescent, whose youthful face gave the S-shaped scar on his cheek an even more disturbing air; burly Mike with his look of perpetual bewilderment; and Martin, the joker, a strapping redhead of uncertain age, whose leathery skin reflected the ravages of a life spent working out in all weathers. It felt strange to Tom that whereas in Murray's fictional world they would all have laid down their lives for him, in the real world he was not so sure they would not slit his throat for a promise of food or money. After all, what did he know about them except that, like him, they were penniless? They had gone out drinking together several times; first to celebrate their more than satisfactory debut performance, then to mark the success of the one given in honor of Her Majesty the Queen, for which they had received double wages, and lastly, having developed a liking for these binges, they had gone out carousing to celebrate their third triumphant performance in advance. That riotous spree had ended like the others in Mrs. Dawson's bawdy house.

But if anything, these revelries had only made Tom realize he should avoid keeping company with these fellows, or they would end up landing him in trouble. With the exception of Martin Tucker—who, despite his fondness for pranks, seemed the most decent—he saw them as a bunch of untrustworthy delinquents. Like him, they lived from hand to mouth, doing odd jobs—although from hearing them speak, it was clear they were not above breaking the law if there was money to be earned. Only a few days before, Jeff Wayne and Bradley Holloway had asked him to play a part in one of their shady dealings—a house in Kensington Gore that looked easy to break into. He had refused to go along, not so much because for the past few weeks he had promised himself to make every effort to earn an honest living, but because when it came to breaking the law, he preferred to act alone: he knew from experience he had more chances of survival if he watched his own back. If you depended only on yourself, no one could betray you. He had slipped into his shirt and begun doing up the buttons when out of the corner of his eye he saw Gilliam coming over. He was so nervous he nearly pulled off one of the buttons.

"I wanted to thank you personally, Tom," said Gilliam, beaming contentedly and stretching out his hand. Tom shook it, forcing a smile. "You realize none of this would be possible without you. Nobody could play Captain Shackleton better than you."

Tom tried to look pleased. Was Murray making a veiled reference to Perkins? From what he had heard, Perkins had been the man hired to play Shackleton before him, who when he discovered what Murray was up to, realized his silence was worth more than the salary Murray intended paying him, and he went to his office to tell him as much. His attempt at blackmail had not ruffled Gilliam Murray, who simply told him if he did not agree with the pay he was free to go, adding in a tone of wounded pride that his Captain Shackleton would never have stooped so low. Perkins smiled ominously and left his office, announcing his intention to go directly to Scotland Yard. He was never seen again. Following his crude effort at extortion, Perkins had simply vanished into thin air, but Tom and the others suspected Murray's thugs had taken care of him before he got anywhere near Scotland Yard. They could not prove it, but they had no desire to put Murray to the test. This was why at all costs Tom had to keep his meeting with Claire Haggerty a secret. If anyone found out that a passenger had seen his face, it was the end for him. He knew Murray would not be content to simply dismiss him. He would take drastic measures, as he had done with poor Perkins. The fact that he was not to blame was irrelevant: his mere existence would be a constant threat to Murray's scheme, a threat he would have to deal with urgently. If Murray ever found out, Tom would end up like Perkins, however big and strong he might be.

"You know, Tom," said Gilliam, "when I look at you I see a true hero."

"I just try to play the part of Captain Shackleton as best I can, Mr. Murray," Tom replied, trying to stop his hands from shaking as he pulled on his trousers.

Gilliam gave what sounded like a growl of pleasure.

"Well, just keep it up, lad, keep it up," he urged, amused.

Tom nodded.

"Now, if you'll excuse me," he said, pulling on his cap, "I'm in a bit of a hurry."

"You're leaving?" said Gilliam, disappointed. "Won't you stay for the jollities?"

"I'm sorry, Mr. Murray, I really have to go," replied Tom.

He snatched his bundled-up jacket, taking care not to let Murray see the parasol, and headed for the door that led from the dressing room into the alley at the back of the building. He had to get out of there before Gilliam noticed the beads of sweat on his brow.

"Tom, wait!" cried Murray.

Tom looked back, his heart knocking in his chest. Gilliam gazed at him solemnly for a moment.

"Is she pretty?" he finally asked.

"I beg your pardon?" Tom stammered.

"The reason you're in such a hurry. Is there a pretty lady waiting to enjoy the company of the savior of the human race?"

"I . . ." Tom stuttered, suddenly aware of the sweat trickling down his cheeks.

Gilliam laughed heartily.

"I understand, Tom," he said, patting him on the back, "you don't like people sniffing around in your private life, do you? Don't worry, you're not obliged to reply. Run along now. And don't forget to make sure no one sees you leave."

Tom nodded mechanically, and moved towards the door, halfheartedly waving good-bye to the others. He stepped out into the alley and hurried as fast as he could towards the main street, where he hid at the corner and paused for a moment, trying to collect his thoughts. He watched the entrance to the alleyway for a few minutes, in case Gilliam sent someone after him, but when no one appeared, he felt reassured. That meant Murray did not suspect anything, at least not for the moment. Tom heaved a sigh of relief. Now he must put his trust in the stars to guide him as far away as possible from the girl called Claire Haggerty. It was then he noticed that in his panic he had forgotten to change his shoes: he was still wearing the brave Captain Shackleton's boots.

XXIV

THE BOARDINGHOUSE ON BUCK-eridge Street was a ramshackle building with a peeling façade, wedged between two taverns that were so noisy it made it hard for anyone trying to sleep on the other side of the partition walls. However, compared to some of the other fleapits Tom had lodged in, the filthy lodgings were the nearest thing to a palace he had known. At that time of day, after twelve, the street was filled with the pungent aroma of grilled sausages from the taverns, which was a constant source of torment for most of the lodgers, whose pockets contained nothing but fluff. Tom crossed the street to the boardinghouse, trying his best to ignore the smell that was making him salivate like a dog, and regretting that out of fear he had passed up the spread Murray had laid out in their honor. It would have filled his belly for days. In the street outside the door to the boardinghouse, he saw the stall belonging to Mrs. Ritter, a mournful-looking widow who made a few pence reading people's palms.

"Good afternoon, Mrs. Ritter," he said with a friendly smile. "How's business today?"

"Your smile's the best thing that's happened to me all day, Tom," the woman replied, cheering up noticeably when she saw him. "No one seems bothered about the future. Have you managed to convince the whole neighborhood not to be curious about what fate has in store for them?"

Tom liked Mrs. Ritter, and from the moment she had set up her miserable little stall there, he had taken it upon himself to be her champion. From scraps of gossip picked up in the neighborhood, Tom had pieced together her tragic story, which might have been the template the Creator used to reproduce unhappy lives, for Mrs. Ritter had apparently been spared no misfortune. He decided the poor woman had undergone more than her fair share of suffering and resolved to help her as best he could. Unfortunately, this stretched little further than stealing apples in Covent Garden or stopping to give her the time of day whenever he went in or out of the boardinghouse, and trying to cheer her up if she was having a bad day. Despite all this, he had never let her read his palm and always gave the same explanation: knowing what fate had in store for him would destroy his curiosity, which was the only thing that got him out of bed every morning.

"I would never try to sabotage your business, Mrs. Ritter," he replied, amused. "I'm sure things will pick up this afternoon."

"I hope you're right, Tom, I hope you're right."

He bade her farewell and began climbing the rickety staircase that led to his room on the top floor of the boardinghouse. He opened the door and carefully examined the room he had been living in for almost two years, as though seeing it for the first time. But, unlike the day the landlady had first showed him the room, he did not size up critically the dilapidated bed, or the worm-eaten chest of drawers, or the flyblown mirror, or even the tiny window overlooking the waterlogged back alley filled with refuse. This time, Tom stood in the doorway and stared at the room as though suddenly aware that the wretched space he could scarcely pay for represented everything he had been able to make of life. And he was struck by the overwhelming certainty that nothing would ever change, that his present existence was so irreversible it would continue silently unraveling into the future without anything happening to mark the passage of time, and only in moments of remarkable lucidity such as these would he realize that life was slipping away from him, like water trickling through his fingers.

But how else could he play the hand he had been dealt? His father had been a miserable wretch who believed he had landed the best job of his life when he was hired to collect the piled-up excrement in the cesspools at the back of people's houses. Each night he ventured forth to unburden the city of its human waste, as though Her Majesty in person would one day thank him for his labors. He was utterly convinced that this loathsome task was the cornerstone upon which the British Empire was founded: how could a country stay on top if it was drowning in its own excrement, he used to say. His greatest aspiration—to his friends' amusement—was to buy a bigger cart that would allow him to shovel more shit than anyone else. If there was one childhood memory etched in Tom's mind it was the unbearable stench his father gave off when he climbed into bed in the early hours, and which Tom tried to fend off by nestling against his mother's chest and breathing in her sweet, smell barely perceptible beneath the sweat from her exhausting toil at the cotton mill. But the foul smell of excrement was preferable by far to the stink of cheap alcohol his father began to bring home with him when the sudden blossoming of the city's sewage system put an end to his absurd dreams. And now Tom could no longer even fend this off with his mother's sweet fragrance, because a sudden outbreak of cholera had torn her from his side. There was more room in the communal bed after that, but Tom slept with one eye open, for he never knew when his father might wake him up with his belt, unleashing his anger at the world on his son's tiny back.

When Tom turned six, his father forced him to go out begging to pay for his liquor. Arousing people's sympathy was a thankless but ultimately undemanding task, and he did not know how much he would miss it until his father demanded he help him in the new job he had obtained thanks to his cart and his ability with a shovel. In this way Tom learned that death could cease to be something abstract and take on form and substance, leaving a chill in his fingers no fire would ever warm. But more than anything, he understood that those whose lives were worth nothing suddenly became valuable in death, for their bodies contained a hidden wealth of precious organs. He helped his father rob graves and crypts for a retired boxer named Crouch, who sold the corpses to surgeons, until during one of his frequent drunken binges his father fell into the Thames and drowned. Overnight, Tom found himself alone in the world, but at least now his life was his own. He was no longer forced to disturb the sleep of the dead. Now he would be the one to decide which path he took.

Stealing corpses had turned him into a strong, alert lad who had no difficulty finding more honest employment, although luck never deigned to shine on him enough to help him escape his hand-to-mouth existence. He had no trouble finding employment as a street sweeper, a pest exterminator, a doorman. He even swept chimneys, until the lad he worked with was caught stealing in one of the houses they were meant to be cleaning, and the pair of them were thrown out on their ears by the servants, not before being given a thrashing. But he put all that behind him the day he met Megan, a beautiful young girl whom he lived with for a few years in a stuffy cellar in Hague Street in Bethnal Green. Megan was not only a pleasant respite from his daily struggle, she taught him to read using old newspapers they fished out of the refuse. Thanks to her, Tom discovered the hidden meaning behind all those strange signs and learned that life beyond his own little world could be just as awful. Unfortunately, there are some neighborhoods where happiness is doomed to failure, and Megan soon ran off with a chair maker who did not know the meaning of hunger.

When she returned two months later, face covered in

bruises and blind in one eye, Tom accepted her back as though she had never left. Although her betrayal had dealt the final blow to a love already strained by circumstance, Tom cared for her day and night, feeding her opium syrup to keep the pain at bay and reading aloud from old newspapers as though he were reciting poetry. And he would have gone on caring for her for the rest of his life, bound to her by a feeling of pity, which in time might have changed back into affection, if the infection in her eye had not meant his bed was once more widened.

They buried her one rainy morning in a small church near the lunatic asylum. He alone wept over her grave. Tom felt they were burying much more than Megan's body that day. His faith in life was buried with her, his naïve belief he would be able to live honorably, his innocence. That day, in the shoddy coffin of the only woman to whom he had dared give the love he had felt for his mother, they were also burying Tom Blunt, for suddenly he did not know who he was. He did not recognize himself in the young man who, that very night, crouched in the dark waiting for the chair maker to come home, in the frenzied creature who hurled himself at the man, throwing him against a wall, in the wild animal who set upon him, beating him into the ground with angry fists. The cries of this man he had never known were also the cries heralding the birth of a new Tom: a Tom who seemed capable of anything, a Tom who could perform deeds such as this without a flicker of conscience, perhaps because someone had extracted it and sold it to the surgeons. He had tried to make an honest living, and life had crushed him as if he were a loathsome insect. It was time he looked for other ways to survive, Tom told himself, gazing down at the bloody pulp to which he had reduced the chair maker.

By the age of twenty, life had instilled a savage harshness in his eyes. Combined with his physical strength, this gave him a disconcerting, even intimidating air, especially as he loped along the streets. And so he had no difficulty in being hired by a moneylender in Bethnal Green, who paid him to bully a list of debtors by day, and who he had no qualms about stealing from at night, as though the morality that had guided his actions in the past had become no more than a useless obstacle preventing him from reaping the benefits of life, in which there was no longer room for anything but self-interest. Life became a simple routine that consisted of perpetrating violence on anyone he was told to, in exchange for enough money to pay for a filthy dank room and the services of a whore when he needed to relax. A life governed by a single emotion, hatred, which he nurtured daily with his fists, as though it were a rare bloom, a vague but intense hatred, exacerbated by a trifle and often responsible for his arrival at the boardinghouse, face black and blue, barred from yet another tavern.

During this period, however, Tom was aware of his numbness, the icy indifference with which he snapped people's fingers and whispered threats in his victims' ears, but he justified his actions by telling himself he had no choice: it was pointless to fight against the current dragging him to where he probably belonged. Like a snake shedding its skin, he could only look away as he relinquished God's mercy on his downward spiral to hell.

Perhaps in the end that was all he was fit for. Perhaps he had been born to break people's fingers, to occupy a place of honor among thieves and wastrels. And he would have reconciled himself to being dragged deeper into the ugly side of life, relinquishing all responsibility, knowing it was only a matter of time before he committed his first murder, had it not been for someone who believed the role of hero suited him better.

Tom had turned up at Murray's offices without knowing anything about the job on offer. He could still remember the look of astonishment on the big man's face as he stood up from his desk when Tom walked in, and how he had begun walking round him, uttering ecstatic cries, pinching his arm muscles and sizing up his jawbone, arms flailing like some demented tailor.

"I don't believe it. You're exactly the way I described you," he declared to the bewildered Tom. "You are Derek Shackleton."

With this he led him down to an enormous cellar where a group of men in strange costumes seemed to be rehearsing a play. That was the first time he met Martin, Jeff, and the others.

"Gentlemen, I'd like to introduce you to your captain," Gilliam announced, "the man for whom you must sacrifice your lives."

And that is how, overnight, Tom Blunt, hired thug, crook, and troublemaker, became the savior of mankind. The job did far more than fill his pockets: it saved his soul from the hellfire where it had been slowly roasting. Because, for some reason, it seemed inappropriate to Tom to go round breaking people's bones now that his mission was to save the world. It sounded absurd, as the two things were perfectly compatible, and yet he felt as though the noble spirit of Derek Shackleton were now glowing inside him, filling the gap from which the original Tom Blunt's soul had been extracted, taking him over serenely, naturally, painlessly. After the first rehearsal, Tom left Captain Shackleton's armor behind but decided to take his character home, or perhaps this was an unconscious act beyond his control. The truth is he liked looking at the world as though he really were its savior, seeing it through the eyes of a hero whose heart was as courageous as it was generous, and that same day he decided to look for honest work, as though the words of the giant named Gilliam Murray had rekindled the tiny flame of humanity that was still flickering in the depths of his soul.

But now all his plans for redemption had been destroyed by that stupid girl. He sat on the edge of the bed and unwrapped the parasol bundled in his jacket. It was doubtless the most expensive thing in his room; selling it would pay his rent for two or three months, he reflected, rubbing the bruise on his side where the bag of tomato juice had been strapped before Martin burst it during their duel. Some good had come out of his meeting with the girl, although it was hard to ignore the tight spot she had put him in. He dreaded to think what would happen if he ever bumped into her in the street. His boss's worst nightmare would come true, for the girl would immediately discover Murray's Time Travel was a fraud. And while that might be the worst consequence, it was not the only one. She would also discover he was no hero from the future, just a miserable wretch who owned nothing but the clothes on his back. And then Tom would be forced with his own eyes to witness her devotion turn to disappointment, possibly even outright disgust, as though she were watching a butterfly change back into a caterpillar. This, of course, was nothing compared to the discovery of the fraud, but he knew he would regret it far more. Deep down, it gave him immense pleasure to remember the woman's entranced gaze, even though he knew it was not directed at him, but at the hero he was impersonating, the brave Captain Shackleton, the savior of the human race. Yes, he wanted Claire to imagine him in the year 2000, rebuilding the world, not sitting in these gloomy lodgings, wondering how much a pawnbroker would give for her parasol.

ANYONE WHO HAS BEEN to Billingsgate fish market in the early hours knows that smells travel faster than light. For, long before the night receives the first flush of dawn, the pungent aroma of shellfish and the overpowering stench of eel filling the fishermen's carts have already mingled with the cold night air. Zigzagging through the oyster stalls and squid sellers hawking their merchandise at three for a penny, Tom Blunt reached the railings at the river entrance, where a crowd of other miserable wretches were flexing their muscles and trying to look enthusiastic, in the hope some kindly skipper would pick them to unload his boat from overseas. Tom hugged his jacket to himself trying to ward off the cold and joined the group of men. He immediately spotted Patrick, a tall youth who was as strapping as he was, with whom by dint of unloading boxes together he had struck up a sort of friendship. They greeted one another with a friendly nod, and like a couple of pigeons puffing up their chests, tried to stand out from the crowd and catch the skippers' eye. Ordinarily, thanks to their glowing physiques, they were both hired straightaway, and that morning was no exception. They congratulated one another with a sly smile and walked towards the designated cargo boat together with the dozen other chosen stevedores.

Tom liked this simple honest work that required no more than strong arms and a degree of agility; not only did it enable him to see the dawn in all its glory above the Thames, but as he began to feel the calming yet vivifying fatigue of physical effort steal over him, he could allow his thoughts to drift down unexpected pathways. It was rather like being on Harrow-on-the-Hill, a small rise in the suburbs of London he had discovered during one of his walks. On top of the hill grew a centuries-old oak surrounded by a dozen graves, as though the dead buried there wanted nothing to do with the others in the tiny adjoining cemetery. He thought of the grassy knoll as his own private sanctuary, a sort of outdoor chapel where he could close his ears to the din of the world. Sometimes when he was up there, he found to his amazement that he was even able to string a few positive thoughts together, which gave him a measure of insight into the usually so elusive meaning of his life. As he sat wondering what sort of life John Peachey, the man buried nearest to the oak, must have led, Tom began to reflect about his own existence as though it belonged to someone else, and to judge it with the same objectivity as that of the deceased stranger.

Once their day was done, he and Patrick sat on a pile of boxes waiting to be paid. The two men usually passed the time chatting about this or that, but Tom's thoughts had been elsewhere all week. This was how long it had been since the unfortunate meeting with Claire Haggerty, and yet still nothing had happened. Apparently, Murray knew nothing about it and possibly never would. Even so, Tom's life would never be the same again. It had already changed. Tom knew London was too big a place for him to run into the girl again, yet he walked around with his eyes wide open, afraid of bumping into her round every corner. Thanks to that stupid girl, he would always be uneasy, always on the alert: he had even considered growing a beard. He shook his head as he reflected how the most trivial act can change your life; why the devil had he not taken the precaution of emptying his bladder before the performance?

When Patrick finally plucked up the courage to chide him gently for his morose silence, Tom stared at him in surprise. It was true he had not tried to hide his anxiety from Patrick, and now he did not know what to say to him. He merely reassured him with a mysterious, doleful smile, and his companion shrugged his shoulders, as if to say he had not meant to poke his nose into Tom's affairs. Once they had been paid, the two men strolled away from the market with the leisurely gait of those who have nothing much else to do for the rest of the day. As they walked, Tom gazed warmly at Patrick, afraid his unwillingness to confide in him might have hurt the lad's feelings. Patrick was only a couple of years younger than him, but his baby face made him look even younger, and Tom could not help instinctively taking him under his wing, like the little brother he never had, even though he knew Patrick could take care of himself. And yet neither of them, whether out of apathy or shyness, had shown any interest in developing their friendship outside the port.

"Today's earnings bring me a little closer, Tom," Patrick suddenly declared in a faintly wistful voice.

"Closer to what?" asked Tom, utterly intrigued, for Patrick had never once mentioned any plans to start a business or marry a woman.

The lad looked at him mysteriously.

"To achieving my dream," he replied solemnly.

Tom was pleased the lad had a dream that would drive him on, a reason to get out of bed in the morning: something lacking in his own life of late.

"And what dream might that be, Patrick?" he asked, knowing the lad was longing to tell him.

Almost reverentially, Patrick pulled a crumpled piece of paper from his pocket and presented it to him.

"To travel to the year 2000 and see the brave Captain Shackleton triumph over the evil automatons."

Tom did not even take the leaflet he knew from memory. He just stared at Patrick glumly.

"Wouldn't you like to know about the year 2000, Tom?" said Patrick, astonished.

Tom sighed.

"There's nothing for me in the future, Patrick," he shrugged. "This is my present, and it's the only thing I want to know about."

"I see," murmured Patrick, too polite to criticize his friend's narrow-mindedness.

"Have you had breakfast yet?" Tom asked.

"Of course not!" he groaned. "I told you, I'm saving up. Breakfast is a luxury I can't afford."

"In that case allow me to treat you," Tom offered, putting a fatherly arm round his shoulder. "I know a place near here where they serve the best sausages in town."

XXV

AFTER ENJOYING A HEARTY BREAK-
fast that would take the edge off their appetite for a week, Tom's pockets were somewhat depleted.
He tried not to reproach himself for his extravagant gesture towards Patrick; he had not been able to resist it, but
next time he must be more careful, for he knew full well
that although these altruistic deeds made him feel good,
they would only be detrimental to him in the long run.
He said good-bye to Patrick, and having nothing better to
do for the rest of the day, made his way towards Covent
Garden, intending to carry on with his charitable deeds by
stealing a few apples for Mrs. Ritter.

It was late morning by the time he arrived, and the
freshest, crispest produce had been snapped up by the
early birds, who came from all over London at the crack
of dawn to stock up their larders. But by the same token,
daylight had removed the eerie atmosphere cast by light
from candles perched on mounds of melted wax, which the
traders stuck on their carts. By now, the market had taken
on the air of a country fair; the visitors no longer looked

like furtive ghosts, but like people strolling about with all the time in the world to make their purchases while, like Tom, they let themselves be captivated by the heady scent of roses, eglantines, and heliotropes wafting from the flower baskets on the western side of the square. Floating along with the crowds filing dreamily between carts laden with potatoes, carrots, and cabbages, a patchwork of color that went all the way down Bow Street to Maiden Lane, Tom tried to locate some of the Cockney girls milling around the stalls with their baskets of apples. Craning his neck, he thought he spotted one on the other side of a mass of people. He tried to get to her before she disappeared again into the crowd, swerving to get past the human wall blocking his way. But this type of abrupt movement, which might have saved Captain Shackleton's life during a skirmish, was unwise in a packed market like Covent Garden. He realized this on slamming into a young woman crossing his path. Reeling from the collision, the woman had to steady herself in order not to end up on the ground. Tom stopped and swung round with the intention of apologizing as politely as possible for having bumped into her. It was then he found himself face to face with the only person in the whole of London he had never wanted to see again, and the world suddenly felt like a tiny, mysterious place, like a magician's hat which could hold everything.

"Captain Shackleton, what are you doing in my time?" asked Claire Haggerty, completely bewildered.

Only inches away from her, Tom received the full impact of the look of devotion that his mere presence triggered in her. He was even able to glimpse the blue of her eyes, a deep, intense blue he knew he would never find anywhere else in the world, however many oceans or skies he saw—a fierce, pure blue, which was probably on the Creator's palette when He colored heaven, and of which her eyes were now the sole custodians. Only when he had managed to break free from her enchanted gaze did Tom realize that this chance encounter could cost him his life. He glanced around to make sure no one was eyeing them suspiciously, but was too dazed to take in what he saw. He fixed his eyes once more on the girl, who was still staring at him overwhelmed with disbelief and emotion, waiting for him to explain his presence there. But what could he tell her without giving away the truth, which would be tantamount to signing his own death warrant?

"I traveled back in time to bring you your parasol," he blurted out.

He immediately bit his lip. It sounded absurd, but it was the first thing that had occurred to him. He watched Claire's eyes grow even wider, and prepared for the worst.

"Oh, thank you, you're so kind," she replied, scarcely able to disguise her joy. "But you shouldn't have taken the trouble. As you can see, I have another," and she showed him a parasol almost identical to the one he had hidden in his chest of drawers. "However, as you've journeyed through time in order to bring it to me, I'll gladly take it back, and I promise I'll get rid of this one."

Now it was Tom's turn to conceal his astonishment at what the girl was saying: she had swallowed his lie completely! Yet wasn't it logical? Murray's pantomime was too convincing for a girl as young as she to question it; Claire believed she had traveled to the year 2000, she truly believed it, and her certainty gave him legitimacy as a time traveler. It was that simple. When he managed to recover from his surprise, he realized she was staring at his empty hands, wondering perhaps why they were not clasping the parasol that had compelled him to journey across an entire century with the sole aim of returning it to her.

"I don't have it with me," he apologized, shrugging foolishly.

She waited, expectantly, for him to come up with an explanation for this, and in that sudden silence enclosing them amid the hustle and bustle, Tom glimpsed the girl's slim, graceful body beneath her robe, and felt painfully aware of how long it had been since he was with a woman. After burying Megan, he had only received the phony tenderness of whores, and had recently forgone even that, considering himself tough enough to do without those bartered caresses. Or so he thought. Now he had in front of him a beautiful, elegant woman, a woman whom a fellow such as he could never hope to possess, and yet she was gazing at him like no other woman ever had. Would that gaze be the tunnel that could lead to his storming the impregnable fortress? Men had risked their lives for much less since the beginning of time. And so, responding to the atavistic desire of his species echoing inside him, Tom did what his reason least advised:

"But I can give it to you this afternoon," he ventured,

"if you'd be kind enough to take tea with me at the Aerated Bread Company near Charing Cross Underground station."

Claire's face lit up.

"Of course, Captain," she replied, excited. "I'll be there."

Tom nodded, gave her a smile purged of all lust, and tried hard to mask his shock, both at her for accepting as much as at himself for having proposed a meeting with the very woman he should flee if he valued his life. Clearly it did not mean that much to him if he was prepared to risk it for a roll in the hay with this vision of loveliness. Just then, someone cried out Claire's name and they turned as one. A fair-haired girl was making her way towards them through the crowd.

"It's my friend Lucy," said Claire, with amused irritation, "she won't let me out of her sight for a second."

"Please, don't tell her I've come here from the future," Tom warned quickly, regaining some of his composure. "I'm traveling incognito. If anyone found out, I'd get into a lot of trouble."

Claire looked at him uncertainly.

"I'll be waiting for you at the tearooms at four o'clock," Tom said brusquely, taking his leave. "But please promise me you'll come alone."

As he thought, Claire promised without demur. Although, owing to his circumstances, Tom had never been to the ABC tearooms himself, he was aware they had been all the rage since the day they opened. For they were the only place two young people could meet without the bothersome presence of a chaperone. He had heard they were airy, pleasant, and warm, and offered tea and buns at an affordable price. Thus, they soon became the perfect alternative to the walks in the cold or meetings in family reception rooms spied upon by the young lady's mother to which young suitors had hitherto been condemned. True, they would be seen, but Tom could think of no better place to meet her—not one where she would have agreed to go unaccompanied.

By the time Lucy reached Claire, Tom had vanished into the crowd. But she still asked her dazed friend who the stranger was she had seen her talking to from a distance. Claire simply shook her head mysteriously. As she expected, Lucy immediately forgot the matter and dragged her over to a flower stall, where they could stock up with heliotropes, bringing the aroma of distant jungles into their bedrooms. And while Claire Haggerty was letting herself be led by the arm and thinking that traveling through time was the most gentlemanly thing anyone had ever done for her, Tom Blunt quickly left Covent Garden Market by the opposite exit, elbowing his way through the crowd and trying not to think of poor Perkins.

HE SLUMPED BACKWARDS ONTO his bed in his lodgings as if he had been shot point-blank. Lying there, he carried on cursing his foolhardy behavior out loud, as he had been doing in the garbled manner of a drunkard all the way home. Had he taken leave of his senses? What the hell did he think he was doing asking the girl to meet him again?

Well, the answer was easy enough. What he wanted was obvious, and it did not involve marveling at Claire's beauty for a couple of hours, like someone admiring an unattainable object in a shop window, tortured by the idea he would never have her. Not on his life: he was going to take advantage of the girl being in love with his other self, the brave Captain Shackleton, to achieve an even greater goal. And he was amazed that for this fleeting pleasure he was prepared to suffer the consequences such an irresponsible course of action would bring, including his probable demise. Did he really value his life so little? he asked himself yet again. Yes, it was sad but true: possessing that beautiful woman was more meaningful to him than anything that might be waiting for him round the corner in his miserable future.

Thinking about it objectively he had to admit that the logical thing to do was not to turn up at the meeting and to avoid trouble. But this was no guarantee against his bumping into the girl again somewhere else and having to explain what he was still doing in the nineteenth century, and even invent some excuse for not showing up at the tearooms. Not going was not the answer, apparently. On the contrary, the only solution he could think of was to go there and cook up a way of avoiding having to explain himself if they bumped into each other again in the future. Some reason why she must not go near him, or even speak to him, he thought to himself, excitedly, as though that were his main reason for seeing her again and not another more vulgar one. All things considered, this meeting might even prove beneficial to him in the long run. Yes, this might be a way of solving the problem once and for all. For it was clear this must be their first and only encounter. He had no choice: he must indulge his desire for the girl on condition that he succeeded in ruling out any possibility of their ever meeting again, nipping any relationship that might grow up between them in the bud. For he could not see how they would keep it secret, conceal it from the multitude of spies Murray had posted all over the city, which would put not only him in danger but her, too. This meeting, then, felt like the last meal of the condemned man, and he resolved to enjoy every minute of it.

When it was time to go, he took the parasol, straightened his cap, and left the boardinghouse. Down in the street, he gave way to an impulse and stopped in front of Mrs. Ritter's stall.

"Good afternoon, Tom," said the old lady.

"Mrs. Ritter," he replied, stretching out his hand, "I think the time has come for us both to see my future."

The old woman glanced up at him in surprise, but at once she gripped Tom's hand and with a wizened finger slowly traced the lines on his palm, like someone reading a book.

"My God, Tom!" she gasped, gazing up at him with mournful dismay. "I see . . . death!"

With a grimace of resigned fortitude, Tom accepted the terrible prediction and withdrew his hand gently from the old woman's clasp. His worst fears had been confirmed. Getting under this woman's skirts would mean death: that was the reward for lust. He shrugged and said good-bye to the alarmed Mrs. Ritter, who doubtless had assumed fate would be kinder to him, then walked down the street towards the tearooms where Claire Haggerty was waiting for him. Yes, there was no doubt about it, he was going to die, but could he call what he had now a life? He smiled and quickened his pace.

He had never felt so alive.

XXVI

WHEN HE ARRIVED, CLAIRE WAS already sitting at one of the small tables at the back of the tearooms, next to a picture window through which the afternoon light filtered onto her hair. Tom gazed at her with awe from the doorway, savoring the knowledge that it was he whom this beautiful young girl was waiting for. Once more, he was struck by her fragile appearance, which contrasted so delightfully with her lively gestures and fervent gaze, and he felt a pleasant stirring inside, in that barren place where he thought nothing would ever grow again. At least he was not completely dead inside, he could still experience emotion. Clutching the parasol in his sweaty palm, he began making his way towards her through the tables, determined to do everything in his power to have her in his arms by the end of the afternoon.

"Excuse me, sir," a young woman on her way out of the tearooms waylaid him, "might I ask where you acquired those boots?"

Taken aback, Tom followed the woman's eyes down to his feet. He almost jumped out of his skin when he saw he was wearing Captain Shackleton's exotic footwear. He stared at the girl, at a loss what to say.

"In Paris," he replied finally.

The young woman appeared content with his reply. She nodded, as if to say such footwear could only come from the birthplace of fashion. She thanked him for the information with a friendly smile and left the tearooms. Tom shook his head and, clearing his throat like a baritone about to walk out on stage, continued across the room towards Claire, who had not yet noticed him and was gazing dreamily out of the window.

"Good afternoon, Miss Haggerty," he said.

Claire smiled when she saw him.

"I believe this is yours," he said, holding out the parasol as if it were a bunch of roses.

"Oh, thank you, Captain," the girl responded, "but, please, take a seat, take a seat."

Tom sat down on the empty chair, while Claire assessed the sorry state of her parasol with slight dismay. After the speedy examination, Claire relegated the object to the side of the table, as though its role in the story were over. She began studying Tom with that strange yearning in her eyes he had noticed during their first meeting, and which had flattered him even though he knew it was not directed at him but at the character he was playing.

"I must compliment you on your disguise, Captain," the girl said, after looking him up and down, "it's truly amazing. You could be an East End barrow boy."

"Er, thanks," Tom stammered, forcing a smile to mask his pique at her remark.

What was he so surprised about in fact? Her comment only confirmed what he already knew: if he was able to enjoy the company of this stuck-up young woman for an afternoon, it was precisely because she believed he was an intrepid hero of the future. And it was precisely thanks to this misunderstanding that he would be able to teach her a lesson, by obtaining from her something which under other circumstances she would never have conceded. He disguised the joy the thought gave him by glancing around the room, taking the opportunity to try to spot one of Gilliam Murray's possible spies among the chattering customers, but he saw no one who struck him as suspicious.

"I can't be too careful," he remarked, turning back to face Claire. "As I said, I mustn't draw attention to myself, and that would be impossible if I wore my armor. That's why I must also ask you not to call me Captain."

"Very well," said the girl, and then, unable to control her excitement at being privy to a secret no one else knew about, added: "I can't believe you're really Captain Derek Shackleton!"

Startled, Tom begged her to be quiet.

"Oh, forgive me," she apologized, her face flushing, "only I'm so excited. I still can't believe I'm having tea with the savior of—"

Luckily, the girl broke off when she saw the waitress coming over. They ordered tea for two and an assortment of cakes and buns. When she had left to fetch their order, they stared at each other in silence for a few moments, grinning foolishly. Tom watched the girl attempt to regain her composure, while he thought of how to steer the conversation onto a more personal footing that would assist his plans. He had chosen the tearooms because there was an inexpensive but clean-looking boardinghouse opposite that had seemed like the perfect venue for their union. Now all he needed to do was employ his powers of seduction, if he had any, to try to get her there. He knew this would be no easy feat: evidently a young lady like Claire, who probably still had her virtue intact, would not agree to go to bed with a man she had only just met, even if she did think he was Captain Shackleton.

"How did you get here?" asked Claire, oblivious to his machinations. "Did you stow away on the *Cronotilus*?"

Tom had to stifle a grimace of irritation at her question: the last thing he wanted while attempting to spin a credible yarn that would enable him to have his way with this lovely creature was to have to justify his earlier fabrication. However, he could scarcely tell her he had traveled back in time in order to return her parasol and expect her simply to accept it, as though it were the most natural thing in the world for people to run back and forth between centuries on unimportant errands. Luckily, the sudden appearance of the waitress bringing their order gave him time to think up an answer that would satisfy Claire.

"The *Cronotilus*?" he asked, pretending he knew nothing of the time tram's existence, for if he had used it to travel back to this century, he would have no choice but to stay there until the next expedition to the year 2000. That was almost a month away, which meant this meeting need not be their last.

"It's the steam tram we traveled to your century in, across that dreadful place called the fourth dimension," Claire explained to him. Then she paused for a few moments before adding: "But if you didn't come here on the *Cronotilus*, then how *did* you get here? Is there some other means of time travel?"

"Of course there's another means, Miss Haggerty," Tom assured her, assuming that if the girl was taken in by Gilliam's hoax, that is to say, if she believed time travel was possible, then the chances were that he could make up any method he liked and she would believe it. "Our scientists have invented a machine that travels through time instantly, without the need for tiresome journeys through the fourth dimension."

"And can this machine travel to any era?" the girl demanded, mesmerized.

"Any time, any time at all," replied Tom casually, as though he were fed up with traveling across the centuries and the creation and destruction of civilizations bored him to tears.

He reached for a bun and munched on it cheerfully, as if to show her that despite all he had seen, he could still enjoy the simplest pleasures of life, such as English baking.

Claire asked: "Do you have it with you? Can you show it to me?"

"Show you what?"

"The time machine you used to travel here."

Tom almost choked on his bun.

"No, no," he declared hastily, "that's out of the question, entirely out of the question."

She responded in a manner that took Tom by surprise, pouting rather childishly and folding her arms stiffly.

"I can't show it to you because . . . it's not something you can see," he improvised, trying to mollify her anger before it set in.

"You mean it's invisible?" the girl looked at him suspiciously.

"I mean, it's not a carriage with wings that flies through time," he explained.

"What is it then?"

Tom stifled a sigh of despair. What was it, indeed, and why could he not show it to her?

"It's an object that doesn't move physically through the time continuum. It's fixed in the future and from there it, well . . . it makes holes we can travel through to other eras. Like a drill, only instead of making holes in rocks . . . it digs tunnels through the fabric of time. That's why I can't show it to you, although I'd like nothing better."

The girl was silent.

"A machine that makes holes in the fabric of time," she finally murmured, intrigued by the idea. "And you went through one of those tunnels and came out today?"

"Yes, that's right," replied Tom halfheartedly.

"And how will you get back to the future?"

"Through the same hole."

"Are you telling me that at this very moment somewhere in London there's a tunnel leading to the year 2000?"

Tom took a sip of tea before replying. He was beginning to tire of this conversation.

"Opening it in the city would have been too obvious, as I'm sure you understand," he said cautiously. "The tunnel always opens outside London, at Harrow-on-the-Hill, a tiny knoll with an old oak surrounded by headstones. But the machine can't keep it open for very long. It will close in a few hours' time, and I have to go back through it before that happens."

With these words, he looked at her solemnly, hoping she would stop plying him with questions if she knew they had so little time together.

"You may think me reckless for asking, Captain," he heard her say after a few moments' reflection, "but would you take me back with you to the year 2000?"

"I'm afraid that's impossible, Miss Haggerty," Tom sighed.

"Why not? I promise I—"

"Because I can't go ferrying people back and forth through time."

"But what's the point of inventing a time machine if you don't use it for—"

"Because it was invented for a specific purpose!" Tom cut in, exasperated by her stubbornness. Was she really that interested in time travel?

He instantly regretted his abruptness, but the harm was done. She looked at him, shocked by his irate tone.

"And what purpose might that be, if you don't mind me asking?" she retorted, echoing his angry voice.

Tom sighed. He sat back in his seat and watched the girl struggling to suppress her mounting irritation.

There was no point in carrying on with this. The way the conversation was headed, he would never be able to coax her over to the boardinghouse. In fact, he would be lucky if she did not walk out on him there and then, tired of his filibustering. What had he expected? He was no Gilliam Murray. He was a miserable wretch with no imagination. He was out of his depth in the role of time traveler. He might as well give up, forget the whole thing, take his leave of the girl graciously while he still could and go back to his life as a nobody: unless of course Murray's thugs had other ideas.

"Miss Haggerty," he began, resolved to end the meeting politely on some pretext, but just then she placed her hand on his.

Taken aback by her gesture, Tom forgot what he had been going to say. He gazed at her slender hand resting gently on his among the cups and saucers, like a sculpture the meaning of which he was unable to fathom. When he raised his eyes, he found her gazing back at him with infinite sweetness.

"Forgive my awkward questions, which no doubt you are not allowed to answer," the girl apologized, leaning delightfully towards him across the table. "It was a very rude way of thanking you for bringing back my parasol. In any case, you needn't tell me what the machine is for, as I already know."

"You do?" said Tom, flabbergasted.

"Yes," she assured him with an enchantingly conceited grin.

"And are you going to tell me?"

Claire looked first to one side then to the other, before replying in hushed tones:

"It's for assassinating Mr. Ferguson."

Tom raised his eyebrows. Mr. Ferguson? Who the devil was Mr. Ferguson, and why did he have to be assassinated?

"Don't try to pretend, Captain," Claire chuckled. "There really is no need. Not with me."

Tom began laughing heartily with her, letting out a few loud guffaws to release the tension accumulated during her interrogation. He had no idea who Mr. Ferguson was, but he sensed that his best bet was to pretend he knew everything about the man down to his shoe size and the type of shaving lotion he used, and pray she would not ask anything about him.

"I can't hide anything from you, Miss Haggerty," he cajoled, "you're far too intelligent."

Claire's face glowed with pleasure.

"Thank you, Captain. But it really wasn't that difficult to guess that your scientists invented the machine in order to travel back to this point in time to assassinate the inventor of the automatons before he could create them, thus preventing the destruction of London and the death of so many people."

Was it really possible to travel back in time in order to change events? Tom wondered.

"You're quite right, Claire. I was sent to kill Ferguson and save the world from destruction."

The girl thought for a few moments before adding:

"Only you didn't succeed, because we witnessed the war of the future with our own eyes."

"Right again, Claire," Tom acknowledged.

"Your mission was a failure," she whispered with a hint of dismay. Then she fixed her eyes on him and murmured: "But why? Because the tunnels don't stay open long enough?"

Tom spread his arms, pretending he was bowled over by the girl's astuteness.

"That's right," he confessed, and with a sudden flash of inspiration, he added: "I made several exploratory journeys in order to try to find Ferguson, but I failed. There wasn't enough time. That's why you might bump into me again in the future, only if you do, you mustn't come up to me because I won't know you yet."

She blinked, trying to grasp his meaning.

"I understand," she said finally. "You made those journeys prior to this one, even though you showed up here days afterwards."

"Exactly," he exclaimed, and encouraged by how much sense this gibberish was apparently making to her, he added: "Although from your point of view this would seem to be my first visit, actually it isn't. I've made at least half a dozen other forays into your time before this one. What's more, this journey, which for you is my first, is also my last, because use of the machine has been prohibited."

"Prohibited?" asked Claire, her fascination growing.

Tom cleared his throat with a gulp of tea, and, emboldened by the mesmerizing effect his words were having on the girl, went on:

"Yes, Claire. The machine was built halfway through the war, but when the mission failed, the inventors forgot about their utopian idea of preventing the war before it broke out and concentrated their efforts instead on trying to win it, and inventing weapons that could cut through the automatons' reinforced armor." The girl nodded, probably recalling the soldiers' impressive guns. "The machine was left to rot, though it was placed under guard to prevent anyone traveling illegally into the past and tampering with anything they felt like. Still, I was able to use it secretly, but I only managed to open the tunnel for ten hours, and I have three hours left before it closes. That's all the time I have, Claire. After that I have to go back to my own world. If I stay here, hero or no hero, they'll find me and execute me for traveling illegally in time. That means, in three hours from now . . . I'll be gone forever."

With these words, he pressed Claire's hand very tenderly, while inwardly applauding his own performance. To his amazement, not only had he solved the problem of possible chance meetings in the future, but had managed to tell her they only had three hours left together before saying good-bye forever. Only three. No more.

"You risked your life to bring me my parasol," she said slowly, as though summing up, as though suddenly she had understood the real dangers Tom had braved.

"Well, the parasol was only an excuse," he replied, leaning over the table and gazing passionately into her eyes.

The moment had come, he said to himself. It was now or never.

"I risked my life to see you again because I love you, Claire," he lied in the softest voice he could muster.

He had said it. Now she must say the same thing to him. Now she must confess she loved him, too, that is, that she loved the brave Captain Shackleton.

"How can you love me, you don't even know me," the girl teased, smiling sweetly.

This was not the response Tom had been hoping for. He disguised his dismay with another gulp of tea. Did she not realize they had no time for anything except giving themselves to one another? He had only three blasted hours! Had he not been clear enough? He replaced the cup in its saucer and glanced out of the window at the boardinghouse opposite, its beds waiting with their clean sheets, ever further out of reach. The girl was right, he did not know her, and she did not know him. And as long as they remained strangers, there was no possibility of their ever ending up in bed. He was fighting a losing battle. But what if they did know each other? he suddenly thought. Did he not come from the future? What was there to stop him claiming that from his point of view they already knew each other? Between this meeting and their encounter in the year 2000, he could make up any number of events it would be impossible for her to refute, he told himself, believing he had finally discovered the perfect strategy for leading her to the boardinghouse, meek as a lamb.

"This time you're wrong, Claire. I know you far better than you think," he confessed solemnly, clasping her hand in both of his, as though it were a wounded sparrow. "I know who you are, your dreams, your desires, the way you see the world. I know everything about you, and you know everything about me. And I love you, Claire. I fell in love with you in a time that doesn't exist yet."

She looked at him, astonished.

"But if we're never to meet again," she mused, "how will we get to know each other? How will you fall in love with me?"

Breaking out in a sudden sweat, Tom realized he had fallen into his own trap. He stifled a curse and, playing for time, gazed at the street outside. What could he say to her now? He watched the carriages go by, indifferent to his distress, making their way through the vendors' barrows. Then his eye fell on the red pillar box on the corner, solid and steadfast, sporting the insignia Victoria Regina on the front.

"I fell in love with you through your letters," he blurted out.

"What letters? What are you talking about?" exclaimed the girl, startled.

"The love letters we've been sending one another all these years."

The young girl stared at him, aghast. And Tom understood that what he said next had to be credible, for it would determine whether the girl surrendered to him forever or slapped him angrily in the face. He closed his eyes and smiled weakly, pretending he was evoking some memory, while he desperately tried to think.

"It happened during my first exploratory journey to

your time," he said finally. "I came out on the hill I told you about. From there I walked to London, where I was able to verify that the machine was completely reliable when it came to opening the hole at the specified date: I had traveled from the year 2000 to November 8, 1896."

"November 8?"

"Yes, Claire, November 8, that's to say, the day after tomorrow," Tom confirmed. "That was my first foray into your century. But I scarcely had time to do anything else, because I had to get back to the hill before the hole closed up again. So I hurried as fast as I could, and I was about to enter the tunnel that would return me to the year 2000, when I saw something I hadn't noticed before."

"What?" she asked, burning with curiosity.

"Under a stone next to the grave marked John Peachey, I found a letter. I picked it up and discovered to my amazement it was addressed to me. I stuffed it in the pocket of my disguise and opened it in the year 2000. It was a letter from a woman I'd never met living in the nineteenth century." Tom paused for dramatic effect, before adding: "Her name was Claire Haggerty, and she said she loved me."

The girl breathed in abruptly, as though gasping for air. Tom watched, a tender smile on his face, as she gulped, attempting to digest what she was hearing, struggling to understand that she was responsible for this whole situation, or would be responsible for it in the future. For if he loved her now it was because she had loved him in the past. Claire stared into her cup, as though she were able to see him in the tea leaves in the year 2000 reading with bewilderment the letter in which a strange woman from another century, a woman who was already dead, declared her undying love for him. A letter she had written. Tom persisted, like the lumberjack who sees the tree he has been hacking away at for hours begin to teeter and despite his exhaustion swings his axe even harder.

"In your letter, you told me we would meet in the future, or more precisely I would meet you, because you had already met me," he said. "You implored me to write back, insisting you needed to hear from me. Although it all seemed very strange to me, I replied to your letter, and on my next visit to the nineteenth century two days later, I left it beside the same tombstone. On my third visit I found your reply, and that's how our correspondence through time began."

"Good God," the girl gasped.

"I had no idea who you were," Tom continued, not wanting to give her any respite, "but I fell in love with you all the same, with the woman who wrote those letters. I imagined your face when I closed my eyes. I whispered your name in my sleep, amid the ruins of my devastated world."

Claire fidgeted in her seat and gave another long, bitter sigh.

"How many letters did we write to each other?" she managed to ask.

"Seven, in all," Tom replied randomly, because it sounded like a good number; not too many and not too few. "We hadn't time to write more before they prohibited the use of the machine, but believe me it was enough, my love."

Upon hearing the captain utter those words, Claire heaved another sigh.

"In your last letter, you named the day we would finally meet. May 20 in the year 2000, the day I defeated Solomon and ended the war. That day I did as you instructed in your letter, and after the duel I looked for a secluded spot among the ruins. Then I saw you, and, as you had described, you dropped the parasol, which I was to return to you using the time machine. Once I reached your era I was to go to Covent Garden Market, where we would meet, and then I was supposed to invite you to tea and tell you everything," Tom paused, before adding wistfully: "and now I understand why. It was so these events would take place in the future. Do you see, Claire? You will write those letters to me in the future because I am telling you now that you will."

"Good God," the woman repeated, almost out of breath.

"But there's something else you need to know," announced Tom, determined to fell the tree with one final blow. "In one of your letters you spoke of how we would love one another this afternoon."

"What?" the girl was scarcely able to stammer in an inaudible voice.

"Yes, Claire, this afternoon we will love one another in the boardinghouse over the road, and in your own words, it will be the most magical experience of your life."

Claire stared at him in disbelief, her cheeks flushing bright pink.

"I can understand why you're surprised, but imagine how I felt. I was astonished when I read the letter in which you described our lovemaking, because for you it was something we'd already done, but as far as I was concerned it hadn't happened yet." Tom paused and smiled sweetly at her. "I've come from the future to fulfill my destiny, Claire, which is to love you."

"But, I—" she tried to protest.

"You still don't understand, do you? We've got to make love, Claire," said Tom, "because in reality we already have."

It was the final axe blow. And, like the oak, Claire teetered on her chair and crashed to the floor.

XXVII

IF SHE HAD WANTED TO DRAW everyone's attention, thought Tom, she couldn't have found a better way. Claire's sudden fainting fit, and the din of the shattering teapot and teacups, dragged with the tablecloth onto the floor, had brought to an abrupt standstill the conversations floating through the air of the tearooms, plunging those present into complete, stunned silence. From his view at the back, where he had been relegated during the ensuing commotion, Tom watched the bevy of ladies rallying round the girl. Like a rescue team with years of practice, they stretched her out on a couch, placed a pile of cushions under her feet, loosened her corset (that diabolical item of clothing entirely to blame for her fainting fit as it had prevented her from breathing in the amount of air necessary for such charged conversations), and went to fetch smelling salts in order to bring her round. Tom watched her come to with a loud gasp. The female staff and customers had formed a sort of matriarchal screen around the girl to prevent the gentlemen in the room from glimpsing more of her flesh than was seemly. A few minutes later he saw Claire stumble through the human wall, pale as a ghost, and peer confusedly around her. He waved at her awkwardly with the parasol. After a few moments' hesitation, the girl staggered towards him through the crowd of onlookers. At least she seemed to recognize him as the person whom she had been taking tea with before she had passed out.

"Are you all right, Miss Haggerty?" he asked when she had succeeded in making her way over to him. "Perhaps a little fresh air would do you good . . ."

The girl nodded and settled her hand on Tom's arm like a tame falcon landing on its owner's glove, as though going outside to get some air and escape from all those prying eyes was the best idea he had ever had. Tom led her out of the tearooms, spluttering an apology for having upset her in that manner. Once outside, they paused on the pavement, unable to help glancing up at the boardinghouse looming across the road. With a mixture of unease and resignation, Claire, whose cheeks had recovered some of their color out in the cold air, studied the place where that afternoon she was fated to give herself to the brave Captain Shackleton, the savior of the human race, a man not yet born, and yet who was standing next to her, as if by magic, trying to avoid her eyes.

"And what if I refuse, Captain?" she spoke as though addressing the air. "What if I don't go up there with you?"

It would be fair to say that the question took Tom by surprise, for, in view of the disastrous conclusion to their meeting, he had given up all hope of accomplishing his wicked aims. However, despite her impressive fainting fit, the girl had forgotten nothing of what he had told her and

was clearly still convinced by his story. Tom had improvised on the blank page of the future a chance encounter, a
romance that would explain what was going to happen, and
even encourage the girl to yield to it without fear or regret,
and to her, this was the only possible outcome. A momen-
tary pang of remorse made him consider the possibility of
helping the girl out of this predicament which she seemed
ready to face as though it were an act of contrition. He could
tell her the future was not written in stone, that she could
choose. But he had invested too much energy in this venture to abandon his prey now she was almost within reach.
He remembered one of Gilliam Murray's pet phrases, and
repeated it in a suitably doom-laden voice:

"I've no idea what effect it would have on the fabric of
time."

Claire looked at him, perplexed, as he shrugged his
shoulders, absolving himself of all responsibility. But
after all, she could not blame him for anything: he was
there because she had told him to come in her letters. He
had traveled through time to perform an act Claire had
told him they had already performed, and with a wealth
of detail, moreover. He had journeyed across time to set
their romance in motion, to trigger off what had already
happened but had not yet taken place. The girl seemed
to have reached the same conclusion: what other choice
did she have, to walk away and carry on with her life,
marry one of her admirers? This was her opportunity to
experience something she had always dreamt of: a great
love, a love that spanned the centuries. Not seizing it
would be like having deceived herself all her life.

"The most magical experience of my life." She smiled. "Did I really write that?"

"Yes," replied Tom emphatically. "Those were your exact words."

The girl looked at him, still hesitating. She could not go to bed with a stranger just like that. Except that this was a unique case: she had to give herself to him or the universe would suffer the consequences. She must sacrifice herself to protect the world. But was it really a sacrifice? she wondered. Did she not love him? Was the flurry of emotions that overwhelmed her soul whenever she looked at him not love? It had to be. The feeling that made her light up inside and go weak at the knees had to be love, because if that was not love, then what was? Captain Shackleton had told her they would make love that afternoon and then she would write him beautiful letters; why resist if that was what she really wanted? Ought she to refuse simply because she was retracing the steps of another Claire who was, after all, she herself? Ought she to refuse because it felt more like an obligation than a genuine desire, a spontaneous gesture? Try as she might, she could find no good reason for not doing what she longed to do with all her heart. Neither Lucy nor any of her other friends would be able to fathom her going to bed with a stranger. In the end, this was precisely what decided the matter for her. Yes, she would go to bed with him, and she would spend the rest of her life pining for him, writing him long beautiful letters soaked with her perfume and her tears. She knew she was both passionate and stubborn enough to keep the flame of her love alive, even though she would never again see the person who had set it ablaze.

It was her fate, apparently. An exceptional fate, not without a hint of tragedy, far more pleasant to bear than the dreary marriage she might enter into with one of her dull suitors. She set her lips in a determined line.

"I hope you aren't exaggerating to avoid a blow to your pride, Captain," she joked.

"I'm afraid there's only one way to find out," Tom parried.

The girl's determination to deal with the situation in such a good-natured fashion was a huge relief to Tom, who no longer felt so bad about having his way with her. He was preparing to enjoy her body by means of a despicable ploy before vanishing from her life forever, and although he considered that the conceited young woman was only getting what she deserved, his own underhanded behavior made him feel surprisingly uneasy. He deduced from his sense of disquiet that he still had some scruples after all. But he felt decidedly less guilty now that the girl also seemed set on deriving unequivocal enjoyment from offering her body to Captain Shackleton, the courageous hero who whispered her name amid the ruins of the future.

Compared to some of the places Tom was used to sleeping in, the boardinghouse was clean, even cozy. The girl might think it drab, unfit for someone of her social class, but at least there was nothing to make her flee in horror. While he was asking about a room, Tom watched the girl out of the corner of his eye as she casually surveyed the pictures decorating the modest hallway. He admired the way she tried to appear blasé, as though spending her afternoons going to bed with men from the future in London boardinghouses was second nature to her. Once he had paid for the room, the two of them climbed the stairs leading to the first floor and went along the narrow corridor. As he watched her walking in front of him with a mixture of boldness and submission, Tom became aware for the first time of what was about to happen. There was no turning back: he was going to make love to the girl, he was going to hold her naked, eager, even passionate body in his arms. His whole body suddenly burned with lust, sending a shudder from head to toes. He tried to contain his excitement as they paused before the door. All at once Claire tensed.

"I know it will be wonderful," she said suddenly, half closing her eyes as if to bolster her courage.

"It will be, Claire," Tom echoed, trying to conceal his eagerness to undress her. "You told me so yourself."

The girl nodded and gave a sigh of resignation. Without further ado, Tom pushed open the door and gestured politely for her to go in before closing it behind them. When they had vanished inside, the narrow corridor was once more deserted. The last rays of the evening sun filtered through the grimy window at the far end. It was a fading light with coppery tones, a soft, pale, almost melancholy glow that shone onto the floating dust particles, turning them into tiny glittering insects. Although, given the leisurely, hypnotic way the particles swirled at random, a spray of pollen might be a more suitable metaphor, do you not agree? From behind a few of the closed doors came the unmistakable sounds of amorous engagement: grunts, stifled cries, and even the occasional hearty slap of a hand on a tender buttock—noises which, added to the rhythmical creaking of bed frames, suggested that the lovemaking going on there was not of a conjugal nature. Mingled with a few of the guests' carnal exploits, other sounds of a less lustful nature, like snippets of conversation or a child crying, helped give the finishing touches to the chaotic symphony of the world. The corridor in the boardinghouse was some thirty yards long and decorated with prints of misty landscapes, with several oil lamps attached to the walls. As was his custom, the landlord, Mr. Pickard (I feel it would be churlish not to introduce him by name even though he will not be appearing again in this tale), was at that very moment preparing to light the lamps, in order not to leave it in darkness, which could have led to all sorts of mishaps when his guests later left the establishment.

Those were his footsteps echoing on the stairs. Each night he found them more difficult to climb, for the years had taken their toll, and recently he could not help giving a triumphant sigh when he reached the top. Mr. Pickard took the box of matches out of his trouser pocket and began lighting the half dozen lamps dotted along the wall in the corridor. He did so very slowly, slipping the match under each lampshade like a skilled swordsman performing a final thrust, and holding it there until the oil-soaked wick caught alight. Time had transformed this gesture into an almost mechanical ceremony he performed mechanically. None of the guests would have been able to tell what Mr. Pickard was thinking as he performed his daily lamp-lighting ritual, but I am not one of the guests and, as with all the other characters in this novel, his innermost thoughts are not off limits to me. Mr. Pickard was thinking about his little granddaughter Wendy, who had died of scarlet fever more than ten years earlier: he could not help comparing the act of lighting those lamps with the manner in which the Creator behaved towards all His creatures, allowing them to burn, then snuffing them out whenever He felt like it, without any explanation or consideration for those He left plunged into darkness. When Mr. Pickard had lit the last lamp, he walked back down the passageway and descended the stairs, exiting this tale as discreetly as he had entered it.

After he had gone, the corridor was once more deserted, although brightly lit. You are probably hoping I will not describe it to you again, but I am afraid I will, as I have no intention of crossing the threshold into the room Tom and Claire are in and rudely intruding on their privacy. Take pleasure in the flickering shadows on the flowery wallpaper, and play at seeing bunnies, bears, and puppy dogs in their shifting shapes as evening turns to night, as—oblivious of man's concerns—minutes turn inexorably into hours, like a snowball rolling down a hill.

I will not ask you how many little animal shapes you managed to see before the door to the room finally opened and Tom stepped out. A smile of satisfaction playing on his lips, he tucked his shirt into his trousers and pulled on his cap. Gently extricating himself from Claire's embrace, he had told her he must go before the hole in time closed up. She had kissed him with the solemnity of one who knows she is kissing the man she loves for the very last time, and with the kiss still imprinted on his lips, Tom Blunt began descending the stairs, wondering how it was possible to feel like the happiest man in the world and at the same time the most despicable creature in the universe.

XXVIII

TWO DAYS HAD GONE BY SINCE their meeting, and, to his surprise, Tom was still alive. No one had shot him in the head as he sat up with a start in his bed, or followed him through the streets waiting to thrust a thirsty blade into his side in the midst of a crowd, or tried to run him down in a carriage, or push him in front of a train. Tom could only presume that this agonizing calm, this excruciating slowness in finishing him off was either their way of tormenting him or that no one was going to make him pay for what he had done. More than once, unable to bear the strain, Tom was on the point of ending it all himself, slitting his throat, or throwing himself off a bridge into the Thames, in the family tradition. Either method seemed a good way of escaping from the apprehension that had even infiltrated his dreams, transforming them into nightmares in which Solomon roamed the streets of London with his metal insect gait, making his way through the crowds thronging the pavements with their hats and coats, and clambering with difficulty up the stairs to his room. Tom awoke when the automaton broke down his door, and for a few bewildered moments believed he really was the brave Captain Shackleton, who had escaped from the year 2000 and was hiding in 1896. He was powerless to dispel those dreams, but if at night he was at the mercy of his fears, in the daytime he was able to overcome them; by keeping a level head, he had managed to compose himself and was even prepared to accept his fate with calm resignation. He would not take his own life. It was far more dignified to die looking his killers straight in the eye, whether they were made of flesh and blood or of cast iron.

Convinced he had not long to live, Tom saw no point in going to the docks to look for work: he could just as well die with empty pockets. And so he spent his days wandering aimlessly around London, like a leaf blown by the wind. Occasionally he would stretch out in some park like a drunk or a vagrant, while in his mind he went over every detail of his encounter with the girl, her ardent caresses, her intoxicating kisses, the passion and ease with which she had given herself to him. Then he told himself again that it had all been worth it, and that he had no intention of putting up any resistance when they came to kill him, to make him pay for that moment of happiness. Part of him could not help considering the bullet that was so long in coming as just punishment for his despicable behavior.

On the third day, his wanderings took him to Harrow-on-the-Hill, the place he usually went to in search of peace. He could think of no better place to wait for his killers, as he tried to understand the random sequence of events that made up his life, to give it some meaning even if he did not believe it. Once he arrived, he sat in the shade of the old oak and breathed in deeply as he cast a dispassionate eye over the city. Seen from the hill, the capital of Empire always looked disappointing to him, like a sinister barge with pointed spires and smoking factory chimneys for masts. He exhaled slowly, trying to forget how famished he was. He hoped they would come for him today, or he would have to steal some food before nightfall to stop his stomach rumbling. Where were Murray's thugs? he wondered for the hundredth time. If they came now he would see them from his vantage point, and he would greet them with his most dazzling smile, unbutton his shirt, and point to his heart to make it easier for them. "Go ahead and kill me," he would say, "don't worry; I won't really kill you later. I'm no hero. I'm just Tom, the despicable wretch Tom Blunt. You can bury me here, next to my friend John Peachey, another wretch like me."

It was at this point that, looking towards the headstone, he noticed the letter tucked under a stone beside it. For a moment he thought he was imagining things. Intrigued, he picked it up and, with an odd sensation of remembering a dream, he saw it was addressed to Captain Derek Shackleton. He hesitated for a moment, not knowing what to do, but of course there was only one thing he could do. As he opened the envelope he could not help feeling he was trespassing, reading someone else's correspondence. He unfolded the sheet of paper inside and discovered Claire Haggerty's neat, elegant handwriting. He began to read slowly, straining to recall the meaning of each letter, declaiming aloud, as though he wanted to explain to the squirrels the travails of men. The letter read as follows:

From Claire Haggerty to Captain Shackleton

Dear Derek,

I was obliged to start writing this letter at least a dozen times before realizing there is only one possible way to begin, and that is to avoid all preliminary explanations and obey the dictates of my heart: I love you, Derek. I love you as I have never loved anyone. I love you now, and I will love you forever. And my love for you is the only thing that keeps me alive.

I can see the surprise on your face as you read these words written to you by an unknown woman, because I assure you I know that face well. But believe me, my sweet: I love you. Or rather, we love each other. For, although it might seem even stranger to you, as you do not know who I am, you love me, too—or you will do in a few hours, or possibly a few moments, from now. However reluctant you are, however incredible all this seems, you will love me. You simply have no choice. You will love me because you already do.

If I allow myself to address you so affectionately it is because of what we have already shared, and because you must know that I can still feel the warmth of your touch on my skin, the taste of you on my lips, I can feel you

inside me. Despite my initial doubts, despite
my young girl's foolish fears, I am overwhelmed
by the love you foresaw, or maybe it is an even
greater love than that, a love so great nothing
will contain it.

Shake your head as much as you like as
you try to understand these ravings, but the
explanation is quite simple. It boils down to
this: what has not yet happened to you has
already happened to me. It is one of the strange
anomalies that occur in time travel, when
journeying back and forth across the centuries.
But you know all about that, don't you? For, if
I am not mistaken, you found this letter next
to the big oak tree when you stepped out of a
time tunnel, so you will not find it so difficult to
believe everything I am telling you. Yes, I know
the place where you come out and your reason
for traveling to my time, and my knowing this
can only mean one thing: that what I am saying
is true, it is not a hoax. Trust me, then, without
reservation. And trust me above all when I tell
you we love each other. Start loving me now
by replying to this letter and reciprocating my
feelings, please. Write me a letter and leave it
beside John Peachey's headstone on your next
visit: that will be our way of communicating
from now on, my love, for we still have six more
letters to write to each other. Are your eyes
wide with surprise? I do not blame you, and yet

I am only repeating what you told me yesterday. Please write to me, my love, for your letters are all I have left of you.

Yes, that is the bad news: I will never see you again, Derek, which is why I cherish your letters. I shall go directly to the point: the love we are going profess to one another is the result of a single encounter, for we shall meet only once. Well, twice actually, but the first time (or the last time if we follow the chronology our love has turned on its head) will only last a few minutes. Our second meeting, in my time, will last longer and be more meaningful, for it will feed the love that will rage in our hearts forever, a love our letters will keep alive for me and will initiate for you. And yet if we respect time, I will never see you again. You, on the other hand, do not yet know me, even though we made love together less than a few hours ago. Now I understand your nervousness yesterday when we met at the tearooms: I had already stirred you with my words.

We will meet on May 20 in the year 2000, but I will tell you all about that first meeting in my last letter. Everything will begin with that meeting, although, now I think about it, I realize that cannot be true because you will already know me through my letters. Where does our love story begin, then? Here, with this letter? No, this is not the beginning either. We are trapped in a circle, Derek, and no one knows where a circle begins. We can only follow the circle until it closes, as I am doing now, trying to stop my hand from trembling. This is my role, the only thing I have to do, because I already know what you will do: I know you will reply to my letter, I know you will fall in love with me, I know you will look for me when the time comes. Only the details will come as a surprise to me.

I suppose I should end this letter by telling you what I look like, my way of thinking and seeing the world, as during our meeting in the tearooms when I asked you how you could possibly love me without knowing me, and you assured me you knew me better than I could ever imagine. And you knew me of course through my letters, so let us begin: I was born on March 15, 1875, in West London. I am slim, of medium height, I have blue eyes and black shoulder-length hair, which, contrary to the norm, I wear loose. Forgive my brevity, but describing myself physically feels like an undignified exercise in vanity. Besides, I would rather tell you more about my inner soul. I have two older sisters, Rebecca and Evelyn. They are both married and live in Chelsea, and it is by comparing myself to them that I can best give you an idea of what I am like. I have always felt different. Unlike them, I have found it impossible to adapt to the time I live in. I do not know how to explain this to you, Derek, but my time bores me. I feel as though I am watching a comedy at the theater and everybody else is laughing. Only I am impervious to the supposed hilarity of the characters' remarks. And this dissatisfaction has turned me into a problem child, someone it is best not to invite to parties, and who must be kept under watch during family get-togethers, for I have ruined more than one by breaking the norms that dictate the behavior of the society I live in, to the astonishment of the guests.

Something else that makes me feel very different from the other young women I know is my lack of interest in getting married. I loathe the role women are supposed to fulfill in marriage and for which my mother tries so hard to groom me. I can think of no better way to destroy my free spirit than to become a sensible housewife who spends her days drilling the moral values she has learned into her children and ordering servants around, while her husband goes out into the world of work, that dangerous arena from which women, universally deemed too sensitive and delicate, have been quietly banished. As you can see, I am independent and adventurous, and, although this might strike you as incongruous, I do not fall easily in love. To be honest, I never thought I would be able to fall in love with anyone the way I have fallen in love with you. I had honestly begun to feel like a dusty bottle in a wine cellar waiting

to be uncorked at a special occasion that never
arrived. And yet, I suppose it is owing to my very
nature that all this is happening.

I will come here to fetch your letter the day
after tomorrow, my love, just as you told me I
would. I am longing to hear from you, to read
your words of love, to know you are mine even
though we are separated by an ocean of time.

Yours evermore,

C.

Despite the effort involved in reading, Tom reread
Claire's letter three times, with the exact look of surprise the girl had predicted, though for quite different
reasons, of course. After the third reading, he replaced
it carefully in the envelope and leaned back against the
tree, trying to understand the contradictory feelings the
pages stirred in him. The girl had swallowed every word
and had come all that way to leave him a letter! He realized that while for him it was all over, for her it was
only just beginning. He saw now how far his adventure
had gone. He had played with the girl without stopping
to think of the consequences it might have, and now he
"knew" what they were. Yes, this letter unintentionally
revealed to him the effect his misbehavior had had on his
victim, and he would rather not have known. Not only
had Claire believed his cock-and-bull story to the point
of obediently following the next step in the sequence of
events, but their physical encounter had been the breath
of life her nascent love had needed in order to catch fire,

apparently taking on the proportions of an inferno. And now the blaze was consuming her, and Tom marveled not only that one brief encounter could produce so much love, but that the girl was prepared to devote her life to keeping it alive, like someone stoking a fire in the forest to keep wolves at bay.

What amazed him most of all, though, was that Claire was doing all this for him, because she loved him. No one had ever expressed such love for him before, he reflected, because it no longer mattered that all the girl's love was directed towards Captain Shackleton: the man who had bedded her, undressed her tenderly, taken her gently, was Tom Blunt. Shackleton was a mere act, an idea, but what Claire had really fallen in love with was his way of acting him. And how did that make him feel? he asked himself. Should being loved so unreservedly and passionately produce the exact same feelings in him, like his reflection appearing the moment he leant over a pond? He was unable to answer that question. And besides, there was not much point in speculating about it, as he would probably be dead by the end of the day.

He glanced again at the letter he was holding. What was he supposed to do with it? Suddenly, he realized there was only one thing he could do: he must reply to it, not because he intended to take on the role of starstruck lover in this story he had unthinkingly set in motion, but because the girl had insinuated she would be unable to live without his letters. Tom imagined her traveling there in her carriage, walking to the top of the little hill, and finding no reply from Captain Shackleton. He was convinced

Claire would be unable to cope with this sudden twist in the plot, this unexpected, mysterious silence. After weeks of going to Harrow and leaving empty-handed, he could imagine her taking her own life in the same passionate way she had decided to love him, perhaps by plunging a sharp dagger through her heart or downing a flask of laudanum. And Tom could not let that happen. Whether he liked it or not, as a result of his little game, Claire Haggerty's life was in his hands. He had no choice.

As HE WALKED BACK to London across country, keeping away from the roads, pausing and tensing at the slightest sound, he realized something had changed: he no longer wanted to die. And not because his life suddenly seemed more worth living than before, but because he had to reply to the girl's letter. He had to keep himself alive in order to keep Claire alive.

Once in the city, he stole some writing paper from a stationer's shop, and, satisfied that Gilliam's thugs had not followed him nor were posted round his lodgings, he locked himself away in his room in Buckeridge Street. Everything seemed quiet. The usual afternoon noises wafted up to his window from the street, a harmonious melody in which no discordant notes were struck. He pushed the chair up to the bed to make an improvised desk, and spread the paper out on the seat together with the pen and ink he had purloined. He took a deep breath. After half an hour of grappling with the page, deeply frustrated, he realized writing was not as easy as he had imagined. It was far more arduous than reading. He was appalled to discover it was impossible for him to transfer the thoughts in his head onto paper. He knew what he wanted to say, but each time he started a sentence his original idea seemed to drift away and become something entirely different. He still remembered the rudiments of writing that Megan had taught him, but he did not know enough grammar to be able to form proper sentences, and, more importantly, he did not know how to express his ideas with the same clarity as she had. He gazed down at the indecipherable jumble of letters and crossings out that defiled the pristine page. The only legible words were the "Dear Claire" with which he had so optimistically begun his missive. The rest was simply a pitiful demonstration of a semi-illiterate man's first attempt at writing a letter. He screwed up the sheet of paper, bowing to the inevitable. If Claire received a letter like this she would end up taking her own life anyway, incapable of understanding why the savior of mankind wrote like a chimpanzee.

He wanted to reply, yet was unable to. But Claire had to find a letter at the foot of the oak tree in two days' time, or she would end up taking her own life! Tom lay back on the bed, trying to gather his thoughts. Clearly he needed help. He needed someone to write the letter for him, but who? He did not know anyone who could write. It could not be just any person, for example, a schoolteacher whom he could force to write it, threatening to break the man's fingers if he refused. The chosen person not only had to be able to write properly, he had to have enough imagination to play a spirited part in the charade. And on top of that, he needed to be capable of corresponding with the girl in the same passionate tone. Who could he find who possessed all those qualities?

It came to him in a flash. He leapt to his feet, thrust aside the chair, and pulled open the bottom drawer of his chest of drawers. There it was, like a fish gasping out of water: the novel. He had purchased it when he first started working for Murray, because his boss had told him it was thanks to this book that his business had been such a success. And Tom, who had never owned a book in his life, had gone out and bought it straightaway. Actually reading it, however, had been too exacting a task for Tom, and he had given up after the third page; yet he had held on to it, not wanting to resell the book because in some sense he owed who he was now to that author. He opened the book and studied the photograph of the writer on the inside flap. The caption below said he lived in Woking, Surrey. Yes, if anyone could help him it had to be the fellow in the photograph, this young man with birdlike features named H. G. Wells.

WITH NO MONEY TO hire a carriage and reluctant to risk hiding on a train bound for Surrey, Tom concluded that the only way for him to reach the author's house was by walking. The three-hour coach ride to Woking would take him three times as long on foot, so that if he left straightaway, he would reach his destination in the early hours of the morning, obviously not the best time to turn up unexpectedly at someone's house, except in case of an emergency, which this was. He put Claire's letter in his pocket, pulled on his cap, and left the boardinghouse for Woking without a second thought. He had no choice and was not in the least daunted by the walk. He knew he could count on his sturdy legs and stamina to complete the marathon journey without weakening.

During his long walk to the author's house, while he watched night spread itself lazily over the landscape, and glanced over his shoulder every now and then to make sure neither Murray's thugs nor Solomon were following him, Tom Blunt toyed with different ways of introducing himself to Wells. In the end, the one he decided was the cleverest also sounded the most far-fetched: he would introduce himself as Captain Derek Shackleton. He was sure the savior of mankind would be far better received at any time of the day than plain old Tom Blunt, and there was nothing to stop him successfully playing the role off-stage as he had already done with Claire. As Shackleton, he could also tell the author the same tale he had told the girl and show him the letter he had found when he came through the hole on his first visit to their time. How could this Wells fellow not be taken in if he himself had written a novel about time travel?

If he were to make his story believable, though, Tom would need to think up a good reason why neither he nor anyone else from the future was able to write the letter himself. Perhaps he could explain that in the year 2000, long before the war began, man had fallen out of the habit of writing, because the task had been given to automaton scribes. In any event, introducing himself as

Captain Shackleton still seemed like the best plan: as he would later rescue the planet from the automatons, it felt preferable for the famous hero of the future to ask for help in order to save his beloved than for a nobody to wake up the famous author to beg him to get Tom out of the predicament his desire for sex had got him into.

When he arrived in Woking in the early hours, the place was immersed in an idyllic calm. It was a cold but beautiful night. Tom spent almost an hour reading letter boxes before coming to the one marked Wells. He was standing in front of a darkened three-story house enclosed by a not too high fence. After studying the author's house for a few moments, Tom took a deep breath and climbed over the fence. There was no point in waiting any longer.

He crossed the garden reverentially, as though he were walking into a chapel, climbed the steps to the front door, and was about to ring when his hand stopped short of the bell chime. The echo of a horse's hooves shattering the nocturnal silence made him freeze. He turned slowly as he heard the animal draw near, and almost immediately saw it stop outside the author's house. A shiver ran down his spine as he watched the rider, barely more than a shadow, dismount and open the gate. Was it one of Murray's thugs? The fellow made a swift gesture that left him in no doubt, pulling a gun from his pocket and pointing it straight at him.

Tom instantly dived to one side, rolling across the lawn and disappearing into the darkness. Out of the corner of his eye he watched the stranger try to follow his sudden movement with the gun. Tom had no intention of making himself an easy target. He leapt to his feet and in two strides had reached the fence. He was convinced he would feel the warm sting of the bullet entering his back at any moment, but apparently he was moving too quickly, and it did not happen. He clambered over the fence and pelted down the street until he reached the fields. He ran for at least five minutes. Only then, panting for breath, did he allow himself to stop and look behind him to see whether Gilliam's thug was following him. All he could see was black night enfolding everything. He had managed to lose him. He was safe, at least for the moment, for he doubted that his killer would bother looking for him in that pitch-blackness. He would no doubt go back to London to report to Murray. Feeling calmer, Tom found a place behind some bushes and settled down for the night. In the morning, after making sure the thug had really gone, he would return to the author's house and ask for his help, as planned.

XXIX

"YOU SAVED A MAN'S LIFE USING YOUR imagination," Jane Wells had said to her husband only a few hours earlier, and her words were still echoing in his head as he watched the dawn light flood in through the tiny attic window, revealing the contours of the furniture and their two figures intertwined like a Greek statue on the seat of the time machine. When he had suggested to his wife they might find a use for the seat, this was not exactly what he had had in mind, but he had thought it best not to upset her, and especially not now. Wells gazed at her tenderly. Jane was breathing evenly, asleep in his arms after giving herself to him with renewed enthusiasm, reviving the almost violent fervor of the first months. Wells had watched this passion ebb away with the resigned sorrow of one who knows only too well that passionate love does not last forever; it merely transfers to other bodies. But there was no law, apparently, against its embers being rekindled by a timely breeze, and this discovery had left a rather foolish grin on the author's face which he had not seen reflected in any of his mirrors for a long time. And it was all due to the words floating in his head: "You saved a man's life using your imagination," words that had made him shine once more in Jane's eyes, and which I trust you have also remembered, because they link this scene and Wells's first appearance in our tale, which I informed you would not be his last.

When his wife went down to make breakfast, the author decided to remain sitting on the machine a while longer. He took a deep breath, contented and extraordinarily at ease with himself. There were times in his life when Wells considered himself an exceptionally ridiculous human being, but he seemed now to be going through a phase where he was able see himself in a different, more charitable, and why not say it, a more admiring light. He had enjoyed saving a life, as much because of Jane's unexpected offering as for the fantastic gift he had been given as a result: this machine that had arisen from his imagination, this ornate sleigh that could travel through time, at least this was what they had made Andrew Harrington believe. Contemplating it now by daylight, Wells had to admit that when he had given it that cursory description in his novel, he never imagined it might turn out to be such a beautiful object if someone actually decided to build it. Feeling like a naughty child, he sat up ceremoniously, placed his hand with exaggerated solemnity on the glass lever to the right of the control panel, and smiled wistfully. If only the thing actually did work. If only he could hop from era to era, travel through time at his whim until he reached its farthest frontier—if such a thing existed—go to the place where time began or ended. But the machine could not be used for that. In fact, the machine had no use at all. And now that he had removed the gadget that lit the magnesium, it could not even blind its occupant.

"Bertie," Jane called from downstairs.

Wells leapt up with a start, as though ashamed for her to discover him playing with his toy. He straightened his clothes, rumpled from their earlier passionate embraces, and hurried downstairs.

"There's a young man to see you," Jane said, a little uneasily. "He says his name is Captain Derek Shackleton."

Wells paused at the foot of the stairs. Derek Shackleton? Why did the name ring a bell?

"He's waiting in the sitting room. But he said something else, Bertie," Jane went on, hesitatingly, unsure what tone of voice she should adopt to express what she was about to say: "He says he's from . . . the year 2000."

From the year 2000? Now Wells knew where he had heard that name before.

"Ah, in that case it must be very urgent," he said, grinning mysteriously. "Let's hurry and find out what the gentleman wants."

With these words, he strode towards the tiny sitting room, shaking his head in amusement. Next to the chimneypiece, too nervous to sit down, Wells discovered a young man dressed in modest clothing. Before saying anything, he looked the man up and down, amazed. He was quite simply a magnificent specimen of the human race, with his statuesque muscles, noble face, and eyes brimming with ferocity like a cornered panther.

"I'm George Wells," he introduced himself, once he had finished his examination. "How may I help you?"

"How do you do, Mr. Wells," the man from the future greeted him. "Forgive me for barging in on you so early in the morning, but it's a matter of life or death."

Wells nodded, smiling inwardly at the rehearsed introduction.

"I'm Captain Derek Shackleton and I've come from the future. From the year 2000 to be precise." The young man stared at him expectantly, waiting for him to respond.

"Does my name ring a bell?" he asked, on seeing the author was not overly surprised.

"Naturally, Captain," Wells replied, grinning slightly as he riffled through a wastepaper basket next to a set of book-lined shelves. A moment later, he extracted a ball of scrunched-up paper, which he unfolded and handed to his visitor, who cautiously took it from him. "How could the name not ring a bell? I receive one of these leaflets every week without fail. You are the savior of the human race, the man who in the year 2000 will free our planet from the yoke of the evil automatons."

"That's right," the young man ventured, slightly unnerved by the author's mocking tone.

A tense silence followed, during which Wells simply stood, hands in pockets, contemplating his visitor with a disdainful air.

"You must be wondering how I traveled to your time," the young man said finally, like an actor obliged to prompt himself in order to be able to carry on his performance.

"Now you mention it, yes," said Wells, without attempting to show the slightest curiosity.

"Then I'll explain," said the young man, trying to ignore Wells's manifest indifference. "When the war first started, our scientists invented a machine capable of making holes in time, with the aim of tunneling from the year 2000 to your time. They wanted to send someone to kill the man who made automatons and prevent the war from happening. That someone is me."

Wells carried on staring at him solemnly for a moment. Finally he let out a guffaw that took his visitor aback.

"I'll grant you have an impressive imagination, young man," he said.

"You don't believe me?" the other man asked, although the tinge of regret in his voice gave his question the air of bitter acknowledgment.

"Of course not," the author declared cheerily. "But don't be alarmed, it's not because you failed to make your ingenious lie sound convincing."

"But, then . . ." the youth stammered, bewildered.

"The problem is I don't believe it's possible to travel to the year 2000, nor that man will be at war with the automatons then. The whole thing is just a silly invention. Gilliam Murray may be able to fool the whole of England, but he can't fool me," exclaimed Wells.

"So . . . you know the whole thing is a fraud?" murmured the young man, utterly flabbergasted.

Wells nodded solemnly, glancing at Jane, who also looked bewildered.

"And you're not going to denounce him?" the lad asked finally.

The author heaved a deep sigh before giving his reply, as though the question had been eating away at him for too long.

"No, I haven't the slightest intention of doing so," he replied. "If people are prepared to part with good money to watch you defeat a lot of pseudo-automatons, then maybe they deserve to be swindled. And besides, who am I to deprive them of the illusion of having traveled to the future? Must I destroy their fantasy simply because someone is getting rich from it?"

"I see," murmured the visitor, still mystified, and then with a hint of admiration he added: "you're the only person I know who thinks it's all a hoax."

"Well, I suppose I have a certain advantage over the rest of humanity," replied Wells.

He smiled at the youth's increasingly bemused face. Jane was also giving him puzzled looks. The author heaved a sigh. It was time he shared his bread with the apostles, and then they might help him bear his cross.

"A little over a year ago," Wells explained, addressing them both, "shortly after *The Time Machine* was published, a man came here wanting to show me a novel he had just written. Like *The Time Machine*, it was a piece of science fiction. He asked me to read it and if I liked it to recommend it to my editor, Henley, for possible publication."

The young man nodded slowly, as though he had not quite understood yet what all this had to do with him. Wells turned around and began scouring the books and files lining the sitting room shelves. Finally he found what he had been looking for—a bulky manuscript, which he tossed onto the table.

"The man's name was Gilliam Murray, and this is the novel he gave me that October afternoon in 1895."

With a wave of his hand he invited the lad to read the title page. The young man moved closer to the manuscript and read aloud clumsily, as though chewing each word:

"*Captain Derek Shackleton: The True Story of a Brave Hero of the Future*, by Gilliam F. Murray."

"Yes," confirmed Wells. "And do you want to know what it's about? The novel takes place in the year 2000 and tells the story of a battle between the evil automatons and the human army led by the brave Captain Derek Shackleton. Does the plot ring a bell?"

The visitor nodded, but Wells deduced from his confused expression that he still did not fully understand what he was getting at.

"Had Gilliam written this novel after he set up his business, I would have no other reason, besides my natural skepticism, to question the authenticity of his year 2000," he explained. "But he brought me his novel a whole year before! Do you understand what I'm saying? Gilliam has staged his novel, and you are its main protagonist."

He picked up the manuscript, searched for a specific page, and, to the young man's dismay, started to read out loud:

"Captain Derek Shackleton was a magnificent specimen of the human race, with his statuesque muscles, noble face, and eyes brimming with ferocity like a cornered panther."

The lad blushed at the description. Was that what he looked like? Did he really have the eyes of a cornered animal? It was quite possible, for he had been cornered since birth, by his father, by life, by misfortune, and lately by Murray's thugs. He stared at Wells, not knowing what to say.

"It's a ghastly description by a talentless writer, but I have to confess you fit the part perfectly," said Wells, hurling the manuscript back onto the table with a gesture of utter contempt.

A few moments passed in which no one spoke.

"Even so, Bertie," Jane finally stepped in, "this young man needs your help."

"Oh, yes. So he does," responded a reluctant Wells, who assumed that with his masterful exposure of Murray he had resolved the reason for the visit.

"What's your real name?" Jane asked him.

"Tom Blunt, ma'am," replied Tom, bowing politely.

"Tom Blunt," Wells echoed mockingly. "It doesn't sound quite so heroic, of course."

Jane shot him a reproachful look. She hated it when her husband resorted to sarcasm to compensate for the terrible feeling of physical inferiority that usually assailed him when he was in the presence of someone bigger than himself.

"Tell me, then, Tom," Wells went on, after clearing his throat, "how may I help you?"

Tom sighed. No longer a brave hero from the future, just a miserable wretch, he stared down at his feet, ceaselessly wringing his hat as though trying to squeeze it dry, and attempted to tell the couple everything that had happened since his pressing need to empty his bladder had compelled him to find a quiet place on the set of the year 2000. Trying not to gabble, he told them about the girl named Claire Haggerty who had appeared out of nowhere just after he had taken off his helmet and armor, how she had seen his face, and the problems that would cause him. He was obliged to tell them about the unpleasant ways Murray had of assuring his cast of actors did not give away the hoax, and about what had happened to poor Perkins.

His speculations caused the author's wife to gasp in horror, while Wells simply shook his head as if to say he had expected as much of Gilliam Murray. Tom then told them how he had bumped into Claire Haggerty at the market and had made her agree to meet him, driven, he confessed shamefully, by his male instinct. He described how he was then forced to make up the story about the letters in order for her to agree to go with him to the boardinghouse. He knew he had done wrong, he told them, not daring to raise his eyes from the floor, and he regretted it, but they should not waste time judging his behavior because his actions had given rise to unforeseen consequences. The girl had fallen in love with him, and, believing every word to be true, had duly written the first letter, which she had left at Harrow-on-the-Hill. He fished the letter out of his pocket and handed it to Wells, who took it from him, stunned at everything he was hearing.

The author unfolded the letter and, after clearing his throat noisily, began reading aloud so that his intrigued wife could also know what it contained. He tried to read in a modulated voice, like a priest reciting the lesson, but could not avoid his voice catching when he read out certain passages. The emotions expressed were so beautiful he could not help feeling a pang of resentment towards the young man in front of him, who had undeservingly become the object of a love so absolute it forced him to question his own emotions, to reconsider his whole way of experiencing love. The look of compassion that had overtaken Jane's face confirmed his wife was feeling something similar.

"I tried writing to her," said Tom, "but I can barely even read. I'm afraid if there's no letter waiting for her on the hill tomorrow, Miss Haggerty might do something foolish."

Wells had to admit it was most likely, given the feverish tone of her missive.

"The reason I came here was to ask you to write to her on my behalf," the young man went on to confess.

Wells looked at him, incredulous.

"What did you say?"

"Three letters, that's all, Mr. Wells. It's nothing for you," pleaded the youth, and then after a moment's thought, he added: "I can't pay you, but if you ever have a problem that can't be dealt with in a civilized way, just call on me."

Wells could scarcely believe his ears. He was about to say he had no intention of getting involved in this mess, when he felt Jane's hand pressing his firmly. He turned to look at his wife, who smiled at him with the same dreamy expression she wore when she finished one of her beloved romantic novels; then he looked back at Tom, who in turn was gaping at him expectantly. And he realized he had no choice: he must once more save a life using his imagination. He gazed for a long time at the pages he was holding, covered in Claire Haggerty's neat, elegant script. Deep down, he had to confess he found it tempting to carry on this fantastic story, to pretend to be a brave hero from the future caught up in a bloody war against the evil automatons, and even to tell another woman he loved her passionately, and with the approval of his own wife. As though suddenly the world had decided to nurture man's deepest feelings, instead of keeping them in check, giving rise to a harmonious cohabitation on a planet cleansed of jealousy and prejudice, where licentious behavior had been sublimated into an almost tender, respectful friendship. The challenge excited him enormously, it was true, and as he had no choice but to accept it, he cheered himself with the notion that he might find corresponding with the unknown young woman at once amusing and exciting.

"Very well," he agreed reluctantly. "Come back tomorrow morning and you'll have your letter."

XXX

HE FIRST THING WELLS DID WHEN he was left alone in the sitting room while Jane accompanied the young man to the door was to place Gilliam Murray's manuscript once more out of his field of vision. Although he had not let it show, he found the appalling manner in which Gilliam kept his masquerade going deeply disturbing. Naturally, the man had to surround himself with people who could keep their mouths shut, and although he could have achieved this with incentives, threats seemed to work much better. The discovery that Gilliam resorted so casually to such gruesome methods sent a shiver down his spine; not for nothing was the man his adversary, or at least that was what his behavior seemed to indicate. He picked up the leaflet Gilliam sent him religiously every week and looked at it with distaste. Sickening though it was, Wells had to accept that it was all his fault. Yes, Murray's Time Travel existed thanks to him, thanks to the decision he had made.

He had only had two meetings with Gilliam Murray, but for some men that was enough to establish an enmity.

And Gilliam was one of those, as Wells soon discovered. Their first meeting had taken place in that very room one April afternoon, he recalled, glancing with horror at the wing chair into which Gilliam Murray had squeezed his bulky frame.

From the moment he had appeared in the doorway with his visiting card and his unctuous smile, Wells had been in awe of his huge oxlike body, although even more astonishing was the extraordinary weightlessness of his movements, as though his bones were hollow. Wells had sat down in the chair facing him, and while Jane served the tea, the two men had studied one another with polite discretion. When his wife had left the room, the stranger gave him an even broader syrupy smile, thanked him for agreeing to see him at such short notice, and, without pausing for breath, showered him with rapturous adulation for his novel *The Time Machine*. However, there are those who only admire a thing in order blow their own trumpet, to show off their own understanding and intelligence to others, and Gilliam Murray belonged to this group of men. He launched into a furious eulogy of the novel, extolling with lofty speech the symmetry of its structure, the power of its imagery, even the color of the suit he had chosen for his main character. Wells simply listened courteously and wondered why anyone would choose to waste their morning inundating him with praise when they could put it all in a polite letter like the rest of his admirers. He weathered the glowing tributes, nodding uncomfortably, as one caught in an irksome yet harmless shower of rain, praying that the tedious panegyric would soon end and he could go back to his work.

However, he soon discovered it had been no more than a preamble aimed at smoothing the man's way before he decided to reveal the real reason for his visit. After finishing his fulsome speech, Gilliam plucked a voluminous manuscript from his briefcase and placed it delicately in Wells's hands, as though he were handing over a sacred relic or a newborn infant. *Captain Derek Shackleton: The True Story of a Brave Hero of the Future*, Wells read, dumbfounded. He could no longer recall how they had agreed to meet again a week later, after the giant wheedled him into promising to read his novel, and if he liked it, to recommend it to Henley.

Wells embarked upon the task of plowing through the manuscript that had unexpectedly come into his hands, like someone undergoing torture. He had no desire to read anything issuing from the imagination of that self-important braggart whom he considered absolutely incapable of interesting him, and he was not mistaken. The more he read of the pretentious prose, the more his mind became fogged with boredom, and he quickly made a conscious decision never again to meet any of his admirers. Gilliam had given him an overwritten, monotonous piece of tripe; a novel which, in common with the many that were swamping bookshop windows, had copied the one he had written speculating about the future. Such novels were brimming with mechanical artifacts, veritable paper depositories of junk, which, drawing inspiration from the growing impact of science, exhibited every type of outlandish machine aimed at satisfying man's most secret longings. Wells had read none of them, but Henley had related many of their hilarious plots to him over a meal; such as those of the New Yorker Luis Senarens, whose main characters explore the planet's far-flung territories in airships, abducting any indigenous tribe they happen across on the way. The one that had stuck in his mind was about a Jewish inventor who built a machine that made things grow bigger. The image of London attacked by an army of giant wood lice, which Henley had described to him with contempt, had actually terrified Wells.

The plot of Gilliam Murray's novel was equally painful. The pompous title concealed the madcap visions of an unhinged mind. Gilliam argued that as the years went by, the automatons—those mechanical dolls sold in some Central London toy shops—would eventually come to life. Yes, incredible though it might seem, beneath their wooden skulls an almost human form of awareness would begin to stir, so human in fact that the astonished reader would soon discover that the automatons harbored a deep resentment towards man for the humiliating treatment they had endured as his slaves. Finally, under the leadership of Solomon, a steam-powered automaton soldier, they swiftly and mercilessly decided the fate of the human race: extermination. Within a few decades the automatons had reduced the planet to a mound of rubble and mankind to a handful of frightened rats, from amongst whose ranks, however, arose the brave Captain Shackleton. After years of futile combat, Shackleton finally put an end to the automaton Solomon's evil plans, defeating him in a ridiculous sword fight. In the final mind-boggling pages of his already preposterous tale, Gilliam had the temerity to draw an embarrassing moral from his story, with which he hoped to give the whole of England—or at any rate the toy manufacturers—something to think about: God would end up punishing man if he went on emulating Him by creating life—if indeed these mechanical creations could be described as possessing such a thing, Wells reflected.

It was possible a story like this might work as satire, but the problem was Gilliam took it terribly seriously, imbuing it with an air of solemnity which only made the plot seem even more ludicrous. Gilliam's vision of the year 2000 was utterly implausible. In all other respects, his writing was infantile and verbose in equal measure, the characters were poorly drawn, and the dialogue dull as dishwater. All in all, it was the novel of someone who believes anyone can be a writer. It was not that he strung words together willy-nilly without any aesthetic pretensions; if he had, it would have made for dull but palatable reading. No, Gilliam was one of those avid readers who believed good writing was akin to icing a cake—a conviction that resulted in overblown, horribly flowery prose that was full of ridiculous verbal displays, indigestible to the reader. When Wells reached the final page he felt aesthetically nauseated. The only fate the novel deserved was to be flung on the fire; furthermore, if time travel were to become the order of the day, Wells would be honor-bound to journey into the past and beat the fellow to a pulp before he was able to disgrace future literature with his creation. However, telling the truth to Gilliam Murray was an experience he had no wish to undergo, especially since he could get out of it simply by handing the novel over to his editor Henley, who would certainly reject it, but with none of the recriminations that would fall upon Wells.

When the day came for his next appointment with Murray, Wells still had not decided what to do. Gilliam arrived at the house with enviable punctuality, a triumphant smile on his face, but Wells immediately sensed the barely controlled anxiety beneath his cloying politeness. Gilliam was plainly desperate to hear his verdict, but both men were obliged to follow the rules of etiquette. Wells made small talk as he guided him into the sitting room, and they sat down while Jane served tea. The author took advantage of this moment of silence to study his nervous guest, who was pressing his fleshy lips into a serene smile. Then, all of a sudden, Wells was filled with a sense of his own power. He, more than anyone, knew of the sense of hope involved in writing a novel and the insignificance of that illusion in the eyes of others, who judged the work on its merits, not on how many sleepless nights had gone into its creation. As Wells saw it, negative criticism, however constructive, was invariably painful for a writer. It always came as a blow, whether he responded to it like a brave wounded soldier or was cast into the abyss, his fragile pride in shreds.

And now, as if by magic, Wells held this stranger's dreams in his hand. He had the power to shatter them or to let them live. In the end, this was the choice before him, he realized; the novel's wretched quality was irrelevant, and in any case that decision could be left to

Henley. The question was whether he wanted to use his
authority for good or not, whether he wanted to witness
this arrogant creature's response to what was in essence
the simple truth, or whether on the contrary he preferred
to fob him off with a pious lie so he could carry on believing he had produced a worthwhile piece of writing, at
least until Henley's diagnosis.

"Well, Mr. Wells?" Gilliam asked as soon as Jane had
left the room. "What did you think of my novel?"

Wells could almost feel the air in the room tremble,
as though reality itself had reached a crossroads and the
universe was awaiting his decision to know which path to
go down. His silence was like a dam, a dike holding back
events.

And still today Wells was not sure why he had taken
the decision he had. He felt no real preference; he could
have chosen either way. He was sure of one thing, though:
it was not out of cruelty. If anything, he was simply curious to see how the man sitting opposite him would react
to such a brutal blow. Would he conceal his wounded
pride, politely accept Wells's opinions, or break down in
front of him like a child or a man condemned to death?
Perhaps he would fly into a rage and hurl himself at Wells
with the intention of strangling him, a distinct possibility Wells could not rule out. Whichever way he dressed
it up, it was an empirical exercise, a simple experiment
on the soul of that poor wretched man. Like the scientist who must sacrifice the rat in pursuit of his discovery,
Wells wanted to measure the capacity for reaction in this
stranger, who by asking him to read his manuscript had

given Wells an immense power over him, the power to act like the executioner of the despicable society in which they lived.

Once Wells had decided, he cleared his throat and replied in a courteous, almost cold voice, as though he were indifferent to the harmful effect his words might have on his visitor:

"I read your work with great care, Mr. Murray, and I confess I did not enjoy any part of it. I found nothing in it to praise, nothing to admire. I have taken the liberty to speak to you in this way because I consider you a colleague and I believe that lying to you would do you no good whatsoever."

The smile on Gilliam's face vanished in a second, and his huge paws gripped the arms of the chair. Wells studied his shifting facial expression even as he carried on wounding him, extremely courteously:

"In my opinion, not only have you started out with a rather naïve premise, but you have developed it in a most unfortunate way, stifling its few possibilities. The structure of your narrative is inconsistent and muddled, the episodes are linked only tenuously, and in the end one has the impression that events occur higgledy-piggledy, without any inner cohesion, simply because it suits you. This tiresome randomness of the plot, added to your writing style—worthy of some legal clerk who admires Jane Austen's romantic novels—inevitably produces boredom in the reader, or if not, then a profound aversion to what he is reading."

At this point, Wells paused for a moment to study his

guest's contortions with scientific interest. The man must be a block of ice not to have exploded with rage at such remarks, he thought. Was Gilliam a block of ice? He watched Murray's attempts to overcome his bewilderment—chewing on his lip, opening then clenching his fists, as though he were milking an invisible udder—and predicted that he was about to find out.

"What are you talking about?" Murray finally burst out, sitting up straight, seized by a rage that made the tendons in his neck bulge. "What kind of reading have you given my work?"

No, Gilliam was not a block of ice. He was pure fire, and Wells instantly realized he would not fall apart. His visitor was one of those people whose pride was so monumental that in the long run they were morally invincible; they were so full of themselves they believed they could achieve anything through simple pigheadedness, whether this was building a birdhouse or writing a science fiction novel. Unfortunately for Wells, Gilliam had not been content to build a bird box. He had decided to employ his efforts in showing the world what an extraordinary imagination he had, how easily he was able to juggle with the words accumulated in a dictionary, and that he had been endowed with many if not all the writerly characteristics that appealed to him. Wells tried hard to remain poised while his guest, shaking with rage, labeled his remarks as foolish. Watching him waving his arms about wildly, Wells began to regret the choice he had made. Clearly, if he carried on in that vein, demolishing his novel with scathing remarks, the situation could only get worse. But what else could he do? Must he retract everything he had said for fear the fellow might tear his head off in a fit of rage?

Luckily for Wells, Gilliam suddenly appeared to calm down. He took a few breaths, twisted his head from side to side, and rested his hands in his lap in a stubborn attempt to regain his composure. His painstaking effort at controlling himself felt to Wells like a sort of caricature of the actor Richard Mansfield's amazing transformation at the Lyceum Theatre during the performance of the play *Dr. Jekyll and Mr. Hyde* a few years earlier. He let him go on without interruption, secretly relieved. Gilliam seemed ashamed at having lost his temper, and the author realized that here was an intelligent man burdened with a passionate temperament, a fiery nature which drove him to those excesses of rage that he had undoubtedly learned to control over the years, achieving a level of restraint of which he should feel proud. But Wells had touched his sore point, wounded his vanity, reminding him his self-control was by no means infallible.

"You may have been lucky enough to write a nice novel everybody likes," Gilliam said when he had managed to calm down, although the tone of his voice was still belligerent, "but clearly you are incapable of judging the work of others. And I wonder whether this might not be because of envy. Is the king afraid the jester might usurp his throne and do a better job as ruler than he?"

Wells smiled to himself. After the outpouring of rage came a false serenity and a change in strategy. The man had just reduced Wells's novel—praised to the skies days before—to the category of popular fiction and had found an explanation for Wells's opinions that bore no relation to his own lack of literary talent—in this case envy. However, this was preferable to having to put up with his angry outbursts. They were now entering the domain of verbal sparring, and Wells felt a rush of excitement, for this was an area in which he felt particularly at ease. He decided to speak even more plainly.

"You are perfectly at liberty to think what you like about your own work, Mr. Murray," he said calmly. "But I imagine that if you came to my house to ask my opinion, it is because you deemed me sufficiently knowledgeable in such matters to value my judgment. I regret not having told you what you wanted to hear, but those are my thoughts. For the reasons I already mentioned, I doubt that your novel would appeal to anyone, although in my view the main problem with it is the implausibility of your idea. Nobody would believe in the future you have described."

Gilliam tilted his head to one side, as though he had not heard properly.

"Are you saying the future I describe is implausible?" he asked.

"Yes, that's exactly what I'm saying, and for various reasons," Wells coolly replied. "The notion that a mechanical toy, however sophisticated, could come to life is unimaginable, not to say ludicrous. Equally implausible is the suggestion that a world war could take place in the coming century. It will never happen. Not to mention other details you have overlooked, for example, that the inhabitants of the year 2000 are still using oil lamps, when anybody can see that it is only a matter of time before electricity takes over. Even fantasy must be plausible, Mr. Murray. Allow me to take my own novel as an example. In order to describe the year 802,701 all I did was to think logically. The division of the human race into two species, the Eloi, languishing in their mindless hedonism, and the Morlocks, the monsters living below ground, is an example of one possible outcome of our rigid capitalist society. By the same token, the future demise of the planet, however demoralizing, is based on complex predictions made by astronomers and geologists and published daily in journals. This constitutes true speculation, Mr. Murray. Nobody could accuse my 802,701 of being implausible. Things may turn out quite differently, of course, especially if other as yet unforeseeable factors come into play, but nobody can rule out my vision. Yours, on the other hand, does not bear up under scrutiny."

Gilliam Murray looked at him in silence for a long time, until finally he said:

"Perhaps you are right, Mr. Wells, and my novel does need a thorough overhaul in terms of style and structure. It is a first attempt, and naturally I couldn't possibly expect the result to be excellent or even passable. But what I cannot tolerate is that you cast doubt on my speculations about the year 2000. Because in that case you are no longer judging my literary abilities, you are simply insulting my intelligence. Admit it; my vision of the future is as plausible as any other."

"Permit me to disagree," Wells replied coldly, judging

that at this point in the conversation the time for mercy had passed.

Gilliam Murray had to repress another access of rage. He twisted in his seat, as though he were suffering from convulsions, but in a matter of seconds he managed to recover his relaxed, almost blasé demeanor. He studied Wells with amused curiosity for a few moments, as though he were a strange species of insect he had never seen before, then let out a thunderous guffaw.

"Do you know what the difference is between you and me, Mr. Wells?"

The author saw no reason to reply and simply shrugged.

"Our outlook," Gilliam went on. "Our outlook on things. You are a conformist and I am not. You are content to deceive your readers, with their agreement, by writing about things that might happen in the hope that they will believe them. But you never lose sight of the fact that what you are writing is a novel and therefore pure make-believe. I, however, am not content with that, Mr. Wells. The fact that my speculations took the form of a novel is purely circumstantial, because all it requires is a stack of paper and a strong wrist. And to be honest, it matters very little to me whether my book is published or not, because I suspect I would not be satisfied with a handful of readers who enjoy it, debating about whether the future I describe is plausible or not, because they will always consider it an invention of mine. No, I aspire to much more than being recognized as an imaginative writer. I want people to believe in my invention without realizing it's an invention, to believe the year 2000 will be exactly as I have described it. And I will prove to you I can make them believe it, however implausible it might seem to you. Only I shan't present it to them in a novel, Mr. Wells; I shall leave those childish things to you. You carry on writing your fantasies in books. I will make mine a reality."

"A reality?" asked Wells, not quite grasping what his guest was driving at. "What do you mean?"

"You'll see, Mr. Wells. And when you do, if you are a true gentleman, you will perhaps offer me an apology."

With that, Gilliam rose from his chair and smoothed down his jacket with one of those graceful gestures that startled everyone in such a bulky man.

"Good day to you, Mr. Wells. Don't forget me, or Captain Shackleton. You'll be hearing from us soon," he said, as he picked up his hat from the table and placed it nimbly on his head. "There's no need to see me to the door. I can find my own way out."

His departure was so sudden that Wells was left sitting in his chair, at a loss, unable to stand up even after Murray's footsteps had died away and he heard him shut the front gate. He remained seated for a long time in the sitting room pondering Murray's words, until he told himself that this egomaniac did not deserve another moment of consideration. And the fact that he heard nothing from him in the ensuing months finally made him forget the disagreeable encounter. Until the day when he received the leaflet from Murray's Time Travel. Then Wells realized what Gilliam had meant by "I will make mine a reality." And, apart from a few scientists and doctors who kicked up a fuss in the newspapers, the whole of England had fallen for his "implausible" invention, thanks in part to Wells himself having raised people's expectations with his novel *The Time Machine*, an added irony that irritated him all the more.

From then on, every week without fail he received a leaflet inviting him to take part in one of the bogus expeditions to the year 2000. That crook would have liked nothing more than to have the very man who had unleashed the current obsession for time travel endorse his company by sanctioning the elaborate hoax, which, naturally, Wells had not the slightest intention of doing. The worst of it, though, was the message underlying the polite invitations. Wells knew Gilliam was certain he would never accept, and this turned the invitations into a mockery, a taunt on paper that was also a threat, for the fact that the leaflets were delivered by hand suggested Murray himself, or one of his men, placed them in Wells's letter box. In any event, it made no difference, since the objective was the same: to show Wells how easy it was to loiter around his house unseen, to make sure he knew he had not been forgotten, to remind him he was being watched.

But what most infuriated Wells in this whole affair was that, however much he wanted to, he could not denounce him, as Tom had suggested, for the simple reason that Gilliam had won. Yes, he had proved that his future was plausible, and, rather than sweep the pieces off the board in a fit of rage, Wells must sportingly accept defeat. His integrity prevented him from doing anything except stand by while Murray made a fortune. And the situation appeared to amuse Murray enormously, for by placing the leaflets religiously in his letter box, not only was he reminding Wells of his victory, he was also defying the author to unmask him.

"I will make my fantasies a reality," he had said. And, to Wells's astonishment, he had done so.

XXXI

HAT AFTERNOON WELLS WENT for a longer bicycle ride than usual, and without Jane. He needed to think while he pedaled, he told her. Dressed in his favorite Norfolk jacket, he rode slowly and silently along the Surrey byways while his mind, oblivious to the action of his legs, reflected on how to reply to the letter penned by the naïve girl named Claire Haggerty. According to the imaginative tale Tom had concocted in the tearooms, their correspondence would consist of seven letters, of which he would write three and Claire four, and in the last she would ask him to travel through time to return her parasol. Otherwise, Wells was free to write whatever he liked, provided it did not contradict Tom's story. And he had to admit, the more he thought about it the more intriguing he found the semiliterate young lad's tale. It was evocative, beautiful, but above all plausible— assuming of course the existence of a machine capable of digging holes through the fabric of time and linking eras, and also of course, if Murray's view of the future were true. This was the part Wells liked least: Gilliam Murray being somehow mixed up in this, as he had been in saving the wretched Andrew Harrington's soul. Were their lives destined to carry on being entwined, like creeping ivy? Wells felt distinctly odd now that he was stepping into the role of Captain Derek Shackleton, the character his adversary had invented. Would he be the one responsible for breathing the gift of life into that empty shell, like the God of the Old Testament?

Wells arrived home after his ride pleasantly exhausted and with a rough idea of what he was going to write. He scrupulously set out his pen, an inkwell, and a sheaf of paper on the kitchen table, and asked Jane not to disturb him for the next hour. He sat at the table, drew a deep breath, and began penning his first ever love letter:

> Dear Claire,
>
> I, too, have been obliged to begin this letter several times over before realizing that, however strange it might seem to me, I can only begin by declaring my love to you, exactly as you requested. Although I have to confess to begin with I did not believe myself capable, and I used up several sheets trying to explain that what you were asking me to do in your letter was to make a leap of faith. I even wrote: How can I fall in love with you if I have never even seen you, Miss Haggerty? Yet, despite my understandable wariness, I had to face the facts: you insisted I had fallen in love with you. And why should I doubt you, since I did indeed discover your

letter beside the big oak tree when I came out of the time tunnel from the year 2000. I need no further evidence, as you rightly say, to see that in seven months we will meet and love will blossom between us. And if my future self—which is still me—falls in love with you as soon as he sets eye on you, why shouldn't I? Otherwise I would be doubting my own judgment. Why waste time, postponing feelings I am inevitably going to experience?

Then again, you are only asking me to make the same leap of faith you yourself made. During our meeting in the tearooms you were obliged to have faith in me, you were obliged to believe you would fall in love with the man sitting opposite you. And you did. My future self is grateful to you for that, Claire. And the self who is writing these lines, who has yet to savor the softness of your skin, can only reciprocate that trust, believe that everything you say is true, that everything you say in your letter will happen because in some way it has already happened. That is why I can only begin by telling you Claire Haggerty, whoever you are, that I love you. I love you from this very moment until the end of time.

Tom's hand trembled as he read the author's words. Wells had thrown himself wholeheartedly into the enterprise: not only had he respected Tom's improvised tale and the history of the character he was playing, but, to judge from his words, he seemed as much in love with the girl as she was with him, with Tom that was, or more precisely with the brave Captain Shackleton. He knew it was only pretense, but the author's skill at deception went far beyond Tom's own impoverished feelings, even though these should have been more intense since he rather than Wells had lain with the girl. If the day before Tom had wondered whether the fluttering feeling in his chest was love, now that he had the yardstick of the author's words to measure it by, he was certain of it. Did Tom feel the emotions Wells attributed to Shackleton? After a few moments' reflection, Tom concluded the only one answer to that tortuous question was no, he did not. He could never keep a love like that alive for someone he was never going to see again.

He placed the letter next to John Peachey's headstone and began the walk back into London. He was pleased with how it had turned out, although a little disconcerted by Wells's request to Claire near the end, which Tom considered worthy of a degenerate. He recalled the final paragraph with deep displeasure:

> I am longing as I have never longed for
> anything before for time to speed up, counting
> the seconds between now and our first meeting in
> seven months' time. Although I must confess that
> as well as being anxious to meet you, Claire, I am
> also fascinated to know how you will travel to my
> era. Is such a thing really possible? For my part, I
> can only wait and do what I have to do, that is to
> say, reply to your letters, complete my part of the

circle. I hope this first letter does not disappoint you. Tomorrow I will leave it beside the oak tree when I arrive in your time. My next visit will be two days later, and I know that by then another letter from you will be awaiting me. You may find this request impertinent, my love, but could I ask you to describe our amorous encounter to me? Remember I must wait many months before I experience it, and although I assure you I will be patient, I cannot imagine a more wonderful way to endure that wait than to read over and over again the things I will experience with you in the future. I want to know everything, Claire, so please, spare me no detail. Describe to me the first and only time we make love, because from now I will experience it through your words, my darling Claire. Things here are hard to bear. Our brothers perish by the thousand under the superior power of the automatons, who raze our cities as though they wanted to destroy everything we have built, every trace of our civilization. I do not know what will happen if my mission fails, if I am unable to stop this war from happening. In spite of all this, my love, I can only smile as the world crumbles around me because your undying love has made me the happiest person on earth.

D.

Claire clasped the letter to her pounding heart. She had so yearned for someone to write such words to her, words that took her breath away and made her pulse quicken. Now her wish had come true. Someone was telling her their love for her transcended time itself. Dizzy with happiness, she took a sheet of paper, placed it on her writing desk, and began to describe to Tom all the things which out of respect for their privacy I drew a veil over:

Oh Derek, my darling Derek: you have no idea how much it meant to me finding your letter where it was supposed to "be," and to find it imbued with such love. It was the final incentive I needed in order to accept my fate without demur. And the very first thing I will do, my love, is to comply with your request, even though I shall no doubt blush with shame. How could I refuse to share intimacies with you which are ultimately yours? Yes, I shall tell you how everything happens, even though in doing so I will be dictating your actions, the way you will behave, such is the strangeness of all this.

We will make love in a room in Pickard's boardinghouse, directly opposite the tearooms. I will agree to go with you there after deciding to trust you. In spite of this, you will notice how terrified I am as we walk down the corridor to the room. And this is something I would like to explain to you, my love, now that I have the opportunity. What I am about to say might surprise you, but in my own time, girls are brought up to repress their instincts, especially in well-to-do families like mine. Unfortunately, it is widely believed that the sole purpose of the sexual act should be procreation, and while men are allowed to express the pleasure they derive from physical contact, provided of course they do so respectfully and with moderation, we women must show perfect indifference, as our enjoyment is considered immoral. My mother has upheld this narrow-minded attitude all her life, and the same can be said of most of my married women friends. However, I am different, Derek. I have always hated this absurd inhibition in the same way I detest crochet and needlework. I believe we women have as much right as you men to experience pleasure and express it freely as individuals. Moreover, I do not believe a woman needs to be married to a man in order to engage in intimate relations with him: in my view it is enough for her to be in love with him. These are my beliefs, Derek, and as I walked down the corridor in the boardinghouse, I suddenly realized the time had come for me to find out whether I was capable of putting them into practice or had merely been lying to myself, and whether my fear was only a sign of my complete ignorance of such matters.

Now you know, and I imagine that is why you treated me so gently and tenderly, but let us not get ahead of ourselves. Let me reveal everything step by step in an orderly fashion, and, out of respect for you, I shall do so using the future tense, as from your point of view none of this has as yet happened. Well, I will not put it off any longer.

The room in the boardinghouse will be very small but cozy. The winter evening will almost have set in, which is why you will first hurry to light the table lamp. I shall watch you from the doorway, unable to move a muscle. Then you will look at me warmly for a few moments, before walking towards me very slowly with a calming smile, like someone afraid of scaring off a nervous cat. When you are near me, you will gaze into my eyes, whether to read what is in them or for me to read what is in yours I do not know. Then you will lean very slowly towards my mouth, so slowly I will be able to perceive your warm breath, the warmth of the air inside you, before feeling your lips firmly and at the same time gently pressing against mine. This subtle contact will unsettle me for a few moments, and then it will be transformed into my first kiss, Derek. And although I will have spent many nights anticipating what it will feel like, I will only have imagined the spiritual side, the supposed floating feeling it gives you, but it will never have occurred to me to consider the physical side, the soft, pulsating warmth of someone else's lips on mine. But little by little I will give myself over to this sensual touch, and I will respond to you with the same tenderness,

sensing that we are communicating in a much
deeper, more sincere way than with words, that
we are putting all of ourselves into that tiny
physical space. Now I know nothing brings two
souls together more than the act of kissing, of
awakening desire for one another.

Then a pleasant tickling sensation will
ripple over my flesh, penetrating my skin and
overwhelming me inside. Is this rush of sensations
what my mother and my most prudish friends try
so hard to suppress? I will experience it, Derek. I
will taste it, delight in it, and cherish it, my love,
in the knowledge that I will be experiencing it for
the first and last time, for I will know that after
you there will be no other men and I must live
off these feelings for the rest of my life. Then the
floor will give way beneath my feet and except for
the pressure of your hands around my waist I will
almost believe I am floating.

Then you will take away your lips, leaving
the imprint of your mouth on mine, and you
will look at me with tender curiosity while I try
to regain my breath and my composure. And
then? It will be time for us to undress and lie
down together on the bed, only you will seem as
hesitant as I, unable to take the first step, perhaps
because you think I will be afraid. And you will
not be mistaken, my love, because I have never
undressed in front of a man before, and all at
once I will feel nervous and bashful and wonder

whether taking off our clothes is really necessary. According to my aunts, my mother kept her marriage vows without my father ever having seen her naked. In keeping with the customs of her generation, Mrs. Haggerty lay down in her petticoats with a hole in her undergarments revealing the scented opening where my father was permitted entry. But it will not be enough for me simply to lift my skirts, Derek. I will want to enjoy our physical contact to the full, and therefore I will overcome my shame and begin to undress, fixing you with a gentle, solemn look.

I will begin by taking off my feather hat, which I will hang on the stand, then I will slip off my jacket, my blouse with its high neck collar, my overcorset, my corset, my overskirt, my skirt, my bustle, and my petticoats, until all I am left wearing is my slip. Still gazing at you tenderly, I will pull down the shoulder straps so the garment slides off my body, like snow slipping off a fir tree, and lies in a furl at my feet. Then, like a final act of a long-drawn-out ritual, I will slip out of my drawers, offering myself to you utterly naked, placing my body at your disposal, surrendering myself to the touch of your hands and your lips, giving myself completely, knowing it is to the right man, to Captain Derek Shackleton, the liberator of the human race, the only man with whom I could ever have fallen in love.

And you, my love, you will watch the

elaborate process, like someone waiting for a
beautiful figure to emerge from a block of marble
as it is teased out by the artist's chisel. You will
see me walking towards you, and will quickly
take off your shirt and trousers, as if a gust had
torn them from a washing line. Then we will
embrace, the warmth of our bodies mingling in
a happy union, and I will feel your fingers, so
accustomed to touching hard metal and weapons,
exploring my body, sensitive to its delicacy, with
exhilarating slowness and respectful tenderness.
Then we will lie on the bed gazing into one
another's eyes, and my hands will search your
stomach for the scar from the bullet with which
Solomon tried to kill you, and which you survived
as one recovers from a fever, only I will be so
nervous I won't be able to find it. Then your
mouth, moist and eager, will cover me with
kisses, leaving a trail of saliva, and once you have
thoroughly charted my body, you will enter it
slowly, and I will feel you moving inside me with
such gentleness. But despite the care you take,
your intrusion will cause me to feel a sudden
sharp pain inside, and I will cry out softly and
even pull your hair, although immediately it will
turn into a bearable, almost sweet ache, and I will
become aware of something dormant inside me
beginning to stir.

How can I describe to you what I will feel
at that moment? Imagine a harp marveling at

the notes it produces when a pair of hands pluck it for the first time. Imagine a burning candle, whose melted wax trickles down the candlestick, oblivious to the flame above, and forms a beautiful latticed pattern at the base. What I am trying to say to you, my love, is that until that moment, I will not have known it is possible to feel such exquisite rapture, the ecstatic pleasure that will radiate through my whole body from a place somewhere inside me, and although at first my bashfulness will force me to grit my teeth, to attempt to stifle the gasps that will rise from my throat, I will end up abandoning myself to that overpowering joy, I will let myself be swept away by that torrent of icy fire, and will proclaim my pleasure with passionate cries, announcing the awakening of my flesh. And I will be insatiable, I will clutch you to me, trapping you with my legs, because I want you to stay inside me forever, because I will be unable to understand how I could have lived all that time without feeling you thrusting sweetly into me. And when, after the final ecstasy, you slip out of me, leaving a crimson trail across the sheets, I will suddenly feel incomplete, bereft, lost. With my eyes closed, I will savor the echo of joy you have left inside me, the delicious memory of your presence; and when this has slowly faded, I will be overwhelmed by a feeling of extraordinary loneliness, but also of infinite gratitude at having

discovered in myself a creature perfectly adapted
to bliss, capable of enjoying the loftiest and
most earthly pleasures. Then I will reach out,
searching for the feel of your skin bathed in my
sweat, your skin that still quivers and burns,
like the strings of a violin after a concerto, and I
will gaze at you with a radiant smile of gratitude
for having revealed to me who I am, everything I
did not yet know about myself.

Tom was so moved and surprised, he had to stop reading. Had he really unleashed all these feelings in the girl?
Leaning back against the tree, almost out of breath, he
let his gaze wander over the surrounding fields. For him,
the carnal act with her had been a pleasant experience he
would always remember, but Claire spoke of it as though
it had been sublime and unforgettable, like the foundation
stone which as the years passed would hold up the cathedral of her love. Feeling even more of a savage than he really was, Tom sighed and went on reading:

I was going to tell you now how I traveled
to your time, Derek, but when I remember that
during our meeting at the tearooms you still did
not know how we do it, I feel compelled to keep
it a secret in order not to change things that have
already happened. What I can tell you is that last
year, an author called H. G. Wells published a
wonderful novel, *The Time Machine*, which made
us all dream about the future. And then someone

showed the machine to us. I can tell you no more
than that. But I will make it up to you by saying
that, although your mission in my time will fail,
and the machine in which you travel here will
be prohibited, the human race will win the war
against the automatons, and it will be thanks
to you. Yes, my love, you will defeat the evil
Solomon in an exciting sword fight. Trust me, for I
saw it with my own eyes.

> Your loving
> C.

Wells placed the letter on the table, trying not to show
how it had aroused him. He glanced at Tom silently, gesturing almost imperceptibly with his head that he could
leave. Once he was alone, he picked up the letter to which
he had to reply, and flushed with excitement as he reread
the detailed account of their meeting at the boardinghouse. Thanks to this girl, he finally understood women's
experience of pleasure, the sensation that crept over them
with intriguing slowness, overwhelming them completely
or scarcely touching them. How sublime, resplendent, and
infinite their enjoyment was compared to that of men, so
vulgar and crude, little more than a spurt of joy between
their legs. But was this the same for all women, or was she
special, had the Creator fine-tuned this particular girl's
sensitivity to such an astonishing degree? No, doubtless
she was a perfectly ordinary creature who simply enjoyed

her sexuality in a way other women of her class would consider brazen. Her simple decision to undress in front of Tom already showed an audacious spirit, a determination to experience to the full every possible sensation arising from the sexual act.

Upon realizing this, Wells felt saddened, annoyed even by the chaste manner in which the women in his life had given themselves to him. His cousin Isabel was one of those who resorted to the hole in the undergarment, presenting him with only her sex, which to Wells seemed like some terrifying entity, a sort of sucking orifice that appeared to have come from some other planet. Even Jane, who was less inhibited in such matters, had never allowed him to see her completely naked, thus sparing him the need to try to discover the shape of her body with his hands. No, he had never been lucky enough to meet a woman blessed with Claire's delightful nature. There were no limits to what he could have done with a girl as easy to win over as she. It would have been enough to extol the therapeutic virtues of sex for women in order to convert her into an eager adept of carnal pleasure, a modern-day priestess ready to give and receive pleasure freely. She would have become a champion of copulation, preaching door-to-door that regular sexual activity improved women's physiques, gave them a mysterious glow, softened their expressions, and even rounded off any of their bodies' unsightly angularities. With a woman like that, he would certainly be a contented man, relaxed, his appetites sated, a man who could put his mind to other things, throw himself into his interests, freed from the relentless male itch that began in adolescence and stayed with him until senility finally rendered his body useless. It was no surprise, then, that Wells immediately envisaged the girl named Claire Haggerty in his bed, without any clothes veiling her slender form, allowing him to stroke her with feline abandon, intensely enjoying the same caresses that scarcely elicited a polite sigh from Jane. It seemed incongruous to him that he should understand this unknown woman's pleasure, while that of his wife remained a mystery to him.

Suddenly, he remembered that Jane was waiting somewhere in the house for him to give her the next letter to read. He left the kitchen to go and look for her, taking deep breaths on the way to calm his excitement. When he found her in the sitting room reading a book, he put the sheet of paper on the table without a word, like leaving a poisoned chalice then waiting to see the effect it had on one's victim. For there was no doubt the letter would affect Jane, as it had affected him, forcing her to question her approach to the physical side of love in the same way that the last letter had made her question the way she experienced its spiritual side. He walked out into the garden to breathe in the night air and gazed up at the pale full moon laying claim to the sky. In addition to the sense of insignificance he always felt beneath the heavens, he was aware of his own clumsiness in comparison to the far more direct, spontaneous way others had of relating to the world, in this case the girl named Claire Haggerty. He remained in the garden for a long while, until he thought it was time to see the effect the letter had produced on his wife.

He walked slowly through the house, with almost ghostlike footsteps, and, unable to find her in the sitting room or in the kitchen, he went on upstairs to the bedroom. There was Jane standing by the window, waiting for him. The moonlight framed her naked, tempting body. With a mixture of astonishment and lust, Wells examined its elements, its proportions, the supple wisdom with which her womanly parts, always glimpsed separately or divined through fabric, formed a greater landscape, creating a liberated, otherworldly being that looked as though it might fly away at any moment. He admired her soft, malleable breasts, her painfully narrow waist, the placid haven of her hips, the dark woolliness of her pubis, her feet like small, appealing animals. Jane was beaming at him, delighted to feel herself the object of her husband's astonished gaze. Then the writer knew what he must do. As though obeying an invisible prompter, he tore off his clothes, also exposing his nakedness to the light of the moon that instantly outlined his skinny, sickly-looking frame. Husband and wife embraced in the middle of their bedroom, experiencing the touch of each other's skin in a way they never had before. And the sensations that followed also seemed magnified, for Claire's words etched in their memories redoubled the dizzying effect of each caress, each kiss. Real or imagined, they abandoned themselves hungrily, passionately, anxious to explore each other, to venture outside the boundaries of their familiar garden of delights.

Later on, while Jane slept, Wells slipped out of their bed, tiptoed into the kitchen, took up his pen, and began to rapidly fill the paper, prey to an uncontrollable sensation of euphoria.

> My love,
>
> How I long for the day when at last I shall
> be able to experience all the things you have
> described to me. What can I say except that I
> love you and I shall make love to you exactly as
> you describe? I shall kiss you tenderly, caress you
> softly and reverently, enter you as gently as I can,
> and, knowing as I do everything you are feeling,
> my pleasure will be even more intense, Claire.

Tom read Wells's passionate letter with suspicion. Even though he knew the author was pretending to be him, he could not help thinking those words might just as well have come from both of them. Wells was evidently enjoying all this. What did his wife think of it? Tom wondered. He folded the letter, replaced it in the envelope, and hid it under the stone next to the mysterious Peachey's tomb. On the way back, he went on mulling over the author's words, unable to help feeling as if he had been left out of a game he himself had invented, relegated to the mere role of messenger.

> I love you already, Claire, I love you already.
> Seeing you will simply be the next phase. And
> knowing we will win this bloody war gives
> me renewed joy. Solomon and I locked in a
> sword fight? Until a few days ago, I would have

wondered whether you were quite sane, my love; I could never have imagined we would settle our differences with such a prehistoric weapon. But this morning, picking through the ruins of the History Museum, one of my men came across a sword. He deemed the noble relic worthy of a captain, and, as though obeying your command, solemnly presented me with it. Now I know I must practice with it in preparation for a future duel, a duel from which I shall emerge victorious, for knowing that your beautiful eyes are watching me will give me strength.

All my love from the future,

D.

Claire felt her knees go weak, and, lying down on her bed, she luxuriated in the wave of sensations the brave Captain Shackleton's words had unleashed in her heart. While he had been dueling with Solomon he had known she was watching him, then . . . The thought made her slightly dizzy again, and she took a moment to recover. Suddenly, it dawned on her she would receive only one more letter from her beloved. How would she survive without them?

She tried to put it out of her mind. She still had to write two more letters. As she had promised, she would only tell him about their encounter in the year 2000 in her last letter, but what about the one she had to write now? She realized, somewhat anxiously, that for the first time she was free to write what she liked. What could she say to her beloved that she had not already said, especially considering that everything she wrote must be carefully examined in case it conveyed information that might jeopardize the fabric of time, apparently as fragile as glass? After some thought, she decided to tell him how she spent her time now, as a woman in love without a lover. She sat at her desk and took up her pen:

My darling,

You cannot know how much your letters mean to me. Knowing I shall only receive one more makes me feel dreadfully sad. However, I promise I will be strong, I will never falter, never stop thinking of you, feeling you near me every second of each long day. It goes without saying that I will never allow another man to tarnish our love, even though I will never see you again. I prefer to live from my memories of you, despite the best efforts of my mother to marry me off to the wealthiest bachelors in the neighborhood—naturally I have told her nothing of you (my love would seem like a waste of time to her, for she would see you as no more than a pointless illusion). She invites them to our house and I receive them courteously, of course, and then amuse myself by inventing the most outrageous reasons for rejecting them, which leaves my mother speechless. My reputation is growing worse by the day: I am doomed to become a spinster and a disgrace to my family. But why should I care a fig for what others think?

I am your beloved. The brave Captain Derek
Shackleton's beloved, although I have to hide my
feelings for you.

Apart from these tedious meetings, I devote
the rest of my time to you, my love, for I know
how to sense your presence swirling around
me like a fragrance even though you are many
years away from me. I feel you near me always,
watching me with your gentle eyes, although
at times it saddens me not to be able to touch you,
that you are no more than an ethereal memory,
that you cannot share anything with me. You
cannot slip your arm through mine in Green Park,
or hold my hand as we watch the sun go down
over the Serpentine, or smell the narcissi I grow
in my garden, whose scent, my neighbors say, fills
the whole of St. James's Street.

Wells was waiting in the kitchen, as before. Tom silently handed him the letter, and left before the writer
could ask him to. What was there to say? Although in the
end he knew it was untrue, he could not help feeling as
though Claire were writing to the author instead of to
him. He felt like the intruder in this love story, the fly in
the soup. When he was alone, Wells opened the letter and
began to devour the girl's neat handwriting:

In spite of all this, Derek, I shall love you
until my dying day, and no one will be able to
deny that I have been happy. And yet, I have to

confess it is not always easy. According to you,
I will never see you again, and the thought is
so unbearable that, despite my resolve, I try to
make myself feel better by imagining you might
be mistaken. That does not mean I doubt your
words, my love, of course not. But the Derek who
uttered them in the tearooms was only guided by
what I am saying now, and it is possible the Derek
who hurried back to his own time after making
love to me in the boardinghouse, the Derek who
is not yet you, will be unable to bear not seeing
me again and will find a way of coming back to
me. What that Derek will do, neither you nor I
can know, for he is outside the circle. This is my
only hope, my love—a naïve one perhaps, but
necessary all the same. I dearly hope I may see
you once more, that the scent of my narcissi will
lead you to me.

Wells folded the letter, put it back in its envelope, and
laid it on the table, where he stared at it for a long time.
Then he stood up, walked round the kitchen in circles, sat
down, stood up again, and walked round in circles some
more, before finally leaving for Woking station to hire a
cab. "I'm going to London to settle some business," he told
Jane, who was working in the garden. During the journey,
he tried to calm his wildly beating heart.

At that hour of the afternoon, St. James's Street
seemed lulled by a peaceful silence. Wells ordered the cab-
driver to stop at the entrance to the street and asked him

to wait for him there. He straightened his hat and adjusted his bow tie, then greedily sniffed the air, like a bloodhound. He concluded from his inhalations that the faint, slightly heady odor reminiscent of jasmine, which he detected through the smell of horse dung, must be narcissi. The flower added a symbolic touch to the scene which pleased Wells, for he had read that, contrary to popular belief, the name narcissus derived not from the beautiful Greek god but from the plant's narcotic properties. The narcissus bulb contained hallucinogenic opiates, and this oddity struck Wells as terribly appropriate: were not all three of them (the girl, Tom, and himself) caught up in a hallucination? He studied the long, shady street and set off down the pavement with the leisurely air of one out for a stroll, although as he approached the apparent source of the aroma, he began to notice his mouth becoming dry. Why had he come there, what did he hope to gain? He was not sure exactly. All he knew was that he needed to see the girl, to give the recipient of his passionate letters a face, or, failing that, to glimpse the house where she penned her beautiful letters. Perhaps that would be enough.

Before he knew it, Wells found himself standing in front of an undeniably well-tended garden with a tiny fountain on one side, and enclosed by a railing at the foot of which lay a carpet of pale yellow flowers with large petals. Since the street boasted no other garden that could rival its beauty, Wells deduced that the narcissi before him, and the elegant town house beyond, must be those of Claire Haggerty, the unknown woman he was pretending to love with a fervor he did not show the woman he truly loved. Not wishing to give too much thought to this paradox, which was nonetheless in keeping with his contradictory nature, Wells approached the railings, almost thrusting his nose through the bars in an attempt to glimpse something behind the leaded windowpanes that made sense of his urgent presence there.

It was then he noticed the girl looking at him slightly perplexed from a corner of the garden itself. Realizing he had been caught red-handed, Wells tried to act naturally, although his response was anything but natural, especially since he realized straightaway that the girl staring at him could be none other than Claire Haggerty. He tried to gather himself even as he gave her a docile, absurdly affable grin. "Magnificent narcissi, miss," he declared in a reedy voice. "One can smell their aroma from the end of the street." She smiled and came a little closer, enough for the author to see her beautiful face and delicate frame. Here she was at last, before his eyes, albeit fully clothed. And she was indeed a vision of loveliness, despite the slightly upturned nose that marred her serene beauty reminiscent of a Greek sculpture, or perhaps because of it. This girl was the recipient of his letters, his make-believe lover.

"Thank you, sir, you're very kind," she said, returning the compliment. Wells opened his mouth as if to speak but hurriedly closed it again. Everything he wanted to tell her went against the rules of the game he had consented to play. He could not say that although he might appear an insignificant little man, he was the author of those words without which she claimed she could not live. Nor could he tell her he knew in precise detail her experience of sexual pleasure. Still less could he reveal that it was all a sham, urge her not to sacrifice herself to a love that only existed in her imagination, for there was no such thing as time travel, no Captain Shackleton waging war on the automatons in the year 2000. Telling her it was all an elaborate lie which she would pay for with her life would be tantamount to handing her a gun to shoot herself through the heart. Then he noticed she had begun giving him quizzical looks, as if his face seemed familiar. Afraid she might recognize him, Wells hurriedly doffed his hat, bowed politely, and continued on his way, trying not to quicken his pace. Intrigued, Claire watched for a few moments as he vanished into the distance, then finally shrugged and went back inside the house.

Crouched behind a wall on the opposite pavement, Tom Blunt watched her go back in. Then he emerged from his hiding place and shook his head. Seeing Wells appear had surprised him, although not excessively. The author would likewise not have been surprised to find him there. Apparently, neither of them had been able to resist the temptation to look for the girl's house, the location of which she had subtly revealed in the hope that if Shackleton came back he could find her.

Tom returned to his lair in Buckeridge Street unsure what to think of Wells. Had the author fallen in love with her? He did not think so. Maybe he had gone there out of simple curiosity. If he were in Wells's shoes, would he not also have wanted to put a face to the girl whom he addressed using words he would probably never utter to his own wife? Tom fell back on the bed feeling completely exhausted, but his anxiety and permanent state of tension prevented him from sleeping more than a couple of hours, and before dawn, he set off once more on the long journey to the writer's house. These walks were keeping him more fit than the training sessions he was put through by Murray, whose hired assassin had again not shown up to punish his flagrant breaking of the rules. Even so, Tom had no intention of lowering his guard.

Wells was waiting for him on the doorstep. He did not look rested either. His face was crumpled, and his eyes had dark shadows under them, although they were twinkling mysteriously. Doubtless he had been awake all night writing the letter he now had in his hand. When he saw Tom, he greeted him with a slow nod and held out the missive, avoiding looking him in the eye. Tom took it from him, and, similarly unwilling to break the silence charged with tacit understanding, turned to go back the way he had come. Then he heard Wells say: "Will you bring her last letter even though it needs no reply?" Tom turned and looked at the author with a profound sense of pity, although he did not know whether he felt sorry for Wells or himself, or possibly for Claire. At length he nodded glumly and left the house. Only when he was at a comfortable distance did he open the envelope and begin to read.

My love,

There are no narcissi in my world, nor the least trace of any flower, and yet I swear that when I read your letter I can almost smell their

fragrance. Yes, I can envisage myself standing
beside you in the garden you speak of, which I
imagine carefully tended by your lily-white hands
and perhaps lulled by a babbling fountain. In some
way, my love, thanks to you, I can smell them
from here, from time's distant shore.

Tom hung his head, imagining how moved the girl would
be by these words, and he felt pity for her again, and in the
final analysis, an overwhelming sense of self-disgust. The
girl did not deserve to be deceived like this. The letters
might save her life, but in the end they were only repairing the harm he had so selfishly caused, merely to quench
the fire between his legs. He felt unable simply to congratulate himself for preventing her suicide and forget the
whole thing, while Claire was ruining her life because of a
lie, burying herself alive due to an illusion. The long walk
to Harrow helped him gather his thoughts, and he concluded that the only reparation he could make that would
ease his conscience would be actually to love her, to make
into a reality the love for which she was willing to sacrifice
herself, to bring Shackleton back from the year 2000, to
make him risk life and limb for her, exactly as Claire was
hoping. That was the only thing that would completely
atone for his wrongdoing. But it was also the one thing he
was powerless to do.

He was reflecting about this when, to his astonishment, he caught sight of the girl under the oak tree. Despite the distance, he recognized her at once. He stopped
in his tracks, stunned. Incredible as it seemed, Claire was

there, at the foot of the tree, shielding herself from the sun with the parasol he had traveled through time to bring her. He also glimpsed the coach at the bottom of the hill, and the coachman nodding off on his perch. He quickly hid behind some bushes before one or other of them sensed his presence. He wondered what Claire was doing there, but the answer was obvious. Yes, she was waiting for him, or rather, she was waiting for Shackleton to step through a hole in the air from the year 2000. Unable to resign herself to living without him, the girl had decided to act, to defy fate, and what simpler way of doing so than by going to the place where the captain emerged to collect her letters. Desperation had compelled Claire to make a move that infringed the rules of the game. And, watching her from behind the bushes, Tom kicked himself for not having foreseen this possibility, especially as the girl had given him ample proof of her courage and intelligence.

He remained in hiding almost the entire morning, watching gloomily as she circled the oak tree, until finally she grew tired, climbed into her carriage, and went back to London. Then Tom finally emerged from his hiding place, left the letter under the stone, and made his own way back to the city. As he walked, he remembered the tormented words Wells had used to end his final letter:

A terrible sorrow overwhelms me when I
realize this is the last letter I am going to write
you, my love. You yourself told me it was, and
I believe you are right about that, too. I would
love nothing more than for us to go on writing to

one another until we meet next May. However,
if there is one thing I have learned from all
this, it is that the future is predestined, and
you have already experienced it. And so I can
only suppose something will happen to stop me
from sending you more letters; possibly use of
the machine will be banned and my hitherto
unsuccessful mission called off. I feel torn, as I
am sure you can imagine: On the one hand, I
am happy to know that for me this is not a last
farewell, for I shall see you again very soon. On
the other, my heart breaks when I think that
you will never hear from me again. But this does
not mean my love for you will die. It will live,
Claire, I promise you, for one thing I am sure of
is my love for you. I shall carry on loving you
from my flowerless world.

    D.

The tears rolling down her cheeks, Claire sat at her
desk, took a deep breath, and dipped her pen into the inkwell.

This, too, is my last letter, my love, and
although I would like to begin by telling you
how much I love you, I must be honest with
myself and confess to you shamefacedly that a
few days ago I did a reckless thing. Yes, Derek,
apparently I am not as strong as I thought, and
I went to the oak tree to wait for you to appear.

Living without you is too painful. I needed to see you, even if it altered the fabric of time. I waited all morning, but you did not come, and I could not escape my mother's watchful eye any longer. It is difficult enough not to arouse Peter the coachman's suspicions. He already looks at me strangely each time I ask him to bring me here, but has so far kept my secret from my mother. How do you suppose he would have reacted if he had seen you step out of the oak tree as if by magic? I expect they would have discovered everything and it would have caused some sort of disaster in time.

I realize now it was foolish and irresponsible of me. Yes, for even if Peter had seen nothing, our impromptu meeting would still have changed the fabric of time. You would not see me for the first time on May 20 in the year 2000, and everything would instantly turn upside down, and nothing would happen as it is meant to. But luckily, although I would have liked nothing more, you did not appear, and so there is nothing to regret. I imagine you arrived in the afternoon, for the next day your beautiful, final letter was there. I hope you can forgive my foolishness, Derek, which I am confessing to you because I do not wish to hide any of my faults from you. And in the hope of moving you to forgive me still further, I am sending you a gift from the bottom of my heart, so that you will know what a flower is.

After writing this, she stood up, took her copy of *The Time Machine* from the bookshelf, opened it, and removed the narcissus she had pressed between its pages. When she had finished the letter, she touched the delicate petals to her lips and carefully slid the flower into the envelope.

Peter asked no questions this time either. Without waiting for her to tell him, he set off for Harrow-on-the-Hill. When they arrived, Claire walked up to the oak tree and discreetly hid the letter under the stone. Then she glanced around at the landscape, aware of saying good-bye to the place that had been the setting for her happiness those past few days, to those peaceful meadows, vibrantly green in the morning sun, to the distant cornfields, a streak of gold marking the horizon. She gazed at John Peachey's headstone and wondered what sort of life this stranger had lived, whether he had known true love or died without ever experiencing it. She gulped a mouthful of air and almost thought she could perceive her beloved Derek's odor, as though his numerous appearances had left a trace behind in that sacred place. It was all in her imagination, she said to herself, the result of her desperate longing to see him. And yet she must accept reality. She must prepare to spend the rest of her life without him, to be content to listen out for the echo of his love resonating from the other side of time, for possibly she would never see him again. That afternoon, or tomorrow, or the next day, an invisible hand would seize her last letter, and after that there would be no others, only solitude unfurling at her feet like a carpet stretching to infinity.

She returned to the carriage and climbed in without giving Peter any orders. With a resigned look, the coachman set off for London as soon as she was comfortably seated. Once the coach had vanished into the distance, Tom lowered himself from the branch he had clambered onto and dropped to the ground. From there he had been able to see her for the last time; he could even have touched her just by stretching out his hand, but he had not allowed himself to. And now, having indulged his whim, he must never go near her again. He took the letter from under the stone, leant against the tree, and began reading, a pained expression on his face.

As you rightly imagined, Derek, they will soon prohibit the use of the machine. There will be no more journeys through time for you until you defeat the evil Solomon. After that, you will decide to risk your life by secretly using the machine to travel to my time. But let us not get ahead of ourselves; let me at last tell you about our first meeting and what you must do afterwards. As I told you, it will take place on May 20 in the year 2000. That morning, you and your men will mount a surprise attack on Solomon. At first glance, and despite the astute positioning of your men, you will not come out of the skirmish with the upper hand, but have no fear, for at the end of it Solomon will suggest resolving the conflict with a sword fight. Accept his offer without hesitation, for you will win the duel. You will be a hero, and this combat that puts an end to the automatons' supremacy over the human race will be hailed as the dawn of a new era, so much so that it will be regarded as a perfect tourist destination for time travelers from my time, who will eagerly flock there to witness it.

I will go on one of those trips, and, concealed behind a pile of rubble, I will watch you fight Solomon, but when the duel is over, instead of going back with the others, I will hide among the ruins, intending to stay behind in your world, because, as you know, my own holds no attraction for me. Yes, thanks to the dissatisfaction that has dogged me all my life, and which I never suspected would lead to anything, you and I will meet. I must warn you though that our meeting will not be as romantic as it ought to have been; on the contrary, it will be rather embarrassing, particularly for you, Derek, and recalling it still brings a smile to my lips. But I suppose I should say no more about your indecorous behavior, as I can only assume it would influence your actions. All you need to know is that during that brief encounter, I will drop my parasol, and although you will travel across time in order to meet me and make love to me, returning it will be the excuse you give so that I agree to meet you at the tearooms. Naturally, in order for all this to happen as it is supposed to, in order to complete the circle in which we are trapped, you must appear in my time before we begin writing to each other—there would be no point in your doing so afterwards, for as you know, it is you who will

encourage me to write to you. You must appear
on exactly November 6, 1896, and look for me at
Covent Garden Market at twelve o'clock, in order
to ask me to meet you that same afternoon. The
rest you know. If you do as I say, you will preserve
the circle, and everything that has happened
already will happen once more.

That is all, my love. In a few months' time,
our love story will begin for you. But for me it
ends here, when I put the last full stop on this
page. However, I will not say a final farewell and
so deny all hope of our seeing one another again,
because as I told you before, I live in the hope of
your coming back to find me. All you have to do is
follow the scent of the flower in the envelope.

With all my love,

C.

Wells let out a sigh of dismay as he folded the letter
Tom had brought him and placed it on the table. Then
he took the envelope and tipped it over his open palm,
but there was nothing inside. What had he expected? The
flower was not for him. And, sitting there in the kitchen,
touched by the rays of the evening sun, he realized his expectations had been too high. Although he appeared to be,
he was not the protagonist of that romance spanning time.
Wells saw himself, empty hand absurdly outstretched as
though checking to see if it was raining inside the house,
and he could not help feeling as if he were the intruder in
this story.

XXXII

VERY CAREFULLY, TOM SLIPPED the delicate flower between the pages of the only book he owned, his battered copy of *The Time Machine*. He had decided to let Wells keep Claire's letters, as a sort of thank-you gift for services rendered, but mainly because in the end he considered they belonged to the writer. In the same way, he had held on to the narcissus he found in the final envelope, because he believed it was meant for him. And, after all, its perfume conveyed more meaning to him than her letters.

He lay back on his bed, and wondered what Claire Haggerty would do now that the letter writing was over and she was officially in love with a man from the future. He imagined her thinking of him each day, as she had predicted in her letters, from dawn to dusk, year in, year out, indifferent to the fact that real life, the one she ought to be living, was slipping away from her. This cruel fate, to which he had contributed, or rather which he had orchestrated, made him deeply unhappy, but he could think of no way of putting things right without making them worse. His only consolation was that in her letters Claire had assured him she would die happy. And perhaps, in the end, nothing else mattered. She probably would be happier in this impossible love affair than if she married one of her insipid suitors. If so, why did it matter if her happiness was based on a lie, provided that she never found out, died without knowing she had been deceived, ended her days believing she had been loved by Captain Derek Shackleton?

He stopped thinking about the girl's fate and focused on his own. He had sworn to himself he would stay alive until he had saved Claire's life, and he had succeeded by staying hidden and sleeping outside in the fields. But now he was ready for death; he was even looking forward to it. There was nothing left for him to do in life except struggle to survive, which felt like a terribly exhausting and in the end pointless exercise, and far harder to achieve with the memory of Claire piercing his heart like a painful splinter. And yet twelve days had gone by since his meeting with the girl in the tearooms, in full view of the whole of London, and Gilliam's hired assassin had still not managed to find him. He could not count on Solomon either, who apparently preferred to haunt his dreams. But someone had to kill him, or he would end up dying of hunger. Perhaps he ought to make things easier for his killer? Added to this was another consideration: rehearsals would soon begin for the third expedition to the year 2000, which was in less than a fortnight. Was Gilliam waiting for him to show up at Greek Street, to kill him in his lair with his own bare hands? Turning up to the first rehearsal was as good as placing his head voluntarily in the lion's mouth, but despite everything, Tom knew that was what he would do, if only to solve once and for all the riddle of his existence.

Just then someone hammered on his door. Tom sprang to his feet but made no move to open it. He stood waiting, every muscle in his body tensed, ready for anything. Had his time come? he thought. A few moments later, the barrage of thuds resumed.

"Tom? Are you there, you miserable scoundrel?" someone outside roared. "Open up or I'll have to knock down the door."

He instantly recognized Jeff Wayne's voice. He put Wells's book in his pocket and somewhat reluctantly opened the door. Jeff burst into the room and gave him a bear hug. Bradley and Mike greeted him from the landing.

"Where have you been hiding the last few days, Tom? The boys and I have been looking everywhere for you . . . Woman trouble, was it? Well, that doesn't matter now, we've found you, and just in time. We're going to celebrate in style tonight, thanks to our good old friend Mike," he said, pointing to the giant, who was waiting in the doorway looking as gormless as ever.

As far as Tom could gather from Jeff's muddled explanation, some days earlier Murray had paid Mike to do a special job for him. He had played the role of the infamous Jack the Ripper, the monster who had murdered five prostitutes in Whitechapel in the autumn of 1888.

"Some are born to play heroes, while others . . ." Jeff

jeered, shrugging his shoulders. "In any case, he got the lead role and that calls for a proper splurge, wouldn't you say?"

Tom nodded. What could he do? This was clearly not Mike Spurrell's idea but had been cooked up by Jeff, who was always ready to spend other people's money. Tom had no desire to go with them, but he knew he did not have the strength to resist. His companions all but dragged him downstairs to one of the adjoining taverns, where the trays of sausages and roast meat spread out on the table in the private room finally overcame his feeble resistance. Tom might not care for their company, but his stomach would never forgive him if he walked away from all that food. Laughing loudly, the four men sat down at the table and gorged themselves, while making fun of Mike's assignment.

"It was a difficult job, Tom," the big man groaned. "I had to wear a metal plate over my chest to stop the bullet. It's not easy pretending to be dead trussed up like that!"

His companions burst out laughing again. They ate and drank until most of the food was gone and the wine had begun to take effect. Then Bradley stood up, turned his chair around, and, placing his hands on the back as though leaning on a pulpit, gazed at his companions with exaggerated solemnity. There always came a time during their drunken sprees when Bradley would display his talent for mimicry. Tom leaned back in his chair, resigned to watching the performance, thinking that at least he had satisfied his hunger.

"Ladies and gentlemen, all I wish to say is that you are

about to participate in the most astonishing event of the century: today you are going to travel through time!" the lad declared in pompous tones. "Don't look so astonished. Murray's Time Travel is not satisfied simply to take you to the future. No, thanks to our efforts you will also have the opportunity to witness possibly the most important moment in the History of Mankind, an unmissable event: the battle between the brave Derek Shackleton and the evil automaton Solomon, whose dreams of conquest you will see perish beneath the captain's sword."

His companions all clapped and roared with laughter. Encouraged by their response to his performance, Bradley leant his head back and put on a grotesquely wistful face.

"Do you know what Solomon's great mistake was? I shall tell you, ladies and gentlemen: his mistake was that he picked the wrong lad in order to perpetuate the species. Yes, the automaton made a bad choice, a very bad choice. And his mistake changed the course of History," he said with a smirk. "Can you imagine a more terrible fate than having to fornicate all day long? Of course, you can't. Well, that was the poor lad's fate." He spread his arms and nodded in a mock gesture of regret. "But not only did he carry it off, he also managed to grow stronger, to study the enemy, who watched him copulating every night with great interest, before going to the city to approve the newly fabricated automaton whores. But the day the woman gave birth, the lad knew he would never see his son grow up—his son who had been brought into the world to fornicate with his own mother, thus initiating a vicious circle that would perpetuate itself through the seed of his seed. However, the lad survived his execution, brought us together, and gave us hope . . ." He paused for effect for a moment, then added: "Only he still hasn't taught us how to fuck properly!"

The laughter grew louder. When it had subsided, Jeff raised his tankard.

"To Tom, the best captain we could ever have!"

They all raised their tankards to toast him. Surprised by his companions' gesture, Tom could scarcely conceal his emotion.

"Well, Tom, I suppose you know what happens now, don't you?" Jeff said, clapping his shoulder once the cheers had died down. "We heard a rumor about some new merchandise at our favorite whorehouse. And they've got almond-shaped eyes, do you hear me, almond-shaped eyes!"

"Have you ever slept with an Asian woman, Tom?" asked Bradley.

Tom shook his head.

"Well, no man should die without trying one, my friend!" Jeff guffawed, as he rose from the table. "Those Chinese girls can give pleasure in a hundred ways our women know nothing about."

They made an almighty din as they left the tavern. Bradley led the procession, vaunting the Chinese prostitutes' numerous virtues, much to the delight of Mike, who smacked his lips in anticipation. According to Bradley, Asian women were not only obliging and affectionate but had supple bodies they could contort into all sorts of positions without injuring themselves. Despite the list of attractions, Tom had to suppress a groan. If he wanted any woman to make love to him just then, it was Claire, even if she did not have almond-shaped eyes or an unnaturally flexible body. He remembered the intensity of her response when he had taken her, and wondered what his companions, those coarse ruffians, would think if he told them there was another way of feeling that was more sublime and exquisite than the primitive pleasure they knew.

They hailed a cab and clambered aboard, still laughing. Mike squeezed his large frame in next to Tom, almost pinning him against the door, while the other two men sat facing them. Jeff, who was behaving in an overexcited, rowdy manner, gave the order for the cab to set off. Reluctant to join in the general gaiety, Tom gazed out of the window at the succession of streets, alarmingly deserted at that time of night. Then he realized the driver had taken a wrong turn: they were going towards the docks, not the brothel.

"Hey, Jeff, we're going the wrong way!" he cried out, trying to make himself heard above the racket.

Jeff Wayne turned and looked at him sternly, letting his laughter die menacingly in his throat. Bradley and Mike also stopped laughing. A strange, intense silence enveloped them, as though someone had dredged it up from the ocean floor and poured it into their carriage.

"No, Tom, we're not going the wrong way," Jeff finally said, contemplating him with an ominous smile.

"But we are, Jeff!" insisted Tom. "This isn't the way to—"

Then he understood. How had he not seen it before: their exaggerated high spirits, the toast that felt more like a farewell, their tense demeanor in the carriage . . . Yes, what more proof did he need? In the funereal silence that had descended inside the carriage, the three men looked at him with an air of false calm, waiting for him to digest the situation. And, to his surprise, Tom discovered that now the time had finally arrived for him to die, he no longer wanted to. Not like this. Not at the hands of these casual assassins, who were simply demonstrating Gilliam Murray's unlimited power, the fact that he could turn anyone into a murderer with a handful of banknotes. He was glad at least that Martin Tucker, whom he had always considered the most decent among them, was not there, that he had been incapable of turning his back on his friend and perpetrating this cheerful collective crime.

Tom heaved a sad sigh, disillusioned by the fickleness of the human spirit, and he gazed at Jeff with an air of disappointment. His companion shrugged, refusing any responsibility for what was about to happen. He was opening his mouth, perhaps to remark that such was life or some other cliché, when a blow to his throat from Tom's boot stopped him, crushing him against the seat. Taken aback by the kick, Jeff let out a loud grunt of pain which instantly turned into a high-pitched whistle. Tom knew this would not put him out of action, but the attack had been sudden enough to take them all by surprise. Before the other two could react, he elbowed the bewildered Mike Spurrell in the face as hard as he could. The blow dislocated Mike's jaw, and a spurt of blood from his split lip hit the window. Undaunted by Tom's violent response, Bradley pulled a knife from his pocket and pounced on him. Although supple and quick, fortunately he was the weakest of the three. Before the weapon could reach him, Tom grabbed his arm and twisted it violently until he dropped the knife. Then, since the move had placed Bradley's head only a few inches from his leg, Tom kneed him brutally in the face, hurling him back against his seat, where he lay slumped, blood streaming from his nose. In a matter of seconds, he had overpowered all three men, but Tom scarcely had time to congratulate himself on his swift, punishing action, when Jeff, who had by then recovered, flew at him with a savage roar. The force of the attack flung Tom back against the cab door, the handle of which dug into his right side like a blade. They wrestled awkwardly for a few moments in the reduced space, until Tom felt something crack behind him. He realized the door had given way, and seconds later found himself dangling in midair, clutching onto Jeff ridiculously as the cab raced on. When he hit the ground, Tom had all his breath knocked out of him. The impact of their fall caused the two men to carry on rolling for a few moments, until it finally disentangled them from their grotesque lover's embrace.

When everything stopped spinning, Tom, whose whole body was aching terribly, tried to heave himself to his feet. A few yards off, Jeff, alternately cursing and howling, was trying to do the same. Tom realized it would be one against one until the others arrived, and that he must take advantage of this. But Jeff was too quick for him. Before he was fully on his feet, Jeff charged at him violently, propelling him back to the ground. He felt his spine crack in several places, but even so, as his companion's hands grappled with his own to try to grab his throat, Tom managed to place his foot on Jeff's chest and push him off. Jeff flew backwards, but Tom felt a searing pain as his thigh muscle ripped under the strain. He ignored it and struggled to his feet, before his adversary this time. The cab had stopped in the distance, one door hanging like a broken wing, and Bradley and Mike were already rushing back towards them. Quickly calculating the odds, Tom decided his best bet was to run away from a fight he could only lose, so he dashed towards the busier streets, away from the deserted docks.

He had no idea where this sudden urge to live had sprung from, when only hours before he had longed for death's eternal oblivion. In any event, he ran as fast as his racing heart and the throbbing pain in his thigh would permit, struggling to find his bearings in the pitch-black night. Hearing his pursuers close behind him, Tom dived into the first side street he came to, which unhappily for him proved to be a dead end. He swore at the wall standing in his way and turned slowly around, resigned to his fate. His companions stood waiting for him at the entrance to the alleyway. Now the real fight began, he said to himself, and strolled casually towards where his executioners were waiting, trying hard not to limp and clenching his fists by his sides. He knew he stood no chance against three of them, but that did not mean he was going to throw in the towel. Would his desire to stay alive prove stronger than their desire to kill him?

Tom walked up to them and gave an ironical bow.

He did not have Captain Shackleton's sword, but he felt as though the man's spirit was beating in his breast. It's better than nothing, he thought to himself. The dim light from the nearest streetlamp barely illuminated the scene, and their faces remained in shadow. No one said a word, for there was nothing more to say. Jeff gave the order, and his men slowly fanned out, like prizefighters sizing up their opponent. Since none of them took the initiative, Tom assumed they were giving him the chance to initiate the one-sided combat. Who would he go for first? he wondered, as his companions slowly circled him. He stepped towards Mike, fists raised, but at the last moment, made a feint and threw the punch at an unsuspecting Jeff. The blow hit him full in the face, knocking him to the ground. Out of the corner of his eye, Tom saw Bradley's attack coming. He dodged the punch, and when Bradley was squarely in front of him, plunged his fist into the lad's stomach, doubling him up in pain. He was not so lucky with Spurrell, whose hammer blow was deadly. The world went fuzzy, Tom's mouth filled with blood, and he had to make a superhuman effort to stay on his feet. But the giant showed him no mercy. Before Tom had time to recover, Spurrell threw another punch, this time right on the chin. There was an ominous crack and Tom went spinning to the ground. Almost immediately, he felt the toe of a boot sink ruthlessly into his side, threatening to shatter his ribs, and Tom realized they had him. The fight was over. From the hail of blows raining down on him, he deduced that Bradley and Jeff had joined in the beating. On the floor beside him, through the dense fog of his pain, he could make out Wells's book, which must have fallen out of his pocket during the brawl. Claire's flower had escaped from its pages and lay incongruously on the filthy ground, a pale yellow brightness that looked as though it would be snuffed out at any moment, like his life.

XXXIII

WHEN AT LAST THE BEATING STOPPED, Tom clenched his teeth and, ignoring the pain, reached out to try to grasp Claire's flower, but was unable to because at that moment someone grabbed his hair and tried to pull him up.

"Nice try, Tom, nice try," Jeff Wayne whispered in his ear, accompanying his words with what sounded like a snigger or perhaps a groan. "Unfortunately, your efforts were wasted. You're going to die anyway."

Jeff ordered Mike Spurrell to take hold of Tom's feet, and he felt himself being borne aloft by his executioners to a place which, on the brink of losing consciousness, scarcely mattered to him. After a few minutes of being bumped and jolted, his companions tossed him on the ground as if he were a bundle of rags. When Tom heard the sound of lapping water and boats knocking together, his worst fears were confirmed: they had brought him back to the docks, probably because they planned to throw him in the river. But for the moment no one did or said anything. Tom was trying to slip into oblivion, but the sensation of something soft, warm, and not unpleasant touching his swollen cheeks prevented him. It felt as if one of his companions had decided to prepare him for death by wiping the blood from his wounds with a cloth dipped in tar.

"Eternal, come here at once!" he heard someone shout.

The sensation stopped instantly, and then through the vibrations in the ground Tom could hear the heavy yet delicate tread of footsteps slowly approaching the scene.

"Stand him up," the voice commanded.

His companions yanked him roughly to his feet, but Tom's legs would not support him and gave way instantly, causing him to slump to his knees with the almost sensual limpness of a puppet whose strings have been cut. A hand grasped his collar to prevent him from keeling over completely. Once he had overcome his dizziness and was able to focus, Tom watched impassively from his kneeling position as Gilliam Murray made his way slowly towards him, his dog circling at his feet. He wore the slightly irritated expression of someone who has been dragged from his bed in the middle of the night for no good reason, as though it had escaped his memory that he was the one behind the ambush. He stopped a few yards in front of Tom and looked at him for a moment, smirking disdainfully, taking pleasure in his pathetic state.

"Tom, Tom, Tom," he said at last, in the tone of someone scolding a child. "How has it come to this unpleasant situation? Was it really so difficult to follow my instructions?"

Tom remained silent, not so much because the question was rhetorical, but because he doubted whether he could utter a word, with his swollen lips and mouth full of blood and pieces of broken tooth. Now that he could focus, he glanced around and saw that they were indeed at the docks, only a few yards from the quayside. Besides Gilliam, who was standing in front of him, and his companions waiting behind him for their orders, there seemed not to be another soul in sight. It would all take place in the strictest intimacy. That was how nobodies met their end, discreetly, without any fuss, like refuse tossed in the river in the middle of the night while the world is sleeping. And no one would notice his absence the next day. No one would say, Hold on, where's Tom Blunt? No, the orchestra of life would carry on playing without him, because in reality his part had never been important to the score.

"Do you know what's so amusing about this whole thing, Tom?" said Murray calmly, moving closer to the edge of the quay and gazing absentmindedly into the murky river. "It was your lover who gave you away."

Again, Tom said nothing. He simply stared at his boss, whose eyes were still contemplating the Thames, that bottomless coffer where he stored anything that posed a problem. A moment later, Murray smirked at him once more with a mixture of pity and amusement.

"Yes, if she hadn't come to my office the day after the expedition asking for the address of one of Captain Shackleton's descendants, I would never have found out about your affair."

He paused again to give Tom time to digest what he had just told him. Evidently, as Murray had suspected, the girl had never mentioned this to him. And why should she? From Tom's point of view, it was unimportant, of course. For Gilliam it had been a fortuitous blunder.

"I had no idea what the girl's game was," he said, walking back over to Tom with mincing, almost ballet dancer's, steps. "I gave her an evasive reply and sent her packing, but I was curious, so I had one of my men follow her just to be on the safe side—you know how much I dislike people poking their noses in my affairs. But Miss Haggerty didn't seem interested in snooping, quite the contrary, isn't that so? I confess to being astonished when my informant told me she had arranged to meet you at the ABC tearooms, and afterwards . . . Well, I don't need to tell you what happened afterwards at the Pickard boardinghouse."

Tom lowered his head, in a gesture that could equally have been embarrassment or vertigo.

"My suspicions were justified," Gilliam went on, amused by Tom's awkwardness, "but not in the way I had imagined. I thought of killing you there and then, despite my admiration for the way you had used the situation to your advantage. But then you did something completely unexpected: you visited Wells's house, and that aroused my curiosity even more. I wondered what you were up to. If you intended telling the writer it was all a hoax, you had gone to the wrong person. As you immediately discovered, Wells is the only person in the whole of London who is aware of the truth. But no, you had a far nobler purpose."

As Gilliam spoke, he paced back and forth in front of Tom, hands behind his back. His movement made the boards on the quayside squeak unpleasantly. Eternal sat a few feet away, fixing him with a vaguely curious look.

"After leaving Wells's house, you went to Harrow-on-the-Hill. There you hid a letter under a stone, which my spy brought to me immediately. And when I read it I understood everything." He gazed at Tom with mock compassion. "I have to confess I was most amused by your letters, which my informant took from underneath the stone and put back before whoever was to collect them that day arrived. Except for the last one, of course, which you whisked away so fast I had to steal it off Wells while he was out on that ludicrous machine known as a bicycle he likes to ride around on."

He stopped pacing and studied the river again.

"Herbert George Wells," he whispered, scarcely able to contain his contempt. "The poor fool. I can't deny I was tempted to tear up all his letters and rewrite them my-self. I only refrained from doing so because Wells would never have found out, which would have been the same as if I had done nothing. But let's not talk about that any-more," he declared, suddenly brightening up and turning once more to face his victim. "You couldn't care less about petty rivalries between writers, could you, Tom? Yes, I greatly enjoyed reading your letters, one passage in par-ticular, as I'm sure you can imagine. I believe it was very instructive to us all. However, now that the final install-ment has been written, the little old ladies will shed bitter tears over the lovers' tragic fate, and I am free to kill you."

He crouched down before Tom and, lifting his chin, raised his head with almost maternal tenderness. The blood streaming from Tom's split lip soiled his fingers and he pulled out a handkerchief and cleaned it off absentmindedly, still gazing intently at Tom.

"Do you know something, Tom?" he said. "In the end, I'm deeply grateful for all your efforts not to reveal my hoax. I realize you are partially blameless. But only partially. True, this foolish girl started everything. Yet you could have let it go, and you didn't, did you? I sympathize, believe me: I'm sure the girl was worth taking all those risks for. However, you see why I can't let you go on living. We each have our role to play in this tale. And sadly for you, mine consists of killing you. And how could I resist the perfect irony of giving the job to your faithful soldiers of the future."

With these words, he directed a twisted smile at the men looming behind Tom. He studied Tom again for a long time, as though giving one last thought to what he was about to do, perhaps mulling over another possible course of action.

"I have no choice, Tom," he said finally, shrugging his shoulders. "If I don't kill you, sooner or later you'll look for her again. I know you will. You'll look for her because you're in love with her."

On hearing this, Tom could not help gazing at Murray in surprise. Was it true? Was he really in love with Claire? This was a question to which he had never given much thought, because, whether or not he loved her or she had just been a passing fancy, an opportunity he was loathe to pass up, he still had to keep away from her. However, now he had to admit that if Gilliam were to let him live, the first thing he would do would be to look for her, and that could only mean his boss was right: he was in love with her.

Yes, he realized with astonishment, he loved her, he loved Claire Haggerty. He had loved her from the moment he saw her. He loved the way she looked at him, the touch of her skin, the way she had of loving him. It felt so good to let himself be enveloped by the protective mantle of that immense unconditional love, that magic cape shielding him from life's coldness, the icy indifference of every day that made his soul tremble, the incessant wind filtering through the shutters and seeping into his innermost depths. And he realized that he wanted nothing more than to be able to love her with the same intensity, to feel he was fulfilling man's highest, most noble achievement, the one he had been born for, the one that satisfied him and made him happy: to love, to love truly, to love for no other reason than the joy of being able to do so. This was what drove him on, this was his reason for living, because although he might be unable to leave his mark on the world, he could make someone else happy, and that was the most important thing, the most important thing was to leave his mark on another person's heart. Yes, Gilliam was right; he would look for her because he wanted her to be with him, because he needed her by his side in order to become someone else, to escape from who he was. Yes, he would look for her, whether to delight in the joys of spring together or to plunge into the abyss. He would look for her because he loved her. And somehow this lessened the lie Claire was living. For, in the end, the girl's love was reciprocated, and Tom's love, like Shackleton's, was also unattainable, lost in the ether, unable to find its way to her. What did it matter if they lived in the same time or even in the same city, that festering turn-of-the-century London, if they were to remain as far apart as if they were separated by an ocean of time.

"But why drag things out?" he heard Murray say, oblivious to his thoughts. "It would make for a worse, far less exciting ending to the story, don't you think? It's best if you disappear, Tom, for the story to end the way it's supposed to. The girl will be far happier in any case."

Gilliam Murray lifted his huge body to its full height and gazed down at Tom once more with scientific interest, as though he were something floating in a bottle of formaldehyde.

"Don't harm her," Tom stammered.

Gilliam shook his head, pretending to be shocked.

"Of course I won't, Tom! Don't you see? With you out of the way, the girl is no threat to me. And, believe it or not, I have my scruples. I don't go round murdering people just for the fun of it, Tom."

"My name is Shackleton," said Tom between gritted teeth, "Captain Derek Shackleton."

Murray burst out laughing.

"Then you needn't be afraid, for I guarantee you will rise from the dead."

With these words, he gave Tom one last smile and gestured to his companions.

"All right, gentlemen. Let's get this over with and go to bed."

Following Murray's command, Jeff and Bradley

scooped Tom up off the ground, while Mike Spurrell brought over a huge block of stone with a piece of rope tied round it which they fastened to Tom's feet. Then they bound his hands behind his back. Gilliam watched the proceedings with a satisfied smile.

"Ready, boys," said Jeff, after making sure the knots were secure. "Let's do it."

Once more, Jeff and Bradley carried Tom shoulder high over to the edge of the quay, while Mike held onto the stone that would anchor him to the riverbed. Tom gazed blankly at the murky water. He was filled with the strange calm of someone who knows his life is no longer in his own hands. Gilliam walked over to him and squeezed his shoulder hard.

"Good-bye, Tom. You were the best Shackleton I could hope to find, but such is life," he said. "Give my regards to Perkins."

Tom's companions swung his body and at the count of three tossed both him and the stone into the Thames. Tom had time to fill his lungs with air before hitting the surface of the river. The ice-cold water came as a shock, dispelling the lethargy pervading his body. He was struck by fate's final irony: what good was it to feel so awake now that he was about to drown? He sank in a horizontal position to begin with, but the weight of the stone soon pulled him upright, and he plummeted with astonishing speed to the bottom of the Thames. He blinked several times, trying to glimpse something through the greeny-brown water, but there was not much to see besides the bottoms of the boats floating above and a flickering halo of light cast by the quay's only streetlamp. The stone quickly hit the river-bed and Tom remained floating above it, suspended by ten inches of rope, like a child's kite, buffeted by the current. How long could he go without breathing? he wondered.

What did it matter? Was it not absurd to struggle against the inevitable? Even though he knew it would only postpone death, he pressed his lips tightly together. Again that painful instinct to survive, but now he had under-stood this sudden will to live: he had discovered that the worst thing about dying was not being able to change what he had been, that when he died, others would only see the repulsive tableau into which his life was going to solidify. He remained hanging upright for what felt like an excru-ciating eternity, lungs burning, temples throbbing deaf-eningly, until the urgent need to breathe compelled him against his will to open his mouth. Water began filling his throat, streaming merrily into his lungs, and everything around him became even fuzzier. Then Tom realized this was it: in a few seconds he would lose consciousness.

In spite of this, he had time to see the figure appear. He watched him emerge from the swirling fog in his brain mist and walk towards him along the riverbed with his heavy metal footsteps, oblivious to the water all around him. Tom assumed that the lack of oxygen to his brain had allowed the automaton to escape from his dreams and move around in the real world. He was too late, though; Tom had no need of him, he was quite capable of drown-ing without his help. Or perhaps he had simply come for the pleasure of watching him die, face to face in the river's murky depths.

But to his surprise, when the automaton finally reached his side, he gripped Tom's waist with one of his metal arms, as if to lead him in a dance, while with the other he tugged at the rope around his feet until he loosened it. Then he heaved Tom up towards the surface, where Tom, still semiconscious, could see the bottoms of the boats and the shimmering streetlamp gradually looming larger. Before he knew it, his head emerged above the water.

The night air coursed into his lungs, and Tom knew this was the true taste of life. He breathed in greedily, spluttering like a hungry infant choking on its food. He allowed his enemy to hoist his near-lifeless body onto the quayside, where he lay on his back, dizzy and numb with cold. He felt the automaton's hands pressing repeatedly down on his chest. The pumping helped him spew out the water he had swallowed. When there seemed to be no more, he coughed a few times, bringing up some congealed blood, and could feel life slowly seeping back into his limp form. He was overjoyed to discover he was alive again, to feel life's soft pulse flowing through him, filling him voluptuously, like the river water had done only moments before. For a split second, he even felt the illusion of immortality, as though such a close brush with death, having felt the Grim Reaper's chill fingers closing around him, had in some way acquainted him with it, so that its rules no longer applied to him. Somewhat recovered, Tom forced himself to smile at his savior, whose metallic head was floating above him, a dark spherical object lit by the single streetlamp on the quay.

"Thank you, Solomon," he managed to splutter.

The automaton unscrewed his head.

"Solomon?" He laughed. "It's a diving suit, Tom."

Although his face remained in the shadow, Tom recognized Martin Tucker's voice, and he was overwhelmed with happiness.

"Have you never seen one before? It lets you walk underwater, just like strolling in a park, while someone pumps air through a tube from the surface. We have Bob to thank for that and for winching us both up onto the quay," explained his companion, pointing towards a figure out of Tom's field of vision. Then, after putting the helmet to one side, Martin lifted Tom's head and examined it with the carefulness of a nurse. "'Struth, the boys did a good job. You're in a right state. Don't be angry with them, though. They had to make it look realistic in order to dupe Murray. And I think it worked. As far as he's concerned, they've done the job and are no doubt receiving their dues right this minute."

Despite his swollen lips, Tom grimaced in surprise. So it had all been a charade? Apparently so. As Murray had explained to him before having him thrown him in the Thames, he had hired Tom's companions to kill him. But they were not as heartless as Tom had thought, even though they were not well enough off to refuse his money. If they were clever, they could put on another performance, Tucker must have suggested—this burly fellow who was now brushing back Tom's hair from his bloodied brow, and gazing down at him with fatherly affection.

"Well, Tom, the performance is over," he said. "Now that you're officially dead, you're free. Your new life begins tonight, my friend. Make the most of it, as I am sure you will."

He squeezed Tom's shoulder in a gesture of farewell, smiled at him one last time, and vanished from the quay leaving an echo of metallic footsteps lingering behind him. After he had gone, Tom lay still, in no hurry to get up, trying to assimilate everything that had happened. He took a deep breath, testing his sore lungs, and looked up at the heavens arching above him. A beautiful pale yellow full moon lit up the night sky. It grinned down at him, like a death's head that had threatened to swallow him only to breathe new life into him, for, incredible though it might seem, everything had been resolved without his having to die—at least not in reality, for his body was supposedly now lying at the bottom of the Thames. His body was racked with pain and he felt weak as a kitten, but he was alive, alive! Then a feeling of wild delight overwhelmed him, compelling him to get up off the cold ground, where if he lay much longer in those wet clothes he would catch pneumonia. He struggled to his feet and limped away from the docks. His bones were bruised but not broken. His companions must have taken care not to injure any of his internal organs.

He glanced around him. The place was deserted. At the entrance to the cul-de-sac where the fight had started, lying next to Wells's novel, he saw the flower Claire had given him. He picked it up gently and held it in the palm of his hand, as one holds a compass indicating which way to follow.

THE SWEET, FRAGRANT SCENT of narcissi, faintly reminiscent of jasmine, guided him slowly through the labyrinth of the night, pulling him gently like the sea's undertow, drawing him towards an elegant house immersed in silence. The fence around it was not too high, and the vines adorning its façade seemed there for the sole purpose of making it easier for the most daring men to climb to the window of the girl sleeping in a bed where there was no longer any room for dreams.

Tom gazed with infinite tenderness at the girl who loved him as no one had ever loved him before. From her open lips came short, soft sighs as though a summer breeze were wafting through her. He noticed her right hand clutched around a piece of paper on which he could make out Wells's minuscule handwriting. He was about to wake her with a caress when she opened her eyelids slowly, as though he had roused her simply by gazing at her body. She did not appear in the least surprised to see him standing beside her bed, as if she had known that sooner or later he would appear, guided by the scent of her narcissi.

"You've come back," she whispered sweetly.

"Yes, Claire, I've come back," he replied in the same voice. "I've come back for good."

She smiled serenely at him, realizing from the dried blood streaking his lips and cheeks how much he loved her. She stood up and, with the same calmness, walked towards his open arms. And as they kissed, Tom understood that, regardless of what Gilliam Murray thought, this was a far more beautiful ending than the one where they never met again.

PART THREE

Distinguished gentlemen and
impressionable ladies, we have
arrived at the closing pages
of our thrilling tale.

What marvels are there
still in store for you?

If you wish to find out, make sure
your attention does not stray from
these pages for an instant, because
in an even more amazing discovery
you will be able to travel in time
to your heart's content, into the
past as well as to the future. Dear
reader, if you are no coward, dare
to finish what you have started!

We can guarantee
this final journey
is well worth the effort.

XXXIV

INSPECTOR COLIN GARRETT OF Scotland Yard would have been pleased if the sight of blood did not make him feel so queasy that each time his job obliged him to look at a dead body he had to leave the scene to be sick, especially if the cadaver in question had been subjected to a particularly dreadful attack. However, sadly for him, this was such a regular occurrence that the inspector had even considered the possibility of forgoing breakfast, in view of how little time the meal actually remained in his stomach. Perhaps it was to compensate for this squeamishness that Colin Garrett had been blessed with such a brilliant mind. At any rate, that was what his uncle had always told him—his uncle being the legendary Inspector Frederick Abberline, who some years previously had been in charge of hunting down the vicious murderer Jack the Ripper. Such was Abberline's belief in his nephew's superior brainpower that he had practically delivered the boy himself to Scotland Yard's headquarters with an impassioned letter of recommendation addressed to Chief

Superintendent Arnold, the austere, arrogant man in charge of the detective squad. And, during his first year there, Garrett had to acknowledge that, to his surprise, his uncle's trust in him had not proved unfounded. He had solved a great many cases, apparently with very little effort, since moving into his office overlooking Great George Street. He had done so without ever leaving his office. Garrett would spend long nights in his cozy refuge, collecting and fitting together the pieces of evidence his subordinates brought to him, like a child absorbed in doing a jigsaw puzzle, avoiding as much as he could any contact with the raw, bloody reality that pulsated behind the data he handled. A sensitive soul like his, despite being twinned with a superior brain, was unsuited to fieldwork.

And of all the infernos raging behind his office door, perhaps morgues were the places that showed off the grittier side of crime to most flamboyant effect, its tangible side, its unpleasantly real, physical side that Garrett tried so hard to ignore. And so, each time he was forced to view a body, the inspector would give a resigned sigh, pull on his hat, and set off for the loathsome building concerned, praying he would have time to flee the autopsy room before his stomach decided to heave up his breakfast, bespattering the pathologist's shoes.

The corpse he was meant to examine that morning had been discovered in Marylebone by the local police, who had handed the case over to Scotland Yard when they found it impossible to identify what kind of weapon had inflicted the wound on the victim—apparently a tramp.

Garrett imagined the Bobbies doing this with a wry smile, content to give the brain boxes in Great George Street a sufficiently puzzling case to make them earn their salary. It had been Dr. Terence Alcock, waiting for him at that very moment at the entrance to the York Street morgue, wearing a bloodstained apron, who had confessed that they were faced with a mystery that he for one found completely baffling. And when a man as well versed as the pathologist, who was fond of airing his knowledge at every opportunity, admitted defeat so openly, it made Garrett think he was confronted by a truly interesting case. This was the sort you might expect to find in a novel featuring his hero Sherlock Holmes, not in real life, where more often than not criminals showed a distinct lack of imagination.

To Garrett's astonishment, the pathologist greeted him with a grim expression and guided him in solemn silence down the corridor to the autopsy room. He immediately understood that the inexplicable wound had vexed him to the point of clouding his usually excellent humor. Despite the rather alarming appearance that having only one eyebrow gave him, Dr. Alcock was a cheerful, garrulous fellow. Whenever Garrett appeared at the morgue, Alcock always greeted him in a jovial manner, reciting in a singsong voice the order in which he considered it most appropriate to examine the abdominal cavity: peritoneum, spleen, left kidney, suprarenal gland, urinary tract, prostate gland, seminal vesicles, penis, sperm cord . . . a litany of names ending with the intestines. He left that part for last for reasons of hygiene, he explained, because handling their contents was a revolting job. And I, who see everything whether I want to or not, as I have repeatedly reminded you throughout this tale, can confirm that, notwithstanding his propensity for bluster, in this instance the doctor was definitely not exaggerating. Thanks to my supernatural ability to be in all places at once, I have seen him more than once in this unpleasant situation, covering himself, the corpse, the dissecting table, and even the floor of the autopsy room with excrement, although out of concern for your sensibilities I shall refrain from any closer description.

This time, however, as he walked down the long corridor, the pathologist had a melancholy air and did not reel off his usual list, which Garrett, thanks to his prodigious memory, had often caught himself singing under his breath, usually when he was in a good mood. At the end of the corridor, they reached a large room where an unmistakable aroma of decaying flesh lingered in the air. The place was lit by several four-branched gas lamps hanging from the ceiling, although Garrett thought these were not enough for such a large room and only made it seem even grimmer. In the semidarkness, he could scarcely see more than two yards in front of him.

Rows of cabinets filled with surgical instruments lined the brick walls, together with shelves lined with bottles containing mysterious opaque liquids. On the far wall was a huge basin, where on more than one occasion he had seen Dr. Alcock rinsing the blood off his hands, like someone practicing a macabre ritual ablution. In the center of the room, on a sturdy table lit by a single lamp, was a figure with a sheet draped over it. The pathologist, who always wore his sleeves rolled up, something Garrett found deeply disturbing, gestured to him to approach the table. Like a sinister still life, on a stand next to the body lay an assortment of dissecting knives, blades for cutting through cartilage, a cutthroat razor, various scalpels, a few hacksaws, a fine chisel and accompanying hammer for boring into the cranium, a dozen needles threaded with catgut suture, a few soiled rags, some scales, an optical lens, and a bucket filled with pinkish water, which Garrett tried to not look at.

Just then, one of the pathologist's assistants opened the door hesitantly, but the doctor shooed him away angrily. Garrett remembered hearing him rail against the foppish youngsters they sent fresh out of university, who wielded an autopsy knife as though it were a pen, moving only their hand and wrist rather than their whole arm, and making timid, small cuts as if they were preparing a meal. "They should leave that type of slicing to the people who give public demonstrations in the amphitheaters," Dr. Alcock declared. He was a believer in bold incisions, long, deep cuts that tested the resilience of an arm or a shoulder's musculature.

After heading off the interruption, the doctor drew back the sheet covering the body on the slab. He did so without ceremony, like a magician wearily performing the same trick for the thousandth time.

"The subject is a male aged between forty and fifty," he said in a flat monotone, "height five foot seven, fragile-boned, with reduced amounts of subcutaneous fat and muscle tissue. The body is pale in color. As for the teeth, the incisors are present, but several molars are missing, and most of those remaining contain cavities and are covered in a darkish layer."

After presenting his report, he paused, waiting for the inspector to stop staring up at the ceiling and to decide to look at the corpse.

"And this is the wound," he declared enthusiastically, attempting to coax Garrett out of his passivity.

Garrett gulped air and allowed his eyes to descend slowly towards the cadaver, until his astonished eyes came to rest on the enormous hole in the middle of the chest.

"It is a circular opening, twelve inches in diameter," explained the pathologist, "which you can look straight through as if it were a window, as you will see if you lean over."

Reluctantly, Garrett bent over the huge hole, and indeed was able to glimpse the table through it.

"Whatever caused the wound, besides badly scorching the skin around the edges, pulverized everything in its path, including part of the sternum, the rib cage, the mediastinum, the lungs, the right ventricle of the heart, and the corresponding section of the spinal cord. What little survived, like some pieces of lung, fused with the thoracic wall. I have yet to carry out the postmortem, but this hole was clearly the cause of death," the pathologist pronounced, "only I'll be hanged if I know what made it. The poor wretch looks as if he's been pierced by a tongue of flame, or if you prefer, by some sort of heat ray. But I don't know any weapon capable of doing this, except perhaps the Archangel Michael's flaming sword."

Garrett nodded, struggling with his rebellious stomach.

"Does the body present any other anomalies?" he asked, by way of saying something, feeling the sweat begin to pearl on his forehead.

"His foreskin is shorter than average, barely covering the base of the glans, but without any sign of any scarring," the pathologist replied, flaunting his professional knowledge. "Apart from that the only anomaly is this accursed hole big enough for a poodle to jump through."

Garrett nodded, disgusted by the image the pathologist had conjured up, and with the feeling he knew more about the poor wretch than was necessary for his investigation.

"Much obliged to you, Dr. Alcock. Let me know if you discover anything new or if you think of anything that may have caused this hole," he said.

At this, he hurriedly took his leave of the pathologist and walked out of the morgue, as upright as he could. Once he reached the street, he dove into the nearest alleyway he could find and brought up his breakfast between two piles of refuse. He emerged, wiping his mouth with his handkerchief, pale but recovered. He paused for a moment, gulped air, then breathed out slowly, smiling to himself. The singed flesh. The grisly hole. He was not surprised the pathologist was unable to identify the weapon responsible for this ghastly wound. But he knew exactly what it was.

Yes, he had seen the brave Captain Shackleton wielding it in year 2000.

I T T O O K H I M A L M O S T two hours to persuade his superior to sign an arrest warrant for a man who had not yet been born. As he stood outside the door to his office, swallowing hard, he knew it was not going to be easy. Chief Superintendent Thomas Arnold was a close friend of his uncle, and had accepted Garrett with good grace into his team of detectives, although he had never shown him anything other than distant politeness, with an occasional outburst of fatherly affection whenever he solved a difficult case. The young inspector had the feeling that when his superior walked past his office and saw him with his head down, he was smiling at him with the same discreet satisfaction as if he were looking at a coal stove in good working order.

The only time his affable smile faded had been the day Garrett went into his office following his trip to the year 2000 to recommend an urgent ban on the production of automatons and the confiscation of those already in circulation, which he said should be stored somewhere, anywhere where they could be watched, in a pen surrounded by barbed wire, if necessary. Chief Superintendent Arnold thought the idea was completely ludicrous. He was only a year away from retirement, and the last thing he wanted was to make life difficult for himself by advocating preventative measures against some far-fetched threat he himself had not foreseen. But because the new recruit had more than proved his astuteness, he reluctantly agreed to ask for a meeting with the commissioner and the prime minister to discuss the matter. On that occasion, the command that had come down to Garrett from the hierarchy was a clear refusal: there would be no halt to the production of automatons or any attempt to prevent them from infiltrating into people's homes under the guise of their innocent appearance, regardless of whether a century later they were going to conquer the planet or not. Garrett pictured the meeting between those three unimaginative men incapable of seeing further than the end of their noses. He was sure they dismissed his request amid scathing remarks and guffaws. This time, however, things would be different. This time they could not look the other way. They could not wash their hands of the matter, arguing that by the time the automatons rebelled against man they would be resting peacefully in their graves, for the simple reason that on this occasion the future had come to them: it was acting in the present, in their own time, that very part of time they were supposed to be protecting.

Even so, Chief Superintendent Arnold put on a skeptical face the moment Garrett began explaining the affair. Garrett considered it a privilege to have been born in an era when science made new advances every day, offering them things their grandparents had never even conceived of. He was thinking not so much of the gramophone or the telephone as of time travel. Who would have been able to explain to his grandfather that in his grandson's time people would be able to journey to the future, beyond their own lifetimes, or to the past, back through the pages of history? Garrett had been excited about traveling to the year 2000 not so much because he was going to witness a crucial moment in the history of the human race—the end of the long war against the automatons—but because he was more conscious than ever that he lived in a world where, thanks to science, anything seemed possible. He was going to travel to the year 2000, yes, but who could say how many more epochs he might visit before he died? According to Gilliam Murray, it was only a matter of time before new routes opened up, and perhaps he would have the opportunity to glimpse a better future, after the world had been rebuilt, or to travel back to the time of the pharaohs or to Shakespeare's London, where he could see the playwright penning his legendary works by candlelight. All this made his youthful spirit rejoice, and he felt continually grateful towards God, in whom, despite Darwin's policy of vilification, he preferred to continue to believe; and so each night, before going to bed, he beamed up at the stars, where he imagined God resided, as if to say he was ready to marvel at whatever He deigned to show him. It will come as no surprise to you, then, that Garrett did not pay any heed to people who mistrusted the discoveries of science, still less to those who showed no interest in Gilliam Murray's extraordinary discovery, as was the case of his superior, who had not even bothered to take time off to visit the year 2000.

"Let me see if I've understood you correctly. Are you telling me this is the only lead you have in this case, Inspector?" Chief Superintendent Arnold said, waving the advertisement for Murray's Time Travel Garrett had given him. He jabbed his finger at the little illustration showing the brave Captain Shackleton shooting a hole in an automaton with a ray gun.

Garrett sighed. The fact that Chief Superintendent Arnold had not been on any of the expeditions to the future meant he was forced to fill him in on the subject, and so he wasted several minutes explaining in general terms what was happening in the year 2000 and how they had traveled there, until he reached the part that really interested him: the weaponry used by the human soldiers. Those guns were capable of cutting through metal, and so it was not impossible to imagine that used on a human the effect might be very similar to what he had seen on the body in the Marylebone morgue. As far as he was aware, no weapons in their own time could cause such a horrific wound, a fact he could see was borne out by Dr. Alcock in his autopsy report. At this point, Garrett presented his theory to Arnold: one of these men from the future, possibly the one named Shackleton, had stowed away on the *Cronotilus* when he and the others had traveled back to their time, and was now on the loose in the year 1896 armed with a lethal weapon. If he were right, they had two choices: they could search the whole of London for Shackleton, which might take several weeks, with no guarantee of success, or they could save themselves the trouble by arresting him where they knew he would be on May 20 in the year 2000. Garrett only had to go there with two police officers, and arrest him before he was able to travel back to their own day.

"What's more," he added, in a last-ditch attempt to convince his superior, who was shaking his head, visibly perplexed, "if you give me permission to arrest Captain Shackleton in the future, your department will be in line for all kinds of plaudits, because we will have achieved something truly groundbreaking: arresting a murderer before he is able to commit a crime, thus preventing it from happening."

Chief Superintendent Arnold gazed at him in disbelief.

"Are you telling me that if you travel to the year 2000 and arrest this murderer, his crime will be . . . rubbed out?"

Garrett understood how difficult it was for a man like Chief Superintendent Arnold to grasp something like this. No one would find it easy to understand the implications of what he was saying, unless they stayed awake all night as he did, mulling over the paradoxes time travel might give rise to.

"I'm convinced of it, Chief Superintendent. If I arrest him before he commits the crime, it will inevitably change the present. Not only will we be arresting a murderer, we'll be saving a life, because I assure you the tramp's corpse will vanish from the morgue in a flash," Garrett declared, unsure himself of exactly how this would happen.

Thomas Arnold pondered for a few moments the praise Scotland Yard would earn from such temporal acrobatics. Luckily, the chief superintendent's limited imagination was unable to comprehend that once the murderer was arrested, not only would the corpse disappear, but so would everything relating to the crime, including the interview taking place at that very moment. There would be no murder to solve. In short: they would earn no plaudits because they would have done nothing. The consequences of arresting Shackleton in the future, before he traveled into the past to commit his crime, were so unpredictable that Garrett himself, as soon as he paused to analyze them for a moment, found them dizzying. What would they do with a murderer whose crime no one remembered because he had been arrested before he committed it? What the devil would they accuse him of? Or perhaps Garrett's journey into the future would also be flushed away down the giant cosmic drain where everything that had been prevented from happening disappeared? He did not know, but he was certain he was the instrument to set everything in motion.

After two hours of discussion, the dazed Chief Superintendent Arnold had ended the interview with a promise to Garrett that he would meet the commissioner and the prime minister that very afternoon and explain the situation to them as best he could. Garrett thanked him. This meant the following day, if no problems arose, he would receive the warrant to arrest Shackleton in the year 2000. Then he would go to Murray's Time Travel to see Gilliam and demand three seats on the next voyage of his *Cronotilus*.

AS ONE MIGHT EXPECT, while Garrett waited he mulled over the case. On this occasion, however, rather than attempt to solve it by analyzing the various elements, which was pointless as he had already found the murderer, he simply marveled at its extraordinary ramifications, as if he were examining a web spun by a new species of spider. And for once Garrett was not sitting in his office thinking these thoughts, but on a bench on the pavement opposite a luxurious house on Sloane Street. This was the abode of Nathan Ferguson, the pianola manufacturer, whom, unfortunately, owing to his friendship with his father, Garrett had known all his life. Garrett had his doubts whether this odious fellow was in fact largely responsible for the devastating war of the future as that foul-mouthed young Winslow had suggested in jest, but he had nothing against spending the evening enjoying a bunch of grapes while he watched his house to see whether anyone suspicious came prowling around. If they did, it would no doubt save him a trip to the future. But it was quite possible too that Ferguson's only function in the vast scheme of the universe was as a manufacturer of those absurd pianolas, and that Captain Shackleton was at that very moment stalking someone else's house. Why else would he have killed the tramp? What could that poor wretch's life have meant to the captain? Had he been an unfortunate casualty, an accident, or was there more to the cadaver lying in the morgue than met the eye? Was it perhaps a key piece in the puzzle of the future?

Garrett was absorbed in these thoughts but was forced to end them when he saw the door to the house open and Ferguson step out. The inspector rose from his bench and ducked behind a tree from where he had a clear view of what was happening on the pavement opposite. Ferguson paused to put on his top hat and survey the night with a triumphant expression. Garrett saw that he was elegantly turned out and assumed he must be on his way to some dinner or other. After pulling on his gloves, Ferguson closed the door behind him, descended the flight of steps, and began strolling down the street in a leisurely way. Apparently, wherever he was headed must be near enough for him not to summon his carriage. Garrett wondered whether to follow him or not. Before he had a chance to decide what action to take, just as Ferguson was passing the flower beds bordering the lawn in front of his house, a shadow emerged silently from among the bushes. It was wearing a long coat and a cap pulled down over its face. Garrett did not need to see who it was; he knew. He was the first to be astonished that his theory had proved correct.

With a determined gesture, the figure pulled a pistol out of its coat pocket and aimed it at Ferguson as he strolled along oblivious of what was going on behind his back. Garrett responded with alacrity. He leapt out from behind the tree and raced across the street. He was aware that surprise was his strongest weapon against Shackleton, who was twice his size and strength. The sound of Garrett's footsteps alerted the shadow, who watched his swift approach with visible alarm, while still training the gun on Ferguson. Garrett hurled himself at Shackleton with all his might, grabbing him round the waist, and the two of them fell through the bushes into the garden. The inspector was surprised at how easily he was able to pin down Shackleton, but quickly realized that this was because he was lying on top of a beautiful young woman, whose mouth was within kissing distance of his.

"Miss Nelson?" he stammered, at a loss.

"Inspector Garrett!" she exclaimed, equally nonplussed.

Garrett's face flushed bright red. He leapt up, disentangling himself from their unseemly embrace, then helped her to her feet. The revolver lay on the ground, but neither of them hurried to pick it up.

"Are you all right?" asked the inspector.

"Yes, I'm fine, don't worry," the girl replied, gasping and pulling an annoyed face. "I don't think I've broken any bones, in spite of everything."

Lucy brushed the mud off her clothes, and let down her hair from the bun it had been wound up in that had come loose during the fall.

"Forgive me for charging at you like that, Miss Nelson," Garrett apologized, entranced by the lovely golden cascade resting on her shoulders liked honey spilling from a jar. "I'm truly sorry, but . . . if I'm not mistaken, you were going to shoot Mr. Ferguson."

"Of course I was going to shoot Mr. Ferguson, Inspector! I haven't been hiding in the bushes all evening for nothing," the girl replied sulkily.

She bent down to retrieve the pistol, but Garrett was quicker than she was.

"I think I'd better keep this," he said, grinning apologetically. "But tell me, why kill Mr. Ferguson?"

Lucy sighed, and stared distractedly at the ground for a few moments.

"I'm not the shallow girl everyone thinks I am, you know," she said in a wounded voice. "I care about the world just as much as anyone else. And I intended to prove it by stopping the man responsible for the war of the future."

"I don't think you're shallow," said Garrett. "And anyone who does is an ass."

Lucy beamed, flattered by the inspector's remark.

"Do you really mean that?" she said demurely.

"Of course, Miss Nelson," said the inspector, smiling shyly back at her. "But don't you think there are better ways of proving it than by staining those lovely hands of yours with blood?"

"I suppose you're right, Mr. Garrett," Lucy admitted, gazing at the inspector in admiration.

"I'm so glad you agree," said Garrett, genuinely relieved.

They stood in silence gazing at each other awkwardly for a few seconds.

"What now, Inspector?" she said at length, her face a picture of innocence. "Are you going to arrest me?"

Garrett sighed.

"I suppose I should, Miss Nelson," he acknowledged reluctantly, "however . . ."

He paused for a moment, weighing up the situation.

"Yes?" said Lucy.

"I'm prepared to forget all about it if you promise not to shoot anyone again."

"Oh, I promise, Inspector!" said the girl, overjoyed. "Now, kindly give me the pistol so I can put it back in my father's drawer before he notices it's missing."

Garrett paused, but in the end handed it to her. When she took it, their fingers touched; they lingered for a moment sharing a sense of delight. Garrett cleared his throat as Lucy slipped the gun into her coat pocket.

"Will you allow me to walk you home, Miss Nelson?" he asked, not daring look her in the eye. "It is unwise for a young lady to be out alone at this hour, even if she does have a gun in her pocket."

Lucy smiled, charmed by Garrett's offer.

"Of course, I will," she said. "You're very kind, Inspector. What's more, I don't live far from here and it's a lovely evening. It'll make a pleasant walk."

"I'm sure it will," Garrett replied.

XXXV

HE NEXT MORNING, IN THE PRI-
vacy of his office, Inspector Colin Garrett
ate his breakfast with a dreamy look on his face. Naturally, he was thinking of Lucy Nelson, her lovely eyes, her
golden tresses, the way she had smiled at him when she
asked whether she could write him a letter. At that moment, a constable barged in with a warrant signed by the
prime minister requesting he set off for the future to arrest a man who had not yet been born. Suffering from the
effects of being in love, which, as you know, more often
than not put one in a daze, the inspector did not realize
the letter's significance until he found himself in the cab
being driven to Murray's Time Travel.

Garrett's legs had turned to jelly the first time he had
crossed the threshold of Murray's headquarters, clutching
the money his father had left him that was to be transformed into something straight out of a dream: a ticket to
the future, to the year 2000. This time he did so with a resolute stride, even though he had something just as incredible in his jacket pocket, a warrant that seemed all the more

extraordinary considering it was for the arrest of a phantom. And Garrett was convinced that if time travel were to become routine, this would be the first in a long line of similar warrants enabling police officers to make arrests in different eras, provided that the crimes were committed in the same place: London. When he had scrawled his signature on the slip of paper Garrett was carrying in his inside pocket, the prime minister, doubtless unawares, had taken an epoch-making step, blazed a new trail. As Garrett had predicted, science and its amazing creations would beat the rhythm to which humanity would dance.

But this warrant would also allow Garrett certain liberties in space. Like not being forced to languish in some waiting room until that busiest of men, Gilliam Murray, deigned to see him. Invested with the power conferred on him by the scrap of paper in his inside pocket, Garrett marched straight past the secretaries guarding Murray's privacy, and, ignoring their objections, went up the stairs to the first floor, then along the corridor lined with clocks, and breezed in to Murray's office, a bevy of breathless assistants in his wake. Gilliam Murray was lying on the carpet playing with a huge dog. He frowned slightly when he saw Garrett come in without knocking, but the inspector did not allow himself to be intimidated. He knew his behavior was more than justified.

"Good morning, Mr. Murray. Inspector Colin Garrett of Scotland Yard," he introduced himself. "Forgive me for barging in like this, but there's an urgent matter I need to discuss with you."

Murray rose to his feet very slowly, eyeing the inspector suspiciously before dismissing his assistants with a wave of his hand.

"You needn't apologize, Inspector, any matter you deal with must by definition be urgent," he said, offering him an armchair as he crammed his huge frame into one opposite.

Once they were seated, Murray picked up a small wooden box from the table between their two chairs, opened it, and, in a brisk, friendly manner that contrasted with his initial aloofness, offered Garrett a cigar. The inspector refused politely, smiling to himself at Murray's brusque change of attitude, reflecting how swiftly he must have weighed up the pros and cons of getting on the wrong side of an inspector from the Yard and decided that playing up to him was a far better strategy. It was thanks to this that Garrett was sitting in a comfortable armchair and not on the footstool next to it.

"So, you don't like smoke?" remarked Murray, putting the box back on the table and picking up a cut-glass decanter containing a peculiar blackish substance, which he poured into two glasses. "Perhaps I can tempt you to a drink."

Garrett balked slightly at the glass of dark liquid Murray was holding out to him. But Murray grinned amiably, encouraging him to try it as he took a swig of his. Garrett did the same and felt the strange beverage sting his throat as it went down, the tears starting to his eyes.

"What is it, Mr. Murray?" he asked, perplexed, unable to refrain from letting out a loud belch. "A drink from the future?"

"Oh, no, Inspector. It's a tonic made from coca leaves

and cola seeds invented by a chemist in Atlanta. It's all the rage in the United States. Some people prefer taking it with a little soda, like me. I expect they'll soon be importing it over here."

Garrett put down his glass on the table, disinclined to take another sip.

"It has a peculiar flavor. I don't imagine people will take to it very easily," he predicted, for the sake of saying something.

Murray smiled his assent, emptied his glass, and, visibly eager to ingratiate himself, asked:

"Tell me, Inspector, did you enjoy your trip to the year 2000?"

"Very much, Mr. Murray," replied Garrett in earnest. "What's more, I'd like to take this opportunity to say that I fully endorse your project, regardless of what some newspapers say about the impropriety of visiting a time that doesn't belong to us. I have an open mind, and I find the idea of time travel enormously appealing. I eagerly await the opening up of new routes to other eras."

Murray thanked Garrett for his comments with a modest smile, then sat expectantly in his chair, no doubt inviting the inspector to reveal the reason for his visit. Garrett cleared his throat and came straight to the point:

"We live in fascinating but tremendously volatile times, Mr. Murray," he said, reeling off the little preamble he had prepared. "Science drives events, and mankind must adapt. Above all, if our laws are to remain effective, we must update them to suit the changing face of the world. Even more so when it comes to time travel. We are at the dawn of an extraordinary era of discovery that will doubtless redefine the world as we know it, and whose inherent dangers are impossible, or extremely difficult, to judge. It is precisely these dangers I came here to speak to you about, Mr. Murray."

"I couldn't agree with you more, Inspector," Murray conceded. "Science will change the face of the world, and oblige us to modify our laws, and even many of our principles, the way that time travel is already doing. But, tell me, what are these dangers you wish to speak to me about? I confess you've aroused my curiosity."

Garrett sat up in his chair and cleared his throat once more.

"Two days ago," he said, "the police discovered a man's body in Manchester Street, Marylebone. He was a tramp, but the injury that killed him was so extraordinary they handed the case over to us. The wound consists of an enormous hole twelve inches wide that goes straight through his chest and is singed at the edges. Our pathologists are baffled. They claim no weapon exists that is capable of inflicting such an injury."

Garrett made a dramatic pause before fixing Murray with a solemn stare, and adding:

"At least not here, not in the present."

"What are you suggesting, Inspector?" asked Murray, in a casual manner that did not correspond with the way he was fidgeting in his chair.

"That the pathologists are right," replied Garrett, "such a weapon hasn't yet been invented. Only I've seen it, Mr. Murray. Guess where?"

Murray did not reply but looked at him askance.

"In the year 2000."

"Really," murmured Murray.

"Yes, Mr. Murray. I'm convinced this wound can only have been inflicted by the weapon I saw the brave Captain Shackleton and his men using. The heat ray that can pierce armor."

"I see . . ." Murray muttered as if to himself, staring into space. "The weapon used by the soldiers of the future, of course."

"Precisely. I believe one of them, possibly Shackleton, traveled back on the *Cronotilus* without being noticed and is roaming our streets at this very moment. I've no idea why he killed the tramp or where he is hiding now, but that doesn't matter: I don't intend to waste time searching the whole of London for him when I know exactly where he is." He pulled a piece of paper from his inside pocket and handed it to Murray. "This is a warrant signed by the prime minister authorizing me to arrest the murderer on May 20 in the year 2000, before he can even commit his crime. It means I'll need to travel with two of my officers on the expedition leaving in a week's time. Once we arrive in the future, we'll separate from the others so that we can spy on the passengers from the second expedition and discreetly detain anyone who attempts to stow away on the *Cronotilus.*"

As he spoke, it dawned on the inspector that if he lay in wait for the passengers of the second expedition he would unavoidably see himself. He only hoped it would not repulse him as much as the sight of blood. He glanced at Murray, who was carefully studying the warrant. He was silent for so long it occurred to Garrett he might even be examining the consistency of the paper.

"But have no fear, Mr. Murray," he felt obliged to add, "if Shackleton does turn out to be the murderer, my arresting him after his duel with Solomon won't affect the outcome of the war. It will still end in victory for the human race, and it won't affect your enterprise, either."

"I understand," murmured Murray without looking up from the document.

"May I count on your cooperation, Mr. Murray?"

Murray slowly raised his head and looked at Garrett with what for a moment the inspector imagined was contempt, but he soon realized his mistake when Murray quickly beamed at him, and replied:

"Certainly, Inspector, certainly. I shall reserve three seats for you on the next expedition."

"I'm most grateful to you, Mr. Murray."

"And now, if you'll excuse me," said Murray, standing up and handing him back the document. "I'm extremely busy."

"Of course, Mr. Murray."

Slightly taken aback by the way Murray had abruptly ended the interview, Garrett rose from his armchair, thanked him once more for his cooperation, and left his office. A smile played across the inspector's lips as he walked along the interminable corridor lined with clocks. By the time he reached the stairs he was in an excellent mood and began chanting to himself:

"Peritoneum, spleen, left kidney, suprarenal gland, urinary tract, prostate gland . . . ," he sang.

XXXVI

NOT EVEN THE TOUCH ON THE skin of the delicious breeze heralding the arrival of summer, nor caressing a woman's body, nor sipping Scotch whiskey in the bathtub until the water goes cold, in short, no other pleasure Wells could think of gave him a greater sense of well-being than when he added the final full stop to a novel. This culminating act always filled him with a sense of giddy satisfaction born of the certainty that nothing he could achieve in life could fulfill him more than writing a novel, no matter how tedious, difficult, and thankless he found the task, for Wells was one of those writers who detest writing but love "having written."

He pulled the last folio from the carriage of his Hammond typewriter, laid it on top of the pile, and placed his hand on it with a triumphant smile, like a hunter resting his boot on a lion's head, because for Wells the act of writing was much like a struggle, a bloodthirsty battle with an idea that refuses to be seized. An idea that nonetheless originated with him; and perhaps that was the most frustrating thing of all, the eternal yawning gap between the fruit of his efforts and his initial goal, which admittedly was always more instinctive than deliberate. He had learned from experience that what he succeeded in putting down on paper was only ever a pale reflection of what he had imagined, and so he had come to accept that this would only be half as good as the original, half as acceptable as the flawless, unachievable novel that had acted as a guide, and which he imagined pulsating mockingly behind each book like some ghostly presence. Even so, here was the result of all those months of toil, he told himself; and it felt wonderful to see transformed into something palpable what had been, until he typed that last full stop, no more than a vague premise. He would deliver it to Henley the next day and could stop thinking about it.

And yet such doubts never arose in isolation. Once more, Wells wondered, as he sat beside his pile of typed folios, whether he had written the book he had been meant to write. Was this novel destined to figure in his bibliography, or had it been engendered by accident? Was he responsible for writing one novel and not another, or was this also controlled by the fate that governed men's lives? He was plagued by doubts, although one caused him particular distress: was there a novel lurking somewhere in his head that would allow him to express the whole of what was really inside him? The idea he might discover this too late tormented him: that as he lay on his deathbed, before his last gasp, the plot of an extraordinary novel he no longer had time to write would rise from the depths of his mind, like a piece of wreckage floating up to the sea's surface. A novel that had always been there, awaiting him, calling out to him in vain amid the clamor, a novel that would die with him, for no one but he could write it, because it was like a suit made to measure just for him. He could think of nothing more terrifying, no worse fate.

He shook his head, driving out these distressing thoughts, and glanced up at the clock. It was past midnight. That meant he could write November 21, 1896, next to his signature on the end page of the novel. Once he had done this, he blew lovingly on the ink, rose from his chair, and picked up the oil lamp. His back was stiff, and he felt terribly tired, yet he did not go into the bedroom, where he could hear Jane's steady breathing. He had no time for sleep; he had a long night ahead of him, he told himself, a smile playing across his face. He padded down the corridor in his slippers, lighting his way with the lamp, and began to climb the stairs to the attic, trying to avoid making the steps creak.

Waiting for him, shiny and magnificent, shimmering in the celestial moonlight filtering in through the open window, stood the machine. He had grown attached to his secret ritual, although he did not know exactly why he derived such enjoyment from the silly, harmless prank that consisted of sitting on the machine while his wife was asleep below him. Perhaps because it made him feel special, even though he knew it was only a sophisticated toy. The maker had considered every detail: the machine might not be able to travel in time, but thanks to a clever mechanism, any date could be set on the control panel, the fictitious destinations of impossible passages through the fabric of time.

Until now, Wells had only set the date to distant times in the future—including to the year 802,701, the world of the Eloi and the Morlocks—times so remote that life as he knew it could only appear completely alien, painfully incomprehensible; or to times in the past he would like to have known, such as the time of the druids. But that night, with a roguish grin, he adjusted the numbers on the control panel to May 20 in the year 2000, the date on which the impostor Gilliam Murray had chosen to stage the greatest ever battle of the human race—that pantomime which to his astonishment all England had been fooled by, thanks in part to his own novel. He found it ironic that he, the author of a novel about time travel, was the only person who thought it was impossible. He had made all England dream but was immune to his own creation.

What would the world really look like in a hundred years' time? he wondered. He would have liked to travel to the year 2000, not just for the pleasure of seeing it, but to take photographs with one of those newfangled cameras so that he could come back and show the unsuspecting crowds queuing up outside Murray's offices what the true face of the future looked like. It was a pipe dream, of course, but there was nothing to stop him from pretending he could do it, he told himself, settling back in his seat and ceremoniously pulling the lever down, experiencing the inevitable frisson of excitement he felt whenever he performed the gesture.

However, to his astonishment, this time when the lever stopped, a sudden darkness fell on the attic. The flecks of moonlight shining through the window seemed to withdraw, leaving him in total darkness. Before he was able to understand what the devil was going on, he was overcome by a dreadful feeling of vertigo and a sudden giddiness. He felt himself floating, drifting through a mysterious void that could have been the cosmos itself. And as he began to lose consciousness, all he managed to think was that either he was having a heart attack or he really was traveling to the year 2000 after all.

HE CAME TO PAINFULLY slowly. His mouth was dry, and his body felt strangely sluggish. Once he could focus properly, he realized he was lying on the floor, not in his attic but on a piece of wasteland covered in stones and rubble. Disorientated, he struggled upright, discovering to his annoyance that each time he moved he felt a terrible shooting pain in his head. He decided to stay sitting on the ground. From there he glanced around with awe at the devastated landscape. "Was this the London of the future?" he thought. Had he really traveled to the year 2000? There was no sign of the time machine, as if the Morlocks had spirited it away inside the sphinx. After his careful inspection, he decided the time had come for him to stand upright, which he did with great difficulty, like Darwin's primate crossing the distance separating him from man. He was relieved to find he had no broken bones, although he still felt unpleasantly queasy. Was this one of the effects of having crossed a century in his time carriage? The sky was covered with a dense fog that left the landscape in a pale twilight, a gray blanket dotted with red from the dozens of fires burning on the horizon. The crows circling above his head were an almost obligatory feature of the desolate scene, he reflected. One flew down, alighting very close to where he was sitting, and made a macabre tapping sound as it began pecking stubbornly at the rubble.

On closer examination, Wells saw with horror that the bird was trying to bore through a human skull with its beak. This discovery caused him to recoil a few paces, a rash response in that hostile environment. The next thing he knew, the ground gave way beneath him, and he realized too late that he had woken up at the top of a small incline, down which he was now unhappily tumbling. He landed with a thump, coughing and spluttering as he breathed in some of the thick dust cloud shrouding him. Irritated by his own clumsiness, Wells rose to his feet. Luckily, he had no broken bones this time either, although as a crowning humiliation, his trousers had been torn in several places, leaving part of one scrawny white buttock exposed.

Wells shook his head. "What more could go wrong?" he thought, dusting himself down as best he could. As the dust settled, he stood stock still, contemplating aghast the figures slowly emerging from the gloom. Staring back at him in ghostly silence, were an army of automatons. There were at least a dozen of them, all with the same inscrutable, intimidating expression, even the one standing slightly to the fore, who was wearing an incongruous gold crown. They looked as though they had halted in their tracks when they saw him roll down the incline. A terrible panic gripped Wells's insides as he realized where he was. He had traveled to the year 2000, and, amazingly enough, it was exactly as Gilliam Murray had portrayed it in his novel, for there in front of him, before his very eyes, stood Solomon himself, the evil king of the automatons responsible for all the devastation around them. His fate was sealed: he was going to be shot by a mechanical toy. There, in the very future he had refused to believe in.

"I imagine right now you must be wishing Captain Shackleton would appear, correct?"

The voice did not come from the automaton, although at that stage nothing would have surprised him, but from somewhere behind Wells. He recognized it instantly. He would have liked never to have to hear it again, but somehow, perhaps because he was a writer, he had known that sooner or later he would bump into Murray again; he knew the story they were both taking part in needed a satisfying conclusion, one that would not frustrate the readers' expectations. Wells would never have envisaged the encounter taking place in the future, though, for the simple reason that he had never believed in the possibility of traveling into the future. He turned around slowly. A few yards away, Gilliam Murray was watching him, an amused grin on his face. He was wearing a purple suit and a green top hat, like a human descendant of those beautifully plumed biblical birds of paradise. Sitting on its haunches next to him was an enormous golden-colored dog.

"Welcome to the year 2000, Mr. Wells," Murray said, jovially, "or should I say to *my* vision of the year 2000."

Wells looked at him suspiciously, one eye on the eerily frozen group of automatons drawn up before them as though posing for a portrait.

"Are you afraid of my nice automatons? But how can you be scared of such an unconvincing future?" Gilliam asked sarcastically.

He walked slowly towards the automaton at the front of the group, and, grinning deliberately at Wells, like a child about to perpetrate some mischief, placed his fleshy hand on its shoulder and gave it a push. The automaton keeled over backwards, crashing noisily into the one behind it, which in turn toppled onto the one next to it, and so on until one after the other they collapsed onto the ground. They fell with the fascinating slowness of a glacier breaking off. When it was finally over, Gilliam spread the palms of his hands as if to apologize for the din.

"With no one inside, they're just hollow shells, mere disguises," he said.

Wells gazed at the pile of upturned automatons, then looked back at Gilliam, struggling with his dizzying feeling of unreality.

"Forgive me for bringing you to the year 2000 against your will, Mr. Wells," apologized Murray, feigning dismay. "If you'd accepted one of my invitations, it wouldn't have been necessary, but as you didn't, I had no alternative. I wanted you to see it before I closed it down. And so I had to send one of my men to chloroform you while you were asleep, although from what he told me, you occupy your nights with other things. He got a real shock after he'd climbed through the attic window."

Murray's words shed a welcome light on the author's

whirling thoughts, and he lost no time in tying up the necessary loose ends. He realized immediately he had not traveled to the year 2000, as everything appeared to indicate. The machine in his attic was still just a toy, and the razed city of London was no more than a vast stage set designed by Gilliam in order to hoodwink people. No doubt, on seeing him enter the attic, Gilliam's henchman had hidden behind the time machine and waited, unsure of what to do, perhaps weighing up the possibility of carrying out Murray's orders using force. But fortunately, he had not needed to resort to an ignoble act of violence, as Wells himself had given the man the perfect opportunity to use the chloroform-soaked handkerchief he no doubt had at the ready by sitting in the time machine.

Of course, once he realized he was standing on a simple stage set and that he had not undergone some impossible journey through time, Wells felt greatly relieved. The situation he found himself in was by no means pleasant, but at least it was logical.

"I trust you haven't harmed my wife," he said, not quite managing to sound threatening.

"Have no fear," Gilliam reassured him, waving a hand in the air. "Your wife is a deep sleeper, and my men can be very quiet when they have to be. I'm sure that the lovely Jane is at this very moment sleeping peacefully, oblivious to your absence."

Wells was about to make a riposte but finally thought better of it. Murray was addressing him with the rather overblown arrogance of people in high places who have the world at their feet. Evidently, the tables had turned

since their last meeting. If during the interview at the author's house in Woking, Wells had been the one wielding
the scepter of power like a child brandishing a new toy,
now it was Murray who held it between his fleshy fingers.
Over the intervening months, Murray had changed: he
had become an altogether different creature. He was no
longer the aspiring writer obliged to kneel at his master's
feet, he was the owner of the most lucrative business in
London before whom everyone grotesquely bowed down.
Wells, of course, did not think he deserved any kind of
adulation, and if he allowed him to use that superior tone,
it was because he considered Murray was entitled to do
so: after all, he was the outright winner of the duel they
had been fighting during the past few months. And had
not Wells used a similar tone when the scepter had been
in his hands?

Gilliam Murray spread his arms wide, like a ringmas-
ter announcing the acts at a circus, symbolically embracing the surrounding devastation.

"Well, what do you think of my world?" he asked.

Wells glanced about him with utter indifference.

"Not bad for a glasshouse manufacturer, don't you
agree, Mr. Wells? That was my occupation before you gave
me another reason to go on living."

Wells could not fail to notice the responsibility Murray
had so happily chosen to ascribe to him in the forging of
his destiny, but he preferred not to comment. Undeterred
by Wells's frostiness, Murray invited him with a wave of
his arm to take a stroll through the future. The author
paused for a moment, then reluctantly followed.

"I don't know whether you're aware that glasshouses are a most lucrative business," said Murray once Wells had drawn level with him. "Everyone nowadays sets aside part of their garden for these cozy spaces, where grown-ups like to relax and children play, and it is possible to grow plants and fruit trees out of season. Although my father, Sebastian Murray, had, as it were, loftier ambitions."

They had scarcely walked a few paces when they came to a small precipice. Unconcerned about taking a tumble, Murray began trotting absurdly down the incline, arms stretched out at his sides to keep his balance. The dog bounded after him. Wells let out a sigh before beginning the descent, taking care not to trip over the mangled bits of pipe and grinning skulls poking out of the ground. He did not wish to fall over again. Once was quite enough in one day.

"My father sensed the beginning of a new future in those transparent houses rich people erected in their gardens," Murray shouted out to him as he went ahead down the incline, "the first step towards a world of translucent cities, glass buildings that would put an end to secrets and lies, a better world where privacy would no longer exist!"

When he reached the bottom, he offered his hand to Wells, who declined, not bothering to conceal his impatience at the whole situation. Murray seemed not to take the hint, and resumed their stroll, this time along an apparently gentler path.

"I confess that as a child I was fascinated by the glorious vision that gave my father's life meaning," he went on. "For a while I even believed it would be the true face of the future. Until the age of seventeen, when I began working with him. It was then that I realized it was no more than a fantasy. This amusement for architects and horticulturalists would never be transformed into the architecture of the future, not only because man would never give up his privacy in the interests of a more harmonious world, but because architects themselves were opposed to the glass and iron constructions, claiming the new materials lacked the aesthetic values that, they maintained, defined architectural works. The sad truth was that, however many glass-roofed railway stations my father and I built up and down the country, we could never usurp the power of the brick. And so I resigned myself to spending the rest of my life manufacturing fancy glasshouses.

"But who could content themselves with such a petty, insignificant occupation, Mr. Wells? Not I, for one. Yet I had no idea what would satisfy me either. By the time I was in my early twenties I had enough money to buy anything I wanted, however whimsical, and as you might expect, life had begun to feel like a card game I had already won and was beginning to tire of. To cap it all, around that time my father died of a sudden fever, and as I was his only heir I became even richer. But his passing also made me painfully aware that most people die without ever having realized their dreams. However enviable my father's life may have seemed from the outside, I knew it hadn't been fulfilling, and mine would be no different. I was convinced I would die with the same look of disappointment on my face. I expect that's why I turned to reading, so as to escape the dull, predictable life unfolding before me. We all begin reading for one reason or another, don't you think? What was yours, Mr. Wells?"

"I fractured my tibia when I was eight," said the author, visibly uninterested.

Gilliam looked at him slightly surprised for a moment, then finally smiled and nodded.

"I suppose geniuses like you have to start young," he reflected. "It took me a little longer. I was twenty-five before I began exploring my father's ample library. He had been widowed early on and had built another wing onto the house, probably in order to use up some of the money my mother would otherwise have helped him to spend. Nobody but me would ever read those books. So I devoured every one, every single one. That was how I discovered the joys of reading. It's never too late, don't you agree? Although I confess, I wasn't a very discerning reader. Any book about lives that weren't my own was of some interest to me. But your novel, Mr. Wells . . . your novel captivated me like no other! You didn't speak of a world you knew, like Dickens, or of exotic places such as Africa or Malaysia, like Haggard or Salgari, or even of the moon, like Verne. No, in *The Time Machine* you evoked something even more unattainable: the future. Nobody before you had been audacious enough to visualize it!"

Wells shrugged off Murray's praise and carried on walking, trying not to trip over the dog, which had the irritating habit of zigzagging across his path. Verne, of course, had beaten him to it, but Gilliam Murray need not know that. Murray resumed, again heedless of the author's lack of interest:

"After that, as you know, doubtless inspired by your novel, a spate of authors hastened to publish their visions of the future. Suddenly, the bookshop windows were crammed with science fiction novels. I bought as many as I could, and after several sleepless nights spent devouring them in quick succession, I decided this new genre of literature would be my only reading."

"I'm sorry you chose to waste your time on such nonsense," muttered Wells, who considered these novels a regrettable blot on the fin-de-siècle literary landscape.

Taken aback once more, Gilliam glanced at him before letting out a loud guffaw.

"Oh, I know these potboilers have little merit," he agreed, when he had stopped laughing, "but I couldn't care less about that. The authors of this nonsense, as you call it, possess something far more important to me than the ability to create sublime sentences: namely a visionary intelligence that amazes me and which I wish I had. Most of these works confine themselves to describing a single invention and its effect on mankind. Have you read the novel about the Jewish inventor who devises a machine that magnifies things? It's a truly awful book, and yet I confess the image of an army of giant stag beetles swarming across Hyde Park truly terrified me. Thankfully, they are not all like that. Such ravings apart, some present an idea of the future whose plausibility I enjoyed exploring. And there was something else I couldn't deny: after enjoying a book by Dickens, for example, it would never have occurred to me to try to imitate him, to see whether I was capable of concocting a story about the adventures of a street urchin or the hardships of a boy forced to work in a blacking factory, because it seemed to me anyone with a modicum of imagination and time would be able to do that. But to write about the future . . . Ah, Mr. Wells, that was different. To me, that seemed a real challenge. It was an undertaking that required intelligence, man's capacity for deduction. Would I be capable of creating a believable future? I said to myself one night after finishing another of those novels. As you will have guessed, I took you as my example, because, besides our common interests, we are the same age. It took me a month to write my novel about the future, a piece of science fiction that would display my insight, my powers of invention. Naturally, I made every effort to write well, but I was more interested in the novel's prophetic side. I wanted my readers to find my vision of the future plausible. But most of all, I valued the opinion of the writer who had been my guiding light. Your opinion, Mr. Wells; I wanted you to be as intellectually stimulated by my novel as I had been by yours."

The two men's eyes met in a silence broken only by the distant cawing of crows.

"But as you know, it didn't happen like that," Gilliam lamented, unable to prevent himself shaking his head in sorrow. The gesture moved Wells, as he considered it the only sincere one Murray had made since they set off on their walk.

They had come to a halt next to a huge mound of

rubble, and there, hands dug into the pockets of his loud jacket, Gilliam paused for a few moments staring down at his shoes, clearly distressed, perhaps waiting for Wells to place his hand on his shoulder and offer words of solace, which, like the shaman's chant, would soothe the painful wound Wells himself had inflicted on Murray's pride that afternoon long ago. However, the author simply studied him with the disdain of the poacher watching a rabbit struggle in a trap, aware that while seemingly responsible for what was happening, he was a simple mediator, and the animal's torment was dictated by the cruel laws of nature.

Having realized that the only person capable of alleviating his hurt seemed unwilling to do so, Gilliam smiled grimly and carried on walking. They went down what was to judge by the grandiose wrought-iron gates and the palatial remains of the buildings amid the rubble, a luxurious residential street evoking a life that seemed incongruous amidst all that devastation, as though man's proliferation on the planet had been no more than a divine blunder, a ridiculous flowering, doomed to perish under the elements.

"I shan't try to deny that at first I was upset when you doubted my abilities as a writer," Gilliam acknowledged in a voice that oozed like treacle from inside his throat. "Nobody enjoys having their work pilloried. But what most vexed me was that you questioned the plausibility of my novel, the future I had so carefully contrived. I admit my response was entirely unacceptable, and I wish to take this opportunity to apologize for having attacked your novel the way I did. As I'm sure you'll have guessed, my opinion of it hasn't changed. I still consider it the work of a genius," Gilliam said, laying a faintly ironic emphasis on the final words. He had recovered his conceited smirk, but Wells had glimpsed a chink in his armor, the crack that from time to time threatened to bring this powerful colossus crashing down, and in the face of Murray's intolerable arrogance, Wells felt almost proud to have been the cause of it.

"That afternoon, however, I was unable to defend myself other than like a cornered rat," Wells heard Gilliam justify himself. "Happily, when I finally managed to recover, I could see things in a different light. Yes, you might say I experienced a kind of epiphany."

"Really," commented Wells, with dry irony.

"Yes, I'm sure of it. Sitting opposite you in that chair, I realized I'd chosen the wrong means of presenting my idea of the future to the world; in doing it through a novel, I was condemning it to being mere fiction, plausible fiction, but fiction all the same, as you had done with your future inhabited by Morlocks and Eloi. But what if I were able to put my idea across without confining it to the restrictive medium of the novel? What if I could present it as something real? Evidently, the pleasure of writing a believable piece of fiction would pale beside the incredible satisfaction of having the whole country believe in the reality of my vision of the year 2000. But was this feasible? the businessman in me asked. The conditions for realizing such a project seemed perfect. Your novel, Mr. Wells, had sparked off a polemic about time travel. People in clubs and cafés talked of nothing else but the possibility of traveling into the future. It is one of life's ironies that you fertilized the ground for me to plant my seed. Why not give people what they wished for? Why not offer them a journey to the year 2000, to 'my' future? I wasn't sure I'd be able to pull it off, but one thing was certain: I wouldn't be able to go on living if I didn't try. Purely by accident, Mr. Wells, the way most things happen in life, you gave me a reason to carry on, a goal which, were I to achieve it, would give me the longed-for fulfillment, the elusive happiness I could never obtain from the manufacture of glasshouses."

Wells was compelled to lower his head in order to conceal his sense of sympathy towards Murray. His words had reminded Wells of the extraordinary chain of events that had delivered him into the loving arms of literature, away from the mediocrity to which his not so loving mother had sought to condemn him. And it had been his way with words, a gift he had not asked for, that had spared him the need to find a meaning to his life, had exempted him from having to tread the path taken by those who had no idea why they had been born, those who could only experience the conventional, atavistic joy found in everyday pleasures such as a glass of wine or a woman's caress. Yes, he would have walked among those redundant shadows, unaware that the longed-for happiness he had scarcely glimpsed during his fits of melancholy lay curled up in a ball on the keys of a typewriter, waiting for him to bring it to life.

"On my way back to London I began thinking," he heard Murray say. "I was convinced people would believe the impossible if it were real enough. In fact, it was not unlike building a glasshouse: if the glass part of the structure were elegant and beautiful enough, nobody would see the solid iron framework holding it up. It would appear to be floating in the air as if by magic. The first thing I did the next morning was to sell the business my father had built up from scratch. In doing so, I felt no regret, in case you were wondering, quite the opposite if anything, because with the money from the sale I would be able literally to build the future, which, ultimately, had been my father's dream. From the proceeds, I purchased this old theater. The reason why I chose it was because right behind it, looking out over Charing Cross Road, were two derelict buildings which I also bought. The next step, of course, was to merge the three buildings into one by knocking down the walls in order to obtain this vast space. Seen from the outside, no one would think it was big enough to house a vast stage set of London in the year 2000. Yet in less than two months, I created a perfect replica, down to the smallest detail, of the scene in my novel. In fact, the set isn't nearly as big as it looks, but it seems immense if we walk round it in a circle, don't you think?"

Is that what we've been doing, walking round in a circle? Wells thought, containing his irritation. If so, he had to acknowledge that the intricate layout of the debris had taken him in completely, for it made the already sprawling stage set appear even more gigantic, and he would never have imagined it could fit inside a modest theater.

"My own team of blacksmiths made the automatons that gave you such a fright a while ago, as well as the armor worn by Captain Shackleton's human army," Gilliam explained, as he guided Wells through a narrow ravine created by two rows of collapsed buildings. "At first I thought of hiring professional actors to dramatize the battle that would change the history of the human race, which I myself had staged so that it would look as appealing and exciting as possible. I immediately discarded the idea because I felt that stage actors, who are famous for being erratic and vain, would be incapable of giving a realistic portrayal of brave, battle-hardened soldiers in an army of the future. More importantly, I thought that if they began to have qualms about the morality of the work they had been hired to do, they would be harder to silence. Instead, I employed a bunch of bruisers who had far more in common with the veterans they were supposed to portray. They didn't mind keeping the heavy metal armor on during the entire performance, and they couldn't have cared less about my scheme being fraudulent. In spite of all that, I had a few problems, but nothing I wasn't able to sort out," he added, smiling significantly at the author.

Wells understood that with this twisted grin Murray meant to tell him two things: firstly, that he knew about his involvement in the relationship between Miss Haggerty and Tom Blunt, the young man who had played Captain Shackleton, and secondly, that he was behind Tom's sudden disappearance. Wells forced his lips into an expression of horrified shock, which appeared to satisfy Gilliam. What Wells wanted more than anything was to wipe the arrogant smirk off the man's face by informing him that Tom had survived his own death. Tom himself had told Wells this only two nights earlier when he showed up at his house to thank him for all he had done for him and to remind him if he ever needed a pair of strong arms, he could call on him.

THE RAVINE OPENED OUT onto what looked like a small square where a few gnarled, leafless trees still grew. In the middle of the square, Wells noticed something resembling an overly ornate tramcar, whose sides were covered in a mass of chrome-plated tubes. Sprouting from these were dozens of valves and other elaborate accessories, which, on closer observation, Wells thought could only be for decoration.

"And this is the *Cronotilus*, a steam-driven tram that seats thirty," declared Gilliam proudly, banging one of its sides. "The passengers embark in the room next door, ready to travel into the future, unaware that the year 2000 is in a large adjoining space. All I have to do is to transport them here. This distance you see, about fifty yards," he said, gesturing towards some doorway hidden by fog, "represents a whole century to them."

"But how do you simulate the effect of traveling through time?" asked Wells, unable to believe Murray's customers would be satisfied by a simple ride in a tramcar, however ostentatious.

Gilliam grinned, as though pleased at his question.

"My hard work would all have been for nothing if I'd failed to find a solution to this niggling problem you so rightly identified. And I assure you it gave me many sleepless nights. Evidently, I couldn't show the effects of traveling into the future as you did in your novel, with snails that moved faster than hares or the moon going through all its phases in seconds. Therefore, I had to invent a method of time travel that didn't need me to show such effects, and which, in addition, had no basis in science, for I was certain that once I told the newspapers I could travel to the year 2000, every scientist up and down the country would demand to know how the devil such a thing was done. A real dilemma, wouldn't you say? And after giving the matter careful thought, I could think of only one method of traveling in time that couldn't be questioned scientifically: by means of magic."

"Magic?"

"Yes, what other method could I resort to if the scientific route wasn't open to me? And so I invented a fictitious biography for myself. Before going into the time travel business, instead of manufacturing dreary glasshouses, my father and I ran a company that financed expeditions, like the scores of others that exist today, intent on disclosing all the world's mysteries. And, like everybody else, we were desperate to find the source of the Nile, which legend situated in the heart of Africa. We had sent our best explorer there, Oliver Tremanquai, who, after many grueling adventures had made contact with an indigenous tribe capable of opening a portal into the fourth dimension by means of magic."

With these words, Gilliam paused, smiling scornfully at the author's attempts to hide his disbelief.

"The hole was a doorway onto a pink, windswept plain where time stood still," he went on, "which was no more

than my portrayal of the fourth dimension. The plain, a
sort of antechamber to other eras, was peppered with holes
similar to the portal connecting it to the African village.
One of these led to May 20 in the year 2000, on the very
day the humans fought the decisive battle for the survival
of their race against the automatons, amid the ruins of a
devastated London. And, having discovered the existence
of this magic hole, what else could my father and I do but
steal it and bring it to London in order to offer it to the
subjects of Her Imperial Majesty? So that's what we did.
We locked it in a huge iron box built for the occasion and
brought it here. And, voilà, I had found the solution, a way
of traveling in time that involved no scientific devices. All
you had to do to journey into the future was pass through
the hole into the fourth dimension aboard the *Cronotilus*,
cross part of the pink plain, and step through another hole
into the year 2000. Simple, isn't it? In order to avoid having
to show the fourth dimension, I inhabited it with terrifying, dangerous dragons, creatures of such horrific appearance I was forced to black out the windows in the *Cronotilus*
in order not to alarm the passengers," he said, inviting the
author to examine the porthole-shaped windows, painted
black as he had said. "And so, once the passengers had
climbed aboard the time tram, I carried them, using oboes
and trombones to conjure up the roars of the dragons roaming the plain. I've never experienced the effect from inside
the *Cronotilus*, but it must be very convincing, to judge by
the pallor on many passengers' faces when they return."

"But if the hole always comes out in this square at the
exact same moment in the year 2000 . . ." Wells began.

"Then each new expedition arrives at the same time as the previous ones," Gilliam cut across him. "I know, I know, that's completely illogical. And yet time travel is still such a young idea, not many people have considered the many contradictions it can give rise to. If the portal into the fourth dimension always opens onto the exact same moment in the future, obviously there should be at least two *Cronotiluses* here, as there have been at least two expeditions. But as I already said, Mr. Wells, not everyone notices such things. In any event, as a precaution against any questions the more inquisitive passengers might have posed, I instructed the actor who played the guide to explain to them as soon as they arrived in the future, before they even stepped out of the vehicle, that we drove each *Cronotilus* to a different place, precisely in order to avoid this eventuality."

Murray waited to see if Wells felt like asking any more questions, but the author appeared immersed in what could only be described as pained silence, a look of impotent sorrow on his face.

"And," Gilliam went on, "as I had anticipated, as soon as I advertised my journeys to the year 2000 in the newspapers, numerous scientists asked to meet me. You should have seen them, Mr. Wells. They came in droves, barely able to conceal their contempt, hoping I would show them some device they could gleefully demolish. But I was no scientist. I was just an honest businessman who'd made a chance discovery. Most of them left the meeting indignant, visibly frustrated at having been presented with a method of travel they had no way of questioning or refuting: you either believe in magic or you don't. Some, however, were thoroughly convinced by my explanation, like your fellow author, Conan Doyle. The creator of the infallible Sherlock Holmes has become one of my most vigorous defenders, as you will know if you've read any of the numerous articles he devotes to defending my cause."

"Doyle would believe in anything, even fairies," said Wells derisively.

"That's possible. As you have seen yourself, we can all be deceived if the fraud is convincing enough. And to be honest, far from upsetting me, the regular visits I received from our skeptical men of science gave me great pleasure. Actually, I rather miss them. After all, where else would I have found a more attentive audience? I enjoyed enormously relating Tremanquai's adventures over and over: as you will have guessed, they were a veiled homage to my beloved Henry Rider Haggard, the author of *King Solomon's Mines*. In fact, Tremanquai is an anagram of one of his best-known characters, Quatermain, the adventurer who—"

"And none of these scientists demanded to see the . . . hole?" interrupted Wells, still disinclined to believe it had all been so easy.

"Oh yes, of course. Many refused to leave without seeing it. But I was prepared for that. My instinct for survival had warned me to construct a cast-iron box identical to the one in my story, supposedly containing the portal to the fourth dimension. I presented it to anyone who wanted to see it, and invited them to go inside, warning them I would have to close the door behind them, because, among other things, the box was a barrier that prevented the ferocious dragons entering our world. Do you think any of them dared to go in?"

"I imagine not," responded Wells, despondently.

"That's correct," affirmed Murray. "In fact, the entire artifice is based on a box, in which the only thing lurking is our deepest fears. Don't you think it's both poetic and exciting?"

Wells shook his head with a mixture of sadness and disbelief at the gullibility of his fellow men, but above all at the scientists' lack of spirit, their spinelessness when it came to risking their lives in the service of empirical truth.

"So, Mr. Wells, that is how I transport my customers into the future, escaping the time continuum only to plunge back into it somewhere else, like salmon swimming their way upstream. The first expedition was a resounding success," Murray boasted. "I confess to being surprised at how readily people were taken in by my hoax. But then, as I said before, people see what they wish to see. However, I scarcely had time to celebrate, for a few days later the Queen herself asked to see me. Yes, Her Majesty in person requested my humble presence at the palace. And I'd be lying if I didn't say I went there prepared to receive my just desserts for my impudence. To my astonishment, however, Her Majesty wanted to see me for a very different reason: to ask if I would organize a private trip to the year 2000 for her."

Wells stared at him, flabbergasted.

"That's right, she and her entourage wanted to see

the war of the future that the whole of London was raving about. As you can imagine, I wasn't too keen on the idea. Not only because, naturally, I would be expected to organize the performance free of charge, but, given the distinguished nature of our guests, it had to be carried off to perfection. In other words, as convincingly as possible. Luckily, there were no mishaps. I think I can even say it was our best performance. The distress on Her Majesty's face when she saw London razed to the ground spoke for itself. But the following day, she sent for me a second time. Again, I imagined my fraud had been discovered, and again I was astounded to discover the reason for this new summons: Her Majesty wished to make a generous donation to enable me to carry on my research. It's the honest truth: the Queen herself was willing to finance my swindle. She was keen for me to carry on studying other holes, to open up other routes to other times. But that wasn't all. She also wanted me to build her a summer palace inside the fourth dimension so that she could spend long periods there, with the aim of escaping the ravages of time and prolonging her life. Naturally, I accepted. What else could I do? Although, of course, I haven't been able to finish building her palace and I never will. Can you think why?"

"It must be because the work is continually being delayed by attacks from the ferocious dragons that live in the fourth dimension," replied Wells, visibly disgusted.

"Precisely," declared Gilliam, beaming. "I see you're beginning to understand the rules of the game, Mr. Wells."

The author refused to humor him, instead staring at

the dog, which was furiously scrabbling in the rubble a few yards from them.

"Not only did the fact that Her Majesty was taken in by my deception line my pockets, it also banished my fears. I immediately stopped fretting over the letters that appeared like clockwork in the newspapers written by scientists accusing me of being a charlatan: in any case, people had stopped paying them any attention. Even the swine that kept smearing cow dung on the front of the building no longer bothered me. Actually, at that point, there was only one person who could have exposed me, and that was you, Mr. Wells. But I assumed that if you hadn't already, you never would. And I confess I found your attitude worthy of admiration, that of a truly sporting gentleman who knows when he has lost."

With a smug grin on his face, Murray gestured to Wells to carry on walking with him. They left the square in silence, the dog tagging along behind, and turned into one of the streets obstructed by mounds of rubble.

"Have you stopped to consider the essence of all this, Mr. Wells?" asked Murray. "Look at it this way: what if I had presented this as a simple play I had written about the future instead of passing it off as the real year 2000? I would have committed no offense, and people would have flocked to see it anyway. But I assure you that when they arrived home, none of them would have felt special, or seen the world in a different light. In reality, all I'm doing is making them dream. Isn't it a shame to think I could be punished for that?"

"You'd have to ask your customers whether they would

be prepared to pay as much to watch a simple play," replied the author.

"No, Mr. Wells. You're wrong. The real question you'd have to ask them is whether they'd prefer to discover this had all been a hoax and get their money back, or, on the contrary, whether they'd prefer to die believing they had visited the year 2000. And I can assure you, the majority would prefer not to know. Aren't there lies that make life more beautiful?"

Wells gave a sigh but refused to acknowledge that in the end Murray was right. Apparently, his fellow men preferred to believe they lived in a century in which science could ferry them to the year 2000, by whatever means, than to be trapped in a time from which there was no hope of escape.

"Take young Harrington, for example," Murray went on, with a playful grin. "Do you remember him? If I'm not mistaken, it was a lie which saved his life. A lie in which you agreed to participate."

Wells was about to remark that there was a world of difference between the purpose behind one lie and the other, but Murray headed him off with another question.

"Are you aware that it was I who built the time machine you keep in your attic, the little toy that pleases you so much?"

This time Wells was unable to conceal his amazement.

"Yes, I had it especially made for Charles Winslow, the wretched Andrew Harrington's cousin," Gilliam chuckled. "Mr. Winslow came on our second expedition, and a few days later he turned up at my offices asking me to organize a private trip for him and his cousin to the year 1888, the Autumn of Terror. They assured me money was no object, but unfortunately I was unable to satisfy their whim."

Murray had wandered off the main road towards a pile of debris beyond which a row of shattered rooftops was visible in the distance, darkened by a few clouds looming above.

"But Mr. Winslow's reason for wanting to travel into the past was so romantic it moved me to help them," said Murray sarcastically, even as, to Wells's horror, he began scrambling up the hill of rubble. "I explained to him he could only make the journey in a time machine like the one in your novel, and together we hatched a plot, in which, as you know, you played the leading role. If Mr. Winslow managed to persuade you to pretend you had a time machine, I would not only produce a replica of the one in your novel, I would also provide him with the actors necessary to play the parts of Jack the Ripper and the whore he murdered. You must be wondering what made me do it. I suppose devising hoaxes can become addictive. And I won't deny, Mr. Wells, that it amused me to involve you in a pantomime similar to the one I had already orchestrated, to see whether you'd agree to take part in it or not."

Wells was scarcely able to pay attention to what Murray was saying. Clambering up the hill, as well as requiring a good deal of concentration, was making him feel distinctly uneasy, for the distant horizon had begun drawing nearer until it was within arm's length. Once they reached the summit, Wells could see that what was in front of them was no more than a painted wall. Astonished, he passed his hand over the mural. Gilliam looked at him affectionately.

"Following the success of the second expedition, and although things had calmed down a lot, I couldn't help wondering whether there was any sense in carrying on with all this now that I had more than proved my point. The only reason I could think of to justify the effort it would take to organize a third expedition," he said, recalling with irritation Jeff Wayne's pompous delivery of Shackleton's lines, and how scrawny he looked brandishing his rifle on top of the rock, "was money. But I'd already made enough for a dozen lifetimes, so that was no excuse either. On the other hand, I was sure my critics would sooner or later mount a concerted attack on me that not even Conan Doyle would be able to head off."

Murray seized the door handle protruding from the wall, but made no attempt to turn it. Instead, he turned to Wells, a contrite look on his face.

"Doubtless I should have stopped then," he said with regret, "setting in motion the plan I'd prepared even before creating the company: I would stage my own accidental death in the fourth dimension, eaten alive by one of my imaginary dragons before the eyes of a group of employees who, filled with grief, would see to it that the newspapers were informed of the tragic news. While I began my new life in America under another name, all England would mourn the passing of Gilliam Murray, the man who had revealed the mysteries of the future to them. However, despite the beauty of such an ending, something compelled me to carry on with my deception. Do you want to know what that was, Mr. Wells?"

The writer merely shrugged.

"I'll do my best to explain, although I doubt you will understand. You see, in creating all of this not only had I proved that my vision of the future was plausible, I had become a different person. I had become a character in my own story. I was no longer a simple glasshouse manufacturer. In your eyes, I'm no more than an impostor, but to everyone else I'm a time lord, an intrepid entrepreneur who has braved a thousand adventures in Africa and who sleeps every night with his magical dog in a place where time has stopped. I suppose I didn't want to close the company down because that meant being an ordinary person again—a terribly rich but terribly ordinary person."

And with this, he turned the knob and stepped into a cloud.

WELLS FOLLOWED HIM A few seconds later, behind the magical dog, only to discover his bad-tempered face multiplied by half a dozen mirrors. He was in a cramped dressing room full of boxes and frames, hanging from which were several helmets and suits of armor. Gilliam was watching him from a corner, a serene smile on his lips.

"And I suppose I'll deserve what I get, if you refuse to help me," he said.

There it was at last. As Wells had suspected, Murray had not gone to all the trouble of bringing him there simply to offer him a guided tour. No, something had happened and Gilliam had come unstuck. And now Murray needed his help. This was the pièce de résistance he was expecting his guest to swallow after having force-fed him with explanations. Yes, he needed his help. Alas, the fact that Murray had never stopped addressing him in that condescending, almost fatherly tone suggested he had no intention of deigning to beg him for it. He simply assumed he would get it. For Wells it only remained to be seen what kind of threat the charlatan would use to extort it.

"Yesterday, I had a visit from Inspector Colin Garrett of Scotland Yard," Murray went on. "He is investigating the case of a tramp found murdered in Marylebone, not exactly an unusual occurrence in that neighborhood. What makes this case so special is the murder weapon. The corpse has a huge hole right through the chest, which you can look through as if it were a window. It appears to have been caused by some sort of heat ray. According to the pathologists, no weapon capable of inflicting such a wound exists. Not in our time, anyway. All of which has led the young inspector to suspect that the wretched tramp was murdered with a weapon of the future, specifically one of the rifles used by Captain Shackleton and his men, whose devastating effects he was able to observe when he formed part of the second expedition."

He took a rifle out of a small cupboard and handed it to Wells. The writer could see that the so-called weapon was simply a piece of wood with a few knobs and pins added for show, like the accessories on the tram.

"As you can see, it's just a toy. The automatons' wounds are produced by tiny charges hidden under their armor. But for my customers, of course, it's a weapon, as real as it is powerful," Murray explained, relieving Wells of the fake rifle and returning it to the closet with the others. "In short, Inspector Garrett believes one of the soldiers of the future, possibly Captain Shackleton himself, traveled back to our own time as a stowaway on the *Cronotilus*, and all he can think of is to travel on the third expedition to apprehend him before he does so, and thereby prevent the crime. Yesterday he showed me a warrant signed by the prime minister authorizing him to arrest a man who from where we're standing hasn't even been born yet. The inspector asked me to reserve three seats on the third expedition for him and two of his men. And, as I'm sure you'll understand, I was in no position to refuse. What excuse could I have made? And so in ten days' time the inspector will travel to the year 2000 with the intention of arresting a murderer, but what he'll in fact do is uncover the greatest swindle of the century. Perhaps, given my lack of scruples, you think I could get out of this fix by handing one of my actors over to him. But to make that believable, not only would I have to produce another *Cronotilus* out of thin air, I would also have to get round the difficult problem of Garrett seeing himself as part of the second expedition. As you can appreciate, all that is far too complicated even for me. The only person who can prevent Garrett from traveling to the future as he intends is you, Mr. Wells. I need you to find the real murderer before the day of the third expedition."

"And why should I help you?" asked Wells, more resigned than threatening.

This was the question they both knew would bring everything out into the open. Gilliam walked towards Wells, an alarmingly calm smile on his face, and, placing a plump hand on his shoulder, steered him gently to the other side of the room.

"I've thought a great deal about how to answer that question, Mr. Wells," he said in a soft, almost sweet-sounding voice. "I could throw myself on your mercy. Yes, I could slump to my knees and beg for your help. Can you imagine that, Mr. Wells? Can you see me sniveling like a child, tears dripping onto your shoes, crying out loud that I don't want my head chopped off? I'm sure that would do the trick: you think you're better than me and are anxious to prove it." Gilliam smiled as he opened a small door and propelled Wells through it with a gentle shove. "But I could also threaten you, by telling you that if you refuse to help me, your beloved Jane will no doubt suffer a nasty accident while out on her afternoon bicycle ride in the suburbs of Woking. I'm sure that would also do the trick. However, I've decided instead to appeal to your curiosity. You and I are the only ones who are aware this is all a big farce. Or, to put it another way: you and I are the only ones who are aware that time travel is impossible. And yet someone has done it. Doesn't that make you curious? Will you just stand by and watch while young Garrett devotes all his energy to pursuing a fantasy when a real time traveler could be roaming the streets of London?"

Gilliam and Wells stared silently at one another.

"I'm sure you won't," Gilliam concluded.

And with these words, he closed the door of the future and deposited Wells back on November 26, 1896. The writer suddenly found himself in the dank alleyway behind Murray's Time Travel, where a few cats were foraging among the rubbish. He had the impression that his trip to the year 2000 had been a dream. On impulse, he thrust his hands into his jacket pockets, but they were empty: no one had slipped a flower into them.

XXXVII

*W*HEN WELLS CALLED IN TO SEE him the next day at his office, Inspector Colin Garrett gave him the impression of being a shy, delicate young lad everything appeared too big for, from the sturdy desk where he was at that moment eating his breakfast, to his brown suit, and especially the murders, burglaries, and other crimes spreading like unsightly weeds all over the city. If he had been interested in writing a detective novel, like those his fellow novelist Doyle penned, for example, he would never have described his detective as looking anything at all like the nervous, frail-looking young man in front of him, who, to judge by the excited way he shook Wells's hand, was particularly susceptible to the reverential zeal of hero worship.

Once he was seated, Wells stoically endured with his usual modest smile the outpouring of praise for his novel *The Time Machine*, although, to give the young inspector his due, he ended his eulogy with a most novel observation.

"As I say, I enjoyed your novel enormously, Mr. Wells,"

he said, pushing aside his breakfast plate somewhat ashamedly, as though wishing to remove the guilty evidence of his gluttony, "and I regret how hard it must be for you, and for all authors of futuristic novels, not to be able to keep on speculating about the future now that we know what it is like. Otherwise, if the future had remained unfathomable and mysterious, I imagine novels that predict tomorrow's world would have ended up becoming a genre in themselves."

"I suppose so," Wells agreed, surprised at the young inspector having thought of something that had never even occurred to him.

Perhaps he was wrong after all to judge him on his youthful appearance. Following this brief exchange, the two men simply smiled affably at one another for the next few moments, as the sun's rays filtered through the window, bathing them in a golden light. Finally, Wells, seeing that no more praise was forthcoming from the inspector, decided to broach the matter that had brought him there.

"Then, as a reader of my work, I imagine it will come as no surprise if I tell you I am here about the case of the murdered tramp," he confessed. "I've heard a rumor that the culprit might be a time traveler, and while I have no intention of suggesting I am an authority on the matter, I think I may be of some assistance."

Garrett raised his eyebrows, as if he had no idea what Wells was talking about.

"What I'm trying to say, Inspector, is that I came here to offer you my . . . support."

The inspector cast him a sympathetic glance.

"You're very kind, Mr. Wells, but that won't be necessary," he said. "You see, I've already solved the case."

He reached into his desk drawer for an envelope and fanned the photographs it contained out on the table. They were all of the tramp's corpse. He showed them to Wells, one by one, explaining in great detail and with visible excitement the chain of reasoning that had led him to suspect Captain Shackleton or one of his soldiers. Wells scarcely paid any attention, as the inspector was merely reiterating what Gilliam had already told him, but became engrossed in studying the intriguing wound on the corpse. He knew nothing of guns, but it did not take an expert to see that the grisly hole could not possibly have been inflicted by any present-day weapon. As Garrett and his team of pathologists maintained, the wound looked as though it had been caused by some sort of heat ray, like a stream of molten lava directed by a human hand.

"As you can see, there is no other explanation," concluded Garrett with a satisfied grin, placing everything back in the envelope. "To be honest, I'm simply waiting until the third expedition leaves. This morning, for example, I sent a couple of officers to the crime scene simply for appearance's sake."

"I see," said Wells, trying not to show his disappointment.

What could he say to convince the inspector to investigate in a different direction without revealing that Captain Shackleton was not a man from the future, and that the year 2000 was no more than a stage set built of the rubble from demolished buildings? If he failed, Jane would almost certainly die. He stifled a gasp so as not to betray his anguish to the inspector.

Just then, an officer opened the door and asked to see Garrett. The young inspector made his excuses and stepped out into the corridor, beginning a conversation with his officer that reached Wells as an incomprehensible murmur. The talk lasted a couple of minutes, after which Garrett came back into the office in a visibly bad mood, waving a scrap of paper in his right hand.

"The local police are a lot of bungling fools," he growled, to the astonishment of Wells, who had not imagined this delicate young lad capable of such an angry outburst. "One of my officers found a message painted on the wall at the scene of the crime which those imbeciles overlooked."

Wells watched him reread the note several times in silence, leaning against the edge of his desk. He shook his head in deep dismay.

"Although, as it turns out, you couldn't have come at a better time, Mr. Wells," he said finally, beaming at the author. "This could almost be taken from a novel."

Wells raised his eyebrows and took the scrap of paper Garrett was holding out to him. The following words were scrawled on it:

The stranger came in early February, one wintry day, through a biting wind and a driving snow, the last snowfall of the year, over the down, walking as it seemed from Bramblehurst railway station.

After reading it, Wells looked up at the inspector, who stared back at him.

"Does it ring any bells?" he asked.

"No," replied Wells, categorically.

Garrett took the note from him and reread it, his head swaying from side to side again, like a pendulum.

"Nor for me," he confessed. "What is Shackleton trying to say?"

After posing the rhetorical question, the inspector appeared to become lost in thought. Wells used the opportunity to rise to his feet.

"Well, Inspector," he said, "I shan't trouble you any longer. I'll leave you to your riddles."

Garrett roused himself and shook Wells by the hand.

"Many thanks, Mr. Wells. I'll call you if I need you."

Wells nodded and walked out of Garrett's office, leaving him pondering, precariously balanced on the corner of his desk. He made his way down the corridor, descended the staircase, and walked out of the police station, hailing the first cab he saw, almost without realizing what he was doing, like a sleepwalker or someone under hypnosis, or, why not, like an automaton. During the journey back to Woking, he did not venture to look out the window even once, for fear some stranger strolling along the pavement or a navvy resting by the side of the road would give him a significant look that would fill him with dread. When he arrived home, he noticed his hands were trembling. He hurried straight along the corridor into the kitchen, without even calling out to Jane to tell her he was back. On the table were his typewriter and the manuscript of his latest novel, which he had called *The Invisible Man*. Pale as a ghost, Wells sat down and glanced at the first page of the manuscript he had finished the day before and which no one but he had ever read. The novel began with the following sentence:

> The stranger came in early February, one wintry day, through a biting wind and a driving snow, the last snowfall of the year, over the down, walking as it seemed from Bramblehurst railway station.

There was a real time traveler, and he was trying to communicate with him. This was what Wells thought when he finally emerged from his daze. And with good reason; why else would the traveler have written on the wall the first lines of *The Invisible Man*, a novel that had not yet been published in his own time, a novel whose existence no one else but he as yet knew about? It was evident that killing a tramp with an unfamiliar weapon had only one purpose: to distinguish that murder from the many others perpetrated each day in the city and to attract the police's attention, but the fragment of his novel left at the scene of the crime could only be a message for him. And although Wells did not rule out the possibility that the tramp's strange chest wound had been inflicted by some present-day instrument Garrett and the pathologists had not yet stumbled upon, obviously no one could have known the beginning of his novel, except a man who came from the future. This fact alone dispelled any lingering doubts Wells might have had that he was dealing with a time traveler. He felt a shudder go through his body at the thought, not only because he had suddenly discovered that time travel, which he had always considered mere fantasy, was possible, or rather, would be possible in the future, but because, for some sinister reason he preferred not to think about, this time traveler, whoever he was, was trying to get into contact with him.

He spent all night tossing and turning, unnerved by the unpleasant feeling of knowing he was being watched and wondering whether he ought to tell the inspector everything, or whether that would anger the time traveler. When dawn broke, he had still not come to any decision. Fortunately, there was no need, as almost immediately an official carriage from Scotland Yard pulled up in front of his house. Garrett had sent one of his officers to fetch him: another dead body had turned up.

Without having breakfasted and still wearing his nightshirt under his coat, the dazed Wells agreed to be driven to London. The coach stopped in Portland Street, where a pale-faced Garrett was waiting for him, alone at the center of an impressive police presence. Wells counted more than half a dozen officers trying desperately to secure the scene of the crime against the crowd of onlookers that had flocked to the area, amongst whom he could make out a couple of journalists.

"The victim was no tramp this time," the inspector said after shaking his hand, "he was the landlord of a nearby tavern, a Mr. Terry Chambers. Although he was undoubtedly killed with the same weapon."

"Did the murderer leave another message?" asked Wells in a faint voice, managing just in time to stop himself from blurting out: "for me."

Garrett nodded, unable to disguise his irritation. Clearly, the young inspector would have preferred Captain Shackleton to find a less dangerous way of amusing himself until he was able to travel to the year 2000 to arrest him. Obviously overwhelmed by the whole incident, he guided Wells to the crime scene, pushing his way through the police cordon. Chambers was propped up against a wall, drooping slightly to one side, with a smoldering hole in his chest. The bricks behind him were clearly visible. Some words had been daubed above his head. His heart pounding, Wells tried not to step on the publican as he leaned over to read the inscription:

Left Munich at 8:35 p.m. on 1st May, arriving at Vienna early next morning: should have arrived at 6:46, but train was an hour late.

When he saw the sentence was not from his novel, Wells let out a sigh of both relief and disappointment. Was the message meant for another author? It seemed logical to think so, and he felt certain the otherwise unremarkable sentence was the beginning of an as yet unpublished novel, which the author had probably just finished. It seemed the time traveler was not only trying to make contact with him, but with someone else as well.

"Do the words ring a bell, Mr. Wells?" asked Garrett hopefully.

"No, Inspector. However, I suggest you publish it in the newspaper. Clearly, the murderer is giving us some sort of riddle, and the more people who see it the better," he said, aware he must do all he could to make this message reach the person to whom it was addressed.

While the inspector kneeled down to examine the corpse at close quarters, Wells gazed distractedly at the crowd on the other side of the cordon. What business could the time traveler have with two nineteenth-century writers? he wondered. As yet he did not know, but there was no doubt he would soon find out. All he had to do was wait. For the moment, the time traveler was the one pulling the strings.

Coming out of his daydream, he suddenly found himself looking at a young woman who was staring back at him. She was about twenty, slender and pale, with reddish hair, and the intentness of her gaze struck Wells as odd. She was wearing an ordinary dress with a cloak over it, and yet there was something strange about her, something about her expression and the way she was looking at him which he was unable to define, but which marked her out from the others.

Instinctively, Wells started towards her. But to his astonishment, his bold gesture scared the girl, who turned on her heel and disappeared into the crowd, her fiery tresses billowing in the breeze. By the time the writer had managed to make his way through the throng, she had slipped away. He peered in every direction but could see no trace of her. It was as though she had vanished into thin air.

"Is something the matter, Mr. Wells?"

The author jumped upon hearing the voice of the inspector, who had come after him, no doubt intrigued by his strange behavior.

"Did you see her, Inspector?" Wells asked, still scanning the street anxiously. "Did you see the girl?"

"What girl?" the young man asked.

"She was standing in the crowd. And there was something about her . . ."

Garrett looked at him searchingly.

"What do you mean, Mr. Wells?"

The writer was about to respond but realized he did not know how to explain the strange impression the girl had made on him.

"I . . . never mind, Inspector," he said, shrugging his shoulders and sighing. "She was probably an ex-pupil of mine, that's why she looked familiar . . ."

The inspector nodded, not very convinced. He clearly thought Wells's behavior odd. Even so, Garrett followed his advice, and the next day the two passages from both his and the unknown author's books appeared in all the London newspapers. And if Wells's suspicions were well founded, the information would have ruined the breakfast of one his fellow authors. Wells did not know who at that precise moment was being seized by the same panic that had been brewing inside him for the past two days, but the realization that he was not the only person the time traveler was trying to contact brought him some relief. He no longer felt alone in all this, nor was he in any hurry to learn what the traveler wanted from them. He was certain the riddle was not yet complete.

And he was not mistaken.

THE FOLLOWING MORNING, WHEN the cab from Scotland Yard pulled up at his door, Wells was already sitting on the porch steps dressed and breakfasted. The third corpse was that of a seamstress by the name of Chantal Ellis. The sudden change in the victim's gender unsettled Garrett, but not Wells, who knew that the corpses were unimportant; they were simple blackboards on which the time traveler scribbled his messages. The words on the wall in Weymouth Street, up against which the unfortunate Miss Ellis was propped, read as follows:

> The story had held us, round the fire, sufficiently breathless, but except the obvious remark that it was gruesome, as, on Christmas Eve in an old house, a strange tale should essentially be, I remember no comment uttered till somebody happened to say that it was the only case he had met in which such a visitation had fallen on a child.

"Does this one ring a bell, Mr. Wells?" asked Garrett, no hope in his voice.

"No," replied the author, omitting to add that the intricate prose struck him as vaguely familiar, although he was unable to identify its author.

While Garrett barricaded himself in the London Library together with a dozen officers, intent on scouring every novel on its shelves for the one from which Shackleton, for some sinister and as yet unknown reason, was quoting, Wells made his way home, wondering how many more innocent victims would die before the traveler's riddle was complete.

The next day, however, no carriage from Scotland

Yard came to fetch him. Did that mean the time traveler had made contact with all his chosen authors? The answer was awaiting him in his letter box. There Wells found a map of London, by means of which the traveler not only indicated the meeting point, but at the same time flaunted his ability to move through the time continuum at will, as the map was dated 1666 and was the work of the Czech engraver Wenceslaus Hollar. Wells admired the exquisite chart representing a city whose countenance was soon to be transformed, for in September of that year London was obliterated by an inferno. If he remembered correctly it had started in a bakery in central London, and, fanned by the neighboring coal, timber, and alcohol warehouses, had spread rapidly, reaching St. Paul's Cathedral and surging over the Roman wall into Fleet Street. But what really astonished Wells was that the map showed no sign of having traveled across two centuries to reach him. Like a soldier holding his rifle aloft as he forges a river, the traveler had protected the map from the ravages of time, saving it from the stealthy caress of the years, the yellow claws of the decades, and the ruinous handling of the centuries.

Having recovered from his astonishment, Wells noticed the circle marking off Berkeley Square and next to it the number 50. This was undoubtedly the place the three authors must visit to meet the traveler. And Wells had to admit he could not have chosen a more appropriate location, for number 50 Berkeley Square was considered the most haunted house in London.

XXXVIII

BERKELEY SQUARE HAD A SMALL park at its center. This was rather gloomy for its size but boasted some of the oldest trees in central London. Wells skirted it almost at a march, glancing with a perfunctory nod toward the languid nymph that the sculptor Alexander Munro had contributed to the relentless melancholy of the landscape, then came to a halt outside a house with the number 50 displayed on its front wall. It was a modest building that looked out of place next to others bordering the square, all of which were designed by well-known architects of the period. It looked as though no one had lived there for decades, and although the façade did not appear too dilapidated, the windows on the upper floors, as well as those downstairs, were boarded up with moldering planks to keep prying eyes from discovering the dark secrets that surely lay within. Was he wise to have come there alone? Wells wondered with an involuntary shudder. Perhaps he should have informed Inspector Garrett, for not only was he about to meet someone who apparently had few scruples when it came to killing ordinary citizens, but he had gone to the meeting with the naïve intention of catching him and handing him over to the inspector on a platter so that he would forget about going to the year 2000 once and for all.

Wells studied the austere front of what was allegedly the most haunted house in London and wondered what all the fuss was about. *Mayfair* magazine had published a highly sensationalist piece about the strange events which had been going on in the house since the start of the century. Everyone who entered it had apparently either died or gone insane. For Wells, who had no interest in the spirit world, the article was no more than a lengthy inventory of gruesome gossip, rumors to which not even the printed word could lend any authority. The articles were full of servant maids who, having lost their wits, were unable to explain what they had seen, or sailors who on being attacked had leapt from the windows and been impaled on the railings below, or the inevitable sleepless neighbors who, during those periods when the house was unoccupied, claimed they could hear furniture being dragged around on the other side of the walls and glimpsed mysterious shadows behind the windows.

This concoction of spine-tingling events had led the building to be classed as a haunted house, the home of a ruthless phantom, and thus the perfect place for young nobles of the realm to show their bravery by spending a night there. In 1840, a rake by the name of Robert

Warboys, who had made a virtue of his skepticism, took up his friends' challenge to sleep the night there in exchange for a hundred guineas. Warboys locked himself in, armed with a pistol and a string attached to a bell at the entrance which he vowed he would ring if he found himself in any difficulty, although he dismissed that possibility with a scornful smirk. Barely a quarter of an hour had passed when the tinkle of the bell was heard, followed by a single shot that shattered the silence of the night. When his friends came running, they found the aristocrat lying on a bed, stone dead, his face frozen in a grimace of horror. The bullet had lodged in the wooden skirting board, perhaps after passing through the specter's vaporous form.

Thirty years later, by which time the house had gained notoriety among the ranks of England's haunted houses, another valiant youth by the name of Lord Lyttleton was brave enough to spend the night there. He was more fortunate, surviving the phantom's assault by firing silver coins at it from a gun he had taken the precaution of carrying with him to bed. Lord Lyttleton claimed he even saw the evil creature fall to the ground, although during the subsequent investigation no body was found in the room, as he himself recounted with palpable unease in the well-known magazine *Notes and Queries*, which Wells had once read with amusement when he came across it in a bookshop. All the rumors and legends were at odds over the origin of the alleged ghost. Some claimed the place had been cursed after hundreds of children had been mercilessly tortured there. Others believed the phantom had been invented by neighbors to explain the bloodcurdling screams of a demented brother a previous tenant kept locked up in one of its rooms and fed through a trapdoor owing to his violent behavior. There were also those—and this was Wells's favorite theory—who maintained the origin of the ghost was a man named Myers, who, finding it impossible to sleep after being jilted on the eve of his wedding, spent his nights desperately traipsing round the house bearing a candle. But during the past decade there had been no further reports of any disturbances in the house, from which it was not unreasonable to assume that the ghost had descended to hell again, bored perhaps by all these young bucks eager to prove their manliness. However, the ghost was the least of Wells's concerns. He had too many earthly cares to worry about creatures from the other world.

He glanced up and down the street, but there was not a soul in sight, and as the moon was in the last quarter, it was absolutely dark, and the night seemed to have taken on that sticky consistency so often described in gothic novels. Since no time was specified on the map, Wells had decided to go there at eight o'clock in the evening because it was the hour mentioned in the second passage. He hoped he was right and would not be the only one to turn up to meet the time traveler. As a precaution, he had come armed, although as he did not have a gun, he had brought his carving knife instead. He had hung it on his back by a piece of string, so that if the traveler decided to frisk him he would not notice the sharp utensil. He had bid Jane farewell like the hero in a novel, with a lingering, unexpected kiss that had startled her at first, but which she had finally accepted with gentle abandon.

WELLS CROSSED THE STREET without further delay, and after taking a deep breath, as though rather than enter the house he were about to plunge into the Thames, he pushed open the door, which yielded with surprising ease. He instantly discovered he was not the first to arrive. Standing in the middle of the hallway, with his hands in the pockets of his immaculate suit as he admired the stairway vanishing into the gloom of the upper floor, was a plump, balding man of about fifty.

Seeing him come in, the stranger turned to Wells and held out his hand, introducing himself as Henry James. So, this elegant fellow was James. Wells did not know him personally, for he was not in the habit of frequenting the sort of club or literary salon which were James's preserve and where, according to what Wells had heard, this prudish man of private means sniffed out the secret passions of his fellow members in order to commit them to paper in a prose as refined as his manners. The difficulty in meeting him did not cause Wells to lose any sleep. Besides, after reading *The Aspern Papers* and *The Bostonians*, Wells felt almost comforted to know that James lived in a world far from his own, for, after plowing laboriously through the two works, Wells concluded the only thing he and James had in common was that they both spent their lives tapping away on typewriters, though he was unaware that his fellow author was now too fastidious to perform such a laborious mechanical task, preferring instead to dictate his work to a stenographer. If Wells recognized any merit in James, it was his undeniable talent for using very long sentences in order to say nothing at all. And James must have felt the same disdain for Wells's work as he felt for James's world of lace handkerchiefs and indolent ladies tormented by unmentionable secrets, because his colleague could not help pulling a face when he introduced himself as H. G. Wells. A number of seconds passed by, during which the two men confined themselves to looking suspiciously at one another until James obviously decided they were about to infringe some obscure law of etiquette and hastened to break the awkward silence.

"Apparently we have arrived at the correct time. Our host was clearly expecting us this evening," he said, gesturing towards the various candelabra distributed around them, which although they did not completely disperse the shadows at least cast a circle of light in the center of the hall, where the meeting was meant to take place.

"It would seem so," Wells acknowledged.

Both men began gazing up at the coffered ceiling, the only thing there was to admire in the empty hallway. But luckily this tense silence did not last long, because almost at once a creaking door announced the arrival of the third author.

The man opening it with the timid caution of someone entering a crypt was also in his fifties. He had a shock of flaming red hair and a neatly clipped beard that accentuated his jaw. Wells recognized him at once. It was

Bram Stoker, the Irishman who ran the Lyceum Theatre, although he was better known in the London clubs as the agent and lapdog of the famous actor, Henry Irving. Seeing him creep in, Wells could not help also recalling the rumors that Stoker belonged to the Golden Dawn, an occult society of which other fellow writers such as the Welsh author Arthur Machen or the poet W. B. Yeats were members.

The three writers shook hands in the circle of light before lapsing into a deep, uneasy silence. James had retreated into his precious haughtiness, while beside him Stoker was fidgeting nervously. Wells was enjoying this awkward meeting of three individuals who apparently had little or nothing to say to one another, despite all three of them, in their own separate ways, devoting their time to the same activity: dredging up their lives on paper.

"I'm so glad to see you're all here, gentlemen."

The voice came from above. As one, the three writers glanced towards the staircase, down which the supposed time traveler was slowly descending, as though relishing the suppleness of his movements.

Wells studied him with interest. He was about forty years old, of medium height and an athletic build. He had high cheekbones, a square chin, and wore a short, clipped beard, whose purpose seemed to be to soften his angular features as much as possible. He was escorted by two slightly younger men, each with a peculiar-looking rifle slung over his shoulder. At least that is what the writers assumed they were, more from the way the men were carrying them than from their appearance, which resembled two crooked sticks made of a strange silvery material. It did not take much intelligence to realize that these were the weapons which emitted the heat ray that had killed the three victims.

The time traveler's ordinary appearance disappointed Wells somehow, as though because he came from the future he ought to have looked hideous, or at the very least disturbing. Had the men of the future not evolved physically, as Darwin had predicted? A few years before, Wells himself had published an article in the *Pall Mall Gazette*, where he envisaged the evolution of man's appearance over the centuries: mechanical devices would finally eliminate the need for limbs; advances in chemistry would render the digestive apparatus obsolete; ears, hair, teeth, and other superfluous adornments would suffer the same fate. Only the two truly vital organs man possessed would survive this slow pruning process: the brain and the hands, which of course would increase in size considerably. The product of such speculation would necessarily be terrifying to behold, which was why Wells felt cheated by the mundane appearance of this man from the future standing in front of him. The traveler, who, to add to his frustration, was dressed like his henchmen in an elegant brown suit, came to a halt and gazed at them in satisfied silence, a mischievous smile playing about his lips. Perhaps the faintly animal look in his intense black eyes and the grace of his gestures were the only qualities that delivered him from ordinariness. But such traits were not exclusive to the future either, for they could be found in some men in the present, which thankfully was inhabited by more athletic, charismatic specimens than those exemplified in the current gathering.

"I imagine this place could not be more to your liking, Mr. James," the traveler remarked, smiling sardonically at the American.

James, a past master at the art of innuendo, smiled back at him coldly but politely.

"I shall not deny you are correct, although if you will allow me, I shall defer my admission, for I shall only be able to give it truthfully if, by the end of this meeting, I consider the outcome a worthy enough recompense for the dreadful toll the journey from Rye has taken on my back," he replied.

The traveler pursed his lips for a few moments, as though uncertain if he had entirely understood James's convoluted response. Wells shook his head.

"Who are you and what do you want from us?" Stoker then asked in a quailing voice, his eyes fixed on the two henchmen, who were looming like a pair of inscrutable shadows at the edge of the lighted area.

The traveler fixed his gaze on the Irishman and studied him with affectionate amusement.

"You needn't address me in that timorous voice, Mr. Stoker. I assure you I only brought you here with the intention of saving your lives."

"In that case, forgive our reticence, but you will understand that murdering three innocent people in cold blood with the sole aim of drawing our attention leads us to doubt your philanthropic intentions," retorted Wells, who was just as capable, when he wanted, of stringing together sentences as tortuous as those of James.

"Oh, that?" said the traveler, waving his hand in the air. "I assure you those three people were going to die anyway. Guy, the tramp in Marylebone, would have been killed the following night in a fight with the one of his fellow vagrants; Mr. Chambers was to have died three days later when someone robbed him outside his tavern; and on the morning of the same day the lovable Mrs. Ellis would have been fatally knocked down by a runaway coach in Cleveland Street. In fact, all I did was bring forward their deaths by a few days. Indeed, the reason why I chose them was because they were doomed to die, and I needed three people I could eliminate with our weapons so that their murders, together with the fragments from your unpublished novels, would be reported in the newspapers where you would learn about them. I knew that once I had convinced you I came from the future, I only had to let you know the meeting place, and your curiosity would do the rest."

"Is it true, then?" asked Stoker. "Do you really come from the year 2000?"

The traveler gave a wry smile.

"I come from a long way beyond the year 2000, where, by the way, there is no war with the automatons. If only those little toys were our main problem—"

"What are you insinuating?" said Stoker incredulously. "Everybody knows that in the year 2000 the automatons will have conquered—"

"What I'm insinuating, Mr. Stoker," the traveler interrupted, "is that Murray's Time Travel is nothing but a hoax."

"A hoax?" the Irishman spluttered.

"Yes, a rather clever hoax, but a hoax all the same, although unfortunately only the passage of time will reveal that," their host informed them, grinning smugly at the three writers. Then he looked again at the Irishman, touched by his gullibility. "I hope you aren't one of Murray's victims, Mr. Stoker."

"No, no . . ." murmured the writer, with gloomy relief, "the tickets are beyond my means."

"In that case you should be happy that at least you haven't wasted your money," the traveler congratulated him. "I am sorry you're so disappointed to discover the journeys to the year 2000 are no more than a charade, but look on the bright side: the person telling you this is a real time traveler: as you will have deduced from the maps I left in your letter boxes, not only do I come from the future, but I am able to move along the time continuum in both directions."

THE WIND WAS HOWLING outside, yet inside the haunted house all that could be heard were the sputtering candle flames that cast suggestive shadows on the walls. The time traveler's voice sounded oddly smooth, as if his throat were lined with silk, when he said:

"But before I tell you how I do it, allow me to introduce myself. I do not want to give you the impression that we in the future have forgotten the basic social graces. My name is Marcus Rhys, and I am, in a manner of speaking, a librarian."

"A librarian?" said James, suddenly interested.

"Yes, a librarian, although at a very special library. But allow me to begin at the beginning. As you have seen, man will gain the ability to travel in time, but don't imagine that where I come from we have time machines like the one in your novel, Mr. Wells, or that time travel is the order of the day. No, during the next century, scientists, physicists, mathematicians all over the world will become embroiled in never-ending debates about the possibility or impossibility of time travel. Theories will abound on how to achieve it, all of which will run up against the immutable nature of the universe, which, regrettably, lacks many of the physical characteristics necessary for them to test their theories. Somehow it seems as though the universe had been created impervious to time travel, as though God Himself had reinforced His creation against this aberration of nature."

The traveler fell silent for a few moments, during which he took the opportunity to scrutinize his audience with his forceful gaze, his eyes as black as two rat holes. "Even so, scientists in my time will refuse to admit defeat and will persist in trying to find a way of fulfilling man's deepest longing: to be able to travel along the time continuum in any direction he pleases. But all their efforts will prove in vain. Do you know why? Because in the end time travel will not be achieved through science."

Then Marcus began pacing around the halo of light, as though to stretch his legs, pretending to be oblivious of the writers' curious stares. Finally, he went back to his position and his face cracked into a smile.

"No, the secret of time travel has always been in our heads," he revealed, almost gleefully. "The mind's capacity is infinite, gentlemen."

The candles continued to sputter as the traveler, with his smooth, downy voice, sympathized with them because science in their time was still a long way from envisaging the enormous potential of the human mind, having scarcely moved on from studying the skull to examining its contents to try to understand the functioning of the brain, albeit through primitive methods such as ablation and applying electrical stimuli.

"Ah, man's brain . . ." he sighed. "The biggest puzzle in the universe weighs only four hundred grams, and it may surprise you to know we use only a fifth of its capacity. What we might achieve if we could use it all remains a mystery even to us. What we do know, gentlemen, is that one of the many marvels hidden beneath its cortex is the ability to travel in time." He paused again. "Although to be honest, even our scientists cannot identify the exact mechanism that enables us to travel along the time continuum. But one thing is clear: man's brain is equipped with some sort of superior awareness that allows him to move through time in the same way as he moves through space. And even though he is far from being able to harness it, he can activate it, which is already a huge accomplishment, as I am sure you can imagine."

"Our brains . . ." whispered Stoker, with childlike awe.

Marcus gazed at him fondly, but did not let this distract him from his explanation:

"We don't know exactly who the first time traveler was, that is to say the first person to suffer a spontaneous displacement in time, as we call it, because the earliest cases were isolated. In fact, if we have any knowledge of those initial displacements it is thanks to the esoteric and other journals devoted to paranormal activity. However, the numbers of people claiming they had suffered such episodes began to increase steadily, although at a slow enough rate for the strange phenomenon to continue to pass unnoticed, except by a handful of mad prophets whom people usually ignore. By the middle of our century, the world suddenly experienced an epidemic of time travelers who appeared to come from nowhere. But the fact is they existed, as if the ability to move along the time continuum were the next step on Darwin's evolutionary ladder. It seemed that, faced with an extreme situation, certain people could activate areas of their brains which snatched them from the present as if by magic, and propelled them forwards or backwards in time. Even though they were still a minority and unable to control their ability, theirs was clearly a dangerous talent.

"As you can imagine, it was not long before the Government created a department responsible for rounding up people showing this ability to study them and help them develop their skills in a controlled environment. Needless to say, registration with the department was not voluntary. What Government would have allowed people who possessed a talent like that to roam free? No, *Homo temporis*, as they came to be referred to, had to be supervised. Be that as it may, the study of those affected did succeed in throwing some light on the strange phenomenon: it was discovered, for example, that the time travelers did not move through the time continuum at a constant speed until the inertia of the impulse was used up and they came to a halt, as in the case of Mr. Wells's machine. Instead, they moved instantaneously from place to place, leaping through the void as it were, only able to control whether they landed in the past or in the future through intuition, as with the initial leap.

"One thing seemed clear: the further they traveled, the more their energy was depleted after the journey. Some took several days to recover, while others remained in a comatose state from which they never recovered. They also discovered that if they concentrated very hard, they could transport objects and even people with them on their leaps through time, although the latter proved doubly exhausting. In any event, once they had understood as much as they could about the mechanism in the mind that enabled people to travel in time, the most pressing question, the one that had given rise to heated debates even before time travel became a reality, still remained to be answered: could the past be changed or was it unalterable? Many physicists maintained that if someone traveled into the past, say, with the intention of shooting someone, the gun would explode in their hands because the universe would automatically realign itself. They assumed the universe must possess some sort of self-awareness designed to protect its integrity, which would prevent the person from dying, because they had not died. However, by means of a series of controlled experiments based on making tiny adjustments to the recent past, they discovered time had no such protective mechanism. It was as vulnerable as a snail without its shell. History, everything that had already taken place, could be changed. And this discovery, as you can imagine, caused an even bigger uproar than time travel itself. Suddenly, man had the power to modify the past. Unsurprisingly, most people saw this as God's way of giving humanity a free hand to correct its mistakes. The logical thing was to prevent past genocides and afflictions, to weed out the errors of history, so to speak, for what lies ahead, gentlemen, is truly dreadful, far worse than in your innocent tale, Mr. Wells. Imagine all the good that time travel could do for humanity. For instance, it would be possible to eradicate the plague that devastated London, causing a hundred thousand deaths before the fire of 1666 ironically stamped it out."

"Or the books in the library at Alexandria that could be saved from being engulfed by flames," suggested James.

Marcus gave a derisive smirk.

"Yes, a million and one things could be done. And so, with the blessing of the people, the Government called on a group of doctors and mathematicians to analyze the set of aberrations that made up the past, in order to decide which acts deserved to be wiped out and to predict how this would affect the fabric of time, for there was no reason to make things worse. However, not everyone was happy, and voices were instantly raised against the Restoration

Project, as it was called. Some considered this happy manipulation of the past that the Government was about to
embark on unethical, and one section of the population did
everything it could to try to sabotage it. This faction—let
us call it conservative—which was gaining more follow-
ers by the day argued that we must learn to live with the
mistakes of the past, for better or for worse. Things being
as they were, the Government found it more and more difficult to continue with the project. Then everything permanently ground to a halt when the time travelers, fearful
of becoming the target of a new wave of hostility, began
fleeing through time in all directions, creating an inevitable wave of panic throughout society. All at once, the past
had become soft clay in the hands of anyone who felt like
altering it for personal gain or simply by accident. Suddenly, the history of the world was in jeopardy."

"But how can we know when someone has altered
the past if in so doing they change the present?" asked
Wells. "We have no way of knowing whether someone is
manipulating history; we would only experience the consequences."

"I applaud your perspicacity, Mr. Wells," said Marcus,
pleasantly surprised by the author's question. "According
to the laws of time, the consequences of any change to the
past are transmitted along the time continuum, modify-
ing everything in their path, like the ripples from a stone
tossed into a pond. Consequently, as you have pointed
out, it would be impossible to detect any manipulation,
because the ripples produced by this change would affect
our present as well as our memories." He paused before

adding, with a mischievous grin, "Unless of course we had a backup copy of the world with which to compare it."

"A backup?"

"Yes, call it what you will," replied the traveler. "I'm referring to a collection of books, newspapers, and other material documenting as exhaustively as possible everything that has happened up until the present, the whole history of mankind. Like a portrait of the true face of the universe, you understand, one that enables us to detect at once any anomaly, however small."

"I see," murmured Wells.

"And this is something the Government has been working on since the first epidemic of time travelers, with the aim of preventing anyone from unlawfully manipulating the past," Marcus declared. "But there was one problem: where could such an archive be kept safe from the harmful ripples caused by any changes?"

The writers gazed at him, enthralled.

"There was only one possible place," the traveler answered his own question. "At the beginning of time."

"The beginning of time?" asked Stoker.

Marcus nodded.

"The Oligocene epoch, the third epoch of the Tertiary period in the Cenozoic era, to be precise, before man had set foot on the Earth, when the world was the preserve of rhinoceroses, mastodons, wolves, and the earliest versions of primates. A period no traveler could go to without linking various leaps—with all the risk entailed, and where there was no reason to go because there was nothing to change. In tandem with the project aimed at training time travelers, the Government had in the strictest secrecy organized what we could call an elite team, made up of the most gifted and loyal travelers. Evidently, the team's mission was none other than to transport the world's memory back to the Oligocene epoch. After countless journeys, the chosen travelers, of which, as you will have guessed, I was one, built a sanctuary there to house the world's knowledge in. The place was also to become our home, for a large part of our lives would be spent in that epoch.

"Surrounded by immense grasslands we were almost afraid to step on, we would live and bring up our children, whom we would teach to use their talent, as we had done, in order to travel through the millennia, keeping watch over history, that timeline which began in the Oligocene epoch and ended at the precise moment when the Government decided to scrap the Restoration Project. Yes, that is where our jurisdiction ends, gentlemen. Any time beyond that moment is unguarded, for it is assumed that the physiognomy of the future can absorb any changes the time travelers might bring about because it occurred after they appeared. The past, on the other hand, is considered sacred and must remain immutable. Any manipulation of it is a crime against the natural order of time."

The traveler folded his arms and paused for a few moments, studying his audience warmly. His voice sounded eager when he took up again:

"We call the place where the world's memory is stored the Library of Truth. I am one of its librarians, the one responsible for guarding the nineteenth century. In order to carry out my task, I travel from the Oligocene epoch to here, stopping off in each decade to make sure everything is in order. However, even I, who am capable of making jumps spanning tens of centuries, find the journey here exhausting. I have to travel more than twenty million years, and the librarians who guard what for you is the future have to cover an even greater distance. That is why the timeline we are protecting is dotted with what we call nests, a secret network of houses and places where we travelers can stop off to make our journeys less exhausting. And this house, of course, is one of them. What better place than a derelict building that will stand empty until the end of the century and is allegedly haunted by an evil ghost that keeps intruders at bay."

Marcus fell silent again, giving them to understand he had finished his explanation.

"And what state is our world in, have you discovered any anomalies?" Stoker asked, amused. "Are there more flies than there should be?"

The time traveler indulged the Irishman's jest but with a strangely sinister chuckle.

"I usually always find some anomaly," he declared in a somber voice. "Actually, my job is rather entertaining: the nineteenth century is one of the time travelers' preferred eras for tampering with, perhaps because in many cases their interference has extreme consequences. And no matter how many of their muddles I sort out, nothing is ever as I left it when I come back. I wasn't expecting it to be any different this visit, of course."

"What has gone wrong this time?" asked James.

Wells could not help noticing the note of caution in the

American's voice, as though he were not completely sure he wanted to know the answer. Might it be the men's clubs, those luxurious redoubts where he took refuge from the loneliness that stuck to him like a birthmark? Perhaps they had never existed prior to a couple of time travelers deciding to found the first one, and now they would all have to close down so that the universe could go back to its original form.

"This may surprise you, gentlemen, but nobody should ever have captured Jack the Ripper."

"Are you serious?" asked Stoker.

Marcus nodded.

"I'm afraid so. He was arrested because a time traveler alerted the Whitechapel Vigilance Committee. Jack the Ripper was caught thanks to this 'witness,' who chose to remain anonymous. But in reality that is not what should have happened. If it hadn't been for the intervention of this time traveler from the future, Bryan Reese, the sailor known as Jack the Ripper, after murdering the prostitute on November 7, 1888, would have boarded a ship bound for the Caribbean as planned. There he would have pursued his bloodlust, murdering several people in Managua. Owing to the distances involved, no one would ever link these crimes with the murdered East End whores. Thus, for the purposes of history, Jack the Ripper would have disappeared off the face of the earth, leaving behind him the unsolved mystery of his identity, over which as much ink would be spilled as the blood that had flowed under his knife, and which throughout the ensuing century would become the favorite pastime of researchers, detectives, and amateurs, who would all root around in Scotland Yard's archives, desperate to be the first to put a face to the shadow time had converted into a gruesome legend. It may surprise you to know that some of the investigations pointed the finger of suspicion at a member of the royal household. It would appear that anyone can have a reason for ripping a whore's guts out. In this case, as you can see, popular imagination outstripped reality. I imagine the traveler responsible for the modification couldn't resist finding out the monster's true identity. And as you deduced, Mr. Wells, no alteration was detected and everyone fell victim to the ripple effect, like the rest of the universe, for that matter. But this is an easy change for me to sort out. In order to set history straight, I only need travel back to November 7 to prevent the time traveler from alerting George Lusk's Vigilance Committee. Perhaps you don't consider this particular change to be for the better, and I wouldn't disagree, but I must prevent it all the same, for, as I explained, any manipulation of the past is a criminal offense."

"Does this mean we are living in . . . a parallel universe?" asked Wells.

Marcus glanced at him in surprise, then nodded.

"It does indeed, Mr. Wells."

"What the devil is a parallel universe?" asked Stoker.

"It is a concept that will not be coined until the next century, well before time travel ceases to be a mere fantasy of writers and physicists," explained the traveler, still regarding Wells with awe. "Parallel universes were meant to be a way of avoiding the temporal paradoxes that might occur if it turned out the past was not immutable, that it could be changed. What would happen, for instance, if someone traveled into the past and killed their grandmother before she gave birth to their mother?"

"He would not be born," replied James hastily.

"Unless his grandmother wasn't really his mother's mother, which would be a roundabout way of finding out that his mother was adopted," Stoker jested.

The traveler ignored the Irishman's observation and went on with his explanation:

"But how could he kill his grandmother if he was never born? Many physicists in my time will argue that the only way around this paradox would be if important changes to the past created parallel universes. After killing his grandmother, the murderer would not vanish from that universe, as one would expect. He would carry on living, only in a different world, in a parallel reality sprouting from the stem of the original universe at the exact moment when he pulled the trigger, changing his grandmother's fate. This theory will be impossible to prove even after time travel becomes a reality with the appearance of time travelers, for the only way to verify whether changes to the past produced parallel worlds or not would be by comparing them with a copy of the original universe, as I explained before. And if we didn't have one now, I wouldn't be here talking to you about the mystery surrounding the identity of Jack the Ripper, because there would be none."

Wells nodded silently, while Stoker and James exchanged puzzled looks.

"But come with me, gentlemen. I'll show you something that will help you understand."

XXXIX

*W*ITH AN AMUSED GRIN ON HIS lips, the time traveler began to climb the stairs. The writers hesitated for a moment, then followed him, escorted by his two henchmen. On the top floor, Marcus led them with his athletic gait to a room containing a bookcase on one wall filled with dusty books, a couple of dilapidated chairs, and a ramshackle bed. Wells wondered whether this was the bed in which Sir Robert Warboys, Lord Lyttleton, and the other plucky young nobles had boldly confronted the ghost, but before he had a chance to search the skirting board for signs of a bullet, Marcus pulled on a lamp attached to the wall and the fake bookcase opened in the middle to reveal a spacious room beyond.

The traveler waited for his henchmen to scuttle through the shadows and light the lamps in the room, before he beckoned the authors in. As James and Stoker seemed reluctant to do so, Wells took the lead and ventured into the mysterious place with cautious, mouselike steps. Next to the entrance he discovered two huge oak tables piled with books, annotated notebooks, and newspapers from the period; no doubt this was where the traveler examined the face of the century, in search of possible inaccuracies. But at the back of the room, he glimpsed something that aroused his interest far more. It was some kind of spider's web made out of multicolored pieces of cord, hanging from which was a collection of newspaper cuttings. James and Stoker had also noticed the network of strings, towards which the traveler was now walking, jerking his head for them to follow.

"What is it?" asked Wells, drawing level with him.

"A map of time," replied Marcus, beaming with pride.

Wells gazed at him in surprise, then stared once more at the shape the colored strings made, studying it more carefully. From a distance, it looked like a spider's web, but now he could see the design was more like a fir tree or fish bone. A piece of white cord, approximately five feet above the floor, was stretched from wall to wall, like a master rope. The ends of the green and blue colored strings hanging from the white cord were tacked to the sidewalls. Each string, including the master rope, was festooned with newspaper clippings. Wells ducked his head, venturing among the news items hanging like washing on a line, and began browsing some of the headlines. After Marcus nodded his approval, the two other writers followed suit.

"The white cord," explained the traveler, pointing at the master rope, "represents the original universe, the only one that existed before the travelers began meddling with the past. The universe it is my task to protect."

At one end of the white cord, Wells noticed a photograph shimmering faintly. Surprisingly it was in color and showed a splendid stone and glass building towering beneath a clear blue sky. This must be the Library of Truth. At the other end of the cord hung a cutting announcing the discontinuation of the Restoration Project and the passing of a law prohibiting any change in the past. Between these two items hung a forest of clippings apparently announcing important events. Wells was familiar with many of these and had lived through some, like the Indian uprising and so-called Bloody Sunday, but as the cord stretched further into the future, the headlines became more and more incomprehensible. He felt suddenly dizzy as he realized these were things that had not yet happened, events that lay in wait for him somewhere along the time continuum, most of them strangely sinister.

Before resuming his examination, Wells glanced at his companions to see whether they were experiencing the same mixture of excitement and dread as he himself. Stoker appeared to be concentrating on one particular cutting, which he was reading, mesmerized, while, after an initial cursory glance, James had turned his back on the map, as though this frightening, incomprehensible future felt less controllable than the reality it was his lot to inhabit and in which he had learned to navigate like a fish in water. The American appeared greatly relieved to know that death would preclude him from having to live in the terrifying world charted on the map of time. Wells also tried to tear his eyes away from the rows of cuttings, fearing his behavior might be affected by knowing about future events, and yet a perverse curiosity compelled him to devour as many headlines as he could, aware he had been given an opportunity many would kill for.

He could not help pausing to read one news item in particular, concerning one of the first ever cases of spontaneous time travel, or so he deduced from the esoteric title of the journal. Beneath the sensationalist headline: "A Lady Time Traveler," the article described how when employees at Olsen's department store went to open the shop on the morning of April 12, 1984, they discovered a woman inside. At first, they thought she was a thief, but when asked how she came to be in the store the woman said she had just appeared there. According to the article, the most extraordinary thing about the case was that the unknown woman claimed she came from the future, as the style of her clothing made clear—from the year 2008, to be exact. The woman maintained her house had been broken into by burglars, who had chased her into her bedroom, where she had managed to lock herself in. Terrified by the battering on the door as her assailants tried to break it down, the woman suddenly felt giddy. A second later, she found herself in Olsen's department store, twenty-four years earlier in time, stretched out on the floor and bringing up her supper. The police were unable to interrogate the woman because, following her initial, rather confused declarations, she mysteriously disappeared once more. Could she have gone back to the future? the journalist speculated darkly.

"The Government suspects it all began with this woman," Marcus announced, almost reverentially. "Have you asked yourselves why some people and not others are able to travel in time? Well, so has the Government, and genetic testing provided the answer: apparently, the time travelers had a mutant gene, a concept still unknown to you. I think it will be a few years yet before it comes into use after a Dutch biologist coins the phrase. But it seemed very likely this gene was responsible for the travelers' ability to connect with the area of the brain which for the rest of the population remained switched off. Research showed that the gene was handed down from generation to generation, meaning all the travelers shared the same distant ancestor. The Government never managed to discover who the first carrier was, although they thought it might be this woman. It is widely believed she had a child with a man who was possibly also able to travel in time, and that their offspring inherited a reinforced gene, establishing a line of time travelers who, by mixing with the rest of the population, would decades later trigger the epidemic of time travelers. However, every effort to find her has failed. The woman vanished hours after turning up at Olsen's department store and hasn't been seen since, as the article says. I won't deny some of us time travelers, including myself, worship her like a goddess."

Wells smiled, peering affectionately at the photograph of the ordinary-looking woman, obviously confused and afraid, unable to believe what had happened to her, whom Marcus had elevated to the status of Goddess of Time Travel. No doubt she had suffered another spontaneous displacement and was wandering around lost in some other distant era, unless, faced with the prospect of losing her mind, she had chosen to kill herself.

"Each of the other strings represents a parallel world," said Marcus, requiring the writers' attention once more. "A deviation from the path that time ought to have taken. The green strings represent universes that have already been corrected. I suppose I keep them for sentimental reasons, because I have to admit I found some of the parallel worlds enchanting, even as I was working out ways of restoring them to the original."

Wells glanced at one green string from which dangled several celebrated photographs of Her Gracious Majesty. They looked identical to the ones of her he had seen in his own time, except for one small detail: the Queen had an orange squirrel monkey perched on her shoulder.

"This string represents one of my favorite parallel universes," said Marcus. "A squirrel monkey enthusiast had the eccentric idea of persuading Her Majesty that all living creatures radiate a magnetic energy that can be transmitted to other beings to therapeutic effect, in particular the squirrel monkey, which according to him worked wonders on people suffering from digestive problems and migraines. Imagine my surprise when browsing the newspapers of the period I found this startling addition to the photographs of the Queen. But that was not all. Thanks to Her Majesty, carrying a monkey around on your shoulder became a fad, and a walk through the streets of London turned into a rather amusing spectacle. Unfortunately, reality was far less exciting and had to be reestablished."

Wells looked out of the corner of his eye at James, who appeared to heave a sigh, relieved at not having to live in a world where he was forced to go around with a monkey on his shoulder.

"The blue strings, on the other hand, represent the timelines I have not yet corrected," Marcus went on to explain. "This one represents the world we are in now, gentlemen, a world identical to the original, but where Jack the Ripper did not mysteriously disappear after murdering his fifth victim, thus becoming a legend, but where he was caught by the Whitechapel Vigilance Committee after perpetrating his crime."

The writers gazed curiously at the string to which Marcus was referring. The first cutting related the event that had caused this bifurcation: Jack the Ripper's capture. The next cutting described the subsequent execution of the sailor Bryan Reese, the man who murdered the prostitutes.

"But as you can see, this is not the only blue string," said the traveler, fixing his attention on another cord. "This second string represents a bifurcation that has not yet taken place, but will happen in the next few days. It concerns you, gentlemen. It is why you are here."

Marcus tore off the first cutting from the string and kept it momentarily concealed from his guests, like a poker player pausing before he reveals the card that will change the outcome of the game.

"Next year, a writer named Melvyn Frost will publish three novels that will bring him overnight fame and secure him a place in literary history," he announced.

He paused, observing his guests one by one, until his eye rested on the Irishman.

"One of them will be *Dracula*, the novel you have just finished, Mr. Stoker."

The Irishman looked at him with astonishment. Wells watched him curiously. Dracula? he said to himself. What was the meaning of that strange word? He did not know, of course, nor did he know much about Stoker, save for the three or four already mentioned facts. He could never have imagined, for instance, that this unassuming, methodical man who observed society's norms, this man who by day adapted with tragic subservience to the frenetic social life of his conceited employer, at night indulged in endless drinking sessions run by whores of every category and condition, wild orgies whose admirable aim was to alleviate the bitterness of a marriage, which, following the birth of his son Irving Noel, had turned into a sham.

"Although you do not know it yet, Mr. Stoker, although you would never dare even dream of it, your novel will become the third most popular book in the English language, after the Bible and Shakespeare's *Hamlet*," the traveler informed him. "And your Count Dracula will enter by right into the pantheon of literary legends, where he will become a truly immortal creature."

Stoker swelled with pride at the discovery that in the future the traveler came from, his work would be regarded as a classic. His novel would elevate him to a prominent position in the pantheon of present-day authors, exactly as his mother had predicted after reading his manuscript, in a note he had carried round in his pocket ever since. And did he not deserve it? he said to himself. He had spent six long years working on the novel, ever since Dr. Arminius

Vambéry, lecturer in Eastern languages at the University of Bucharest and an expert on the occult, had loaned him a manuscript in which the Turks spoke of the cruel practices of the Prince of Wallachia, Vlad Tepes, better known as Vlad the Impaler owing to his custom of impaling prisoners on pointed stakes and imbibing a cup of their blood as he watched them die.

"Another of Frost's novels is entitled *The Turn of the Screw*," Marcus went on, turning to the American. "Does the name ring a bell, Mr. James?"

The American looked at him in mute surprise.

"Of course it does," said Marcus. "As you can tell from his response, this is the novel Mr. James has just finished, a charming ghost story that will also become a classic."

Despite his consummate skill at dissimulating his feelings, James was unable to hide his pleasure at discovering the happy fate of his novel, the first he had chosen not to hammer out with his own fingers, preferring to hire the services of a typist instead. And perhaps for that very reason, because of the symbolic distance created between him and the paper, he had ventured to speak of something as intimate and painful as his childhood fears. Although he suspected it might also have had something to do with his decision to give up residing in hotels and guest houses and settle in the beautiful Georgian house he had acquired in Rye. It was only then, when he found himself in his study, the autumn sunlight shimmering around the room, a delicate butterfly fluttering at the windowpane, and a stranger hanging on his every word, fingers poised over the keys of the monstrous machine, that James had found the courage to write a novel inspired by a story the Archbishop of Canterbury had told him long before, about two children who lived in an isolated country house where they were haunted by the evil spirits of departed servants.

"And Frost's third novel," said Marcus, turning to address Wells, "could be none other than *The Invisible Man*, the work you have just finished, Mr. Wells, the hero of which will also find his place in the pantheon of modern legend, beside Mr. Stoker's Dracula."

Was it his turn now to swell with pride? Wells wondered. Perhaps, but he could find no reason to do so. All he wanted to do was to sit in a corner and weep, and to carry on weeping until not a drop of water was left in his body, because he was only able to see the future success of his novel as a failure, in the same way he considered *The Time Machine* and *The Island of Dr. Moreau* had also failed. Rattled off at the same speed as, alas, he felt obliged to write all his works, *The Invisible Man* was yet another novel that conformed to the guidelines set down for him by Lewis Hind: a science fiction novel intended as a cautionary tale about the dangers of misusing scientific knowledge. This was something Jules Verne had never ventured to do, always portraying science as a sort of transparent alchemy at man's disposal. Wells, on the other hand, could not share the Frenchman's unquestioning optimism, and had therefore produced another dark tale about the abuses of technology, in which a scientist, after managing to make himself invisible, ends up losing his mind. But it was clear no one would perceive the real message in his work, for, as Marcus had hinted, and as he had seen for himself by reading some of the horrific news items hanging from the master rope, man had ended up harnessing science for the most destructive purpose imaginable.

Marcus handed the clipping to Wells, to read and pass on to the others. The author felt too dejected to wade through the handful of tributes that appeared to make up the bulk of the article. Instead, he confined himself to glancing at the accompanying photograph, in which the fellow Frost, a small, neat-looking man, was leaning absurdly over his typewriter, the prolific source from which his supposed novels had emanated. Then he passed the cutting to James, who cast a scornful eye over it before handing it to Stoker, who read it from beginning to end. The Irishman was the first to break the deathly silence that had descended on the room.

"How could this fellow have had the same ideas for his novels as we did?" he asked, completely baffled.

James gave him the contemptuous look he would give a performing monkey.

"Don't be so naïve, Mr. Stoker," he chided him. "What our host is trying to tell us is that Mr. Frost didn't write these novels. Somehow he stole them from us before we published them."

"Precisely, Mr. James," the time traveler affirmed.

"But how will he stop us from suing him?" the Irishman persisted.

"I'm sure you don't need me to tell you that, Mr. Stoker," replied Marcus.

Wells, who had managed to thrust aside his despair and take an interest in the conversation again, was suddenly struck by a ghastly thought.

"If I'm not mistaken, what Mr. Rhys is trying to tell us," he explained, with the aim of dispelling the fog the others were in, "is that the best way to silence a person is by killing him."

"By killing him?" declared Stoker, horrified. "Are you saying this fellow Frost is going to steal our works and then . . . kill us?"

"I'm afraid so, Mr. Stoker," Marcus confirmed, accompanying his words with a solemn nod. "When, after arriving in your time, I came across the news item about a mysterious fellow named Melvyn Frost who had published these novels, I hastened to learn what had become of you, their real authors. And I'm sorry to have to tell you this, gentlemen, but all three of you are going to die next month. You, Mr. Wells, will break your neck in a cycling accident. You, Mr. Stoker, will fall down the stairs of your theater. And you, Mr. James, will suffer a heart attack in your own home, although, needless to say, your death, like those of your colleagues, will also be murder. I don't know whether Frost plans to carry out the deeds himself or to hire someone else, although judging from Frost's frail physique, I would incline towards the latter. In fact, Frost is a typical instance of a time traveler who, afraid to return to his own time, chooses a particular time in the past in which to settle down and build a new life. All perfectly understandable and legitimate. The problem arises because the majority of these time exiles consider earning a living in the traditional sense, by the sweat of their brow—utterly absurd, when their knowledge of the future could make them rich. Most give themselves away when they modify the past in order to implement their moneymaking schemes, like this fellow Frost. Otherwise, it would be impossible for us to trace them. But I didn't bring you here to torment you with tales of your imminent demise, gentlemen, rather to try to prevent it from happening."

"Can you do that?" Stoker asked, suddenly hopeful.

"Not only can I, but it is my duty, for your deaths represent a significant change to the century I have been assigned to protect," replied Marcus. "My sole aim is to help you, gentlemen, I hope I've convinced you of that. And that includes you too, Mr. Wells."

Wells gave a start. How did Marcus know he had come to the meeting filled with misgivings? He found the answer when he followed the direction the traveler and his two henchmen were looking. All three of them were staring at his left shoe, where the knife he had strapped to his back was peeping out. It seemed the knot he had tied had been a little precarious. Shamefaced, Wells picked up the knife and slipped it into his pocket, while James shook his head disapprovingly.

"All of you," the traveler went on, attaching no further importance to the matter, "will live for many more years in your original universe and will continue delighting your faithful readers, of whom I consider myself one, with many more novels. Forgive me, though, if I refrain from telling you any details about your future, so that once we have resolved this small matter, you will continue to act naturally. In fact, I ought to have intervened without revealing myself to you, but this fellow Frost is devilishly clever and will eliminate you so stealthily that the information I need in order to prevent your deaths, such as the exact time you were pushed down the stairs, Mr. Stoker, will not appear in the newspapers. I only know the days on which you will suffer your respective accidents, and in your case, Mr. James, I won't even know that, because no one will notice you are dead until a neighbor discovers you body."

James nodded ruefully, perhaps aware for the first time of the utter loneliness enveloping his life, an entrenched loneliness that would make of his death a silent act, unseen by the world.

"Let us say that bringing you here was a desperate measure, gentlemen, for I could think of no other way to prevent your deaths than by asking for your cooperation, which I feel sure will be forthcoming."

"Naturally," said Stoker hastily, apparently physically ill at the thought he could be dead in a few days. "What do we have to do?"

"Oh, it's quite simple," said Marcus. "Providing this fellow Frost cannot find your manuscripts, he won't be able to kill you. I therefore suggest you bring them to me at the first opportunity. Tomorrow, if at all possible. This simple act will create another bifurcation in the timeline, because Frost will not have killed you. Once I am in possession of the novels, I shall travel forward to the year 1899, and take another look at reality in order to decide what to do next."

"I think it's an excellent plan," said Stoker. "I shall bring you my manuscript tomorrow."

James agreed to do the same, and although Wells had the impression they were mere pawns in a game of chess between Marcus and this fellow Frost, he had no choice but to consent. He felt too disoriented by events to try to think of a better way than the one Marcus was proposing. And so, like the others, he agreed to bring him his manuscript the next morning, although if Marcus finally apprehended Frost and unraveled the muddle of the future, it did not guarantee he would be able to ride his bicycle in complete safety without first resolving the matter pending with Gilliam Murray. And to do this he had no choice but to help Inspector Garrett catch Marcus, the very man who was trying to save his life.

BUT IF THERE WAS a more difficult undertaking than capturing a time traveler, it was undoubtedly catching a cab in London in the early hours of the morning. James, Stoker, and Wells spent almost an hour scouring the area around Berkeley Square without success. Only when they decided to walk towards Piccadilly, shivering with cold and cursing their luck, did they catch sight of a berlin. They gave a start as it emerged from the thick fog that had settled over London, rolling along the street towards them almost solely thanks to the horse's own efforts, because the driver was half-asleep on his perch. It would have passed straight by them, like a visitation from the beyond, had the driver not finally noticed the redheaded giant blocking the street and waving his arms wildly. After the cab came to a hasty halt, the three men spent what seemed like an eternity trying to explain their itinerary to the driver: first, he would take Stoker to his house, then drop James off at his hotel, and finally leave London for Woking, where Wells lived. When the driver signaled that he had understood the route by blinking a couple of times and grunting, the three men clambered into the carriage, flopping onto the seat amid loud sighs, like castaways having finally reached shore after spending days in a lifeboat.

Wells longed for some peace and quiet so that he could reflect on the events of the past few hours, but when Stoker and James launched into a discussion about their respective novels, he realized he would have to wait a little while longer. He did not mind them leaving him out; in fact, he was relieved. Apparently, they had nothing to say to a writer of escapist literature who in addition came to meetings with a kitchen knife strapped to his back. He was not in the slightest bit interested in what they had to say either, and so he tried to stay out of the conversation by gazing through the window at the turbulent swirls of mist, but he soon found that Stoker's voice, when not cowed by fear, was too loud to ignore even if he wanted to.

"What I'm trying to achieve with my novel, Mr. James," the Irishman explained, waving his arms in the air, "is a deeper, richer portrayal of that elegant embodiment of Evil, the vampire, whom I have attempted to divest of the burden of the romantic aesthetic that turned him into little more than a grotesque sex fiend incapable of inspiring anything more than a sensual thrill in his victims. The protagonist of my novel is an evil vampire, whom I have endowed with the original attributes found in the myth of folklore, although I confess to having added a few of my own, such as his having no reflection in mirrors."

"But if you embody it, Mr. Stoker, Evil loses most of its mystery, and its potency!" exclaimed James in an offended tone that took his fellow writer by surprise. "Evil should always manifest itself in the subtlest way. It must be born of doubt, inhabit the shadowy realm between certainty and uncertainty."

"I'm afraid I don't really understand what you mean, Mr. James," murmured the Irishman once the other man appeared to have calmed down.

James let out a long sigh before agreeing to expand a little more on the sensitive subject, but Wells could tell from the bewildered look on Stoker's face that the Irishman was growing more and more confused as the other man spoke. It is no surprise, then, that when they stopped in front of Stoker's house, the red-haired giant had the air of someone punch-drunk as he stepped out of the cab. The situation only grew worse after Stoker's desertion (for this is precisely how Wells experienced it) as the two men found themselves brutally exposed to silence—a silence that the urbane James naturally felt obliged to break by engaging Wells in a shallow discussion about the different kinds of material that could be used to upholster carriage seats.

When Wells was finally alone in the coach, he raised his arms to heaven in thanks, then eagerly became lost in his deliberations as the cab gradually left the city behind. He had many things to think about, he told himself. Yes, matters of great import, ranging from the future he had glimpsed in the clippings, which he was unsure whether to forget or to commit to memory, to the exciting idea that someone had thought of charting time as though it were a physical space. Only this was a region that could never be properly charted, because there was no way of knowing where the white cord ended. Or was there? What if the time travelers had journeyed far enough into the future to discover the edge of time, the end of the thread, just as the traveler in his novel had tried to do? But did such a thing exist? Was there an end to time, or did it carry on forever? If it did end, then it had to happen at the exact moment when man became extinct and no other species was left on the planet, for what was time if there was no one to measure it, if there was nothing to experience its passing? Time could only be seen in the falling leaves, a wound that healed, a woodworm's tunneling, rust that spread, and hearts that grew weary. Without anyone to discern it, time was nothing, nothing at all.

Although, thanks to the existence of parallel worlds, there would always be someone or something to make time believable. And there was no doubt that parallel worlds existed. Wells knew this for sure now: they sprouted from the universe like branches from a tree at the minutest change to the past, just as he had explained to Andrew Harrington in order to save his life less than three weeks earlier. And discovering this gave him more satisfaction than any future success of his novel, because it spoke of his powerful intuition, the effective, even precocious workings of his brain. Perhaps his brain lacked the mechanism that enabled Marcus to travel in time, but his powers of reasoning set him apart from the masses.

He recalled the map the traveler had shown them, the figure made of colored strings representing the parallel universes Marcus had untangled. It suddenly struck him that the map was incomplete, because it only included worlds created by the travelers' direct interventions. But what of our own actions? The parallel universes not only grew from their wicked manipulations of the hallowed past, but from each and every one of our choices. He imagined Marcus's map with this new addition, the white cord weighed down by a sudden flowering of yellow strings representing the worlds created by man's free will.

Wells emerged from these reflections as the cab pulled up in front of his house. He climbed out, and, after tipping the driver generously for having made him leave London in the small hours of the morning, he lifted the latch, and entered the garden wondering whether it was worth going to bed or not, and what effect it might have on the fabric of time if he decided to do one thing or the other.

It was then he noticed the woman with the fiery red hair.

XL

THIN AND PALE, HER REDDISH HAIR glowing on her shoulders, like embers escaped from a fire, the girl looked at him with that peculiar gaze that had caught his attention a few days before, when he had noticed her among the crowd of onlookers milling around the scene of Marcus's third crime.

"You?" exclaimed Wells, stopping in his tracks.

The girl said nothing. She simply walked over to where he was standing as silently as a cat and held something out to him. The author saw it was a letter. Puzzled, he took it from the girl's lily-white hand. *To H. G. Wells. To be delivered on the night of November 26, 1896,* he read on the back. So, this girl, whoever she might be, was some sort of messenger.

"Read it, Mr. Wells," she said, with a voice that reminded him of the sound of the early afternoon breeze rustling the net curtains. "Your future depends on it."

With that, the woman walked away towards the gate, leaving him motionless in the doorway, his face frozen in a frown. When he managed to rouse himself, Wells turned and ran after the woman.

"Wait, Miss . . . "

He came to a halt halfway. The woman had disappeared: only her perfume lingered in the air. And yet Wells could not recall having heard the gate squeak. It was as though after handing him the letter, she had literally vanished without trace.

He stood stock still for a few moments, listening to the silent throb of night and breathing in the unknown woman's perfume until finally he decided to enter the house. He made his way as quietly as possible to the sitting room, lit the little lamp, and sat down in his armchair, still startled by the appearance of the girl, whom he could have mistaken for one of Doyle's fairies had she measured eight inches and worn a pair of dragonfly wings on her back. Who was she? he wondered. And how had she suddenly vanished? But it was foolish to waste time surmising when he would no doubt find the answer within the envelope he was holding. He tore it open and took out the pages it contained. He shuddered when he recognized the handwriting, and, his heart in his mouth, began to read:

Dear Bertie,

    If you are reading this letter, then I am right, and in the future time travel will be possible. I do not know who will deliver this to you, I can only assure you she will be a descendant of yours, and of mine, for as you will have guessed from

the handwriting, I am you. I am a Wells from the
future. From a very distant future. It is best you
assimilate this before reading on. Since I am sure
the fact that our handwriting is identical will
not be enough to convince you, as any skilled
person could have copied it, I shall try to prove
to you that we are one and the same person by
telling you something only you know about. Who
else knows that the basket in the kitchen full of
tomatoes and peppers is not just any old basket?
Well, is that enough, or must I be crude and
remind you that during your marriage to your
cousin Isabel, you masturbated while thinking
about the nude sculptures at the Crystal Palace?
Forgive me for alluding to such an upsetting
period of your life, only I am certain that, like
the secret meaning the basket has for you, it is
something you would never mention in any future
biography, proving beyond doubt that I am not
some impostor who has found out everything
about you. No, I am you, Bertie. And unless you
accept that, there is no point in reading on.

Now I shall tell you how you became me.
The three of you will be in for a nasty surprise
tomorrow when you go to give Marcus your
manuscripts. Everything the traveler has told
you is a lie, except that he is a great admirer
of your work. That is why he will be unable to
stop himself from smiling when you deliver his
precious haul to him in person. Once this is done,

he will give the order to one of his henchmen,
who will fire at poor James. You have already
seen what their weapons can do to a human body
so I shall spare you the details, but it is not hard
to imagine that your clothes will be sprayed
with a grisly spatter of blood and entrails. Then,
before either of you have a chance to react, the
henchman will fire again, this time at a stunned
Stoker, who will suffer the same fate as the
American. After that, paralyzed with fear, you
will watch as he takes aim at you, except that
before he pulls the trigger, Marcus will stop him
with a gentle wave of his hand. And he will do
this because he respects you enough not to want
to let you die without telling you why. After all,
you are the author of *The Time Machine*, the novel
that started the vogue for time travel. At the
very least he owes you an explanation, and so,
before his henchman kills you, he will go to the
trouble of telling you the truth, even if it is only
to hear himself recount aloud how he managed to
outsmart the three of you. Then he will confess
to you, as he bounces round the hallway in that
ridiculous way of his, that he is not a guardian of
time, and that in fact, had it not been for a chance
encounter, he would have known nothing of the
existence of the Library of Truth or that the past
was being guarded by the State.

     Marcus was an eccentric millionaire, a
member of that select group of people who go

through life doing only what they wish to, and who had been obliged to let the Government study him when they opened the Department of Time. He had not found the experience too objectionable, despite being forced to rub elbows with people from all walks of life. It was a small price to pay for finding out the cause of his ailment (which is what he assumed it was after suffering a couple of spontaneous displacements at moments of extreme tension) and above all if he could discover the exciting possibilities it opened up. When the department was closed down, Marcus decided to hone the skills he had already learned to control remarkably well by doing some sightseeing through time. For a while, he devoted himself to traveling back into the past at random, wandering through the centuries until he grew tired of witnessing historic naval battles and witches being burnt at the stake, and tired of impregnating the bellies of Egyptian whores and slave girls with his seed of the future.

It was then it occurred to him to use his talents to take his passion for books to the limit. Marcus had a fabulous library in his house containing a fortune in sixteenth-century first editions and incunables, but suddenly his collection of books seemed to him ridiculous and utterly worthless. What good was it to him to own a first edition of Lord Byron's *Childe Harold's Pilgrimage* if in the end the verses he was reading could be perused by anyone else's eyes? It would be quite different if he possessed the only copy in the world, as if the poet had written it exclusively for him. With his newly discovered abilities this was something he could achieve quite easily. If he traveled back in time, stole one of his favorite author's manuscripts before he published it, and then killed the writer, he would be able to build up a unique library of works no one else knew even existed. Murdering a handful of writers in order to add a private literary archive to his library did not bother him in the slightest, for Marcus had always thought of his favorite novels as originating out of nowhere, independently of their authors, who were human beings, and like all human beings, pretty despicable. Besides, it was too late for him to start having scruples, especially since he had amassed his fortune in a way conventional morality would doubtless have deemed criminal. Happily, he no longer need judge himself by others' moral codes, for he had long ago elaborated his own morality. He had been obliged to do so to be able to get rid of his stepfather in the way that he had. Still, even though he poisoned him the moment he included Marcus's mother in his will, this did not stop him from going to put flowers on his stepfather's grave every Sunday. After all, he had him to thank for who he was, even though the vast fortune he had inherited from this brutal, uncouth man was

nothing compared to the legacy from his real
father: the precious gene that enabled him to
travel in time, placing the past at his feet.

He began dreaming of his unique library,
on whose shelves *Treasure Island*, the *Iliad*, and
Frankenstein, or his three favorite novels by
Melvyn Aaron Frost, would sit secretly side by
side. He picked up a copy of *Dracula* by Frost
and studied his photograph carefully. Yes, the
sickly little man with eyes that oozed corruption,
showing he was as riddled with vices and
weaknesses as any other, and only worthy of
admiration when he had a pen in his hand, would
be the first of a long list of writers who would
meet their end in a series of freak accidents that
would help Marcus amass his phantom library.

With this in mind, he traveled to our time
accompanied by two of his men, arriving a few
months before Frost's rise to fame. He needed
to find him, make sure he had not delivered
his manuscripts to his editor, and force him
at gunpoint to hand over the only thing that
differentiated him from all the other wretches
who gave the world a bad name. Then he would
end Frost's ridiculous life by staging some sort
of accident. But to his surprise, he could find no
trace of Melvyn Frost. No one seemed to have
heard of him. It was as though he had never
existed. How could he possibly have guessed
that Frost was also a time traveler and would

only reveal his identity once he was in possession
of your works? But Marcus had no intention of
leaving empty-handed. This was the writer he had
chosen in order to start his literary bloodbath,
and he would find him come hell or high water.
His plan was not notable for its subtlety: the only
thing he could think of to force Frost out into
the open was to kill three innocent bystanders
and write the opening sentence of each of his
three novels at the scene of each crime, lifting
them from the published copies he had brought
with him. This could not fail to arouse Frost's
curiosity. As Marcus had predicted, it was
not long before the passages appeared in the
newspapers. But still Frost did not come forward,
seemingly not taking the hint.

By turns desperate and infuriated, Marcus
lay in wait day and night with his men at the
scenes of the crimes, but to no avail, until a man
in the crowd caught his eye. It was not Frost, and
yet his presence gave Marcus a similar frisson of
excitement. He had been staring like any other
spectator at Mrs. Ellis's slender corpse, which
hours before he himself had propped up against
the wall, and at the inspector from Scotland Yard
standing next to the dead woman, a young man
who appeared to be trying not to vomit, when
he noticed the middle-aged man on his right.
He was wearing all the typical accoutrements
of the period: an elegant blue suit, a top hat, a

monocle; and a pipe was hanging out of his mouth,
all of which revealed themselves to Marcus to
be part of a deliberate disguise. Then he noticed
the book the man was carrying. It was Melvyn
Frost's hitherto unpublished novel *The Turn of the
Screw*. How could this man possess a copy of it?
Clearly, he was a fellow time traveler. Scarcely
able to contain his excitement, Marcus discreetly
watched as the man compared the beginning of
the novel with the passage Marcus had scribbled
on the wall, and then frowned, surprised to find
they were identical.

When he slipped the book into his pocket and
began to walk away, Marcus decided to follow
him. Unawares, the stranger guided him to a
deserted-looking house in Berkeley Square, which
he entered after making sure no one was watching.
Seconds later, Marcus and his men forced their
way inside. In no time they overpowered the
stranger. It took only a few blows for him to
confess how he came to be in possession of a
book that did not yet exist. This was when
Marcus found out about the Library of Truth and
everything else. He had traveled there in order to
murder his favorite author and become his only
reader, but had ended up discovering much more
than he had bargained for.

The name of the fellow in front of him with
the bloody nose and two black eyes was August
Draper, the real librarian responsible for guarding

the nineteenth century. He had gone there in
order to repair changes made to the fabric of
time when a traveler named Frost murdered
the authors Bram Stoker, Henry James, and H.
G. Wells, and published their novels in his own
name. Marcus was astonished to find that Melvyn
Frost was not the real author of his favorite
novels, that they were the works of the three
writers his hostage had mentioned, who although
in Marcus's reality had died just as they were
becoming famous, in the original universe had
gone on to write many more novels. Almost as
astonished as he was to learn that Jack the Ripper
had never been caught. Marcus felt an almost
metaphysical revulsion when he realized he had
simply been traveling between parallel universes
created at will by other travelers like him, but
who, unlike him, had not been content merely to
fornicate with Egyptian slave girls. However, he
tried to put it out of his mind and concentrate on
Draper's explanations. The stranger planned to
rectify the damage, warning the three authors
what was about to happen by leaving a copy
of their respective novels published under the
name Melvyn Frost in each of their letter boxes,
together with a map showing them where they
could meet him. He was about to set his plan
in motion when news of Marcus's mysterious
murders began appearing in the papers, and this
led him to go to the scene of one of the crimes.

You can imagine what happened next: Marcus killed him in cold blood and decided to step into his shoes and pass himself off to you as the real guardian of time.

These are the facts, and if you study them carefully, certain things become clearer. For example, did it not strike you as odd that Marcus chose such an indiscreet way of contacting you, by reports in the press and alerting every policeman in the city with the brutal murder of three innocent people?—who, by the way, I doubt very much were going to die anyway in a few days' time. But what you think now is irrelevant, actually: you should have thought of it then, and you did not. You cannot imagine how much it pains me to tell you this, Bertie, but you are not as intelligent as you think you are.

Where was I? Oh yes. You will listen to Marcus's explanation, eyes fixed on his henchman's weapon pointing at you as your heart begins to beat faster and faster, the sweat starts to pour down your back, and you even begin to feel overcome with a strange dizziness. I imagine if you had been shot as promptly as James and Stoker were, nothing would have happened. But Marcus's lengthy explanation had enabled you to "prepare yourself," so to speak, and when he had finished his little talk, and his henchman took a step forward and aimed at your chest, all of your built-up tension exploded, and a flood

of light enveloped the world. For a split second,
you became weightless, released from your own
body that felt more than ever like an unnecessary
shell, a focus for pain and futile distractions, and
you had the impression of being a creature of
the air. But a moment later the weight of your
body returned, like an anchor securing you to
the world, and although you were relieved to feel
solid again, it also left you with a vague sense
of nostalgia for the fleeting experience of being
out of your body. You found yourself once more
trapped inside the organic casing that contained
you while blinkering your vision of the universe.
A sudden surge of vomit filled your throat, and
you released it with violent retching. When your
stomach stopped heaving, you dared look up,
unsure if Marcus's henchman had already fired
or was relishing drawing out the moment. But
there was no weapon aimed at you. In fact, there
was no one around you, no trace of Marcus, or his
henchmen, or Stoker, or James. You were alone
in the darkened hallway, for even the candelabra
had disappeared. It was as if you had dreamed
the whole thing. But how could such a thing have
happened? I'll tell you, Bertie: simply because you
were no longer you. You had become me.

So now, if you have no objection, I shall
carry on narrating events in the first person.
To begin with, I did not understand what had
happened. I waited for a few moments in the by

now pitch-black hallway, trembling with fear and
alert to the slightest sound, but all around me
was silence. The house was apparently empty.
Presently, as nothing happened, I ventured out
into the street, which was equally deserted.
I was utterly confused, although one thing
was clear: the sensations I had experienced
were too real to have been a dream. What had
happened to me? Then I had an intuition. With
trepidation, I plucked a discarded newspaper out
of a refuse bin and after verifying the date with
amazement, realized my suspicions were true:
the unpleasant effects I had felt were none other
than those of spontaneous time travel. Incredible
though it may seem, I had traveled eight years
back in time, to November 7, 1888!

I stood in the middle of the square for a few
moments, stunned, trying to take in what had
happened, but I did not have much time, for I
suddenly remembered why that date seemed
so familiar: it was the day Jack the Ripper
had murdered young Harrington's beloved in
Whitechapel and was subsequently captured
by the Vigilance Committee, who had gone
to Miller's Court after being alerted by a time
traveler who . . . was it me? I wasn't sure, but
there seemed to be every indication it was.
Who else could have known what was going to
happen that night? I glanced at my watch. In less
than half an hour the Ripper would commit his

crime. I had to hurry. I ran in search of a cab,
and when at last I found one I told the driver
to take me to Whitechapel as fast as he could.
As we crossed London towards the East End, I
could not help wondering whether it was I who
had changed history, who had made the whole
universe abandon the path it was on, and take this
unexpected detour represented by the blue string,
moving further and further away from the white
cord, as Marcus had explained to us; and if so, had
I done so by my own free will or simply because it
was preordained, because it was something I had
already done?

As you will imagine, I arrived in Whitechapel
in a state of extreme agitation, and once there
I did not know what to do: naturally, I had no
intention of going to Dorset Street alone to
confront the bloodthirsty monster; my altruism
had its limits. I burst into a busy tavern crying
out that I had seen Jack the Ripper at the Miller's
Court flats. It was the first thing that came into
my head, but I suspect whatever I had done
would have been the right thing to do. This was
confirmed to me when a stocky fellow with a
shock of blond hair named George Lusk sprang
out from among the throng of customers gathered
round me, and, twisting my arm behind my
back and pressing my face against the bar, said
he would go and take a look, but that if I was
lying I would live to regret it. After this display

of strength, he released me, gathered his men together, and headed towards Dorset Street in no particular haste. I went as far as the door, rubbing my arm and cursing the brute who was about to take all the credit. Then, amongst the crowd out in the street, I glimpsed young Harrington. Pale as a ghost, he was stumbling through the crowd, a dazed expression on his face, burbling incoherently and every now and then shaking his head. I understood that he must have just discovered the disemboweled corpse of his beloved. He was the image of despair. I wanted to comfort him; I even took a few steps towards him, but I stopped when I realized I had no memory of having performed this kindly gesture in the past, and so I confined myself to watching him until he disappeared down the end of the street. My hands were tied: I had to follow the script; any improvisation on my part could have had an incalculable effect on the fabric of time.

Then I heard a familiar voice behind me, a silky voice that could belong to only one person: "Seeing is believing, Mr. Wells." Marcus was leaning against the wall, clutching his rifle. I looked at him as though he had stepped out of a dream. "This is the only place I could think of to look for you, and I was right to follow my instinct: you are the traveler who alerted the Vigilance Committee which then captured Jack the Ripper,

changing everything. Who would have thought
it, Mr. Wells? Although I imagine that's not
your real name. I expect the real Wells is lying
dead somewhere. Still, I'm beginning to grow
accustomed to the masked ball time travelers'
actions have transformed the past into. And the
fact is I couldn't care less who you are, I'm going
to kill you anyway." With that, he smiled and
aimed his gun very slowly at me, as though he
were in no hurry to finish me off, or wanted to
savor the moment.

But I was not just going to stand there
and wait for him to blast me with his heat
ray. I wheeled round and ran as fast as I could,
zigzagging down the street, playing the role of
quarry to the best of my ability in that game
of cat and mouse. Almost at once, a ray of lava
shot over my head, singeing my hair, and I could
hear Marcus's laughter. Apparently, he meant to
have some fun before murdering me. I continued
running for my life, although as the seconds
passed, this felt like an ever more ambitious
endeavor. My heart was knocking against my
chest, and I could sense Marcus advancing
casually behind me, like a predator intent on
enjoying the hunt. Luckily, the street I had run
down was empty, so no innocent bystanders
would suffer the deadly consequences of our game.
Then another heat ray passed me on the right;

shattering part of a wall; after that, I felt another one cleave the air on my left, blowing away a streetlamp in its path.

At that moment, I saw a horse and cart emerge from one of the side streets, and, not wanting to stop I speeded up as fast as I could, just managing to pass in front of it. Almost at once, I heard a loud explosion of splintering wood behind me, and I realized Marcus had not hesitated to fire at the cart blocking his way. This was confirmed to me when I saw the flaming horse fly over my head and crash to the ground a few yards ahead of me. I dodged the burnt carcass as best I could, and leapt into another street, aware of a wave of destruction being unleashed behind me. Then, after turning down another side street, I caught sight of Marcus's elongated shadow thrown onto the wall in front of me by a streetlamp. Horrified, I watched him stop and take aim, and I realized he was tired of playing with me. In less than two seconds I would be dead, I told myself.

It was then that I felt a familiar dizziness coming over me. The ground beneath my feet vanished for a moment, only to reappear a second later with a different consistency, as daylight blinded me. I stopped running and clenched my teeth to prevent myself from vomiting, blinking comically as I tried to focus. I succeeded just in time to see a huge metal machine bearing down on me. I hurled myself to one side, rolling several times on the ground. From there, I looked up and saw the fiendish machine continue down the street while some men who were apparently traveling inside shouted at me that I was drunk. But that noisy vehicle was not the only one of its kind. The whole street thronged with the machines, hurtling along like a stampede of metal bison. I picked myself up off the ground and glanced about me, astonished but relieved to see no sign of Marcus anywhere. I grabbed a newspaper from a nearby bench to see where my new journey in time had brought me, and discovered I was in 1938. Apparently, I was becoming quite skilled at it: I had traveled forty years into the future this time.

I left Whitechapel and began wandering in a daze through that strange London. Number 50 Berkeley Square had become an antiquarian bookshop. Everything had changed, and yet happily it still seemed familiar. I spent several hours wandering aimlessly, watching the monstrous machines crisscrossing the streets; vehicles that were neither drawn by horses nor driven by steam—whose reign, contrary to what people in your time imagined, would end up being relatively brief. No time had passed for me, and yet the world had lived through forty years. Yes, I was surrounded by hundreds of new inventions, machines testifying to man's indefatigable imagination, despite the fact that the director of the New York patent office had called for its closure at the end of your century, because, he claimed, there was nothing left to invent.

Finally, weary of all these marvels, I sat down on a park bench and reflected about my newly discovered condition as time traveler. Was I in Marcus's future, where there would be a Department of Time I could turn to for help? I did not think so. After all, I had only traveled forty years into the future. If I was not the only time traveler there, the others must have been as lost as I was. Then I wondered whether if I activated my mind again, I could travel back to the past, to your time, to warn you about what was going to happen. But after several failed attempts to reproduce the same impulse that had brought me there, I gave up. I realized I was trapped in that time. But I was alive, I had escaped death, and Marcus was unlikely to come looking for me there. Should I not be happy about that?

Once I had accepted this, I set about finding out what had happened to my world, but above all, what had become of Jane and all the other people I knew. I went to a library and after hours spent searching through newspapers, I managed to form a general idea of the world I was living in. With great sorrow, I discovered not only that the world was moving stubbornly towards a world war, but that there had already been one some years earlier, a bloody conflict involving half the planet in which eight million people had died. But few lessons had been learned, and now, despite its graveyards piled with dead, the world was once more teetering on the brink. I recalled some of the clippings I had seen hanging from the map of time, and understood that nothing could prevent this second war, for it was one of those past mistakes which the people of the future had chosen to accept. I could only wait for the conflict to begin and try my best to avoid being one of the innumerable corpses that would litter the world a few years on.

I also found an article that both bewildered and saddened me. It was the twenty-fifth anniversary of the death of Bram Stoker and Henry James, who had died attempting to spend the night confronting the ghost in number 50 in Berkeley Square. That same night another equally tragic event in the world of letters had occurred: H. G. Wells, the author of *The Time Machine*, had mysteriously disappeared and was never seen again. Had he gone time traveling? the journalist had asked ironically, unaware of how close he was to the truth. In that article, they referred to you as the father of science fiction. I can imagine you asking what the devil that term means. A fellow named Hugo Gernsback popularized it in 1926, using it on the cover of his magazine *Amazing Stories*, the first publication devoted entirely to fiction with a scientific slant in which many of the stories you wrote for Lewis Hind were reedited, together with those of Edgar Allan Poe, and, of course, Jules Verne, who competed with you for the title of father of the genre. As Inspector Garrett had predicted, novels that envisioned future worlds had ended up creating a genre of their own, and this was largely thanks to his discovery that Murray's Time Travel was the biggest hoax of the nineteenth century. After that, the future went back to being a blank space no one had any claims on, and which every writer could adorn as he liked, an unknown world, an unexplored territory, like those on the old nautical maps, where it was said monsters were born.

On reading this, I realized with horror that my disappearance had sparked off a fatal chain of events: without my help, Garrett had been unable to catch Marcus and had gone ahead with his plan to visit the year 2000 and arrest Captain Shackleton, thus uncovering Gilliam's hoax, resulting in his being sent to prison. My thoughts immediately turned to Jane, and I scoured hundreds of newspapers and magazines, fearing I might come across a news item reporting the death of H. G. Wells's "widow" in a tragic cycling accident. But Jane had not died. Jane had gone on living after her husband's mysterious disappearance. This meant Gilliam had not carried out his threat. Had he simply warned her to convince me to cooperate with him? Perhaps.

Or perhaps he just had not had time to carry out his threat, or had wasted it searching for me in vain all over London to ask why on earth I was not trying to discover the real murderer. But despite his extensive network of thugs, he had failed to find me. Naturally, he had not thought to look in 1938. In any case, Gilliam had ended up in prison, and my wife was alive. Although she was no longer my wife.

Thanks to the articles about you, I was able to form an idea of what her life was like, what it had been like after my sudden upsetting departure. Jane had waited nearly five years in our house in Woking for me to come back, and then her hope ran out. Resigned to continuing her life without me, she had returned to live in London, where she had met and married a prestigious lawyer by the name of Douglas Evans, with whom she had a daughter they named Selma. I found a photograph of Jane as a charming old lady who still had the same smile I had become enamored of during our walks to Charing Cross. My first thought was to find her, but this of course was a foolish impulse. What would I say to her? My sudden reappearance after all this time would only have upset her otherwise peaceful existence. She had accepted my departure, why stir things up now? And so I did not try to find her, which is why from the moment I disappeared, I never again laid eyes on the sweet creature who must at this very moment be sleeping right above your head. Perhaps my telling you this will prompt you to wake her up with your caresses when you finish reading the letter. It is something only you can decide: far be it from me to meddle in your marriage. But of course, not looking for her was not enough. I had to leave London, not just because I was afraid of running into her or into one of my friends, who would recognize me immediately, since I had not changed, but purely for my own self-protection: it was more than likely Marcus would carry on trolling the centuries for me, searching through time for some trace of my existence.

I assumed a false identity. I grew a bushy beard and chose the charming medieval town of Norwich as the place where I would discreetly start to build a new life for myself. Thanks to what you had learned at Mr. Cowap's pharmacy, I found work at a chemist's, and for a year and a half I spent my days dispensing ointments and syrups, and my nights lying in my bed listening to the news, alert to the slow buildup of a war that would redefine the world once more. Of my own free will I had decided to live one of those redundant, futile lives that I had always been terrified my mother's stubbornness would finally condemn me to, and I could not even compensate for its simplicity by writing for fear of alerting

Marcus. I was a writer condemned to live like someone who had no gift for writing. Can you imagine a worse torture? Nor can I. Yes, I was safe, but I was trapped in a dismal life, which made me wonder at times whether it was worth the trouble of living. Happily, someone came along to brighten it up: she was called Alice, and she was beautiful. She entered the chemist's one morning to buy a bottle of aspirin—a preparation of acetylsalicylic acid marketed by a German company that was very popular at the time—and when she left, she took my heart with her.

Love blossomed between us amazingly quickly, outstripping the war, and by the time it broke out, Alice and I had much more to lose than before. Luckily, it all seemed to be taking place far away from our town, which apparently presented no threat to Germany, whose new chancellor intended to conquer the world under the dubious pretext that the blood of a superior race pulsed through his veins. We could only glimpse the terrible consequences of the conflict through the ghastly murmurings carried to us on the breeze, a foretaste of what the newspapers would later report, but I already understood this war would be different from previous ones, because science had changed the face of war by presenting men with new ways of killing one another. The battle would now take place in the skies. But do not think of dirigibles firing at one another to see who could

burst the enemy's hydrogen balloons first. Man
had conquered the skies with a flying machine
that was heavier than air, similar to the one Verne
had envisaged in his novel *Robur the Conqueror*,
only these were not made of papier-mâché glued
together, and they dropped bombs. Death came
from above now, announcing its arrival with
a terrifying whistle. And although, because of
complex alliances, seventy different countries had
been drawn into the atrocious war, in no time
England was the only country left standing, while
the rest of the world contemplated, astonished, the
birth of a new order.

Intent on breaking England's resistance,
Germany subjected our country to a remorseless
bombardment, which, while to begin with was
confined to airfields and harbors (in keeping
with the curious code of honor that sometimes
underlies acts of war), soon spread to the cities.
After several weeks of repeated bombing, our
beloved London was reduced to smoking rubble,
from which the dome of St. Paul's Cathedral
emerged miraculously, the embodiment of our
invincible spirit. Yes, England resisted, and even
counterattacked with brief sallies over German
territory. One of these left the historic town of
Lübeck, on the banks of the River Trave, partially
destroyed. In angry retaliation, the Germans
decided to increase their attacks twofold. Even so,
Alice and I felt relatively safe in Norwich, a town

of no strategic interest whatsoever. Except that
Norwich had been blessed with three stars in the
celebrated Baedeker guide, and this was the one
Germany consulted when it resolved to destroy
our historical heritage. Karl Baedeker's guide
recommended visiting its Romanesque cathedral
and its twelfth-century castle, as well as its many
churches, but the German chancellor preferred to
drop bombs on them.

The intrusion of the war took us by surprise
as we listened to Bishop Helmore's sermon in the
cathedral. Sensing it would be one of the enemy's
prime targets, the bishop urged us to flee the house
of God, and while some people chose to remain—
whether because they were paralyzed by fear or
because their faith convinced them there could be
no safer refuge, I do not know—I grabbed Alice's
hand and dragged her towards the exit, fighting
my way through the terrified crowd blocking the
nave. We got outside just as the first wave of bombs
began to fall. How can I describe such horror to
you? Perhaps by saying that the wrath of God
pales beside that of man. People fled in panic in all
directions, even as the force of the bombs ripped
into the earth, toppling buildings and shaking the
air with the roar of thunder. The world fell down
around us, torn to shreds. I tried to find a safe
place, but all I could think of as I ran hand in hand
with Alice through the mounting destruction was
how little we valued human life in the end.

Then, in the middle of all that frenzied running, I began to feel a familiar dizziness stealing over me. My head began to throb, everything around me became blurred, and I realized what was about to happen. Instantaneously, I stopped our frantic dash and asked Alice to grip my hands as tightly as she could. She looked at me, puzzled, but did as I said, and as reality dissolved and my body became weightless for a third time, I gritted my teeth and tried to take her with me. I had no idea where I was going, but I was not prepared to leave her behind the way I had left Jane, my life, and everything that was dear to me. The sensations that subsequently overtook me were the same as before: I felt myself float upwards for a split second, leaving my body then returning to it, slipping back between my bones, except that this time I could feel the warm sensation of someone else's hands in mine. I opened my eyes, blinking sluggishly, struggling not to vomit. I beamed with joy when I saw Alice's hands still clasping mine. Small, delicate hands I would cover with grateful kisses after we made love, hands joined to slender forearms covered in a delightful golden down. The only part of her I had managed to bring with me.

I buried Alice's hands in the garden where I appeared in the Norwich of 1982, which did not look as if it had ever been bombed, except for the monument to the dead in the middle of one of its squares. There I discovered Alice's name, among the many others, although I always wondered whether it was the war that killed her, or Otto Lidenbrock, the man who loved her. In any event, it was something I was condemned to live with, for I had leapt into the future to escape the bombs. Another forty years: that seemed to be as far as I could jump.

The world I now found myself in was apparently wiser, intent on forging its own identity and displaying its playful, innovative spirit in every aspect of life. Yes, this was an arrogant world that celebrated its achievements with a child's jubilant pride, and yet it was a peaceful world where war was a painful memory, a shameful recognition that human nature had a terrible side which had to be concealed, if only under a façade of politeness. The world had been forced to rebuild itself, and it had been then, while clearing the rubble and gathering up the dead, while putting up new buildings and sticking bridges back together again, patching up the holes that war had wreaked on his soul and his lineage, that man had become brutally aware of what had happened, had suddenly realized that everything which had seemed rational at first had become irrational, like a ball at which the music abruptly stops. I could not help rejoicing: the zeal with which those around me condemned their grandfathers' actions convinced me there would be no more wars like the one I had lived through. And I will tell you I was also right about that. Man can learn, Bertie, even if, as with circus animals, it has to be beaten into him.

In any event, I had to start again from scratch, to build another wretched life from the very beginning. I left Norwich, where I had no ties, and went back to London, where, after being astounded by the advances of science, I tried to find a job that might be suitable for a man from the Victorian age going by the name of Harry Grant. Was I doomed, then, to wander through time, floating from one period to another like a leaf blown in the wind, alone forever? No, things would be different this time. I was alone, yes, but I knew I would not be lonely for very long. I had a future appointment to keep, one that did not require me to travel in time again. This future was close enough for me to wait until it came to me.

But apparently, before that, the mysterious hand of fate had made another appointment for me, with something very special from my past. And it happened at a cinema. Yes, Bertie, you heard right. It is hard to exaggerate the extent to which cinema will develop from the moment the Lumière brothers first project images of workers leaving their factory at Lyon Monplaisir. No one in your time had any inkling of the enormous

potential of their invention. However, once the
novelty wears off, people will soon tire of images
of men playing cards, scampering children, and
trains pulling into stations—everyday things
they can see, from their windows and with
sound—and they will want something more
than dull social documentaries accompanied by
the absent tinkle of a piano. That is why the
projector now tells a story on the empty screen.
To give you an idea, imagine one of them filming
a play that does not have to take place on a
stage raised in front of rows of seats, but can use
anywhere in the world as its setting. And if in
addition I tell you that the director can narrate
the story using not just a handful of painted
backdrops but a whole arsenal of techniques,
such as making people vanish in front of our
eyes by means of manipulating images, you will
understand why the cinema has become the most
popular form of entertainment in the future, far
more so than the music hall. Yes, nowadays an
even more sophisticated version of the Lumière
brothers' machine makes the world dream,
bringing magic into their lives, and an entire
industry commanding enormous sums of money
has grown up around it.

However, I am not telling you all this for pure
pleasure, but because sometimes these cinema
stories are taken from books. And this is the
surprise, Bertie: in 1960, a director named George

Pal will turn your novel *The Time Machine* into
a film. Yes, he will put images to your words.
They had already done this with Verne, of course,
but that in no way diminished my joy. How can
I describe what I felt when I saw the story you
had written take place on screen? There was
your inventor, whom they had named after you,
played by an actor with a determined, dreamy
expression, and there, too, was sweet Weena,
played by a beautiful French actress whose face
radiated a hypnotic calm, and the Morlocks, more
terrifying than you could ever have imagined, and
the colossal sphinx, and dependable, no-nonsense
Filby, and even Mrs. Watchett, with her spotless
white apron and cap. And as one scene succeeded
another, I trembled with emotion in my seat at
the thought that none of this would have been
possible if you had not imagined it, that somehow
this feast of images had previously been projected
inside your head.

   I confess that, at some point, I looked away
from the screen and studied the faces of the people
sitting near me. I imagine you would have done
the same, Bertie. I know more than once you
wished you had that freedom, for I still remember
how downcast you felt when a reader told you
how much they had enjoyed your novel, without
your being able to see for yourself how they had
responded to this or that passage, or whether they
had laughed or wept in the proper places, because

in order to do so you would have had to steal into their libraries like a common thief. You may rest assured: the audience responded exactly as you had hoped. But we must not take the credit away from Mr. Pal, who captured the spirit of your novel brilliantly. Although I will not try to hide the fact that he changed a few things in order to adapt it to the times, essentially because the film was made sixty-five years after the book was written, and part of what for you was the future had already become the past. Remember, for example, that despite your concern over the ways man might use science, it never even occurred to you that he might become embroiled in a war that would engulf the entire planet. Well, he did, not once but twice, as I have already told you. Pal made your inventor witness not only the First and Second World Wars, he even predicted a third in 1966, although fortunately in that case his pessimism proved unfounded.

As I told you, the feeling I experienced in that cinema, hypnotized by the swirling images that owed so much to you, is beyond words. This was something you had written, yes, and yet everything that appeared on the screen was unfamiliar to me, everything that is except the time machine, your time machine, Bertie. You cannot imagine how surprised I was to see it there. For a moment I thought my eyes were playing tricks on me. But no, it was your machine,

gleaming and beautiful, with its graceful curves,
like a musical instrument, betraying the hand
of a skilled craftsman, exuding an elegance the
machines in the period I had been cast adrift in
had lost. But how had it ended up there, and where
could it be now, twenty years after the actor called
Rod Taylor who played you first climbed out of it?

After several weeks spent scouring the
newspapers at the library, I managed to trace its
eventful journey. I discovered that Jane had not
wanted to part with it and had taken it with her
to London, to the house of Evans, the lawyer,
who would contemplate with resignation the
intrusion into his home of the absurd, seemingly
useless piece of junk, which, to cap it all, was a
symbol to his new wife of her vanished husband. I
pictured him unable to sleep at night, circling the
machine, pressing the fake buttons and moving
the glass lever to satisfy himself it did not work,
and wondering what mystery was contained
in this object his wife referred to as the time
machine, and why the devil it had been built, for
I was sure Jane would have explained nothing to
him, considering the machine part of a private
world Evans the lawyer had no business knowing
about.

When, many years later, George Pal began
preparations for his film, he ran into a problem:
he did not find any of the designs his people had
come up with for the time machine convincing.

They were clunky, grotesque, and overelaborate.
None of the models bore any resemblance to the
elegant, stately vehicle in which he envisaged
the inventor traveling across the vast plains
of time. That is why it seemed to him nothing
short of a miracle when a woman named Selma
Evans, close to bankruptcy after squandering
the small fortune she had inherited from her
parents, offered to sell him the strange object her
mother had dusted every Sunday in a languid,
ceremonious manner that made little Selma's
hair stand on end almost as much as it did that
of Evans the lawyer. Pal was stunned: this was
exactly what he had been looking for. It was
beautiful and majestic and had the same lively
air as the toboggans he had ridden as a boy. He
remembered the wind whipping his face as he
sped down the slopes, a wind that had taken on a
magical quality over time, and he imagined if you
traveled through time in that machine you would
feel the same wind lashing your face. But what
really decided him was the little plaque on the
control panel that said: manufactured by
H. G. Wells. Had the author really built it
himself? And if so, why? This was an insoluble
mystery, as Wells had disappeared in 1896, just as
he was becoming famous. Who knows how many
more remarkable novels he might have given the
world? However, although he did not know why
the machine had been built, Pal sensed it could

not be put to better use than in his film, and so he convinced the production studio to buy it. That is how your machine gained the fleeting immortality of the silver screen.

Ten years later, the studios organized a public auction of scenery and other props from several of its productions, including the time machine. It sold for ten thousand dollars, and the buyer went round the United States showing it in every town, until finally, after getting his money's worth from it, he sold it to an antiquarian in Orange County. And that was where Gene Warren, one of the technicians on Pal's film, stumbled on it in 1974. It was sitting in a corner, rusty and neglected, with all the other junk. The seat had long since been sold. Warren bought it for next to nothing, and set about lovingly restoring the toy that had come to mean so much to everyone who had worked on the film: he repainted all the bars, repaired the broken parts, and even made a replacement seat from memory. Once fully restored, the machine was able to continue its journey, being displayed in fairs and events with a science fiction theme, and even occasionally being driven by an actor dressed as you. Pal himself appeared sitting on it on the front cover of *Starlog*, smiling like a boy about to ride his toboggan down a snowy slope. That year, Pal even sent out Christmas cards to his friends of Santa Claus riding on your time machine. As you can imagine, I followed its progress like a loving

father contemplating the adventures of a son who
has lost his way, knowing that sooner or later he
will return to the fold.

And on April 12, 1984, I kept my appointment
at Olsen's department store. There she was,
confused and scared, and I was the one who
whisked her out from under the noses of the press,
by holding her hand and whispering in her ear, "I
believe you because I can also travel in time." We
left the store through the emergency exit, taking
advantage of the ensuing chaos. Once in the
street, we scrambled into the car I had hired and
made our way to Bath, where a few weeks before
I had acquired a charming Georgian house. There
I intended us to make our home, far from London
and all those time travelers from the future, who
would doubtless be searching for her under orders
from the Government, which had decreed her
sacrifice as the only way of eradicating the root of
the problem.

At first, I was not sure I had done the right
thing. Should I have been the one to rescue her
from Olsen's, or had I usurped the role of another
time traveler from the future who had proclaimed
himself the savior of the Madonna of Time? The
answer came a few days later, one bright spring
morning. We were painting the sitting room walls,
when suddenly a little boy of about three or four
materialized on the carpet, gave a loud chortle,
as though tickled with joy, then disappeared

again, leaving behind a piece of the puzzle he
had been playing with on the carpet. Following
that brief and unexpected glimpse of a son we
had not yet conceived, we understood that the
future began with us, that we were the ones who
would produce the mutant gene which, years,
or possibly centuries later, would enable man to
travel in time. Yes, the epidemic of time travelers
Marcus had told us about would quietly originate
in that secluded house, I said to myself, stooping
to pick up the piece of puzzle left behind on the
carpet, like an unconscious gift from our son. I
kept this fragment of the future in the kitchen
larder, among the tins of beans, knowing that in
a few years' time it would help me understand
the puzzle someone would give to the boy I had
glimpsed on the carpet at the precise moment in
which it was supposed to happen.

After that, there is not much more to tell. She
and I lived happily ever after like the characters
in a fairy tale. We enjoyed life's small pleasures,
attempting to live as quiet and uneventful a life
as possible so that neither of us would suffer an
inopportune displacement that would separate us
in time. I even indulged myself and bought your
time machine when Gene Warren's son put it up
for sale, although I had absolutely no need of it,
because I traveled through time like everyone
else now, letting myself be swept along by the
delightful flow of the days, while my hair began

falling out and I found it more and more difficult
to climb the stairs.

I suppose a mark of the calm happiness we
enjoyed were our three children, one of whom we
had already met. Needless to say, their gift for
time travel was far greater than ours. They were
never in complete control of their ability, but I
knew their descendants would be, and I could
not help smiling when I saw our genes begin to
propagate as they went out into the world. I did
not know how many generations it would take
before the Government finally noticed the time
travelers, but I knew it would happen sooner or
later. That was when I had the idea of writing you
this letter with the aim of entrusting it to one
of my grandchildren, who in turn would pass it
down to one of his, until it reached someone who
would be able to carry out my request: to deliver
it to the author H. G. Wells, the father of science
fiction, on the night of November 26, 1896. And
I imagine that if you are reading it now, then I
was right about that, too. I have no idea who will
deliver this letter to you, but as I said before, he
or she will be our own flesh and blood. And when
that happens, as you will have guessed, these
words will already be the voice of a dead man.

Perhaps you would have preferred it if I had
not written you any letter. Perhaps you would
have liked it better if I had let you meet your
fate unprepared. After all, what awaits you is

not all that bad and even contains moments of
happiness, as you have seen. But if I wrote to you,
it is because somehow I feel this is not the life
you should live. Indeed, perhaps you should stay
in the past, living happily with Jane and turning
me into a successful writer who knows nothing
about journeys through time, not real ones
anyway. For me it is too late, of course; I cannot
choose a different life, but you can. You can still
choose between your life and the life I have just
recounted to you, between going on being Bertie
or becoming me. In the end, that is what time
travel gives us, a second chance, the opportunity
to go back and do things differently.

I have given a great deal of thought to what
might happen if you decide not to go to the
meeting with Marcus tomorrow. If you do not
go, no one will point a gun at you, your brain
will not be activated, and you will not travel
through time, and therefore you will neither bring
about the Ripper's capture, nor will you meet
Alice, nor flee the German bombardment, nor
rescue any woman at Olsen's department store.
And without you, the mutant gene will not be
created, and so there will be no time travelers
and no Marcus to travel into the past to kill you,
and I imagine everything that happened from the
moment he murdered the tramp in Marylebone
will disappear from the time continuum as
though a huge broom had swept it away. All the

colored strings dangling from the white cord of
the map of time would vanish, for no one would
have created any parallel universe where Jack the
Ripper had been caught, or where Her Gracious
Majesty went around with a squirrel monkey on
her shoulder. Good God, the map of time itself
would disappear! Who would be there to create
it? As you can see, Bertie, if you decide not to go,
you will annihilate an entire world. But do not
let this put you off. The only thing that would
remain unchanged would be a certain woman's
appearance at Olsen's department store in 1984,
although no one will take her by the hand and
lead her away to a beautiful Georgian house where
she will live happily ever after.

And what would happen to you? I imagine you
would go back to the moment just before your life
was altered by your own time traveling. Before
Murray's thug chloroforms you? Almost certainly,
because if Marcus never traveled to your time and
did not kill anyone, Garrett would never suspect
Shackleton, and Gilliam would not send his thug
to abduct you so that you could save his bacon,
and therefore no chloroform-soaked handkerchief
would be placed over your face on the night of
November 20, 1896. Be that as it may, however far
back you go, I do not imagine you will experience
any of the physical effects of time travel: you will
simply disappear from one place and reappear
in another as if by magic, without being aware

of any transition, although of course you will
remember nothing of what you experienced after
that moment. You would not know that you had
traveled in time or that parallel universes exist. If
you decide to change what happened, this is what
will occur, I fear: you will know nothing of me.
It would be like reversing the moves in a game
of chess until you find the one that began the
checkmate. At that point, if instead of the bishop
you ought to move, you decide to use your rook,
the game will take a different turn, just as your
life will tomorrow if you do not go to the meeting.

And so everything depends on you, Bertie.
Bishop or rook. Your life or mine. Do what you
believe you have to do.

Yours ever,
Herbert George Wells

XLI

AND WHAT ABOUT PREDESTINA-
tion? Wells wondered. Perhaps he was fated to
travel in time, first to 1888, then to the beginning of that
atrocious war that would involve the entire planet, and
so on, exactly as he had told himself in the letter. Perhaps
he was fated to produce the first race of time travelers.
Perhaps he had no right to change the future, to prevent
man from being able one day to travel in time because he
refused to sacrifice his own life, because he wanted to stay
with Jane in the past it had taken him so long to arrange to
his liking. For wanting to go on being Bertie.

However, this was not only a consideration about the
morality of his choice, but about whether he really had a
choice. Wells doubted he could solve the problem simply by
not turning up at the meeting, as his future self had suggested. He was certain that if he did not go, sooner or later
Marcus would find him and kill him in any case. In the
end, he was sure that what he was about to do was his only
choice, he said to himself, clutching the manuscript of *The
Invisible Man*, as the cab skirted Green Park on its way to

Berkeley Square, where the man who intended to kill him was waiting.

After he had finished reading the letter, he had put it back in the envelope and sat for a long time in his armchair. He had been irritated by the tone of mocking condescension the future Wells had used to address him, although he could hardly reproach him for it, given that the author of the letter was he himself. Besides, he had to recognize that if he had been in the future Wells's shoes, considering all he had gone through, he would have found it difficult to avoid that patronizing tone towards his callow past self, someone who had scarcely taken his first steps in the world. But all that was immaterial. What he needed to do was assimilate as quickly as possible the astonishing fact that he himself was the author of that letter, in order to focus on the really important question: what should he do about it? He wanted his decision to take into account what he thought was the almost metaphysical principle of the matter.

Which of the two lives branching off beneath him was the one he really ought to live? Which path should he venture down? Was there any way of knowing? No, there was not. Besides, according to the theory of multiple worlds, changes to the past did not affect the present, but created an alternative present, a new universe that ran alongside the original, which remained intact. Accordingly, the beautiful messenger who had crossed time to give him the letter had crossed into a parallel universe, because in the real world no one had walked up to him outside his house. Consequently, even if he did not go to the meeting, in the world in which he did not receive the letter, he would. His other life, then, the one in which the epistolary Wells had lived, would not disappear. It was redundant, therefore, to regard the act of not bowing to fate as some sort of miscarriage of time.

He must simply choose the life that most appealed to him without splitting moralistic hairs. Did he want to stay with Jane, write novels, and dream about the future, or did he aspire to the life of that distant, future Wells? Did he want to go on being Bertie, or to become the link between *Homo sapiens* and *Homo temporis*? He had to admit he felt tempted to surrender quietly to the fate described in the letter, to accept that life punctuated by exciting episodes such as the bombardment of Norwich, which, why deny it, he would not have minded experiencing secure in the knowledge he would come out of it alive. It would be like rushing around calmly while bombs dropped out of the sky, admiring the terrifying force of man's insanity, the hidden depths of beauty in that display of destruction. Not to mention all the wonders he would be able to see on his journeys into the future, brimming with inventions even Verne could not have imagined. But that would mean giving up Jane, and, more importantly, literature, for he would never be able to write again. Was he prepared to do that? He thought about it for a long time, before finally making up his mind. Then he went up to the bedroom, woke Jane with his caresses, and in the anguished, oppressive darkness of the night, which felt exactly like being down a mole hole, he made love to her as if for the last time.

"You made love to me as if for the first time, Bertie," she said, pleasantly surprised, before falling asleep again.

And hearing her breathe softly by his side, Wells understood that, as so often happened, his wife knew what he wanted much better than he did, and that if only he had asked her, he could have saved all that time he had taken coming to a decision which, in addition, now proved to be the wrong one. Yes, he told himself, sometimes the best way to find out what we want is to choose what we do not want.

HE PUSHED ASIDE THESE thoughts when the cab pulled up in front of number 50 Berkeley Square, the most haunted house in London. Well, the moment had finally arrived. He took a deep breath, climbed out of the carriage, and made his way slowly towards the building, savoring the aromas floating in the afternoon air and carrying the manuscript of *The Invisible Man* tucked under his arm. On entering, he discovered Stoker and James already there, engaged in a lively conversation with the man who was about to kill them in the halo of light cast by the candelabra dotted about the hallway. From then on, every time he heard some columnist praising the American's uncanny powers of observation, he would be unable to stop himself guffawing.

"Ah, Mr. Wells," cried Marcus on seeing him, "I was beginning to think you weren't coming."

"Forgive the delay, gentlemen," Wells apologized, glancing despondently at Marcus's two henchmen, who were firmly planted at the edge of the rectangle of light on the floor, waiting for Marcus to give them the order to finish off the foolish trio.

"Oh, that doesn't matter," said his host, "the important thing is you've brought your novel."

"Yes," said Wells, waving the manuscript idiotically.

Marcus nodded, pleased, and pointed at the table beside him, signaling to him to leave it on top of the two already there. Rather unceremoniously, Wells added his own to the pile, then stepped back a few paces. He realized this placed him directly in front of Marcus and his henchmen, and to the right of James and Stoker, an ideal position if he wanted to be shot first.

"Thank you, Mr. Wells," said Marcus, casting a satisfied eye over the spoils on the table.

He will smile now, thought Wells. And Marcus smiled. He will stop smiling now and look at us, suddenly serious. And he will raise his right hand now. But it was Wells who raised his. Marcus looked at him with amused curiosity.

"Is something wrong, Mr. Wells?" he asked.

"Oh, I hope nothing is *wrong*, Mr. Rhys," replied Wells. "But we'll soon find out."

With these words, he let his hand fall in a sweeping motion, although owing to his lack of experience at making gestures of this kind, it lacked authority, looking more like the action of someone swinging a censer. Even so, the person who was supposed to receive the message understood. There was a sudden noise on the upper floor, and they raised their heads as one towards the stairwell, where something which for the moment they could only describe as vaguely human came hurtling towards them. Only when the brave Captain Shackleton landed on the ground in the middle of the circle of light did they realize it was a person.

Wells could not help smiling at the position Tom had taken up, knees bent, muscles tensed, like a wild cat ready to pounce on its prey. The light from the candelabra glinted on his armor; the metal shell covered him from head to toe, except for his strong, handsome chin. He struck a truly heroic figure, and Wells understood now why Tom had asked his former companions to get him the armor, which they had stolen from Gilliam Murray's dressing room that very morning. While the others were still trying to understand what was going on, Shackleton unsheathed his saber, performed a perfect flourish in the air and, following the movement through, plunged the blade into the torso of one of the two henchmen. His companion tried to take aim, but the distance between them was too short for him to maneuver, which gave the captain ample time to draw the sword from his victim's stomach and swing round gracefully. The henchman watched with horrified fascination as Shackleton raised his sword, slicing the man's head off with a swift two-handed blow. Still gaping in terror, the head rolled across the floor, disappearing discreetly into the gloomy edge of the circle of light.

"Have you brought an assassin with you, Wells?" James exclaimed, scandalized by the bloody spectacle taking place before him.

Wells ignored him. He was too busy following Tom's movements. Marcus finally responded. Wells saw him retrieve one of his men's weapons from the floor and aim it at Tom, who, gripping his bloody saber, was that very moment turning towards him. They stood at least four paces apart, and Wells realized with horror that the captain would be unable to cover this distance before the other man fired. And he was not mistaken: Tom barely managed to take a step before receiving the full blast of the heat ray in his chest. The captain's armor shattered, like a crab shell hit by a hammer, and he was thrown backwards, his helmet flying off as he fell. The force of the shot sent him rolling across the floor until he finally came to a stop, a smoldering crater in his chest, his handsome face lit up by the nearby candelabra. Blood trickled from his mouth, and only the candle flames glinted now in his beautiful gray-green eyes.

Marcus's roar of triumph broke the silence, forcing Wells to take his eyes off Tom and fix them on him. Marcus surveyed the three corpses strewn around him with amused incredulity. He nodded his head slowly for a few moments, then turned towards the writers huddled together on the far side of the hallway.

"Nice try, Wells," he said, walking over to them with his springy gait, a ferocious grin on his face. "I have to admit you took me by surprise. But your plan has merely added a few more bodies to the count."

Wells did not reply. He felt suddenly dizzy as he watched Marcus raise his weapon and point it at his chest. He assumed it was the feeling announcing he was about to travel through time. So he would be going to the year 1888 after all. He had done his best to prevent it, but apparently his fate was sealed. There probably did exist a parallel universe where Shackleton had been able to finish off Marcus, and where he would not travel in time and could go on being Bertie, but unfortunately he was not in that universe. He was in one very similar to that of the future Wells, where he would also travel eight years into the past, but where Captain Shackleton had died, pierced by a heat ray.

Realizing he had failed, Wells could only smile sadly, as Marcus slid his finger towards the trigger. At that very moment, a shot rang out, but a shot fired from an ordinary pistol. Then it was Marcus's turn to smile sadly at Wells. A moment later, he lowered his weapon and let it drop to the floor, as though he had suddenly decided it was worthless. With the languid voluptuousness of a puppet whose strings have been cut one by one, Marcus slumped to his knees, sat down, and finally toppled over onto the floor, his blood-spattered face still smiling. Behind him, a smoking gun in his hand, Wells saw Inspector Colin Garrett.

Had the inspector been following him all along? he wondered, bemused by the young man's sudden appearance. No, that was impossible, for if Garrett had been spying on him in the original universe, that is to say in the universe where Wells would inevitably travel in time and would write himself a letter, the inspector would have burst in and seized Marcus once Wells had vanished into thin air; and even if Marcus had succeeded in escaping, whether through time or space, Garrett would have discovered everything, whereas Wells knew this was not the case because his future self had read a news item reporting the strange deaths of the authors Bram Stoker and Henry

James after a night spent in the haunted house at Berkeley Square. Evidently, if Garrett had seen what happened, that article would not have existed. Accordingly, Inspector Garrett had no business being in that universe any more than in the previous one. The only new card on the table was Shackleton, whom Wells had enlisted in his battle with fate. Garrett's presence, therefore, could only have been determined by Shackleton, leading the writer to conclude that he was the person the inspector had followed there.

And, incidentally, he was correct in this assumption, for I, who see everything, can confirm that not two hours before, after a delightful stroll in the company of Miss Nelson, Garrett had bumped into an enormous fellow in Piccadilly. Following the violent collision, the inspector had turned to apologize, but the man was in too much of a hurry even to stop. This strange haste was not the only thing that aroused Garrett's suspicion; he was also puzzled by the curious solidity of the man's body, which had left his shoulder smarting painfully. Such was the force of the blow that Garrett had even thought the fellow must be wearing a suit of armor under his long coat. A minute later, this thought did not seem so foolish. Gazing down at the stranger's bizarre footwear, he realized with a shudder who it was he had just bumped into. His jaw dropped, scarcely able to believe it. Trying to keep calm, he began tailing Shackleton cautiously, his trembling hand clasping the pistol in his pocket, unsure of what to do next. He told himself the best thing would be to follow Shackleton for a while, at least until he discovered where he was going in such a hurry. By turns excited and calm, Garrett followed him down Old Bond Street, holding his breath each time the dead leaves rustled like old parchment under his feet, and then down Bruton Street, until they reached Berkeley Square. Once there, Shackleton had paused in front of what looked like a deserted building and then began scaling its façade until he disappeared through a window on the top floor. The inspector, who had watched his climb from behind a tree, was unsure how to proceed. Should he follow him in? Before he had time to answer his own question, he noticed a carriage pull up in front of the dilapidated building, and, adding to his surprise, out of it stepped the author H. G. Wells, who walked very calmly up to the house and went in through the front door. What was going on between Wells and the man from the future? Garrett wondered, perplexed. There was only one way to find out. He crept across the street, scaled the front of the building, and climbed in through the same window Shackleton had disappeared through moments before. Once inside the darkened building, he had witnessed the entire scene unnoticed. And now he knew Shackleton had not come from the future in order to perpetrate Evil with impunity, as he had first thought, but to help Wells do battle against the time traveler named Marcus, whose wicked plan, as far as the inspector could tell, had been to steal one of Wells's works.

Wells watched the inspector kneel beside Tom's corpse and gently close his eyes. Then Garrett stood up, grinned his inimitable boyish grin, and said something. Wells, though, could not hear him, because at that very moment the universe they were in vanished as if it had never existed.

XLII

WHEN HE PUSHED THE LEVER ON the time machine forward as far as it would go, nothing happened. Wells only needed to glance about him to see that it was still November 20, 1896. He smiled sadly, although he had the strange sensation that he had been smiling like that long before he touched the lever and confirmed what he already knew, that despite its majestic beauty, the time machine was simply a toy. The year 2000—the genuine year 2000, not the one invented by that charlatan Gilliam Murray—was beyond his reach. Like the rest of the future, in fact. No matter how many times he performed the ritual, it would always be make-believe: he would never travel in time. No one could do that. No one. He was trapped in the present from which he could never escape.

Gloomily, he climbed off the machine and walked over to the attic window. Outside, the night was quiet. An innocent silence enveloped the neighboring fields and houses tenderly, and the world appeared exhausted, terribly defenseless, at his mercy. He had the power to change the trees around, paint the flowers different colors, or carry out any number of outrageous acts with total impunity, for, as he gazed out over the sleeping universe, Wells had the impression of being the only man on earth who was awake. He had the feeling that if he listened hard enough he could hear the roar of waves crashing on the shores, the grass steadily growing, the clouds softly chafing against the membrane of the sky, and even the creak of age-old wood as the planet rotated on its axis. And his soul was lulled by the same stillness, for he was always overcome with an intense calm whenever he put the final full stop to a novel, as he had recently done with *The Invisible Man*. He was back at the point of departure, at the place that filled writers with dread and excitement, for this was where they must decide which new story to tackle of the many floating in the air, which plot to bind themselves to for a lengthy period; and they had to choose carefully, study each option calmly, as though confronted with a magnificent wardrobe full of garments they might wear to a ball, because there were dangerous stories, stories that resisted being inhabited, and stories that pulled you apart while you were writing them, or, what was worse, fine-looking clothes fit for an emperor that turned out to be rags. At that moment, before reverently committing the first word to paper, he could write anything he wanted, and this fired his blood with a powerful sense of freedom, as wonderful as it was fleeting, for he knew it would vanish the moment he chose one story and sacrificed all the others.

He contemplated the stars dotted across the night sky with an almost serene smile. He felt a sudden pang of fear. He remembered a conversation with his brother Frank a few months before, during his last visit to the house in Nyewood where his family had washed up like flotsam. When the others had gone to bed, he and Frank had taken their cigarettes and beers out onto the porch, for no other reason than to stand in awe under the majestic sky studded with stars like a brave general's uniform. Beneath that blanket, which allowed them a somewhat immodest glimpse of the universe's depths, the affairs of man seemed painfully insignificant and life took on an almost playful air. Wells swigged his beer, leaving Frank to break the atavistic silence that had settled over the world. Despite the blows life had dealt him, whenever Wells came to Nyewood he always found his brother brimming with optimism, perhaps because he had realized it was the only way he could stay afloat, and he sought to justify it in tangible ways, for example, in the pride any man should feel at being a subject of the British Empire. Perhaps this explained why Frank had begun to extol the virtues of colonial policy, and Wells, who detested the tyrannical way in which his country was conquering the world, had felt compelled to mention the devastating effects of British colonization on the five thousand aborigines in Tasmania, whose population had been decimated. Wells had tried to explain to an inebriated Frank that the Tasmanians had not been won over by values superior to their own indigenous culture, but had been conquered by a more advanced technology. This made his brother laugh. There was no technology in the known world more advanced than that of the British Empire, he declared with drunken pomposity. Wells did not bother to argue, but when Frank had gone back inside, he remained gazing uneasily up at the stars. Not in the known world perhaps, but what of the others?

He studied the firmament once more now with the same sense of unease, in particular the planet Mars, a tiny dot the size of a pinhead. Despite its insignificant appearance, his contemporaries speculated about the possible existence of life on the planet. The red planet was shrouded in the gauze of a thin atmosphere, and although it lacked oceans, it did have polar ice caps. Astronomers everywhere agreed that of all the planets apart from Earth, Mars possessed the conditions most advantageous for the creation of life. And for some this suspicion had become a certainty when, a few years earlier, the astronomer Giovanni Schiaparelli had discovered grooves on its surface that might be canals, undeniable evidence of Martian engineering. But what if Martians existed and were not inferior to us? What if, unlike the indigenous peoples of the New World, they were not a primitive people eager to welcome a missionary visit from Earth, but a more intelligent species than man, capable of looking down their noses at him in the same way he did at monkeys and lemurs? And what would happen if their technology allowed them to travel through space and land on our planet, motivated by the same conquering zeal as man? What would his compatriots, the great conquerors, do if they encountered another species that sought to conquer them, to destroy their values and their self-respect as they did those of the peoples they invaded, applauded by people like his brother? Wells stroked his moustache, reflecting on the potential of this idea, imagining a surprise Martian attack, steam-propelled cylinders raining down on Woking's sleepy commons.

He wondered whether he had stumbled upon the theme of his next novel. The buzz of exhilaration he felt in his brain told him he had, but he was worried about what his editor would say. Had he heard right? A Martian invasion was what he had come up with, after inventing a time machine, a scientist who operated on animals to make them human, and a man suffering from invisibility? Henley had praised his talent after the excellent reviews of his last book, *The Wonderful Visit*. Agreed, he did not do science the way Verne did, but he used a kind of "implacable logic" that made his ideas believable. Not to mention his prodigious output of several novels a year. But Henley seriously doubted whether books pulled out of a hat like that were true literature. If Wells wanted his name to endure longer than a new brand of sauce or soap, he must stop wasting his considerable talent on novels which, while undeniably a feast for the imagination, lacked the necessary depth to really impress themselves on his readers' minds. In brief: if he wanted to be a brilliant writer, and not just a clever, competent storyteller, he must demand more of himself than dashing off little fables. Literature was more than that, much more. True literature should rouse the reader, unsettle him, change his view of the world, give him a resolute push over the cliff of self-knowledge.

But was his understanding of the world profound enough for him to unearth its truths and transmit them to others? Was he capable of changing his readers with what he wrote? And if so, into what? Supposedly into better people. But what kind of story would achieve that; what should he write in order to propel them towards the self-knowledge of which Henley spoke? Would a slimy creature with a slavering mouth, bulbous eyes, and slippery tentacles change his readers' lives? In all probability, he thought, if he portrayed the Martians in this way the subjects of the British Empire would never eat octopus again.

Something disturbed the calm of the night, stirring him from his meditations. This was no cylinder falling from the sky, it was the Scheffer boy's cart. Wells watched it pull up in front of his gate, and smiled when he recognized the sleepy young lad up on the driver's seat. The boy had no objection to getting up early to earn a few extra pennies. Wells made his way downstairs, grabbed his overcoat, and left the house quietly, so as not to wake up Jane. He knew his wife would disapprove of what he was doing, and he could not explain to her either why he had to do it, despite being aware it was not the behavior of a gentleman. He greeted the lad, cast an approving eye over the cargo (he had excelled himself this time), and clambered onto the driver's seat. Once he was safely installed, the lad snapped the reins and they set off towards London.

During the journey, they scarcely exchanged a few pleasantries. Wells spent most of the time silently absorbed in fascinated contemplation of the drowsy, defenseless world around him, crying out to be attacked by creatures from space. He glanced out of the corner of his eye at the Scheffer boy and wondered how such a simple soul, for whom the world probably only extended as far as the horizon, would react to an invasion of extraterrestrials. He imagined a small huddle of country folk approaching the place where a Martian ship had landed, nervously waving a white flag, and the extraterrestrials responding to the innocent greeting by instantaneously annihilating them with a blinding flame, a sort of heat ray that would raze the ground, leaving a burning crater strewn with charred corpses and smoldering trees.

When the cart reached the slumbering city, he stopped imagining Martian invasions to concentrate on what he had come to do. They drove through a maze of streets, each one more deserted than the last, the clatter of hooves shattering the silence of the night, until they reached Greek Street. Wells could not help grinning mischievously when the boy stopped the cart in front of Murray's Time Travel. He glanced up and down the street, pleased to see no one was about.

"Well, my boy," he said, climbing down, "let's go to it."

They each took a couple of buckets from the back of the cart and approached the front of the building. As quietly as possible, they plunged the brushes into the buckets of cow dung and began daubing the walls round the entrance. The repellent task took no more than ten minutes. Once they had finished, a nauseating stench filled the air, although Wells breathed it in with great delight: it was the smell of his rage, the loathing he was obliged to suppress, the never-ending directionless anger bubbling up inside him. Startled, the boy watched him inhale the foul odor.

"Why are you doing this, Mr. Wells?" he ventured to ask.

For a moment, Wells stared at him with furious intent. Even to such an unthinking soul, devoting one's nights to a task that was as eccentric as it was disgusting must have appeared ridiculous.

"Because between doing something and doing nothing, this is all I can do."

The lad nodded in bewilderment at this gibberish, no doubt wishing he had not ventured to try to understand the mysterious motivations of writers. Wells paid him the agreed sum and sent him back to Woking, telling him he still had a few errands to run in London. The boy nodded, visibly relieved at not having to consider what these might be. He leapt onto his cart and, after geeing up the horse, disappeared down the end of the street.

XLIII

WELLS CONTEMPLATED THE OR-
nate façade of Murray's Time Travel and
wondered again how this modest theater could possibly
contain the vast stage set Tom had described to him of a
devastated London in the year 2000. Sooner or later, he
would have to try to get to the bottom of the mystery,
but for the moment, he must forget about it if he did not
want his adversary's unarguable shrewdness to put him
in a bad mood. Determined to push the thought aside,
he shook his head and stood admiring his work for a few
moments. Then, satisfied at a job well done, he began
walking in the direction of Waterloo Bridge. He knew
of no better place from which to observe the beautiful
spectacle of morning. Cracks of light would soon begin to
appear in the dark sky as dawn broke through, and there
was nothing to stop him dallying for a few moments to
witness the colorful duel before going to Henley's office.

In fact, any excuse was good enough to delay his meeting with his editor, for he felt certain Henley would not
be overly pleased with the new manuscript. Of course, he

would agree to publish it, but this would not spare Wells from having to listen to one of Henley's sermons aimed at steering him into the fold of authors destined to pass into the annals of literary history. And why not accept his advice for once? he suddenly thought. Why not give up writing for naïve readers easily convinced by any adventure story, or any story that shows a modicum of imagination, and write for more discerning readers, those, in short, who reject the entertainments of popular fiction in favor of more serious, profound literature that explains the universe to them and even the precariousness of their existence in the centuries to come? Perhaps he should resolve to write another kind of story altogether, one that would stir his readers' souls in a different way, a novel that would be nothing short of a revelation to them, just as Henley wanted.

Immersed in these thoughts, Wells turned down Charing Cross Road and headed for the Strand. By that time, a new day was slowly dawning around him. The black sky was gradually dissolving, giving way to a slightly unreal dark blue that instantly paled on the horizon, taking on a soft violet tint before turning orange. In the distance, the author could make out the shape of Waterloo Bridge growing more and more distinct as the darkness faded, slowly invaded by the light. A series of strange, muffled noises reached his ears, making him smile contentedly. The city was beginning to stir, and the isolated sounds hanging in the air would soon be transformed into the honest, relentless flow of life, an earsplitting din which might arrive at the outer reaches of space transformed into a pleasant buzz of bees, revealing that the third largest planet in the solar system was very much inhabited.

And although as he walked towards the bridge Wells could see nothing beyond what was in front of him, somehow he felt as though he were taking part in a huge play which, because every single inhabitant of the city was cast in it, seemingly had no audience. Except perhaps for the clever Martians, busy studying human life the way man peered down a microscope at the ephemeral organisms wriggling around in a drop of water, he reflected. And in fact, he was right, for as he threaded his way along the Strand, dozens of barges loaded with oysters floated in eerie silence along the ever more orange-tinted waters of the Thames, on their way from Chelsea Reach to Billingsgate Wharf, where an army of men hauled the catch onto land. In wealthy neighborhoods, fragrant with the aroma of high-class bakeries and violets from the flower sellers' baskets, people abandoned their luxurious houses for their no less luxurious offices, crossing the streets that had begun filling up with cabriolets, berlins, omnibuses, and every imaginable type of wheeled vehicle, jolting rhythmically over the paving stones, while above them, the smoke from the factory stacks mingled with the mist rising from the water to form a shroud of dense, sticky fog, and an army of carts drawn by mules or pushed manually, brimming with fruit, vegetables, eels, and squid, took up their positions at Covent Garden amid a chaos of shouts.

At the same hour, Inspector Garrett arrived before

finishing his breakfast at Sloane Street, where Mr. Ferguson was waiting to inform him rather anxiously that someone had taken a potshot at him the night before, poking his pudgy thumb through the hole it had made in his hat. Garrett examined the surrounding area with a trained eye, searching among the bushes around Ferguson's house, and could not prevent a tender smile spreading across his face when he discovered the charming kiwi bird someone had scratched in the dirt. Looking up and down the street to make sure no one was watching, he quickly erased it with his foot before emerging from the bushes, shrugging his shoulders. Just as he was telling Ferguson with an expression of feigned bewilderment that he had found no clues, in a room at a boardinghouse in Bethnal Green, John Peachey, the man known as Tom Blunt before drowning in the Thames, embraced the woman he loved, and Claire Haggerty let herself be wrapped in his strong arms, pleased he had fled the future, the desolate year 2000, to be with her. At that very moment, too, standing on top of a rock, Captain Derek Shackleton declared in a grating voice that if any good had come of the war it was that it had united the human race as no other war had ever done before, and Gilliam Murray shook his head mournfully, telling himself this was the last expedition he would organize, that he was tired of fools and of the heartless wretch who kept smearing his building with dung, that it was time to stage his own death, to pretend he had been devoured by one of the savage dragons that inhabited the fourth dimension, dragons between whose razor-sharp teeth Charles Winslow was that very instant being torn to ribbons in his dreams, before waking up with a start bathed in sweat, alarming the two Chinese prostitutes sharing his bed with his cries, at the same time as his cousin Andrew, who was just then leaning on Waterloo Bridge watching the sun rise, noticed a familiar-looking fellow with bird-like features coming towards him.

"Mr. Wells?" he called out as the man drew level.

Wells stopped and stared at Andrew for a few moments, trying to remember where he had seen him before.

"Don't you remember me?" said the young man. "I'm Andrew Harrington."

As soon as he heard the name, Wells remembered. This was the lad whose life he had saved a few weeks before, preventing him from killing himself thanks to an elaborate charade that had allowed him to confront Jack the Ripper, the murderer who had terrorized Whitechapel in the autumn of 1888.

"Yes, Mr. Harrington, of course I remember you," he said, pleased to see the young man was still alive and his efforts had not been in vain. "How good it is to meet you."

"Likewise, Mr. Wells," said Andrew.

The two men stood in silence for a moment, grinning idiotically.

"Did you destroy the time machine?" enquired Andrew.

"Er . . . yes, yes," stammered Wells, and quickly tried to change the subject. "What brings you here? Did you come to watch the dawn?"

"Yes," the other man confessed, turning to look at the

sky, which just then was a palette of beautiful orange and purple hues. "Although in actual fact I'm trying to see what's behind it."

"What's behind it?" asked Wells, intrigued.

Andrew nodded.

"Do you remember what you told me after I came back from the past in your time machine?" he said, rummaging for something in his coat pocket. "You assured me I'd killed Jack the Ripper, in spite of this newspaper clipping contradicting it."

Andrew showed Wells the same yellowed cutting he had presented to him in the kitchen of his house in Woking a few weeks before. "Jack the Ripper Strikes Again!" the headline announced, going on to list the ghastly wounds the monster had inflicted on his fifth victim, the Whitechapel prostitute whom the young man loved. Wells nodded, unable to help wondering, as everyone did in those days, what had happened to the ruthless murderer, why he had suddenly stopped killing and had disappeared without a trace.

"You said it was because my action had caused a bifurcation in time," Andrew went on, slipping the cutting back in his pocket. "A parallel world, I think you called it, a world in which Marie Kelly was alive and living happily with my twin. Although, unfortunately, I was in the wrong world."

"Yes, I remember," said Wells cautiously, uncertain what the young man was driving at.

"Well, Mr. Wells. Saving Marie Kelly encouraged me to forget about suicide and to carry on with my life. And that is what I am doing. I recently became engaged to an adorable young woman, and I am determined to enjoy her company and to savor the small things in life." He paused and looked up at the sky again. "And yet I come here each dawn to try to see the parallel world you spoke of, and in which I am supposedly living happily with Marie Kelly. And do you know what, Mr. Wells?"

"What?" asked the writer, swallowing hard, afraid the young man was about to turn round and punch him, or seize him by the lapels and throw him into the river, out of revenge for having deceived him in such a childish way.

"Sometimes I can see her," said Andrew, in an almost tremulous whisper.

The author stared at him, dumbfounded.

"You can see her?"

"Yes, Mr. Wells," the young man affirmed, smiling like one who has had a revelation, "sometimes I see her."

Whether or not Andrew really believed this or had chosen to believe it Wells did not know, but the effect on the young man appeared to be the same: Wells's fabrication had preserved him, as in a bed of ice. He watched the young man contemplating the dawn, or perhaps what was "behind" it, an almost childlike expression of ecstasy illuminating his face, and could not help wondering which of them was more deluded: the skeptical writer, incapable of believing the things he himself had written, or the desperate young man, who in a noble act of faith had decided to believe Wells's beautiful lie, taking refuge in the fact that no one could prove it was untrue.

"It's been a pleasure meeting you again, Mr. Wells," Andrew suddenly said, turning to shake his hand.

"Likewise," replied Wells.

After they had said good-bye, Wells stood for a few moments watching the young man cross the bridge unhurriedly, swathed in the golden light of dawn. Parallel worlds. He had completely forgotten about the theory he had been obliged to make up to save the young man's life. But did they really exist? Did each of man's decisions give rise to a different world? In fact, it was naïve to think there was only one alternative to each predicament. What about the unchosen universes, the ones that were flushed away; why should they have less right to exist than the others? Wells doubted very much whether the structure of the universe depended on the unpredictable desires of that fickle, timid creature called man. It was more reasonable to suppose that the universe was far richer and more immeasurable than our senses could perceive, that when man was faced with two or more options, he inevitably ended up choosing all of them, for his ability to choose was simply an illusion. And so, the world kept splitting into different worlds, worlds that showed the breadth and complexity of the universe, worlds that exploited its full potential, drained all of its possibilities, worlds that evolved alongside one another, perhaps only differentiated by an insignificant detail such as how many flies were in each, because even killing one of these annoying insects implied a choice: it was an insignificant gesture that gave birth to a new universe all the same.

And how many of the wretched creatures buzzing

around his windows had he killed or allowed to live, or simply mutilated, pulling off their wings while he thought about how to resolve a dilemma in one of his novels? Perhaps this was a silly example, reflected Wells, as such an action would not have changed the world in any irreversible way. After all, a man could spend his entire life pulling off flies' wings without altering the course of history. But the same reasoning could be applied to far more significant decisions, and he could not help remembering Gilliam Murray's second visit. Had Wells not also been torn between two possible choices, and, intoxicated with power, had he not opted to squash the fly, giving rise to a universe in which a company offering trips to the future existed, giving rise to the absurd universe in which he was now trapped? But, what if he had opted instead to help Murray publish his novel? Then he would be living in a world similar to the one he was in now, only in which the time travel company did not exist, a world in which one more book would have to be added to the necessary bonfire of scientific novels: *Captain Derek Shackleton, The True and Exciting Story of a Hero of the Future*, by Gilliam F. Murray.

And so, since an almost infinite number of different worlds existed, Wells reflected, everything that could happen did happen. Or, what amounted to the same thing: any world, civilization, creature it was possible to imagine already existed. And so, for example, there was a world dominated by a nonmammalian species, another by birdmen living in huge nests, another in which man used an alphabet to count the fingers on his hand, another in which sleep erased all memory and each day was a new life, another in which a detective called Sherlock Holmes really did exist, and his companion was a clever little rascal called Oliver Twist, and still another in which an inventor had built a time machine and discovered a nightmarish paradise in the year 802,701. And taking this to its limit, there was also somewhere a universe governed by laws different from those Newton had established, where there were fairies and unicorns and talking mermaids and plants, for in a universe where anything was possible, children's stories were no longer inventions, but copies of worlds their authors, by some quirk of fate, had been able to glimpse.

Did no one invent anything, then? Was everyone merely copying? Wells wondered. The writer pondered the question for a while, and given it is becoming clear this particular tale is drawing to a close, I shall use the time to bid you farewell, like an actor waving good-bye to his audience from the stage. Thank you very much for your attention, and I sincerely hope that you enjoyed the show . . . But now let us return to Wells, who recovered with a start owing to an almost metaphysical shudder running down his spine, because his wandering thoughts had led him to pose another question: What if his life were being written by someone in another reality, for instance, in the universe almost exactly like his own in which there was no Time Travel company and Gilliam Murray was the author of dreadful little novels? He gave serious thought to the possibility of someone copying his life and pretending it was fiction. But why would anyone bother? He was not material for a novel. Had he been shipwrecked on a tropical island, like Robinson Crusoe, he would have been incapable of even making a clay gourd. By the same token, his life was too dull for anyone to transform it into an exciting story.

Yet undeniably the past few weeks had been rather eventful: in a matter of a few days, he had saved Andrew Harrington's and Claire Haggerty's lives by using his imagination, as Jane had taken care to point out in a somewhat dramatic manner, as though she had been addressing a packed audience he could not see in the stalls. In the first case, he had been forced to pretend he possessed a time machine like the one in his novel, and in the second that he was a hero from the future who wrote love letters. Was there material for a novel in any of this? Possibly. A novel narrating the creation of a company called Murray's Time Travel, in which he, unfortunately, had played a part, a novel that surprised its readers towards the middle when it was revealed that the year 2000 was no more than a stage set built with rubble from a demolition (although this, of course, would only be a revelation to readers from Wells's own time). If such a novel survived the passage of time, and was read by people living after the year 2000, there would be nothing to reveal, for reality itself would have given the lie to the future described in the story. But did that mean it was impossible to write a novel set in Wells's time speculating about a future that was already the author's past? The thought saddened him. He preferred to believe his readers would understand they were meant to read the novel as if they were in 1896, as if they, in fact, had experienced a journey through time.

Still, since he did not have the makings of a hero, he would have to be a secondary character in the novel, someone to whom others, the story's true protagonists, came to for help.

If someone in a neighboring universe had decided to write about his life, in whatever time, he hoped for their sake that this was the last page, as he very much doubted his life would carry on in the same vein. He had probably exhausted his quota of excitement in the past two weeks, and from this point on his life would proceed once more in peaceable monotony, like that of any other writer.

He gazed at Andrew Harrington, the character with whom he would have started this hypothetical novel, and, as he saw him walk away bathed in the golden glow of dawn, perhaps with a euphoric smile playing about his lips, he told himself that this was the perfect image with which to end the tale. He wondered, as if somehow he were able to see or hear me, whether at that very moment someone was not doing precisely that, and then experiencing the rush of joy every writer feels when finishing a novel, a happiness nothing else in life can bring, not sipping Scotch whiskey in the bathtub until the water goes cold, nor caressing a woman's body, nor feeling the touch on the skin of the delicious breeze heralding the arrival of summer.

ACKNOWLEDGMENTS

Writing is the loneliest profession in the world. Those of us who choose to earn our living this way accept that from the outset. I imagine that if we wanted to be surrounded by people, we would be tourist guides or pianists in hotel bars. Even so, with this novel I wanted to experiment, to see whether it was possible to write with others. And thanks to two people who are very special to me, I have discovered that it is, as I have never felt less alone than while writing this book.

One of these people is my friend and fellow author Lorenzo Luengo, who watched over this novel as though it were his own, reading through each section I sent him carefully and dispassionately, offering advice about character and plot, as well as details about the period, urging me on when my stamina began to flag, and showing his belief in the project when my own faltered. Thanks to his generous help, not only did I learn about writing a novel, I learned the meaning of the word *friendship*. And I can only show my gratitude by adding his name to these pages that owe so much to him, as well as making him a gift of the squirrel monkey he became so fond of.

Thanks to Judith Curr, publisher of Atria Books, to Johanna Castillo and Amy Tannenbaum, and to the Time Mappers Group for their support.

Take a sneak peek at
Félix J. Palma's next novel . . .

the

MAP *of the* SKY

HE DEMON FROM THE STARS WAS nowhere to be found. After hacking the surgeon to pieces, the monster had apparently vanished into thin air. There was no trace either of any damage to the ship's hull, no hole through which the Martian, or whatever it was, could have slipped aboard the *Annawan*. Incredible though it might seem, the creature had found a way to enter and leave without being seen. Unnerved, MacReady's only answer was to double the number of lookouts. He even posted a few men outside on the ice, forming a ring around the ship.

But, regrettably, his strategy did nothing to wipe the fear from the eyes of the sailors, who went on searching the ship obsessively and grilling Carson about what he had seen. They needed to know what the monster that had come down from the stars to destroy them looked like. But Carson's account was only sketchy. The sailor had been stretched out on one of the cots in the infirmary, semiconscious from the laudanum, so that he felt the teeth of the saw as little more than a pleasant, harmless tickle, even though the surgeon was about to take off his right foot below the ankle, when a huge shadow entered the room and hurled itself at the unwitting Doctor Walker. In a matter of seconds, the apparition had torn the surgeon to shreds, pieces of him flying about the room in a hail of bloody lumps of flesh and broken bone. Unsure if this was a hallucination caused by the laudanum, or, however insane it seemed, if it was really happening, the horrified Carson prepared himself to meet the same fate, wondering whether he would feel anything more than a pleasant tickle, when the creature began to dismember him. But luckily for Carson, his fellow sailors' screams had alerted the demon, and it had fled the room. Carson could only offer a vague and incomplete description of the monster that added nothing new to the information Peters had gleaned from its footprints. The Martian, indeed, did have claws, not hooves, and was terrifying to behold, but they could get no more information out of Carson, not even about the color of its skin. Carson was a man of few words, who knew when to unfurl a sail to make the most of the wind, but whose vocabulary was too limited to describe a creature which probably resembled nothing he had ever seen before. When Carson had recovered from the shock, they dressed the tiny incision on his foot made by the saw, although none of them dared finish the amputation the doctor had started. They left him in the infirmary, hoping for a miracle or that a game of cards would decide who would wield the saw and put an end to Carson's suffering.

The following morning, they buried the remains of Doctor Francis Walker in the ice, in a coffin expressly built by the carpenters, although what they placed inside it was little more than a smattering of fragments. They dug a grave in the ice with shovels and pickaxes, and they lowered the box into it, draped in a flag. Marking his final resting place was a simple stone, with the following inscription:

In memory of Doctor Francis T. Walker, who departed this life on 4 March 1830 A.D. on board the Annawan, *at the age of thirty-four years.*

Peters took it upon himself to drive the headstone into the ice with an enormous mallet. They performed the ceremony close to the ship, and although it was meant to be a solemn affair they could not help carrying it out as quickly as possible, since no one wanted to spend too long exposed to that bitter cold, especially when the monster responsible for what happened to the doctor was still at large.

AFTER THE BURIAL, REYNOLDS retired to his cabin, and, lying on his bunk with his eyes closed, he mulled over recent events. After seeing the doctor's broken body it was logical to assume the monster had no interest in fraternizing with them, but rather seemed hell-bent on death and the annihilation of all forms of life, whether of polar bears or skilled surgeons. Still, Reynolds had not given up his idea of conversing peaceably with it. Must he rule out that option simply because the monster had not shown Doctor Walker the proper respect? Perhaps it had felt threatened by the frail-looking surgeon. Or perhaps it still had not grasped that they, too, were intelligent beings, and that it could therefore communicate with them if it so wished. Perhaps to the monster they were simple cockroaches, so that it had no moral scruples about crushing them. Reynolds abandoned that line of reasoning when he realized he was simply trying to find a way of justifying the monster's violent behavior, whereas perhaps what he ought to be doing was accepting the fact that, for whatever reason, the demon was intent on destroying them, giving them no choice but to kill it before it killed them. Although he could not be sure of that either. They lacked information, and staying posted around the ship, ready to blast away anything on the snow that moved, whatever its size or shape, was clearly not the best way to get any. The explorer sighed and sat upright in his bunk. Something prevented him from giving up hope of communicating with a being from another planet. Perhaps they would succeed if they dealt with the situation a little more calmly instead of giving way to panic. They had the opportunity to establish diplomatic, peaceful relations with another world! They should not rule out that possibility simply because they did not yet know what they were up against, he told himself. Reynolds stood up and, brimming with resolve, made his way to Captain MacReady's cabin to discuss the matter with him.

MacReady greeted him with his usual apathy. The captain's cabin was almost four times bigger than that of Reynolds, spanning the breadth of the ship's stern. It boasted a substantial library, and an enormous food store crammed with hams, cheeses, pots of marmalade, sacks of tea, bottles of excellent brandy, and other delicacies paid for out of the captain's own pocket. But more significant, it was fitted with its own privy, where MacReady could relieve himself away from the stresses and strains of his position. Reynolds envied him this tiny closet on the starboard side, which he considered a great luxury, a slice of civilization as comforting as it was incongruous. The captain offered him a glass of brandy and gestured wearily toward a chair.

"Well, Reynolds, to what do I owe the honor of your visit?" he said sardonically as soon as his visitor had sat down.

The explorer gazed pityingly at this giant of a man who, despite being aware he was defeated, utterly overwhelmed by circumstances, insisted on exerting his authority with a kind of crude malevolence. For perhaps the ship becoming icebound was a foreseeable event, a setback which years of experience had prepared the captain to face with professional equanimity, imagining perchance that the arrival of summer would bring the long awaited miracle: the thaw that would liberate them. Yes, the accursed ice pack would eventually break up, and the *Annawan*, less damaged than they had feared, would be free to sail away from there, down the channels that would widen with their passage, in a genuine apotheosis of human will, but above all in a celebration of life, shared by ducks and puffins flocking gaily overhead, as well as shoals of cod and herring and even Arctic whales, which would escort them home in a majestic convoy. Reynolds took a sip of brandy, and went straight to the point:

"Captain, I think we need to talk about the strategy we should follow in the current circumstances."

"The strategy we should follow?" MacReady repeated in astonishment, looking Reynolds up and down as if he had just walked in wearing a clown's outfit. "What the hell are you talking about?"

"It is very simple, Captain. As organizer of this

expedition, I am the one in charge of any discoveries we might make along the way, and although we are clearly no closer to finding the passage to the Hollow Earth than we were when we left New York, we are nevertheless on the brink of one of the most significant discoveries in the history of mankind, one which I believe requires us to establish a plan of action and a set of criteria."

MacReady carried on gaping at the explorer for a few moments, before throwing his head back and letting out a loud guffaw. Spluttering, he dried his eyes with his chubby fingers, and, regaining his composure, declared:

"For heaven's sake, Reynolds: you never cease to amaze me! So you want us to discuss criteria . . . Well, mine are very simple. As soon as that thing, whatever it is, shows its ugly face around here, my men and I will shove a musket up its backside, cut its head off as a memento, and providing its flesh isn't too disgusting, we'll feed it to the dogs. That's my plan of action in the *current circumstances*. In the meantime, if you wish to carry on playing explorer, be my guest, only kindly do it in the confines of your cabin so that you don't get in the way."

Reynolds had to make a supreme effort to keep calm. He knew the captain would not make it easy for him, but he had gone there with a clear purpose, and he refused to allow MacReady's continual provocation to deflect him. He took another sip of brandy and waited for a few moments before responding, resorting this time to flattery:

"Captain," he said, "you are not a simple drunken sailor, like the rest of the crew. You are a gentleman, an experienced ship's captain, and intelligent enough I am sure to grasp the magnitude of what is going on. I have been speaking with Sergeant Allan, who as you know is a man of letters, well versed in, er, astronomy, and he agrees with me that the creature doubtless comes from Mars. Do you realize what this thing is we are fighting? A Martian, captain! A being from another planet! I refuse to believe you do not appreciate the enormous significance of such a discovery, and how reckless it would be of us not to consider carefully every possible alternative. Allow me to give you an example: if we kill the creature before communicating with it, how will we know where it comes from? And more important, if all we take with us to New York is a strange animal's head, how will we prove the thing really is from another planet? It won't give scientists much to go on, will it, Captain? And this leads to my next request. I would like you to organize another expedition to the flying machine."

"Are you out of your mind?" said MacReady, genuinely taken aback. "I've no intention of sending my men out there with that thing lurking in the snow. I would be sending them to their death. Besides, that machine is impossible to open, we can't even touch it, or perhaps you've forgotten what happened to you." MacReady tilted his chin toward the explorer's still bandaged hand. "And anyway, why the devil would we want to do that?"

"Primarily because if we manage to get inside the machine we will probably find some information about the creature that is attacking us," Reynolds explained patiently. "This could prove essential if on the one hand the creature's intentions are peaceful and we simply need to learn how to communicate with it, and on the other if they are not, because we may find some clue as to how to destroy it, a weapon even." Seeing that the captain was still staring blankly at him, Reynolds realized he must take a different approach, and so he tried enticement. "Supposing that were the case, I mean, supposing we had no choice but to kill the creature, and, assuming we succeeded, and then the ice thawed and we sailed home, don't you think we would be entitled to some compensation for all we had been through? For I assure you, if we arrive in New York with the Martian's head, together with some proof from the machine that this is indeed a being from another planet, we will be showered with more money and recognition than you can imagine."

"I still don't know if you are a visionary, a complete idiot, or both, Reynolds," MacReady said. "To begin with, I don't understand how you can go on doubting the creature's intentions after the *courteousness* he showed poor Doctor Walker. I assure you I need no further proof. I know exactly how we should *communicate* with that thing. As for the flying machine . . . how the devil do you intend to get inside it? Through sheer brain power?"

"I don't know, Captain," Reynolds confessed, irritated by the officer's mocking tone. "We could try blowing it up with dynamite . . ."

The captain shook his head, as though he were conversing with a lunatic, and a sullen silence descended on the two men. Reynolds tried to think. He was running out of ideas.

"I've never understood men like you, Reynolds," MacReady suddenly murmured absentmindedly, gently swirling his brandy. "What is it you want? To be remembered by History? Of what use is that to a God-fearing Christian once the maggots have finished with him? I told you the other day, Reynolds: I don't give a fig about your Hollow Earth. The same goes for that creature's origins. It could come from Mars or Jupiter or any other planet for all I care. My job is to bring this ship and her crew safely back to New York, and I'll be well paid if I do. That's all I care about, Reynolds: saving my skin and getting my money."

"I refuse to believe you have no other desires in life," Reynolds hissed, with as much contempt as he could muster.

"Why, of course I do. I dream of a cottage in the country, with a garden full of tulips."

"Tulips?" the explorer asked in astonishment.

"Yes, tulips," the captain repeated, defensively. "My mother was Dutch, and I still remember her planting them in our garden when I was a child. I hope to have saved enough by the time I retire to live a quiet life and devote myself to growing tulips. And I assure you, I won't give up until I have grown the most beautiful tulip on our side of the Atlantic. I shall name it after my mother, and enter it in all the flower shows. That's all I want, Reynolds: a beautiful tulip garden and a sitting room with a fireplace, above which I shall hang the head of the monster you are so intent on communicating with."

Reynolds gazed at him in silence for a while, trying to thrust aside the alarming image of the captain, a pair of pruning shears in one hand and a basket of tulips in the other. Could a brute like MacReady hold a tulip without crushing it? And if his tulip failed to win, would he take it with a smile, or would he shoot the judges? The explorer leaned back in his chair, trying to gather his thoughts, while taking another sip from his glass. He had to admit that whereas he had failed to win over the captain with his arguments, MacReady had almost succeeded in convincing him with his. What did he hope to find inside the flying machine? Perhaps it would be best if he took the captain's advice and saved his skin so he could return to Baltimore and carry on with his dreary, pedestrian life. Compared to what he was going through on that vast expanse of ice it did not seem half so bad, and maybe if he took up gardening it would be easier to bear. He set his glass down on the table, surprised that part of him longed to surrender to that life. But the other part, the part that had poisoned him with dreams of glory, and had brought him there, sank its fangs into him once more. What the devil was he thinking? He had not come all this way for nothing!

"Tell me, Captain, has it not occurred to you that the creature may be unaware that it is behaving in a malevolent fashion?" he blurted out, in a tone of bitterness, born of despair. "Perhaps the monster's thought patterns are so different from ours that it sees what it has been doing as comparable to crushing a spider underfoot or pulling up weeds." He paused to allow MacReady to digest his words, then added: "Can you really not see what I am driving at, Captain? Whether we intend to communicate with the creature or to kill it, clearly we must first understand it. Moreover, I am sure any one of the sailors will readily accompany me to the machine when I explain it's our only hope of survival."

MacReady stared at him coolly.

"Have you quite finished?" he asked, addressing the explorer with unnerving slowness. "Good! Now listen to me, Reynolds. I shall ignore your veiled threat of mutiny, for which I could have you locked up in the ship's hold until you rot. But, although you don't deserve it, I shall be lenient, and simply inform you that the circumstances of the expedition have changed radically. We are now in a state of emergency, which gives me complete control over this vessel, whether you like it or not. You no longer have any say in the matter. From now on, I decide what action we take against the ruthless enemy that is attacking us. We shall wait for it to come after us, that is what we shall do. If you disagree and want to return to the flying machine, I shan't try to stop you. Take as many weapons from the armoury as you can carry, but don't count on the support of any of my men. They will stay on the ship with me, waiting for that thing."

At first, Reynolds had no idea how to respond. With obvious satisfaction, MacReady had relieved him of his authority, thereby leaving him with only one possible line of attack.

"I can assure you that when we reach New York," he said, "I intend to hold you fully responsible for the failure of this expedition: I shall accuse you of causing the ship to become icebound through your inept navigation, of refusing to explore the area in search of the passage to the center of the Earth, and, above all, Captain, I shall hold you to account for every death that occurs from now on, including that of the first visitor from space ever to set foot on our planet."

Reynolds fell silent, glowering at the captain. He bitterly regretted having to resort to threats, but that stubborn, arrogant devil had proved immune to every other approach. It seemed however that even this outburst did not have the slightest effect on MacReady, who simply sighed wearily.

"Reynolds, you are the stupidest man I have ever met," he said. "And I have nothing more to say to you. This conversation has already gone on too long, and we have both made our positions clear. With all due respect, I shan't deny that your wild fantasies have been a source of great amusement to certain gentlemen and myself. But this is no time for laughter, and the last thing I need on board now is a buffoon."

Reynolds stared at the captain openmouthed.

"If that is all, Reynolds," said MacReady, standing up and turning his back on the explorer, "kindly allow me to carry on with my duties. Go ahead with your plan if you want, but don't even think about approaching my men."

Speechless, Reynolds contemplated the captain's broad back. There was no point insisting. He let out a grunt of frustration and rose to his feet.

"As you wish, Captain. But you can forget about ever naming a tulip after your mother," he retorted.

And he walked out of the cabin, slamming the door behind him.